SelectEditions

SelectEditions

BY READER'S DIGEST

THE READER'S DIGEST ASSOCIATION, INC.
MONTREAL • PLEASANTVILLE, NEW YORK

READER'S DIGEST SELECT EDITIONS

Vice President, Books & Home Entertainment: Deirdre Gilbert

The condensations in this volume have been created by The Reader's Digest Association, Inc., by special arrangement with the publishers, authors, or holders of copyrights.

With the exception of actual personages identified as such, the characters and incidents in the fictional selections in this volume are entirely the products of the authors' imaginations and have no relation to any person or event in real life.

CONTENTS

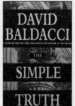

TOM CLANCY

RAINBOW SIX

It's a new kind of terrorism—secret, scientific, global.

No country can escape it.

And only the Rainbow team can stop it.

"It's a thrill ride."
—*USA Today*

SETTING UP

JOHN Clark had more time in airplanes than most licensed pilots, and he knew the statistics as well as any of them, but he still didn't like the idea of crossing the ocean in a twin-engine airliner. Four was the right number of engines, he thought, because losing one meant losing only twenty-five percent of the aircraft's available power, whereas on this United 777 it meant losing *half*. Maybe the presence of his wife, one daughter, and a son-in-law made him a little itchier than usual. No, that wasn't right. He wasn't itchy, not about flying anyway. It was just a lingering . . . what? he asked himself. Next to him, in the window seat, Sandy was immersed in a mystery, while he was trying to concentrate on the current issue of *The Economist* and wondering what was putting the cold-air feeling on the back of his neck. He sipped his glass of white wine, shook his shoulders, and went back to the article on how peaceful the new world was.

Right. Well, yes, he had to admit that things were a lot better than they'd been for nearly all his life. No more swimming out of a submarine to do a collection on a Russian beach, or up a fetid river in North Vietnam to rescue a downed aviator. Someday maybe he'd do a book. Problem was, who'd believe it? And would the CIA ever allow him to tell his tales except on his deathbed? He was not in a hurry for that, not with a grandchild on the way. He grimaced, unwilling to contemplate that development. Patsy must have gotten pregnant on their wedding night, and Ding glowed more about it than she did.

John looked back to business class—the curtain wasn't in place yet—and there they were, holding hands. The flight attendant made the rounds, removing his wineglass as the aircraft taxied out to the runway. Her last stop was by Alistair, over on the left side of the first-class cabin. John caught his eye and got a funny look back. The Brit, too? Wasn't that something? Neither of them had ever been accused of nervousness.

Alistair Stanley had been a major in the Special Air Service (SAS) before being permanently seconded to the Secret Intelligence Service (SIS). His position had been much like John's—the one you called in to take care of business when the gentler people got skittish. Al and John had hit it off right away on a job in Romania eight years before, and the American was pleased to be working with him again, even if they were both too old now for the fun stuff. Administration wasn't exactly John's idea of a job, but he had to admit he wasn't twenty anymore, or thirty, or even forty. It was remarkable enough, he told himself, that he was still alive.

The airliner started moving. The usual sensation came, like being pressed back into the seat of a sports car jumping off a red light, but with more authority. A little voice in John's head said, "Rotate," and the floor came up under his feet. The body of the aircraft followed the nose into the sky, and the flight began properly.

"On our way, honey," Sandy said, taking a second away from her book.

John smiled. "Who done it?"

"Not sure yet, but probably the wife."

"Yeah, divorce lawyers are so expensive."

Sandy chuckled and went back to the story as the stewardesses got up from their seats to resume drink service. Clark finished *The Economist* and started *Sports Illustrated*. Darn, he'd be missing the end of the football season. That was one thing he'd always tried to keep track of, even when off on a mission. He'd been a pretty good linebacker in high school, and Indiana University had shown some interest in him. Then he'd decided to forgo college and join the navy, as his father had before him, though Clark had become a SEAL rather than a skimmer sailor on a tin can.

"Mr. Clark?" The stewardess delivered the dinner menu. "Mrs. Clark?"

One nice thing about first class—the flight crew pretended you had a name. John had gotten an automatic upgrade because of frequent-flier miles. The menu, he saw, was pretty good. He settled back and rolled up the sleeves of his shirt. These flights always seemed overheated to him.

The captain got on the intercom next, interrupting all the personal movies on the mini-screens. They were following a southerly routing to take advantage of the jet stream. That, Captain Will Garnet explained, would cut their time to Heathrow by forty minutes. He didn't say it would also make for a few bumps. Airlines tried to conserve fuel, and forty-five minutes' worth would put a gold star in his copybook. Well, maybe just a silver one.

It started on the left side of the aircraft. The man was dressed properly, wearing a jacket. That was what got John's attention. Most people took them off as soon as they sat down, but—

It was a Browning automatic, with a flat black finish that said "military" to Clark and, less than a second later, to Alistair Stanley. A moment later two more men appeared on the right side, walking right next to Clark's seat.

"Damn," he said so quietly that only Sandy heard him. Why had he packed his side arm in his carry-on and stowed it in the overhead? What a rookie mistake! He had only to look to his left to see the same expression on Alistair's face. Two of the most experienced pros in the business.

"John . . ."

"Just relax, Sandy," her husband replied quietly. He sat back. Three of them. One was taking a stewardess forward, where she unlocked the door to the flight deck. John watched them go through and close the door. The other two stood forward, where they could see down both aisles of the aircraft.

Only three? Might there be a backup guy disguised as a passenger? That was the one who controlled the bomb—if there was a bomb—and a bomb was the worst thing there could be. A pistol bullet might punch a hole in the skin of the aircraft, forcing a rapid descent, but nobody died from that. A bomb would kill everyone aboard, probably . . . better than even money. Clark hadn't gotten old by taking that sort of chance.

By now the bad guy would have gotten onto the radio and passed along the bad news of the day, and the director of security for United—Clark knew him, Pete Fleming, former deputy assistant director of the FBI—would call his former agency and get *that* ball rolling, to include notification of the CIA and the State Department, the FBI Hostage Rescue Team in Quantico, and Delta Force down at Fort Bragg. Pete would also pass along the passenger list, with three names circled in red, and *that* would make the troops at Langley and Foggy Bottom wonder about a security leak. John dismissed that. This was a random event.

It was time to move a little. Clark turned his head toward Domingo "Ding" Chavez, just twenty feet away. When eye contact was established, he touched the tip of his nose as though to make an itch go away. Chavez did the same . . . and he was still wearing his jacket. He was more used to hot weather, John thought, and probably felt cold on the airplane. Good. He'd still have his Beretta .45. Ding knew what was going down and had the good sense to do nothing about it . . . yet. How might he react with his pregnant wife sitting next to him? Domingo was smart and cool under pressure, but he was still Latino, a man of no small passion.

THE guy at the head of the left-side aisle was going over the passenger list. He started moving, and fifteen feet later he was looking down at the woman in the window seat next to Alistair. "Who are you?" he demanded in Spanish.

The lady replied with a name John didn't catch—a Spanish name. Alistair was leaning back in his seat, staring with wide blue eyes up at the guy with the gun.

A scream came from the back of the aircraft. "Gun, that's a gun!" a man's voice shouted. Now everybody would know, John thought.

The right-aisle guy knocked on the cockpit door and stuck his head in to announce this good news.

"Ladies and gentlemen, this is Captain Garnet. I, uh, am instructed to tell you that we are deviating from our flight plan. We have some guests aboard who have told me to fly to Lajes, in the Azores. They say they have no desire to hurt anyone, but they are armed, and First Officer Renford and I are going to do exactly what they say. Please remain calm. I will be back to you later." His voice was as cool as the smoke off dry ice.

Lajes, in the Azores, Clark thought. Former U.S. Navy base. Still active? The left-side guy had spoken in Spanish. Basques? That was still perking over in Spain. The woman, who was she? Early fifties, well turned out. The Spanish ambassador to Washington was male. Might this be his wife?

The left-side man shifted his gaze a seat. "Who are you?"

"Alistair Stanley," was the reply. There was no sense in Alistair's lying, Clark knew. They were traveling openly. "I'm British," he added in a quaky voice. "My passport's up in the—" He reached up and had his hand slapped down by the guy's gun.

Nice play, John thought, even if it hadn't worked. Alistair might have gotten the bag down, produced the passport, and then had his gun in his lap. Alistair was up to speed. The three wolves didn't know the sheep herd had three dogs in it. Big ones.

More Spanish from the left side. "Where is your husband?" he demanded. They wanted him, not her. Bad intelligence, guys, Clark thought. The two he could see were talking to each other quietly, but the body language said it all. They were annoyed. So he had three (or more?) angry terrorists with guns on a two-engine airplane over the North Atlantic at night. They were late twenties, Clark thought. Old enough to be technically competent but young enough to need adult supervision.

The air changed then and not for the better. Number 2 went into the cockpit and stayed for several minutes. When he reappeared, he went back to Number 3 instead of taking his post to cover the right-side aisle. They spoke in raspy whispers that Clark understood in context if not content. Nobody's really in charge, he decided. Three free agents with guns in an airplane. It was time to start being afraid. Clark closed his eyes and took a deep breath.

Number 2 headed aft to look at the woman sitting next to Alistair. He just stood there for a few seconds, then looked at Alistair. "Who are you?" he demanded.

"I told your friend, old man. Alistair Stanley. I have my passport in my carry-on bag if you wish to see it."

"Yes. Show it to me!"

"Of course, sir." In elegantly slow movements the former SAS major opened the overhead bin and extracted his black carry-on bag. He unzipped the side compartment and pulled the passport out, handed it over, then sat down, holding the bag in his lap.

Number 2 looked at the passport and tossed it back into the Brit's lap while John watched. Then he stormed away to speak with Number 3 again. Alistair let out a long breath and looked around the cabin, finally catching John's eye. These three were dumb. They hadn't had an intelligence team in place to tell them their primary target hadn't made the flight, and so here they were, committed to a mission that was already blown. Soon they'd realize that their guns were the only power they had and that they might as well start using them.

Clark couldn't just sit here and wait for them to start killing people. It took five minutes more until Number 2 decided to talk some more with Number 3. When he did, John turned to catch Ding's eye again, swiping one finger across his upper lip as though to stroke a mustache he'd never grown. Chavez cocked his head as though to reply, "You sure?" but he took the sign. He loosened his seat belt and reached behind his back with his left hand, bringing his pistol out before the alarmed eyes of his six-weeks-pregnant wife. Domingo touched her right hand with his to reassure her, covered the Beretta with a napkin in his lap, and waited for his senior to make the play.

Clark unbuckled his seat belt and started to stand.

"You!" Number 2 called from forward. "Sit still!"

"Hey, look, I, uh, had a few drinks, and—well, I gotta go. How about it? *Por favor,*" John added sheepishly.

"No. You will stay in your seat!" Number 2 raced aft, gun in front, stopping just short of pressing it against John's chest. Sandy's eyes were wide. She'd never seen her husband do anything dangerous, but this wasn't the husband who had slept next to her for twenty-five years. This was the other Clark, the one she knew about but had never seen.

"Look, I go in there, and I come back, okay? Please don't make me wet my pants, okay?"

What turned the trick was Clark's size. He was just under six two, and his forearms, visible with the rolled-up sleeves, were powerful. Number 2 was smaller by four inches and thirty pounds, but he had a gun, and making bigger people do one's wishes is always a treat for bullies. So he gripped John by the arm and pushed him roughly aft, toward the right-side lavatory. John cowered and went, his hands above his head.

"Hey, *gracias,* amigo, okay?" Clark opened the door. Dumb as ever, Number 2 actually allowed him to close it. John did what he'd asked permission to do, then washed his hands and took a brief look in the mirror. Hey, Clark, you still got it? he asked himself. Okay, let's find out. He slid the locking bar loose and pulled the folding door open with a grateful look on his face. "Hey, uh, thanks."

"Back to your seat."

"Wait. Let me get you a cuppa coffee, okay? I—" John took a step aft, and Number 2 was dumb enough to follow him; then he reached for Clark's shoulder and turned him around.

"Buenas noches," Ding said quietly from less than ten feet away, his gun aimed at the side of Number 2's head. The man's eyes caught the blue steel, and the distraction was just right. John's right hand came around, the back of his fist catching the terrorist in the right temple. The blow was enough to stun.

"Miguel!" Number 3 called loudly.

Clark moved to the left side, pausing to get a cup of coffee from the machine, complete with saucer and spoon. He then reappeared in the left-side aisle and moved forward. "He said to bring you this. Thank you for allowing me to use the bathroom," John said in a shaky voice.

"Miguel!" Number 3 called again.

"He went back that way. Here's your coffee." John took a few steps forward, hoping this amateur would continue to act like one. He did, coming toward him. John allowed the cup and saucer to shake in his hand, and just as Number 3 reached him, Clark dropped both of them on the floor and dived down to get them, about half a step behind Alistair's seat. Number 3 bent down as well. It would be his last mistake. John grabbed the pistol and twisted it into its owner's belly. It might have gone off, but Alistair's own Browning crashed down on the back of the man's neck, and Number 3 went limp. Alistair snapped his fingers at the nearest stewardess. "Rope, cord, anything to tie them up, quickly!"

John collected the pistol. In two more seconds he'd fieldstripped the weapon and tossed the pieces at the feet of Alistair's traveling companion, whose brown eyes were wide and shocked. "Sky marshals, ma'am. Please be at ease," Clark explained. A few seconds after that, Chavez appeared, dragging Number 2 with him. The stewardess returned with a spool of twine.

"Ding, front office!" John ordered him.

"Roge-o, Mr. C." Chavez moved forward, his Beretta in both hands, and stood by the cockpit door. On the floor, Clark did the wrapping, tying the hands of the terrorists as tight as he could.

"One more, John," Alistair breathed.

"You want to keep an eye on our two friends."

"A pleasure."

John walked forward, still unarmed. His junior was still at the door, pistol aimed upward in both hands, eyes on the door. "How we doing, Domingo?"

"Cockpit ain't a real good place to start a gunfight, John. Let's invite him aft."

It made sense. Clark hopped aft to retrieve the cup and saucer. "You!" He gestured to the other stewardess. "Call the cockpit and tell the pilot to tell our friend that Miguel needs him."

She did exactly as she was told, lifting the phone and passing along the message. A few seconds later the door opened, and Number 1 looked out. The stewardess pointed to John.

"Coffee?"

It only confused him, and he took a step aft toward the large man with the cup. His pistol was aimed at the floor.

"Hello," Ding said from Number 1's left, placing his pistol against his head. "Drop the gun!"

"It is best you do what he says," John added in his educated Spanish, "or my friend will kill you." Number 1's eyes darted around the cabin, looking for his colleagues, but they were nowhere to be seen. John reached for the gun and took it from an unresisting hand. This he placed in his waistband, then dropped the man to the floor to frisk him, while Ding's gun rested at the back of the terrorist's neck.

John waved to the first stewardess, who had come up with the twine. A moment later he stood and walked into the cockpit. "Captain?"

"Who are you?"

"Where's the nearest military airfield?"

"RCAF Gander," the copilot—Renford, wasn't it?—replied.

"Well, let's go there. Cap'n, the airplane is yours again. We have all three of them tied up."

"Who are you?" Will Garnet asked again rather forcefully.

"Just a guy who wanted to help out," John replied with a blank look, and the message got through. Garnet was ex–air force. "Can I use your radio, sir?"

The captain pointed to the fold-down jump seat and showed him how to use the radio. "This is United flight niner two zero," Clark said. "Who am I talking to? Over."

"This is Special Agent Carney of the FBI. Who are you?"

"Carney, call the director and tell him Rainbow Six is on the line. Situation is under control. We're heading for Gander."

"Rainbow?"

"Just like it sounds, Agent Carney." Clark looked down to see his hands shaking a little now that it was over. Well, that had happened once or twice before.

"Niner two zero, niner two zero, this is Agent Carney again. Stand by for the director."

There was a click and a brief crackle. "John?" a new voice asked.

"Yes, Dan."

"What gives?"

"Three of them, Spanish speaking, not real smart. We took them down."

"Alive?"

"That's affirmative," Clark confirmed. "Zero casualties. I told the pilot to head for RCAF Gander. We're due there in—"

"Niner zero minutes," the copilot said.

"Hour and a half," John went on. "Have the Mounties collect our bad boys, and call Andrews. We need transport to London."

"Okay, John. Anything else?"

"Yeah, send me a few hours of sleep, will ya?"

"Anything you want, pal," the FBI director replied with a chuckle, and the line went dead.

THEY'D been doing it for some time. The powder-blue vans— there were four of them—circulated throughout New York City, picking up homeless people and shuttling them to dry-out centers run by the corporation. The kindly operation had made local television over a year ago and garnered the corporation a few dozen friendly letters. The people they helped weren't compelled to get aboard. The volunteers asked, politely, if they wanted a clean bed for the night, free of charge. Those who declined were given blankets. Some preferred to stay out, deeming it a sort of freedom, but with dropping autumn temperatures more did not. It was approaching midnight, and presently there were ten of them in the van, and that was all it could hold. None of them knew this was the *fifth* of the four vans operating, though they found out something was a little different when the attendant leaned back from the front seat and handed out bottles of an inexpensive California burgundy— a better wine than they were used to drinking and one to which something had been added.

By the time they reached their destination, ten miles west of Binghamton, in the hill country of central New York State, all were asleep. They were sprayed in the face from a squeeze bottle much like that used to clean windows, then given steel bracelets numbered one to ten. Those with even numbers got injections in the arm. The odd-numbered control group did not. With this task done, the ten homeless were carried off to a bunk room to sleep off the wine and the drugs. The van that had delivered them headed west for a return to its regular duties. The driver hadn't even known what he'd done except drive.

THEY landed at RAF Northholt, a military airfield just west of London. As the U.S. Air Force G-IV taxied to the ramp, the rain started, making for a proper welcome to British soil. It was a hundred-yard walk to the reception building, where a British official stamped their passports.

Three cars waited outside, all of them black Daimler limousines, which headed off the base, south for Hereford. This was proof that he was a civilian bureaucrat, Clark told himself in the lead car. Otherwise they'd have used helicopters. But Britain wasn't entirely devoid of civilization. They stopped at a McDonald's for Egg McMuffins and coffee. Sandy snorted at the cholesterol intake. She'd been chiding John about it for months. Then she thought about the previous night. "Who were they, John?"

"Who? The guys on the plane?" He got a nod. "Probably Basque separatists. They were after the Spanish ambassador, but he wasn't aboard." An inner smile. Boy, did they ever pick the wrong flight!

"What'll happen to them?" Sandy persisted.

"There's an international treaty. The Canadians will ship them back to the States for trial—federal court. They'll be behind bars for a long time."

"First time in a long time something like that happened."

"Yep." He agreed. You had to be a real dolt to hijack airplanes, but dolts, it appeared, were not yet an endangered species. That was why he was the Six of an organization called Rainbow.

"THERE is good news and there is bad news," the memo he'd written had begun. As usual, it wasn't couched in bureaucratese, a language Clark had never learned despite his thirty years in the CIA.

With the demise of the Soviet Union and other nations with political positions adverse to American and Western interests, the likelihood of a major international confrontation is at an all-time low. But many experienced and trained international terrorists still roam the world, and some nations still make use of these "free agents" for more narrow political goals.

The most obvious solution to this problem will be a new multinational counterterrorist team. I propose the code name Rainbow. I further propose that the organization be based in the United Kingdom. The reasons for this are simple: (1) The U.K. currently owns and operates the Special Air Service, the world's foremost—that is, most experienced—special-operations agency. (2) London is the world's most accessible city in terms of commercial air travel. (3) The legal environment is particularly advantageous, due to press restrictions possible under British law but not American.

For all of these reasons the proposed special-operations team will be composed of U.S., U.K., and selected NATO personnel, with full support from national intelligence services.

And he'd sold it, Clark told himself with a wispy smile. It had helped that CIA director Ed Foley had backed him up in the Oval Office. The new agency, Rainbow, was blacker than black, its American funding directed through the Department of the Interior by Capitol Hill, then through the Pentagon's Office of Special Projects, with no connection whatsoever to the intelligence community. Fewer than a hundred people knew it existed, and Clark was the boss. The only bad news was that he was now a suit. He'd have an office and two secretaries instead of going out to run with the big dogs. Well, if he couldn't run with the dogs, he would play with them. He would be a *colonel,* not a general, Clark told himself. He'd be with the troops as much as possible, running, shooting, and talking things over.

Meanwhile, I'm a captain, Ding was telling himself in the next car behind while eagerly taking in the countryside. He'd be under John, Mr. C., leading one of the strike teams, and in effective rank, that made him a captain, which was about the best rank to have in the army—high enough that the NCOs respected you and low enough that you played with the troops. He'd volunteered for this to stay with Mr. C. Someone had to look after the boss. The airplane had surprised him. Mr. C. hadn't had his weapon handy. Even John Clark was getting old. Must have been the first operational mistake he'd made in a long time.

Ding looked at Clark's daughter, who was dozing next to him. The pregnancy was taking it out of Patsy and doing so in unpredictable ways. Sometimes she bubbled with activity. Other times she just vegetated. Well, she was carrying a new little Chavez in her belly, and that made everything okay—better than okay. A miracle. Ding leaned over to kiss her lightly on the cheek.

FOR the moment Rainbow H.Q. was at Hereford, headquarters of the British army's 22nd Special Air Service Regiment. The base looked like any other, Ding decided. Only the signs were different, and some of the spelling. His car ended up in officer country by a modest house, and he noticed that John's car kept going another couple of blocks toward a larger house. Well, colonels lived better than captains. Ding opened the door, twisted out of the car, and headed for the trunk—excuse me, he thought, boot—to get their luggage. Then came a surprise.

"Major Chavez?" a voice asked.

"Uh, yeah?" Ding said, turning. Major? he wondered.

"I'm Corporal Weldon. I'm your batman." The corporal was much taller than Ding's five feet seven and beefy-looking. He bustled past his assigned officer and manhandled the bags out of the trunk/boot. "Follow me, sir." Ding and Patsy did.

Three hundred meters away, it was much the same for John and Sandy, though their staff was a sergeant and a corporal, the latter female and blond. Sandy's first impression of the kitchen was that British refrigerators were tiny and that cooking in here would be something of an exercise in contortion. She was a little slow to catch on that she'd touch an implement in this room only at the sufferance of Corporal Anne Fairway.

"Where's the local hospital?" Sandy asked her.

"About six kilometers away, mum." Fairway hadn't been briefed that Sandy Clark was a highly trained ER nurse and would be working in the hospital.

John checked out his study. The computer was in place, tempested, he was sure, to make certain that people couldn't park a few hundred yards away and read what he was typing. Of course, getting that close would be a feat. The perimeter guards had struck John as competent. While his batman got his clothes squared away, John hopped into the shower. Twenty minutes later, wearing a blue pin-striped suit, a white shirt, and a striped tie, he appeared at the front door, where a car waited to whisk him off to his headquarters.

"Have fun, honey," Sandy said with a kiss.

IT TURNED out his office was less than two miles from his house, in a two-story brick building surrounded by workers. Alistair Stanley was waiting for him inside.

"The building dates back to 1947," Alistair said. "It was unused for some years and won't be finished for another week or so. Come, I'll take you to your office."

They headed down the corridor, and Alistair opened the door to John's office, where John saw two secretaries, both in their late thirties. Alice Foorgate and Helen Montgomery stood and introduced themselves with charming smiles. Stanley's XO (executive officer) office was adjacent to Clark's, which contained a huge desk, a chair, and the same kind of computer as in John's CIA office—tempested here, too, so people couldn't monitor it electronically. John took a breath before trying out the swivel chair and decided to doff his jacket first. Sitting in a chair with a suit coat on was something he'd never really learned to enjoy. He waved Alistair to the seat opposite the desk. "Where are we?"

"Two teams fully formed. Chavez will have one. The other will be commanded by Peter Covington. Father was colonel of the Twenty-second. Marvelous lad. Ten men per team, as agreed."

"The shooters?"

"Top-drawer, John. As good as any I've ever worked with."

"Intel?"

"All excellent. The chief of that section is Bill Tawney, an SIS man for thirty years, supported by Dr. Paul Bellow—Temple University, Philadelphia. Was a professor there until your FBI seconded him. Smart chap. Principled, also. He flies in tomorrow."

"What's my status here?"

"General officer—brigadier at least, maybe a two-star. I seem to be a colonel—chief of staff," Stanley said.

"Al, you know what I really am—was, I mean?"

"You were a SEAL, a navy chief boatswain's mate, I believe, with the Navy Cross, Silver Star with a repeat cluster, Bronze Star with Combat-V and three repeats, and three Purple Hearts. And all that's before the Agency took you in and gave you no less than four Intelligence Stars." Stanley said all this from memory. "Rescuing Koga and taking Daryei out were brilliant jobs, in case I never told you. We do know a little bit about you and your young Chavez. The lad has enormous potential if he's as good as I've heard."

"YO, DING!" a familiar voice called. Chavez looked to his left in surprise.

"Oso! What are you doing here?" Both men embraced.

"The Rangers were getting boring, so I shipped up to Bragg for a tour with Delta, and then this came up on the scope and I went after it. You're the boss for Team Two?" First Sergeant Julio "Oso" Vega asked.

"Sorta-kinda," Ding replied, shaking the hand of an old friend and comrade. "Ain't lost no weight, man. Oso, you *eat* barbells?"

"Gotta keep fit, sir," replied a man for whom a hundred morning push-ups didn't generate a drop of sweat. "Come on, I'll intro you to the team. We got some good troops, Ding."

Team 2, Rainbow, had its own building—brick, single story, and fairly large, with a desk for every man. The team was composed exclusively of NCOs, mainly senior ones: four Americans, four Brits, a German, and a Frenchman. Sergeant Louis Loiselle was the nearest. Short and dark-haired, he was a former member of the French parachute forces. Like all the men, Loiselle was a weapons expert and, his file said, a brilliant marksman with pistol and rifle. Feld-webel Dieter Weber was next, also a paratrooper and a graduate of the German army's Burger Führer, or Mountain Leader school, one of the physically toughest schools in any army in the world. And he looked it. Six three, blond-haired, and fair-skinned, he might have been on an SS recruiting poster sixty years earlier. His English, Ding learned at once, was better than his own. Weber was one of the team's two long-rifle men. Sergeant First Class Homer Johnston was the other. A mountaineer from Idaho, he'd taken his first deer at the age of nine. He was a former Green Beret and Delta member, like Chavez's friend Oso Vega.

The shooters, as Ding thought of them, the guys who went into the buildings to do business, were Americans and Brits. Steve Lincoln, Paddy Connolly, Scotty McTyler, and Eddie Price were from the SAS. They'd all been there and done that in Northern Ireland. Mike Pierce, Hank Patterson, and George Tomlinson mainly had not, be-cause the American Delta Force didn't have the experience of the SAS. Every one of them was taller than "Major" Chavez. Every one was tough. Every one was smart, and with this realization came an oddly deflating feeling that despite his own field experience, he'd have to earn the respect of his team and earn it fast. "Who's senior?"

"That's me, sir," Eddie Price said. He was the oldest of the team, forty-one, and a sergeant major. Like the rest in the bull pen, he was wearing nonuniform clothes, though they were all wearing the same nonuniform things, without badges of rank.

"Okay, Price. Have we done our P.T. today?"

"No, Major, we waited for you to lead us out," Sergeant Major Price replied with a smile that was ten percent manners and ninety percent challenge.

Chavez smiled back. "Well, I'm a little stiff from the flight, but maybe we can loosen that up. Where do I change?" Ding asked, hop-ing his last two weeks of five-mile runs would prove to be enough.

DING cut the run off at three miles, which they'd done in twenty minutes. Good time, he thought, somewhat winded, until he turned to see his men about as fresh as they'd been at the beginning.

The run had ended at the weapons range, where targets and arms were ready. A longtime Beretta aficionado, Chavez had decided that his men would use the recent Beretta .45 as their personal side arm, along with the Heckler & Koch MP-10 submachine gun. Without saying anything, Ding picked up his weapon, donned his ear protectors, and started going for the silhouette targets set five meters away. *There,* he saw, all eight holes in the head. But Dieter Weber, next to him, had grouped his shots in one ragged hole, and Paddy Connolly had made what appeared to be one not-so-ragged hole less than an inch across, all between the target's eyes, without touching the eyes themselves.

"Told you they were good, Ding," said First Sergeant Vega.

"How long they been here?"

" 'Bout a week. Used to running five miles, sir," Julio added with a smile.

Formerly a squad leader in the 7th Light Infantry Division, Ding had been one of the toughest soldiers in his country's uniform, which was why John Clark had tapped him for a job in the Agency—and in *that* capacity he'd pulled off some tough missions in the field. It had been a very long time since Domingo Chavez had felt the least bit inadequate about anything. But now quiet voices were speaking into his ear.

THEY awoke late, one at a time, over a period of about an hour. For the most part, they just lay there in bed, some of them shuffling off to the bathroom, where they found Tylenol for the headaches they all had. In the adjoining room of the facility in central New York State was a breakfast buffet with pans full of scrambled eggs, pancakes, sausage, and bacon. They met their captor after breakfast.

"What is this place?" asked the one known to the staff as Subject 4. It sure wasn't any Bowery mission he was familiar with.

"My company is undertaking a study," the host said from behind a tight-fitting mask. "You gentlemen will be part of that study. You will be staying with us for a while. During that time you will have clean beds, clean clothes, good food, good medical care, *and*"—he pulled a wall panel back—"whatever you want to drink." In the wall alcove were three shelves of every manner of wine, beer, and spirit, with glasses, water, mixes, and ice.

"You mean we can't leave?" Subject 7 asked.

"We would prefer that you stay," the host said somewhat evasively. He pointed to the liquor cabinet. "Anyone care for a morning eye-opener?"

It turned out it wasn't too early in the morning for any of them. The additional drug in the alcohol was quite tasteless.

CHAPTER 1
―――――――――
SADDLING UP

THE first two weeks started off pleasantly enough. Chavez was now running five miles without any discomfort and shooting better, though not as well as Paddy Connolly and Hank Patterson, both of whom must have been born with pistols in their cribs, Ding decided after firing three hundred rounds per day to try to equal them. He checked his watch and headed out into the bull pen. On the way, he drew his pistol and belt. The next stop was what the Brits called a robing room, except there were no robes, but instead coal-black fatigue clothes complete with body armor.

Team 2 was all there, relaxed and joking quietly before the day's exercise. "Team Two, we ready?" Chavez asked.

"Yes, sir!" came the chorused reply.

With that, Ding led them outside and ran them half a mile to the shooting house. Johnston and Weber were already on the scene, at opposite corners of the rectangular structure.

"Command to Rifle Two Two," Ding said into his helmet-mounted microphone. "Anything to report?"

"Negative, Two Six. Nothing at all," Weber reported.

"Rifle Two One?"

"Six," Johnston replied, "I saw a curtain move. Instruments show four to six voices inside, speaking English."

"Roger," Ding responded, the remainder of his team concealed behind a truck. The raid had been fully briefed. Ding waved for the team to move.

Paddy Connolly took the lead, racing to the door. Just as he got there, he let go of his H&K and let it dangle on the sling while he pulled the Primacord from the fanny pack hanging from his body armor. He stuck the explosive to the doorframe by its adhesive and pushed the blasting cap into the top-right corner. A second later he moved right ten feet, holding the detonator control up in his left hand. "Let's go!" Ding shouted.

As the first of them bolted around the truck, Connolly thumbed the switch and the doorframe disintegrated, sending the door flying inward. The first shooter, Sergeant Mike Pierce, disappeared into the smoking hole, with Chavez right behind him.

The inside was dark, the only light coming through the shattered doorway. Pierce scanned the room, found it empty, then lodged himself by the doorway into the next room. Ding ran into that first, leading his team. There they were, four targets and four hostages. Chavez brought his MP-10 up and fired two silenced rounds into the left-most target's head. He saw the rounds hit right between the blue-painted eyes, then traversed right to see that Steve Lincoln had gotten his man. In less than a second the lights came on. It was over—elapsed time from Primacord explosion, seven seconds. Eight seconds had been programmed for the exercise. Ding safed his weapon.

"Damn it, John!" he said to the Rainbow commander.

Clark stood, smiling at the target to his left, less than two feet away, the two holes drilled well enough to ensure certain, instant death. He wasn't wearing protective gear. Neither was Stanley, at the far end of the line. "Seven seconds. That'll do, I guess. Five would be better," John observed.

"Mark us down fully mission-capable, Mr. C.," Chavez said with a confident smile. "How'd Team One do?"

"Two tenths of a second faster," John replied, glad to see the diminutive leader of Team 2 deflate a little. "And thanks."

"What for?"

"For not wasting your father-in-law." John clapped him on the shoulder and walked out of the room.

"SO, DMITRIY," the man said, "where and how do we begin?"

They'd met by a fortunate accident, both thought (albeit for very different reasons), in Paris at some sidewalk café. One had noted that the other was Russian and wanted to ask a few questions about business in Russia. Dmitriy Arkadeyevich Popov, a former KGB colonel scouting for opportunities in the world of capitalism, had quickly determined that this American had a great deal of money and was therefore worthy of stroking. He had answered the questions openly, leading the American to deduce his former occupation. The language skills (Popov was fluent in English, French, and Czech) had been a giveaway, as had Popov's knowledge of Washington, D.C. As usual, one thing had led to another: first the exchange of business cards, then a trip to America first class on Air France as a security consultant and a series of meetings that had moved ever so subtly in a direction that came as a surprise to the Russian.

"You actually worked with terrorists?" the American had asked.

It was necessary for Popov to explain the proper ideological context. "You must remember that to us they were not terrorists at all. They were fellow believers in world peace and Marxism-Leninism and, truth be told, useful fools, all too willing to sacrifice their lives in return for a little support of one sort or another. Idealists are foolish people, are they not?"

"Some are," his host admitted, nodding for his guest to go on.

"They believe all the rhetoric, all the promises. Don't you see? I, too, was a party member. I attended the meetings, paid my party dues. But really, I was KGB. I traveled. I *saw* what life was like in the West. Better food, better clothes, better everything. Unlike these foolish youths, I knew what the truth was."

"So what are they doing now?"

"Hiding," Popov answered.

"I wonder . . ."

"Wonder what?"

"If one could still contact them."

"Most certainly. My contacts"—he tapped his temple—"well, such things do not evaporate."

"Well, Dmitriy," the American had said, "how about dinner?"

By the end of dinner Popov was earning one hundred thousand dollars per year as a special consultant.

It was ten months later now, again in Paris.

"You have to do it face to face?" the American asked.

A gentle laugh. "My dear friend, one does not arrange such a thing with a fax. But the risk is only a small one. The meet will be in a safe place. They know me only by a password and code name and, of course, the currency."

"How much?"

Popov shrugged. "Oh, shall we say five hundred thousand dollars? In cash, of course."

The host scribbled a quick note and handed the paper across. "That's what you need to get the money." And with that, things began. Morals were variable things. Dmitriy's main principle was to earn a living.

"You know that this carries a certain degree of danger for me, and as you know, my salary—"

"Your salary just doubled, Dmitriy."

A smile. Even the Russian Mafia didn't advance people as quickly as this.

THE communications room was on the second floor of the Rainbow headquarters building. It had the usual number of teletype machines for the various world news services, plus TV sets for CNN, Sky News, and a few other broadcasts. These were overseen by people the Brits called "minders," who were overseen in turn by a career intelligence officer. The one on this shift was an American air force major from the National Security Agency.

Major Sam Bennett had acclimated himself to the environment. The duty here was pretty easy. General Clark seemed a decent boss. And Bill Tawney, the British intelligence team boss, was about the best Bennett had ever seen—quiet, thoughtful, and smart.

"Major!" a voice called from one of the news printers. "We have a hostage case in Switzerland."

"What service?" Bennett asked on the way over.

"Agence France-Press. It's a bank," the corporal reported as Bennett came close enough to read but couldn't, since he didn't know French. The corporal translated. Bennett lifted a phone and pushed a button.

"Mr. Tawney, we have an incident in Bern. Unknown number of criminals have seized the central branch of the Bern Commercial Bank. There are some civilians trapped inside."

"Thank you, Major Bennett." Tawney killed the line and dialed the British embassy in Geneva to ask for an evaluation of the situation. He then went upstairs to watch TV.

Behind the Rainbow headquarters building were four large satellite dishes trained on communications satellites hovering over the equator. A direct news feed from the local Swiss station showed the outside of an institutional-looking building. The voice was that of a reporter talking to his station, not to the public. A linguist stood by to translate. " 'No, I have no idea. The police haven't talked to us yet,' " the translator said in a dull monotone. Then a new voice came on the line. "Cameraman," the translator said. "Sounds like a cameraman— There's something—"

The camera zoomed in, catching a shape, a human shape wearing something over his head, a mask of sorts.

"What kind of gun is that?" Bennett asked.

"Czech Model 58," Tawney said at once. Bill Tawney was about John Clark's age, with brown, thinning hair and an unlit pipe in his mouth. A former member of Britain's Secret Intelligence Service (SIS), he was a field spook who'd come inside after ten years working the streets behind the Iron Curtain.

"What gives, Bill?" Tawney and Bennett turned to see Clark. "Your secretary said you had a developing situation here."

"We may," the intel chief replied. "I have the Geneva station sending two men over to evaluate it. Who's the go team?"

"Team Two, Chavez and Price. How long before you think we declare an alert?"

"We could start now," Bill answered, even though it was probably nothing more than a bank robbery gone bad.

Clark pulled a mini-radio from his pocket and thumbed it on. "Chavez, this is Clark. You and Price report to communications right now."

"I WONDER what this is about," Ding observed to his command sergeant major. Eddie Price, he'd learned in the past three weeks, was as good a soldier as he was ever likely to meet: cool, smart, quiet, with plenty of field experience.

"I expect we'll find out, sir," Price responded. Officers felt the need to talk a lot, he knew. Proof of that came at once.

"How long you been in, Eddie?"

"Nearly thirty years, sir. I enlisted as a boy soldier—age fifteen. Parachute regiment. Came over to SAS when I was twenty-four. Been here ever since."

"Well, Sar Major, I'm glad to have you with me," Chavez said as they entered the communications room.

"Thank you, sir," the sergeant major replied. Decent chap, this Chavez, he thought. Perhaps even a good commander, though that remained to be seen.

"Hey, Mr. C., what gives?" Domingo asked his boss.

"Domingo, there's a chance we may have a job for your team. Bern, Switzerland. Bank robbery gone bad, hostage situation." Clark pointed at the TV screens.

If nothing else, it was good as a practice alert. The preplanned mechanisms were now moving. On the first floor, tickets had already been arranged on no fewer than four flights from Gatwick to Switzerland, and two helicopters were on the way to Hereford to ferry his men to the airport with their equipment. British Airways had been alerted to accept sealed cargo—inspecting it for the international flight would just have gotten people excited. If the alert went further, Team 2 members would change into civilian clothes, complete with ties and suit jackets.

"Not much happening now," Bill Tawney said. "Sam, can you roll the earlier tapes?"

"Yes, sir." Major Bennett keyed one up and hit the PLAY button on the remote.

"Czech 58," Price said immediately. "Odd weapon for a Swiss bandit."

"Why?" Clark asked.

"They make far better weapons in Switzerland, sir, for their territorials. Their citizen soldiers stow them in their closets, you see. Should not be all that difficult to steal several."

"How good are the Swiss cops?" Chavez asked Price.

"Very good indeed, sir, but not a great deal of experience with a serious hostage event."

"That's why we have an understanding with them," Tawney put in.

"Yes, sir." Price leaned back, reached into his pocket, and took out his pipe. "Anyone object?"

Clark shook his head. "No health nazis here, Sergeant Major. What do you mean by a 'serious' hostage event?"

"Committed criminals, terrorists." Price shrugged. "The sort who kill hostages to show their resolve." *The sort we go in after and kill,* Price didn't have to add.

The protocol on this was both simple and complex. Rainbow had an understanding with the Swiss government. If the local police couldn't handle it, they'd bump it up to the canton—state—level, which would then decide whether to bump it up to the central government, whose ministerial-level people could then make the Rainbow call. The "help" call would come through the British Foreign Office. Until the call was made, the Swiss would tell them nothing.

For another half hour the TV screens showed very little beyond an empty city street. Then a senior police officer walked into the open, holding a cellular phone. His body language was placid at first. Abruptly it changed. Eddie Price tensed in his chair.

" 'Was that a shot?' " the translator said, relaying the words of one of the reporters on the scene.

Less than a minute later one of the bank's glass doors opened, and a man in civilian clothes dragged a body onto the sidewalk. It seemed to be a man, but his head was a red mass. The civilian got the body all the way outside and froze the moment he set it down.

Move right; go to your right, Chavez thought as loudly as he could from so far away. Somehow the thought must have gotten there, for the man stood stock-still for several seconds and then went to the right. He was now invisible from the interior of the building.

"Good move, old man," Tawney observed quietly. "Now we'll see if the police can get you into the clear."

"Mr. Tawney, a call for you on line four," the intercom called.

The intelligence chief walked to a phone and punched the proper button, then hit the speaker switch on the phone. It was the two men from the Geneva station, now in Bern. The local police, they said, were out of their depth and sending up to the canton for advice.

"Mr. C.?" Chavez said from his chair.

"Tell the choppers to spool up, Ding. You're off to Gatwick. Hold there for further instructions."

"Roger that, Mr. C. Team Two is moving."

Chavez walked down the stairs with Price behind him. They jumped into their car and were at Team 2's building in under three minutes. "People, if you're watching the telly, you know what's happening. Saddle up. We're choppering to Gatwick." They'd just headed out the door when a brave Swiss cop managed to get the civilian to safety.

THE helicopter ride to the airport was just twenty-five minutes. At the British Airways terminal Chavez watched his men load their gear into a cargo container that would be first off when the plane arrived at Bern. But they still had to wait for the go-mission order. Chavez flipped open his cellular phone and thumbed speed-dial number one.

"Clark," the voice said after the encryption software clicked in.

"Ding here, John. The call from London come yet?"

"Still waiting, Domingo. We expect it shortly. The canton bumped it upstairs. Their Justice Minister is considering it now."

"Well, tell the worthy gentleman that this flight leaves in two zero minutes, and the next one after that is ninety minutes."

"I hear you, Ding. We have to hold."

Chavez swore in Spanish. He knew it. He didn't have to like it. "Roger, Six. Team Two is holding on the ramp at Gatwick."

"Roger that, Team Two. Rainbow Six, out." Clark looked over at Bill Tawney. "Bill," he said, "we have twenty minutes to get them off the ground. After that, over an hour delay."

Tawney nodded and called his contact in the Foreign Ministry. From there it went to the British ambassador in Geneva. Word came back in fifteen minutes: *"Ja."*

"We have mission approval, John," Tawney reported.

Clark hit the speed-dial number two button on his phone.

"Chavez," a voice said over considerable background noise.

"We have a go mission," Clark said. "Acknowledge."

"Team Two copies go mission. Team Two is moving."

"That's affirmative. Good luck, Domingo."

"Thank you, Mr. C."

THE last man aboard the aircraft was Tim Noonan, the team's technical wizard. Not a wizened techno-nerd, Noonan had played defensive back at Stanford before joining the FBI and had taken weapons training with the team to fit in. Six feet, two hundred pounds, he was larger than most of Ding's shooters, but he was a better-than-fair shot.

Dr. Paul Bellow settled into his window seat with a book extracted from his carry-on bag. It was one of his own—his first, in fact—the one that had gotten him into this business. He glanced at the title, *The Enraged Outlook: Inside a Terrorist Mind.* It wouldn't hurt to refresh his memory. The rest of the team just leaned back, enjoying the comfort of their first-class seats.

The British Airways flight touched down two minutes early, then taxied to the gate. Exiting the Jetway, Chavez saw a chauffeur sort of man holding a sign with the proper name on it. He walked up to him. "Waiting for us?"

"Yes, sir. Come with me?"

Team 2 followed him into what seemed a conference room. In it was a uniformed police officer. "You are . . ." he said.

"Chavez." Ding stuck his hand out. "Domingo Chavez."

"Spanish?" the cop asked in considerable surprise.

"American. And you, sir?"

"Roebling, Marius," the man replied when all the team was in the room and the door closed. "Come with me, please." Roebling opened a far door, which led outside to some stairs. A minute later they were in a minibus heading onto a highway. Ding looked back to see another truck, doubtless carrying their gear.

"Okay, what can you tell me?"

"Nothing new. We are speaking with them over the phone. No names. They've demanded transport to this airport and a flight out of the country. No destination as of yet."

"Okay, what did the guy who got away tell you?"

"There are four of them. They speak German. They are armed with Czech weapons, and it would seem they are not reluctant to make use of them."

The minibus and truck pulled up to a secondary school a block from the bank, and Team 2 walked into the gymnasium area, which was secured by uniformed cops. The men changed into their gear in a locker room and walked back into the gym to find Roebling with an additional garment for them to wear—a black pullover with POLIZEI printed on it in gold lettering. It was a useful subterfuge.

The men and their gear reboarded the minibus, which deposited them around the corner from the bank, invisible both to the terrorists and the TV news cameras. The long-rifle men, Johnston and Weber, were walked to preselected perches—one overlooking the rear of the bank, the other diagonally facing the front. Both men unfolded the bipod legs on their gunstocks and started surveying the target building. They determined the range to target and dialed it into their telescopic sights, then lay down on the foam mattresses they'd brought. Their immediate mission was to observe and report.

Noonan set up his laptop computer and started looking over the building blueprints so he could input them into his system. In thirty minutes he had a complete electronic map of the target building. Everything but the vault combination, he thought with a smile. Then he erected a whip antenna and transmitted the imagery to the team's other three computers.

Chavez, Price, and Bellow walked to the senior Swiss policeman on the scene. Greetings were exchanged. Price set up his computer and put in a CD-ROM disk with photos of known terrorists.

The man who'd dragged the body out was one Hans Richter, a German national from Bonn who banked here for his Swiss-based trading business. "Did you see their faces?" Price asked.

"Yes." A shaky nod. Price started flashing photos of known German terrorists. "*Ja, ja,* that one. He is the leader."

"You are quite sure?"

"Yes, I am."

"Ernst Model, formerly of Baader-Meinhof." Price scrolled down. "Nearly captured in Hamburg, 1987. Killed two policemen to make his escape. Communist trained. Last suspected to be in Lebanon. Okay." Price scrolled down some more.

"That one . . . possibly."

"Erwin Guttenach, also Baader-Meinhof. Background also murder. Oh, yes, he's the chappie who kidnapped and killed a board member of BMW in 1986. Kept the ransom. Four million D-marks," Price added.

Bellow looked over his shoulder. "What did he say on the phone?"

"We have a tape," the cop replied.

"Excellent! But I require a translator."

"Doc, a profile on Ernst Model. Quick as you can." Chavez turned. "Noonan, can we get some coverage on the bank?"

"No problem," the tech man replied.

"Okay, people, let's move," Chavez ordered. Noonan went off to his bag of tricks. Bellow headed around the corner with Herr Richter and a Swiss cop to handle the translation. That left Chavez and Price alone.

"Eddie, am I missing anything?"

"No, Major," Sergeant Major Price replied.

"Okay, number one, my name is Ding. Number two, you have more experience in this than I do. If you have something to say, I want to hear it *right now,* got it? I need your brains, Eddie."

"Very well, sir—Ding." Price managed a smile. His commander was working out rather nicely. "What's the plan if the opposition starts shooting out of hand?"

"Tell Louis Loiselle, two flash-bangs at the front door, toss four more inside, and we blow in like a tornado."

POPOV STOOD IN THE CROWD of onlookers. He hadn't known the Swiss police had such a well-trained counterterrorist squad. As he watched, the commander was crouching close to the front of the bank building, and another, his second-in-command probably, was heading around the corner to the rest of the team. His first impression of Model had been correct. The German's IQ was little more than room temperature. But he was not entirely impractical. Ernst had wanted to see the money, six hundred thousand dollars in D-marks. Popov smiled, remembering where it had been stashed. It was unlikely that Ernst would ever see it again. Killing the hostage so early—foolish but not unexpected. He was the sort who'd want to show his resolve and ideological purity, as though anyone cared about that today! Popov grunted to himself and lit a cigar.

NOONAN crept along the outside wall of the bank, below window level. At every window he raised his head slowly to see if the interior curtains allowed any view of the inside. The second one did, and there Noonan affixed a lens, roughly the shape of a cobra's head but only a few millimeters across, which led by fiber-optic cable to a TV camera set in his black bag around the corner. He placed another at the lower corner of the bank's glass door, then worked his way back, crawling to a place where he could stand. That done, he walked around the block to repeat the procedure from the other side of the building, where he was able to make three placements. He also positioned microphones to pick up sound. "Okay," the techie said in his place on a side street. All the video displays were up and running. The size of the lenses didn't make for good imagery despite the enhancement program built into his computer. "Here's one shooter . . . and another." They were within ten meters of the front of the building. The rest of the people visible were sitting on the white marble floor, in the center for easy coverage. "The guy said four, right?"

"Yeah," Chavez answered. "But not how many hostages."

"Okay, this is a bad guy, I think, behind the teller places. Hmph, looks like he's checking the cash drawers." Noonan switched displays on the computer screen. "I got blueprints of the building, and this is the layout."

"Ceiling construction?" Chavez asked.

"Rebarred concrete slab, forty centimeters thick. Same with the walls and floor. This building was made to last."

"So we can go in the front door or the back door, and that's it. And that puts number four bad guy at the back door. Okay, Eddie, we blow the rear door with Primacord—three men in that way. Second later we blow the front glass doors, toss flash-bangs, and move in. You and me go left. Louis and George go right."

Price nodded. "Who leads the rear-entry team?"

"Scotty, I think. Paddy does the explosives." Chavez made a mental note that the sub-teams had to be more firmly established.

"Vega?"

"Oso backs us up." Julio Vega had become their heavy-machine gunner, slinging a laser-sighted M-60 7.62-mm machine gun for really serious work. There wasn't much use for that now, and wouldn't be unless everything went to hell. "The question now is when." Ding checked his watch. "Back to the doc."

BELLOW was walking Herr Richter through the event for the sixth time when Chavez and Price showed up again.

"His eyes are blue, like ice. Like ice," Richter repeated. "He is not a man like most men. He should be in a cage with the animals at the Tiergarten." The businessman shuddered involuntarily.

Roebling came over carrying his cell phone. "It is time," he said, "to speak with them again."

"Doc?" Ding asked Bellow.

"My preliminary profile on Model says he's quick to use violence. If he threatens to kill, we have to believe he's not kidding. I do not expect negotiations to be very useful. I think it is likely that an assault resolution will be necessary."

Chavez frowned. Trained as he was, he wasn't all that eager to take this one on. He'd seen the interior pictures. There had to be twenty, perhaps thirty, people inside, with three people in their immediate vicinity holding fully automatic weapons. If one of them went rock-and-roll on his Czech machine gun, a lot of those people wouldn't make it home.

Dr. Bellow conferred with Roebling, then turned to Chavez. "Model's getting aggressive. He says he'll kill a hostage in thirty minutes unless we get him a car to a helicopter pad a few blocks from here, and from there to the airport. After that he kills a hostage every fifteen minutes. He's not kidding, Ding. He shoots the first one at eight thirty."

"What are the cops saying back?"

"What I told them to say: It takes time to arrange all of that; give us a hostage or two to show good faith. But Ernst is losing control, very unhappy with how things turned out. Like a spoiled kid with nothing under the tree on Christmas morning."

"Super." Ding keyed his radio. "Team, this is Chavez. Stand to." He'd been trained in what to expect. One ploy was to deliver the car. It'd be too small for all the hostages, and you could take the bad guys down on the way out with rifle fire. But he had only two snipers, and their rifle bullets would blast through a terrorist's head with enough leftover energy to waste two or three people beyond him. No, he had to take his team in while the hostages were still on the floor, below the line of fire.

Chavez and Price crawled to the door from the left. Louis Loiselle and George Tomlinson did the same from the other side. At the rear Paddy Connolly attached a double thickness of Prima-cord to the doorframe, inserted the detonator, and stood away, with Scotty McTyler and Hank Patterson nearby. "Rear team in place, Leader," Scotty told them over the radio.

"Roger that. Front team is in place," Chavez replied.

"Okay, Ding." Noonan's voice came over the command circuit. "TV one shows a guy brandishing a rifle, walking around the hostages on the floor. If I had to bet, I'd say it's Ernst. One more behind him and a third to his right. Hold. He's on the phone now. I hear him talking to the cops, getting ready to pick a hostage to whack. He's going to give out his name first. Nice of him."

"Okay, people, it's just like the exercises," Ding told his troops. "Stand by." He looked up to see Loiselle and Tomlinson trade a look. Louis would lead, with George behind. Chavez would let Price take the lead.

"Ding, he just grabbed a guy, standing him up. On the phone again. The hostage is Dr. Mario Donatello, a medical school professor. I think it's showtime," Noonan concluded.

"Chavez to Team, we are ready to rock. Stand by. Paddy, hit it!"

A loud metallic crash shook the whole world. Price and Loiselle had placed their flash-bangs at the brass lower lining of the door and punched the switches on them as soon as they heard the first detonation. Instantly the glass doors disintegrated into thousands of fragments, which mainly flew into the bank lobby in front of a blinding white light and an end-of-the-world noise. Price darted in, with Chavez behind.

Ernst Model was right there, his weapon's muzzle pressed to the back of Dr. Donatello's head. He'd turned to look at the back of the room when the first explosion had happened, and as planned, the second one, with its immense noise and blinding flash of magnesium powder, had disoriented him. The captive had reacted, too, dropping away from the gunman, giving the intruders a blessedly clear shot. Price depressed the trigger of his MP-10 for a quick three-round burst into the center of Model's face.

Chavez, immediately behind him, spotted another gunman. He was facing away, but he still held his weapon, and rules were rules. Chavez double-tapped the gunman's head, then traversed his weapon right to see that the third terrorist was already on the floor, a pool of red streaming from his head. "Clear!" Chavez shouted.

"Clear!" "Clear!" "Clear!" the others agreed. Loiselle raced to the back of the building, with Tomlinson behind him. Before they'd gotten there, the black-clad figures of McTyler and Patterson appeared, their weapons immediately pointing up at the ceiling: "Clear!" Chavez moved farther left to the teller cages, leaping over the barrier to check for additional people. None. "Clear here! Secure the area!"

By this time some Swiss cops were entering the bank. The hostages were pushed toward the front, a shocked bunch of citizens still disoriented by what had happened, some bleeding from the head or ears from the flash-bangs and flying glass.

"What about the back door?" Ding asked Paddy Connolly.

"Come and see." The former SAS soldier led Ding to the back

room. It was a bloody mess. Perhaps the subject had been resting against the doorframe. It seemed a logical explanation for the fact that no head was visible on the corpse, and only one shoulder. The double thickness of Primacord had been a little too powerful, but Ding couldn't say that. A steel door and frame had demanded it.

THERE were cheers on the street outside as the hostages came out. So, Popov thought, the terrorists he'd recruited were dead fools now. No real surprise there. The Swiss counterterror team had handled the job well, as one would expect of Swiss policemen. One of them came outside and lit a pipe. How very Swiss! Popov thought. Probably climbs mountains for personal entertainment.

The Russian got into his rented Audi and drove to the half-baked safe house Model had set up. The black leather suitcase with the D-marks would be inside. He had a noon flight back to New York tomorrow. Before that he had to open a bank account here in Bern, a city well suited for the task.

CHAPTER 2
TRUE BELIEVERS

CHAVEZ and most of the rest of Team 2 woke up when the airliner touched down at Heathrow. It was after eleven at night, and all the men were tired after a day that had started with the usual P.T. and ended with real mission stress. It wasn't rest time yet, though. Once back at Hereford, they all gathered in the bull pen. Alistair Stanley and Team 1 leader Peter Covington were there. It was time for the after-action review, or AAR.

"Okay, people," Clark said as soon as they'd sat down. "Good job. Now, what did we do wrong?"

Paddy Connolly stood. "I used too much explosives on the rear door. Had there been a hostage immediately inside, he would have been killed," the sergeant said honestly. "I assumed the doorframe was stouter than it actually was." Then he shrugged. "I do not know how to correct for that."

John nodded. "Neither do I. Any problems shooting?"

"No." This was Chavez. "The interior was lighted. The bad guys were standing up like good targets. The shots were easy." Price and Loiselle nodded agreement.

"Ding, you sent Price in first. Why?" This was Stanley.

"Eddie's a better shot, and he has more experience. I trust him a little more than I trust myself—for now," Chavez added.

John turned to Paul Bellow. "Any observations, Doc?"

"John, we need to follow the police investigation of these subjects. Were they terrorists or robbers? We need to find out. We were not able to conduct negotiations in this case, but in the future we'll need more translators. My language skills are not up to what we need."

Clark saw Stanley make a note of that. Then he checked his watch. "Okay. We'll go over the videotapes tomorrow morning. For now, good job, people. Dismissed." He watched as the men filed out, leaving him alone with Stanley. "Well, Al?" he asked.

"Your Chavez is all he was reported to be. Clever of him to let Price take the lead. He doesn't let ego get in the way. I like that in a young officer. He'll do. So will the team."

"Lessons learned?"

"Dr. Bellow's was the best. We need more and better translators if he's to be involved in negotiations. I'll work on that tomorrow. Oh, yes, that Noonan lad—"

"A late addition. He was a techie with the FBI. They used him on the Hostage Rescue Team for technical backup. Sworn agent, knows how to shoot," Clark explained. "Good all-around man to have with us."

"He did a nice job planting his video-surveillance equipment. On the whole, John, full marks for Team Two."

"Nice to see that everything works, Al."

"Until the next one."

A long breath. "Yeah." But Rainbow was now certified. And so, Clark knew, was he.

THE SOCIETY OF CINCINNATUS owned a large house on Massachusetts Avenue that was frequently used for the semiofficial dinners that were so vital a part of the Washington social scene and allowed the mighty to cross paths and validate their status over drinks and small talk. The new President made that somewhat difficult, of course, with his . . . eccentric approach to government, but no person could really change that much in this city, and the new crop in Congress needed to learn how Washington really worked.

As a White House adviser, Carol Brightling was one of the new important people. A divorcée for over ten years, she had no less than three doctorates, from Harvard, CalTech, and the University of Illinois, thus covering both coasts and three important states, which guaranteed her the instant attention of six Senators and a larger number of Congressmen, all of whom had votes and committees.

"Catch the news?" the junior Senator from Illinois asked her over a glass of white wine.

"What do you mean?"

"Switzerland. Either a terrorist thing or a bank robbery. Nice takedown by the Swiss cops."

"Boys and their guns," Brightling observed dismissively.

"It made for good TV."

"So does football," Brightling noted with a gentle, nasty smile.

"True. Why isn't the President supporting you on global warming?" the Senator asked next, wondering how to crack her demeanor.

"Well, he isn't *not* supporting me. The President thinks we need some additional science on the issue."

"And you don't?"

"Honestly, no. I think we have all the science we need."

Carol Brightling had been a surprise appointment to the White House staff, her politics very different from the President's, respected as she was in the scientific community for her environmental views. It had been an adroit political move—probably engineered by White House Chief of Staff Arnold van Damm, arguably the most skillful political operator in this city of maneuvering—and had secured for the President the qualified support of the environmental movement.

"Does it bother you that the President is out in South Dakota slaughtering geese?" the Senator asked with a chuckle as a waiter replaced his drink.

"*Homo sapiens* is a predator," she replied, scanning the room.

"Oh, that's your ex-husband over there in the corner, isn't it?" the Senator asked.

"Yes." Her voice showed no emotion as she turned in another direction. Having spotted him, she needed to do no more. Both knew the rules. No lengthy eye contact and certainly no words.

"I had the chance to put money into Horizon Corporation two years ago. I've kicked myself quite a few times since."

"Yes, John has made quite a pile for himself, twisting science the way he has."

And well after their divorce, so she didn't get a nickel out of it. Probably not a good topic for conversation, the Senator thought at once. "You don't approve?"

"Restructuring DNA in plants and animals—no. Nature has evolved without our assistance. I doubt it needs our help."

" 'There are some things man is not meant to know'?" the Senator asked with a chuckle.

"The problem, Senator Hawking, is that nature is complex. When we change things, we cannot easily predict the ramifications. It's called the law of unintended consequences. In the case of recombinant DNA we can more easily change the genetic code than we can evaluate the effects those changes will cause a century from now."

Which point was difficult to argue with, the Senator conceded gracefully. With that observation the Senator made his excuses and headed off to join his wife.

"THERE'S nothing new in that point of view." John Brightling's doctorate in molecular biology came from the University of Virginia, along with his M.D. "It started with a guy named Ned Ludd a few centuries ago. He was afraid the Industrial Revolution would end the cottage-industry economy in England. And he was right. But what replaced it was better for the consumer, and that's why we call it progress!" John Brightling, billionaire, was holding court before a small crowd of admirers.

One of the audience started to object. "But the complexity—"

"Happens every day, madam. Every second, in fact. And so do the things we're trying to conquer. Cancer, for example. Cancer is a *genetic* disease. The key to curing it is in the human genome. And my company is going to find that key! Aging is the same thing. Salk's team at La Jolla found the kill-me gene more than fifteen years ago. If we can find a way to turn it off, then human immortality can be real. Madam, does the idea of living forever in a body of twenty-five years' maturity appeal to you? It appeals to me," he said with a warm smile. With sky-high salaries and promises of stock options his company had assembled an incredible team of talent to look at that particular gene. The profits that would accrue from its control could hardly be estimated.

"You think you can do it?" a Congresswoman from San Francisco asked. Women of all sorts found themselves drawn to this man. Money, power, and movie-star good looks made it inevitable.

John Brightling smiled broadly. "Ask me in five years. We know the gene. We need to learn how to turn it off. It's like setting off with Magellan. We aren't sure what we're going to find, but we know it'll all be interesting."

"And profitable?" a new Senator from Wyoming asked.

"That's how our society works, isn't it? We pay people for doing useful work. Is this area useful enough?"

"If you bring it off, I suppose it is." This Senator was himself a physician, a family practitioner who knew the basics but was well over his head on the deeply scientific side. The objective of Horizon Corporation was well beyond breathtaking, but he would not bet against them. They'd done too well developing cancer drugs and synthetic antibiotics. In fact, about the only thing in which John Brightling had failed was his marriage. Well, Carol Brightling was also pretty smart but more political than scientific, and perhaps her ego, capacious as everyone in this city knew it to be, had quailed before the greater intellectual gifts of her husband. Only room in town for one of us, the doctor from Wyoming thought with an inner smile. And Brightling, John, seemed to be doing better in that respect than Brightling, Carol. At the former's elbow was a very pretty redhead drinking in his every word, while the latter had come alone and would be leaving alone for her apartment in Georgetown. Well, the Senator-M.D. thought, that's life.

FOR street people who were often as contentious and territorial as junkyard dogs, this group was remarkably sedate, Dr. John Killgore thought. The large quantities of good booze helped, as did the sedative. The physicals had gone well. They were all healthy-sick people, outwardly fairly vigorous but inwardly all with physical problems ranging from diabetes to liver failure. Not the best example of humanity he'd ever seen. Yet the Project had managed to change them quite a bit. All bathed regularly now and dressed in clean clothes and watched TV. But always they drank, and the sedative he gave them calmed them further, limiting any altercations that his security staff would have to break up. It worried the epidemiologist that their guest–test subjects were seriously impaired street alcoholics. The advantage of using them, of course, was that they wouldn't be missed.

Killgore didn't have to be here, and it troubled his conscience to look at them so much, but they were *his* lab rats, and he was supposed to keep an eye on them, and so he did, behind a mirror, while he did his paperwork and listened to Bach on his portable CD player.

DAILY P.T. started at 0630 and concluded with the five-mile run, timed to last forty minutes. This morning it ended at thirty-eight minutes, and Chavez wondered if his team had an additional spring in their step from the successful mission. If so, was that good or bad? Killing fellow humans wasn't supposed to make you feel good, was it? A deep thought for a foggy English morning.

By the end of the run everyone had a good sweat, which the hot showers took care of. As Team 2 leader, he rated his own private facility, and he took the time to admire his body, always an object of pride for Domingo Chavez. Yeah, the exercise that had been so tough the first week had paid off. He hadn't been much tougher than this in Ranger school at Fort Benning. And he'd been—

what?—twenty-one then and one of the smallest men in the class. It was something of an annoyance to Ding that, tall and rangy like her mom, Patsy had half an inch on him. But Patsy only wore flats, which kept it respectable, and nobody messed with him. He had the look of a man with whom one did not trifle.

Back home, Patsy was already dressed in her greens. She was on an ob-gyn rotation at the moment, scheduled to assist on a cesarean section at the local hospital, where she was completing what in America would have been her year of internship. Next would be her pediatric rotation, which struck both of them as totally appropriate. Already on the table for him was bacon and eggs.

"I wish you'd eat better," Patsy observed.

Domingo laughed, reaching for his morning paper. "Honey, my cholesterol is one three zero, my resting heart rate is fifty-six. I am a lean, mean fighting machine, Doctor!"

"But what about ten years from now?" Patricia Chavez, M.D., asked.

"I'll have ten complete physicals between now and then, and I will adjust my lifestyle according to how those work out," Domingo Chavez, master of science (international relations), answered, buttering his toast. The bread in this country, he'd learned, was just fabulous. Why did people knock English food? He began reading the front-page story on the previous day's events in Bern.

DR. CAROL Brightling awoke, patted her only companion, a calico cat named Jiggs, and stepped into the shower. Ten minutes later, with a towel wrapped around her head, she opened the door and got the morning papers. The coffee machine had already made its two cups of Mountain Grown Folger's, and in the refrigerator was the plastic box full of melon sections. Next she switched on the radio to catch the morning edition of *All Things Considered,* beginning her news fix, which would go on through most of the day. Her job in the White House was mainly reading, and today she had to meet with that bozo from the Department of Energy who still thought it important to build H-bombs, which she would advise the President against, which advice he would probably decline.

This President was anything but an environmental President. Worse, he was using her as political camouflage. That appalled her, or would have under other circumstances. But here she was, a senior adviser to the President of the United States. *That* meant she saw him a couple of times per week. It meant he *read* her policy recommendations. It meant she had *access* to the media's top-drawer people, was free to pursue her own agenda . . . within reason.

But she paid a price, she thought, reaching down to scratch Jiggs's ears.

"So, Mr. Henriksen, who were they?" the *Fox News* morning anchor asked his guest expert.

"We don't know much beyond the name of the purported leader, Ernst Model. Model was once part of the Baader-Meinhof gang, the notorious German communist terrorist group from the '70s and '80s. Baader-Meinhof used kidnappings to extort money from their victims' corporate and family ties."

"So was this a terrorist incident or just a bank robbery?"

"No telling as yet, but I would not discount robbery as a motive. One of the things people forget about terrorists is that they have to eat, too, and you need money to do that."

"How would you rate the takedown?"

"Pretty good. The TV coverage shows no errors at all."

"Your company, Global Security, trains local police forces in SWAT tactics, doesn't it?"

"Yes, it does. And we could use this Swiss operation as a textbook example of how it's done," Henriksen said—because his corporation trained foreign police forces as well, and being nice to the Swiss wouldn't hurt his bottom line one bit.

"Well, Mr. Henriksen, thanks for joining us this morning. International terrorism expert William Henriksen, CEO of Global Security, Inc., an international consulting firm. It's twenty-four minutes after the hour." In the studio Henriksen kept his professional face on until five seconds after the light on the nearest camera went out. At his corporate headquarters they would have already taped this interview to add to their vast library. GSI was known over most of the world, and their introductory tape included snippets from many such interviews. This one had gone well, he thought.

POPOV'S four-engine Airbus A-340 touched down on time at JFK International. You could always trust the Swiss to do everything on time. His first-class seat was close to the door, which allowed him to be the third passenger out; then he went to claim his bags and go through the ordeal of U.S. Customs. A short while later a cab dropped him off at his employer's office.

"SO HOW did it go?" the boss asked.

"Much as I expected," Popov replied. "They were foolish—really rather amateurish despite all the training we gave them back in the '80s. I told them to feel free to rob the bank as cover for the real mission."

"Which was?"

"To be killed. At least, that is what I understood your intentions to be, sir." His words occasioned a smile of a sort Popov wasn't used to.

"What happened to the money?" the boss wanted to know.

A diffident reply: "I'm quite sure the Swiss will find a use for it." Certainly his banker would. "Surely you did not expect me to recover it?"

A shake of the boss's head. "No, not really, and it was a trivial sum anyway."

Trivial sum? No Soviet-employed agent had ever gotten so much in a single payment. Ernst Model had been an amateur, but this man was not. Something to keep in mind, the former spy told himself in large red mental letters.

There followed a few seconds of silence. Then, "I require another operation."

"What, exactly?" Popov asked, and got the answer immediately.

THE problem was environmental tolerance. They knew the baseline organism was as effective as it needed to be. It was just so delicate. Exposed to air, it died far too easily. They weren't sure why exactly, and the uncertainty had been a great annoyance until a member of the team had come up with a solution. They'd used genetic-engineering technology to graft cancer genes into the organism. The results had been striking. The new organism was far stronger. The proof was on the electron microscope's TV screen. Tiny strands exposed to air and light for ten hours before being reintroduced into the culture dish were replicating themselves into millions more little strands, which had only one purpose—to eat tissue. In this case it was kidney tissue, though liver was just as vulnerable. Because it was her project, the technician got to name it.

Shiva, she thought. The most complex of the Hindu gods, by turns the Destroyer and the Restorer, who controlled poison meant to destroy mankind, and one of whose consorts was Kali, the goddess of death herself. Shiva. *Perfect.*

She took a sample of Shiva, sealed in a stainless steel container, and walked down the corridor to another lab. "Hi, Maggie," the head of that lab said in greeting. "Got something for me?"

"Hey, Steve." She handed the container over. "This is the one."

"What are we calling it?" Steve took the container and set it on a countertop.

"Shiva, I think."

"Sounds ominous," Steve observed with a smile.

"Oh, it is," Maggie promised. Steve was the company's best man on vaccines. "Ten hours in the open, and it shows good UV tolerance. Not too sure about direct sunlight, though."

"What about the atomization system?"

"Still have to try it," she admitted, "but it won't be a problem." Both knew the organism should easily tolerate passage through the spray nozzles of a fogging system—which would be checked in one of their big environmental chambers.

"Thanks, Maggie." Steve turned his back and inserted the container into one of the laboratory glove boxes to open it in order to begin his work on the vaccine. Much of the work was already done. The baseline agent was well known, and the government had funded his company's vaccine work after the big scare the year before. And Steve was known far and wide as one of the best around for generating, capturing, and replicating antibodies to excite a person's immune system. Now he turned back to his worktable and computer keyboard and made some notations. The Project allowed only computers for recordkeeping, and all the notes were electronically encrypted.

"Getting the aircraft is your business. Where to fly it—that we can help with," Popov assured his host.

"Where?" the host, Hans Fürchtner, asked.

"The key is to become lost to air-traffic-control radar and to travel far enough that fighter aircraft cannot track you, then to land in a friendly place," Popov explained.

"The world is awash with radar systems," the host objected.

"True," Popov conceded, "but air-traffic radars do not see aircraft. They see the return signals from aircraft radar transponders. Only military radars see the aircraft themselves, and what African country has a proper air-defense network? Your escape is not a problem *if* you get as far as an international airport, my friend. That," he reminded them, "is the difficult part. Once you disappear over Africa— Well, that is your choice, then."

"A pity about Ernst," the host said quietly.

"Ernst was a fool!" his lady friend, Petra Dortmund, countered with an angry gesture. "He should have robbed a smaller bank. He was trying to make a statement." Popov had known Petra Dortmund only by reputation until today. She had been pretty once, but now her once blond hair was dyed brown, and her thin face was severe, the cheeks sunken and hollow, the eyes rimmed in dark circles. She was almost unrecognizable, which explained why European police hadn't snatched her up yet, along with her longtime lover, Hans Fürchtner, who had gone the other way. Fürchtner, a good thirty kilos overweight, looked like a banker now, fat and happy, no longer the driven, committed Communist he'd been in the '70s and '80s—at least not visibly so. They lived in the mountains south of Munich, and because both of them painted, neighbors thought them to be artists. It was a hobby unknown to their country's police.

Fürchtner and Dortmund must miss the safe houses in the old East Germany, the DDR, Dmitriy Popov thought, where serious intelligence officers had fed them information with which to plan their operations. They had accomplished several decent operations, the best being the kidnapping and interrogation of an American sergeant who serviced nuclear artillery shells. This mission had been assigned them by the Soviet GRU. Much had been learned from it. The sergeant's body had later been discovered in the mountains of Bavaria, apparently the result of a nasty traffic accident.

"So what is it that you want to learn?" Petra asked.

"Electronic access codes to the international trading system," said Popov.

"So you, too, are a common thief now?" Hans asked.

"A very uncommon thief, my sponsor is. If we are to restore a socialist, *progressive* alternative to capitalism, we need funding and we need to instill a certain lack of confidence in the capitalist nervous system, do we not?" Popov paused. "You know who I am. You know where I worked. Do you think I have forsaken my beliefs?"

"You ask us to give up much," Hans Fürchtner pointed out.

"You will be properly provided for. My sponsor—"

"Who is that?" Petra asked.

"This you may not know," Popov replied quietly. "Operational security is paramount. You are supposed to know these things," he reminded them. They took the mild rebuke well, as he'd expected. These two fools were true believers, as Ernst Model had been, though they were somewhat brighter and far more vicious.

"So, Iosef Andreyevich," Hans said—they knew Popov by one of his many cover names, in this case Iosef Andreyevich Serov—"when do you wish us to act?"

"I will call in a week. If you are willing—"

"We are," Petra assured him. "We need to make our plans."

"Then I shall call you in a week for your schedule."

IT WAS odd the way it worked. Peter Covington's Team 1 was now the go team, ready to depart Hereford at a moment's notice, while Chavez's Team 2 stood down for two weeks. But it was the latter that was running complex exercises, while the former did little but morning P.T. and routine marksmanship training. They were worried about a training accident that could hurt or even cripple a team member, thus breaking up a field team at a delicate moment.

That was the problem with this sort of work, Chavez knew. Rainbow members had been selected for many reasons, not least of which was their brutally competitive nature. Every man pushed himself to the limit in everything. It made for injuries. Three more days to go for Team 1, and then, Chavez knew, it would be his turn.

He entered the headquarters building, returning the salute of the guard as he went inside. The Brits sure saluted funny, he thought. Once inside, he found Major Bennett at his desk. "Hey, Sam."

"Good morning, Ding. Coffee?" the air force officer asked.

"No, thanks. Anything happening anywhere?"

A shake of the head. "Quiet day."

Bennett was working on his computerized list of known terrorists, shifting through photos and summaries of what was known about these people—generally, not much.

"What's this?" Ding asked, pointing at the computer.

"A new toy we're using. Noonan got it from the FBI. It ages the subject photos. This one is Petra Dortmund. We only have two photos of her, both almost fifteen years old. So I'm aging her by fifteen years. Nice thing about women—no beards," Bennett observed with a chuckle. "Check out the eyes."

"Not a girl I'd try to pick up in a bar," Chavez observed.

CHAPTER 3
FINANCE

POPOV stepped off his airliner and walked onto the concourse like any other businessman, carrying his attaché case with its combination lock and not a single piece of metal inside, lest some magnetometer operator ask him to open it and so reveal the paper currency inside. Terrorists had really ruined air travel for everyone, the former KGB officer thought to himself. But traveling by train was *so* boring.

Hans Fürchtner was at his designated location, reading *Der Spiegel* and wearing the agreed-upon brown leather jacket. He saw Popov carrying his black case in his left hand, striding down the concourse. Fürchtner finished his coffee and followed Popov into the parking garage. Fürchtner's car was in a distant corner on the first level, a blue Volkswagen Golf.

"Grüss Gott," Popov said, on sitting in the right-front seat.

"Good morning," Fürchtner replied in English.

The Russian dialed the combinations into the locks of the case, opened the lid, and placed it in his host's lap. "You should find everything in order."

"It's heavy," Fürchtner observed.

"True," Dmitriy Arkadeyevich agreed. "But it could be worse. I might have paid you in gold," he joked, then decided to make his own play. "Too heavy to carry on the mission?"

"It *is* a complication, Iosef Andreyevich."

"Well, I can hold the money for you and deliver it to you upon the completion of your mission. Though, honestly, it makes me nervous to travel with so much cash. What if I am robbed?" he said theatrically.

Fürchtner found that very amusing. "Here, in Österreich, robbed on the street? My friend, these capitalist sheep are very closely regulated," he said.

"Besides, I do not even know where you will be going, and I really do not need to know—at this time anyway," Popov said.

"The Central African Republic is our ultimate destination."

"Well, my friend, it is your decision." Popov patted the attaché case still open in Fürchtner's lap.

The German considered that for half a minute or so. "I have seen the money," he concluded to his guest's utter delight. Fürchtner lifted a thousand-note packet of the cash and riffled it like a deck of cards before putting it back. Next he scribbled a note and placed it inside the case. "Here is the address. We will be there starting late tomorrow, I imagine."

Popov wondered about that. He'd be surprised if they even boarded an aircraft, much less got it to Africa. But Hans and Petra were believers. "Are you sure, my friend?" he asked.

"*Ja,* I am sure." Fürchtner closed the case, reset the locks, and passed it to Popov.

The Russian accepted the responsibility with proper gravity. "I will guard this carefully." All the way to my bank in Bern. Then he extended his hand. "Good luck, and please be careful."

"*Danke.* We will get you the information you require."

THE home of Erwin Ostermann was a former baronial schloss, or castle, thirty kilometers outside Vienna. A dwelling of six thousand square meters divided into three floors, on a thousand hectares of land, it was totally in keeping with Ostermann's stature in the financial community. It was magnificent, Hans Fürchtner thought, just the sort of thing for an arrogant class enemy.

Pulling up close to the schloss, Fürchtner stopped the rented Mercedes and turned right, as though looking for a parking place. Coming around the rear of the building, he saw Ostermann's Sikorsky S-76B helicopter. Good. They'd be using that later. Fürchtner continued the circuit of the schloss and parked about fifty meters from the main entrance. "Are you ready, Petra?"

"*Ja,*" was her tense reply. It had been years since either had run an operation. They started walking to the front door when a delivery truck came up. Its doors opened, and two men got out, carrying large boxes in their arms. One waved to Hans and Petra to go up the stone steps, which they did. Hans hit the button, and a moment later the door opened.

"*Guten Tag,*" Hans said. "We have an appointment with Herr Ostermann."

"Your name?"

"Bauer," Fürchtner said. "Hans Bauer."

"Flower delivery," one of the other two men said.

"Please come in. I will call Herr Ostermann," the butler—whatever he was—said.

"*Danke,*" Fürchtner replied, waving for Petra to precede him through the ornate door. The deliverymen came in behind, carrying their boxes. The butler closed the door, then turned to walk left toward a phone. He lifted it. Then he stopped. There was a pistol in the woman's hand aimed right into his face.

"What is this?"

"This," Petra Dortmund replied with a warm smile, "is my appointment." It was a Walther P-38 automatic pistol.

The butler swallowed hard as he saw the deliverymen open their boxes and reveal light submachine guns, which they loaded in front of him. One of them opened the front door and waved. In seconds two more young men entered, both similarly armed.

Fürchtner took a few steps to look around. There were no other servants in view, though he could hear a distant vacuum cleaner. He turned to the two most recent arrivals and pointed them west on the first floor. The kitchen was that way, and there would doubtless be people there to control.

"Where is Herr Ostermann?" Petra asked next.

"He is not here. He—"

This occasioned a movement of her pistol right against his mouth. "His automobiles and helicopter are here. Now tell us where he is."

"In the library, upstairs."

"*Gut.* Take us there," she ordered. The butler looked into her eyes for the first time and found them far more intimidating than the pistol in her hand. He nodded and turned toward the main staircase, which was gilt, with a rich red carpet held in place with brass bars, sweeping on an elegant curve to the right as they climbed to the second floor. Ostermann was a quintessential capitalist who'd made his fortune trading shares in various industrial concerns. A string puller, Petra Dortmund thought, a *Spinne,* a spider, and this was the center of his web.

At the top of the staircase the butler turned right, leading them down a wide hall into a large room. Three people were there, a man and two women, working away at computers. "This is Herr Bauer," the butler said in a shaky voice. "He wishes to see Herr Ostermann."

"You have an appointment?" the senior secretary asked.

"You will take us in *now,*" Petra announced. Then the gun came into view, and the three people stopped what they were doing and looked at the intruders with open mouths and pale faces.

Ostermann's home was several hundred years old but not entirely a thing of the past. The male secretary, an executive assistant, was named Gerhardt Dengler. Under the edge of his desk was an alarm button. He thumbed this hard and long while he stared at the visitors. The wire led to the schloss's central alarm panel and from there to the alarm company. Twenty kilometers away, the employees at the central station responded by calling the office of the *Staatspolizei.* Then one of them called the schloss for confirmation.

"May I answer it?" Gerhardt asked Petra. He got a nod and lifted the receiver. "Herr Ostermann's office."

"Hier ist Traudl," the alarm company's secretary said.

"Guten Tag, Traudl. Hier ist Gerhardt," the executive assistant said. "Have you called about the horse?" That was the phrase for serious trouble.

"Yes. When is the foal due?" she asked.

"A few more weeks. We will tell you when the time comes."

"Danke, Gerhardt. Wiedersehen."

With that, he hung up. "It is about the horses," he explained to Petra. "We have a mare in foal and—"

"Silence," Petra said quietly, waving for Hans to approach the double doors into Ostermann's office. Then she pointed to the executive assistant. "Your name is . . ."

"Dengler," the man replied. "Gerhardt Dengler."

"Take us in, Herr Dengler," she suggested in a strangely childlike voice.

Gerhardt walked slowly to the double doors, his movements wooden. He turned the knobs and pushed, revealing Ostermann's office. The desk was huge and sat on a red wool rug. A tall man with regal gray hair and a trim figure sat with his back to them, examining a computer display. "Herr Ostermann?" Dengler said.

"Yes, Gerhardt?" When there was no response, the man turned in his swivel chair. "What is this?" he asked, his blue eyes going very wide when he saw the guns. "Who—"

"We are commanders of the Red Workers' Faction," Petra informed the trader. "And you are our prisoner. We will be taking a trip. If you behave yourself, you will come to no harm. If you do not, you and others will be killed. Is that clear?" To make sure it was, she again aimed her pistol at Dengler's head.

Ostermann's face contorted itself into shock and disbelief. *This* could not be happening. Not here, not in his own office. Next came the outraged denial of the facts he could see before him and then came fear. The process lasted five or six seconds. It was always the same. Petra had seen it before, but she'd forgotten the sheer joy of the power she held in her hands. How had she ever gone so long without exercising it?

"What do you want of me?" Ostermann asked finally.

"We want your personal access codes to the international trading network," Fürchtner told him.

"What do you mean?"

"The computer access codes which tell you what is going on."

"But those are public. Anyone can have them."

"Yes, certainly they are. That is why everyone has a house like this one." Petra managed an amused sneer.

"Herr Ostermann," Fürchtner said patiently, "we know there is a special network for people such as you so that you can take advantage of special market conditions and profit by them. You think us fools?"

Oh, my Lord, they think I have access to something that does not exist, and I will never be able to persuade them otherwise. Ostermann's face was now as pale as his white Turnbull and Asser shirt.

CAPTAIN Willi Altmark parked his Audi radio car behind a tree, almost totally concealed from the house. The first order of police business was to check the license-plate numbers of the vehicles parked close to the house. The automobile was a rental. The truck tags had been stolen two days before. He then made a call to one of Herr Ostermann's business associates. He needed to know how many employees might be in the building. He also had the phones tapped. Incoming calls were given busy signals, and outgoing calls would be recorded at the central telephone exchange, but there had been none, which suggested to Captain Altmark that the criminals were all inside, since they were not seeking external help. Unless they were using cellular phones. He didn't have the equipment to intercept those.

He soon had three additional police cars under his command. One of these looped around the property. The first thing he learned was that Ostermann owned a helicopter, an American-made Sikorsky S-76B. The landing pad was two hundred meters from the house, a good three hundred meters from the tree line. This meant that some really good riflemen were needed, but his preset response team had them. Then he received a very surprising radio call from the head of the *Staatspolizei*.

THE stewardess hadn't received instructions to get Team 2 off more quickly than anyone else, but she suspected there was something odd about them. They had not been on her computerized manifest, and they were politer than the average business travelers. Their appearances were unremarkable except all looked very fit, and all had arrived together in a single bunch. They left together, too, most giving her a smile on the way out of the 737. "*Au revoir,* madam," the last one said as he passed with a very Gallic evaluative sweep of her figure and a charming smile.

"Louis," an American voice observed, "you don't ever turn it off, do you?"

"Is it a crime to look at a pretty woman, George?" Loiselle asked with a wink.

Three minutes later they were in a pair of vans heading off the flight line with a police escort. Twenty minutes after that the vans stopped outside the main entrance to Schloss Ostermann.

Two in a row for Team 2, Chavez thought. Terrorist incidents weren't supposed to happen so closely together, were they? He walked over to the senior officer. "Hello, I am Major Chavez. This is Dr. Bellow and Sergeant Major Price."

"Captain Wilhelm Altmark," the man said.

"What do we know?"

"We know there are two criminals inside, probably more. You know what their demands are?"

"Airplane to somewhere was the last I heard. And a list of prisoners to be released. Midnight deadline?"

"Correct. No changes in the past hour."

"How will we get them to the airport?" Ding asked.

"Herr Ostermann has a private helicopter and pad about two hundred meters behind the house."

"Flight crew?"

"We have them over there." Altmark pointed.

"Who's been speaking with them?" Dr. Bellow asked from behind the shorter Chavez.

"I have," Altmark replied.

"Okay, we need to talk, Captain."

Chavez headed over to a van where he could change along with the rest of the team. For this night's mission—the sun was just setting—they wore mottled green coveralls over their body armor. Weapons were issued and loaded. Ten minutes later the team was at the edge of the tree line, everyone with binoculars, checking out the building. "Where you want us, boss?" Homer Johnston asked Chavez.

"Far side, both sides, cross fire on the chopper pad. Right now, people, and when you're set up, give me radio calls to check in. You know the drill," Chavez said, then turned to Altmark. "Do we have a layout of the house?"

"Layout?" the Austrian cop asked.

"Diagram, map, blueprints," Ding explained.

"Ach, yes, here." Altmark led them to his car. Blueprints were spread on the hood. "Here, as you see, forty-six rooms, not counting the basements."

"It's as big as a castle," Ding observed.

"That is what the word 'schloss' means, Herr Major," Altmark informed him.

"Doc?"

Bellow came over. "From what Captain Altmark tells me, they've been pretty businesslike to this point. No hysterical threats. They gave a deadline of midnight for movement to the airport, else they say they will start killing hostages. Their language is German, with a German accent, you said, Captain?"

Altmark nodded. "*Ja.* They are German, not Austrian. We have only one name, Herr Wolfgang, and we have no known criminal terrorist by that name or pseudonym. Also, he said they are of the Red Workers' Faction, but we have no word on that organization either."

Neither did Rainbow. "So we don't know very much?" Chavez asked Bellow.

"Not much at all, Ding."

"Full moon tonight," Price observed. "And not much cloud cover."

"Yeah," Ding noted in some discomfort when he looked up at the sky. "Captain, do you have searchlights we can use?"

"The fire department will have them," Altmark said.

"Could you please order them brought here?"

"*Ja.*"

"We'll give these people what they want and let them think that they are in control . . . until it is time for us to take control."

THINGS had gone well to this point, Hans and Petra thought. They had their primary hostage under tight control, and his lackeys were now in the same room, with easy access to Ostermann's personal bathroom. Hostages needed such access; otherwise it stripped them of their dignity and made them desperate. Desperate people did foolish things, and what Hans and Petra needed at the moment was control over their every action.

SERGEANT First Class Homer Johnston was in his gillie suit, an overall-type garment made of rags sewn on a gridded matrix, whose purpose was to make him appear to be a bush or a pile of leaves or compost—anything but a person with a rifle. The rifle was set up on its bipod, the hinged flaps on the front and back lenses of his telescopic sight flipped up. He'd picked a good place to the east of the helicopter pad that would allow him to cover the entire distance between the helicopter and the house. He thumbed his radio microphone. "Lead, Rifle Two One."

"Rifle Two One, Lead."

"In place and set up. I show no movement in the house."

"Rifle Two Two, in place and set up. I also see no movement," Sergeant Dieter Weber reported from his spot, two hundred and fifty-six meters from Johnston.

"Achtung," a voice called. Johnston turned to see an Austrian cop approaching. *"Hier,"* the man said, handing over some photos and withdrawing rapidly. Johnston looked at them. Good. Shots of the hostages, but none of the bad guys. Well, at least he'd know whom *not* to shoot. "Dieter?" he said over his direct radio link.

"Yes, Homer?"

"They get you the photos?"

"Yes, I have them."

"No lights inside."

"Ja. Our friends are being clever."

EDDIE Price scanned the blueprints. "It's a bloody nightmare on the inside, Ding," he said.

"That's the truth. Lots of places for the bad guys to hide and snipe at us. We'd need our own chopper to do this right." But they didn't have a helicopter. That was something to talk with Clark about. Rainbow hadn't been fully thought through. "I'm thinking about letting them walk to the helicopter and taking them down that way rather than forcing our way in."

Noonan came over. "Dark and cold enough for the thermal viewers to start working," he said helpfully.

"Yeah." Chavez picked up his radio mike. "Team, Lead, go thermal." Then he turned. "What about cell phones?"

Noonan could do little more than shrug. There were now something like three hundred civilians gathered around, as well as the local TV people. If one of them had a cell phone and someone inside did as well, all that person outside had to do was dial his buds on the inside to tell them what was going down.

"Tim, make a note for when we get back about dealing with cellular phones and radios outside the objective. Captain Altmark! The lights, are they here yet?"

"Just arrived, *ja*. We have three sets." Altmark pointed.

Chavez told him where he wanted them.

THE thermal viewers relied on difference in temperature to make an image. The evening was cooling down rapidly and with it the stone walls of the house. Dieter Weber made the first spot. "Lead, Rifle Two Two. I have a thermal target first floor, fourth window from the west."

"Okay! That one's in the kitchen." It was the voice of Hank Patterson, who was hovering over the blueprints. "Can you tell me anything else, Dieter?"

"Negative. Just a shape," the German sniper replied.

"This is Pierce. I have one—first floor, second window from east wall."

KLAUS Rosenthal was Ostermann's head gardener and at seventy-one the oldest member of the domestic staff. His wife was at home in her bed, with a nurse in close attendance handling her medications, and worrying about him, he was sure, and that worry could be dangerous to her. Hilda Rosenthal had a heart condition. Klaus was in the kitchen along with the rest of the domestic staff. He'd been getting a glass of water when these swine had stormed in, their weapons showing. The close one was either a Berliner or from West Prussia, judging by his accent, and he'd recently been a skinhead, or so it appeared from the uniform-length stubble on his head. A product of the DDR, the now defunct East Germany. One of the new Nazis who'd grown out of that fallen communist nation. Rosenthal had met the old ones at Belzec concentration camp as a boy. He closed his eyes. He still had the nightmares that went along with the five-digit number tattooed on his forearm. The other staff members, all Christians, had never experienced this, but Klaus Rosenthal had, and he knew what to expect.

DING ordered the lights switched on at eleven twenty. The front and both sides of the schloss were bathed in yellow-white light but not the back, which projected a triangular shadow all the way to the helicopter and beyond into the trees. "Oso," Chavez said, "get over to Dieter and set up close to there."

"Roger." First Sergeant Vega hoisted his M-60 onto his shoulder and made his way through the woods.

Louis Loiselle and George Tomlinson had the hardest part. They were dressed in their night greens. The coveralls over their black ninja suits looked like graph paper, light green background crosshatched in darker green lines. The blazing lights would help. Aimed at and somewhat over the schloss, they created an artificial well of darkness into which the green suits should disappear. Tomlinson and Loiselle moved out from different directions, keeping inside the triangular shadow all the way in. It took them twenty minutes of crawling.

"EXCELLENT," Fürchtner said shortly before midnight. He could barely see the turning rotor, but the blinking flying lights told the tale. "So we begin. Herr Ostermann, stand up!"

Petra Dortmund made her way downstairs ahead of the important hostages. She frowned, wondering if she should be disappointed that they'd not killed a hostage to show their resolve. That time could come later, when they started the serious interrogation aboard the airliner. She activated her radio and called the rest of her people. They were assembling in the foyer as she came down the main staircase, along with the six hostages from the kitchen area.

THEY were taking him, Rosenthal knew, to die, and as in his nightmares of Belzec he was doing nothing! The realization caused a crippling wave of headachelike pain. His body twisted left, and he saw the main food-preparation table—and on it a small paring knife. In that moment he made his decision and snapped up the knife, tucking it up his right sleeve. Perhaps fate would give him a chance. If so, Klaus Rosenthal promised himself, this time he'd take it.

"TEAM Two, this is Lead," Chavez said over the radio links. "We should have them start to come out shortly. Everybody check in."

"Rifle Two One," Homer Johnston said. His night-vision system was now attached to his telescopic sight and trained on the building's rear doors.

"Rifle Two Two," Weber called in a second later.

"Oso," Vega reported. He licked his lips as he brought his weapon up to his shoulder, his face covered with camouflage paint.

"Connolly."

"Lincoln."

"McTyler."

"Patterson."

"Pierce." They all reported from their spots on the grass.

"Price," the sergeant major reported from the left-side front seat of the helicopter.

"Okay, Team, we are weapons-free. Normal rules of engagement in effect. Stay sharp, people," Chavez added unnecessarily. His position was eighty yards away from the helicopter, marginal range for his MP-10, with his night-vision goggles (NVGs) aimed at the building.

"Door opening," Weber reported a fraction before Johnston.

"I have movement," Rifle Two One confirmed.

"Captain Altmark, this is Chavez. Kill the TV feed now," Ding ordered on his secondary radio.

The police captain shouted an order at the TV director. The cameras would stay on but would not broadcast, and the tapes from this point on were considered classified. The signal going out on the airways merely showed talking heads.

"Door open now," Johnston said from his sniper perch. "I see one subject, female, dark hair, holding a pistol. Hostage in view. It's Little Man," he said, meaning Dengler. Ostermann was Big Man, and the female secretaries were Blondie and Brownie, so named for their hair color. They didn't have photos for the domestic staff, hence no names for them. Known bad guys were "subjects." They hesitated at the door. Johnston centered the crosshair reticle on the face. "Come on out, honey," he breathed. "Dieter?" he asked, keying his radio.

"On-target, Homer," Rifle Two Two replied. "We know this face, I think. . . . Lead, Rifle Two Two—"

"Rifle Two, Lead."

"The female subject—we have seen her face recently. Baader-Meinhof, Red Workers' Faction, partnered with a man. Marxist, experienced terrorist, killed an American soldier, I think."

Price broke in, thinking about the computer-morphing program they'd played with earlier in the week. "Petra Dortmund, perhaps?"

"*Ja!* That is the one! And her partner is Hans Fürchtner," Weber replied. *"Komm 'raus, Petra,"* he went on in his native language. *"Komm zu mir, Liebschen."*

SOMETHING was bothering her. She could see the helicopter with its blinking lights and turning rotor, but her foot did not want to make the move out of the schloss. Her blue eyes screwed up. The trees were lit so brightly by the lights on the far side of the house, with their shadows stretching out to the helicopter like black fingers, and maybe the thing that discomforted her was the deathlike image before her. Then she shook her head, disposing of the thought. She yanked at her two hostages and made her way down the six granite steps to the grass.

"MALE subject in view—Fürchtner," Johnston said over the radio. "He has Big Man with him . . . and Brownie also, I think."

"Agree," Weber said, staring through his ten-power sight. "Subject Fürchtner, Big Man, and Brownie are in sight. Fürchtner appears to be armed with pistol only. Starting down the steps now. Another subject at the door, armed with submachine gun. Two hostages with him."

"They're being smart," Chavez observed. "Coming in groups."

As they approached the chopper, Eddie Price got out of the helicopter and opened both side doors for loading. He'd already stashed his pistol in the map pocket of the left-side copilot's door. He was wearing a blue shirt with wings pinned above the breast pocket and a tag that announced his name as Tony. A wireless earpiece gave him the radio link to the rest of the team, along with a microphone chip inside his collar.

"Brush your hair if you can hear me," Chavez told him from his position. A moment later he saw Price's left hand go up nervously to push his hair back from his eyes. "Okay, Eddie. Stay cool, man."

"Armed subject at the door with three hostages," Weber called. "No, no. Two armed subjects with three hostages. Hostage Blondie is with this one. Old man and middle-aged woman, all dressed as servants."

"At least one more bad guy," Ding breathed, and at least three more hostages to come. "Helicopter can't carry all of them." What were they planning to do with the extras? Kill them?

"I see two more armed subjects and three hostages inside the back door," Johnston reported.

"That's all the hostages," Noonan said. "Total of six subjects, then. How are they armed, Rifle One?"

"Submachine guns. Look like Uzis."

"Riflemen, take aim on Subject Dortmund," Chavez said.

"On-target," Weber managed to say first. Johnston swiveled to take aim a fraction of a second later, the crosshair reticle centered just above and between Petra Dortmund's eyes as she walked to the helicopter, not knowing that two sniper rifles followed her head every centimeter of the way. The important part came when she got to the chopper. If she went around the right side, Johnston would lose her, leaving her to Weber's rifle. If she went left, then Dieter would lose her to his rifle. She seemed to be favoring . . . Yes, Dortmund walked to the left side of the aircraft.

"Rifle Two Two off-target," Weber reported at once. "I have no shot at this time."

"On-target. Rifle Two One is on-target," Johnston assured Chavez. H'm, let Little Man in first, honey, he thought.

Petra Dortmund did just that, pushing Dengler in the left-side door ahead of her, probably figuring to sit in the middle herself, so as to be less vulnerable to a shot from outside. A good theoretical call, Homer Johnston thought, but off the mark in this case.

Gerhardt Dengler strapped himself in under the aim of Petra's pistol, commanding himself to be brave. Then he looked forward and felt hope. The pilot was the usual man, but the copilot was not. Their eyes met, and Dengler looked down and out of the aircraft, afraid that he'd give something away.

Good man, Eddie Price thought.

"Riflemen, do you have your targets?" Chavez asked.

"Rifle Two One, affirmative. Target in sight."

"Rifle Two Two, negative. I have something in the way. Recommend switch to Subject Fürchtner."

"Okay, Rifle Two Two, switch to Fürchtner. Rifle Two One, Dortmund is all yours."

"Roger that, Lead," Johnston confirmed.

Okay, Chavez thought, we have Subject 1 in the chopper and a gun on her. Subject 2 was in the open, two thirds of the way to the chopper and a gun on him. Two more bad guys were approaching the halfway point, with Mike Pierce and Steve Lincoln within forty meters, and the last two subjects they'd managed to identify still in the house, with Louis Loiselle and George Tomlinson in the bushes right and left of them. His plan was holding up. The key now was the final team of subjects.

ROSENTHAL saw the snipers. It was to be expected, though it had occurred to no one. He was the head gardener. The lawn was his, and the odd piles of material left and right of the helicopter were things that didn't belong. He'd seen the TV shows and movies. This was a terrorist incident, and the police would respond. And there were two *things* on his lawn that hadn't been there in the morning.

"HERE they come," George Tomlinson announced when he saw a woman's leg step out of the house, followed by a man's, then a woman's. "One subject and two hostages out. Two more hostages to go."

FÜRCHTNER was almost there, heading to the right side of the helicopter, to the comfort of Dieter Weber. But then he stopped, seeing inside the open right-side door to where Gerhardt Dengler was sitting, and decided to go to the other side.

"Off-target. Rifle Two Two is off the subject," Weber announced rather loudly over the radio circuit.

"Retarget on the next group," Chavez ordered.

"Done," Weber said. "I'm on the lead subject, group three."

"Rifle Two One, report!"

"Rifle Two One tight on Subject Dortmund," Homer Johnston replied.

"Ready here!" Loiselle reported next from the bushes at the back of the house. "We have the fourth group now."

Chavez took a deep breath. All the bad guys were now in the open, and now it was time. "Okay, Lead to Team, execute, execute!"

SEVEN meters behind their targets Loiselle and Tomlinson lined up their tritium-lit sights. Both subjects were taller than their hostages, which made things easy. Both MP-10 submachine guns were set on three-round burst. Both sergeants fired at the same instant, and both bodies dropped limp to the grass.

"This is George. Two subjects dead!" Tomlinson called over the radio as he started running to the hostages who were still walking toward the helicopter.

HOMER Johnston's right index finger pushed gently back on the set trigger. The bullet drove through the thickest part of Petra Dortmund's skull.

EDDIE Price pulled his pistol from the map pocket in the left-side door of the aircraft and dived out the helicopter's autolike door, aiming it one-handed at Hans Fürchtner's head, firing one round just below his left eye. Fürchtner fell to the ground, his hand still holding Erwin Ostermann's upper arm and pulling him down somewhat until the fingers came loose.

THAT left two. Steve Lincoln took careful aim from a kneeling position, then stopped as his target passed behind the head of an elderly man wearing a vest. Weber got the other one, whose head exploded like a melon from the impact of the rifle bullet.

Rosenthal saw the head burst apart, but the large stubbly head next to his was still there, a machine gun still in his hand—and nobody was shooting at this one. Then Stubble Head's eyes met his, and there was fear/hate/shock there, and Rosenthal's stomach turned to ice. All time stopped around him. The paring knife came out of his sleeve and into his hand, which he swung wildly, catching the back of Stubble Head's left hand. Stubble Head's eyes went wider as the elderly man jumped aside. That cleared the way for Steve Lincoln, who fired a three-round burst.

"CLEAR!" Price called. "Clear aircraft!"
"Clear house!" Tomlinson announced.
"Clear middle!" Lincoln said last of all.

THE cops were swarming in now, plus a covey of ambulances with blinking blue lights. Captain Altmark arrived at the helicopter with Chavez at his side. Price walked toward them, fishing in his pocket for his curved briar pipe, which he lit with a kitchen match, his never-changing ritual for a mission completed.

Mike Pierce was assisting the hostages, all sitting for the moment while Steve Lincoln stood over them, his MP-10 out and ready. But then a gaggle of Austrian police exploded out the back door, telling him there were no terrorists left inside the building. With that, he safed his weapon and came up to the elderly gent. "Well done, sir," he told Klaus Rosenthal.

"Ja," was all Rosenthal was able to say, and that took three breaths.

Pierce reached down to shake his hand. It hadn't really mattered very much, but resistance by a hostage was rare, and it had clearly been a gutsy move by the old gent.

"Amerikaner?"

"Sh." Sergeant Pierce held a finger up to his lips. "Please don't tell anyone, sir."

Twenty minutes later Team 2 was back at the assembly point, packing their gear for the ride to the airport. The TV lights and cameras were running but rather far away. The team was relaxing now, the stress bleeding off with the successful completion of their mission. Price puffed on his pipe outside the van, then tapped it out on the heel of his boot before boarding.

CHAPTER 4
COVERAGE

THE television coverage was out before Team 2 flew into Heathrow. Fortunately, the video of the event was hampered by the schloss's great size and the fact that the *Staatspolizei* kept the cameras well away from events. About the only decent shot was of a team member lighting a pipe, followed by Captain Wilhelm Altmark's summary of events for reporters. A special team of his country's police had dealt efficiently with the incident at Schloss Ostermann, he said, rescuing all of the hostages. No, unfortunately, no criminals had been arrested.

Popov turned his TV back to a cable channel. He hadn't learned much of anything, but he was a trained intelligence officer and therefore a thorough man. He poured himself an Absolut vodka to drink neat—he missed the superior Starka brand he would have had in Russia—and decided to obtain videotapes of the two terrorist incidents so he could study them.

In the hotel room with him was the attaché case filled with D-mark banknotes, which he would take to Bern the following day for deposit in his account before flying back to New York.

"THIS seems to work," Steve said quietly.

"How many strands fit inside?" Maggie asked.

"Anywhere from three to ten."

"And how large is the overall package?"

"Six microns. Would you believe it? The packaging is white in color, so in a water-spray environment it's just about invisible." The individual capsules couldn't be seen with the naked eye. Better still, their weight was such that they'd float in air about the same as dust particles, as readily breathable as secondhand smoke in a singles bar.

Once in the body, the coating would dissolve and allow the release of the Shiva strands into the lungs, where they could go to work.

SUBJECT 4 was the first, as expected. He was fifty-three years old, and his liver function was so far off the scale as to qualify him for a high place on the transplant list at the University of Pittsburgh medical center. His name was Chester something, Dr. John Killgore remembered.

Killgore entered the room and came over to the man's bunk. "Not feeling good, Chester?" Killgore asked from behind his mask.

"Stomach. Can't keep stuff down. Feel crummy all over."

"Well, come along with me, and we'll see what we can do."

"You say so, Doc," Chester replied.

Outside the door they put him in a wheelchair. It was only fifty yards to the clinical side of the installation. Two orderlies lifted Subject 4 onto a bed and restrained him with Velcro ties. Then one of the orderlies took a blood sample. Ten minutes later Killgore tested it for Shiva antibodies, and the sample turned blue, as expected. Chester, Subject 4, had less than a week to live—not as much as the six to twelve months to which his alcoholism had already limited him, but not really all that much of a reduction, was it? Killgore started an IV and hung a morphine drip that soon had Chester unconscious and even smiling slightly. Good. Subject 4 would die in relative peace. More than anything else, Dr. Killgore wanted to keep the process orderly.

Chester's early response to the virus had been a little unsettling— only half the time programmed—but it had been brought about by his grossly reduced liver function. It couldn't be helped. Some people would get hit sooner than others because of differing physical vulnerabilities, so the outbreak would start unevenly. It shouldn't matter in the eventual effects, though it would alert people sooner than he hoped it would. That would cause a run on the vaccines Steve Berg and his shop were developing. Vaccine A would be widely distributed after the rush to manufacture it, while vaccine B would go only to those people who were supposed to survive, people who understood what it was all about.

Killgore shook his head. There was a lot left to be done and, as usual, not enough time to do it.

"MAY I ask a question?" Popov asked in New York.

"Sure," the boss said, suspecting what it would be.

"What is the purpose of all this?"

"You really do not need to know at this time," was the expected reply to the expected question. "What went wrong in this case?"

Popov shrugged. "They were willing, but they made the mistake of underestimating the skill of the police response."

"It was the Austrian police?"

"So the news media said. I did not press my investigation further. Should I have done so?"

A shake of the head. "No. Just idle curiosity on my part."

So you don't care if these operations succeed or fail, Popov thought. Then why do you fund them? There was no logic to this.

"Stay in the city for a few days. I will call you when I need you."

"As you say, sir." Popov left the office and caught the next elevator to street level. Once there, he decided to walk south along Fifth Avenue to the public library with the lion statues in front.

Popov hadn't done this kind of research in ages, but he remembered how. His employer had been written about more than many politicians, Popov discovered—which was only just, as this man did far more important things. He was a genius both in his scientific field and in running a major corporation. But the news articles didn't help Popov much. There was little about his personal life except that he'd been divorced. A pity. His former wife seemed both attractive and intelligent, judging by the photos and appended information on her. Maybe two such intelligent people had difficulty staying together.

But there was nothing to connect the man with terrorists.

Popov had to admit that he really didn't know what sort of man he was working for, which was more than troubling. His life was now in pawn to a man whose motivations he didn't understand. Well, the former KGB officer thought as he returned the last of the periodicals to the clerk, there was an easy solution to that. He'd always have a bag packed and two false identities ready.

THE FOURTH MAN OFF THE Boeing 757 out of Raleigh-Durham was dressed in marine class-A's, with four-and-a-half rows of ribbons on his olive-colored uniform blouse. Lieutenant Colonel Daniel Malloy's blue-gray eyes saw the card with "Malloy" printed on it, and he headed for it, half-dragging his canvas bag with him. "Nice to be met," he observed. "Who are you guys?"

"John Clark."

"Domingo Chavez." Handshakes were exchanged. Chavez and Clark had come together to meet him. They were dressed in civilian clothes.

"Chopper is waiting. Car's this way." Clark headed through a side door of Heathrow's terminal 3 to a waiting car. The driver took Malloy's bag and tossed it into the boot for the half-mile drive to a waiting British army Puma helicopter. They loaded into the back, and the Puma lifted off.

"What's this all about?" Malloy asked.

"What did they tell you?"

"Pack underwear for a week," he replied, a twinkle in his eye.

"There's a nice department store a few miles from the base."

"Hereford?"

"Good guess, Colonel," Chavez responded. "Been there?"

"Lots of times. And you can call me Bear."

It fit, both men decided of their visitor. He was Clark's height, six one, and bulky, as though he pumped barbells for fun and drank his share of beer afterward.

"Well, Bear, you're going to be working with us, probably," Clark told him.

"Who's 'us,' sir?"

"We're called Rainbow, and we don't exist."

"Vienna?" The way they both blinked was answer enough. "Okay, that looked a little slick for cops. What's the makeup of the team?"

"NATO, mainly Americans and Brits, but others, too," John told him. "I'm a simulated two-star. Ding here is a simulated major. What are you current in?"

"H-60, Hueys, and H-53s. The Night Stalker, of course, but not many of them around. None based over here that I know of." The Puma turned then, circling, then flaring to settle into the Hereford pad. "I can also handle the MH-47 if I have to, General."

"The name's John, Mr. Bear," Clark said with a smile. He knew a pro when he saw one.

"I'm Ding," Chavez said.

The helicopter settled down. The crew chief jumped out to pull the sliding doors open. Malloy grabbed his bag, stepped down, and walked to the Rover parked just off the pad. The Rover took them to what looked like a headquarters building instead of his guest housing. Whoever they were, they were in a hurry.

"Nice office, John," he said, looking around on the inside. "I guess you really are a simulated two-star."

"I'm the boss," Clark admitted, "and that's enough. Coffee?"

"Always," Malloy confirmed, taking a cup. "Thanks."

"How many hours?" Clark asked next.

"Total? Sixty-seven forty-two last time I added it up. Thirty-one hundred of that is special operations. And oh, about five hundred combat time: Grenada, Lebanon, Somalia, couple of other places. I suppose you need a delivery boy, right?"

"Something like that. Ding, let's run Mr. Bear through the Vienna field operation."

"Roge-o, Mr. C." Chavez unrolled the big photo of Schloss Ostermann on Clark's conference table and started his brief as Stanley and Covington came in to join the conference.

Malloy was intrigued. Whoever these people were, they had serious horsepower. His orders to fly to England had come directly from "Big Sam" Wilson himself, commander in chief of the Special Operations Command at MacDill Air Force Base, outside Tampa, and the people he'd met so far looked fairly serious.

"Well, Mr. Bear, what do you think?" Rainbow Six asked. "The air force is going to lend us an MH-60 for you to play with."

"Neighborly of them. What about my family? Is this TAD?"

"No. It's a permanent duty station for you. They'll come over on the usual government package. So you want to work with us?"

The question surprised Malloy. "This is a volunteer outfit?"

Clark nodded. "Every one of us."

"Well, how about that," Malloy said. "Okay, sign me up."

IL'YCH Ramirez Sanchez was not a happy man. The cell in the Le Sante prison was not calculated to make him so. Once the most feared terrorist in the world, he'd had every police and intelligence service on his trail, and he laughed at them all from the security of his safe houses in the former Eastern Europe . . . until Eastern Europe had fallen and with it the nation-state support for his revolutionary acts. And so he'd ended up in Sudan, where he'd decided to take his situation more seriously. He'd gone to a trusted physician for some cosmetic surgery, had general anesthesia, and awakened aboard a French jet, strapped to a stretcher, with a Frenchman saying, *"Bonjour, Monsieur Chacal,"* with the beaming smile of a hunter who'd just captured the most dangerous of tigers with a loop of string. Tried, finally, for the murder of a cowardly informant and two French counterintelligence officers in 1975, he'd defended himself with panache, keeping his dignity throughout, but inwardly he'd felt the pain of a trapped animal. The ultimate result had hardly been a surprise.

The prison had already been a hundred years old on the day of his birth, and it was built along the lines of a medieval dungeon. His small cell had but a single window, and he was not tall enough to see out the bottom of it. He was as alone as a man could be. The whole world knew that Carlos the Jackal was caged forever and could therefore be forgotten.

Forgotten? That was the most hurtful part of all. He made a mental note to contact his lawyer.

IT WAS a beautiful thing to watch, even in the dark. The MH-60K Night Hawk helicopter came in at about thirty miles per hour, almost two hundred feet over the ground, approaching the range building from the south, into the wind, traveling smoothly, not at all like a tactical deployment maneuver. Under the helicopter was a dark nylon rope, about one hundred and fifty feet long, barely visible with the night-vision goggles, and at the end of it were Peter Covington and two other Team 1 members, dangling free below the black Sikorsky in their black ninja suits. The helicopter proceeded in evenly until its nose crossed the building's wall. Then the nose came up, and the aircraft flared, slowing rapidly. The people attached to the rope swept forward, as though on a child's swing, and then, at the limit of the arc, they swung backward. The backward swing froze them still in the air, their rearward velocity almost exactly matching the remaining forward motion of the helicopter, and then they were on the roof, almost as though they'd stepped off a stationary object. Instantly Covington and his men unclipped their quick-release attachments and dropped down. The helicopter resumed its forward flight. Anyone on the ground would scarcely have known that the aircraft had done anything but fly at a steady pace over the building.

"Awfully good," Al Stanley breathed. "Not a sound."

"He is as good as he says," Clark observed.

As though hearing the remarks, Malloy brought the helicopter around, flashing a thumbs-up out the window to the two men on the ground as he headed off to orbit the area for the remainder of the simulation.

Twenty minutes later in the officers club Malloy said, "The aircraft is nicely set up." He was wearing his green Nomex flight suit, with a yellow scarf around his neck, like a good aviator, though it struck Clark as odd.

"What's with the necktie?"

"Oh, this? It's the A-10 scarf. One of the guys I rescued in Kuwait gave it to me. I figure it's lucky, so I wear it on missions."

"How hard is it to do that transition maneuver?" Covington asked.

"Your timing has to be pretty good, and you have to read the wind. You know what helps me prepare for it?"

"Tell me," Clark said.

"Piano playing." Malloy sipped at his pint of bitter and grinned. "Don't ask me why, but I always fly better after I've played some. Maybe something to do with getting the fingers loose. Anyway, that chopper they lent us is set up just right. Control cables have the right tension; throttles are just so. You can sweet-talk to her, and she listens real nice."

"Like a good rifle," one of the others observed.

"Roger that," Malloy said, saluting with his pint.

"I WANT to get out of this place," the Jackal told his attorney.

"I understand that, my friend," the lawyer replied with a look around the room. It was the law in France, as in America, that conversations between clients and attorneys were privileged and could not be recorded or used in any way by the state, but neither man really trusted the French to abide by that law, especially the DGSE, the French intelligence service, which had been so instrumental in bringing Il'ych to justice.

Well, there were other people talking in this room, and there were no obvious shotgun microphones here—and the two had not taken the seats offered by the prison guards, opting instead for ones closer to the windows because, they'd said, they wanted the natural light.

"I must tell you that the circumstances of your conviction do not lend themselves to appeal," the lawyer advised.

"I am aware of that. I need you to make a telephone call." The Jackal gave him a name and a number. "Tell him that it is my wish to be released and that the rewards will be great." It was suspected that Il'ych Ramirez Sanchez had a goodly sum of money squirreled away as a result mainly of his attack on the OPEC ministers in Austria almost twenty years earlier. "If he has an immediate reply, you will convey it to me," the Jackal told him. There was still an intensity to his eyes, something cold and distant—but even so, he was right there looking deep into his interlocutor and telling him what must be. The lawyer knew that he would pass along the message.

CONSTRUCTION was about ninety percent complete. There were twenty sections around the site—twenty blocks of land, one square mile each, mainly flat, with a four-lane paved road leading north to Interstate 70. The last two miles of the highway were set up without a median strip, the rebarred concrete paving a full thirty inches deep, as though it had been built for airplanes to land on—big ones, Charlie Hollister, the construction superintendent, had observed.

The buildings were fairly pedestrian except for their environmental-control systems, which were so state of the art that the navy could have used them on nuclear submarines. It was all part of the company's leading-edge posture on its systems, a top executive had told him on his last visit.

Building 1 was already complete—three weeks early. It was specced for a full 1.3 pounds of overpressure. They'd told Hollister it was tornado protection, and that sorta-kinda made sense. Kansas was tornado country. But it could also make for sick-building syndrome. Buildings with overly good environmental isolation kept flu germs in and helped colds spread like a prairie fire. Well, that had to be part of the idea, too. The company worked on drugs and vaccines and stuff, and that meant that this place was like a germ-warfare factory, didn't it? So it made sense to keep stuff in—and keep stuff out, right?

Three hundred million dollars total was going into this project. The buildings were huge. You could convert them to living space for three or four thousand people, the super thought. The site had its own power plant, and despite the local lake, there were no fewer than ten twelve-inch artesian wells drilled down into—and *past*—the Cherokee Aquifer, which local farmers used to water their fields. That was enough water to supply a small city! But the company was footing the bill, and he was getting his usual percentage of the total job cost to bring it in on time, with a substantial bonus for coming in early, which he was determined to earn. Then he'd take the family to Disney World for two weeks of Mickey and golf.

"FEELING bad, Pete?" Dr. Killgore asked.

"Must be the flu or something. I feel beat-up all over."

"Let's give it a look, then." Killgore stood, donning a mask and latex gloves. "Gotta take a blood sample, okay?"

"Sure, Doc."

Killgore gave him the usual stick inside the elbow and filled four 5-cc test tubes. Next he checked Pete's eyes and mouth and did the normal prodding, which drew a reaction over the liver.

"Ouch! That hurts, Doc. Like you just stabbed me with a knife."

"Sorry, Pete. How about here?" The physician probed lower.

"Not as sharp, but it hurts a little. Somethin' I ate, maybe?"

"Could be. I wouldn't worry too much about it," Killgore replied. So Pete would be number two. Bad luck, Pete, Killgore thought. "Let me give you something to take the edge off." He pulled open a drawer on the wall cabinet. Five milligrams, he thought, filling the plastic syringe to the right line, then turning and sticking the vein on the back of the hand.

"Oooh!" Pete said a few seconds later. "That feels okay. Lot better, Doc. Thanks." The rheumy eyes went wide, then relaxed.

Heroin was a superb analgesic. Pete would feel just fine for a while. Killgore took the blood samples off for testing. In thirty minutes he was sure. The antibody tests still showed positive, and microscopic examination showed what the antibodies were fighting against . . . and losing to.

Only two years earlier, people had tried to infect America with the natural version of this bug, this "shepherd's crook," some had called it. Adding the cancer DNA had made this negative-strand RNA virus more robust, but the best news was that the genetic engineering had more than tripled the latency period. Once thought to be four to ten days, now it was almost a month. Maggie really knew her stuff, and she'd even picked the right name for it. Ebola-Shiva was nasty.

That concluded Killgore's work for the day. He made his way outside. The evening air was chilly and clean and pure. Well, as pure as it could be in this part of the world. There were a hundred million cars in the country, all spewing their complex hydrocarbons into the atmosphere. Killgore wondered if he'd be able to tell the difference in two or three years when all that stopped. In the glow of the building lights, he saw the flapping of bats. Cool, he thought. One rarely saw bats. They must be chasing insects.

There would be birds up there, too. Owls especially, magnificent raptors of the night. Killgore felt far more kinship for the wild predators than he did for the prey animals. But that was to be expected, wasn't it? He did have kinship with the predators, those wild, magnificent things that killed without conscience, because Mother Nature had no conscience at all. She gave life with one hand and took it back with the other. The ageless process of life—that had made the earth what it was. Men had tried so hard and so long to change it, but other men now would change it back quickly and dramatically, and he'd be there to see it. Pollution would stop, and the land would soon be covered with life, as Nature intended, with him and his colleagues there to see the magnificence of the transformation. And if the price was high, then the prize it earned was worth it. The earth belonged to those who appreciated and understood her. Chester and Pete would not have understood, but then they'd never understood much of anything, had they?

"THERE will be thousands of Frenchmen there," Juan, a Basque, said. "Half of them will be children. If we wish to liberate our colleagues, the impact must be strong. This should be strong enough."

"Where will we go afterward?" René asked.

"The Bekáa Valley is still available, and from there, wherever we wish. I have good contacts in Syria still, and there are always options. But first we must plan the mission in every detail. Esteban, you will get yourself a job there. You, too, Andre."

"We'll need more men. At least ten more."

"Men can be hired. We need only promise them the right amount of money," Esteban, another Basque, pointed out.

"They must be faithful men," René told them forcefully.

"They will be faithful enough," Esteban said. "I know where to go for them."

They were all bearded. It was the easiest disguise to adopt, and though the national police in their countries had pictures of them, the pictures were all of shaven young men. A passerby might have thought them to be artists, the way they looked and the way they all leaned inward on the table to speak with intense whispers. Perhaps they were arguing over some political issue, the waiter thought, or some confidential business matter. He couldn't know that he was right on both counts.

"BUT this is an environmental disaster waiting to happen!" Carol Brightling insisted.

"Carol," Arnold van Damm, the White House chief of staff, replied. "I know what your concerns are, but the president of Atlantic Richfield has promised me personally that this will be a clean operation. So, no, the President will *not* withdraw his support for this drilling project. It makes economic sense for the country." They were discussing Bill S-1768, which would authorize the Department of the Interior to auction off the drilling rights in an area of more than a thousand square miles east of Alaska's Prudhoe Bay.

"I have to talk to him personally," the science adviser insisted.

"No." The chief of staff shook his head emphatically. "There is only one position in this building, and that position is what the President says it is. Whether you believe in it or not, you will say publicly that you think that drilling that oil is a good thing for America and for the environment. Do you understand that?"

"No, Arnie, I won't!" Brightling exclaimed.

"Carol, you will. And you will do it convincingly. If, that is, you like working here."

"Are you threatening me?"

"No, Carol, I am not threatening you. I am explaining the rules. You knew those rules when you came on board. Now it's time for a gut check. Will you live by the rules or won't you?"

Her face was red. She hadn't learned to conceal her anger, the chief of staff saw, and that was too bad. You couldn't afford to get angry over minor items. And this was a minor item. When you found several billion barrels of oil in a place that belonged to you, you drilled. It was as simple as that. It would remain that simple as long as the voters drove automobiles. "Well, Carol?"

"Yes, Arnie, I know the rules, and I will live by the rules."

"Good. I want you to prepare a statement this afternoon for release next week. Thanks for coming over," he said in dismissal.

Back in her office, Dr. Brightling turned on her computer and called up her word-processing program. She took a deep breath and began drafting her defense of something that, after all, would never happen, would it?

No, she told herself, it would never happen.

CHAPTER 5

SWORD OF THE LEGION

THE theme park had learned well from its more famous model. It had hired away a dozen senior executives, their lavish salaries paid for by the park's Persian Gulf financial backers, who had already exceeded their fiscal expectations and looked forward to recouping their total investment in less than six years.

Those investments had been considerable, since they were determined not merely to emulate the American corporation but to exceed it in every respect. The castle in *their* park was made of stone, not fiberglass. The circular railroad used two real steam locomotives, and there was talk of extending the line to the international airport, which the Spanish authorities had modernized to support the theme park— as well they might: Worldpark, as it was called, provided twenty-eight thousand full-time and ten thousand more part-time jobs. Guests flew in from all over Europe, or took the trains, or came down on bus tours to stay at the large, comfortable hotels. On a good day they spent ten *million* dollars in cash and far more than that in plastic.

A thoroughly modern facility, every attraction, ride, and food outlet was monitored by a master command center. Mike Dennis, the operations director, had been hired away from Orlando. While he missed the friendly managerial atmosphere there, the running of Worldpark had been the challenge he'd waited for all his life. This was his baby, Dennis told himself, looking out the battlements of the tower. His office and the command center were in the castle keep, the tall tower in the twelfth-century fortress they'd built. Under the main concourses was a subterranean labyrinth where the support services operated. Running it was the equivalent of being mayor of a not-so-small city. That he did his job well meant he'd earned the million-dollar bonus that had been delivered to him only five weeks earlier. Now, if only his kids could get used to the local schools. . . .

ANDRE had been assigned, fortuitously, to the security department, the notional Worldpark *policía,* which meant that he wore a light blue shirt and dark blue trousers with a vertical blue stripe, carried a whistle and a portable radio, and spent most of his time telling people where the rest rooms were. He'd gotten this job because he was fluent in French, Spanish, and English and thus could be helpful to the majority of the visitors.

Esteban, Andre saw, was in his usual place, selling his helium-filled balloons. Bread and circuses, they both thought. The vast sums expended to build this place—and for what purpose? To give the children of the working classes a brief few hours of laughter before they returned to their dreary homes?

The children loved it, of course. He passed a crowd of them there now, pulling the hands of their parents, dressed in their shorts and sneakers, with helium-filled balloons tied to their little wrists. And there was a special one, a little girl in a wheelchair, wearing the special-access button that told ride attendants to allow her on without the need to stand in line. She was probably dying from cancer, Andre thought, sent here by some charity modeled on the American Make-A-Wish Foundation, which paid for the parents to bring their dying whelp here for one first and last chance to see the trolls and other cartoon characters.

An amazing place, Andre thought. He punched his time card and changed his clothes. It had been a good day. His wanderings had confirmed his previous observations of the park. He now knew how to accomplish the mission.

That night he would make the first of several international calls.

"THIS will do it," Tim Noonan said, walking into the morning meeting.

"What's 'this'?" John Clark asked the technical expert.

Noonan held up a computer floppy disk. "It's just a hundred

lines of code, not counting the installation stuff. Phone cells all use the same computer program to operate. When we get to a place, I just insert this in their drives and upload the software. Unless you dial in the right prefix to make a call—777, to be exact—the cell will respond that the number is busy. So we can block any cellular calls into our subjects from some helpful soul outside and also prevent them from getting out. It's called Cellcop, and it'll work anywhere in the world."

"Good one, Tim," Clark said.

BY EARLY morning, after the telephone calls were made, people rented cars with false IDs and drove south from France to Spain and were waved through the border checkpoints, usually with a friendly smile. Travel agents had already made the necessary reservations.

For Juan check-in at the hotel was handled with mechanical precision. He took his card-key and nodded his thanks at the pretty female clerk, then hoisted his bags and headed off to his room. He'd just finished unpacking when a knock came at the door.

"Bonjour." It was René. The Frenchman came in and sat on the bed, stretching as he did so. "Are you ready, my friend?" he asked in Spanish.

"Sí," the Basque replied. He didn't look especially Spanish. His hair was on the red side of strawberry blond, his features handsome, and his beard neatly trimmed. Never arrested by the Spanish police, he was bright, careful, and thoroughly dedicated, with two car bombings and a murder to his credit. René, too, had done this sort of thing before, most often murders on crowded streets. Action Directe had been largely, but not completely, broken up by the French police. The captured men hadn't betrayed their at-large comrades despite the pressure of their uniformed countrymen—and perhaps some of them would be released as a result of this mission, though the main objective was to release their comrade Carlos. It would not be easy to get him out of Le Sante, René thought, rising to look out the window at the train station used by people going to the park. But he saw the children there, waiting for their ride in, and there were some things no government could overlook.

Two buildings away, Jean-Paul was looking out at the same scene and contemplating much the same thoughts. Jean-Paul and his friends *knew* the rightness of their cause and their beliefs. Someday people *would* see the path of justice offered by socialism. Someday.

THE meeting place was prearranged. The Dive Bomber ride used as its symbol the German Ju-87 Stuka. Although the swastika on the tail had been thoughtfully deleted, it ought to have greatly offended Spanish sensibilities. Did no one remember Guernica, that first serious expression of Nazi *Schrecklichkeit,* when thousands of Spanish citizens had been massacred? Was historical appreciation that shallow here? Evidently it was. People raced off the top-hanging coaster to rejoin the line to ride it again.

Jean-Paul, René, and Juan appeared almost together, all sipping soft drinks. They and the six others were marked by the hats they'd bought at the entrance kiosk. Andre nodded to them, rubbing his nose as planned. René came over to him.

"I get off at 1800 hours," Andre said. "Dinner as planned?"

"Yes."

"All are ready?"

"Entirely ready, my friend."

"Then I will see you at dinner." Andre nodded and walked off, continuing his patrol as he was paid to do.

As operations officer for Action Directe for over a decade, Andre had planned and executed a total of eleven murders. This mission, however, would be by far the grandest of all. Affixed to the wall of his flat was a map of Worldpark: way in, way out. Where to take the hostages. How to get everyone out. Andre had gone over it repeatedly, looking for weaknesses. The Spanish national police, the Guardia Civil, would respond to this mission, and Andre did not take police lightly. They'd almost killed him twice in France, but that was because he'd made mistakes. Not this time.

He knew that the park would be busy tomorrow as people checked into hotels in preparation for the Good Friday holiday weekend. He also knew that a major French arms manufacturer, Thompson CSF, would be sending six hundred employees and their families.

Some of the workers, and therefore their children, would be known and important to the French government. It could not be better.

SANDY Clark served the main course, a fine roast beef. John rose to get the carving knife. Patsy, their daughter, thought briefly about mad-cow disease but decided her mother had cooked the meat thoroughly. Besides, she liked good roast beef, cholesterol and all, and her mom was the world's champ at making gravy.

"How's it going at the hospital?" Sandy asked her physician daughter.

"OB is pretty routine. I've kinda hoped for a placenta previa, maybe a placenta abrupta to see if we have the drill down, but—"

"Don't wish for those, Patsy. I've seen them happen in the ER. *Total* panic."

"Well, if you know what you're doing—"

"If you know what you're doing, it's still tense. Routine is fine with me," Sandy Clark went on. "I love a quiet night."

"Voice of experience," John Clark observed.

"Makes sense to me," Domingo Chavez agreed, stroking his wife's arm. "How's the little guy?"

"Kicking up a storm right now," Patsy replied, moving her husband's hand to her belly. It never failed, she saw. The way his eyes melted when he felt the movement in her womb.

"Well, no nasty surprises when the time comes, okay?" Chavez said. "I don't want to faint or anything."

"Right!" Patsy laughed. "You? Faint? My commando?"

"You never know, honey," her father observed, taking his seat. "I've seen tough guys fold before."

"Not this one, Mr. C.," Domingo noted with a raised eyebrow.

"You guys are more like firemen than commandos," Sandy said from her seat. "The way you just hang around until something happens."

"And if the fire never starts, it's okay with us," Domingo agreed.

"You really mean that?" Patsy asked.

"Yes, honey," her husband told her. "Going out isn't fun. We've been lucky so far. We haven't lost a hostage."

"But that'll change," Rainbow Six told his subordinate.

"Not if I have anything to say about it, John." Chavez went on, "Noonan came over today. Says he's got a new toy."

"What's it do?" John asked.

"It finds people."

"How?"

"Tracks the human heart up to five hundred meters away."

"What?" Patsy asked. "How's it do that?"

"Not sure, but Noonan says the guys at Fort Bragg are real enthusiastic about it. He asked the headquarters people to send us a demo."

"We'll see," John said, buttering his roll.

"Team Two is lean and mean now," Chavez said. "We always were, but I don't see us getting any better than we are now. Same with Peter's bunch. Specially with Malloy on the team now."

"Ready to kill people?" Patsy asked dubiously. Much as she loved her husband, it was hard sometimes for her to be a physician, dedicated to saving life, and yet be married to a man whose purpose often seemed to be the taking of it.

"No, honey, ready to rescue people," he corrected her. "That's the job."

THE company outing for Thompson CSF had been planned for some months. The three hundred children had been working overtime to get a week ahead in their schoolwork, and the event had business implications as well. Thompson had installed computerized control systems in the park. It was part of the company's transition from being mainly a military-products producer to a more generalized electronics-engineering firm. The new systems could monitor activities throughout the establishment, transmitting their data through ether-space rather than over copper landlines, which saved a few million francs.

In recognition of the successful fulfillment of the contract, Thompson management had cooperated with Worldpark to arrange this company picnic. Everyone in the group, children included, wore red T-shirts with the company logo on the front. They were moving toward the center of the park in a group escorted by six of the park trolls, two Roman legionnaires, and one lion-skinned *aquilifer,* carrying the gold eagle, the hallowed emblem of the VI Legio Victrix, now quartered at Worldpark, Spain, as its antecedent had been under the Emperor Tiberius in A.D. 20.

Mike Dennis watched them on his office TV monitors. The Roman soldiers were a signature item for his theme park and, for some reason, had proved to be wildly popular. Francisco de la Cruz—Pancho to his friends—was leading the parade. Francisco was a retired sergeant in the Spanish army's paratroops, and the guy just grooved to leading parades. Over fifty, with burly arms and a heavy beard, he could be intimidating to the little kids. But Francisco had a way of scooping them up like a bearish grandfather and putting them instantly at ease. The kids especially liked playing with the red horsehair plume atop his iron helmet. Dennis made a mental note to have lunch with the man sometime soon. Francisco ran his little department well and deserved some attention from topside.

Dennis glanced at the notes on his desk. He had to give a welcoming speech to the Thompson guests, to be followed by a parade of the trolls. He jumped at the shattering staccato of Jean-Paul's submachine gun firing a long burst up into the air. In the castle courtyard people turned and cringed instinctively at the same time. They did little for the first few seconds but look in shock at the shooter in their midst and at the others withdrawing their weapons from their backpacks.

Francisco de la Cruz recognized the shape of an Israeli Uzi submachine gun, and his twenty-plus years of uniformed service flashed into his consciousness. Two meters behind that bearded criminal he started moving. Claude, one of René's group, caught the movement, and he turned to see— What was this? A man wearing Roman armor was moving toward him.

Centurion de la Cruz acted on some sort of soldierly instinct that had transformed itself from the era to which his uniform belonged to where he was this noon. His right hand pulled the *spatha* from its scabbard high up on his right side, and the shield came up, its center iron boss aimed at the muzzle of the Uzi as the sword came straight in the air. He'd had this sword custom-made by a distant cousin in Toledo. It was formed of laminated carbon steel, just as the sword of El Cid had once been, and it had an edge fit to shave with. Suddenly he was a soldier again, and he had an armed enemy before him. The distance was less than two meters now, and gun or not, he was going to—

Claude fired off a quick burst into the center of his advancing target, but that happened to be the three-centimeter-thick iron boss of the *scutum,* and the bullets deflected off it.

De la Cruz felt the impact of the bullet fragments peppering his left arm, but the stings of insects would have felt worse as he closed in, and his right sword-arm came left, then right, catching the *cabrón's* upper arm. And for the first time in his life Centurion Francisco de la Cruz drew blood in anger.

Claude felt the pain. His right arm moved, and his finger depressed the trigger, and the long burst hit de la Cruz's left leg, causing the centurion to scream in pain as he went down, his second, lethal slash of the sword missing the man's throat by a whisker.

Mike Dennis ran to the window. His eyes saw a number of men with guns surrounding the sea of red shirts, and they herded them now, like sheepdogs, toward the castle courtyard. Dennis turned. "Security lockdown *now!*" he called to the man on the master control board, and with a mouse click the castle's doors were dead-bolted. "Call the police!" Dennis ordered next. That was also preprogrammed. An alarm system fired off a signal to the nearest police barracks. The park's internal response to the signal was also preprogrammed. All park rides would be stopped at once, and people would be informed that the park was closing due to an unexpected emergency.

THE children were not as overtly frightened as their parents, perhaps thinking that this was one of the magic things to be expected at the park. But fear is contagious, and the children quickly saw that emotion in their parents' eyes. One by one they held tight to hands and legs, looking about at the adults who were moving quickly now around the red-shirted crowd, holding things that looked like guns.

René was in command. He moved toward the castle entrance, clear of the nine others who were holding the crowd in place. "Two!" he called. "Select our guests!"

Two was Jean-Paul. He grabbed the arm of a four-year-old French girl.

"No!" her mother screamed. Jean-Paul pointed his weapon at her, but she stood her ground, holding both shoulders of the child.

"Very well, I will shoot her." In less than a second his Uzi was against the little girl's light brown hair. The mother screamed all the louder, but she pulled her hands back.

"Walk over there," Jean-Paul told the child firmly, pointing to Juan. The little girl did so, looking back at her mother while the armed man selected more children.

Andre went to a little Dutch girl in a wheelchair. ANNA, her special-access name tag read. He pushed Anna's father away from the wheelchair and shoved it off toward the castle.

"My child is ill," the father protested in English.

"Yes, I can see that," Andre replied in the same language, moving off to select the other sick child in the area. What fine hostages these two would make.

"You swine!" this one's mother snarled at him. For her trouble she was clubbed by the extended stock of Andre's Uzi, which broke her nose and bathed her face in blood. "Mummy!" the little boy screamed as Andre one-handed his wheelchair up the ramp to the castle. The child turned in his chair to see his mother collapse. A park employee knelt down to assist her, but all she did was scream for her son: "Tommy!"

To her screams were soon added those of more parents, all of them wearing the red T-shirts of the Thompson company. The armed men and their hostages withdrew into the castle, leaving the rest to stand there, stunned.

"They're coming here," Mike Dennis said. He was talking on the phone now to the captain of the local Guardia Civil barracks.

"Get clear," the captain told him. "We need you and your people to assist us. Leave now!"

Dennis replaced the phone, turning to look at the fifteen-person staff in the command center. "People, everybody, follow me. We're heading for the backup command center. Right now."

The castle, real as it appeared, was not real. It had been built with the modern conveniences of elevators and fire stairwells. The former were probably compromised, Dennis thought, but one of the latter descended to the underground. He walked to a fire door and opened it, waving for his employees to head that way. This they did, the last tossing him keys on the way through. When Dennis left, he locked this door behind him, then raced down the four levels of spiral stairs. Another minute and he was in the underground, which was already crowded with employees and guests hustled out of harm's way by uniformed park personnel. The alternate Worldpark command post was actually outside the park grounds, just at the end of the underground. He ran there and keyed up his castle office on his monitor.

"THIS way," Andre told his comrades. The door was locked, however. He fired his pistol at the doorknob, which bent from the impact but remained locked. Then René tried his Uzi, which wrecked that portion of the door and allowed him to pull it open. Andre led them upstairs, then kicked in the door to the command center—empty. He swore foully at that discovery.

"I see them on the monitor!" Dennis said. He again had the captain of the Guardia Civil on the phone. "One man—two—six men with guns. They have kids with them!" One of them walked up to a surveillance camera, pointed his pistol, and the picture vanished. Dennis worked other camera controls to see what was happening in his park. Rage was now replacing shock.

IN HIS office Captain Dario Gassman called Madrid to make his first report. He had a crisis plan for his barracks. Ten cars and sixteen men were now racing toward Worldpark. Their first mission was to establish a perimeter, with orders to let no one in or out. How many more men would he need? Captain Gassman wondered. But things were already leaving his hands. The senior Thompson executive was on his cell phone talking with his corporate headquarters in France, a call quickly bucked up to the chairman, who called the Defense Minister, and that got things rolling very rapidly indeed.

"YES, this is John Clark," Rainbow Six said into the phone. "Yes, sir. Where is that exactly? . . . I see. . . . How many? . . . No, sir, we cannot move until the host government makes the request. Thank you, Minister." Clark changed buttons on his phone. "Al, get in here."

"GOOD Lord, I took the family there last year," Peter Covington said. "You could use up a whole battalion retaking the place. It's a nightmare—lots of buildings, lots of space, multilevel. I think it even has an underground service area."

"Maps, diagrams?" Clark asked his secretary Alice Foorgate.

"I'll see," she replied, leaving the conference room.

"What do we know?" Chavez asked.

"Not much, but the French are pretty worked up, and they're requesting that the Spanish let us in and—"

"This just arrived," Mrs. Foorgate said, handing over a fax.

"List of hostages—all kids, ages four to eleven. Thirty-three of them." Clark handed it to Alistair Stanley.

"Both teams, if we deploy," the Scotsman said immediately.

"Yeah." Clark nodded. Then the phone beeped.

"Phone call for Mr. Tawney," a female voice announced on the speaker.

"This is Tawney," the intelligence chief said on picking up the receiver. "Yes, Roger. . . . Yes, we got a call from . . . Oh, I see. Very well, Roger. Thank you." Tawney hung up. "The Spanish government has requested that we deploy at once."

"Okay, people," John said. "Saddle up."

THE park command center was better than anything he'd hoped for, René thought. He was learning to use the computer system to select TV cameras that seemed to cover the entire grounds. Nobody would get close to the castle without his knowledge. Excellent.

In the secretaries' room just through the door, Andre had the children sitting on the floor in one tight little knot, except for the two in their wheelchairs, whom he'd placed against the wall. The children were uniformly wide-eyed, but at the moment they were quiet, which suited him. "Stay still," he told them in French, then backed to the door into the command center. "One," he called.

"Yes, Nine," René answered.

"Things are under control here. Time to make a call?"

"Yes," One agreed. He took his seat and picked up a phone, then examined the buttons, and finding a likely one, he pressed it.

"Yes?"

"Who is this?"

"I am Mike Dennis. I am managing director of Worldpark."

"*Bien.* I am One, and I am now in command of your park."

"Okay, Mr. One. What do you want?"

"You have the police here?"

"Yes, they are here now."

"Good. I will speak with their commander, then."

"Captain?" Inside the alternate park command post Dennis waved. Gassman stepped over to his desk.

"I am Captain Dario Gassman of the Guardia Civil."

"I am One. I have taken over thirty hostages."

"Do you have a request for me?"

"I do not make requests. I give orders. Do you understand?" René asked in English.

"*Sí, comprendo.*"

"Our hostages are French. You will establish a line of communication with the French embassy in Madrid. This affair is between us and the French. Do you understand that?"

"Senor One, this is Spanish soil."

"Be that as it may, you will open a telephone link to the French embassy at once," René told him before hanging up.

IT WAS noisy in the back. The four Allison engines screamed as they accelerated the MC-130 down the runway; then the aircraft rotated abruptly, jumping into the sky for its flight to Spain. Clark and Stanley were in the communications compartment forward, where a fax had just arrived from Paris. It was another list of hostages, and this time Clark took the time to read the names, and part of his mind tried to conjure up faces to go with them, knowing he'd be wrong in every case but doing it even so. Thirty-three children surrounded by men with guns, numbering at least six, maybe more. They were still trying to develop that information. Nothing in this business ever went fast enough.

Clark walked aft to check on the Rainbow team. The men had suited up in their black Nomex, then settled into their seats, buckling their belts. Most had closed their eyes and affected sleep, but mainly they didn't sleep, merely sat with eyes closed, seeking and sometimes finding an hour's peace amid the screeching noise of the turboprop engines. These men were professional enough to know that the stress would come in its own good time. In that moment John Clark, long before a chief SEAL, U.S. Navy, was struck with the honor he held, commanding such men as these. They didn't make men any better, and his two leaders, Chavez and Covington, had trained them to a razor's edge of perfection.

"John!" Stanley called, heading aft with a new fax. "The terrorists have contacted the French ambassador. Here's what they're asking for."

"Anybody we know?"

"Il'ych Ramirez Sanchez is at the top of the list."

"Carlos?" Dr. Bellow jumped up from his seat and took the fax, scanning it before handing it over to Clark. "We're dealing with ideological ones again, John, just like Vienna, but they have a definite fixed objective." He checked his watch and grunted. "Next time, a faster airplane."

"Be cool, Doc," Clark told him, knowing that Paul Bellow would have the toughest job from the moment they got to the objective. He had to read minds, evaluate the terrorists' resolve, and, hardest of all, predict their actions.

"HOW long?" Esteban asked René.

"They will take time," One replied. "Remember that their strategy is to lengthen the process to wear us down, weaken our resolve.

Against that we have the ability to force the issue by killing a hostage. Above all, we must control the pace of events. For now we will let them take their time." René walked to the corner to see how Claude was doing. There was a nasty gash on his arm from that fool of a Roman soldier, the only thing that had gone wrong. Claude would need stitches. It was bad luck but not that serious, except to Claude, who was in considerable pain.

HECTOR Weiler, the park physician, spent most of his time putting Band-Aids on skinned knees and elbows, though there was a photo on his wall of the twins he'd delivered after a pregnant woman had been foolish enough to ride the Dive Bomber. There was now a sign at the entrance warning against that. Francisco was a lucky man, the doctor thought. At least six shots had been fired at him, and though the first three had merely resulted in fragment-peppering on his left arm, one of the second bursts had hurt his leg badly. A broken tibia would take a long time to heal.

"I could have killed him," the centurion groused through the anesthesia. "I could have taken his head off, but I missed!"

"Not with the first one," Weiler observed, seeing the red crust on the sword that now lay in the corner of the treatment room.

"Tell me about him," Captain Gassman ordered as he entered the room.

"Forties, early forties," de la Cruz said. "My height plus ten or twelve centimeters. Brown hair, brown beard, some speckles of gray in it. Dark eyes," the former sergeant reported. "There were others. I saw four, maybe more."

"Who are they?" the surgeon asked, not looking up from his work.

"We think they are French, but we are not sure," the captain of the Guardia Civil answered.

"THIRTY-FIVE hostages," Colonel Tomas Nuncio told Clark as the car started rolling. "Thirty-three of them are French children." Nuncio had come by helicopter from Madrid. Behind him were three Spanish army trucks with Clark's people and their equipment aboard.

"I've seen the list," Clark said. "Who are the other two?"

Nuncio looked down in distaste. "Sick children. A girl from Holland and a boy from England, both in wheelchairs. All the rest are children of workers for Thompson, the French defense equipment company."

"How many people do you have on the scene?" Clark asked.

"Thirty-eight, with more coming. We have an inner perimeter established and traffic control."

"Reporters—what about them?"

"We are stopping them at the main gate. I will not give these swine a chance to speak to the public," Colonel Nuncio promised. He'd already lived up to what John expected of the Guardia Civil. His hat was something out of another century, but the cop's blue eyes were cold and hard as he drove his radio car out onto the interstate-type highway. Fifteen kilometers later Nuncio took the last exit before the one that went into the park. Presently they were parked outside what appeared to be a tunnel with a steel door sitting partially open. Nuncio popped open his door, and Clark did the same, then walked quickly into the entrance.

"Your Spanish is very literate, Senor Clark. But I cannot place your accent."

"Indianapolis," John replied. It would probably be the last light moment of the day. "How are the bad guys talking to you?"

"What language, you mean? English so far."

And *that* was the first good break of the day. For all his expertise, Dr. Bellow's language skills were not good.

The park's alternate command center was a mere twenty meters inside the tunnel. The door was guarded by yet another Civil Guard, who opened it and saluted Colonel Nuncio.

"Senor Clark, this is Captain Gassman." Handshakes were exchanged, and Gassman waved them to the conference table in the middle of a room lined with TV cameras and other electronic gear. A large map of the park was laid out.

"The criminals are all here," Gassman said, tapping the castle in the middle of the park. "We believe there to be ten of them and thirty-five hostages, all children. My contact is a man, probably a Frenchman, calling himself One."

Clark nodded. "What about blueprints?"

"Here," a park engineer said, sliding the castle blueprints onto the table. "Windows here, here, here, and here. Stairs and elevators as marked." Clark referenced them against the map. "They have stair access to the roof and good line of sight everywhere."

"If I want to keep an eye on things, what's the best place?"

"The Dive Bomber ride, top of the first hill."

"Good. Can you get from here to there unseen?"

"The underground, but there're TV cameras in it." The engineer traced his hand over the map. "Here, here, another one there. Better to walk on the surface, but dodging all the cameras won't be easy."

"Can you turn them off?"

"We can override the primary command center from here."

"But if we do that, it might annoy our friends in the castle," John noted. "Okay, we need to think that one through."

"Hey, John."

Clark turned. It was Chavez, with Covington right behind him. Both team leaders strode in, wearing their black assault gear and looking to the others in the room like angels of death. They came to the conference table and started looking at the diagrams.

"Domingo Chavez, this is Colonel Nuncio and Captain Gassman."

"Good day," Ding said in his Los Angeles Spanish, shaking hands. Covington did the same, speaking his own language.

"Sniper perch here?" Ding asked at once, tapping the Dive Bomber. "I saw the thing from the parking lot. Can I get Homer there unobserved?"

"We're working on that right now."

Tim Noonan came in next, his backpack full of electronics gear. "Okay, this looks good," he observed, checking the TV screens.

"Our friends have a duplicate facility here."

"Oops," Noonan said. "Okay. First I want to shut down the cell phone nodes."

"What?" Nuncio asked. "Why?"

"In case our friends have a pal outside, sir," Clark answered.

"Ah. Can I help?"

Noonan answered. "Have your people go to each node, and

have the technicians insert these disks into their computers."

"Filipe!" Nuncio turned and snapped his fingers. A moment later his man had the disks and orders, and was leaving the room with them as Team 1 and Team 2 entered, crowding around the conference table.

"Bad guys and hostages here," John told them, pointing at the castle blueprints.

"Who's been talking to them?" This was Dr. Bellow.

"I have," Captain Gassman answered. Bellow grabbed him and walked him to the corner for a quiet chat.

"First of all, overwatch," Chavez said. "We need to get Homer to the top of that ride unseen. How do we do that?"

"There's people moving around on the TV screens," Johnston said, turning to look. "Who are they?"

"Park people," Dennis said, "making sure all our guests are out."

"Okay, then that's what I am—coveralls, toolbox, and all. You have the rides running?"

"No. They're all shut down."

"The more things moving, the more they have to watch," Sergeant Johnston told his boss.

"I like it," Chavez agreed, looking up at Clark.

"So do I. Mr. Dennis, turn them all on if you would, please."

"They have to be started up individually. We can turn them off from here by killing the power, but we can't turn them on."

"Then get your people out to do it. Sergeant Johnston will go with your man to the coaster. Homer, set up there."

"How high will I be?"

"About one hundred forty meters above the ground."

"Fair enough. Where do I change?"

"This way." The engineer led him out the door.

"When's Malloy get here?" Covington asked.

"Another hour or so," Clark answered.

Chavez and Covington got park maps—the same ones sold to park guests, with the camera positions hand-marked with black sticky dots. An electric cart—actually a golf cart—met them out in the corridor and whisked them outside, then back into the park on a surface road.

Covington navigated from the map, avoiding camera positions as they made their way along the back-lot areas of Worldpark.

The smell of the food from the concession stand made Chavez a little hungry. "Getting in there's going to be fun, man."

The castle certainly looked real enough, over fifty meters square and about the same in height. "How big do those windows look to you, Peter?"

"Big enough, Ding."

"Yeah, I think so, too." And already a plan was coming together in the two minds. "I hope Malloy is well rested."

Sergeant Homer Johnston, now wearing park coveralls over his ninja suit, popped out of the ground fifty meters from the Dive Bomber. He walked toward it, escorted by a park employee who was also a ride operator for this attraction.

"I can take you to the top and stop the car there."

"Great." It sure looked like a long way to climb. They walked under the canopied entrance, and Johnston sat in the lead seat on the right, his gun case on the seat next to his. "Go," he told the operator. The gang of three-seat cars stopped just at the crest. Johnston wriggled out, taking his gun case with him. This he set in an equipment bay, opening it to extract a rubber mat, and a gillie blanket to drape over himself. He took his time setting the mat down. The decking was perforated steel, and lying there would be uncomfortable. He deployed the blanket atop his prone frame. It was essentially a light fishing net covered with green plastic leaves. Then he set up his rifle on its bipod and took out his binoculars. His personal radio microphone dangled in front of his lips. "Rifle Two One to Command."

"This is Six," Clark responded.

"Rifle Two One in place, Six. I can see the whole roof of the castle and the doors to the elevator and stairwell."

"Good. Keep us posted."

"Roger that, boss. Out." Just then the car he'd ridden up in wheeled forward and dropped from sight.

"MY GOVERNMENT will *not* negotiate with these creatures!" the French Minister of Justice insisted over the telephone.

"Yes, sir, I understand that," Dr. Bellow said, "but I need to know what leeway, if any, you will give me as a negotiating position. That could include taking this Sanchez guy out of prison and bringing him here as . . . well, as bait."

"Do you recommend that?" the minister asked.

"I am not sure yet. I haven't spoken with them. For the moment I must assume that we are dealing with serious people who are willing to kill hostages."

"Children?"

"Yes, Minister, we must consider that a real threat." That generated a silence that lasted for a full ten seconds.

"I must consider this. I will call you later."

"Thank you, sir." Bellow hung up and looked up at Clark.

"They don't know what to do. Neither do I yet."

"Okay, so what's our play?"

"Put 'em in the dark for starters."

Clark turned. "Mr. Dennis, can we cut the electricity to the castle?"

"Yes," the park engineer answered for his boss. "But there's emergency lights in the stairwells. They click on when the power goes down. There's two in the command center, too. But they'll lose the TVs."

"Doc?" John asked Bellow, getting a nod. "Okay, pull the plug."

"Let's see how long this takes," Bellow said quietly.

It took five seconds. Dennis's phone rang.

"Yes?" the park manager said into the speakerphone.

"Why did you do that? The power went off."

Dr. Bellow leaned over the speaker. "I am Dr. Bellow. Who am I talking to?"

"I am One. I am in control of Worldpark. Who are you?"

"Paul Bellow. I have been asked to speak with you."

"Ah, the negotiator. Excellent. Turn the power back on."

"Before we do that," Bellow said, "I would like to know who you are. You have my name. I do not have yours."

"I told you, I am One. You will call me Mr. One."

"Okay, Mr. One, if you insist. You can call me Paul."

"Turn the electricity back on, Paul."

"In return for which you will do what, Mr. One?"

"In return for which I will abstain from killing a child—for the moment," the voice added coldly.

"You do not sound like a barbarian, Mr. One, and the taking of a child's life is a barbaric act."

"I have told you what I require. Do it." The line went dead.

"Bad," Bellow breathed. "He knows the playbook. He knows what we're trying to do—on my side, I mean."

"ANDRE," René called from his desk, "select a child."

He'd already done that and pointed to the little Dutch girl, Anna, in her wheelchair, wearing her special-access button. René nodded, checked his watch, and decided to wait ten minutes.

"THE trick will be to get close enough," Covington said.

"Yeah." Chavez nodded. They'd circulated carefully to the other side of the castle now. They could hear the Dive Bomber ride running behind them. There was a good forty meters of open ground all around the castle.

Both men took their time, examining everything from the little man-made streams to the bridges over them. They could see the windows into the command center where the terrorists were.

"Two groups, up and down," Covington said. "But we need something to tell us about that room."

"THAT camera is dead. They shot it out," Dennis said. "We have a tape of him doing it."

"Show me," Noonan commanded.

The room's layout was not unlike that of the backup command center, Tim Noonan saw in the fifty seconds of tape they had. The children were in the corner opposite the camera. Maybe they'd even stay there. "Anything else? Audio systems, a microphone?"

"No," Dennis replied. "We have phones for that."

"Yeah." The FBI agent nodded resignedly, knowing he would have to put a device on the building. "I have to figure a way to spike it, then." Suddenly the phone rang.

"Yes, this is Paul," Bellow said instantly.

"Paul, this is One. I told you to restore power."

"Working on that, but the police here are fumbling around."

"I am not a fool, Paul. I say it one last time: Turn the electricity back on immediately."

"Mr. One, we're working on it. Please be patient." Bellow's face was sweating now, and though he knew why, he hoped he was wrong.

"ANDRE," René said.

The former park security guard walked over to the corner. "Hello, *mon petit chou.* I think it is time for you to go back to your mother."

"Oh?" the child asked. She had china-blue eyes and light brown hair, nearly blond in fact. Her skin had the pale, delicate look of parchment. Andre walked behind the chair, taking the handles and wheeling her to the door.

The elevator outside had a default setting. It could go down on battery power. Andre pushed the chair inside, flipped off the red EMERGENCY switch, and pressed the number one button. The doors closed, and the elevator went down. A minute later the doors opened. The castle had a wide walk-through corridor that allowed people to transit from one part of Worldpark to another, and a mosaic that covered the arching walls. There was also a pleasant westerly breeze, and the Frenchman wheeled Anna right into it.

"COMMAND, this is Rifle Two One. I see a guy pushing a wheelchair with a kid in it coming out the west side of the castle." Johnston set his binoculars down and got on his rifle, centering the crosshairs on the man's temple, his finger lightly touching the set trigger. "Rifle Two One is on-target."

"Weapons tight," was the reply from Clark.

"Roger, Six. Weapons tight." Sergeant Johnston took his finger out of the trigger guard. What was happening here?

Chavez and Covington had an easy direct line of sight. The little girl was slumped to her left in the chair, trying to look back at the man pushing her. He was about forty, a mustache but no beard, average in height, weight, and build.

"Where is Momma?" Anna asked in the English she'd learned in school.

"You will see her in a moment," Andre promised. He wheeled her around the curving entrance to the castle. It circled around a statue, took a gentle upward turn, then led down to the courtyard. Andre stopped the chair in the middle of the path and looked around. There had to be policemen out here, but he saw nothing. He reached into his belt, took out his pistol, and—

"Gun! He's got a pistol out," Homer Johnston reported urgently. "He's gonna—"

The gun fired into Anna's back, driving straight through her heart. Her head dropped forward.

Covington drew his Beretta. It would not have been an easy shot, but he had nine rounds in his pistol and that was enough.

"Weapons tight!" the radio earpiece thundered. "Do not fire," Clark ordered.

The Englishman holstered his pistol, watching the man turn and walk back into the shelter of the stone castle.

"There was nothing we could have done, John. Not a thing," Bellow said.

"Now what?" Clark asked.

"Now I guess we turn the power back on."

As they watched the TV monitors, Dr. Hector Weiler raced to the child.

Chavez and Covington watched from a closer perspective. Weiler wore a white lab coat, the global uniform for physicians, and his race to the child ended abruptly as he touched the warm but still body. The slump of his shoulders told the tale, even from fifty meters away. Chavez walked over. In this moment Ding remembered that his wife held a new life in her belly. The little girl's face was at peace now, as though asleep, and he could not hold his hand back from touching her soft hair. "What's the story, Doc?"

The physician bit his lip and looked up. "She was quite ill. I have a file on her back at my office. When these children come here, I get a summary of their condition. She was dying, but not yet completely without hope." He'd never known rage, but now he did. "Will you kill them?"

Chavez looked up. There were no tears in his eyes. Perhaps they'd come later, he thought, his hand still on the child's head. Her hair wasn't very long, and he didn't know that it had grown back after her last chemotherapy protocol. He did know that she was supposed to be alive, and that in watching her death, he had failed to do that which he'd dedicated his life to doing. *"Sí,"* he told the doctor. "We will kill them."

THAT'LL do, Malloy thought, surveying the still wet paint on the side of the Night Hawk. POLICÍA, the lettering said. He and his two-man flight crew, Lieutenant Harrison and Sergeant Jack Nance, had stopped at a French military airfield outside Bordeaux for refueling, since he lacked the external fuel tanks used to ferry the Night Hawk long distances. Now in Spain at last, Malloy lifted the aircraft into the sky, then keyed his tactical radio. "Rainbow, this is the Bear. Over."

"Bear, this is Rainbow Six, reading you five by five. Over."

"Bear's in the air, sir. Be there in seven minutes."

"Roger. Please orbit the area until we tell you otherwise. The subjects are all in the castle. Be advised they have killed a hostage—a little girl," John Clark said.

In the helicopter Malloy's head didn't move at the news. "Roger, okay, Six. We will orbit and observe. Over."

Malloy dipped the nose and headed into the gathering darkness. The sun was almost down now, and the park lights in the distance were all coming on.

CHAVEZ and Covington returned to the alternate command center. The men were quiet, Chavez saw. Their faces were like stone, only their eyes moving back and forth between the castle blueprints and the TV monitors. It must have been very hard on Homer Johnston, Ding thought. Homer had kids. He could have transported the subject into the next dimension as easily as blinking his eyes. But no, that would not have been smart. The men hadn't been ready for even an improvised assault, and anything that smacked of improvisation would only get more children killed. A phone rang. Bellow got it, hitting the speaker button. "Yes?" the doctor said.

"We regret the incident with the child, but she was soon to die anyway. Now, when will our friends be released?"

"Paris hasn't gotten back to us yet," Bellow replied.

"Tell Paris that unless the aircraft bringing our friends is ready for us to board in one hour, we will kill a hostage and then another every hour until our demands are met."

"That is unreasonable, Mr. One. Even if they brought all of them out of their prisons *now,* it would take at least two hours to get them here. Your wishes cannot make an airplane fly faster."

That generated a thoughtful pause. "Very well. We will commence the shooting of hostages in three hours from now. . . . No. I will start the countdown on the hour. That gives you an additional twelve minutes. I will be generous. Do you understand?"

"Yes. You say that you will kill another child at 2200 hours and another one every hour after that."

"Correct. Make sure Paris understands." And the line went dead.

"Well?" Clark asked.

"John, you don't need me for this. It's clear they'll do it."

"WHAT is that?" Esteban asked. He walked to the window to see. "Helicopter!"

"Oh?" René went there also. The windows were so small he had to move the Basque aside. "Yes, I see. The police have them. This is not a surprise. But get up to the roof, Esteban, with a radio, and keep us informed."

"COMMAND, Rifle Two One," Johnston called a minute later. "I got a guy on the castle roof. One man, armed. He's circulating around. . . . Yeah, looking over the edge, looking down."

"Roger that, Rifle Two One."

"RENÉ," Andre called from in front of a TV screen, "look."

There were two Guardia cops moving to a place fifty meters from the castle. René nodded and picked up his radio. "Three!"

"Yes, One."

"Police approaching the castle. Keep an eye on them."

"I will do that, One," Esteban promised.

"OKAY, they're using radios," Noonan said, checking his scanner. "Citizens-band walkie-talkies, set on channel sixteen."

"No names, just numbers?" Chavez asked.

"So far. Our point of contact calls himself One, and this guy is Three. Okay, does that tell us anything?"

"Radio games," Dr. Bellow said. "Right out of the playbook. They're trying to keep their identities secret from us."

"Okay, will the French deal?"

A shake of the head. "I don't think so. The minister, when I told him about the Dutch girl, said Carlos stays in the jug no matter what. And he expects us to resolve the situation successfully, and if we can't, his country has a team of its own to send down."

"So we've gotta have a plan ready by 2200."

John stood up straight and turned to look at his two team leaders. "Okay. You got two hours to plan it and one more to set it up. We go at 2200 hours."

"We need to know more about what's happening inside," Covington told Clark.

"Agreed. Noonan, what can you do?"

The FBI agent looked down at the blueprints, then over at the TV monitors. The best news he'd seen so far was that the castle windows made for two blind spots. Better yet, they could control the lights that bled energy into both of them. He walked over to the park engineer next. "Can you switch off these lights along here?"

"Sure. When?"

"When the guy on the roof is looking the other way. And I need somebody to back me up," Noonan added.

"I can do that," First Sergeant Vega said, stepping forward.

FIFTEEN minutes later Noonan was in his night costume, the two-shade greens they'd used in Vienna. His Beretta .45 automatic, with suppressor, was in a large shoulder holster over his body armor, and he had a backpack slung over one shoulder. "Vega, ready to take a little walk?"

"You betcha," Oso replied, glad at last to be doing *something* on a deployment. As much as he liked being responsible for the team's heavy machine gun, he'd never gotten to use it and, he thought, probably never would. He followed Noonan out the door, then outside. "Ladder?" he asked.

"Tool-and-paint shop fifty yards from where we're going. I asked. They have what we need."

It was a fast walk, dodging through a few open areas visible to the fixed cameras. The shop had no sign on it. Noonan slipped the ground-bolted door, and they walked in. Vega pulled a thirty-foot extension ladder off its wall brackets. "This ought to do."

"Yeah." They went outside. Movement would now be trickier. "Noonan to Command."

"Six here."

"Start doing the cameras, John."

In the command center, John Clark pointed to the park engineer. There was danger here but not much, they hoped. The castle command center, like this one, had eight TV monitors, which were hardwired into more than forty cameras. You could have the computer flip through them in an automatic sequence, or you could select cameras for special use. With a mouse click one camera was disabled. If the terrorists were using the automatic sequence, as seemed likely, they probably would not notice that one camera's take was missing.

"Okay, twenty-three is off, Noonan."

"We're moving," Noonan said. They walked twenty meters and stopped. "Okay, we're at the popcorn concession."

The engineer flipped camera 23 back on, then turned off 21.

"Twenty-one is off," Clark reported next. "Rifle Two One, where's the guy on the roof?"

"West side, just lit up a smoke. Staying still at the moment," Sergeant Johnston reported.

"Noonan, you are clear to move."

"Moving now," the FBI agent replied. He and Vega double-timed it across the stone slabs, their rubber-soled boots keeping their steps quiet. At the side of the castle were some large boxwoods. Carefully Noonan and Vega angled the ladder up, setting it behind a bush. Vega pulled the rope to extend the top portion, stopping it just under the window.

"Watch your butt, Tim," Oso whispered.

"Always." Noonan went up quickly for the first ten feet, then slowed to a vertical crawl. Patience, Tim told himself. Plenty of time to do this. It was the sort of lie that men tell themselves.

"OKAY," Clark heard Johnston say. "He's going up the ladder now. The roof guy is still on the opposite side, fat, dumb, and happy."

"Bear, this is Six. Over," John said, getting another idea.

"Bear copies, Six."

"Play around a little on the west side. Draw some attention."

"Roger that."

Malloy stopped his endless circling, leveled out, and then eased toward the castle. He stopped his approach at about two hundred meters. He wanted to get their attention, not to spook them. Through his night-vision goggles the colonel saw the guy on the roof turn to watch.

"Six, Bear. I have the bastard's attention."

NOONAN took off his Kevlar helmet and edged his face to the window. It was made of irregular glass segments held in place by lead strips, just like in the castles of old. Okay. He reached into his backpack and pulled a fiber-optic cable with the same cobra-head arrangement he'd used in Bern. "Noonan to Command, you getting this?"

"That's affirmative," Clark replied. The picture he saw was distorted, but you quickly got used to that. It showed four adults, but more important, it showed a crowd of children sitting on the floor in the corner, close to two doors with labels. The toilets, he realized. "Looks good, Tim. Looks very good."

"Okay." Noonan glued the tiny instrument in place and headed down the ladder. His heart was racing faster than it ever did on the morning three-mile run. At the bottom he and Vega hugged the wall.

T<small>HE SENTRY WAS TIRED OF</small> looking at the chopper, Johnston saw. "Our friend's moving east on the castle roof. Noonan, he's coming your way."

"Let's go," Noonan told Vega.

"The ladder?" They'd laid it behind the bushes on its side.

"Leave it." Noonan ran off in a crouch, reaching the concession stand in a few seconds. "Noonan to Command. Time to do the cameras again."

"Camera twenty-one is down. Get moving, Tim."

Seconds later they were in a safe position. Noonan leaned against a building wall and took a long breath. "Thanks, Julio."

"Anytime, man," Vega replied. And with that, they headed back to the underground command post.

"Blow the windows? Can we do that, Paddy?" Chavez was asking when they got there.

Paddy Connolly was wishing for a cigarette. He'd quit years before, but at times like this it seemed to help the concentration. "Six windows, three or four minutes each. No, I think not, sir. I can give you two—if we have the time."

"How sturdy are the windows?" Clark asked. "Dennis?"

"Metal frames set into the stone," the park manager said.

"Wait." The engineer turned a page on the castle blueprints. "Here's the specs. They're held in by grouting only. You should be able to kick them in, I think."

The "I think" part was not as reassuring as Ding would have preferred, but how strong could a window frame be with a two-hundred-pound man swinging into it with two boots leading the way?

"What about flash-bangs, Paddy?"

"We can do that," Connolly answered.

Chavez leaned over the plans. "You'll have time to blow two windows. This one and this one." He tapped the prints. "We'll use flash-bangs on the other four and swing in a second later. Eddie here, me here, Louis here. George, how's the leg?"

"Marginal," Sergeant Tomlinson replied with painful honesty. He'd strained his Achilles tendon in training, and it was still far from healed. He'd have to kick through a window, drop to a concrete floor, then come up shooting. And the lives of children were at stake. He couldn't risk it. "Better somebody else, Ding."

"Oso, think you can do it?" Chavez asked.

"Oh, yeah," Vega replied, trying not to smile. "You bet, Ding."

"Okay, Scotty here, and Mike take these two windows," he said to Pierce and McTyler. "What's the exact distance from the roof?"

That was on the blueprints. "Sixteen meters exactly from the level of the roof. Add another seventy centimeters to allow for the battlements."

"The ropes can do that easily," Eddie Price decided. The plan was coming together. He and Ding would get between the kids and the bad guys, shooting as they went. Vega, Loiselle, McTyler, and Pierce would be tasked to killing the subjects in the castle's command room. Covington's Team 1 would race up the stairs from the underground to intercept any subjects who ran out and to back up Team 2 if something went wrong on their assault.

"Let's kill the lights," Covington said. "Disorient them."

"Okay. The emergency lights will come on, but we'll still kill the lights right before we hit, just to distract them. Anything else?" Ding asked.

Major Covington nodded. "It ought to work."

Both men looked at Clark.

"Okay," he said. "Dr. Bellow, tell Mr. One that the French have caved, and their friends will be here."

"YES?" René said.

"Il'ych Sanchez is being released from Le Sante prison in about twenty minutes. Six of the others too, but there's a problem on the last three. I'm not sure what that is. They'll be taken to Charles de Gaulle Airport and flown here on an Air France Airbus 340. We think they'll be here by 2240. How will we get you and the hostages to them for the flight out?" Bellow asked.

"You will bring a bus to the castle. We will take ten or so of the children with us and leave the rest here as a show of good faith. Tell the police that any treachery will have severe consequences." René set the phone down and stood. "My friends, Il'ych is coming. The French have granted our demands."

MALLOY headed back to the airfield for refueling, which took half an hour. While there, he heard what was going to happen. In the back of the Night Hawk the crew chief, Sergeant Jack Nance, set the ropes to fifty-foot lengths exactly and hooked them into eye-bolts on the chopper's floor. Like Malloy and the copilot, Lieutenant Harrison, Nance had a pistol holstered on his left side. He never expected to use it and was only a mediocre shot, but it made him feel like part of the team. He supervised the refueling, capped the tank, and told Colonel Malloy the bird was ready.

"OKAY, people, let's move," Chavez told his team. Those directly involved in the rescue operation headed out to where one of the Spanish army trucks stood. They boarded it, and it drove off, looping around into the massive parking lot.

Dieter Weber selected a sniper perch opposite Sergeant Johnston's position, on top of the flat roof of a theater building, only a hundred and twenty meters from the castle's east side. Once there, he unrolled his foam mat, set up his rifle on the bipod, and started training his ten-power scope over the castle's windows. "Rifle Two Two in position," he reported to Clark.

"Very well. Report as necessary."

THE parking-lot lights went off at once. The truck, also with lights out, stopped next to a light standard. Chavez and his team jumped out. Ten seconds later the Night Hawk came in, touching down with the rotor still turning. The side doors opened, and the shooters clambered aboard. Without a word Malloy pulled the collective and climbed back into the sky.

"Bear, this is Six," Clark called on the radio.

"Bear copies, Six. Over."

"We execute in five minutes."

"Roger that. We party in five." Malloy turned in his seat. Chavez nodded, holding up one hand, fingers spread.

IN THE UNDERGROUND PETER Covington led three of his men toward the castle stairwells while the park engineer selectively killed off the surveillance cameras. His explosives man set a small charge on the fire door at the bottom and nodded at his boss. "Team One is ready."

"Rifle Two One is ready and on-target," Johnston said.

"Rifle Two Two is ready, but no target at this time," Weber told Clark.

"Three, this is One," the scanner crackled.

"Yes, One," the man atop the castle replied.

"The bus should be here in fifteen minutes. Stay alert."

"Okay," Noonan said. "That's a time stamp. Mr. One calls Mr. Three about every fifteen minutes. Never more than eighteen, never less than twelve. So—"

"Yeah." Clark nodded. "Move it up?"

"Why not?" Stanley said.

"Rainbow, this is Six. Move in and execute. Say again, execute!"

ABOARD the Night Hawk, Sergeant Nance moved left and right, sliding the side doors open. The shooters hooked up their zip-line rope to D rings on their belts. All of them turned inward, getting up on the balls of their feet, so their backsides were now dangling outside the helicopter.

"ANDRE, go down and look at the courtyard," René ordered. His man moved at once, holding his Uzi in both hands.

"Somebody just left the room," Noonan said.

"Rainbow, this is Six. Subject has left the command center."

Eight, Chavez thought. Eight subjects to take down. The other two would go to the long-rifle men.

THE last two hundred meters were the hard ones, Malloy thought. His hands tingled on the cyclic control stick. He dropped his nose, heading toward the castle. Without the anticollision lights the aircraft would only be a shadow. Better yet, the four-bladed rotor made a nondirectional sound. Someone could hear it, but locating the source was difficult. He needed that to last only a few more seconds.

"RIFLE TWO ONE, stand by."

Johnston's breathing became regular, and his elbows moved slightly, so that only bone, not muscle, was in contact with the mat under him. The mere passage of blood through his arteries could throw his aim off. His crosshairs were locked just forward of the sentry's ear. "On-target," he reported.

"Fire," the earpiece told him.

"Say good night, Gracie," a small voice in his mind whispered. His finger pushed back gently on the set trigger, which snapped cleanly. The body dropped straight down like a puppet with cut strings. No one inside would hear the shot, not through thick windows and stone walls from over three hundred meters away.

"Rifle Two One, target is down," Johnston reported.

"THAT'S a kill," Lieutenant Harrison breathed over the helicopter's intercom.

"Yep," Malloy agreed, easing back on the cyclic. "Sergeant Nance—*now!*" In the back, Nance pushed outward. The helicopter was still slowing, nose up now as Malloy performed the rocking-chair maneuver to perfection.

Chavez pushed off with his feet and went down the zip-line. In less than two seconds his rubber-soled black boots came down lightly on the flat roof. He immediately loosened his rope and turned to watch his people do the same. Eddie Price ran over to the sentry's body and turned, making a thumbs-up for his boss.

"Six, this is Team Two Lead. On the roof. The sentry is dead," he said into his microphone. "Proceeding now." With that, Chavez turned to his people, waving his arms to the roof's periphery. The Night Hawk was gone into the darkness.

The castle roof was surrounded by battlements, vertical rectangles of stone behind which archers could shelter while loosing their arrows at attackers. Each man had one such shelter assigned. They looped their rappelling ropes around them, then stepped into the gaps. When all of them were set up, they held up their hands. Chavez did the same, then dropped his as he kicked off the roof and slid down the rope to a point one meter to the right of a window, using his feet to stand off the wall. Paddy Connolly came down on the other side, reached to apply his Primacord around the edges, and inserted a radio detonator on one edge. Then Paddy moved to his left, swinging on the rope as though it were a jungle vine to set the explosives on one more window. Other team members took flash-bang grenades and held them in their hands.

"Two Lead to Six. Lights!"

In the command center, the engineer again shut off power to the castle.

The windows went dark. Then the wall-mounted emergency lights came on, just like miniature auto headlights, not enough to light the room properly. The TV monitors went dark. René reached for a phone. If they wanted to play more games, then . . . He thought he saw movement outside the window.

"Team Two, this is Lead. Five seconds, four, three." At three, the men holding the flash-bangs pulled the pins and set them right next to the windows, then turned aside. "Two, one, *fire!*"

Sergeant Connolly pressed his button, and two windows were sundered from the wall by explosives. A fraction of a second later three more windows were blown in by a wall of noise and blazing light. They flew across the room in a shower of glass, missing the children in the corner by three meters.

Next to Chavez, Sergeant Major Price tossed in another flash-bang, which exploded the moment it touched the floor. Then Chavez pushed outward from the wall, swinging into the room through the window, his MP-10 up and in both hands. He hit the floor badly, falling backward, then felt Price's feet land on his left arm. Chavez rolled and jolted to his feet, then moved to the kids. They were screaming with alarm, but he couldn't worry about them just yet.

Price scanned the room. There. It was a bearded one, holding an Uzi. Price extended his MP-10 to the limit of the sling and fired a three-round burst into his face from three meters away.

Oso Vega had kicked his window loose on leg power alone, and he landed right on top of a subject, rather to the surprise of both, but Vega was ready for surprises. Oso's left hand slammed out and hit the terrorist in the face with enough force to split it open into a bloody mess that a burst of three 10-mm rounds only made worse.

René was at his desk, the phone in his hand, his pistol on the table before him. He was reaching for it when Pierce fired into the side of his head.

In the far corner Ding came to one knee, his weapon up while his eyes scanned for targets. The semidarkness of the room was alive now with moving shadows.

One subject in the corner got his Uzi up. Chavez and Price both engaged him, then McTyler did as well. The terrorist crumpled.

Another terrorist had opened a door and raced through it. This one ran down, away from the shooting, turning one corner, then another, and tried to stop when he saw a black shape on the steps. It was Peter Covington, leading his team up. Covington took aim and fired when the surprised-looking face entered his sights. Then he resumed his race topside, with four men behind him. Just as Covington came in, Vega was circulating about, kicking the weapons away from every body. After five seconds he shouted, *"Clear!"*

ANDRE was outside, in the open, and all alone. He turned to look up at the castle.

"Dieter!" Homer Johnston called.

"Yes!"

"Can you take his weapon out?"

The answer was an exquisitely aimed shot that tore Andre's gun from his hands. From his perch four hundred meters away Johnston took careful aim and fired his second round of the engagement. It would forever be regarded as a very bad shot. Half a second later the 7-mm bullet struck the subject six inches below the sternum.

For Andre it seemed like a murderously hard punch. His screech ripped across the one hundred acres of Worldpark.

"COMMAND, this is Chavez. Mission accomplished. The kids— Uh-oh, we got one kid hurt here. Looks like a scratch on the arm. The rest of 'em are all okay. Subjects all down for the count, Mr. C. You can turn the lights back on."

As Ding watched, Oso Vega leaned down and picked up a little girl. "Hello, *querida*. Let's find your *mamacita,* eh?"

Eddie Price reached into his pocket and pulled out his pipe and a pouch of good Cavendish tobacco.

HOMER Johnston fairly ran down the steps of the Dive Bomber ride, then raced the few hundred meters to the castle. A doctor was there, wearing a white coat and looking down at the man Johnston had shot. "How is he?" the sergeant asked. The man's hands were holding his belly and were covered with blood.

"He will not survive," Dr. Weiler said. He had no chance, and all Weiler could do was give him morphine for the pain.

"That's the one shot the little girl," Johnston told the doctor. "I guess my aim was a little off." He looked down into the open eyes and grimacing face that let loose another moaning scream. Ten seconds later the rifleman turned away.

In the medical office, there were a lot of kids wide-eyed in shock. The Rainbow troopers fussed over them. One bandaged the only wound—a scratch, really—on a young boy.

Centurion de la Cruz was still there. The troops in black stripped off their body armor, and he saw on their uniform jackets the jump wings of paratroopers—American, British, and German. "Who are you?" he asked in Spanish.

"I'm sorry, I can't say," Chavez replied. "But I saw what you did on the videotape. You did well, Sergeant."

"So did you, ah—"

"Chavez. Domingo Chavez."

"The children—were any hurt?"

"Just the one over there."

"And the criminals?"

"They will break no more laws, amigo," Team 2 Lead told him.

"*Bueno.* I must—" He stood and hobbled out the door. He came back five minutes later, following John Clark, and holding—

"What is that?" Chavez asked.

"The eagle of the legion, VI Legio Victrix," the centurion told them. "The victorious legion. Senor Dennis, *con permiso?*"

"Yes, Francisco," the park manager said with a serious nod.

"With the respect of my legion, Senor Chavez. Keep this in a place of honor."

Ding took it. The thing must have weighed twenty pounds, plated as it was with gold. It would be a fit trophy for the club at Hereford. "We will do that, my friend."

The stress was bleeding off now, to be followed as usual by elation and fatigue. The troopers looked at the kids they'd saved, soon to be reunited with their parents.

"Time to leave," John said.

Out in the open, his pipe now filled, Eddie Price took a match from his pocket and struck it on the stone wall of the medical office, lighting the curved briar pipe for a long, victorious puff.

CHAPTER 6

DISCOVERY

THE successful conclusion of the Worldpark operation turned out to be a problem for Colonel Tomas Nuncio, the senior officer of the Guardia Civil on the scene. Assumed by the local media to be the officer in command of the operation, he was besieged with requests for details and videotapes for the TV reporters. The colonel decided to release Worldpark's own video coverage, as it showed very little. The most dramatic part had been the descent of the shooting team from the helicopter to the castle roof, then from the roof to the windows. That lasted a mere four minutes, and the distance of the cameras from the scene of action prevented the recognition of the rescue team. Nothing of the shooting inside the control room had been taped, because the terrorists had themselves wrecked the surveillance camera inside the facility. The elimination of the castle-roof sentry had been taped but was not released due to its gruesome nature, and the killing of the last terrorist, the one who had killed the little Dutch girl, was withheld for the same reason. The rest was released to news agencies for broadcast around the world.

It was eight o'clock in the evening when Dmitriy Arkadeyevich Popov saw it in his New York apartment. He smoked a cigar and sipped a vodka while his VCR taped it for later examination. The assault phase, he saw, was expert. The flashes of light from the explosives were dramatic and singularly useless for showing him anything, and the parade of the rescuers was as predictable as the dawn, their springy steps, their slung weapons, their arms full of small children. The trailing footage showed them walking off to a building where there must have been a physician to care for the child who'd sustained a minor injury, as the reporters said. Then, later, the troops had come outside, and one of them had swiped an arm against the stone wall of the building, lighting a match, which he used to light a pipe.

Popov blinked hard, leaning forward in his seat. The camera didn't zoom in, but the soldier/policeman in question was clearly smoking a curved pipe. Popov rewound the tape, ejected it, and then reached for a different tape. He inserted it into the VCR, then fast-forwarded to the end of the incident in Bern, where— Yes, a man had lit a pipe. He got the tape of the press coverage from the Vienna incident, and yes, at the end a man had lit a pipe, holding the pipe in exactly the same way.

Popov searched for other facts from the visual information he had. The pipe smoker was often attended by a shorter man. And there was another man, a large, muscular one, who in two of the tapes carried a heavy machine gun but in the third was carrying a child instead. So there were two and maybe a third man who had appeared in Bern, Vienna, and Spain. In every case the reporters had credited the rescue to local police, but no, that wasn't the truth, was it? So who were these people who arrived with the speed and decisiveness of a thunderbolt—in *three* different countries—twice to conclude operations he had initiated and once to settle one begun by others. Who those initiators had been, he didn't know, nor did he especially care. The reporters said they'd demanded the release of his old friend Carlos the Jackal. What fools. The French would as soon toss Napoleon's corpse from the Hôtel des Invalides as give up that murderer. Popov shook that thought off. He'd learned something of great importance this night, and to celebrate, he poured himself another vodka.

PETE was in real agony now, Dr. Killgore saw. It was time to move him. This he ordered at once, and two orderlies came in dressed in protective gear to load the wino onto a gurney for transport to the clinical side. Killgore followed his patient. The orderlies loaded Pete onto a bed, next to which was an electronically operated "Christmas tree" medication dispenser. Killgore got the IV plugged into Pete's major vein. Then he keyed the electronic box, and seconds later the body relaxed with a large bolus of medication while the Shiva continued to eat him alive from the inside out. Another IV would be set up to feed him with nutrients to keep his body going, along with various drugs. None were expected to work on the Shiva, but all had to be tested to make sure they didn't, lest there be a surprise when the epidemic spread. Vaccine B was expected to work, and that was being tested now with a new control group of people kidnapped from Manhattan bars. There was more sympathy for this group of test subjects. They were not winos. No, they were healthy people, eight women and three men. Eleven was actually one more than they'd planned, but after kidnapping them, you couldn't very well give them back.

The abductions had been expertly done. Letters of resignation had been sent when necessary, with signatures expertly forged and plausible explanations included. Still, Killgore didn't like it, but Shiva needed to be tested on a set of healthy subjects. And so did the vaccines. Eight of the eleven healthy subjects would be vaccine testers. Five with vaccine A, three with vaccine B. At least three would live, observed Dr. Killgore. Much of what the Project did might be distasteful, but it would still be done. The planet was dying and had to be saved, and there was only one way to do it, because too many others had no more understanding of the system than the lower animals. Only man could hope to understand the great balance. Only man had the responsibility to sustain that balance, and if that meant the reduction of his own species, well, everything had its price.

The Project would save Nature herself, and the Project was made of relatively few people, less than a thousand, plus those who had been selected to survive and continue the effort. The Project's installation in Kansas would grow all the grain they needed, and there would be cattle as well, until the buffalo spread out.

The Project would support itself by hunting for much of its meat. Needless to say, some members objected to that. They objected to killing anything, but cooler and wiser heads had prevailed on that issue. Man was both a predator *and* a toolmaker, and so guns were okay, too.

Cereals and vegetables would be grown by the farmers. They'd all eat well and live in harmony with Nature. It was a beautiful future to look forward to, though the initial four to eight months would be pretty dreadful. Humanity as the dominant force on the planet had to die, to be replaced by Nature herself, with just enough of the right people to observe and appreciate what she was and what she did.

"GOOD morning, Dmitriy," the boss said, coming into his office early.

"Good morning, sir," the intelligence officer said, rising to his feet as his employer entered the anteroom.

"What do you have for me?" John Brightling asked, unlocking his office door and going in.

"Something very interesting," Popov said. "On video."

"Okay, let's see it." He sat down in his swivel chair while Popov went to the far wall and slid back the wood panel that covered the electronics equipment. He retrieved the remote control and keyed up the large-screen TV and VCR. Then he inserted a videocassette.

"This is the news coverage of Bern," he told his employer. The tape ran for only thirty seconds before he stopped it, ejected the cassette, and inserted another. "Vienna," he said then, hitting the PLAY button. Another segment, which ran less than a minute. This he also ejected. "Last night at the park in Spain." This segment lasted just over a minute before he stopped it.

"What did you see, sir?"

"Some guy smoking. The same guy, you're saying?"

"Correct. It would appear that the same special-operations group responded to all three incidents. That is very interesting."

"Why?"

Popov took a patient breath. This man may have been a genius in some areas, but in others he was a babe in the woods. "Sir, there is now a team of special-operations troops operating in Europe. Such a group has never been admitted to in the press. It is, therefore, a 'black' group, highly secret. Now," Popov went on, "I have some questions for you."

"Okay." The boss nodded.

"Did you know of this team? Did you know they existed?"

A shake of the head. "No."

"Is it possible for you to find out some things about them?"

A shrug. "Maybe. Why is it important?"

"That depends on another question. Why are you paying me to incite terrorists to do things?" Popov asked.

"You do not have a need to know that, Dmitriy."

"Yes, sir, I do. One cannot stage operations against sophisticated opposition without some idea of the overall objective."

It occurred to Popov's employer that his existence was somewhat in pawn to this Russian ex-spook. He could deny everything the man might say, and he even had the ability to make the man disappear, but Popov might well have told others or even left a written record. Of course, there *was* a trail of sorts that a very clever investigator *might* be able to trace back closely enough to him to cause concern. The problem with electronic banking was that there was always a trail of electrons, and bank records were both time-stamped and amount-specific—enough to make some connection appear to exist.

"Dmitriy, will you let me think about that?"

"Yes, sir. Of course. I merely say that if you want me to do my job effectively, I need to know more. Show those tapes to people in your confidence, and see if they think the information is significant. Then call me when you need me, sir."

"Thanks for the information." He waited for the door to close. In his desk he had a beeper number for Bill Henriksen, president of Global Security. This he called, keying in his private line. Four minutes later the phone rang.

"Yeah, John, what is it?"

"Bill, I need to see you in my office ASAP."

"Give me twenty minutes."

Henriksen walked into the office eighteen minutes after the call. "What gives?"

"Watch this," John told him, flipping his office TV to the VCR and running the released tape of Worldpark. Then he had to rise and switch to the cassette of Vienna. Thirty seconds of that and then Bern. "So what do you think?"

"The same team on all three?" Henriksen wondered aloud. "The KGB guy you found—is he the guy who twigged to this?"

"Yep." A nod. "It worries him. Does it worry you?"

The former FBI agent grimaced. "Not sure. I want to know more. I'll talk to some contacts, rattle a few bushes. Thing is, if there is a black special-ops team out there, I should have known about it. What else did Popov say to you?"

"He wants to know why I'm having him do these things."

"That's the problem with spooks. They like to know things."

"What if we have to take him out?"

Another grimace. "You want to be careful doing that. Spooks are trained to be cautious. This operation is not without its dangers, John. How close are we to having the technical—"

"Very close. The test program is moving along nicely. Another month or so and we'll know all we need to know."

"Well, all I have to do is get the contract for Sydney. I'm flying down tomorrow. These incidents won't hurt. Run that tape again, the one of the Spanish job."

John inserted the tape and rewound it back to the beginning of the released TV coverage. It showed the assault team zip-lining down from the helicopter.

"I missed that," the expert admitted.

"What?"

"That's not a police chopper. It's a Sikorsky H-60. The H-60 has never been certified for civilian use. See how it's got 'Police' painted on the side? It isn't a police chopper, John. It's military. And if this is a refueling probe," he said, pointing, "then it's a special-ops bird. *That* means U.S. Air Force, man. That also tells us where these people are based—England or Germany. The air force has a special-ops wing based in those two countries. Your friend Popov is right. There *is* a special bunch of people handling these things. But who are they?"

"It's important?"

"Potentially, yes. What if the Aussies call them in to help out on the job I'm trying to get? That could screw up the whole thing."

"You rattle your bushes. I'll rattle mine."

"Right."

"HEY, Bill," Gus Werner said on the telephone from his office in the Hoover Building. "What's happening?"

"Catch the TV this morning?" Henriksen asked.

"You mean the thing in Spain?" Werner asked.

"That wasn't the Spanish cops, Gus. I know how they train. Not their style, man. So who was it? Delta, SAS, HRT?"

Gus Werner's eyes narrowed. Now assistant director of the FBI, he'd once been the special agent in charge of the FBI's elite Hostage Rescue Team. Bill Henriksen had once worked for him; then he left the Bureau to start his own consulting company. But once FBI always FBI, and so now Bill was fishing for information. "I really can't talk about that one, buddy."

"Classification issues?"

"Something like that," Werner allowed.

A chuckle. "Well, that tells me something, eh?"

"No, Bill, it doesn't tell you anything at all."

"You always were a straight shooter," Henriksen agreed. "Well, whoever they are, I'm glad they're on our side. Tell them one thing, though, if you get a chance."

"What's that, Bill?" was the noncommittal response.

"If they want to look like the local cops, they ought not use a U.S. Air Force helicopter. I'm not stupid, Gus."

Oops, Werner thought. He'd allowed that one to slip through. "Anybody else catch on to that?"

"Not that I know of, but tell them to be a little more careful."

"I'll do that," Werner promised, making a note.

"Black project," Henriksen told himself after hanging up. Whoever those people were, they had FBI connections. What else could he figure? How about where they were based? To do that . . . Yes. All he needed was a start time for the three incidents, then figure when it was the cowboys showed up, and from that he could make a pretty good guess as to their point of origin. Airliners traveled at about five hundred knots, and that made the travel distance— England, Henriksen decided. The Brits had all the infrastructure in place, and security at Hereford was pretty good.

What if the team deployed to Melbourne? Would that hurt anything? It surely wouldn't help, especially if there was an FBI agent on the team. He'd spent fifteen years in the Bureau, and Henriksen was under no illusions about those men and women. They had eyes that could see and brains that could think. And so his strategy to raise the world's consciousness of the terrorist threat—and help himself get the Melbourne job—might have gone an unplanned step further. But the law of unintended consequences could hit anyone, couldn't it? That's why he was in the loop. It was his job to deal with the unintended things. He'd confirm it from written records on the Bern and Vienna incidents. His staff covered all counterterror operations as a normal part of doing business, and he could call contacts in Switzerland and Austria.

The really bad news was that he had to fly off to Australia in less than a day and would himself be unable to do any more gathering. Well, he'd have dinner tonight with his boss to pass along what he knew, and maybe that ex-KGB guy on the payroll could pursue it. He'd performed pretty well to this point. A pipe smoker. It never ceased to amaze Henriksen how such little things could break open a case. You just had to keep your head up and eyes open.

THE CABINET MEETING ENDED early, and people headed out of the building. "Hi, George." Dr. Brightling greeted the Secretary of the Treasury.

"Hey, Carol, trees hugging back yet?" he asked with a smile.

"Always." She laughed in reply to this ignorant plutocrat. "Catch the TV report on that thing in Spain?"

"Worldpark? What about it?"

"Who were those masked men?"

"Carol, if you have to ask, then you're not cleared into it."

"I don't want their phone number, George," she replied, allowing him to hold open the door for her. "And I *am* cleared for just about everything."

Treasury Secretary George Winston had to admit that this was true. The President's science adviser was cleared into all manner of classified programs, including weapons, nuclear and otherwise. She was entitled to know about Rainbow if she asked. He just wished she hadn't asked. Too many people knew as it was. He sighed. "We set it up a few months ago. It's black, okay? Special-operations group, works out of England, mainly Americans and Brits, but others, too. The idea came from an Agency guy the boss likes."

"What's it called?"

"Rainbow. Because of the multinational nature."

"Well, whoever they are, they scored some points last night. You know, I really ought to get briefed on this. I *can* help, you know."

"So tell the boss you want in," the Secretary of the Treasury suggested as he opened his car door for the two-block ride back to his department. He waved at her as his driver pulled off.

"Rainbow," Brightling said to herself as she walked across West Executive Drive. Was it worth taking it a step further? The funny part about dealing with classification issues was that if you were inside, then you were inside. Reaching her office, she inserted the plastic key into her STU-4 secure telephone and dialed the CIA director's private line.

"Yeah?" a male voice answered.

"Ed, this is Carol Brightling."

"Hi. How'd the Cabinet meeting go?"

"Smooth, like always. I have a question for you."

"What's that, Carol?" the director of Central Intelligence asked.

"It's about Rainbow. That was some operation in Spain."

"Are you in on that?" Ed Foley asked.

"How else would I know the name, Ed? I know one of your people set it up. Can't remember the name, the guy the President likes so much."

"Yeah, John Clark. He was my training officer once, long time ago. What's your interest?"

"The new tactical-radio encryption systems the National Security Agency is playing with. Do they have it yet?"

"I don't know. Are they ready for prime time?"

"Should be in another month. E-Systems will be the manufacturer, and I thought they ought to be fast-tracked into Rainbow."

The DCI reminded himself that he should pay more attention to the work done at the National Security Agency. "Not a bad idea. I'll look into it. Thanks, Carol."

"Anytime, Ed, and maybe get me fully briefed into the program someday, eh?"

"Yeah. I'll send a guy down to get you the information you need. Bye, Carol."

The secure line was broken. Carol smiled at the phone. It was so easy to get information if you spoke the right language.

"THE interleukin isn't doing anything," Dr. John Killgore said, looking away from the monitor. "Shiva just laughs at it and moves on. This is one scary bug, Steve. Is vaccine B ready?"

Steve Berg nodded. "Yes. I had my injection a few hours ago. Ready for yours?"

"And vaccine A?"

"In the freezer, ready for mass production as soon as people need it. We'll be able to turn it out in thousand-liter lots per week. Enough to cover the planet."

"Can anybody else—"

"No way. Not even Merck can move that fast. And even if they did, they'd have to use our formula, wouldn't they?"

That was the ultimate hook. If the plan to spread Ebola-Shiva around the globe didn't work as well as hoped, then the entire world would be given vaccine A, which Antigen Laboratories, a division of Horizon Corporation, just happened to be working on as part of its corporate effort to help the third world, where all the hemorrhagic fevers lived. Steve Berg had published papers on these diseases, so the medical world wouldn't be surprised to learn that Horizon/Antigen had a vaccine in the works. They'd even test the vaccines in laboratories and find that sure enough, the liquid had all manner of antibodies. But they'd be the wrong antibodies, and the live-virus vaccine would be a death sentence to anyone who had it enter his system. The time from injection to onset of frank symptoms was programmed at four to six weeks.

A beeper went off. Killgore turned to look at the control panel. "It's Ernie, Subject Five. Looks like cardiac arrest," he said.

"What are you going to do?" Steve Berg asked.

Killgore stood. "Make sure he's dead."

"IT's called Rainbow," John Brightling told them, having gotten the best information of the day. "It's based in England. It was set up by a CIA guy named John Clark, and he's evidently the boss."

"That makes sense," said Henriksen. "Multinational, right?"

"I think so," Brightling confirmed.

"Yes," Dmitriy Popov said, picking at his Caesar salad. "Some sort of NATO unit, I imagine, based at Hereford. What do you want me to do about it?"

"We need to learn more," Henriksen said.

"How do we do that?" Brightling asked.

"It is not difficult," Popov assured him. "Once you know where to look, you merely go there and look."

POPOV boarded the morning Concorde flight for London. He'd never flown the Concorde before, and he found the interior of the aircraft cramped, though the legroom was all right. He settled into seat 4-C. Meanwhile, at another terminal, Bill Henriksen was in a first-class seat in an American DC-10 for his trip to Los Angeles.

William Henriksen, Dmitriy Arkadeyevich Popov thought, formerly of the FBI's Hostage Rescue Team and an expert on counter-terrorism, president of an international security company, now headed off to Australia to seek a consulting contract for the next Olympics. How did that factor into what Popov had been doing for John Brightling's Horizon Corporation? How did an expert on the mission side of terrorism and an expert on counterterrorism factor into the same plan? What were they up to? Popov shook his head.

The not knowing worried him. The KGB had never encouraged curiosity, but even they knew intelligent people had to be told something, and so with mission orders had usually come some kind of explanation, and at the least he'd always known that he was serving the interests of his country. He didn't know what he was doing now. He'd take the money and do the job, but for the first time he was uneasy, and the feeling was not a pleasant one.

"SO HOW does this thing work, Tim?"

Noonan moved his hand away, but the pointer stayed right on Chavez. "This is slick. It tracks the electromagnetic field generated by the human heart. It's a unique low-frequency signal. Doesn't even get confused by animals."

The gadget looked like a ray gun from a '30s science fiction movie, with a slim antenna wire out the front and a pistol grip underneath. It swung on a frictionless bearing, drawn to the signal it received. Noonan moved away from Chavez and Covington and headed for the wall. There was a secretary sitting right . . . there. The gadget locked onto her. As he walked, it stayed pointed at her through the blank wall.

"It's like a divining rod," Peter observed.

"Does look that way, doesn't it? No wonder the army wants this baby. Forget about being ambushed. This thing'll find people underground, behind trees, in the rain—wherever."

"What's it for?" Chavez asked.

"Search and rescue—firemen in a burning building, avalanche victims, lots of things, Ding. The Delta guys have fallen in love with it. Still a little hard to use, and it can't tell range yet, but all they have to do is modify the antenna for greater gain, then link two of the detectors with a GPS locator and triangulate. They say this one can lock onto a person at five hundred meters."

"But what good will it be for us? It can't tell a hostage from a terrorist," Chavez pointed out.

"It can tell you where the bad guys are *not*," Noonan said.

THE Brown Stallion was the name of the pub right next door to Popov's motel. It was only half a kilometer from the main gate at Hereford, and it seemed like a good place to start. Popov ordered a pint of Guinness and sipped at it, surveying the room. A television was on, carrying a soccer match between Manchester United and the Rangers from Scotland. Popov watched and listened to the chitchat around the room. He was trained to be patient. The game ended in a 1–1 tie around the time Popov ordered a second pint.

"Tie, stinking tie," one man observed at the bar seat next to Popov's.

"That's sport for you, Tommy. At least the chaps down the road never tie—and never lose."

"How are the Yanks fitting in, Frank?"

"Good bunch, that lot. Very polite. I had to fix the sink for one of the houses today." The plumber finished off his pint of lager and called for another.

"You work on the base?" Popov asked the plumber.

"Yes. Have for twelve years, plumbing and such."

"Good lot of men, the SAS," the Russian offered in his best British blue-collar accent. "So some Americans are based there now, eh?"

"Yes. About ten of them and their families."

"I may know one of them—chap name of Clark, I think," Popov offered as a somewhat dangerous ploy.

"Oh? He's the boss. Wife's a nurse in the local hospital. Haven't met him, but they say he's a very serious chappie. Must be to command that lot."

"Were they involved in the showdown in Spain last week?"

"Well, they don't tell us any of that, see, but"—the plumber smiled—"I saw a Hercules fly out of the airstrip the day it happened, and they were back in their club late that night, looking very chuffed with themselves."

Popov drained his glass and paid the bill. It had been a pretty good night, and he didn't want to press his luck. So the wife of John Clark was a nurse at the local hospital, eh? He'd have to check that out.

CHAPTER 7

CONTACTS

SO WHAT can you offer us?" the police superintendent asked.

Bill Henriksen liked the Australians. They came right to the point. They were sitting in an office in Canberra, Australia's capital, with the country's senior cop and some people in military uniforms. "Well, first of all, you know my background." He'd already made sure of that. His FBI experience and the reputation of his company were also well known. "You know I work with the FBI and sometimes even with Delta at Fort Bragg. I have contacts, good ones. Furthermore, I work with all the hardware suppliers. I can connect you with H&K for the new MP-10 that our guys like. But anyone can get guns for you. I also do business with all the electronics companies. I know what's happening in communications and surveillance equipment. Your SAS is weak in that area, according to my contacts. I can fix that. In addition, my people can train you on the new equipment. I have a team of former Delta and HRT people, including Dick Voss, the regimental sergeant major from the Special Operations Training Center at Fort Bragg. He's the best in the world, and he works for me."

"I've met him," the Aussie SAS major noted. "Yes, he's very good indeed."

"You've all seen the upsurge of terrorist activity in Europe,"

Henriksen went on, "and that's a threat you need to take seriously for the Olympics. Your SAS people don't need any advice on tactics, but what my company can do is to get you state-of-the-art electronics gear and train your troops on it. There's no other company in the world with our expertise."

"What do you know about the European incidents?" the Aussie SAS officer asked.

Henriksen affected a sensitive look. "Much of what I know is, well, off the record, if you know what I mean."

"We all have security clearances," the cop told him.

"Okay, but you see, the problem is, I am *not* cleared into this stuff, exactly, and— Oh, what the heck. The team doing the takedowns is called Rainbow. It's a black operation composed mainly of Americans and Brits, with some other NATO nationalities tossed in. They're based in the U.K. at Hereford. Their commander is an American CIA type, guy name of John Clark. They evidently have diplomatic agreements in place to operate all over Europe when the countries with problems invite them in. Has your government talked to anyone about them?"

"We're aware of it," the chief cop replied. "What you said is correct in all details. In honesty, I didn't know the name of the commander. Anything else you can tell us about him?"

"I've never met the man, but his operational people have shown what they can do. Anyway, that's what I bring to the party, boys. My people and I can be down here to assist your people in three or four days from the moment you say come."

There were no additional questions. The top cop seemed properly impressed, and the SAS major even more so.

"Thanks very much indeed for coming," the policeman said.

It was hard not to like the Aussies, and their country was still largely in a pristine state, Henriksen thought as he looked across the table at his hosts. But he couldn't think of them as fellow human beings, could he? They were competitors, rivals for the ownership of the planet, but unlike himself, they were poor stewards. There were relatively few people in Australia, but even that small number had still managed to upset the ecosystem. Maybe that was a sign that man simply couldn't be trusted anywhere, he thought, even a few of them in a whole continental landmass. And so the Project was needed here as well. A pity.

POPOV, his wide-brimmed brown hat in his lap, was sitting in the train on the way back to Hereford, leafing through the pages just relayed from Moscow. His former colleague Ivan Petrovich Kirilenko had been as good as his word, Dmitriy Arkadeyevich saw with pleasure. In exchange for Popov's information about a certain black operation based in England, the KGB's Station London *rezident* had furnished his organization's dossier on Clark, John T., senior CIA field officer.

The manila envelope had come with unusual speed from number 2 Dzerzhinsky Square, and the report ran to twenty single-spaced pages. His former agency in Moscow had paid quite a bit of attention to John Clark. There were three photographs of him. They'd even taken the time to learn about his family. Two daughters, one still in college in America and one a physician now married to Domingo Chavez—*another* CIA field officer—who, Popov saw, was evidently partnered with the older officer. Might this Chavez be in England, too? Chavez's wife was a physician. Clark's wife, Popov knew, was a nurse at the local hospital. Wasn't *that* interesting?

"YES, this is Henriksen," he said into the hotel phone.

"This is Bob Aukland," the voice said. He was the senior cop at the meeting, Bill remembered. "I have good news for you."

"Oh? What might that be, sir?"

"The name's Bob, old man. We spoke with the minister, and he agrees that we should award Global Security the consulting contract for the Olympics."

"Thank you, sir. When can I go out to the facility?"

"I'll fly you down myself tomorrow afternoon."

"Excellent, Bob. What about your SAS people?"

"They'll be at the stadium as well. They want to see that new communications equipment you told them about."

"E-Systems has just started manufacturing it for our Delta people.

Six ounces per unit, real-time 128-bit encryption. Near impossible to intercept. Anyone trying to listen in would hear only static."

"DR. CHAVEZ, please," Popov told the operator at the hospital.

"Wait, please," the voice replied. It took seventy seconds.

"Dr. Chavez," a voice said.

"Oh, sorry, I have the wrong number," Popov said, and cradled the phone. Excellent. Both Clark's wife and daughter worked at the local hospital. That confirmed that this Domingo Chavez was over in Hereford as well. It had been a good week for the intelligence officer, and now it was time to leave. He packed his clothes, wondering what use his employer would make of the things he'd learned.

"FOR what do we deserve this honor, Ed?" Clark asked.

"You have a fairy godmother at the White House. The first thirty radio sets go to you. Ought to be there in two days," the director of Central Intelligence told Rainbow Six.

"Who at the White House?"

"Carol Brightling, presidential science adviser. After the World-park job she suggested you get these new radios."

"She's not cleared into us, Ed," Clark remembered. "At least, I don't remember her name on the list."

"Well, somebody must have told her something, John. When she called, she knew the code word. Anyway, getting you this gear was a good call on her part. I talked to Sam Wilson down at Special Operations Command, and his people have signed off on it with enthusiasm. Jam-proof, encrypted, and light as a feather." As well it ought to be at seven thousand dollars per set.

"Okay. Two days, you said?"

"Yep. Oh, one other thing."

"What's that?"

"Tell Noonan his letter about that people-finder gadget has generated results. The company's sending a new unit for him to play with—four of them, as a matter of fact. Improved antenna and GPS locator, too."

"Okay, I'll pass that along to Tim."

"WHAT'S THIS FOR?" Henriksen asked innocently.

"A fog-cooling system. We got it from your chaps," Aukland said.

"Huh? I don't understand," the American replied.

"One of our engineers saw it in . . . Arizona, I think. It sprays a very fine water mist, has the same effect as air-conditioning but with negligible energy expenditure."

"Ah," Bill Henriksen said, doing his best to act surprised. "How widely distributed is the system?"

"Just the tunnels and concourses. The architect wanted to put it all over the stadium, but people objected, said it would interfere with cameras," Aukland answered. "Too much like a real fog."

"Okay. I think I need to look at that."

"Why?"

"Well, sir, it's a heck of a good way to deliver a chemical agent, isn't it?" The question took the police official seriously aback.

"Well, yes, I suppose it would be."

"Good. I have a guy in the company, former officer in the U.S. Army Chemical Corps. I'll have him check it out ASAP."

"Yes, that is a good idea, Bill. Thank you," Aukland said, kicking himself for not thinking of that on his own.

"Does it get that hot here?"

"Oh, yes, quite. We expect temperatures in the nineties. The architect said that this was an inexpensive way to cool the spectators down. It feeds off the fire sprinkler system. It's been installed for over a year. We test it periodically. American company, can't recall the name at the moment."

Cool-Spray of Phoenix, Arizona, Henriksen thought. He had the plans for the system in his office. It had been seen as a godsend for the Project from the first moment. Here was the place. Soon would come the time.

"HIS wife is a nurse at the local community hospital," Popov told his boss, "and his daughter is a medical doctor—married to one of the other team members—working at the same hospital. She is Dr. Patricia Chavez. Her husband is Domingo Chavez, also a CIA field officer now assigned to this Rainbow group. Both Clark and Chavez are highly experienced intelligence officers. It would be dangerous to underestimate them," Popov concluded.

"Okay, so we know about them. Is it possible they know about us?" John Brightling asked.

Possible, but unlikely, Popov thought. "If that were the case, you would have agents of your FBI in here to arrest you—and me—for criminal conspiracy. I am not being followed. Well, I do not think I am."

That shook his employer, Popov saw. He'd just admitted he was not perfect. His former supervisors in the KGB would have known it and accepted it as a normal risk of the intelligence trade.

"What are the risks?"

"If you mean what methods can be used against you?" Popov said, and Brightling nodded. "That means your phones could be tapped, and—"

"My phones are encrypted. My consultants tell me—"

Popov cut him off with a raised hand. "Sir, do you really think your government allows the manufacture of encryption systems that it cannot itself break?"

"Huh? What do you mean? I've been told this system I have could not be broken, because it is a 128-bit—"

"Ah, yes, the STU-3 standard. That system has been around your government for about twenty years. Your people have changed to STU-4. Do you think they made that change merely because they wanted to spend money, Dr. Brightling?"

"So people could be listening in on every call I make?"

Popov nodded. "Of course. Why do you suppose all of our substantive conversations have been made face to face?" He was really shaken, Dmitriy Arkadeyevich saw. The genius *was* a babe in the woods. "Now, perhaps, is the time for you to tell me why I have undertaken these missions for you."

He couldn't tell Popov, Brightling knew. He didn't know Popov's views on the environment and nature, so he couldn't predict the Russian's reaction to the Project. Popov was dangerous to him in many ways, like a falcon trained to the fist but still a free agent. Not for the first time Brightling thought about having Bill

Henriksen take care of this potential problem. He'd know how.

Assets, Brightling thought next. What could he do to make his position and his Project more secure? If this Rainbow was a problem, would it be possible to strike at it directly? Destroy it? "I have to think that one through first, Dmitriy," he said finally.

Popov nodded soberly, wondering what thoughts had gone through his employer's mind in the fifteen seconds he'd taken to consider the question.

"YES, Minister. . . . Excellent, thank you," Bob Aukland said into his cellular phone. He thumbed the END button and put the phone back into his pocket; then he turned to Bill Henriksen. "Good news. We'll have that Rainbow group down to consult on our security as well."

"Oh?" Bill observed. "Well, I guess it can't hurt all that much."

"Nose a little out of joint?" the cop asked.

"Not really." He lied. Once more the law of unintended consequences had risen up to bite him.

Henriksen caught the Qantas flight for Los Angeles and spent the better part of a day in his first-class seat, considering what he knew. The plan for the Olympics was essentially in the bag. He'd have one of his men check out the fogging system and thereby get himself in place for the delivery on the last day. It was that simple. The operational concept had been brilliant—mainly his from the beginning. John Brightling had merely funded it. Getting the terrorists to operate in Europe had raised the international consciousness about the threat, and *that* had allowed his company to get the contract to oversee security for the Olympics. But then this Rainbow team had appeared and handled three major incidents—and who had instigated the third one? he demanded of himself—so well that now the Australians had asked *them* to come down for a look. And if they came down, they might wonder about chemical weapons and—

Relax, he told himself as the stewardess came around with drinks and he had a glass of wine. Relax. But no, he couldn't do that. If his man was stopped, even by accident, the entire Project could be uncovered. And *that* would mean more than failure. It would mean lifelong imprisonment at best. No, he was committed to the Project for more than one reason. It was his task to save the world first of all. And second, he wanted to be around to enjoy what he'd had a hand in saving.

And so risks of any type were unacceptable. He had to eliminate them. The key to that was the Russian, Popov. He wondered what that spook had discovered on his trip to England. With the right information he could devise a plan to deal with that Rainbow bunch directly. Wouldn't that be interesting?

POPOV was eating dinner alone in a disreputable-looking restaurant at the southern end of Manhattan. But the vodka here was superb, and as usual, a few drinks helped him think abstractly.

What did he know about John Brightling? Well, the man was a scientific genius and very impressive in his business skills. He had good connections in the community of people admitted into classified matters. This Rainbow group was evidently black, but he'd gotten its name and the name of its commander in a day. Just one day, Popov reminded himself. That was beyond impressive. It was startling. Yet when Popov had informed Brightling of the flaws in his communications security, the man had become frightened. He ought to have warned him earlier, Dmitriy Arkadeyevich realized, but operational security was not all that bad. Only two people knew what was happening. Well, probably that Henriksen fellow as well. But Bill Henriksen was former FBI, and if he was an informer, they'd all be in jail now. The FBI would not allow things to proceed any further unless there was some vast criminal conspiracy yet to be uncovered.

What was going on here? Was Brightling a spy, feeding information to a foreign government? But in return for what? How could anyone, government or not, bribe a billionaire? No, money was out. What did that leave?

There was a classic acronym for the reasons for making treason against your native land: MICE—or money, ideology, conscience, and ego. Money was out. Brightling had too much of that. Ideology was always the best motivation for a traitor/spy—people would risk their lives far more readily for their closely held beliefs than for filthy lucre—but what ideology did this man have? Next came conscience. But conscience against what? What wrong was he trying to right? That left ego. Well, Brightling had a capacious ego, but ego assumed the motive of revenge against some more powerful person or institution that had wronged him. Who could possibly have hurt billionaire John Brightling so much that his material success was not a sufficient salve against the wound? Popov waved to the waiter for another vodka. No, money was out. So was ego. That left ideology and conscience.

In his career in the KGB, Popov had played the game against world-class adversaries and never once failed in an assignment. As a result, he considered himself a clever sort. That made the current impasse all the more frustrating. He had over a million dollars in a Bern bank. He had the prospect of more in due course. He'd set up two terrorist missions that had accomplished their goal. Or had they? His employer evidently thought so, despite the tactical failure of both. But he knew even less now, Dmitriy Arkadeyevich told himself. And the less he knew, the unhappier he became.

THEY practiced the breathing exercises. Ding found it amusing, but he was also persuaded that it was necessary. Tall and rangy though Patsy was, she was not the athlete he'd become to lead Team 2. She had to practice how to breathe to make the baby come more easily, and so they sat on the floor of their house, both with their legs spread, huffing and puffing as though to destroy the home of a mythical pig. It was all he could do not to laugh. "Deep cleansing breath," he said after timing the notional contraction. Then he reached for her hand and bent forward to kiss it. "How we doing, Pats?"

"I'm ready, Ding. I just want it to happen and be over."

"Worried?"

"Well," Patsy Clark Chavez, M.D., replied, "I know it's going to hurt some, and I'd just as soon have it behind me, y'know?"

"Yeah." Ding nodded. The anticipation of unpleasant things was usually worse than their realization. Maybe that was why second deliveries were almost always easier than the first. You knew what to expect, knew that though it was uncomfortable, you'd make it through and have a baby at the end of it. That was the key for Domingo. To be a father! To have a child. To begin the greatest of all adventures, raising a new life, making some mistakes but learning from them and ultimately presenting to society a new, responsible citizen to carry on. Yes, there was much to look forward to, Ding told himself, still holding Patsy's hand in his own. "Scared?"

"Not scared. A little nervous," Patsy admitted.

"Honey, if it were all that hard, how come there's so many people in the world?"

"Spoken like a man," Dr. Patricia Chavez noted. "It's easy for you to say. You don't have to do it."

"I'll be there to help," her husband promised.

"You better be!"

THE information was very interesting, Henriksen thought. This Russian was pretty good. And with the information he recalled his idea from the Qantas flight. "Dmitriy," he asked, "do you have contacts in Ireland?"

Popov nodded. "Yes, several of them."

Henriksen looked over at John Brightling for approval and got a nod. "How would they like to get even with the SAS?"

"That has been discussed many times, but it is not practical. It is like sending a robber into a guarded bank. No, it is like sending a robber into the government agency which prints the money. There are too many defensive assets to make the mission practical."

"But what if we could draw them into the open and then stage our own little surprise for them?"

"It is still a very dangerous mission."

"Very well. What is the current condition of the IRA?"

Popov leaned back in his chair. "They are badly split. Some factions want peace. Some want the disorders to continue. The reasons are both ideological and personal. Ideological insofar as they truly believe in their objective of overturning both British rule in Northern Ireland and the Republican government in Dublin and estab-

lishing a 'progressive socialist' government. They are committed
Marxists—actually more Maoist than Marxist."

"And the personal side?" Brightling asked.

"To many people a revolutionary is a romantic character, a person who believes in a vision of the future and is willing to risk his
life for it. From that comes his social status. To lose that status in-
jures the former revolutionary. He must now work for a living, drive
a truck or whatever—"

"Do you know these people?" Henriksen asked pointedly.

"Yes. I met many in the Bekáa Valley in Lebanon, where they
trained with other 'progressive elements.' And I have traveled to
Ireland to deliver messages and money to support their activities."
Popov looked at the other two men in the room. "What would you
have them do?"

"It's not so much a question of what as of how," Bill told the Russian. "You know, when I was in the Bureau, we used to say the IRA
had the best terrorists in the world—dedicated, smart, and utterly
vicious."

"I would agree."

"How would they view this mission?"

"What mission is that?" Dmitriy asked, and then Bill explained
his concept. The Russian listened politely before responding. "That
would appeal to them, but the dangers are very large."

"What would they require to cooperate?"

"Money and other support—weapons, explosives, the things they
need to carry on their operations. Several million dollars, I should
say—at the least, that is."

"Call it five million?" John Brightling asked.

"That should be enough," Popov said after a moment's reflection.
"Plus the psychological attraction of bearding the lion so close to
his own den. But I can offer no promises. These people make their
own decisions."

"How quickly could you arrange the meeting?"

"Two days, perhaps three, after I arrive in Ireland."

"Get your tickets," Brightling told him decisively.

Five million dollars, Popov thought to himself. If he could bank that, he'd have the resources he needed to live in comfort forever. But how could he defraud the IRA out of the money detailed to them? Well, that might easily come to him.

THE initial meeting took place in a park. Popov had checked the telephone book and called the number for one Patrick X. Murphy. "Hello, this is Joseph Andrews. I'm trying to find Mr. Yates," he'd said.

There was silence as the man on the other end of the phone had searched his memory for the code phrase.

After ten seconds or so he'd fished it out. "Ah, yes, Mr. Andrews. We haven't heard from you in some time."

"I just arrived in Dublin this morning, and I'm looking forward to seeing him. How quickly can we get together?"

"How about one this afternoon?" And then had come the instructions. So here he was, wearing his raincoat and wide-brimmed fedora hat, carrying a copy of the *Irish Times* in his right hand and sitting on a particular bench close to an oak tree.

"Joe!" a happy voice said.

Popov looked up to see a fortyish man with a beaming smile. "Patrick!" he responded, shaking his hand. "It's been a long time." Very long, as he'd never met this particular chap before, though they exchanged greetings like old friends. With that, they walked off to O'Connell Street, where a car was waiting. Popov and his new friend got into the back, and the driver took off, checking his rearview mirror carefully as he took several random turns. Well, Dmitriy thought, the Provisional wing of the Irish Republican Army was as ruthless as any terrorist organization in the world, and these PIRA soldiers hadn't lived to their current ages by being careless. For his part Popov just sat back and relaxed. After forty minutes of weaving through the city, they came to a commercial building and looped around into an alley. There the car stopped, and they got out to enter a door in a blank brick wall.

"Iosef Andreyevich Serov," a voice said calmly in the darkness. Then a face appeared.

"Sean, it has been a long time." Popov extended his hand.

"Eleven years and six months, to be exact," Sean Grady agreed, taking the hand and shaking it warmly. "Come this way."

Grady directed him to a small room with a table and a few chairs. There was tea brewing. The Irish hadn't lost their sense of hospitality, Dmitriy Arkadeyevich saw, removing his coat and dumping it on an armchair. Then he sat down.

"What can we do for you?" Grady asked. He was nearly fifty, Popov saw, but the eyes retained their youth and dedicated look.

"Before we get to that, how are things going for you, Sean?"

"They could be better. Some of our former colleagues in Ulster are committed to surrendering to the British crown."

"Thank you," Popov said to the one who gave him a cup of tea. He took a sip before speaking. "Sean, you know, from the first time we met in Lebanon, I have respected your commitment to your ideals. I am surprised that so many others have wavered."

"It's been a long war, Iosef, and I suppose not everyone can maintain his dedication. And more is the pity, my friend." His voice was singularly devoid of emotion. His face wasn't so much cruel as blank.

"There is a new counterterror team in England," Dmitriy said.

"Oh?" The revelation surprised Grady.

"Yes. It is called Rainbow. It is a joint effort of the British and the Americans. It was they who handled the jobs at Worldpark, Vienna, and Bern."

"What do you know about this new group?"

"Quite a lot." Popov handed over his written summary.

"Hereford," Grady observed. "We've been there to look, but it is not a place one can easily attack."

"I know that, Sean, but with proper planning we think it possible to strike a hard blow. You see, both the wife and daughter of the Rainbow group commander, this American, John Clark, work at the nearby hospital. They would be the bait."

"Bait?" Grady asked.

"Yes, Sean." And then Popov went on to describe the mission.

"Colonel Serov, you propose that we undertake a major risk."

Dmitriy nodded. "Yes, that is true, and it is for you to decide if the risk is worth the rewards." Popov did not have to point out that this mission, if successful, would not only catapult Grady to the forefront of IRA commanders but also perhaps poison the peace process between the British government and the "official" faction of the PIRA. To be the man who humbled the SAS on their own turf would win him such prestige as no Irish revolutionary had enjoyed since 1920.

"Iosef Andreyevich, unfortunately, we do not have the resources to consider such a mission as this."

"I understand that. What resources do you require, Sean?"

"More than you can offer."

"Five million American dollars in a numbered Swiss account," Popov said evenly, and this time he saw emotion on Grady's face.

"Six," Grady said, just to take control of the agenda.

That suited Popov fine. "Very well. I suppose I can offer six. How quickly will you need it?"

"How quickly can you deliver it?"

"A week, I think. How long for you to plan the operation?"

Grady thought for a few seconds. "Two weeks." He already knew much of the area around Hereford. That he had not been able to conduct an attack in earlier days hadn't prevented him from thinking—dreaming—about it. "One other thing," he said. "How good are your contacts with drug dealers?"

Popov was shocked, though he didn't react visibly. Grady wanted drugs to sell? That was a huge change in the PIRA's ethos. In earlier years the Provos had made a point of killing or knee-capping drug dealers as a means of showing they were worthy of community support. "I have some indirect contacts, I suppose. What would you require?"

"Cocaine. A large quantity of it, preferably pure."

"To sell here?"

"Yes. Money is money, Iosef," Grady pointed out. "And we need a continuing income to maintain operations."

"I make no promises, but I will see what I can do. Weapons?"

"That is not a concern," Grady assured him.

BILL Henriksen was assembling his team. He figured ten men, all briefed on the Project. Foremost among them would be Lieutenant

Colonel Wilson Gearing, formerly of the U.S. Army Chemical Corps. A genuine expert on chemical weapons, he would be the delivery-man. The rest would consult with the locals and tell them things they already knew, enforcing the international rule that an expert was somebody from out of town. The Australian SAS would listen politely and maybe even learn a thing or two, especially when his people brought down the new radio gear from E-Systems and Dick Voss trained the Aussies on them. After that they'd be able to watch the Olympics close-up, which would be an interesting fringe benefit for his people, some of whom, he was sure, were real sports fans.

So THIS project was done. Charlie Hollister looked over the buildings, the roads, the parking lots, and the ersatz airplane runway whose construction he'd supervised here on the Kansas plains. The company car pulled up to his 4 × 4 and stopped, and then Hollister was surprised. The guy who got out was the big boss, John Brightling himself. He'd never met the chairman of the corporation, though he had seen the face on TV.

"Mr. Hollister, I presume?"

"Yes, sir." He took the extended hand and shook it. "It's all done as of today, sir."

"You beat your promise by two and a half weeks," Brightling observed.

"The toughest part was the environmental systems. That's the most demanding set of specifications I've ever seen. What's the big deal, Dr. Brightling?"

"Well, some of the things we work with demand full isolation."

"But the whole building?" Hollister asked. Rarely was any large structure designed to be completely airtight.

"Well, we just wanted it done our way. And you've earned your bonus. The money will be in your account by the close of business tomorrow."

"Suits me, sir." Hollister fished in his pocket for the master key that would open any door in the complex. It was a little ceremony he always performed when he finished a project. He handed it over. "Well, sir, it's yours now."

Brightling looked at the electronic key and smiled. This was the last major hurdle for the Project. This would be the home of nearly all his people. A similar but much smaller structure in Brazil had been finished two months earlier, but that one barely accommodated a hundred people. This one could house three thousand. He could sustain his medical research efforts here with his best people—most of them *not* briefed on the Project but worthy of life even so— because that work was heading in some promising directions. So promising that he wondered how long he himself might live here. Fifty years? A hundred? A thousand, perhaps? Who could say?

Olympus, he'd call it, Brightling decided on the spot. The home of the gods, for that was exactly what he expected it to be. From here they could watch the world, study it, enjoy it, *appreciate* it.

GRADY'S face was known in the United Kingdom, but not the red beard and glasses, which, he hoped, would reduce the chance of his being spotted by an alert police constable. The gate into the base at Hereford was just as he'd remembered it, and from there it wasn't a long drive to the hospital, where he examined the roads and parking areas and found them to his liking as he shot six rolls of film with his Nikon. His plan was simple, as all good plans were. As always, surprise would be his primary weapon. He needed that and fifteen good men. The other resources money could purchase, Grady thought as he sat in the hospital parking lot. Yes, this could work. The only question was daylight or nighttime. The latter was the usual answer, but he'd learned the hard way that counterterror teams loved the night because their night-vision equipment made the time of day indistinguishable in a tactical sense. And people like Grady were not trained to operate as well in the dark. It had given the police an enormous advantage recently in Vienna, Bern, and Worldpark. So why *not* try it in broad daylight? It was something to discuss with his friends.

"YES, he will do it," Popov said. They were in a corner booth, and the background music made it a secure place to talk. "He has not confirmed it, but he will." Popov knew the challenge was too great for a man of Grady's ego to walk away from, and the same was true of the reward.

"Who is he?" Henriksen asked.

"Sean Grady. Do you know the name?"

"PIRA. Worked in Londonderry mainly, didn't he?"

"For the most part, yes. He captured three SAS people and disposed of them. Two separate incidents. The SAS then targeted him on three separate missions. Once, they came close to getting him, and they eliminated ten or so of his associates. Then he cleaned out some suspected informers in his unit. He's quite ruthless," Popov assured his associates.

"Does he have enough people?" Henriksen asked.

"I think yes," Dmitriy Arkadeyevich replied. "And he held us up for money. I offered five, and he demanded six, plus drugs."

"Drugs?" Henriksen was surprised.

"We live in a practical world. Grady needs income for his operations," Dmitriy explained. The morality of the issue didn't seem very important to anyone at the table.

"Yeah, well, I suppose we can entertain that request," Brightling said with a small measure of distaste.

"And I assume you will approve the increase he requires."

"What's another million or so?" Henriksen asked with a suppressed grin.

So both of them regarded such a large sum as trivial, Popov saw, and again he was struck in the face with the fact that they were planning something monstrous—but what?

"How do they want it? Cash?" Brightling asked.

"No. I told them it would be deposited in a numbered Swiss account. I can arrange that, though it means I fly to Switzerland again," Dmitriy observed sourly.

"Getting tired of flying?"

"I have traveled a great deal, Dr. Brightling." Popov sighed openly. He was jet-lagged, and it showed for once.

"Call me John."

"John." Popov nodded, seeing some actual affection in his boss for the first time, somewhat to his surprise.

"Where did you grow up?" Brightling asked.

"Moscow. My father was also an officer in State Security. I was educated in Moscow State University. Language and economics."

"Ever get out of the city? You know, like Boy Scouts do here, that sort of stuff?"

Popov smiled, wondering where this was going. But he played along. "One of my happiest memories of childhood—I was in the Young Pioneers. We worked on a state farm for a month, helping with the harvest, living with nature, as you Americans say." And then, at age fourteen, he'd met his first love, Yelena Ivanovna. He succumbed to a brief attack of nostalgia, but clearly they didn't want to hear that story.

"Well, John and I are nature lovers," Bill explained, waving to the waiter for another bottle of wine. "Always have been. All the way back to Boy Scouts—like your Young Pioneers, I suppose."

"The state was not kind to nature in the Soviet Union. Americans have come to Russia to survey the damage and suggest ways to fix the problems of pollution and such."

"It's a global problem," Brightling said. "People don't respect nature the way they should." He went on for several minutes delivering what had to be a brief canned lecture, to which Dmitriy listened politely, all the while wondering why a conversation that had begun with the discussion of a terrorist incident had drifted into this. They were sounding him out, but on what? This nature drivel? He sipped at his wine and stared at his dinner companions.

"Anyway, Dmitriy," Henriksen broke in, "how will we know when Grady wants to go forward?"

"I will call him."

"Well, call him as soon as you think proper. We want this one to run, don't we, John?"

"Yes," Dr. Brightling said definitively as the dessert cart approached the table.

GRADY, they saw, was excited about this mission. It was approaching two in the Dublin morning. The photos had been developed by a friend of the movement, and six of them had been blown up. The large ones were pinned to the wall. The small ones lay in appropriate places on a map on the worktable. "They will approach the hospital from this road. Only one place for them to park their vehicles, isn't there?"

"Agreed," Rodney Sands said, checking angles.

"Okay, Roddy, then we do this. . . ." Grady outlined the plan.

"How do we communicate?"

"Cellular phones with select speed-dial settings."

"Weapons?" Danny McCorley asked.

"We have plenty of those, lad. They will respond with five men, perhaps as many as ten, but no more than that. They've never deployed more than ten or eleven men to a mission, even in Spain. Fifteen of us, ten of them, and surprise works for us."

The Barry twins, Peter and Sam, looked skeptical at first, but if the mission ran according to schedule . . . Yes, it was possible.

"What about the women?" Timothy O'Neil asked.

"What about them? They are our primary targets."

"A pregnant woman, Sean? It will not look good."

"They are Americans, and their husbands are our enemies, and they are bait for getting their men close. We will not kill the women at once, and if circumstances permit, they might well be left alive to mourn their loss, lad," Grady added, just to assuage the conscience of the younger man. Timmy wasn't a coward, but he did have some lingering bourgeois sentimentality.

O'Neil nodded. Grady wasn't a man to cross and was in any case their leader. "I lead the group into the hospital, then?"

"Yes. Roddy and I will remain outside with the covering group."

"Very well, Sean," Timmy agreed, committing himself to the mission now and forever.

GETTING the weapons was the easiest part. For a generation people had shipped arms to the IRA, and the IRA had cached them like squirrels with nuts, burying them for the time when the entire nation would rise up under Provo leadership and drive the English invaders from the sacred soil of Ireland, or something like that, Grady thought. He'd personally buried over three thousand weapons, most of them Russian-made AKMS assault rifles, like this stash in a farm field in County Tipperary. There were a hundred of them, delivered in 1984 along with pre-loaded plastic magazines, twenty per rifle. It was all in a series of boxes, the weapons and the ammunition wrapped in greased paper to protect them against moisture. Grady removed twenty weapons, tearing open each one's paper to check for rust or corrosion. In every case the packing grease was intact, the same as when the weapons had left the factory at Kazan. The AKMS was the updated version of the AK-47, and these were the folding-stock version, much easier to conceal than the full-sized military shoulder weapon. More to the point, this was the weapon his people had trained on in Lebanon. The fifteen he took, along with three hundred thirty-round magazines, were loaded into the back of his truck.

POPOV didn't like the idea of transporting drugs. It wasn't a case of sudden morality, but simply concern about customs officials and luggage-sniffing dogs. But Brightling had provided him with documents showing that the drugs were destined for Horizon Corporation's subsidiary in Dublin. And he'd be flying in a chartered Gulfstream V private jet this time.

Popov was still uneasy. Chartering a private business jet linked Brightling's corporation with him for the first time, as did the protective documentation attached to the cocaine. Brightling was violating the most rudimentary security considerations here. Perhaps his employer planned to have him eliminated? But he didn't think so. Brightling would have to consider the possibility that Popov had left a written record somewhere.

He ran through it again. The operation had grown in magnitude until now he was transporting *cocaine* to make a terrorist happy, *after* transferring six million dollars! To make the drug smuggling easier, he had documentation to justify the drug shipment from one branch of a major corporation to another, tying himself and the drugs to Brightling's company. The only thing that made sense was that this was the last operation. Brightling would be closing things down. To Popov that meant this was his last chance to cash in. And so he found himself hoping that Grady and his band of murderers would come to as shabby an end as the others in Bern and Vienna—and even Spain, though he had had no part in that one. He had the number and control code for the new Swiss account, and in that was enough money to support him for the rest of his life. All he needed was for the Rainbow team to kill them off, and then he could disappear forever. With that hopeful thought in mind Popov started packing. His plane was leaving Teterboro Airport in New Jersey at exactly six p.m.

POPOV managed five hours of sleep on the trip across and was awakened when the flight attendant shook his shoulder twenty minutes out of Shannon. The touchdown was smooth and the rollout brief as the private aircraft approached the general aviation terminal. Barely had it stopped when a uniformed customs official boarded.

"Welcome to Shannon, sir," he said. "May I see your passport, please?"

Popov handed it across.

The bureaucrat thumbed through it. "Ah, you've been here recently. The purpose of your trip, sir?"

"Business. Pharmaceuticals," the Russian added in case the immigration official wanted to open his bags.

"Mm-hmm," the man responded without a shred of interest. He stamped the passport and handed it back. "Anything to declare?"

"Not really."

"Very well. Have a pleasant time, sir."

Something else to learn about capitalism, Dmitriy Arkadeyevich told himself. If you had enough money to travel like a prince, then you couldn't be outside the law. Amazing, he thought. He put on his overcoat and walked out of the aircraft, where a black car was waiting, his bags already loaded into the boot.

"IT REALLY is a waste of time," one of the doctors said at her seat in the conference room. "Subject Four is dead. Just her heart's still beating. We've tried everything. Nothing stops Shiva."

"Except the vaccine B antibodies," Killgore noted.

"Except them," the doctor agreed.

There was agreement around the table. They had literally tried every treatment modality known to medicine. This new version of Ebola hemorrhagic fever, genetically engineered to be hardier than the naturally produced version that still haunted the Congo River valley, was as close to one hundred percent fatal as anything known to medical science, and absent a breakthrough in infectious-disease treatment, nothing would help those exposed to it. Shiva would sweep across the world like a slow-developing storm. Inside of six months the people left alive after the initial release would fall into three categories. First, those who hadn't been exposed in any way. There would be few of them because the first Shiva victims would horrify any human with access to a television, and every nation on earth would gobble up supplies of Steve Berg's vaccine A and inject their citizens with it. The second group would be those rarest of people whose immune systems were sufficient to protect them from Shiva. Happily, most of those would probably die from the ordinary bacterial diseases that accompanied large numbers of unburied dead. The third group would be the few thousand people in Kansas. That group would be composed of active Project members—just a few hundred of them—and their families, as well as other selected scientists protected by Berg's vaccine B.

They would be moving out west to the Kansas facility as soon as they disposed of the one surviving test subject. Then the treatment rooms would be scrubbed down so there would be no lingering Shiva presence. The Project members would be pleased by that, Killgore thought. Shiva was a useful tool for their objective but sufficiently creepy that they'd all be glad when it was gone.

THE ride took half an hour and ended in a farmhouse well off the main road. Two cars were there and a van, with one man standing outside to keep watch. Popov recognized him. It was Roddy Sands, the cautious one of this unit. Dmitriy got out and looked at him without shaking hands. He took the black drug-filled suitcase from the boot and walked in.

"Good morning, Iosef," Grady said in greeting.

Popov handed the bag over. "This is what you requested."

The tone of voice was clear in its meaning. Grady looked his guest in the eye, a little embarrassment on his face. "I don't like it either, but one must have money to support operations."

Popov handed over a slip of paper. "That is the number and activation code for the account in Switzerland. You can make withdrawals only on Monday and Wednesday as an added security measure. The account has in it six million dollars," Popov told him. "When will you move? I will need to know when exactly. There are things I must do."

"The day after tomorrow," Sean said. "The operation will commence at one in the afternoon."

"So soon?"

"Why delay? We have everything we need now that the money is in place."

"OKAY," Sergeant Major Dick Voss told them. "First of all, the sound quality of the E-Systems digital radios is so good you can recognize voices just like a regular conversation in a living room. Second, they're coded so that if you have two teams operating in the field, one team comes in the left ear, the other in the right ear. That's to keep the commander from getting too confused," he explained, to the amusement of the Australian NCOs.

"What's the range?" a senior Aussie NCO asked.

"Up to ten miles, or fifteen thousand meters. The batteries are rechargeable, and every set comes with two spares. Okay, people, let's try them out. Power on/off switch is here. . . ."

"FIFTEEN kilometers, eh?" Colonel Malloy asked at Rainbow headquarters in Hereford, England.

"Right," Tim Noonan said. "This way you can listen to what we're doing on the ground instead of waiting to be told. It fits inside your aircraft headset, and the control button goes down your sleeve into your hand so you can flip it on or off. It also has a listen-only mode. That's the third position here."

"Slick," Sergeant Nance observed. "Be nice to know what's happening on the ground."

"It's still experimental. E-Systems says there may be a few bugs in it, but nobody's found them yet. The encryption system is state of the art. And it's been tested on Night Hawks and Stalkers at Fort Bragg. No problems discovered. This'll make your long-rope deployments go smoother, Bear."

"How so, Noonan?"

"Well, the guys on the end of the rope'll be able to tell you when you're a little high or low."

"Noonan," came the irate reply, "what do you think depth perception is for?"

"Roger that, Bear." The FBI agent laughed.

CHAPTER 8

BROAD DAYLIGHT

THE money made it far easier. Instead of stealing trucks, they could buy them with cashier's checks drawn from an account set up by a person with false papers. The trucks were large Volvo commercial vehicles, straight or nonarticulated trucks with canvas covers over the load area that proclaimed the names of nonexistent businesses.

The trucks came across the Irish Sea to Liverpool on commercial ferries, their interiors laden with cardboard cartons for refrigerators, and passed through British customs with no trouble. They arrived near Hereford just before dusk. The drivers dismounted at a truck stop and headed for a pub.

Sean Grady and Roddy Sands had flown in the same day. They'd passed through customs at Gatwick with false papers. Both rented cars with false credit cards and drove west to Hereford, arriving at the pub before the trucks. "Any problems?" Grady asked the Barry twins.

"None," Sam replied, accompanied by a nod from Peter. Soon

everyone was there, and two groups, one of seven and one of eight, sat in booths sipping their Guinness and chatting quietly.

POPOV told himself he had to watch. He was in London again, checked into a medium-class hotel made from a bunch of renovated row houses. He'd take his rented car. This one he had to see, if only to learn whether he should call the bank and recode the money into his own account and then disappear.

HEREFORD wasn't exactly a sleepy community, but the vehicular traffic didn't make it a bustling metropolis either. Grady was in his rented Jaguar following the trucks to the objective, going more slowly than usual because he'd anticipated thicker traffic and a longer trip in terms of time. He could have moved off at a faster clip and started the mission earlier, but he was a methodical sort, and once his plan was drafted, he tended to stick to it almost slavishly. That way everyone knew what had to happen and when. For the unexpected, every team member carried a cellular phone with speed-dial settings for every other member.

There was the hospital. It sat at the bottom of a shallow slope. The parking lot wasn't very crowded. Maybe the visitors were off having lunch before coming back to see their loved ones.

DMITRIY pulled his rental car over to the side of the road and stopped. He was half a kilometer or so from the hospital, and from the top of this hill he could see the front and the side entrances to the emergency room. He switched the motor off and decided to get his binoculars from the back seat.

He saw three heavy trucks pull up and stop close to the hospital. It was then that Popov had a random thought. Why not call that Clark fellow and warn him of what was to happen? *He,* Popov, didn't want these people to survive the afternoon, did he? If they didn't, then he'd have that five million–plus American dollars. But no. There was the off-chance Grady would get away, and he didn't want to risk being hunted by that vicious Irishman. No, it was better to let this play out without interference, and so he sat in the car, binoculars in his lap, listening to classical music on one of the BBC radio stations.

GRADY got out of his Jaguar near the hospital. He opened the boot, withdrew his parcel, and pocketed the keys. Timothy O'Neil dismounted his vehicle—he'd chosen a small brown van—and stood still in the hospital parking lot, waiting for the other men to join him. Then he thumbed the number one speed-dial setting on his cell phone. Fifty meters away, Grady's phone chirped.

"Yes?"

"We are ready here, Sean."

"Go on, then. We're ready here as well. Good luck, lad."

O'Neil was wearing the brown coveralls of a package delivery-man. He entered the hospital's side entrance carrying a large card-board box, followed by four other men in civilian clothes carrying boxes similar in size but not in color.

POPOV looked into his rearview mirror in annoyance. A police car was pulling over, and a few seconds later a constable got out and walked to his car. "Having a problem, sir?" the cop asked.

"Oh, no, not really. That is, the motor started running badly, so I called the rental company, and they're sending someone out."

"Ah, very good, then." The police constable stretched, and it seemed he'd pulled over as much to get some fresh air as to render assistance to a stranded motorist. The timing, Popov thought, could have been better.

"CAN I help you?" the desk clerk said.

"I have a delivery for Dr. Chavez, and nurse"—he looked down at the slip of paper on the box—"Clark. Are they in this after-noon?" Timmy O'Neil asked.

"I'll fetch them," the clerk said helpfully.

The IRA soldier's hand slid along the inside of the lid, ready to flip the box open. He turned and nodded to the other four, who waited politely in line behind him. O'Neil thumbed his nose, and one of them—his name was Jimmy Carr—walked back outside.

There was a police car there, a Range Rover, white with an orange stripe down the side. The policeman inside was eating a sandwich. He saw the man standing outside the emergency entrance holding what looked like a flower box. Several others had just gone inside holding similar boxes, but this was a hospital, and people gave flowers to those inside. Even so, the man with the large white box was staring at his police automobile. The cop looked back at him, mainly in curiosity, though his cop instincts were beginning to light up.

"I'M DR. Chavez," Patsy said. She was almost as tall as he was, O'Neil saw, and very pregnant beneath her starched white lab coat. "You have something for me?"

"Yes, Doctor, I do." Then another woman approached, and the resemblance was striking. They had to be mother and daughter, and that meant it was time. O'Neil flipped the top off the box and extracted the AKMS rifle. His right hand withdrew one of the magazines and slapped it home into the weapon. Then he changed hands and let his right hand take hold of the pistol grip while his left slapped the bolt back into the battery position. The entire exercise hadn't lasted two seconds.

Patsy and Sandy froze, as people usually do when suddenly confronted with weapons. Their eyes were wide and their faces shocked. To their left someone screamed. Behind this deliveryman three others now held identical weapons, and a routine day in the emergency room changed into something very different.

OUTSIDE, Carr popped open his box, smiling as he aimed it at the Range Rover only twenty feet away. The engine was running, and the cop's first instinct was to get clear and report in. He shifted into reverse and slammed down on the accelerator. The car jolted backward. Carr's response was automatic. He pulled the trigger, firing fifteen rounds into the automobile's windscreen. The Rover swerved and ended up against the brick wall of the hospital. Carr sprinted over and looked inside to see that there was one less police constable in the world.

"WHAT'S THAT?" IT WAS THE helpful roadside cop who asked the rhetorical question. It was rhetorical because automatic weapons fire is not something to be mistaken for anything else. His head turned, and he saw a Range Rover parked near the hospital scream backward, then stop. A man walked up to it, looked, and walked away.

Dmitriy Arkadeyevich sat still, now watching the cop who'd come to his unneeded assistance run back to his vehicle, reach inside, and pull out a radio microphone. Popov couldn't hear what was said, but then he didn't need to.

"WE'VE got them, Sean," O'Neil's voice told him. Grady acknowledged, thumbed the END button, and speed-dialed a number.

"Hello, this is Patrick Casey. We have seized the Hereford Community Hospital. We are holding as hostages Dr. Chavez and nurse Clark, plus numerous others. We will release our hostages if our demands are met. If they are not, it will be necessary for us to kill hostages. We require the release of all political prisoners in Albany and Parkhurst prisons on the Isle of Wight. When they are seen to be released on television, we will leave this area. Do you understand?"

"Yes, I understand," the desk sergeant replied. He didn't, but he had a tape of this call, and he'd forward it to someone who would. Every police station in the world has preset responses for various emergencies. This one had a folder labeled TERRORISM, and moments later the police superintendent pulled it out. The top emergency number went to a desk in the Home Office.

"THIS is John Clark," Rainbow Six said, lifting the receiver.

"This is Frederick Callaway at the Home Office. We have a possible emergency situation," the civil servant said.

"Okay, where is it?"

"Just up the road from you. Hereford Hospital. The voice that called in identified itself as Patrick Casey. That is a code name for PIRA operations."

"Hereford Hospital?" John asked, his hand suddenly cold on the phone. "Hold for a second. I want to get one of my people on this line." John put his hand over the receiver. "Alice! Get Alistair on this one right now!"

"Yes, John?" Alistair picked up.

"Mr. Callaway, this is Alistair Stanley, my second-in-command. Please repeat what you just told me."

He did so, then added, "The voice identified two hostages by name—a nurse Clark and a Dr. Chavez."

John Clark took a deep breath.

"Peter has the go team, John. I'll get them moving."

"Right. Anything else, Mr. Callaway?"

"That is all we have now."

Clark replaced the receiver in its cradle. His mind was racing. Those two names had not been an accident. This was a direct challenge to him and his people. They were using his wife and daughter as a weapon. His next thought was that he would have to pass command over to Al Stanley, and the next that his wife and daughter were in mortal danger, and he was helpless.

"ATTENTION. We have some business," Major Peter Covington told his men. "Get ready to move."

Team 1's members headed to their lockers. Former navy SEAL Miguel "Mike" Chin, Covington's second-in-command, was the first to be suited up. He came to see his boss, who was putting on his body armor. "What gives, skipper?"

"PIRA, local hospital, holding Clark's and Ding's wives as hostages."

"What's that?" Chin asked, blinking hard.

"You heard me, Mike."

"Okay." Chin went back into the squad bay. "Saddle up, people."

Malloy sprinted to his Night Hawk. Sergeant Nance and Lieutenant Harrison were already there. "Let's start 'er up."

"Turning one," Harrison confirmed as Nance strapped on his safety belt.

Malloy keyed his radio. "Command, this is Bear. What do you want us to do? Over."

"Bear, this is Five," Stanley's voice came back, to Malloy's surprise. "We have subjects holding the local hospital. They have Mrs. Clark and Mrs. Chavez as hostages. Your orders are to lift off and orbit the hospital."

"Roger. Copy that. Bear is lifting off now." His left hand pulled the collective, climbing the Sikorsky into the sky.

"AL, I have to let you run this operation," Clark said, standing by his desk and preparing to leave. Dr. Bellow was in the room, along with Bill Tawney, the British intelligence team boss.

"I understand, John. You know how good Peter and his team are."

A long breath. "Yeah."

Stanley turned to the others. "Bill?"

"They used the right code name. Patrick Casey is not known to the press. It's used to let us know their operation is real. Paul?"

"They're telling us they know about Rainbow, that they know who we are and, of course, who *you* are, John. They're announcing their expertise and their willingness to go all the way." The psychiatrist shook his head. "But if they're really PIRA, that means they're Catholic. I can work on that. Let's get me out there and establish contact, shall we?"

TIM Noonan was already in his car, his tactical gear in the back. At least this was easy for him. There were two cell-phone nodes in the Hereford area, and he'd been to both while experimenting with his lockout software. He drove to the farther of the two first and inserted a floppy disk into the computer control system. Two mouse clicks and forty seconds later the system was modified. Only a number with a 777 prefix would be accepted now.

He got back into his car and headed for the other site. Traffic was backing up, and his car didn't have a siren and gumball machine—an oversight he had never considered, to his sudden rage. How had they forgotten that? He pulled to the shoulder, turned on his flashers, and started leaning on the horn as he sped past the stopped cars.

COVINGTON jumped out of a British army truck near where some commercial trucks were parked. The police had established a perimeter to keep the curious at bay. He trotted over to what appeared to be the senior cop at the site.

"THERE they are," Sean Grady said over his phone to Timmy O'Neil. "And they responded quickly," he added. "How are things inside?"

"Too many people for us to control properly, Sean. I have the twins in the main lobby, Jimmy here with me, and Daniel is patrolling upstairs."

"What of your hostages?"

"The women, you mean? They're on the floor. The young one is very pregnant, Sean. She could have it today, looks like."

"Try to avoid that, lad," Grady advised with a smile.

HOUSTON'S first name wasn't really Sam—his mother had named him Mortimer after a favored uncle—but the current moniker had been laid on him during boot camp at Fort Jackson, South Carolina, eleven years before, and he hadn't objected. His sniper rifle was still in its boxy carrying case, and he was looking around for a good perch. Where he was standing wasn't bad, the sergeant thought. His rifle was a virtual twin to that used by his Team 1 mate Homer Johnston, and his marksmanship was just as good. The same was true of Rifle One Two, Sergeant First Class Fred Franklin, a deadly shot out to a mile with his huge MacMillan .50 bolt-action rifle.

"What d'ya think, Sam?"

"I like it here, Freddy. How about you go to that knoll past the helo pad?"

"Looks good to me. Later."

CHAVEZ didn't react much. Instead, he just turned inward. A small man, his body seemed to shrink even further before Clark's eyes. "Okay," he said finally. "What are we doing about it?"

"Team One is there now. We're spectators."

"Head over?"

Clark wavered, which was unusual for him. The best thing to do, one part of his mind told him, was to sit still and wait rather than drive over and torture himself with knowledge that he couldn't do anything about. On the other hand, to stay here and listen to a phone or radio account was far worse. So he walked back to his desk, opened a drawer, and took out his Beretta .45 automatic. Chavez, he saw, had his side arm as well. "Let's go."

"Wait." Chavez lifted Clark's desk phone and called the Team 2 building.

"Sergeant Major Price," the voice answered.

"Eddie, this is Ding. John and I are going to drive over there. You're in command of Team Two."

"Yes, sir, I understand. Team Two is suited up and ready to deploy. Good luck, sir."

"Thanks, Eddie." Chavez hung up. "Let's get going, John."

"WHO is this?"

"This is Superintendent Fergus Macleash," the cop on the other end of the phone circuit responded. "And you are?"

"Patrick Casey will do for now," Grady answered smugly. "Have you spoken with the Home Office yet?"

"Yes, Mr. Casey, I have." Macleash looked at Alistair Stanley and Paul Bellow as he stood at his command post half a mile from the hospital and listened to the speakerphone.

"When will they release the prisoners, as we demanded?"

"Mr. Casey, most of the senior people are having lunch at the moment. The chaps in London are trying to track them down. I haven't spoken with anyone in a position of authority yet, you see."

"You have two hours until we begin eliminating hostages." The line went dead.

"Okay. Next time he calls, I talk to him," Bellow said.

"Peter, this is Stanley," Rainbow Five called over his radio.

"Covington here."

"What have you done to this point?"

"I have both riflemen deployed for overwatch and intelligence gathering, but I'm keeping the rest close. We have no firm esti-mate of the number of subjects or hostages." The voice hesitated before going on. "I recommend we bring Team Two in. This is a large building to cover with only eight men, should we have to move in."

Stanley nodded. "Very well, Peter. I will make the call."

MALLOY could see everything as he orbited the hospital. Some trucks were parked close to the building. Police cars were visible from their flashing blue lights, and they had traffic pretty well stopped. The roads were clogged, at least those leading *to* the hospital. The roads leading away were wide-open. A white TV truck appeared as though by magic, setting up a half mile or so from the hospital on the hilltop where some other vehicles were stopped. Probably rubbernecking, the marine thought. It always happened. Very distasteful and very human.

Popov also saw the white TV truck, which stopped not ten meters from the rear bumper of his rented car.

FINALLY, Noonan said to himself, pulling off the road at the other cell site. He uploaded his spoofing software, then donned his tactical radio set. "Noonan to Stanley. Over."

"This is Stanley."

"Okay, Al. Cell phones are down."

"Very good, Tim. Come this way now."

"Roger. On the way."

"SEAN?"

Grady turned. "Yes, Roddy?"

"There they are," Sands pointed out. The black-clad soldiers were standing behind their British army trucks only a few meters from the Volvo trucks the Irishmen had driven to the site.

"I only count six," Grady said. "We're hoping for ten or so."

"It is a poor time to become greedy, Sean."

Grady thought about that for a second, then checked his watch. He'd allotted forty-five to sixty minutes for this mission. Any more, he thought, would give the other side too much time to get organized. They were within ten minutes of the lower limit. So far, things had gone according to plan. Traffic would be blocked on the roads but only into the hospital, not away from it. He had his three large trucks, Timothy O'Neil's van, and two private cars, all within fifty meters of where he was standing. The crucial part was yet to begin, but his people knew what to do. Grady pulled out his cell phone and hit the speed-dial button for O'Neil.

But it didn't work. Lifting the phone to his ear, all he heard was a busy signal. Annoyed, he thumbed END and redialed and got the same result. "What's this?" he said, trying a third time. "Roddy, give me your phone." Sands offered it, and again Grady got the busy response. Grady had a sudden empty feeling in his stomach. For the mission to work, he had to coordinate his groups. They all knew what to do but not when.

"WE HAVEN'T heard from him in a while," Bellow observed.

"He hasn't given us a phone number yet."

"Try this." Tawney handed over a handwritten list of numbers in the hospital. Bellow selected the main ER number and dialed it on his cell phone, making sure to start with the 777 prefix.

"Yes?" It was an Irish-sounding voice, but a different one.

"I need to talk to Mr. Casey," the psychiatrist said, putting the call on speaker.

"He's not here right now," was the reply.

"So what do I call you?" Bellow asked.

"You can call me Timothy."

"Okay," the doctor said agreeably. "I'm Paul."

"You're an American," O'Neil observed.

"That's right. And so are the hostages, Dr. Chavez and Mrs. Clark. Did you know they are Catholic, just like you?"

"No."

"Well, they are," Bellow assured him. "Mrs. Clark's maiden name is O'Toole. She is an Irish-Catholic American. What makes her your enemy, Timothy?"

"She's— Her husband is— I mean—"

"He's also an Irish Catholic, and to my knowledge he has never taken action against you or your organization. I have trouble under-standing why you are threatening their lives."

"Her husband is the head of this Rainbow mob, and they kill people for the British government."

"No, actually, they do not. Rainbow is a NATO establishment. The last time we went out, we had to rescue thirty children. The people holding them murdered one of the kids, a little Dutch girl named Anna. She was dying, Timothy. She had cancer, but those people weren't very patient about it. One of them shot her in the back and killed her. Not the sort of thing a religious person would do—not the sort of thing a Catholic would do. And Dr. Chavez is pregnant. I'm sure you can see that. If you harm her, you'd be aborting her unborn child. You know what the church says about that. Please, Timothy, think about what you've threatened to do. I have to go now. If I call this number again, will you be there?"

"Yes."

"Good. I'll call back when I have some news for you." Bellow punched the OFF switch. "Good news. Different person, younger. He really *is* Catholic, or at least he thinks of himself that way. That means conscience and rules. I can work on this one."

"But where is the other one?" Stanley asked. "Unless he's not in there at all. He called *us* before, but he hasn't talked to us in quite a while. Shouldn't he be doing so?"

Bellow nodded. "I would have expected that, yes."

"But Noonan has chopped the cell phones," Stanley pointed out. He switched on his tactical radio. "This is Command. Look for someone trying to use a cell phone. We may have two groups of subjects here. Acknowledge."

"Command, this is Covington. Roger."

"INSIDE-OUTSIDE?" John speculated as he and Chavez dismounted their vehicle fifty yards from the green-painted British army trucks that had brought Team 1 to the site. Team 2 was now on its way, in another green truck, with a police escort to speed their way through the traffic.

NOONAN crested the hill and started driving down to where the team was. Bugging the building, his usual job, meant getting close.

But it was broad daylight, and getting close would be difficult, probably beyond the range of possibility until nightfall. He slowed the car for his approach and saw Peter Covington in the distance conferring with his black-clad shooters.

GRADY was at the point of losing his temper. He had a virtually perfect tactical situation but lacked the ability to coordinate his teams. There they were, those Rainbow people, standing in a bunch not a hundred meters from his Volvo trucks. This couldn't last, though. The local police would surely start securing the area soon. The time was right. If he wanted to achieve his goal and make his escape, it had to be now. His gun-containing parcel was sitting on the ground next to his rented Jaguar. He left it there with Roddy Sands and walked to the farthest of the Volvo trucks.

A voice called from the cargo area, "The phones don't work."

"I know. We begin in five minutes."

"Okay, Sean," the voice replied. To punctuate it, Grady heard the cocking of the weapons inside as he walked to the next, delivering the same message. Then the third. There were three men in each truck. The canvas covers over the cargo areas had holes cut in them, and those inside had opened them slightly and were now looking at the soldiers less than a hundred meters away. Grady made his way back to his Jaguar. He checked his watch, looked at Roddy Sands, and nodded.

POPOV was watching with his binoculars. A third military truck came into view. He saw more men sitting in the back, probably reinforcements for the people outside the hospital.

"Excuse me." Popov turned to see a reporter and a cameraman, and he closed his eyes in a silent curse.

"Yes?"

"Could you give us your impressions of what is happening here? First of all, your name and what causes you to be here."

"Well, I—my name—my name is Jack Smith," Popov said in his best London accent. "And I was out here in the country, birding, you see, and . . ."

GRADY BENT DOWN AND opened his parcel, removing the AKMS assault rifle. Then he slapped in the magazine, extended the folding stock, and brought it to his shoulder. A second later he fired into the group of black-clad soldiers. A second after that, the men in the Volvo trucks did the same.

There was no warning at all. Before Team 1 had the time to react, the bullets came in on their bodies. Four men dropped in the first two seconds. By that time the rest had jumped away and down, their eyes looking around for the source of the fire.

Noonan saw them crumple, and it took a second for him to realize what was happening. Then he spoke into his tactical radio: "Warning, Team One is under fire from the rear!" His eyes searched for the source. It had to be there, in that big truck. The FBI agent floored his accelerator, his right hand reaching for his pistol.

MIKE Chin was down with a bullet in each upper leg. The pain paralyzed him for several seconds until training reasserted itself and he tried to crawl to cover. "Chin is hit; Chin is hit," he gasped over the radio, then turned to see another Team 1 member down, blood gushing from the side of his head.

SERGEANT Houston turned away from his scope with the sudden noise of automatic weapons fire. He saw what appeared to be the muzzle of a rifle sticking out the side of one of the trucks, and he swung his rifle up to the right to try to acquire a target.

Roddy Sands saw the movement. The sniper was where he remembered, but covered as he was in his camouflage blanket, it was hard to track in on him. The movement fixed that. Holding low and left, he pulled the trigger.

Houston got one round off, but it went wild as a bullet penetrated his right shoulder, blasting through his body armor, which was sufficient to stop a pistol round but not a bullet from a rifle. His body collapsed, and a second later Houston knew his right arm would not work at all. On instinct he rolled to his left, while his left hand tried to reach across his body for his service pistol.

It was easier for Fred Franklin. Too far away for easy fire from one of the terrorists' weapons, he was also well concealed under his blanket. It took him a few seconds to realize what was going on, but the screams over his radio earpiece told him that some team members had been badly hurt. He swept his scope sight over the area and saw one gun muzzle sticking out the side of a truck. Franklin flipped off his safety, took aim, and loosed his first .50-caliber round of the fight. The big MacMillan sniper rifle sent a two-ounce bullet off at twenty-seven hundred feet per second, covering the distance in less than a third of a second and drilling a half-inch hole into the soft side of the truck, but there was no telling if it hit a target. He swept the rifle left, passing over another big truck. He saw the holes in the cover but nothing inside. More to the left—there, there was a guy holding a rifle and firing—off to where Sam was. Sergeant First Class Fred Franklin worked his bolt, loaded a second round, and took careful aim.

RODDY Sands was sure he'd hit his target, and he was now trying to kill it. To his left Sean was already back in his Jaguar, starting it for the getaway that had to begin in less than two minutes.

Grady heard the engine catch and was turning to look back at his most trusted subordinate when the bullet hit, just at the base of Sands's skull. Team 1 got its first kill of the day.

NOONAN stopped his car inches from the third of the Volvo trucks. He dived out the right-side driver's door and heard the distinctive chatter of Kalashnikov-type weapons. Those had to be enemies, and they had to be close. He held his Beretta pistol in both hands, looked for a second at the back of the truck, and wondered how to— Yes! There was a ladder-handle fixture on the rear door. He slipped a booted foot into it and climbed up, finding a canvas cover roped into place. He forced his pistol into his waistband and withdrew his K-Bar combat knife, slashing at the rope loops, getting a corner free. He lifted it with his left hand, looked inside, and saw three men facing left and doing aimed fire with their weapons. Leaning in, his left hand holding the canvas clear, he aimed with his right hand. The first round was double-action, and his finger pulled the trigger slowly. The head nearest to him snapped to its right, and the body fell. The others were too distracted by the noise of their own weapons to hear the report of the pistol. Noonan adjusted his grip and fired off a second round into the next head. The third man felt the body hit his and turned to look. The brown eyes went wide. He brought his rifle up but not quickly enough. Noonan fired two rounds into his chest. Noonan looked hard at all three targets and, sure they were dead, jumped back off the truck and headed forward to the next. He paused to slap in a fresh magazine, while a distant part of his mind remarked on the fact that Timothy Noonan was on autopilot, moving almost without conscious thought.

Grady floored the gas pedal, hitting the horn as he did so. That was the signal for the others to get clear, including the men inside the hospital, whom he'd been unable to alert with his cell phone.

THE third British army truck stopped a few yards behind Noonan's car. Eddie Price jumped out first, his MP-10 up in his hands; then he crouched, looking around to identify the noise. Whatever it was, it was happening fast, and there was no plan. Mike Pierce came down next to him. "What's happening, Eddie?"

Just then they saw Noonan jump from the Volvo truck and swap out magazines on his pistol. The FBI agent saw them and waved them forward.

"I suppose we follow him," Price said. Louis Loiselle appeared at Pierce's side, and the two started off. Paddy Connolly caught up, reaching into his fanny pack for a flash-bang grenade.

O'NEIL and his four men ran out the emergency-room entrance and made it to their van without being engaged. He'd left the keys in it and had the vehicle moving before the others had a chance to close the doors.

"Warning, warning," Sergeant Fred Franklin called over the radio. "We have bad guys in a brown van leaving the hospital, looks like five of them." Then he swiveled his rifle, took aim just aft of the left-front tire, and fired.

The heavy bullet ripped through the fender, then slammed into the iron block of the six-cylinder engine, penetrating one cylinder. The van swerved left with a sudden loss of engine power. O'Neil tried to restart the engine with no result at all. He didn't know why, but this vehicle was dead and he was stuck in the open.

Franklin jacked in another round. This one was aimed at the driver's head. He centered his sight reticle and squeezed, but at the same moment the head moved and the shot missed. That was something Fred Franklin had never done. He looked on in stunned surprise for a moment, then reloaded.

O'Neil was cut on the face by glass fragments. The bullet had missed him by more than two inches, but the shock of it propelled him out of the driver's seat into the cargo area of the van. There he froze, without a clue as to what to do next.

HOMER Johnston and Dieter Weber still had their rifles in the carrying cases, and since it didn't appear that either would have much chance to make use of them, right now they were moving with pistols only. They watched Eddie Price slash a hole in the rear cover of the second Volvo truck. Paddy Connolly pulled the pin on a flash-bang and tossed it inside. Two seconds later the explosion of the pyro charge blew the canvas cover completely off the truck. Pierce and Loiselle jumped up, weapons ready, but the three men inside were stunned unconscious from the blast.

IN EACH of the three Volvo trucks one of the armed men was also to be the driver. In the foremost of the three, this one was named Paul Murphy, and from the beginning he'd divided his time between shooting and watching Sean Grady's Jaguar. He saw that the car was moving and dropped his weapon to take the driver's seat and start the diesel engine. Sean's right arm came out the window, waving in a circling motion for the truck to follow. Murphy slipped the truck into gear. He turned left to see the brown van Tim O'Neil had been driving stopped cold in the hospital parking lot. His first instinct was to go pick his comrades up, but the turn would have been difficult and Sean was still waving, so he followed his leader. In the back, one of his shooters lifted the rear flap and looked to see the other trucks, but neither was moving and there were men in black clothing there.

One of those was Sergeant Scotty McTyler, and he had his MP-10 up and aimed. He fired a three-round burst at the face in the distance and had the satisfaction of seeing a puff of pink before it dropped out of sight. "Command, McTyler. We have a car and truck leaving the area with subjects aboard!"

POPOV had never seen a battle before, but that was what he watched now. It seemed chaotic. Three people in black were down at the truck from the initial gunfire, and others were moving, apparently in pursuit of the Jaguar and the truck, now exiting the parking lot. Not three meters away the TV reporter was speaking into his microphone, while his cameraman had his instrument locked on events down the hill. Popov was sure it was exciting viewing for everybody in their sitting rooms. He was also sure that it was time for him to leave.

"I GOT 'em," Malloy reported, his eyes locked on the two moving vehicles. "Anybody in command of this disaster?"

"Mr. C.?" Ding asked.

"Bear, this is Six. I am in command now." Clark and Chavez sprinted back to Clark's official car, where both jumped in, and the driver, unbidden, started in pursuit. He was a corporal of military police in the British army. The PIRA's Volvo truck was powerful but no competition for the V-8 Jaguar racing up behind it.

Paul Murphy checked his mirror and was instantly confused. Coming up to join him was a Jaguar visually identical to the— He looked. Yes, Sean was there, up in front of him. Then who was this? He turned to yell at the people in the back but saw that one was clearly dead. The other was just holding on.

"THIS is Price. Where is everyone? Where are the subjects?"

"Price, this is Rifle One Two. We have subjects in the brown van outside the hospital. I took the motor out, so they ain't going nowhere, Eddie."

"Okay." Price looked around. He felt as though he'd been awakened by a tornado and was now looking at his wrecked farm, trying to make sense of what had taken place. One deep breath and the responsibility of command asserted itself: "Connolly and Lincoln, go right. Tomlinson and Vega, down the hill to the left. Patterson, come with me. McTyler and Pierce, guard the prisoners. Weber and Johnston, get down to Team One and see how they are. *Move!*"

"GAME face, Domingo," Clark said, sitting in the left-front seat of the Jaguar.

"I hear you, John," Chavez snarled back.

"Corporal Mole, isn't it?"

"Yes, sir," the driver said without moving his eyes.

"Okay, Corporal, get us up on his right side. We're going to shoot out his right-front tire."

"Very good, sir," was the cool reply. "Here we go."

The Jag leaped forward and in twenty seconds was alongside the Volvo diesel truck. That caught the driver by surprise. Clark and Chavez lowered their windows. The Jag was doing over seventy miles per hour now as they leaned out of the automobile.

From the back seat Chavez saw the face of the man. Fair-skinned and red-haired, a real Paddy, Domingo thought, extending his pistol and aiming at the right-front wheel. "Now!" John called from the front seat. In that instant their driver swerved to the left. Paul Murphy saw the auto jump at him and instinctively swerved hard to avoid it. Then he heard gunfire.

Clark and Chavez fired several times each. Their bullets all hit home just outside the rim of the wheel, and the nearly half-inch holes deflated the tire rapidly. Scarcely had the Jaguar pulled forward when the truck swerved back to the right. The driver tried to break, but that instinctive reaction only made things worse. The Volvo truck dipped to the right, and the right-side front-wheel rim dug into the pavement. The truck flipped over, landed on its right side, and slid forward at over sixty miles per hour. Strong as the body of the truck was, it hadn't been designed for this, and when the roll continued, the truck body started coming apart.

Corporal Mole allowed the Jaguar to slow now, watching the rearview mirror as the Volvo truck rolled like a child's toy, shedding pieces as it did so.

"Stop the car!" Clark ordered.

Mole did better than that, coming to a stop, then backing up to within a few meters of the wrecked truck. Chavez jumped out first, pistol in both hands as he advanced toward the vehicle. "Bear, this is Chavez. You there?"

"Bear copies," came the reply.

"See if you can get the car, will ya? This truck's history, man."

"Roger that. Bear is in pursuit."

"Colonel?" Sergeant Nance said over the intercom. "You see how they did that?"

"Yeah. Think you can do the same?" Malloy asked.

"Got my pistol, sir."

"Well then, it's air-to-mud time." The marine dropped the collective and brought the Night Hawk to a hundred feet over the road. He was behind and down-sun from Grady's Jag. "Right side, Sergeant."

"Yes, sir." Nance slid the door back and knelt on the aluminum floor, his Beretta in both hands.

GRADY bit his lip, seeing that the truck was no longer there, but behind him the road was clear, and ahead as well. He allowed himself a relaxing breath, flexed his fingers on the wheel, and then his peripheral vision caught something black on his left.

Nance thumbed back the hammer and fired. The gun jumped in his hand. He brought it down and kept pulling the trigger. On the fourth round he saw his target jerk to the right and the car swerve into the steel guardrail.

Malloy looked for his flight bag. His Beretta was in there. Harrison handled the landing, bringing the Sikorsky to rest fifty feet from the car. Nance jumped out first, ducking under the turning rotor as he ran to the car's right side. Malloy was two seconds behind him.

"Careful, Sergeant!" Malloy screamed, slowing his advance on the left side. The window was gone except for a few shards still in the frame, and he could see the man inside, still breathing but not doing much else behind the deployed air bag.

"He's still alive!" Nance said in amazement. Moments later Malloy strapped the body into the chopper and took the controls. Inside a minute they were airborne and heading for the hospital.

"LIEBER Gott," Dieter Weber said to himself, seeing the wounds. One Team 1 member was surely dead, having taken a round in the side of his head. Four others right here were hit, three of them in the chest. One of those was Alistair Stanley. "This is Weber. We need medical help here at once," he called over his tactical radio. "Rainbow Five is down."

PRICE heard that. He was now thirty yards from Timothy O'Neil and the brown van. Hank Patterson was at his side, trying to approach without being seen. To his left he could see Oso Vega along with Tomlinson. Off to the right he could see the face of Steve Lincoln. Paddy Connolly would be with him. "Team Two, this is Price. We have subjects in the van. I do not know if we have any inside the building. Vega and Tomlinson, get inside and check."

"Vega here. Roger that, Eddie."

Oso headed for the main entrance with Tomlinson in support, while the other four kept an eye on the brown van. Moving quickly, Vega entered the main lobby and swept his eyes around. Two people screamed to see another man with a gun. As Tomlinson appeared behind him, Vega held up his left hand. "Easy, folks. We're the good guys. Does anybody know where the bad guys are?" Two people pointed to the rear of the building in the direction of the emergency room. Vega advanced to the double doors leading that way and called on his radio. "Command, this is Vega. Hospital lobby is clear, Eddie. Got maybe twenty civilians here to get looked after, okay?"

"I have no people to send you, Oso. We're all busy out here. Weber reports we have some serious casualties."

THE driver was dead, Chavez saw, crushed between the large wheel and the back of his seat from when the Volvo truck had slammed into the guardrail. The body tossed out of the back was dead as well. That left a guy with two broken legs and horrible scrapes on his face, his pain masked by his unconsciousness.

"Bear, this is Six," Clark said.

"Bear copies."

"Can you pick us up? We have an injured subject here."

"I'll be there. We have a wounded subject aboard, too."

"Roger that, Bear." Clark looked west. The Night Hawk was in plain view, and he saw it come straight for his position.

TIMOTHY O'Neil was still in his van wondering what to do.

"Back into the hospital?" one of the men asked.

"But then we're trapped!" Sam Barry objected.

"We're trapped here!" Carr pointed out. "We need to move."

O'Neil thought that made sense. "Okay. I'll pull the door, and you lads run back to the emergency entrance. Ready?" They nodded. "Now!" he rasped, pulling the sliding door open.

Eddie Price observed them from a football field away. "Subjects running back into the hospital. I counted five."

VEGA and Tomlinson were close enough to see people in the emergency room but not the double glass doors that led outside. They heard screams. Vega took off his Kevlar helmet and peeked around the corner. He saw a guy with an AKMS looking around inside the building, and behind him was half the body of someone looking outward. Oso nearly jumped out of his skin when a hand came down on his shoulder. He turned. It was Fred Franklin, without his monster rifle, holding only his Beretta pistol.

"I just heard. Five bad guys there?"

"That's what the man said," Vega confirmed. He waved Tomlinson to the other side of the corridor. "You stick with me, Fred."

"Roge-o, Oso."

Vega took another look. There was Ding's wife, pregnant as she could be in her white coat. He and Chavez went back nearly ten years. He couldn't let anything happen to her. He backed off the corner and waved his arm at her.

PATSY CLARK CHAVEZ, M.D., saw the motion out of the corner of her eye and turned to see a soldier dressed in black. He was beckoning her to him. Slowly she started moving to her right.

"You, stop!" Jimmy Carr called angrily. Then he started moving toward her. Unseen to his left, Sergeant George Tomlinson edged his face and gun muzzle around the corner. Vega's waves grew more frantic, and Patsy kept moving his way. Carr stepped toward her, bringing his rifle up. As soon as he came into view, Tomlinson took aim, and seeing the weapon aimed at Ding's wife, he depressed the trigger gently, loosing a three-round burst.

The silence of it was somehow worse than the loudest noise. Patsy turned to look at the guy with the gun as his head exploded. Jimmy Carr's body fell straight down.

"Come here!" Vega shouted, and she did what she was told, ducking and running toward him. Sergeant Franklin scooped her up and ran down the corridor, carrying her like a toy. In the main lobby he found the hospital security guard and left her with him, then ran back.

"Franklin to Command. Dr. Chavez is safe. We got her to the main lobby. Get some people there, will ya?"

"Price to Team. Where are the subjects?"

"Price, this is Vega. We are down to four subjects. George just dropped one. They are in the emergency room. Mrs. Clark is probably still there. We have their escape route closed. I have Tomlinson and Franklin here. Fred's only got a pistol. Unknown number of hostages. Over."

"I'VE got to get down there," Dr. Bellow said. He was badly shaken. People had been shot within a few feet of him. Alistair Stanley was down with a chest wound, and at least one Rainbow trooper was dead, along with three additional wounded, including Team 1 leader Peter Covington.

"That way." Price pointed to the front of the hospital. A Team 1 member appeared and headed that way as well. It was Geoff Bates, one of Covington's shooters from the SAS. He and Bellow moved quickly.

SOMEHOW JIMMY CARR HAD died without notice. Timothy O'Neil turned and saw him there, his body like the stem for a huge red flower of blood on the dingy tile floor. It was only getting worse. He had three armed men, but he couldn't see around the corner twenty feet away, and surely there were soldiers there. He had no escape.

SANDY Clark watched O'Neil from fifteen feet away. He was a handsome man in his early thirties, holding a weapon in his hands and looking as though he didn't have a friend in the world. But the mother in her told Sandy that her daughter was probably safe now, along with her grandchild. The dead one had called after her, but now he was on the hospital floor, and so Patsy had probably gotten away. That was the best information of the day, and she closed her eyes to whisper a prayer of thanks.

Outside, things were gradually becoming organized. Ambulances were on the scene, plus medical orderlies from the British army. The wounded were being moved to the base hospital at Hereford, and coming in were SAS soldiers, thirty of them, to assist the Rainbow troopers. Colonel Malloy's helicopter set down on the pad at the base, and the two prisoners were taken to the military hospital for treatment.

"HEY, Doc," Vega said to Paul Bellow in greeting.

"Where are they?"

Vega pointed. "Around this corner. Four of them, we think."

"Okay." Bellow took a deep breath. "This is Paul," he called loudly. "Is Timothy there?"

"Yes," came the reply.

"Okay, Timothy, you will not be getting away from here. I think you know that," Bellow observed in as gentle a voice as he could manage.

"I can kill hostages if you don't let me leave."

"Yes, you can do that, but you still won't get away. And what do you gain by murdering people, Tim?"

"The freedom of my country!"

"That is happening already, isn't it?" Bellow asked. "There are peace accords, Tim. And Tim, tell me, what country ever began on a foundation of the murder of innocent people?"

O'Neil looked around at his comrades. They were trapped, and all of them knew it. "We want a bus to take us away!"

"Take you away to where?" the doctor asked.

"Just get us the bus!" O'Neil screamed.

"Okay, I can talk to people about that, but they have to know where the bus is going so the police can clear the roads," Bellow observed reasonably. It was just a matter of time now. Tim wasn't a murderer. He thought of himself as a soldier, and that was different. "Oh, Tim? Could you do something for me?"

"What?"

"Could you let me make sure the hostages are okay? That's something I have to do to keep my boss happy."

O'Neil hesitated.

"Tim, come on. Okay? I'm a physician. I don't carry a gun or anything. You have nothing to be afraid of." Telling them that they had nothing to fear, and thus suggesting that they were unnecessarily afraid, was usually a good card to play. There followed the usual hesitation, confirming that they were indeed afraid—and that meant Tim was rational.

"No, Tim, don't," Peter Barry insisted. "Give them nothing."

"But how will we get the bus if we don't cooperate on something?" O'Neil looked around at the other three. Sam Barry nodded. So did Dan McCorley. "All right," O'Neil called.

Bellow looked at Vega, the senior soldier present.

"Watch your butt, Doc," the first sergeant suggested.

"Always," Paul Bellow assured him. Then he took a deep breath, walked the ten feet to the corner, and turned, disappearing from the view of the Rainbow troopers.

"YOU'RE hurt," Bellow said on seeing Timothy's face.

"It's nothing, just a few scratches."

"Why not have somebody work on it for you?"

"It's nothing," Tim O'Neil said again.

"Okay, it's *your* face," Bellow said, looking and counting four of them, all armed. Only then did he count the hostages. He recognized Sandy Clark. There were seven others, all very frightened. "So what exactly do you want?"

"We want a bus, and we want it quickly," O'Neil replied.

"Okay, but we'll need something in return."

"What's that?" Timothy asked.

"Some hostages to be released," the psychiatrist answered.

"No. We only have eight."

"Look, Tim, you have to offer them something," Bellow said. "It's how the game is played. As a sign of good faith you give me a couple hostages—women, because that looks better." Bellow looked again. Four women, four men. It would be good to get Sandy Clark out.

"And then?"

"And then I tell my superiors that you want a bus and that you've shown good faith. I have to represent you to them, right?"

"Ah, and you're on our side?" another man asked.

"No, I won't say that. Look, I am not going to insult your intelligence. But if you want to get things, you have to deal for them. I'm the go-between."

"Get the bus," Timothy said.

"In return for what?" Paul asked.

"Two women." O'Neil turned. "That one and that one."

"Can they come out with me?" Bellow saw that Timothy had actually indicated Sandy Clark.

"Yes, but get us that bus!"

"I'll do my best," Bellow promised, gesturing at the two women to follow him back around the corner.

"Vega to Command," Oso called on seeing the two women.

"Price to Vega."

"Tell Six his wife and daughter are both safe."

JOHN was back in a truck, with Domingo next to him, heading to the hospital to take charge of the operation. Both heard the radio call. In both cases the heads dropped for a brief moment of relief. But there were six more hostages. "Okay, this is Clark. What's happening now?"

In the hospital, Vega gave his radio set to Dr. Bellow.

"John? This is Paul. There's four of them, all armed. But I've spoken with their leader, and I can work with this kid, John. Give me a couple hours."

"Okay, Doc. What are they asking for?"

"The usual," Bellow answered. "They want a bus."

John thought about that. Make them come outside, and he had riflemen to handle the problem. "Do we deliver?"

"Not yet. We'll let this one simmer a little."

"Okay, Doc, that's your call. See you soon. Out."

Bellow handed the radio back to First Sergeant Vega and returned to the emergency room.

"Where's the bus?" O'Neil demanded.

"Tim, I've talked to my superiors. They're thinking about it."

"Paul, I have six hostages here, and I can—"

"Yes, you can, but Timothy, if you do that, then the soldiers outside come storming in here, and you will be remembered forever as a killer of innocent people, a murderer. Do you really want that, Tim?" Bellow paused. "Oh, by the way, we have Sean Grady in custody."

"What?"

That, Bellow saw, shook Timothy. "Grady was captured trying to escape. He was shot, but he'll survive. They're operating on him right now."

His leader was a prisoner? Tim O'Neil thought. "How do I know you're telling the truth?"

"Tim, in a situation like this, I can't lie. If you caught me in a lie, you'd never believe me again, and that would end my usefulness to my bosses and to you too, wouldn't it?"

Then something good happened. Tim pulled out a cigarette. A sure sign of stress and an attempt to control it.

"HAZARDOUS to your health, boy," Clark observed, looking at the TV picture Noonan had established. The assault plan was ready. Paddy Connolly had line charges set on the windows, both to open an entry path and to distract the terrorists. Vega, Tomlinson, and Geoff Bates, from Team 1, would toss flash-bangs at the same time and dart into the room to take the bad guys down with aimed fire. The only downside was that one of them could turn and hose the hostages as his last conscious act, or even by accident.

"YOU know how this day will end, don't you, Tim?" Bellow offered like a nice fly to a brook trout, wondering if he'd rise to it.

"Yes, Doctor, I do." He paused. "I haven't even fired my rifle today. I haven't killed anyone. Jimmy did," he went on, gesturing to the body on the floor, "but not any of us."

Bingo! Bellow thought. "That counts for something, Tim. You know, the war will be over soon. They're going to make peace. And when that happens, there's going to be an amnesty for most of the fighters. So you have some hope. You all do," Paul told the other three, who were watching and listening . . . and wavering, as their leader was. "Tim, if you set your weapons down, you have my word you will not be hurt."

"And go to prison?" Defiance and anger in the reply.

"Timothy, you can get out of prison someday. You cannot get out of death. Please think about that."

Timothy Dennis O'Neil looked at his fellow PIRA soldiers and saw the same expression that they saw on his face. O'Neil safed his rifle and set it on the floor. The others did the same.

CHAPTER 9
RECOVERY

HEY, baby," Ding said. He'd finally found his wife outside the hospital, surrounded by a ring of SAS troopers. Patsy ran the ten steps to him and hugged her husband as tightly as her swollen abdomen allowed.

"You okay?" Ding asked.

She nodded, tears in her eyes. "You?"

"I'm fine. It was a little exciting there for a while, and we have some people down, but everything's under control now."

"One of them— Somebody killed him, and—"

"I know. He was pointing a weapon at you, and that's why he got himself killed." Tears welled up in his eyes. Ding blinked them away. "How's the little guy?" he asked his wife.

"Feels okay, Ding. Really. I'm okay," Patsy assured him.

"Okay, baby, you're going home." He waved to an SAS trooper. "Take her back to the base, okay?"

"Yes, sir," the sergeant replied. Together they walked her to the parking lot. Sandy Clark was there with John, also hugging and holding hands.

POPOV was most of the way back to London, listening to his car radio. Whoever was briefing the media talked too much. Then he heard that the leader of the IRA raiders had been captured, and Dmitriy's blood turned to ice. If they had Grady, they had the man who knew his cover name, knew about the money transfer. It wasn't time for panic, but it was sure time to get out of the country.

Popov checked his watch. The banks were still open. He lifted his cell phone and called Bern. In minutes the Russian was richer by over five million dollars. Popov took the exit to Heathrow, returned his rental car, and got the last first-class ticket on a British Airways flight to Chicago. Once he got into O'Hare, he'd catch the next flight to New York.

Why go back to New York at all? Why not simply disappear? It was tempting, but no. If nothing else, Popov had to tell Brightling and Henriksen to leave him alone from now on and explain why it was in their interest to do so.

SEAN Grady came out of surgery just after eight in the evening, following three and a half hours on the table. Bellow sat by the bed in the hospital's recovery room waiting for him to awaken. There were police around now, and Clark and Chavez were there too, staring at the man who'd so brazenly attacked their men—and their women.

"Anytime now," Bellow said. Grady's vital signs were coming up.

Bellow consulted the list of IDs that others had drawn up. He hoped the British police and the guys from intelligence had provided him with good data. "Sean?" he said. "Sean, are you awake?"

"Who?"

"It's me. It's Jimmy Carr, Sean. You back with us now, Sean?"

"Where . . . am . . . I?" the voice croaked.

"University Hospital, Dublin, Sean. Dr. McCaskey just finished fixing your shoulder up. You're going to be okay. Does it hurt—your shoulder, Sean?"

"No, no hurt now, Jimmy. How many?"

"How many of us? Ten. Ten of us got away."

"Good." Grady's eyes opened, and he saw someone wearing a surgical mask and cap, but he couldn't focus well. The room . . . Yes, it was a hospital. His throat was sore from the intubation, but it didn't matter. At least Jimmy Carr was here. "Roddy, where's Roddy?"

"Roddy's dead, Sean," Bellow answered. "He didn't make it."

"Not Roddy," Grady breathed.

"Sean, we need some information. We need it quickly. The chap who got us the information—we need to contact him, but we don't know how to find him."

"Iosef, you mean?"

Bingo, Paul Bellow thought. "Yes, Sean. Iosef. We need to get in touch with him."

"The money . . . Swiss Commercial Bank in Bern. Call . . . account number and control number in . . . in my wallet."

Grady's personal possessions were sitting on a portable table. In the wallet, Clark saw, were two hundred and ten British pounds, one hundred and seventy Irish pounds, and several slips of paper. On one yellow Post-it note were two numbers, six digits each.

"Good. Thank you, Sean. And Iosef—what's the rest of his name? How do we get in touch with him?" Bellow's false Irish accent wasn't good enough to pass muster with a drunk, but Grady's condition was far beyond anything alcohol could do to the mind.

"Don't . . . know. Iosef Andreyevich contacts me through the network. Never gave me a way to contact him."

"His last name, Sean. What is it? You never told me."

"Serov. Iosef Andreyevich Serov. Russian . . . KGB chap. Bekáa Valley . . . years ago."

"He gave us good information on this Rainbow mob, didn't he, Sean?"

"How many did we— How many?"

"Ten, Sean. We killed ten of them."

"Good . . . good . . ." Grady whispered from his gurney.

"Now, Sean, this Russian chap. I need to know more."

"Iosef? Good man, got the money and the drugs for us. Six million. Six . . . and the cocaine," Grady added. "Flew into Shannon from America. Well, think it was America."

"Where are the drugs, Sean?"

"Farm—farmhouse." Grady mentioned a town on the Irish west coast and gave a road description.

"What does Serov look like, Sean?"

"Tall as me . . . brown hair, eyes . . . round face. Speaks many languages."

"How we doing, Bill?" Clark whispered to Tawney.

"The name Serov doesn't ring a bell, but Iosef is the Russian version of Joseph. I can check with our files, and we can run these account numbers down."

Clark nodded. "Heck of an interrogation method."

"Never seen this before. Yes, it is."

Just then Grady's eyes opened more. He saw the others around his bed, and his face twisted into a question. "Who are you?" he asked groggily.

"My name is Clark. John Clark, Sean."

The eyes went wide for a second. "But you're—"

"That's right, pal. That's who I am. By the way, Clark is just my working name. Before that it was John Kelly, and my wife's maiden name was O'Toole. Thanks for spilling your guts. We got all of you, Sean. All fifteen dead or captured. I hope you like it here in England, boy. You're going to be here a long, long time."

"OKAY, what do we have?" John asked his senior executives.

"This name, Iosef Serov. It's not on our computer in London," said Cyril Holt, deputy director of the Security Service, once called MI5. "What about the CIA?"

Clark shook his head.

"Well, the description fits this chap." Holt passed a photo across the table. "He's a chap who met with Ivan Kirilenko, the London *rezident,* some weeks ago, John. We believe he was involved in the leak of information on your organization, as you will recall. For him, then, to show up with Grady . . . Well, it fits."

"What else?"

"It turns out that the account number Grady gave us was real enough," Bill Tawney put in. "Actually, it's still an active account. It began with about six million dollars; then several hundred thousand was withdrawn—and then, the very day of the attack at the hospital, all but a hundred thousand was withdrawn and redeposited elsewhere."

"Where?"

"The Swiss say they cannot tell us."

Clark thought for a second. "The Russian?"

Tawney nodded sagely. "Yes, that makes sense, doesn't it? He set them up a numbered account, and when they were taken out, he still had the numbers, didn't he?"

"So he sets them up and rips them off."

"Well, why not?" the intelligence officer asked.

"Okay, let's back up some," John proposed. "This Russian appears, gives them intelligence information on us, funds the operation from somewhere. First question: Where did the money—"

"And the drugs, John. Don't forget that."

"Okay, and the drugs come *from?*"

"On the drug issue," the senior cop present told them, "I forwarded the information to Dennis Maguire—he's chief of the Irish national police, the Garda. They found ten pounds of pure cocaine in the farmhouse Grady told us about. By 'pure' I mean medicinal quality, almost as though it had been purchased from a pharmaceutical house. The street value is enormous. Millions."

Just then Chavez was looking down at the conference table and shaking his head when his beeper went off. He lifted it and saw that it was his home number. He rose from his seat and called on the wall phone. "Yeah, honey?"

"Ding, it's started," Patsy told him calmly. Ding's response was a sudden flip of his heart. "On the way, baby." Ding hung up. "John, I gotta get home. Patsy says it's started."

"Okay, Domingo." Clark managed a smile finally. "Give her a kiss for me."

"Roge-o, Mr. C." And Chavez headed for the door.

"The timing on this thing is never good, is it?" Tawney observed.

"Well, at least something good is happening today." John rubbed his eyes and went on. "Okay. What about the information leak? People, we've been set up. What are we going to do about it?"

IT WAS everything he'd expected—not knowing what to expect—and more, and at the end of it Domingo Chavez held his son in his hands. After a second that seemed to last into weeks he handed the newborn to his wife.

Patsy's face was bathed in perspiration and weary from the five-hour ordeal of delivery, but already the pain was forgotten. The goal had been achieved, and she held her child. The package was pink, hairless, and noisy, the last part assuaged by the proximity of Patsy's left breast, as John Conor Chavez got his first meal. But Patsy was exhausted, and in due course a nurse removed the child to the nursery. Then Ding kissed his wife and walked alongside her bed as she was wheeled to her room. She was already asleep when they arrived. He kissed her one last time and walked outside. Then his car took him to the official home of Rainbow Six.

"Yeah?" John said, opening the door.

Chavez handed over a cigar with a blue ring. "John Conor Chavez, seven pounds eleven ounces. Patsy's doing fine, Gran-pop," Ding said with a subdued grin. After all, Patsy had done the hard part.

There are moments to make the strongest of men weep, and this was one of them. The two men embraced. "Well," John said, reaching into the pocket of his bathrobe for a handkerchief with which he rubbed his eyes. "Who's he look like?"

"Winston Churchill," Domingo replied with a laugh.

AT LA GUARDIA, POPOV HEADED for a cab, on the way out check-ing his inside coat pocket and finding the travel documents that had gotten him across the Atlantic. They had served him well, but they had to go. Emerging into the evening air, he surreptitiously dumped them into a trash container before walking to the cabstand. He was a weary man. He hadn't managed much sleep on the flight, and his body was—how did the Americans put it?—running on empty. Maybe that explained the break with fieldcraft.

Popov was within blocks of his downtown apartment when the waste-disposal crew circulated past the United Airlines terminal to change the trash bags. One at a time they lifted the metal tops off the cans to remove the plastic garbage bags, then dumped the bags into wheeled containers that would later be tipped into trucks for trans-port to a landfill on Staten Island. One can, fifty yards from the cab-stand, didn't sit properly in its holder. When the cleanup man lifted the bag, it caught and ripped, spilling its contents onto the concrete sidewalk. That generated a quiet curse from the worker, who now had to pick up a bunch of objects with his gloved hands. He was halfway through when he saw the crimson cover of a passport. Peo-ple didn't throw those things away, did they? He flipped it open and saw two credit cards inside, stamped with the same name on the passport. Serov, an unusual name. He dropped the whole package into a pocket of his coveralls. He'd bring it by the lost-and-found.

By this time Popov was in his apartment, too tired even to un-pack his bags. He undressed and collapsed on the bed, without even a vodka to help him off to sleep. By reflex he turned on the TV and caught yet another story about the Hereford shoot-out. There was the TV truck whose reporter had tried to interview him. They hadn't used it, but there he was, in profile, twenty feet away, while the reporter gave a stand-up. All the more reason to clear out now, he thought as he drifted off.

"JOHN?"

"Yeah, Bill?" Clark replied tiredly, looking up from his desk and wondering if he'd get to see his grandson that day.

"Our friend Serov has turned up," Bill Tawney, the SIS man said.

"Oh? Where?"

"New York. A British passport was found in a dustbin at La Guardia Airport, along with two credit cards. All in the name of Joseph A. Serov. I called the legal attaché in your embassy in London to have the accounts run. Should have some information from your FBI within the hour."

"Who's handling it in the U.S.?"

"Gus Werner, assistant director, terrorism division. I know Gus. Good chap."

"HELLO, Gus. That was very fast of you," Tawney said a short while later.

"The wonders of the computer age, Bill. This Serov guy flew from Heathrow to Chicago yesterday, about three hours after the fracas you had at Hereford. I have a rental car, a hotel bill, and a flight from Chicago to New York City."

"Address?"

"We're not that lucky. Post-office box in lower Manhattan," the FBI's assistant director told his British counterpart. "Bill, how hot is this?"

"Gus, it's very hot. Sean Grady gave us the name. This Serov chap delivered a large sum of money and ten pounds of cocaine shortly before the attack. We're working with the Swiss to track the money right now. And now it appears this chap is based in America. Very interesting."

"We're going to have to track this mutt down if we can," Werner thought aloud. There was ample jurisdiction for the investigation he was about to open. American laws on terrorism reached across the world. And so did drug laws. "I'm starting the case file myself. The hunt is on for Mr. Serov."

"Excellent. Thank you, Gus."

At his office in FBI headquarters in Washington, Werner consulted his computer for a code word. This case would be classified, and the code word on the file would read . . . No, not that one. He told the machine to pick another. Yes: PREFECT, a word he remembered from his Jesuit high school in St. Louis.

"Mr. Werner?" his secretary called. "Mr. Henriksen on line three."

"Hey, Bill," Werner said, picking up the phone.

"So, DMITRIY, you got back here in a hurry," Brightling observed.

"It seemed a good idea," Popov replied. "The mission was a mistake. The enemy was far too proficient."

"Well, the attack must have shaken them up."

"Perhaps," Popov allowed. Just then Henriksen walked in.

"Bad news," he announced.

"What's that?"

"You goofed up some, Dmitriy."

"Oh? How did I do that?" the Russian asked.

"Not sure, but I was just on the phone with Gus Werner. I asked him about the Hereford incident. He told me they had reason to believe a Russian, possibly based in America, had been in contact with the PIRA. The FBI is working on the case."

"Is this a danger to us?" Brightling asked.

"If they find our friend here," Henriksen replied.

Brightling nodded and thought quickly. "Dmitriy, have you ever been to Kansas?"

HENRIKSEN was being overly cautious, Dmitriy thought as he boarded the business jet at Teterboro Airport in New Jersey. What could the FBI possibly have on him? A name? Credit cards, if they were lucky, and from that his travel records, but none of them would have value in any court of law. Unless Sean Grady positively identified him, he was safe, and Popov thought he could depend on Grady not to cooperate with the British.

A large military-type automobile was waiting for him when he stepped off the aircraft. Darkness hid the landscape, but Popov noticed lines painted on the pavement and wondered if he'd landed on an airport runway or a country road of some sort. In the distance was a huge building, partially lit. More curious than ever, Dmitriy got into the vehicle and headed off toward it. Inside the building a security guard walked him to the elevator and then to his fourth-floor room, which was not unlike a medium-decent hotel room, complete with cooking facilities and a refrigerator. There was a TV and VCR. The tapes in the storage cupboard were nature tapes, he saw. Not a single feature film. How odd. But there was a complete bar, including Absolut vodka, which was almost as good as the Russian kind he preferred. He poured himself a drink and switched on the TV to CNN. He'd explore this place tomorrow, and from the way he was treated, he'd know—

No, there was an even easier way. He lifted his phone, hit 9 to get an outside line, then dialed his apartment in New York. The phone rang four times before his answering machine clicked in. So he had phone access to the outside. That meant he was safe, but he was no closer to understanding what was going on than he'd been during that first meeting with Brightling in France. Now here he was in *Kansas,* U.S.A., drinking vodka and watching television, with over six million American dollars in two numbered accounts in Switzerland. He'd reached one goal. Next he had to meet another. What was this adventure all about? Would he find out here? He hoped so.

"So, COLONEL, what do you think?"

"It's one heck of a stadium," Colonel Wilson Gearing, U.S. Army Chemical Corps, retired, replied. "But it sure gets hot here. I hope this fogging system works, 'cuz if it doesn't, you'll have a lot of heatstroke cases, pal."

"It works," the Aussie cop told him. "It's fully tested."

"Can I take a look? Bill Henriksen wants me to see if it could be used as a chemical-agent delivery system by the bad guys."

"Certainly. This way." They were there in five minutes. The water-input piping was contained in its own locked room. The cop had the key for this, and he took the colonel inside.

"Oh, you chlorinate the water here?" Gearing asked.

"Yes. We don't want to spread germs on our guests, do we?"

"Not exactly," Colonel Gearing agreed, looking at the plastic chlorine container that hung on the distribution piping beyond the pumps. Water was filtered through that before it went into the fogging nozzles that hung in all the concourses and ramps to the stadium bowl. The system would have to be flushed with unchlorinated water before delivery would work, but that was easily accomplished, and the false chlorine container in his hotel room was an exact twin of this one. The contents even looked like chlorine, almost, though the nanocapsules actually contained something called Shiva. Gearing thought about that behind blank brown eyes. He'd been a chemical weapons expert his whole professional life. Well, this wasn't really chemical warfare. It was biowarfare, a sister science of the one he'd studied for over twenty uniformed years. "Is the door guarded?" he asked.

"No, but it is alarmed."

"Can you give me the alarm code for this facility?"

He didn't even hesitate. Gearing was a former staff-grade army officer, after all, and a senior member of the consulting team for security at the Olympic Games. "One one three three six six," the cop told him. Gearing wrote it down, then punched the numbers into the keypad, which armed and then disarmed the system. He'd be able to switch out the chlorine canister very quickly. This would work just fine, just like the model they'd set up in Kansas, on which he and his people had practiced for several days. They'd gotten the swap-out time down to fourteen seconds. Anything under twenty meant that nobody would notice anything remiss in the fog-cooling system because residual pressure would maintain the fogging stream.

Gearing felt a slight chill in his blood. Planning was one thing. Seeing where it would happen for real was something else. This was the place. Here he would start a global plague that would take lives in numbers far too great to tally and, in the end, would leave alive only the elect. It would save the planet—at a ghastly price, to be sure—but he'd been committed to this mission for years. He'd seen what man could do to harm things. He'd been a young lieutenant at Dugway Proving Grounds in Utah when they'd had the well-publicized accident with GB, a persistent nerve agent that had blown too far and slaughtered a few hundred sheep. And neurotoxins were not a pretty death, even for sheep. The news media hadn't even bothered to talk about the wild game that had died a similar ugly death—everything from insects to antelope. It had shaken him that the United States Army could make so grave an error to cause such pain. The things he'd learned later had been worse. For years he'd worked on an effort to manufacture "safe" poisons for battlefield use. The crazy part was that it had all begun in Germany as insecticide research in the 1920s and 1930s. Most of the chemicals used to kill off insects were nerve agents, simple ones that attacked and destroyed the rudimentary nervous systems in ants and beetles, but those German chemists had stumbled upon some of the deadliest chemical compounds ever formulated.

The problem with chemical weapons had always been their distribution—how to spread them evenly across a battlefield, thus exposing enemy soldiers efficiently. That the same chemicals would travel downrange and kill innocent civilians had been the dirty secret that the organizations and the governments that ruled them had always ignored. And they didn't even consider the wildlife that would also be exterminated in vast quantities—and, worse still, the genetic damage those agents caused, because marginal doses of nerve gas, below the exposure needed to kill, invaded the very DNA of the victim, ensuring mutations that would last for generations.

This wasn't quite the same thing. He would not be spreading chemical poisons, but rather tiny virus particles. And the people walking through the cooling fog to the stadium bowl would breathe them in, and their body chemistry would break down the nanocapsules, allowing the Shiva strands to go to work—slowly, of course—and they'd go home to spread the Shiva farther, and in four to six weeks after the Sydney Olympics, the plague would erupt worldwide, and a global panic would ensue. Then Horizon Corporation would announce that it had an experimental A vaccine that had worked in animals and primates—and was safe for human usage—ready for mass production. It would be distributed worldwide, and four to six weeks after injection those people, too, would develop the Shiva symptoms. Before long there would be just a few people left, safe in Kansas and Brazil, the inheritors of a world returning to its natural state. He turned to look at his host. "With your permission I'll have my people keep an eye on this thing."

"Fine," the senior cop agreed.

POPOV HADN'T CLOSED HIS shades the previous evening, and so the dawn woke him rather abruptly. He opened his eyes, then squinted in pain as the sun rose over the Kansas plains. In the medicine cabinet in the bathroom, he found Tylenol and aspirin, and there was ground coffee for the machine in the kitchen area but nothing of value in the refrigerator. So he showered and had his coffee, then went looking for food. He found a cafeteria—a huge one—almost entirely empty of patrons. He got breakfast and sat alone.

"Mr. Popov?" a voice said. Dmitriy turned. "I'm David Dawson, chief of security here. I have a badge for you to wear"—he handed over a white plastic shield that pinned to his shirt—"and I'm supposed to show you around today. Welcome to Kansas."

"Thank you." Popov pinned the badge on. So this place was pass-controlled. How interesting. "So what is this place?"

"Well, Horizon set it up as a research facility. You know what the company does, right?"

"Yes." Popov nodded. "Medicines and biological research."

"Well, this is a research-and-development facility for their work. It was just finished recently. We're bringing people in now."

"Why here, in the middle of nothing?" Popov asked.

"Well, for starters, it's centrally located. You can be anywhere in the country in less than three hours. And nobody's around to bother us. Horizon does lots of work that requires protection."

"Industrial espionage?"

Dawson nodded. "That's right. We worry about that. Finish your breakfast. I'll be back in about fifteen minutes to show you around."

"Thank you," Popov said, watching him walk out of the room. There was a strange institutional quality to this place . . . like a *Russian* facility, Popov thought. It seemed to have no soul at all, no human dimension. Even the KGB would have hung a photo of Lenin on the bare white walls. The former KGB officer worked through his breakfast, his instincts on alert.

"DOMINGO, I need you to take this one," John said.

"It's a long way to go, John, and I just became a daddy," Chavez objected.

"Sorry, pal, but Covington is down. So's Chin. I'm going to send you and four men. It's an easy job, Ding. The Aussies know their stuff, but they asked us to come down and give it a look."

"When do I leave?"

"Tonight, out of Heathrow." Clark held up the ticket envelope.

"Great," Chavez grumbled.

SECURITY was good here, Popov thought as he rode around in another of the military-type vehicles that Dawson called a Hummer. The first thing about security was to have defensive depth. That they had. It was ten kilometers at least before you approached a property line.

"It used to be a number of large farms, but Horizon bought them out a few years ago and started building the research lab."

"You still grow wheat here?"

"Yeah. Got our own elevators over that way." He pointed north. Popov looked that way and saw the massive concrete structures some distance away. Farther north he could barely make out traffic moving on a distant highway.

"That's the northern border," Dawson explained as they passed into nonfarm land.

"What's that?"

"Oh, that's our little herd of pronghorn antelopes." Dawson turned the wheel slightly to go closer. "Those babies can run at forty miles an hour. They also have superb eyesight."

"Difficult to hunt, I imagine. Do you hunt?"

"They are, and I don't. I'm a vegan."

"What?"

"Vegetarian. I don't eat meat or other animal products."

"Why is that, David?" Popov asked. He'd never come across anyone like him before.

"Oh, just a choice I made. I don't approve of killing animals for food or any other reason." He turned. "Not everybody agrees with me, not even here at the Project. Nature is something to be respected, not exploited."

"So you don't buy your wife a fur coat," Popov said, smiling.

"Not hardly." Dawson laughed.

"I've never hunted," Popov said next, wondering what response he'd get. "I never saw the sense in it, and in Russia they've nearly exterminated most game animals."

"So I understand. That's very sad, but they'll come back."

"How? With all the state hunters working to kill them?"

Dawson's face took on a curious expression, one Popov had seen many times before at the KGB. The man knew something he was unwilling to say right now, though what he knew was important somehow. "Oh, there's ways, pal. There's ways."

The driving tour required an hour and a half, at the end of which Popov was mightily impressed. He'd never appreciated the power of a major American corporation. This should have been a government facility, with all the land and the huge building complex. Was Brightling going to move his entire corporation here? So far from all the things civilization offered. Why?

Dawson drove up to the lab building and stopped. "Come with me." Popov followed without asking why.

Inside the lab building there was a desk and a receptionist who knew David Dawson. The two men proceeded unimpeded to the elevators, then up to the fourth floor and right to an office.

"Hi, Doc," Dawson said. "This is Dmitriy. Dr. Brightling sent him to us last night. He's going to be here awhile."

"I got the fax." The physician stood and extended his hand to Popov. "Hi, I'm John Killgore. Follow me." The two went into an examining room, while Dawson waited outside. Killgore told Popov to disrobe down to his underwear, and he proceeded to give him a physical examination, taking blood pressure, checking reflexes, prodding his belly to make sure the liver was nonpalpable. Popov submitted to it all without objection, somewhat bemused by the whole thing. Finally Killgore pulled a vial from the medicine cabinet and stuck a disposable syringe into it.

"What's this?" Dmitriy Arkadeyevich asked.

"Just a booster shot," Killgore explained, setting the vial down. It's a pity, he thought, that the patient couldn't be appreciative for having his life saved.

Popov picked it up and looked at the label, which read "B-2100 11-21-00." He winced when the needle went into his upper arm.

"There, that's done. Has David given you the tour?"

"Yes, and this place reminds me of the many western movies I have seen. When Dawson drove me around, I expected to see cowboys herding cattle and carrying Colt pistols on their belts."

Killgore had a good chuckle at that. "I guess you're a city boy. Well, so was I once, but I've come to love it out here, especially on horseback. Like to go for a ride?"

"I've never sat on a horse," Popov admitted, intrigued by the invitation.

"Well, we have a nice gentle mare. Buttermilk, would you believe?" Killgore paused. "Wow, it's nice to be out here."

"You are a recent arrival?"

"Just last week. I used to be in the Binghamton lab, northwest of New York City," he explained.

"What sort of work do you do?"

"I'm a physician—epidemiologist. I'm supposed to be an expert on how diseases riffle through populations."

"I have a sister who is a pediatrician," Popov tried.

"Oh? Where?"

"In Moscow. Her name is Maria Arkadeyevna. I am Dmitriy Arkadeyevich. Our father was Arkady, you see."

"Was he a doctor, too?" Killgore asked.

Popov shook his head. "No. He was like me, a spy—an intelligence officer for State Security." Popov dropped that in to see how Killgore would react. He figured he didn't need to keep it a secret out here, and it could be useful.

"You were KGB?" the doctor asked, impressed.

It was as though he'd just admitted to being a sports star, Popov saw. "Yes, I was KGB, but with the changes in my country I was, how you say, laid off?"

"What did you do with the KGB?"

"Oh, I met with certain people and groups to discuss matters of mutual interest," Popov replied coyly.

"Like who?"

"I'm not supposed to say. Your Dr. Brightling knows. That's why he hired me."

"So you're part of the Project now?"

"What project? I don't know what that means. John sent me here, but he didn't say why."

Killgore looked uncomfortable. "Well, John will brief you on that when he gets out here, Dmitriy. So you want to go horseback riding in the country?"

"Yes, I'd like that very much," Popov replied, wondering what mine he'd just stepped on. His instincts told him he'd been close to something important.

"Meet me in the cafeteria tomorrow morning, say about seven."

CLARK awoke to the noise and had to think for a second or so to remember that Patsy had moved in with them so as not to be alone and to have her mother's help with J.C., as they were calling him. This time he decided to get up, too, despite the early hour. Sandy was already up, her maternal instincts ignited by the sound of a crying baby. John arrived in time to see his wife hand his newly re-diapered grandson to his daughter. He was a cute little guy, Clark thought, and Ding would be a good father, Clark was sure. He smiled and walked back to bed, trying to remember exactly where Chavez the Elder was at the moment and leaving the women's work to the women of the house.

THE dawn again awoke Popov in his motel-like room. He dressed and headed down to the cafeteria, where he found Dr. Killgore eating breakfast, as promised. "Good morning, John," the Russian said, taking his seat across the table from the epidemiologist.

"Morning, Dmitriy. Ready for your ride?"

"Yes, I think I am. You said the horse was gentle?"

"That's why they call her Buttermilk. Eight-year-old quarter horse mare. She won't hurt you."

"Quarter horse? What does that mean?"

"It means they only race a quarter mile, but you know, one of the richest horse races in the world is for that distance, down in Texas.

I forget what they call it, but the purse is huge. Well, one more institution we won't be seeing much more of," Killgore went on, buttering his toast.

"Excuse me?" Popov asked.

"Hmph? Oh, nothing important, Dmitriy." And it wasn't. The horses would survive for the most part, returning to the wild to see if they could make it after centuries of being adapted to human care. He supposed their instincts, genetically encoded in their DNA, would save most of them. And someday Project members and/or their progeny would capture them, break them, and ride them on their way to enjoy Nature and her ways. The working horses—quarters and Appaloosas—should do well. Thoroughbreds he was less sure of. Killgore finished his breakfast and stood. "Ready?"

"Yes, John." Popov followed him to the doors. Outside, Killgore had his own Hummer, which he drove to the southwest in the clear, bright morning. Ten minutes later they were at the horse barns. He took a saddle from the tack room and walked to a stall whose door had BUTTERMILK engraved on the pine. He opened the door, walked in, saddled the horse, and handed Popov the reins. "Just walk her outside. She won't bite, Dmitriy."

"If you say so, John," the Russian observed dubiously. He was wearing sneakers rather than boots, and he wondered if that was important or not. Dmitriy walked to the barn's large door, and the horse followed quietly into the clear morning air. A few minutes later Killgore appeared astride his horse.

"You know how to get on?" the physician asked.

Popov figured he'd seen enough western movies. He stuck his left foot into the left stirrup and climbed up, swinging his right leg over and finding the opposite stirrup.

"Good. Now just hold the reins and click your tongue like this." Killgore demonstrated.

Popov did the same, and the horse started walking forward.

"There you go, Dmitriy," the doctor said approvingly. "Come on." Killgore's legs thumped in on his mount, making him move a little faster.

It was magnificent, Dmitriy Arkadeyevich thought, and now he understood the ethos of all those bad movies he'd seen. He looked around at the rolling land and somehow felt himself to be a part of it all. "John, I must thank you. This is wonderful," he said sincerely. "Could we do it again?"

"It's part of my morning routine here. Want to join me?"

"Yes, thank you. That is very kind."

"Seven a.m.," Killgore responded with a smile. "Every day."

CHAPTER 10
THE GAMES BEGIN

CHAVEZ did his best not to stumble off the aircraft, somewhat amazed that the cabin crew looked so chipper. Well, they had practice, and maybe they'd adapted to jet lag better than he ever had. He headed for the door with the eagerness of a man being released from a maximum-security prison.

"Major Chavez?" a voice asked in an Australian accent. "G'day, I'm *Lef*tenant Colonel Frank Wilkerson, Australian Special Air Service." He held out his hand.

"Howdy." Chavez grabbed the hand and shook it. "These are my men, Sergeants Johnston, Pierce, Tomlinson, and Special Agent Tim Noonan of the FBI. He's our technical support."

"Welcome to Australia, gentlemen. Follow me, if you please."

It took fifteen minutes to collect all the gear and load it into a minibus. Then they headed for Sydney.

"When do the games start?" Mike Pierce asked.

"Tomorrow," Wilkerson replied. "We've got most of the athletes settled into their quarters, and our security teams are fully manned and trained. We expect no difficulties at all."

The driver turned off the highway, taking an exit that seemed to head into downtown Sydney. Traffic was light. It was around six a.m.

The minibus pulled up to an upscale hotel. "We have an arrange-ment with this one," Wilkerson explained. "The Global Security people are here, too."

"Who?" Ding asked.

"Global Security. They have the consulting contract. Mr. Noonan, you probably know their chief, Bill Henriksen."

"Bill the Tree-hugger?" Noonan managed a strangled laugh. "Oh, yeah, I know him."

"Tree-hugger?"

"Colonel, Bill was a senior guy in Hostage Rescue a few years ago. Competent guy, but one of those nutty environmentalist types. Worries about the ozone layer," Noonan explained.

"I didn't know that about him. Anyway, he seems to know his stuff. Those new radios that E-Systems make, which he got for us—they're marvelous."

The door of the minibus was pulled open by a hotel employee, and the men stumbled out. Colonel Wilkerson must have called ahead, Ding thought a minute later as they were fast-tracked to their rooms—nice ones—for wake-up showers, followed by big breakfasts with *lots* of coffee. As dreadful as the jet lag was, the best way to handle it was to gut through the first day, then try to get a decent night's sleep. At least that was the theory, Ding thought.

THE Irish Garda had almost always cooperated with their British counterparts, and this time was no exception. With information provided by Timothy O'Neil, the senior local Gardai drove at once to Shannon to check for flight records. As far as he was concerned, all he wanted to know was how ten pounds of illegal drugs had entered his country.

The flight-operations office at Shannon had paper records of every flight that arrived or departed from the complex, and with the date the assistant operations manager found the right sheet in under three minutes. Yes, a Gulfstream business jet had arrived early in the morning, refueled, and departed soon after. The air-craft was registered to a large U.S. charter company. The Irish police officer then went to immigration/customs control, where he found that one Joseph Serov had indeed cleared customs on the morning indicated. The Gardai took a photocopy of all relevant documents back to his station, where they were faxed immediately to Garda headquarters in Dublin, then on to London and from there to Washington, D.C.

Thirty minutes later a pair of FBI agents arrived at the office of the charter company at the Teterboro, New Jersey, airport, where they ascertained that the aircraft had been chartered by one Joseph Serov, who'd paid with a certified check drawn on an account at Citibank. The agents went to the bank branch where Serov kept his account and learned that nobody had ever met the man. His address, they found, was the same post-office box that had dead-ended the search for his credit card records.

By this time the FBI had a copy of Serov's passport photo. The case file was growing. Sooner or later they'd find where he'd slipped up, because once you appeared on the FBI's collective radarscope, nine thousand skilled investigators started looking, and they wouldn't stop looking until told to stop.

"HELLO," Popov said.

"Howdy," the man replied. "You're not from here."

"Dmitriy Popov," the Russian said, extending his hand.

"Foster Hunnicutt," the American said, taking it. "What do you do here?"

Popov smiled. "Here, I do nothing at all, though I am learning to ride a horse. I work directly for Dr. Brightling."

"Who? Oh, the big boss of this place?"

"Yes, that is correct. And you?"

"I'm a hunter and guide," the man from Montana replied.

"Good, and you are not a vegan?"

Hunnicutt thought that was pretty good. "Not exactly. But I prefer elk to this mystery meat," he went on, looking down with some distaste at what was on his plate. "I'm partial to bear meat, too."

"That'll annoy a lot of the folks here," Dr. Killgore observed, working on his pasta salad.

"Look, man, hunting is the first form of conservation. Maybe I kill game, but I eat what I kill. I don't kill things just to watch 'em die. Well," he added, "not game animals anyway. There's a lot of ignorant people I wouldn't mind popping."

"You ride, Mr. Hunnicutt?" Killgore asked.

"How else does a man hunt in the West?"

"So you're a hunting guide?"

"Yeah." Hunnicutt nodded. "I used to be a geologist for the oil companies, but then I got tired of helping to kill the planet, y'know, and I took my money and hung it up, like. Built me a cabin in the mountains and took to hunting full-time."

"Oh, you can do that? Hunt full-time, I mean?" Killgore asked.

"That depends. A fish-and-game cop hassled me about it, but well, he stopped hassling me."

From the way he said it, Popov knew that this Hunnicutt person had killed a police officer and gotten away with it. What sort of people did this "project" recruit?

"Anyway, we all ride in the morning. Want to join us?"

"You bet! I never turn that down."

"I have learned to enjoy it myself," Popov put in.

"Dmitriy, you must have some cossack in you." Killgore laughed. "Anyway, Foster, show up here for breakfast a little before seven."

"Deal," Hunnicutt confirmed.

RIDING had become so enjoyable that Popov was waking up just after first light in order to relish it more. And so he was in the cafeteria early, picking his breakfast food—plus a fresh red apple for Buttermilk—just as the kitchen staff set it out. He was halfway through his scrambled eggs when Killgore and the new one, Hunnicutt, approached, carrying their breakfast trays.

"Morning, Dmitriy," the tall hunter said in greeting.

"Good morning, Foster."

"Doc here tells me you were a spy, eh?"

"Intelligence. Yes, that was my job for the Soviet Union."

"So what do you think of Kansas?" Like Popov, Hunnicutt had piled up eggs and bacon. He needed a lot of food to support his frame, Dmitriy imagined.

"Like Russia in many ways—the broad horizons and vast farms, though yours are far more efficient."

"Yeah, we're counting on that to keep us in bread," Hunnicutt agreed, stuffing his face. "We have enough land here to grow plenty, and all the equipment we need. I may be into that myself."

"Oh?"

"Yeah, well, everybody's going to be assigned Project work. We all gotta pull together in the beginning anyway."

Popov didn't ask what he meant, and he remained puzzled as they finished breakfast and walked to Killgore's Hummer. At the horse barn, Popov saddled Buttermilk, fed her the apple from the cafeteria, and took her outside. As he mounted the mare and looked around the green-amber sea that surrounded the facility, Hunnicutt came out on a horse Dmitriy had never seen. On a closer look Popov asked, "Is that a pistol?"

"It's an M-1873, Colt's single-action army revolver," Foster replied, lifting it from his holster. "The gun that won the West."

"Forty-five?" the Russian asked. He'd seen them in movies.

"No, it's a .44-40. Caliber forty-four, with forty grains of black powder. Just about the deadliest cartridge ever made." Hunnicutt replaced the revolver in the leather holster.

It impressed Popov to see it in real life after so many movies. The American hunter even wore a wide-brimmed western hat, and Popov found himself liking the man despite his bombast.

"Come on, Jeremiah," Hunnicutt said to his horse as Killgore entered the corral, and with that, he led them off.

"Your horse?" Popov asked.

"Oh, yeah. A blanket Appaloosa. Bought him off a Nez Percé Indian pal." Foster smiled as they walked out the gate. A man fully in his element, Popov thought.

They went north this morning, close to the interstate highway with its truck traffic. "Where is the nearest town?" Popov asked.

"That way"—Killgore pointed—"about five miles. Not much of a town."

"Does it have an airport?"

"Little one, for private planes only," the doctor replied. "You go east about twenty miles. There's another town with a regional airport, so you can get to Kansas City."

Popov looked off at the highway and saw a Greyhound bus stop at an odd little square hut. "What's that?" he asked.

"Bus stop for the intercity buses," Killgore replied. "You sit there and wait; then you wave for the bus to stop, like the old flag stops for trains."

"Ah." Dmitriy filed that one away and turned his horse to the east. They rode for another hour, then headed back. Killgore rode ahead, so Popov ended up next to Hunnicutt.

"You're doing okay for a tenderfoot," Foster told him.

"I want to do it more, so that I can ride better at a faster pace."

"Well, how about tonight? Just fore sundown, say?"

"Thank you, Foster. Yes, I would like that. Just after dinner?"

"Sure. Meet me around six thirty at the corral."

"Thank you. I will do that," Popov promised. A night ride under the stars. Yes, that should be very pleasant.

CHAVEZ turned in after another long day of watching athletes run and sweat. It had been an interesting couple of weeks, and though he sorely missed Patsy and J.C., he couldn't deny that he was enjoying himself. But soon it would be over. Reporters were tallying up the medals. America had done well, and the Aussies had done spectacularly well, especially in swimming events. Three more days and they'd run the marathon, traditionally the last Olympic event, followed by the closing ceremonies and the dousing of the flame.

The games had been wonderfully managed. Security hadn't had even a hint of a problem. The Aussie cops were competent and numerous, and the Australian SAS backing them up were nearly as good as his own troopers, well supported by the Global Security people, who'd gotten them the same tactical radios that Rainbow used. That company looked like a good vendor, and he thought he might recommend that John talk to them.

About the only bad news was the weather, which had been sultry hot for the entire Olympic Games. That had kept the medics busy at their first-aid heatstroke kiosks. Nobody had died yet, but about a hundred people had been hospitalized. Chavez didn't mind the heat all that much, but like everyone else, he was grateful for the fogging system. His last thought of the night was that he would not have minded having the sunblock concession.

POPOV saddled Buttermilk at about six that evening. Jeremiah, Hunnicutt's horse, was smaller than Buttermilk but appeared more powerful. Hunnicutt showed up, hoisting his large western-style saddle on his shoulder, tossing it atop the blanket Appaloosa stallion, then reaching under to cinch in the straps. His last act, Popov saw, was to strap on his Colt pistol. Then he slid his left foot into the left stirrup and climbed aboard. Jeremiah must have liked to be ridden. The head came up proudly, and the ears swiveled around, waiting for the command of its rider. There was a clucking sound, and the stallion moved out into the corral alongside Popov and Buttermilk.

"He is a fine horse, Foster."

"Best I've ever had," the hunter agreed. He reached down to pat his horse's neck with rough affection. "Jeremiah here even found my gold for me."

"Excuse me? Gold?"

Hunnicutt laughed. "On my spread up in Montana there's a stream coming down from the mountain. I was letting Jeremiah drink one afternoon, and I saw something shiny. It was gold. I figure I got a fair-sized deposit on my land. How big? There's no tellin', and it doesn't matter much anyway."

"Not matter?" Popov turned in the saddle to look at his companion. "Foster, for the last ten thousand years men have killed one another over gold."

"Not anymore, Dmitriy. That's going to end—forever."

"But how? Why?" Popov demanded.

"Don't you know about the Project?"

"A little, but not enough to understand what you just said."

"Dmitriy, human life on the planet is going to come to a screeching halt, boy. They didn't tell you?"

"No, Foster, not that part. Can you tell me?"

What the heck, Hunnicutt thought. The Olympics were almost over, and this Russki understood about nature. "It's called Shiva," he began, and then went on for several minutes.

For Popov it was a time to put his professional face back on. He even managed a smile that masked his inner horror. "But how do you distribute it?"

"Well, you see, Brightling has a company that also works for him—Global Security. The boss is a guy named Bill Henriksen. Anyway, they got the consulting contract with the Aussies for the Olympics, and one of Bill's people will be spreading the Shiva. Something to do with the air-conditioning system at the stadium. They're going to spread it on the last day. Then everyone flies home, and thousands of people take the bug with them."

"But what protects us?"

"You got a shot when you came here, right?"

"Yes. Killgore said it was a booster for something."

"It's a booster, all right. It's the vaccine that protects you against Shiva. I got it, too. That's the B vaccine, pal. There's another one, they tell me, the A vaccine, but that one's not the one you want to get." Hunnicutt went on, "The original outbreak may kill a few million people, but that's mainly psychological. Then Horizon's going to market this A vaccine. It's a live-virus vaccine, like the Sabin polio vaccine. But they've tuned it, like. It doesn't stop Shiva, man. It *spreads* Shiva."

"How do you know all this?" Popov asked.

"I'm one of the guys who helped set up the perimeter security system here. So they told me why the Project *needs* perimeter security. Not many people really understand about saving the planet. I mean, we do this now, or in about twenty years *everything* and *everybody* dies. We can't let that happen, can we?"

"I see your point," Dmitriy Arkadeyevich agreed without choking on his words. "Brightling is a genius to see this, to find a way of solving the problem and then to have the courage to act." Popov hoped his voice wasn't too patronizing, but this man Hunnicutt was a technocrat, not one who understood people.

"Yep. And he has the resources. Setting all this up must have cost near onto a billion dollars—not counting Brazil."

"Brazil?"

"There's a smaller version of the complex down there, somewhere west of Manaus, I think." Hunnicutt clucked and got Jeremiah to go faster, an easy canter that Popov tried to duplicate.

"So you will transform this country to the Old West, eh?" Popov said, looking north to where the interstate highway was.

"That's one of the things we're going to do."

"And you'll carry your pistol everywhere?"

"Revolver, Dmitriy," Foster corrected. "But yeah."

"Foster? Your pistol—may I hold it?"

"Sure." He drew it and passed it across, muzzle up for safety.

Popov felt the weight and the balance. "It is loaded?"

"Nothing much more useless than a handgun that ain't loaded. You want to shoot it? Just cock the hammer back and let go, but make sure your horse is reined in tight. Jeremiah here's used to the noise. That mare might not be."

"I see." Popov took the reins in his left hand to keep Buttermilk in check. Next he extended his right hand and cocked the hammer on the Colt. He took aim at a wooden surveyor's stake and pulled the trigger. Buttermilk jumped slightly with the noise. And the bullet, Popov saw, grazed the two-inch stake, six meters or so away. So he still knew how to shoot.

"Nice, isn't it?" Hunnicutt asked. "If you ask me, the single-action army's got the best balance of any handgun ever made."

"Yes," Popov agreed, "it is very nice." Then he turned. Foster Hunnicutt was seated on his stallion not three meters away. The former KGB officer cocked the hammer again, aimed right at the center of his chest, and pulled the trigger. The body of the hunter stayed erect in the saddle for a few seconds, the eyes wide with shock; then it fell lifelessly backward onto the grassland.

Dmitriy dismounted to make sure Hunnicutt was dead. Then he unsaddled Jeremiah and removed the bridle, surprised that the animal didn't bite him for what he'd just done, but a horse wasn't a dog. He smacked the stallion heavily on the rump, and it trotted off for fifty meters or so, then stopped and started grazing.

Popov remounted Buttermilk and clucked her to a northerly direction. He looked back, saw the lit windows of the Project building complex. He was not a man who believed in God. His education and upbringing had not aimed him in that direction. But he'd learned something important today. He might never know if there was a God, but there were surely devils, and he had worked for them. The horror of that was like nothing he'd ever known as a young colonel of the KGB.

He dismounted Buttermilk a hundred meters from the bus hut, and again he took the time to remove the saddle and bridle, because a saddled, riderless horse was sure to attract notice, but a horse merely walking about on its own probably would not. Then it was just a matter of easing his way through the barbed wire fence and walking to the bus hut, which, he found, was empty.

After ten minutes he walked to the shoulder and held up his hand. A cream-colored Ford pickup eased over to the side of the road. "Where you headin', buddy?" the driver asked. He looked to be a farmer, perhaps sixty years of age.

"The airport in the next town. Can you take me?" Dmitriy said, getting in.

"Sure. I have to get off at that exit anyway. What's your name?"

"Joe—Joseph Demetrius," Popov said, remembering the name on his single remaining credit card.

"Well, I'm Pete. You're not from around here, are you?"

"Not originally. England, actually," Dmitriy went on, trying that accent on for size.

"Oh, yeah? So how'd you get stuck out here, Joe?"

What was the matter with this man? He asked questions like someone from the Second Chief Directorate of the KGB. "My, uh, friend, had a family emergency, and he had to drop me off to wait for a bus."

"Oh." And that shut him up, Popov saw, blessing his most recent lie. *You see, I just shot and killed someone who wanted to kill you and everyone you know. . . .* It was one of those times when the truth simply didn't work.

CAROL BRIGHTLING STOOD IN her office. She'd just printed up a letter to the White House chief of staff saying she'd be taking a leave of absence to work on a special scientific project. She'd done her job for the Project and for the planet, and it was now time for her to leave. It had been so long, so very long, since she'd felt her husband John's arms around her. The divorce had been well publicized. It had had to be. She would never have gotten the White House job if she'd been married to one of the country's richest men. And so she'd forsworn him, and he'd publicly forsworn the movement, the beliefs they'd both held ten years before when they'd formulated the idea for the Project, but he'd never stopped believing, any more than she had. And so she'd gotten a security clearance that gave her access to literally everything, even operational intelligence, which she then forwarded to John when he needed it.

But it had had a price. John had been seen in public with all manner of young women and had doubtless dallied with many of them, for he'd always been a passionate man. But set against that small personal consideration was the Project. Her ten years of sacrifice were over, and the reward for it would be a planet turning back to green, Nature restored to her glory.

ALICE Foorgate came in a few minutes early. She put her purse in a desk drawer and began reviewing her notes on the things that were supposed to happen today. Oh, she saw, a budget meeting. Mr. Clark would be in a foul mood until after lunch. Then her phone rang.

"I need to speak to Mr. John Clark," the voice said.

"May I tell him who's calling?"

"No," the voice said, "you may not."

That made the secretary blink with puzzlement. She placed the incoming call on hold and punched another button.

"A call for you on line one, sir."

"Who is it?" Clark asked.

"He didn't say, sir."

"Okay." John switched buttons. "This is John Clark."

"Good morning, Mr. Clark," the anonymous voice said.

"Who is this?" John asked.

"We have a mutual acquaintance. His name is Sean Grady."

"Yes?" Clark punched the RECORD button.

"You may know my name, therefore, as Iosef Andreyevich Serov. We should meet, Mr. Clark."

"Yes," John replied evenly, "I'd like that. How do we do it?"

"Today, in New York. Take the British Airways Concorde flight one into JFK. I will meet you at the entrance to the Central Park Zoo. I shall be there at eleven exactly. Any questions?"

"I suppose not. Okay, eleven a.m. in New York."

The line went dead, and Clark switched buttons. "Alice, could you have Bill and Alistair join me, please?"

They came in less than three minutes later. "Listen to this one, guys," John said, hitting the PLAY button on the tape machine.

"You're going?" Stanley asked when the tape ended.

"Why not? It gets me out of the budget meeting."

"Quite so, but there could be dangers involved."

"I'll have the FBI send some people to look after me, and I'll have a friend with me," Clark said, meaning his Beretta .45.

DR. KILLGORE came to the cafeteria at his accustomed hour but surprisingly didn't find his Russian friend or Foster Hunnicutt. Well, maybe they'd both slept late. He lingered over breakfast twenty minutes more than usual, then drove to the horse barn. There he found another surprise. Both Buttermilk and Jeremiah were in the corral, neither of them saddled or bridled. He waited outside for another fifteen minutes, wondering if his friends would show up. But they didn't, and he rode off west for his morning tour of the countryside.

THE van crossed the East River and proceeded west through crowded streets. John checked his watch.

"No problem, sir. We'll be about ten minutes early," FBI agent Tom Sullivan told him.

"Good," John replied tensely. It was coming soon now, and he had to get his emotions under control. He had to set aside all thoughts of past dangers to his immediate family. He had to be stone-cold at this meeting. And so, sitting there in the front seat of what appeared to be a Consolidated Edison vehicle, he told himself to relax. Then curiosity took over. This Russian had to know that Clark knew what he'd done, and *still* he'd asked for this meeting. That had to mean something, John told himself as they broke through traffic and turned left onto Fifth Avenue. He checked his watch again. They were fourteen minutes early. The van eased over to the right and stopped. Clark stepped out and headed south on the crowded sidewalk. Two FBI agents also got out, carrying papers and looking rather too obviously like Con Ed employees, John thought. Then he turned right and walked down the stairs to the zoo. It didn't take long.

"Good morning, John Clark," a man's voice said behind him.

"Good morning, Dmitriy Arkadeyevich," John replied without turning.

"Very good," the voice said approvingly. "I congratulate you on learning one of my names."

"We have good intelligence support. What can I do for you?"

"I must first of all apologize for my contacts with Grady."

"What about the other operations?" Clark asked.

"Those did not concern you directly, and only one person was killed."

"But that one was a sick little girl," John observed.

"No. I had nothing to do with Worldpark. The bank in Bern and the stock trader outside Vienna—yes, those were my missions, but not the amusement park."

"You have implicated yourself in three terrorist operations. That is against the law, you know."

"Yes, I am aware of that," the Russian replied dryly.

"So what can I do for you?" John asked.

"It is more what I can do for you, Mr. Clark."

"And that is?" Still he didn't turn.

"I can give you the reason for the missions and the name of the man who instigated it all. It is quite monstrous. I only discovered yesterday what the purpose for all of this is."

"So what is the objective?" John asked.

"To kill almost every human being on the planet."

That made Clark turn to look at the man. "Is this some sort of movie script?" he asked coldly.

"Clark, yesterday I was in Kansas. There I learned the plan for this 'project.' I killed the person who told me, so I could escape. The man I killed was Foster Hunnicutt. I shot him in the chest with his own pistol. From there I went to the nearest highway and begged a ride to the regional airport, from there to Kansas City, and from there to New York. I know you have the power to arrest me. You have security watching us right now. Plus you have me for inciting terrorist incidents and I presume for drug trafficking as well. I know this, yet I have asked for this meeting. Do you suppose that I am joking with you, John Clark?"

"Perhaps not." Rainbow Six looked closely at the man.

"Very well. In that case I propose that you have us taken to a secure place so I can give you the information you need. I require only your word that I will not be detained or arrested."

"You would believe me if I were to say that?"

"You are CIA. You know the rules of the game, do you not?"

Clark nodded. "Okay, you have my word—if you're telling me the truth."

"John Clark, I wish I were not," Popov said. "Truly I wish I were not, *tovarishch.*"

John looked hard into his eyes, and in them he saw fear. No, something deeper than fear. This guy had just called him comrade. "Come on," John told him.

"That's Serov," a female agent said over the radio circuit. "All gift wrapped like a toy from FAO Schwarz. Wait. They're heading this way."

Tom Sullivan saw them walking very quickly to the van.

"You got a safe house around here?" Clark asked.

"Well, yeah, we do, but—"

"Get us there right now," Clark ordered. "You can terminate your cover operation at once. Get in, Dmitriy," he said, opening the sliding door.

CHAPTER 11
DYING FLAME

THE safe house was a four-story brownstone that had been given to the federal government by a businessman whose kidnapped son had been recovered alive by the FBI. Outwardly unremarkable, inside it had an elaborate security system and three rooms, with recording systems and two-way mirrors. It was manned around the clock.

"Okay," Clark said, announcing the date, time, and place. "With me is Colonel Dmitriy Arkadeyevich Popov, retired, of the former Soviet KGB. The subject of this interview is international terrorist activity. My name is John Clark, and I am a field officer of the Central Intelligence Agency. Also here are—"

"Special Agent Tom Sullivan."

"And—"

"Special Agent Frank Chatham."

"Of the FBI's New York office. Dmitriy, would you please begin?" John said.

"THIS is the day, Carol," John Brightling told his ex-wife. "Less than ten hours from now the Project starts."

She dropped Jiggs, her cat, onto the floor and came to embrace him. "Oh, John."

"I know," he told her. "It's been a long time. Couldn't have done it without you."

Henriksen was there, too. "I talked with Wil Gearing twenty minutes ago. He'll be hooking up the Shiva dispenser right before they start the closing ceremonies. The weather is working for us, too. It's going to be another hot one in Sydney, so people'll be camping out under the foggers."

"And breathing heavily," Dr. John Brightling confirmed. That was another of the body's methods for shedding excess heat.

"YOU'RE lucky you got me, John. I was just getting dressed to leave and watch the mara—"

"Shut up and listen to me, Domingo," Clark said harshly.

Chavez got out a pad and took some notes. "Is this for real?" he asked finally.

"We believe it to be, Ding. The guy giving this to me is named Serov, Iosef Andreyevich. He's here with me now."

"Okay, Mr. C. When is this operation supposed to take place?"

"Around the time of the closing ceremonies."

"And you want us to stop it."

"Correct. From now on, all transmissions will be secure."

"You got it. Let me get moving, John."

"Move," the voice told him. "Bye."

First Chavez had to assemble his team. They were all on the same floor, and he knocked on each door and told the NCOs to come to his suite.

"Okay, people, we got a job. Here's the deal." The story was quite incredible, but they were accustomed to hearing and acting upon strange information. "We have to put people in the control room for the fogging system. We'll rotate the duty. George and Homer, you start; then Mike and I will relieve you. Radios will be on at all times. Deadly force is authorized. Let's move, people," Ding told them.

KIRK Maclean was a biochemist and environmental engineer. His job at the Project in Kansas was to keep an eye on the environmental support systems, mainly the air-conditioning and the overpressurization system. His day's work had been easily dealt with. It mainly involved checking dials and recording systems—all of which were stuck in the very center of normal operating ranges—and now he felt like taking a ride. He walked into the transport office, took a set of keys for a Hummer, then headed out to the barn to get his horse. Another twenty minutes and he was cantering across the grassland, heading toward the northern edge of the Project's real estate. About forty minutes into the ride he saw about six buzzards circling something in the tall grass. Six was a lot. Then he realized there were more still as he spotted the black, angular shapes in the grass. Something large had died.

Probably a deer or pronghorn antelope, Maclean thought, heading his horse over that way. But at fifty yards he stopped. Whatever they were eating seemed to be wearing a plaid shirt. He urged his horse closer, and at ten yards the buzzards took notice, first swiveling their odious red heads and cruel black eyes, then hopping away a few feet, then, finally, flapping back into the air. Maclean got closer. He recognized Foster Hunnicutt. It required a few more feet of approach to see the small red circle in the center of the dark shirt. Maclean didn't dismount. He decided to get back to the Project as quickly as his horse could manage.

THE room was grossly nondescript, Chavez saw. Just pipes and a pump, which was running, as the fogging-cooling system had started off from its timer a few minutes before. Chavez's first thought was, What if the bug's already in the system? But no, John had told him the poisoning was to start later in the day.

Noonan bent down to look at the chlorine canister that hung on the piping. "I can see how you switch them out," the FBI agent said. "Looks like a thirty-second job, maybe less. But who would do something like this, Ding? And why?"

"I guess we have to figure that out. But for now we watch this thing like it's the most valuable gadget in the world." Ding turned to look at his men. "George and Homer, you guys stay here. Mike and I will handle things outside. Tim, you stay close, too. We got our radios, and that's how we communicate. Two hours on, two hours off. Questions?"

"Nope," Sergeant Tomlinson said for the rest. "If somebody comes in and tries to fool with this—"

"You stop him, any way you have to."

"Roge-o, boss," George said, and Homer Johnston nodded agreement.

Chavez and the other two went back outside. The stadium had filled up, people wanting to see the start of the marathon. He, Pierce, and Noonan walked to one of the ramps and watched the TVs hanging there. The local Australian commentary was discussing the betting on the event. Smart money seemed to be on a Kenyan, though there was an American who'd blown away the record for the Boston Marathon the previous year by almost half a minute, and a thirty-year-old Dutchman who was the dark horse among the favorites.

"So what do we do now?" Mike Pierce asked.

"Wait. Stand around and wait."

"YOU say he was shot?"

"Sure looked like it," Maclean replied heatedly.

Killgore lifted his phone. "Bill, it's John Killgore. Meet me in the main lobby right away. We have a problem." The physician replaced the phone and rose. "Come on," he said to Maclean.

Henriksen arrived in the lobby of the residential building two minutes after they did, and together they drove in a Hummer north to where the body was. Again the buzzards had to be chased off, and Henriksen, the former FBI agent, walked up to take a look. "He's been shot, all right," he said. "Big bullet, right through the X ring. Who hung out with Foster?"

"The Russian guy. We rode together," Killgore answered.

"Okay, let's find Popov. I think I need to talk to him."

"He didn't show up for breakfast this morning like he usually does," Killgore revealed. "You think he—"

"I don't think anything yet. Let's get the body into the Hummer."

Twenty minutes later they were back in the Project complex. It took half an hour to determine that Popov was nowhere to be found. Okay, Henriksen thought. Popov killed Hunnicutt, then skipped. But why? "What did Popov know?" he asked Killgore.

"Not much. Brightling didn't really brief him. But Foster Hunnicutt knew everything, and he could have told Popov."

"So Popov finds out, gets Foster's revolver, shoots him, and gets out." *Wil Gearing's going to initiate phase one today!* Henriksen realized. He had to talk to Brightling right away.

Both Doctors Brightling were in the penthouse accommodations atop the residence building. Henriksen's news wasn't pleasing to either of them. "How bad is this?" John asked.

"Potentially, it's pretty bad," Bill had to admit.

"How close are we to—"

"Four hours or less," Henriksen replied.

"Does Popov know that?"

"It's possible, but we can't know for sure."

"Where would he have gone?" Carol Brightling asked.

"I don't know—CIA, FBI, maybe. Popov's a trained spook. In his position I'd go to the Russian embassy in D.C. and tell the *rezident*. He'll have credibility there, but the bureaucracy works for us. The KGB can't do *anything* fast, Carol. They'll spend hours trying to swallow whatever he tells them."

"Okay. So we proceed?" John Brightling asked.

A nod. "Yeah, I think so. Look, even if the whole thing comes apart, we turn out the B vaccine instead of the A, and we're heroes. There's no physical evidence that we've done anything wrong—at least none that we can't destroy in a matter of minutes, right?"

That part had been carefully thought through. All of the Shiva virus containers were a two-minute walk from incinerators. The bodies of the test subjects were ashes. There *were* people with personal knowledge of what had happened, but for any of them to talk meant implicating themselves in mass murder.

"Okay." John Brightling looked at his wife. They'd worked too hard and too long to turn back. Husband-physician-scientist traded a look with wife-scientist, and then both looked at their director of security. "Tell Gearing to proceed, Bill."

GEARING packed his clothing in a pair of wheeled suitcases and set them by the door of the room. Then he left his hotel carrying a backpack, like many of the other people on the street, and flagged a cab to the stadium. He paid his fare plus a generous tip, got out, and walked toward the massive concrete bowl. At the entrance he showed his security pass and was waved through. The marathon was about half an hour from its conclusion.

"THAT DUTCHMAN LOOKS pretty tough," Noonan said. Willem terHoost was in the lead and was heading for a record despite the weather conditions.

Chavez checked his watch and reached for his radio microphone. "Command to Tomlinson."

"I'm here, boss," Chavez heard in his earpiece.

"Coming in to relieve you."

"Roger that," the sergeant replied from inside the locked room.

Ding stood, waving for Pierce and Noonan to follow. It was just a hundred feet to the blue door. Ding twisted the knob and went inside. Tomlinson and Johnston had hidden in the shadows in the corner opposite the door. They came out when they recognized their fellow team members. "Stay close and stay alert," Chavez told the two sergeants.

"Roge-o," Homer Johnston said. On his way out he placed his hands over his ears, popping them open to rid himself of the pump noise.

The sound was annoying, Chavez realized in the first few minutes. Not overly loud, but constant, like a beehive.

"Why are we leaving the lights on?" Noonan asked.

"Good question." Chavez walked over and flipped the switch. The room went almost totally dark, with just a crack of light coming in from under the steel fire door.

GEARING was dressed in shorts and low-cut hiking boots, with short socks as well. It seemed the form of dress the locals had adopted for dealing with the heat, and it was comfortable enough, as was his backpack and floppy hat. He paused fifty feet or so from the blue door and asked himself for the thousandth time if he really wanted to do this. There were fellow human beings all around him, people seemingly like himself—but no, they weren't like him. They didn't get it, didn't understand what was important. They didn't see Nature for what she was, and as a result, they lived lives that were aimed at destroying her, driving cars that injected hydrocarbons into the atmosphere, using chemicals that found their way into the water, pesticides that killed birds. They were *killing* Nature. They didn't care. They didn't even try to understand the consequences of what they were doing. And so, no, they didn't have a right to live. With that decided, Wil Gearing resumed his walk to the blue door, fished in his pocket for the key, and inserted it into the knob.

"COMMAND, this is Johnston. You got company coming in! White guy, khaki shorts, red polo shirt, and backpack."

"Heads up," Chavez said in the darkness. There was the sound of a key in the lock; then the door opened, and there was a silhouette, a human shape—a man, Chavez saw as the lights flipped on. A man who knew what he was about. He reached for the wrench hanging on the wall, then shrugged out of his backpack and flipped off the motor switch, ending the whirring. He closed the valve and lifted the wrench to—

"Hold it right there, pal," Chavez said from the shadows.

"Who are you?" the man asked.

"I could ask you the same thing but I know. Your name is Wil Gearing. What are you planning to do, Mr. Gearing?"

"I'm here to swap the chlorine canister on the fogging system," Gearing replied, shaken that this Latino knew his name. Was he part of the Project?

"Oh? Let's see about that, Mr. Gearing. Tim?" Chavez gestured for Noonan to get the backpack. Sergeant Pierce stayed back, his hand on his pistol and his eyes locked on their visitor.

"Sure looks like a normal one," Noonan said. If this was a counterfeit, it was a beaut. He was tempted to open the screw top, but he had good reason not to. Next to the pump motor Chavez took the wrench and removed the existing canister.

"Looks about half full to me, pal. Not time to replace it yet, at least not with something called Shiva. Tim, let's be careful with that."

"You bet." Noonan tucked it back into Gearing's pack and strapped the cover down. "We'll have this checked out. Mr. Gearing, you are under arrest," the FBI agent told him. "You have the right to remain silent. You have the right to have an attorney present during questioning. If you cannot afford an attorney, we will provide you with one. Anything you say can be used against you in a court of law. Do you understand these rights, sir?"

Gearing was shaking now, and he turned to look at the door, wondering if he could . . . He couldn't. Tomlinson and Johnston chose that moment to come in. "Got him?" Homer asked.

"Yep," Ding replied. He pulled his cell phone out and called America. Again the encryption systems went through the synchronization process. "We got him," Chavez told Rainbow Six. "And we got the canister. Now, how do we get home?"

"There's an air force C-17 at Alice Springs. It'll wait for you."

"Okay." Chavez thumbed the END button and turned to his prisoner. "Okay, pal, you're coming with us."

"HE HASN'T called yet," John Brightling observed, checking his watch. The closing ceremonies were under way.

"I know. Let me make a call." Henriksen rose from his seat, pulled a card from his wallet, and dialed a number on the back of it to a cellular phone owned by a senior Global Security employee in Sydney. "Tony? This is Bill Henriksen. I need you to find Wil Gearing and tell him to call me immediately. He has the number. . . . Yes, that's the one. Right now, Tony. . . . Yeah. Thanks."

Down in Sydney, Tony Johnson walked across the street to Wil Gearing's hotel. Defeating the lock was child's play, just a matter of working a credit card into the doorjamb and flipping the angled latch, and then he was inside. And so were Gearing's bags, sitting there by the door. This was odd. Wil's flight was due to go off in twenty minutes. *Where are you, Wil?* Johnson wondered. Then he remembered why he was here, and he lifted the phone.

"What do you mean, Tony?" Henriksen asked, beginning to feel a chill on his skin. "Okay. If you find out anything else, call me here." Henriksen set the phone down and turned to look at the other two. "Wil Gearing's not in his room, but his luggage is."

"What's that mean?" Carol Brightling asked.

"I'm not sure. Hey, maybe he got hit by a car in the street."

"Or maybe Popov spilled his guts to the wrong people, and they bagged him," John Brightling suggested nervously.

"Popov didn't even know his name. Hunnicutt didn't either." But then Henriksen thought, Foster *did* know how the Shiva was supposed to be delivered, didn't he?

"What's the matter, Bill?" John asked, seeing the man's face and knowing that something was wrong.

"John, we may have a problem."

"What problem?" Carol asked.

Henriksen explained, and the mood changed abruptly.

"You mean they might know?"

Henriksen nodded. "That is possible, yes."

"What can we do?" the presidential science adviser asked.

"For starters, we destroy all the evidence. All the Shiva, all the vaccines, all the records. It's all on computer, so we just erase it. We can do that from here."

"They're encrypted, all of them," John Brightling pointed out.

"You want to bet against the code breakers at Fort Meade? I don't," Henriksen told them. "No, those files have to go, John. Without physical evidence they can't hurt you."

"What about witnesses?"

"The most overrated thing in the world is an eyewitness. Any lawyer with half a brain can make fools out of them. Okay, I'm going to my office to get rid of the computer stuff." Henriksen left at once, leaving the two Brightlings behind him.

"John," Carol said in quiet alarm, "what if people find out? Nobody'll understand—"

"Understand that we were going to kill them and their families? No," her husband agreed dryly.

"So what do we do?"

"We fly to Brazil."

IN HIS office Henriksen lit up his personal computer and pulled open an encrypted file. It had telephone numbers and access codes to every computer in Horizon Corporation, plus the names of the files relating to the Project. He accessed them via modem and moved them with mouse clicks into trash cans that shredded the files completely instead of merely removing their electronic address codes. He found that he was sweating as he did so, and it took him thirty-nine minutes. But after that he was certain that he'd completely destroyed them all.

Okay, he asked himself, what else might they have? Gearing's Shiva-delivery canister. Gearing could tell them it had come from Horizon Corporation, but no one working on that segment of the Project would admit to it, so there would be no corroborating evidence to back up the assertion. Work on the A and B vaccines could be explained away as medical research. The Shiva virus and the vaccine would be burned in a matter of hours, leaving no physical evidence.

This was enough. Well, it was almost enough. They still had Gearing, and Gearing, if he talked, could make life very uncomfortable for Brightling and a lot of other people, including himself. They would probably avoid conviction, but the embarrassment of a trial . . . And there was Popov, who could link John Brightling and himself to terrorist acts. The best thing would be to be beyond their reach. That meant Brazil and Project Alternate in the jungles west of Manaus. They could head down there, sheltered by Brazil's wonderfully protective extradition laws, and study the rain forest. He printed a list of true believers—Project members who knew everything, those who, if the FBI interrogated them, could hang them all—and tucked the pages into his shirt pocket. That done, he went back to Brightling's penthouse office. In less than an hour he and the two Brightlings were in the lobby of the residence building, along with fifty-three other loyal Project members. From there a minibus ferried them to four Gulfstream aircraft whose engines were already warm.

It would be a thirty-five-hundred-mile flight to Manaus, they were told on boarding, an easy hop for the Gulfstream V. The lead aircraft was nearly empty, just the Doctors Brightling, Bill Henriksen, and Steve Berg, lead scientist for the Shiva part of the Project. The aircraft lifted off at nine in the morning, local time. Next stop the Amazon Valley of central Brazil.

A car and two agents from the FBI drove out to the Kansas site in time to see the jets lift off, which they duly reported.

"WHAT'S THAT?" AGENT Sullivan asked. Then he turned. "Four jets just left the Kansas location, and they headed off to the south."

"Is there any way to track them?"

Sullivan shrugged. "The air force, maybe."

Clark called Ed Foley at Langley and told the director of Central Intelligence what he knew. "Can we get the air force to track the planes?"

"I can try, John. I'll call the NMCC."

That was not a difficult thing for the director of Central Intelligence to do. The senior duty officer in the National Military Command Center was an air force two-star recently rotated into a desk job after commanding the remaining USAF fighter force in NATO. The general phoned the North American Aerospace Defense Command in Cheyenne Mountain, which had radar coverage over the entire country, and ordered them to identify the four Gulfstreams. That took less than a minute, and a computer command was sent to the Federal Aviation Administration to check the flight plans that had to be filed for international flights. NORAD also told the general that there were *two* E-3B AWACS aircraft aloft at the moment: One was three hundred miles south of New Orleans doing counter-drug operations; the other was just south of Eglin Air Force Base conducting a routine training exercise. With that information he called Langley Air Force Base, got operations, and told them about the DCI's request.

"WE'RE in luck," Ed Foley told Clark. "The air force is chopping an AWACS to us. We can follow them all the way to where they're going." Foley was exaggerating somewhat, since the AWACS radar aircraft would have to refuel on the way. Aerial tanking would interfere with matters, but not very much.

BY THIS time Clark was on a shuttle flight to Reagan National Airport, across the river from Washington. He and Popov were met by a CIA employee whose Company car was parked outside, ready for the twenty-minute ride to Langley and the seventh floor of the Old Headquarters Building. Dmitriy Popov had never expected to be inside this particular edifice, even wearing a VISITOR—ESCORT REQUIRED badge. John handled the introductions.

"Okay, Ed, where are the Gulfstreams now?"

"Over northern Venezuela, heading south, probably for central Brazil. They filed a flight plan for Manaus."

"They told me that there is a facility there like the one in Kansas but smaller," Popov informed his hosts.

"Once we know where they're going, then what?" Clark asked the DCI.

"Not sure," Foley admitted.

"There might not be a good criminal case on this one, Ed," Clark said. "If they're smart, and we have to assume they are, they'll destroy all physical evidence of the crime. That leaves witnesses, but who, do you suppose, is aboard those four Gulfstreams heading into Brazil?"

"Okay, John, so what should we do?"

"Pay them a little visit, maybe?"

"John, I—"

"Do I have your permission to get my people together?"

Foley hesitated, but in the end, he had to yield to the logic of the moment. "Permission granted."

And with that, Clark called Hereford.

ALISTAIR Stanley had bounced back well from his wounds, enough so that he could just about manage a full day in his office without collapsing from exhaustion. His secure phone started chirping, and he reached to answer it.

"Hi, Al, this is John. You sitting down?"

"Yes, John, of course I am, and—"

"Listen up. I'll give you the short version," Clark commanded, and proceeded to do that for the next ten minutes.

"You're sure of this?" Stanley said.

"Very sure, Al. I need you to get our people to Fort Bragg—Pope Air Force Base, North Carolina—with all their gear. We may be taking a trip to the jungle to . . . to, uh, deal decisively with these people."

"TARGET ONE IS DESCENDING," a control officer reported over the aircraft's intercom. The senior controller of the AWACS activated his scope and confirmed the information. He was breaking international law at the moment. The radar aircraft, Eagle Two Niner, hadn't gotten permission to overfly Brazil, but the air-traffic-control radar systems down there read his transponder signal as a civilian air-cargo flight—the usual ruse—and nobody had challenged them yet. Confirming that information, he got on his satellite radio to report to NORAD and, though he didn't know it, on to the CIA.

"THANK you," Bill Henriksen replied upon hearing the information. He replaced the cabin phone and made his way forward to the Brightlings and Steve Berg. "Okay, guys, that was Binghamton. All the Shiva stuff has been burned. There is no physical evidence that the Project ever existed."

"We're supposed to be happy about that?" Carol demanded.

"No, but I hope you'll be happier than you'd be if you were facing an indictment for conspiracy to commit murder, Doctor."

"He's right, Carol," John said, sadness in his voice. Well, he consoled himself, he still had resources, he still had a core of good people, and this setback didn't mean that he'd have to give up his ideals, did it? Below, under the triple-canopy jungle into which they were descending, was a great diversity of life—he'd justified building Project Alternate to his board for that very reason, to find new chemical compounds in the trees and plants that grew only here— maybe a cure for cancer, who could say? He heard the flaps lower, and soon thereafter the landing gear went down. Another three minutes and they thumped down on the road-runway constructed along with the lab and residential buildings.

"OKAY, Target One is on the ground." The controller read off the exact position, which information was relayed to Cheyenne Mountain and from there to DCI Ed Foley, who wrote it all down on a pad.

"John, I have exact lat and longe for where they are. I'll task a satellite to get pictures for us. Should have that in, oh, two or three hours, depending on weather."

"So fast?" Popov asked.

"It's just a computer command," Clark explained. "And the satellites are always up there."

SKIES were blessedly clear over the jungles of central Brazil. The first KH-11D went over at nine thirty at night, local time. Its infrared cameras took a total of three hundred and twenty frames plus ninety-seven more in the visible spectrum. These images were cross-loaded to a communications satellite and from there beamed down to the antenna farm at Fort Belvoir, Virginia. From there they went by landline to the National Reconnaissance Office building near Dulles Airport and from there via another fiberoptic line to CIA headquarters.

"This looks pretty vanilla," the senior duty photoanalyst told them in Foley's office. "Buildings here, here, here, and this one here. Four airplanes on the ground. Private airfield—it's got lights but no ILS gear. I expect the fuel tanks are here. Power plant here, probably a diesel generator system by the look of this exhaust plume. This building looks residential from the window-light pattern. Somebody build a nature resort we're interested in?"

"Something like that," Clark confirmed. "What else?"

"Nothing much for a ninety-mile radius. That's one lonely place, sir. Must have been a real pain to build, isolated as it is."

"Okay. Send us the Lacrosse images, and when we get good visuallight images, I want to see those, too," Foley said.

"We'll have a direct overhead pass on another bird at about zero seven twenty Lima," he said, meaning local time.

"How wide is this runway?" Clark asked.

"Oh, looks like seven thousand feet long by three hundred or so wide, standard width. You could get a fair-sized airplane in there. There's a dock here on the river. It's the Río Negro, not the Amazon itself, but no boats."

"I don't see any telephone or power lines," Clark said.

"No, sir. There ain't none. I guess they depend on satellite and radio comms from this antenna farm." He paused. "Anything else you need?"

"No, and thanks," Clark told the technician.

"Learn anything?" Foley asked.

"Well, we know where they are, and we know about how many of 'em there are."

"You've got a plan already, John," Foley observed. He'd known Clark long enough to recognize that look in his eyes.

"Ed, is this my case to run or isn't it?" he asked the DCI.

"Within reason, John. Let's try not to start a nuclear war or anything, shall we?"

"Ed, can this ever come to trial? What if Brightling ordered the destruction of all the evidence? It's not hard to do, is it? A few buckets of bio-gunk and some computer records. There're commercial programs that destroy files thoroughly enough that you can't recover them ever, right?"

"True, but somebody might have printed stuff up, and—"

"And then what do we have? A global panic when people realize what a biotech company can do if it wants."

"But we can't *murder* these people, John! They're U.S. citizens with rights, remember?"

"I know, Ed. But we can't let them go, and we probably can't prosecute them. What's that leave?" Clark paused. "I'll try something creative."

"What?"

John Clark explained his idea. "If they fight back, well then, it makes things easier for us, doesn't it?"

"Twenty men against maybe fifty?"

"My twenty—actually, more like fifteen—against those feather merchants? Give me a break, Ed."

Foley frowned mightily, worried about what would happen if this ever made the media, but there was no particular reason that it should. "John," he said finally.

"Yeah, Ed?"

"Make sure you don't get caught."

"Never happened yet, Ed," Rainbow Six reminded him.

"Approved," said the DCI, wondering how he'd ever explain this one to the President of the United States.

THE C-17 THUMPED DOWN rather hard at Travis Air Force Base in California. Chavez and his companions were rather seriously disoriented by all the travel, but the walk outside the aircraft was, at least, in pleasantly cool air. He pulled out his cell phone and speed-dialed Hereford, then learned that John was in Langley and dialed that number. "This is Domingo Chavez calling for John Clark."

"Hold, please," Foley's receptionist replied.

"Where are you now?" John asked when he got on the line.

"Travis, north of Frisco. Now where do we go?"

"There's an air force VC-20 waiting at the distinguished visitors terminal."

"Okay, I'll get over that way. We don't have any of our gear with us, John. We left Australia in a hurry."

"I'll have somebody take care of that. Your guest—what's his name? Gearing?"

"That's right. He sang like a canary, John. This thing they planned to do, I mean—"

"I know, Ding. Just get back to D.C., okay?"

"Yes, sir, Mr. C.," Ding acknowledged.

CHAPTER 12

HARMONY

IS THAT *all* you need?" General Sam Wilson asked.

"Yes, General, that should do it."

"Can I ask what it's for?"

"Something covert," he heard Clark reply.

"That's all you're willing to say?"

"Sorry, Sam. Check this out with Ed Foley if you want."

"I guess I will," the general's voice rumbled. But he was a pro and knew the rules. "Okay, let me make some calls."

The first went to Fort Campbell, Kentucky, home of the 160th

Special Operations Aviation Regiment, whose commanding officer, a colonel, made the expected objection, which was expectedly overridden. That colonel then lifted a phone and ordered an MH-60K Night Hawk special-operations helicopter ferried to Pope Air Force Base in North Carolina. The next call went to an air force officer who took his notes and said, "Yes, sir," like the good airman he was. Getting the pieces in place was mainly an exercise in electronics—lifting encrypted phones and giving spooky orders to people who, fortunately, were accustomed to such things.

"BUILDING up those frequent-flier miles, Domingo?" John asked from the concrete.

"I suppose. Am I sprouting feathers yet?" Chavez asked tiredly.

"Only one more hop for now."

This hop was blessedly short and ended at Pope Air Force Base, which adjoins the home of the 82nd Airborne Infantry Division at Fort Bragg, North Carolina, also home of Delta Force and other special-operations units. Three MPs carted Wil Gearing to the base stockade. The rest of the people ended up in bachelor officers quarters, colloquially known as the Q.

Chavez wondered if the clothing he stripped off would ever be clean enough to wear again. He showered and shaved and emerged from the bathroom to find fresh clothing laid out.

"I had the base people run this over," John said.

"Thanks." Chavez put on the white boxers and T-shirt, then dressed in the forest-pattern battle dress uniform—BDU—items laid on the bed, complete to socks and boots.

"Now what, John?"

"Brazil. That's where they all went. We tracked them down, and I have overheads of the place where they're camped out. We're going to settle this thing once and for all, Domingo."

"Suits me, but is it legal?"

"When did you start worrying about that?"

"I'm a married man, John, and a father, remember? I have to be responsible now, man."

"It's legal enough," his father-in-law told the younger man.

CLARK AND ALISTAIR STANLEY, just in from England, were conferring in a room at Joint Special Operations Command Headquarters when Clark's cell phone started chirping. Again he had to wait for the encryption system to handshake with the other end.

"Ed Foley here, John. The sample was examined by the troops up at Fort Dietrick, Maryland. It's a version of the Ebola virus, modified—'engineered' is the term they used—by the addition of cancer genes. They say that makes it more robust. It looks like what your Russian friend told you is fully confirmed."

"What did you do with Dmitriy?" Rainbow Six asked.

"A safe house in Winchester," the DCI replied. "Oh, the FBI tells me that the Kansas State Police are looking for him on a murder charge. Supposedly he killed one Foster Hunnicutt from the state of Montana."

"Why don't you have the Bureau tell Kansas that he didn't kill anybody. He was with me the whole time," Clark suggested. He had already made the conceptual leap of forgetting that Popov had instigated an attack on his wife and daughter. Business, in this case, was business.

"Okay, I can do that." It was a little white lie, Foley agreed, set against a big black truth. These lunatics had not only *wanted* to kill the whole world, they'd had the *ability* to do so.

"Thanks, Ed." Clark killed the phone and looked at Al. "We confirmed the contents of the chlorine canister. They created a modified form of Ebola for distribution. It's time to get moving."

The major aircraft sitting on the Pope Air Force Base ramp was an air force C-5B Galaxy transport, with HORIZON CORPORATION painted in the place of the USAF roundels. Clark and Stanley arrived first. The rest of the troops came by bus, carrying their personal gear.

"OKAY, so that's what seems to have happened," John Brightling told the people assembled in the auditorium. He saw disappointment on their faces but some relief as well. Even true believers had consciences, he imagined. Too bad. "We have destroyed everything of evidentiary value," he went on. "The only records of the Project are what you people have in your heads. In other words, if anybody tries to make a criminal case against us, you just have to keep your mouths shut. Bill?" Brightling gestured to Henriksen, who walked to the podium.

"Okay. You know I used to be in the FBI. I know how they make their criminal cases. Making one against us will not be easy. People, if we stand together, we can't lose."

"And we can also work on Project Two," Brightling said, resuming the podium. "You are some of the smartest people in the world, and our commitment to our ultimate goal has *not* changed. We'll be here for a year or so to find a new way to achieve that to which we have dedicated our lives," he went on, seeing nods. "Okay. It's been a long day. Let's all get some rest. Tomorrow morning I'm going out in the forest to see an ecosystem that we all want to learn about." The applause moved him.

Bill Henriksen came up to John and Carol during the walk to their rooms. "There is one other potential problem."

"What's that?"

"What if they send a paramilitary team here?"

"We fight them," John said. "We have guns here, don't we?"

And that they did. The Project Alternate armory had a hundred German-made G-3 military assault rifles. And quite a few of the people knew how to shoot.

WIL Gearing sat in the C-5 looking at the soldiers, who mainly dozed. Two of them were wide-awake, however, and looking right at him. They were loaded for bear, Gearing saw, lots of weapons evident. Where were they going?

Clark, Chavez, and Stanley were in the compartment aft of the flight deck. The flight crew was regular air force, but they were dressed in civilian clothes so as to make the deception plausible. But who would believe a Lockheed Galaxy was civilian owned despite the alteration in the aircraft's exterior paint job?

"It looks pretty straightforward," Chavez observed. "Question is, will they resist?"

"If we're lucky," Clark responded.

"How many of them?"

"They went down in four Gulfstreams, figure a max of sixteen people each. That's sixty-four, Domingo."

"Weapons?"

"Would you live in the jungle without them?" Clark asked.

"But are they trained?" Team 2's commander persisted.

"Most unlikely. These people will be scientist types, but some will know the woods. Maybe some are hunters. I suppose we'll see if Noonan's new toys work as well as he's been telling us," Rainbow Six replied. They stopped talking as the aircraft jolted somewhat when they flew into the wake turbulence of the KC-10 for aerial refueling.

Malloy was farther aft, looking at the satellite overheads along with Lieutenant Harrison. "Looks easy," the junior officer opined, "but we're going to be close to overloading the aircraft."

"That's why it's got two engines, son," Malloy pointed out.

It wasn't yet dawn when they spotted the runway lights of the airport at Manaus, Brazil, where they were expected. The pilot, a young major, squirmed erect in his front-left seat and slowed the aircraft while the first-lieutenant copilot to his right watched the instruments and called off altitude and speed numbers. Presently he rotated the nose up and allowed the C-5B to settle onto the runway. He had a diagram of the airport, and he taxied off to the far corner of the ramp, then stopped the aircraft and told the loadmaster it was his turn to go to work.

The huge rear doors opened, and the MH-60K Night Hawk was dragged out into the predawn darkness. Sergeant Nance supervised three other enlisted men from the 160th Special Operations Aviation Regiment as they extended the rotor blades from their stowed position and climbed atop the fuselage to make sure the blades were safely locked in place for flight operations. The Night Hawk was fully fueled. Nance installed the M-60 machine gun in its place on the right side and told Colonel Malloy that the aircraft was ready.

The last people off the C-5B were the Rainbow troopers, now dressed in multicolor BDU fatigues, their faces painted in green and brown camouflage makeup. Gearing came down last of all, a black cloth bag over his head so he couldn't see anything.

It turned out that they couldn't get everyone aboard. Vega and four other soldiers were left behind to watch the helicopter lift off just at first light.

I⊤ WAS so much like Vietnam, Clark thought, riding in a helicopter over solid treetops of green. But he was not in a Huey this time, and it had been nearly thirty years since his first exposure to combat operations.

"How we doing, Malloy?" he asked over the intercom.

"Should have it in sight any second. There, lights ahead!"

"Got it." Clark waved for the troops in the back to get ready. "Proceed as planned, Colonel Malloy."

"Roger that, Six." He held course on a heading of two nine six, at seven hundred feet AGL—above ground level—and a speed of one hundred and twenty knots. The lights in the distance seemed hugely out of place, but lights they were, just where the navigation system and the satellite photos said they would be. Soon the point source broke up into separate distinct sources.

"Okay, Gearing," Clark was saying in the back. "We're letting you go to deliver a message to your boss. If he surrenders to us, nobody gets hurt. If he doesn't, things'll get nasty. Understand?"

"Yeah." The head nodded inside the black cloth bag.

Malloy made a fast landing at the west end of the runway—which some construction crew had carved into the jungle—without allowing his wheels to touch the ground. Standard procedure lest there be mines there. Gearing was pushed out the door, and immediately the helicopter lifted back off.

Gearing pulled the bag from his head, spotted the lights for Project Alternate—a facility he knew about but had never visited— and headed there without looking back.

A⊤ THE east end the Night Hawk again came in to hover a foot or so off the ground. The Rainbow troops leaped out and ran into the thick jungle cover a scant hundred yards from the concrete pavement of the runway. The helicopter immediately climbed up for the return trip to Manaus.

THE FRONT DOOR OF THE building was unlocked. Gearing entered an elevator, punched the topmost button, and arrived on the fourth floor. Once there, it was just a matter of opening one of the double doors on the corridor and flipping on a light in what had to be the master suite. The bedroom doors were open, and he walked that way.

John Brightling's eyes reported the sudden blaze of light from the sitting room. He opened them and saw Gearing.

"What are you doing here, Wil?"

"They brought me down, John."

"*Who* brought you down?"

"The people who captured me in Sydney," Gearing explained.

"What?" Brightling stood and put on the robe next to the bed.

"John, what is it?" Carol asked from her side of the bed.

"Nothing, honey, just relax." John went into the sitting room, pulling the doors closed as he did so. "What's going on, Wil?"

"They're here, John. The counterterror people, the ones who went to Australia, the ones who arrested me. They dropped me off by helicopter. Their boss is a guy named Clark. He said to tell you to surrender, or—"

"Or what?" Brightling demanded.

"Or they're going to come in and get us."

"Really?" Brightling had spent two hundred million dollars to build this place—labor costs were low in Brazil—and he considered Project Alternate a fortress. He called Bill Henriksen's room and told him to come upstairs.

"What is it, John?" Henriksen asked. Then he looked at the other man in the room. "Wil, how did you get here?"

While Gearing and Henriksen exchanged information, Brightling switched off the lights, looked out the large windows for signs of activity, and saw nothing at all.

"How many?" Bill was asking.

"Ten or fifteen soldiers. Are you going to surrender?"

"No!" John Brightling snarled. "Bill, what they're doing—is it legal?"

"No, not really. I don't think it is anyway."

"Okay, let's get our people up and armed."

"Right," the security chief said dubiously.

"OH, BABY, talk to me," Noonan said. The newest version of the people-finding system that tracked the electromagnetic field generated by the beating of the human heart was up and running now. He'd spotted two of the receiver units about three hundred yards apart. Each had a transmitter that reported to a unit wired to his laptop computer.

Clark was looking at the computer screen. It showed blips indicating people evenly spaced in their rooms in the headquarters/residential building. Each of the Rainbow troopers had a GPS locator built into his personal radio transceiver, and these also reported to the computer, giving Noonan and Clark exact locations for their own people and locations on those in the building to their left as well.

"I can't tell you what floor they're on," the FBI agent noted, "but look, they've all started moving. I guess somebody woke them up."

"Team Two, this is Command," Clark said into his tactical radio.

"Two Lead here, Command," Chavez replied. "I can see people running out of the building. They appear to be armed with shoulder weapons."

"Roger that. Okay, Ding, we will proceed as briefed."

"Understood, Command." Team 2 was intact except for Julio Vega, who'd just arrived on the second helicopter delivery. Chavez got on his radio and paired his people off with their normal partners. The Team 1 people would be the operational reserve, assigned to Clark at the command post.

Noonan watched the Team 2 shooters move. Each friendly blip was identified by a letter so he'd know them by name. The battery was good for five hours, and he had two spares in his pack.

Pierce and Loiselle took the lead, heading half a kilometer into the jungle. The temperature was rising, and both soldiers were sweating under their camouflage makeup. After ten minutes they found a nice spot, a decent field of fire with a standing tree and a fallen one next to it.

"They've got radios," Noonan reported. "Want me to take them away?" He had his jammer set up already.

Clark shook his head. "Not yet. Let's listen in for a while." The FBI agent flipped the radio scanner to the speaker setting.

"Killgore and Maclean, keep moving north about half a mile, find a place, and sit still there," a voice said.

"Yeah, yeah, okay, Bill," a second voice agreed.

"Listen up, everybody," Bill was saying. "Don't clutter up these radios. Report in when you see something important."

"They're in pairs, moving close together," Noonan said, staring at his screen. "This pair is heading right for Mike and Louis."

Clark looked down at the screen. "Pierce and Loiselle, this is Command. You have two targets approaching you from the south at about two hundred meters."

"Roger, Command. Can we engage?" Pierce asked.

"Affirmative," Clark replied. Then, "Rainbow, this is Six. Weapons are free. I repeat, we are weapons-free at this time."

THIS wasn't so bad, Killgore thought. Plenty of shadows, little in the way of direct sunlight. Except for the bugs, he might have even been comfortable here. The next time he came out, he'd try to spray some repellent, the physician thought as he moved forward. The branch of a bush was in his way. He used his left hand to move it lest he make noise by walking through it.

THERE, Pierce saw. A bush branch had just moved, and there wasn't a breath of wind to make that happen. "Louis," he whispered. When the Frenchman turned, Pierce held up one finger and pointed. Loiselle nodded. "I have a visual target," Pierce reported over his radio. With that, he tightened his grip on the MP-10, centered the target on the sights, and squeezed the trigger. He saw the man's mouth spring open, and then the figure fell. Pierce ran forward, his weapon up, with Loiselle in close support.

Killgore's mind didn't have time to analyze what had happened to him, just the impacts to his chest, and now he was looking straight up into the treetops, where there were small cracks of blue and white from the distant sky. He tried to say something, but he wasn't breathing very well, and when he turned his head a few inches, there was no one there to see. Where was Kirk Maclean? he wondered.

"Wrong playground, partner," Pierce said softly, and then life left the eyes, and he bent down to collect the man's rifle. He looked left to see Loiselle holding an identical rifle in one hand and waving his hand across his throat. His target was dead, too.

HENRIKSEN was just inside the tree line. His radio crackled with voices acknowledging his order. Except two voices were missing. "Killgore and Maclean, report in." Nothing. "Who's closest to them?"

"Me and Dawson," another voice answered.

"Okay, Berg and Dawson, move north. See what you can see."

"PIERCE and Loiselle, Command. Two targets moving toward you, almost due south."

"This isn't very fair," Noonan observed, looking up from his tactical picture.

"Timothy, fair means I bring all my people home alive," Clark responded.

"You say so, boss," the FBI agent agreed. Together he and Clark watched the blips move toward the ones labeled "L" and "P." Five minutes after that both unidentified blips dropped off the screen and did not return.

"That's two more kills for our guys, John."

"This thing's magic," Clark said after Pierce and Loiselle called in to confirm what the instrument had already told them.

"Can you get me on their radio?"

"Easy." Noonan plugged a microphone in. "Here."

"Hi, there," Clark said over the CB frequency.

"Who is this?"

"I'm the guy who's killing your people. The name's Clark. John Clark. Who are you?"

"William Henriksen," the voice shouted back.

"Oh, you're the former Bureau guy. Well, I'm only going to say this once: Put your weapons down, walk into the open, and we won't shoot any more of you."

There was a long silence. Clark wondered what the voice on the other end would do, but after a minute he did what John expected.

"Listen up, everybody. Pull back to the building now!" Henriksen said.

"Rainbow, this is Six. Expect movement back to the building. Weapons are free," he added over the encrypted tactical radios.

The panic in Henriksen's radio call was contagious. Immediately they heard the thrashing sound of people running in the woods, taking direct paths back toward the open. That made an easy shot for Homer Johnston. One green-clad man broke from the trees and ran down the grassy part next to the runway. The weapon he carried made him an enemy, and Johnston dispatched a single round that went between his shoulder blades. The man took one more stumbling step and went down. "Rifle two one, I got one," the sniper called in.

It was more direct for Chavez. Ding was sheltering behind a hardwood tree when he heard noise coming his way. He brought his MP-10 to his shoulder. The man saw him and tried to bring up his rifle. He even managed to fire but shot right into the ground before taking a burst in the face and falling like a sack of beans.

It was like some sort of horrid gladiatorial game for Clark. The unknown blips on the screen of Noonan's computer disappeared as their hearts stopped.

"Vega, start doing windows," he ordered in a calm voice.

"Roger that, Command," Oso replied. He lifted the shoulder stock of his M-60 machine gun and started on the second floor. The weapon traced right to left, shattering glass into the building.

Carol Brightling screamed as the glass from the upstairs windows cascaded like a waterfall in front of her face. "Make them stop!" she cried.

"Give me the radio," Brightling said.

Henriksen handed it to him.

"Cease firing. This is John Brightling. Cease firing, everybody. That means you, too, Clark, okay?"

In a few seconds it stopped, which proved harder for the Project people, since Rainbow had only one weapon firing and Oso stopped immediately on being ordered to.

"Brightling, this is Clark. Can you hear me?"

"Yes, Clark, I hear you."

"Bring all your people into the open, and nobody will get shot."

Brightling walked to the reception desk and spoke over the building's intercom system, calling everyone to the lobby. Then he lifted the portable radio. "We'll be coming out in a second. Give us a chance to get organized."

"This is a mistake, John," Henriksen told his employer.

"This whole thing's been a mistake, Bill," John observed, wondering where he'd gone wrong. As he watched, the black helicopter reappeared and landed about halfway down the runway, as close as the pilot was willing to come to hostile weapons.

PADDY Connolly was at the fuel dump. There was a huge aboveground fuel tank labeled #2 DIESEL. The explosives expert set ten pounds of charges on the opposite side of the tank from the generator plant it served. "Command, Connolly."

"Connolly, Command," Clark answered.

"I'm going to need more," he reported.

"It's on the chopper, Paddy. Stand by."

Clark advanced to the edge of the tree line, a scant three hundred yards from the building. Just beyond him Vega was still on his heavy machine gun, and the rest of his troops were close by. It had been a grim day. Success or not, there is little joy in the taking of life, and this day's work had been as close to pure murder as anything the men had ever experienced.

"Coming out," Chavez said, his binoculars to his eyes.

"Gimme," Clark said, taking the glasses from Domingo. Surprisingly, the first face he could put a name on was Carol Brightling, presidential science adviser. The man next to her would be her former husband, John Brightling, Clark surmised. He could see no one carrying weapons, so he decided it was safe for him to walk out with five members of Team 1 as an escort. The walk took about five minutes, and then he saw John Brightling face to face. "I guess this is your place, eh?"

"Until you destroyed it."

"The guys at Fort Dietrick checked out the canister Mr. Gearing tried to use in Sydney, Dr. Brightling. If you're looking for sympathy, you've called the wrong number."

"So what are you going to do?" Just as he finished the question, the helicopter lifted off and headed for the power plant, delivering the rest of Connolly's explosives.

As it turned out, the hardest thing to take care of was the freezer in the main building. For this Connolly borrowed a Hummer and used it to ferry two oil drums into the building. There being no time for niceties, Connolly simply drove the vehicle through the glass walls. Meanwhile, Malloy and his helicopter ferried half the team back to Manaus and refueled before returning. All in all, it took nearly three hours, during which time the prisoners said virtually nothing. Finally Connolly came striding over to Clark, holding an electronic box in his hand. Clark nodded and cued his tactical radio. "Bear, Command."

"Bear copies."

"Let's get wound up, Colonel."

"Roger that. Bear's on the way."

Clark walked back to where the prisoners were sitting. "We are not going to kill you, and we are not going to take you back to America," he told them. The surprise in their faces was stunning. "Stand up and get undressed, all of you."

"But—"

"Do it!" Clark shouted at them. "Or I will have you shot."

And slowly they did, piling their clothes in the middle of the runway. Carol Brightling, oddly, wasn't the least bit modest about the moment. "Now what?" she asked.

"Okay, here's the score. You want to live in harmony with nature; then go do it. If you can't hack it, the nearest city is Manaus, about ninety-eight miles that way." He pointed, then turned. "Paddy, fire in the hole."

Without a word Connolly started flipping switches on his box.

The first thing to go was the fuel tank. That ignited the diesel fuel, which blew out of the tank like the exhaust from a rocket and propelled the tank straight into the powerhouse, less than fifty meters away. There the tank stopped and ruptured, pouring burning number two diesel fuel over the area. They couldn't see the freezer area in the main building go, but here, as well, the diesel fuel ignited, ripping out the wall of the freezer unit and then dropping part of the building on the burning wreckage. The other buildings went in turn, along with the satellite dishes. Over a period of less than a minute everything useful to life here had been destroyed.

"You're sending us out into the jungle without even a knife?" Henriksen demanded.

"Find some flint rocks and make one," Clark suggested as the Night Hawk landed. "You want to be in harmony with nature, go harmonize." Seconds later he was strapped into the jump seat behind the pilots, and Colonel Malloy lifted off.

Looking down one last time, Clark saw that all the eyes down there were following the Night Hawk as it headed east.

"Maybe a week, Mr. C.?" Ding asked. A graduate of the U.S. Army's Ranger school, he didn't think that *he* could survive very long in this place.

"If they're lucky," Rainbow Six replied.

EPILOGUE
NEWS

THE *International Trib* landed on Chavez's desk after the usual morning exercise routine, and he leaned back comfortably to read it. Life had become boring at Hereford. They hadn't been called away from the base since returning from South America six months earlier.

GOLD MINE IN THE ROCKIES, a front-page story started. A ranch in Montana, the article read, owned by a Russian national, had been found to contain a sizable gold deposit. The place had been bought by Dmitriy A. Popov, a Russian entrepreneur, as a vacation site, and then he'd made the accidental discovery. Mining operations would begin in the coming months. "You see this?" Ding asked Clark.

"Yeah, I read it," John replied, checking out the latest pictures of his grandson on Chavez's desk. "He spent half a million to buy the place from the estate of Foster Hunnicutt. I guess the man told him more than just what Brightling was planning, eh?"

"I suppose." Chavez read on. In the business section he learned that Horizon Corporation stock was heading back up with the release of a new drug for heart disease, recovering from the loss in value that had resulted from the disappearance of its chairman, Dr. John Brightling, several months earlier. Horizon was also working on human longevity and cancer medications, the article concluded.

"John, has anybody gone back to Brazil to—"

"Not that I know of. Satellite overheads show that nobody's cutting the grass next to their airport."

"So you figure the jungle killed them?"

"Nature isn't real sentimental, Domingo. She doesn't distinguish between friends and enemies."

"I suppose not, Mr. C." Even terrorists could do that, Chavez thought, but not the jungle. So who was the real enemy of mankind? Himself, mostly, Ding decided, setting the newspaper down and looking at a photo of John Conor Chavez, who'd just learned to sit up and smile. His son would grow into the brave new world, and his father would be one of those who tried to ensure that it would be a safe one—for him and all the other kids whose main tasks were learning to walk and talk.

in Montana, the article
found to contain a size
by Dmitri A. Popov

TOM CLANCY

JOHN EARLE

It all began in 1984. The Annapolis
Naval Institute Press printed a modest
14,000 copies of a fat novel written by
a fellow in the insurance business.
Word got around that *The Hunt for
Red October* was quite a read—"the
perfect yarn," Ronald Reagan called
it—and the rest is megatechno-thriller
history. These days Clancy's books sell
in the millions worldwide. And the
books are only the beginning. Clancy
also creates computer-game versions
of his novels, which are produced by
another of his ventures, a company
called Red Storm Entertainment.
Movies, too, are likely to follow. Not
by books alone does this author
thrive.

Cloud Nine

LUANNE RICE

*W*ith featherlight quilts and heavenly soft pillows, her shop, Cloud Nine, invites sweet dreams. But what Sarah Talbot longs for are sweet dreams come true: A chance to see her father and teenage son again. A chance to glory in the beauty of her Maine island home. A chance to fall in love . . . before it's too late.

Chapter 1

ANOTHER autumn had come to Fort Cromwell, New York, and Sarah Talbot was there to see it. She sat on the front porch of her small white house, drinking apple-cinnamon tea, wondering what to do next. The college kids next door were washing their car. Spray from the hose misted her face. Wrapped in a red plaid blanket, she tilted her face to the sun and imagined the drops were salt water and she was home on Elk Island.

A blue sedan drove slowly down the street. It looked municipal. FORT CROMWELL VNA was stenciled on the side. When it parked in Sarah's driveway, a small, trim woman in a white coat climbed out.

Sarah smiled. "What are you doing here?" she asked.

"That's a fine greeting," the visiting nurse said.

"I thought you were done with me," Sarah said, unconsciously ruffling her closely shorn hair.

"Done with you? My daughter would kill me. Besides, do you think that's how I treat my friends?"

"I'm your patient, Meg," Sarah said, smiling.

"*Were,* Sarah. Were. We're here to take you for a ride."

"A ride? Where—" Sarah began, glancing at the car and noticing Mimi in the back seat.

"Happy birthday," Meg said, bending down to hug her.

Sarah reached up. She put her arms around the visiting nurse.

Meg's pockets jangled with keys, pens, and a stethoscope. The hug felt good, and Sarah bit her lip. "How did you know?" she asked when they pulled apart. Today was her thirty-seventh birthday. She was having a quiet day: no party, no cards or calls from home. In the car's back window, Mimi was holding up a bright pink sign. In silver glitter she had written MANY HAPPY RETURNS OF THE DAY!

"I read your chart," Meg said, grinning. "Come on."

WILL Burke stood in the hangar, his head under the hood of the Piper Aztec. Fall was his biggest season. He needed all three of his planes serviced and ready to fly. The lake region was a tourist destination, with all the cider mills and foliage trails. He operated fifteen-minute aerial tours, especially popular during the Fort Cromwell Fair. And the end of October brought parents weekends at two area colleges, with scheduled flights back and forth to New York City.

At the sound of tires crunching over the gravel outside, he wiped his socket wrench on a blue rag and placed it on his tall red toolbox. He checked his watch: four o'clock. A friend of his daughter's had booked a quick birthday tour—up and down, a fifteen-minute scenic loop of the lake and mountains. Tucking his work shirt into his jeans, Will walked outside to greet his customers. He didn't really feel like taking a break, but the afternoon was sunny and the fresh air felt good. He found himself smiling as they pulled up.

Meg and Mimi Ferguson got out of the car. His daughter, Susan, sometimes baby-sat for Mimi, and judging from what he remembered, Mimi must be about nine. Then someone new got out—a small, thin woman the size of an underfed teenager. Her skin was pale and translucent, and her head was covered with gray-blond peach fuzz. She looked at the sky with total rapture, as if she hadn't ever seen it so blue before.

"Ready to fly?" he asked.

"Which plane, Mr. Burke?" Mimi asked, excited.

"That one," he said, pointing at the two-seater Piper Cub.

"We can't all fit?" Mimi asked, disappointed.

"Now, Mimi—" Meg began.

"Sorry, Mimi," Will said. "The big plane's getting an oil change. If I'd known—"

"You know what, Mimi?" the thin woman said eagerly. "Why don't you go up for me?"

"It's your birthday flight," Mimi said. "It was my idea, and we want *you* to go."

"Happy birthday," Will said to the woman.

"Thank you." Again, that expression of amazement, as if she had never been so happy. She stared at him directly, and he had that shock he felt when coming upon a person he knew from somewhere, who has undergone a drastic change of appearance. He had seen this woman around town, looking quite different.

"Ready?" he asked.

"I am," she said.

"Let's go." Then, speaking to Mimi, he said, "Hey, Susan's in the office. She'd be glad to see you."

SECRET'S dad had brought her to the airport. Her allergies were out of control, and the school nurse had tried to call her mother, but of course she wasn't home. So Secret had told the nurse to call Burke Aviation and ask for Will. Her father would definitely pick her up. And he had. Now she slouched at his desk, painting her nails. Outside the big window Mimi and her mom and their friend were standing by the landing strip, talking to him. Of all the kids Secret baby-sat for, Mimi was the best. She was a nice little kid. She had dreams and goals, and she knew there was more to life than the school in this one-horse town, just as Secret herself did.

"Hi, Susan," Mimi said, bursting through the door.

"Susan?" Secret said. "There's no Susan here."

"That's right, I forgot," Mimi said, grinning. "Secret. You changed your name. What're you doing?"

"October is the month for witchy doings, and since you know I'm a witch, I'm painting my nails accordingly," Secret said patiently. She wiggled her fingers at Mimi, casting a spell.

"Wow," Mimi said. Secret had used india ink and a crow-quill pen to paint delicate spiderwebs on her pale blue nails.

"You brought that lady here for her plane ride, I see," Secret said, looking out the window again. "Was she surprised?"

"Very surprised," Mimi said. "I'm glad you suggested it."

"Mmm," Secret said. Watching the woman, she noticed a few things: She was too thin, her hair looked terrible, and she had the nicest face Secret had seen in a long time. "Is she really sick?" she asked.

"She *was*," Mimi said. "My mom takes care of lots of people, and for a while she said Sarah was going to die. But now she says she's probably not. I'm really glad, but I don't get it."

"You're too young to get it," Secret said benevolently, although Mimi was older than Secret had been when her brother died. Secret's throat began tickling. Her chest got that heavy feeling, and she reached into her father's top drawer for the inhaler they always kept there. She took a hit.

"Are you okay?" Mimi asked, always worried when Secret had an asthma attack. They had first met because Meg Ferguson was Secret's nurse after a really bad attack, when she needed inhalation therapy for a few days.

"I'm fine."

"Good thing you have your inhaler."

"I didn't have it at school today, so I had to come home early." As soon as she said it, Secret felt bad for lying—to Mimi *and* to the school nurse. She *did* have her inhaler, but she had been bored, feeling lonely, and when the opportunity presented itself with a choking fit, she had asked them to call her father.

Lonely. Secret felt it all the time, down to her toes. She missed her brother. Living with her mother, she missed her father. Right under the same roof Secret missed her mother. Half the time she missed people sitting right next to her. Walking through the mall with girls from her school, she missed her friends, and they were right there.

Like now. Sitting here with Mimi, gazing out at the airstrip, she watched the sick lady with the terrible hair get into the plane with this beautiful, radiant look in her eyes, and Secret missed *her*. Missed her badly, even though Secret had never met her before.

THEY FLEW NORTH. THE PILOT took her over the lake and western ridge, where the leaves blazed in the orange light. The craggy rocks glowed red, and the lake was deep blue-black.

"Ever been up in a small plane before?" the pilot asked.

"Yes," Sarah said.

"Don't know why I thought it was your first time. Mimi and her mom were so excited arranging it for you."

"Maybe I mentioned to Meg that I love flying," Sarah said. "Although I don't do it as much now as I used to. Lots of weekends I'd be on a plane just slightly bigger than this, flying home to Maine from Boston."

"I'm from New England too." He nodded. "That lake's pretty, but it's not—"

"The Atlantic," she said, grinning.

He laughed—the response of a man who had salt water in his veins, who for some reason, like Sarah, had found himself living in upstate New York. "I'm Will Burke," he said.

"Sarah Talbot."

"Hi, Sarah."

"Who was that I saw in the window back at the airport?" Sarah asked. "That young girl looking out?"

"My daughter, Susan," Will said.

"A teenager?"

"Fifteen," he said. "Going on thirty."

"I know the syndrome," Sarah said, glancing east, as if she could see across five states to a tiny island off the coast of Maine.

They kept heading north, even though they had reached the midway point. Down below was an endless pine forest, and the dying sun threw glints of gold in the tall treetops.

Sarah felt her eyes fill with tears. "I didn't think I'd be here," she said. "For another birthday."

Will glanced over. "But you are."

He pulled back on the controls, and the plane began to climb. They left the earth behind, flying straight into the sky. Sarah felt the exhilaration of adventure. The plane dived down. They did one loop-the-loop, then another. Will's hand was so close, she wanted to grab for it. It was a sudden impulse, and it passed. The plane stead-ied off. Sarah's fifteen minutes were up, but they kept flying north for a while longer before they turned for home.

"DID she like her ride?"

Sitting at the kitchen table, reading the evening paper, Will didn't quite hear the question. He had been up since five. "Sorry, Susan," he said, yawning. "Did you ask me something?"

"Susan?" she asked, frowning.

"I mean . . ." He tried to remember. "September?"

"Dad, I haven't been September for weeks. I can't believe you don't even know your own daughter's name. Try Secret."

"That's right," Will said, folding his paper. He didn't understand this name-changing business, and he didn't like it, but his daughter had been traumatized by losing Fred, then the divorce, so he tended to give in on points that didn't seem that important. "Okay, Secret. What was the question?"

"Did she like her ride? That lady."

"Sarah? I think so," Will said, remembering her shining eyes.

"You were gone a long time. Thirty-five minutes."

"My watch must've stopped," Will said, trying not to smile. Any-time his daughter sensed even a glimmer of interest on his part in a woman, she turned ultra-vigilant. She was probably afraid he'd do what her mother had done with Julian: go off skiing for a weekend and come back married.

"Your watch never stops, Dad. You are Mr. Time Man. Zero one hundred hours and counting. You've even got me trained." She glanced at the wall clock, which read six thirty. "Like now, it's eigh-teen thirty. From our years in the navy, right?"

"Well, I guess I lost track of the time."

"You never lose track of the time, Dad. I know that. I just think—" She paused. She had made a big salad for their dinner, and she carried it in a wooden bowl to the table. Lettuce, tomatoes, cucumbers, croutons, and white grapes. She presented it with shy expectation in her wide blue eyes.

"Wow," he said. "That looks great."

"Thank you. Most people wouldn't think of including grapes, but I think they add a lot. Do you?"

"Yes, definitely," he said, knowing he would stop by McDonald's for a double cheeseburger after he drove her home.

"Well, just don't get too attached to her."

"Who?" he asked, knowing.

"That lady. Sarah."

"Honey, I just took her up for a birthday ride. That's all."

"She's sick, Dad. She's all alone in Fort Cromwell, and the Fergusons wanted to make sure her last birthday was happy."

"It wasn't her last birthday," Will said.

"If it was mine, I'd want to know. I'd want to have a great old time. Go back to Rhode Island, for one thing."

"That won't happen for a long time," Will said.

"It did for Fred. His last birthday passed, and he didn't know. When his last day came, he didn't even know *that*. How can it happen, Dad? That you wake up happy and fine one morning, and by fourteen hundred hours you're drowned?" Secret was staring straight at him, no blame in her expression.

"I don't know, sweetheart," Will said, because honesty was the best he could offer her.

"Mom's over it," she said bitterly.

"She'll never get over it. You don't get over losing one of your kids, honey."

"Whenever I mention him, she tells me to shush, it upsets *Julian*. And he's just a rich bastard who spends all his time *car* racing and going to lectures. Is that where they are tonight?"

"Don't say bastard, Susan. A play, I think she said."

"Jerk, then. Idiot. Numskull. Drip. Flaming creep."

"Susan. Secret," Will said wearily. "Stop, okay?"

"Sorry, Dad," she said, drizzling vinegar onto her salad. She had taken only lettuce leaves.

Assuming she had left all the good stuff for him, Will took an extra helping to make her happy. "The grapes were a good call," he said, taking a bite.

"Thank you," she said. "She looked nice."

"Who, honey?"

"That lady, Sarah."

"She was," Will said.

"I hope she's okay," she said. "Because death stinks."

SARAH had begun to open the shop for a few hours every day, usually from ten until two. She loved how the morning sun streamed through the tall windows, throwing light and shadows on the pale yellow walls. Today she felt a little tired. She imagined curling up for a nap in the middle of the things she sold—quilts and pillows, some filled with white down from the geese on her father's saltwater farm in Maine.

The bell above the shop door tinkled. Sarah glanced up from an inventory list and smiled at the two college students who walked in. They stared at her for a second. She felt she still looked weird with her tufty hair. "Hi," she said. "Let me know if I can help."

"We will. Thanks," the taller girl replied, smiling as her friend lay flat on the sample bed that was prettily made up with a fluffy quilt.

"I want this exact bed." The second girl sighed.

"You do?" Sarah asked.

"The linen service at school doesn't exactly provide sumptuous bedding," the tall girl explained. "We're fantasizing."

"Be my guest," Sarah said. "Everyone deserves sweet dreams."

"I don't have a credit card," the other girl said, "but if I call my parents and they give you their account number, can I charge every single thing in your store and take it back to campus?"

"That can be arranged," Sarah said. "I'll deliver it myself in a silver sleigh."

The girl giggled and sighed again.

Sarah remembered her own college days. Too thin sheets and scratchy old blankets had been her inspiration for starting her own business, Cloud Nine. She had dropped out of Wellesley after her freshman year. Opening her first store in Boston, she had stocked it with down products made by her father back on the farm.

The farm had been on the verge of failing. Her mother had died when Sarah was fourteen. Sarah and her father never talked about it, but she knew she had saved him. She had gotten her own financing, expanded into mail order, taken on lines from France and Italy. The original store remained in Boston, but after eight years and the last in a series of ridiculous love affairs Sarah had expanded to this college-rich valley in upstate New York. She had been here for ten years now.

The telephone rang. "Hello, Cloud Nine," she said.

"Happy birthday," the deep voice said.

"Thank you," she said. Her heart contracted. She couldn't talk. She had the feeling that if she breathed, the line would go dead.

"I'm a day late. Sorry."

"That's okay. I didn't even notice," she lied.

"What'd you do? Go out for dinner or something?"

"I took a plane ride," she said. "To see the leaves. All red and orange and yellow, like a big bowl of Trix. I couldn't stop smiling. I mean, flying over this beautiful fall landscape and thinking of Trix. Remember when that was your favorite cereal?"

"Huh. Not really."

"How are you?" she asked. She could picture him standing in the big basement kitchen with a fire burning in the old stone hearth. Closing her eyes, she was back on Elk Island, could see the dark bay, the prim white house, the fields full of white geese.

"Fine."

"Really? Do you still like living there? Because—"

"What about you?" he asked, sounding sullen. "How are you?"

"I'm great." She turned her back so the college girls wouldn't hear. "I finished chemo last month, and my X rays look good. There's no sign of any tumor. I had an MRI, and I'm all clear."

"You're cured?"

"Yes," Sarah said, biting her lip. She knew about statistics, five-year survival rates, worst-case scenarios.

"Good," he said. A long silence passed. "That's good."

"Is your grandfather there?" she asked.

"He's in the barn. I just came in to get some lunch." He cleared his throat. "Just thought I'd call to say happy birthday."

"I'm glad you did, Mike. I miss you. I wish you'd—"

"When're you coming to Maine? I mean, Grandpa was wondering. He told me to say happy birthday. I almost forgot."

"Was it his idea for you to call?" Sarah asked.

"No. It was mine. So when're you going to come?"

"I don't know," she said. The idea of going to the island filled her with more anxiety than she knew was good for her. Her doctor had told her to avoid stress. Just thinking about seeing Mike with her bitter old father sent Sarah's spirit careening.

"Thanksgiving would be good," Mike said.

"We'll see."

An uneasy silence developed between them. Sarah's mind raced with questions, accusations, declarations of love. How could her son have left her to go *there?* From the day of her mother's death Sarah couldn't wait to leave the island. She had let her father down, and even in his bitter silence he refused to let her forget. But Mike had gone to live with him while searching for connections to Zeke Loring, the father who had died before he was even born.

"Excuse me," called the girl who had been lying on the bed. "I think I do want to buy some things. Can we call my mother?"

"I guess I'd better go," Mike said. "Grandpa's waiting for lunch."

"Honey, I'm glad you called. You can't imagine how happy you made me. It's ten times better than any present I ever got."

"Bye, Mom," Mike said.

When she turned back to the girls, she was smiling. Her face was calm as she nodded yes, the girl could call her mother. She was going through the motions of selling a quilt, cultivating the business of the girls at Marcellus College, the students who were her bread and butter.

But her heart was far away with her son, Mike Talbot, her seventeen-year-old dropout, the person Sarah Talbot loved more than her own life, the boy who was single-handedly planning to carry on the family traditions of quilt making and farm saving under the wing of her father, the wrathful George Talbot of Elk Island, Maine.

It was during moments such as this that Sarah, writing a sales ticket for a three-hundred-dollar quilt, wished that she had just let the old farm die.

Chapter 2

SECRET rode her bike through town. The air was freezing cold, and her fingers felt stiff. Sticking out her tongue, she caught the first snowflakes of the year. Her nose and cheeks stung. Halloween had barely passed, and ice had already formed on the lake. Nowhere on earth was colder than Fort Cromwell. Newport had been tropical by comparison.

All the shops looked cozy. Pedaling slower, she looked in each one. A few still had jack-o'-lanterns in the windows. Others had jumped the gun, getting ready for Christmas. The down shop looked especially inviting, with no holiday decorations whatsoever. The sign was enough: a magical cloud and a golden 9. Brass lamps glowed; the quilts appeared thick and enveloping. Wanting to warm up, Secret parked her bike and walked in.

"Hi," the lady called from the back.

"Hi," Secret said. Trying to look like a genuine shopper, she frowned and began looking at price tags.

"Just let me know if you need any help."

"I will," Secret said, earnestly riffling through a bin of small silk-velvet pillows. Spiced cider was brewing somewhere in back.

"Would you like some hot cider?" the voice asked.

"Well, I shouldn't," Secret said, feeling guilty for defrauding the lady. She had absolutely no intention of buying a single thing.

"Are you sure? It's pretty cold out there."

"You can say that again," Secret said.

"Are you sure? It's pretty cold out there."

Secret chuckled. She glanced up, and for the first time she actually saw the shop owner. It was Sarah Talbot, the sick lady, Mimi Ferguson's friend. "Oh, hi," Secret said.

"Hi," Sarah said. "I know you. You were in the airport office the day I took my birthday flight."

"Yes. My father's the pilot."

"An excellent pilot. Are you sure you wouldn't like a little cider?"

"Maybe a little." Secret waited while Sarah filled two brown mugs. "My dad had offers from TWA, Delta. He could fly anywhere, but he likes being his own boss."

"He certainly seemed capable," Sarah said, handing her a mug.

"The navy trained him," Secret said. "But he was a pilot even before that. He was so valuable to the navy; he could do everything. Fly, swim in times of disaster, lead his men. He always kept his head during maneuvers. The Persian Gulf, for example. He was there."

"You sound like a proud daughter," Sarah said. "Upstate New York is pretty far inland for a navy family."

"Yes." Secret felt her asthma just waiting for the next questions: Why are you here? Do you have any brothers or sisters? But the questions never came. Instead, Sarah stuck out her hand.

"We haven't officially met. I'm Sarah Talbot."

"I'm Secret Burke."

"What a beautiful name," Sarah said.

Secret glanced over to see if she was being fake, but Sarah's eyes were full of admiration. "Thank you," Secret said. "I'm actually getting ready to change it. I was thinking of Snow."

Sarah nodded. "Perfect for winter," she said.

"Is Sarah your real name?"

"Yes, it is. I've lugged it around my whole life. In seventh grade I tried out Sadie, but it wasn't me."

"No," Secret agreed. "You are definitely a Sarah." She eyed Sarah appraisingly. "I was just noticing your hair."

"My poor hair," Sarah said, blushing. "Yep, I lost it. It used to be dark brown, and now look. It came in such a funny color."

"You could bleach it," Secret suggested. Beauty tips were one of Secret's best talents. "The way it's growing in, it's so cute and punky. You could get it pure white and look so great."

Just then the bells above the door sounded. A cluster of college girls walked in. Sarah called hello, and they called back.

Secret nestled into her spot on the edge of the bed. Sarah served the college girls cider, but when she was done, she came back to sit beside Secret. Side by side they sipped their drinks. The girls were the paying customers, but Sarah was sitting with Secret. As if she were her friend. As if she were hers alone.

THE Fort Cromwell Fair was always held the Saturday midway between Halloween and Thanksgiving. Everyone went. Sarah had come with Meg and Mimi. They wandered around, gazing at prize pigs and champion steers. Mimi had gotten a camera for her birthday, and she was taking pictures of everything.

"Want to ride the Ferris wheel?" Meg asked.

"You two go ahead," Sarah said. "I'm going to find some hot chocolate." They agreed to meet by the paint-on tattoo booth in an hour. Heading toward the refreshment area, Sarah felt exhilarated. Fairs always did this to her: the crowds, the animals, bells ringing everywhere. She said hello to a few people she knew.

She wore a black bowler hat, black jeans, and Zeke's old leather bomber jacket. She hardly ever wore it when Mike was around. Sarah had so few of Mike's father's things, and they all seemed to stir Mike into asking questions Sarah couldn't answer.

"One hot chocolate," she said to the man behind the counter.

The cardboard cup was scalding hot. Glancing around for napkins, she saw a counter with ketchup and mustard and napkins and straws. A man was blocking her way. Tall and big-shouldered, he was wearing a leather jacket almost exactly like hers.

"Excuse me," she said, leaning around him to get a napkin.

"Hi, Sarah," he said, sounding surprised and happy.

"Hi," Sarah said. It was the pilot, Will Burke. She had worked herself practically under his arm to reach the napkins, and he was holding his hot dog aloft to keep the relish from spilling on her.

He stood back, smiling. "Good to see you," he said.

"You too. How have you been?"

"I've been fine," he said. "How about you?"

"Great," Sarah said. "Really great. What brings you to the fair? Are you here with Secret?"

"Secret?" He frowned. "Oh, Susan. You've met her?"

"She stopped by my store."

He shook his head. "Secret. It gets me every time. We gave her a perfectly nice name. Susan."

Sarah nodded. He looked like a man with something weighing on his mind, but she didn't know him well enough to ask. "She's a nice girl," she said. "No matter what she calls herself."

"So you wouldn't worry about it?"

"Personally, no. I wouldn't."

"Hmm." He frowned again. "Her mother thinks it's a danger sign. Some kind of call for help. I don't know."

"I wouldn't want to second-guess your wife—" Sarah began.

"Ex-wife," Will said.

"But it doesn't seem all that dangerous to me. She's fifteen, trying out new things, just figuring out who she is. You know?"

Will nodded. He obviously felt better, because he started eating his hot dog. His face and hands were weathered. He had curly brown hair, with gray streaks at the temples. For a man who had been in the navy, it looked a little long. His eyes were startling dark blue.

"Is she here?" Sarah asked, looking around.

"Secret?" he asked, grinning. "No, she's home. I'm here for work. I take people up for rides, like the one I gave you."

"That was a great ride. I've thought of it often. It was the first time I knew"—she took a sip of hot chocolate—"that I'm okay again," she said, smiling.

"I'm glad about that," Will said. He touched her arm.

An idea came upon her. It must have been brewing. For the last few nights she had lain awake wondering whether she should go home for Thanksgiving, how she would get there if she did. Now when she asked the question, it seemed as if she had it all planned.

"Do you take long-distance charters? To Maine, for example?"

"Yes," he said. "Lots of times. Where in Maine?"

"Elk Island. It's far up, past Penobscot Bay, almost to Mount Desert. Just a tiny little island way out at sea."

"Does it have an airport?"

"Not much of one. Just a grass strip."

"My planes like grass strips. When do you want to go?"

"That's the thing," she said. "Thanksgiving. I know you probably have plans, so . . . if you're even working that weekend."

"I am," he said.

"Well . . . Do you want to work up a price and let me know?"

"Sounds good," he said. "We'll have to watch the weather. My big plane has the most instruments, but it's more expensive."

She nodded, swallowed hard. Making transportation arrangements brought her one step closer to actually going. Seeing Mike! Her throat vibrated with a laugh, and she started to let it out, until she realized that by returning to Elk Island, she would be facing her father for the first time in many years. He had never gotten over her growing up, leaving the island for college, coming back just long enough to get pregnant and cause a scandal. Trapped by his grief for Sarah's mother, her father just grew more bitter as the years went by. Sarah had tried taking Mike there for summers long ago, but after a while her father's darkness had stopped her.

"I'll call you," she said, shaking Will's hand.

"Right," he said, glancing at his watch. "Guess I'd better get back to work." He started to walk away. Then, turning, he called, "Hey, Sarah."

"What is it?" she asked.

"Secret lives with her mother and stepfather," he said. "I mean, Secret is my family, but she doesn't live with me, and she's having Thanksgiving with Alice. So it's no problem to fly you to Maine."

"Oh," Sarah said. She was trying to think of what to say next when a pack of teenage boys charged by. One of them grabbed her bowler hat. She felt him drag it off her head. The brim scraped her scar, and she felt a flash of pain. The kids dropped it with embarrassment. "Sorry!" one of them yelled. Her mouth dropped open, and for one terrible instant she looked at Will and registered her own shame in his eyes.

Ducking her head so he wouldn't see her cry, she felt his arms come around her. He held her against his chest. "Your hair's pretty," he whispered.

"It's ugly," she wept. "My son's going to hate it."

"No, he won't," Will said.

"He ran away when I got sick," she said. "He's never seen me this way. It'll never grow out by Thanksgiving."

"Well, he'll see you then," Will whispered, his mouth against her ear. "I'm taking you there myself."

"If I even go."

"You'll go," he said. "You won't back out."

"How do you know?" she asked, leaning back to see his eyes.

"Because you're the bravest woman I've ever met," he said.

SECRET sat in the back seat of Julian's Range Rover. She was seething. Her mother and Julian had promised they could go to the fair, but instead they were driving in the opposite direction.

"I can't believe this," Secret said out loud. "You're making me miss the fair for a stupid umbrella stand."

Julian chuckled. Alice gazed at him with a tight-lipped smile, as in, what-an-amusing-child-I-have-don't-be-mad-at-me. Alice was beautiful, a porcelain doll. She had golden hair and a perfect face.

"It's so unfair," Secret said.

"Just be patient," Julian said in the rearview mirror.

"It's not just an umbrella stand," her mother explained. "We're sorry about the fair, honey, but it's a great old carved Victorian thing with hooks and a huge mirror and a bench. It's being auctioned off this afternoon, and it would look great in the south foyer."

"That's the thing about a big house," Julian said. "It needs lots of nice things to fill it up. Now that I have you and your mother with me, I want it to be even more beautiful."

"I'm not materialistic," Secret said. "I don't need *things*." She settled lower into her seat, pulling her Red Sox cap down. Glancing at the back of Julian's head, she wished she had the powers necessary to make him disappear as dramatically as he had arrived.

For a year he had only been her mother's boss. He owned a company called Von Froelich Precision that built racecars for rich guys. Secret's mother had been the secretary, and she was always coming home with stories about the famous people she talked to.

Suddenly, weeks after she started working, she had started talking about Julian Von Froelich nonstop. How he was so *interesting*. While Secret's dad buried himself in the newspaper, Alice was building a new life in the fast lane. Secret and her dad were numb zombies, too busy missing Fred to notice that her mother was leaving their family behind. Secret's parents had gotten divorced a year earlier. Her mother married Julian a month later.

"When will we get to the fair?" Secret said. She wanted to see her father. He was giving sight-seeing rides until three. She checked her watch. "It's nearly fourteen hundred hours."

"People who think small end up with small lives," Julian said.

"I agree," Secret said.

"You're too good for the fair, Susan. It's beneath you. I want to show you beautiful things—"

"I was thinking of something else," Secret said.

"Yeah? What?" Julian asked, meeting her gaze in the mirror. He had eager, puppy-dog green eyes that made her feel terrible. He wanted her to like him, and she never would. He had long dark blond hair that he tied back in a tucked-under ponytail.

"People who buy things all the time," Secret said quietly. "I feel sorry for them."

"Susan," her mother said. "You love shopping. Don't—"

"No, let her talk," Julian said, sounding hurt. "I want to hear."

"Nothing," Secret said, scrunching down. She thought of the carriage house, filled to the brim with rosewood chests, teak benches. "You could open your own shop."

"Yes, but I don't need to," he said.

"Honey, with all the beautiful things Julian gives you, you're not sounding very grateful," Alice said.

"Dad gives me everything I need."

Julian made a sound through his nose.

"What?" Secret asked, feeling something hard in her chest.

"You're right. You're absolutely right," Julian said.

"Then why did you make that noise?" Secret felt the wheezing start.

"Oh, no reason. That's correct. Your father puts clothes on your back. If Cromwell Casuals is okay for you, then fine."

"It is!" Secret nearly screamed.

"You're a little young, Susan, but one day the names Armani and Prada might mean something to you. I want to treat you like a princess. Being a pilot is very cool, but the salary?"

"Julian, I think that's enough," Alice said.

"I just want her to understand the way the world works."

"Don't talk about her father," Alice said, lowering her voice. "Don't say anything bad to her about Will."

But it was too late. Secret was having an asthma attack. She fought to breathe. The air rasped through her mouth, into her lungs. Her chest ached, and her throat stung, but that wasn't the worst part. Secret's heart was being squeezed. Reaching into her pocket, she found her inhaler. Pumping it once, she placed it in her mouth and took a breath. The aerosol hissed. Her mother looked back and with her eyes asked Secret if she was okay. Secret nodded, her eyes glittering with tears. They stared at each other, each wanting something they could never have.

SARAH sat at the edge of the exam table in a paper smock, waiting for Dr. Goodacre to see her. Each monthly visit required long intervals of patience. He was a neurosurgeon, and most of his cases were life or death. He saw the head-on crash victims, the motorcyclists who spun out without their helmets, the people who woke up with brain tumors.

Finally Dr. Goodacre walked through the door. He was tall and extremely thin, dressed in a dark suit covered by a white lab coat. He had short dark hair. Without smiling, he reached behind the door and pulled out Sarah's chart.

"Hello, Sarah." Frowning, he began to read. Sarah was unafraid of his severe expression. Dr. Goodacre had saved her life, and she adored him with all her heart. "Any pain?"

"Only when I touch the scar."

"Numbness? Tingling?"

"No."

"No more seizures?" he asked, reading.

"Not since July." Sarah closed her eyes. She hated seizures. She had had three, including the one that alerted her that something was wrong. Nine months ago she had been perfectly healthy, running seven miles a day, training for her first marathon. One day she woke up on the floor of her shower. The hot water had run out. She couldn't remember getting in, and it took all her strength to crawl to the phone and dial 911.

At first they thought she had had a stroke. She could barely talk. She had double vision. Cardiologists ordered EKGs and EEGs and CT scans. The CT scan revealed seizure activity, and within a day the neurosurgery department found the brain tumor.

"Okay," he said, laying down her chart. He leaned close to look into her eyes. Then: "Sit up straight and close your eyes. Hold your arms straight out in front. Now out to the sides."

Like wings, she thought, like a plane flying to Maine.

"Touch your nose with your left index finger. Now your right. Eyes closed. Very good."

Sarah had first come to Dr. Goodacre for a second opinion. The first doctor had told her that she had osteogenic sarcoma—the most deadly tumor possible—that even with surgery she would have only ten weeks to live. He had suggested she go to Paris, eat her favorite foods, say good-bye to the people she loved.

He had sent her home. In shock, Sarah had curled into a ball. Was this what her mother had gone through? Crying, Sarah had prayed to her. Weak and sick, she had needed a visiting nurse to check on her. Meg Ferguson had come to call. Six days into her death sentence Mike left for Maine. Ten days into it Sarah listened to Meg: Get a second opinion. And Sarah had called Dr. Goodacre.

"I'm thinking about taking a trip," she said to him now.

"You are?" he asked, examining the back of her head.

"To Maine. To see my son."

"Ah," he said, probing her scar. Her tumor had been located in the meninges, the lining between the skull and the brain. It had clung to the sinus nerve, but Dr. Goodacre had gotten ninety-nine percent of it out. To get inside, he had cut a large flap in her scalp. U-shaped, it looked like a big red smile on the back of her head.

"Remember I told you about him?" she asked. "Mike? He left

to live with my father in Maine, right about the time I met you."

"Are you asking me if you should go?" he asked.

"Yes, I am."

"I see no reason why not," he said. He leaned against a low cabinet, and for the first time since entering the exam room, he really looked at her. "Have you asked Dr. Boswell?"

"No. Should I?" Dr. Boswell, Sarah's oncologist, had administered two courses of chemotherapy and overseen the radiation treatment. But Dr. Goodacre was the One. He was the one who had identified her tumor as large-cell lymphoma, eminently less deadly than osteogenic sarcoma.

"I'll have the nurse give her a call," Dr. Goodacre said. "If she has no objection, neither do I."

"Really?" Sarah asked.

"You know the road we face, Sarah. You've responded well."

"I just don't want a recurrence," she said, shivering.

"I know. We can't predict. Your tumor was . . ." The look on his face said it all. She might survive, and she might not. "Be alert. If you have any symptoms of numbness or tingling, call me immediately. But I see no reason for you not to go."

"Thank you," Sarah said, glowing as if she had just won a race.

"I'll see you back here in a month," he said, preparing to leave.

"Dr. Goodacre," Sarah asked, needing to summon up a little courage. She had never asked him anything personal. "How's your father?" The last time she was here, she had heard the nurse saying his father had had a heart attack.

"Better." Dr. Goodacre gave Sarah a curious look. "But he lives in Florida. It falls to my older brother to look after him."

"Does your brother do a good job?" Sarah asked.

"He's an angel," Dr. Goodacre said with passion. He broke into a grin, staring straight into Sarah's eyes. "I wish everyone had someone like him." He lingered for a moment, then walked away. The door closed softly behind him.

Alone in the room, Sarah felt her heart beating fast. She had never had an angel in her life. But then she thought of Will Burke holding her at the fair, flying her home. Taking her to see Mike.

Chapter 3

WILL drove up the long driveway to Windemere Hill through a forest of white pines. Snow had fallen the previous night, and the drive opened onto a wide snow-covered lawn lined with white-capped boxwood hedges. It was late Friday afternoon, and he was there to pick up his daughter.

Julian's imposing stone mansion lorded over the wintry scene. Two old Ferraris and a Porsche 356 were visible in the carriage house. Will parked his car, trying not to feel resentful that one guy should have all this and Alice and Susan too.

Expecting Susan, he was surprised to see Alice walk out the front door. The sight of her made him catch his breath. She was still the most beautiful woman he had ever seen, with her creamy skin, wide almond-shaped blue eyes, and silky golden hair.

"Susan asked me to tell you she'll be a few minutes late," Alice said hurriedly, her arms folded in front of her.

"No problem," Will said. He got out of the car, leaned against the door. He wore jeans and an old green sweater.

"Her asthma's been terrible lately," Alice said. "It's completely psychosomatic. She works herself into attacks just to interrupt whatever's going on. I'm not blaming her. She's been through a lot, but she needs to be the center of attention."

"I did when I was fifteen," Will said, smiling.

"Like *that* ever stopped."

Was she kidding? Will couldn't tell. She was staring at his boots, a pair of old Dunhams. He wondered if she remembered buying them for him their first winter in Fort Cromwell, five long years ago.

"I wanted to ask you about Thanksgiving—" Will began.

Her head snapped up. "She stays with me. We have plans—"

"Whoa," Will said, raising one hand. The smallest conversation became so tense. Every point felt like a negotiation.

"She stays with me on holidays. It was part of the agreement."

"Yes, I know. Relax, Alice. I was just asking. I have a charter to Maine. I just thought you should know I'll be out of town."

Alice nodded, her face stern.

"She'll be okay," Will said. "Secret's going to be fine."

"Secret? Come off it, Will!" Alice exploded. "We named her Susan. Don't indulge this Secret crap. It's really unsettling. Julian thinks she needs more professional help."

"That's a good sign that she doesn't. Didn't you tell him we went through that when we first got to Fort Cromwell?"

"Of course I did. He knows Dr. Darrow." Splaying her fingers with frustration, Alice revealed her jewels: the largest diamond ring Will had ever seen, and a wedding ring–style band of diamonds and emeralds. He exhaled slowly.

"Hi!" their daughter called, bursting through the front door with her knapsack, duffel bag, and a small package. She stood there like a star: radiant smile, theatrical pose, arms open wide to greet her adoring public. Her parents were too upset to even smile. Will held out his arm to embrace her as she ran toward him through the snow.

"Hi, Dad. Can we drive through town? I have something I have to drop off for a friend."

"You bet," he said.

"I'll need a number for wherever you're going on Thanksgiving," Alice said brusquely. "Just in case."

"You're going somewhere for Thanksgiving?" Secret said.

"Just for work," he said.

"You're going to *work* on *Thanksgiving?*"

"I'm flying the Fergusons' friend Sarah Talbot to Maine."

Secret stared at her package. "That's who you're taking?"

"Do you have your inhaler?" Alice asked, pulling her away from Will for a hug.

Seeing his ex-wife hold their daughter brought too much back for Will, and he had to look away. Glancing toward the carriage house, he saw Julian walking out. Time to go.

"You ready, Secret?" Will asked, hoisting her bags.

"Please," Alice said. "I hate that name."

"You don't have to call me Secret," she said. "I'm changing it. As of midnight last night I'm Snow."

"Susan . . ." Alice said dangerously.

"Well, hello," Julian said, walking over. He had the tall, lean look of a man who worked out or ran a lot. He wore an expensive suede jacket with his racecar logo embroidered on the front.

"Hi, Julian," Will said, shaking his hand.

"You know why I'm Snow?" his daughter asked, her voice high and tense. "Because of Freddie. He adored winter. Sledding. Skiing. Remember when we all went to Mount Tom?"

"Susan, honey. Stop—" Alice said.

"He taught me how to make angels in Newport. We lay on our backs in the snow, looking out over the harbor, and we waved at the sky over and over. Remember?"

"I remember," Will said.

"Stop, honey," Alice said, grabbing her wrist, tears rolling down her cheeks. "Changing your name won't bring him back."

"Snow. Falling out of the sky, lying on the docks. He didn't care. He died in September, so I was September, and he kept my secrets, so I was Secret, and he loved, loved, loved snow, so I'm Snow."

"Oh, Lord," Alice said, burying her face in her hands.

"Can't you say something to your daughter?" Julian asked harshly, wrapping his arms around Alice as he glared at Will.

Will didn't speak. He took his daughter's hands, held them in his. She was wild with grief. Looking deep into her eyes, he tried to pull her close, but she wouldn't let him. She faced Julian with hatred in her gaze. "Don't you talk to my dad that way," she said.

"Listen," Julian said. "I've had about as much as I'm going to take with you disrespecting your mother. If your father won't say it, I will. You're hurting your mother, Susan. Cut the damn name crap right now!"

Will didn't even feel it coming. The punch started somewhere in his gut, and by the time it got to his fist, Julian was laid out on his driveway, blood from his nose turning the snow pink.

Will's knuckles hurt. "I'm sorry," he said calmly, standing over his ex-wife's husband. "But I can't have you speaking to my daughter that way."

"Crazy maniac," Julian said, struggling to get up.

Will turned to his daughter, tried to reassure her with a smile.

"Sarah thinks it's a beautiful name," his daughter said, her eyes full of panic, looking as if the world had betrayed her.

"Sarah? Who's Sarah?" Alice asked, but no one answered her.

"Come on, Snow," Will said, his hands shaking. "Time to leave." The two of them climbed into Will's old blue Jeep and drove away.

SARAH had just opened her shop on Saturday morning when she heard the bells above her door tingle. Will Burke and his daughter stood there holding two white bakery bags. "We came last night, but you had already closed," the young girl said.

"You caught me," Sarah said. "I wanted to go to the movies, so I closed early. What do you have there?"

"We brought you breakfast," Will said. He was bundled up in a hunter-green ski jacket. The corners of his blue eyes crinkled in the sunlight.

"You must have read my mind," she said, grinning. "I'm starved."

"Are you really?" the girl asked.

"Yes, Snow," Sarah said.

Snow's intake of breath was loud and dramatic. "How did you know I'd changed my name?"

"You told me you wanted to be Snow for winter, didn't you? Just look outside." Sarah pointed at the snow-covered street.

Snow and her father looked at each other. Some violent feeling was clouding the girl's eyes. She took a deep breath. Removing the plaid muffler from around her neck, she trailed it across the damask-covered bed.

"Let's sit back here," Sarah said, pointing to some chairs and clearing a place on her desk for the doughnuts, coffee, and juice.

"You're going to Maine, I hear," Snow said, placing a small white bag on the desk. Sarah moved to open it, but Snow gestured for her to wait till later. Curious, Sarah slid it aside.

"Maine? Yes, I am," she said.

"The five-day forecast looks cold but clear," Will said, handing her a cardboard cup of coffee.

"Why all the way to Maine?" Snow asked.

"To see my son. Mike."

"He doesn't live with you? Does he live with his father?"

"Snow . . ." Will began.

"That's okay. I love talking about him. About a year ago he dropped out of high school to go home and save my father's farm."

"You grew up on a farm?" Snow asked.

"Yes," Sarah said. She gestured at a pile of quilts stacked in the corner. "See those? They were made on our farm. About eighteen years ago I started a store like this in Boston because the farm was about to go under. My mother had been sick when I was young, and when I was fourteen, she died. My father was . . . distracted. He found someone from Thomaston who wanted to buy all the geese, and he had a man from Camden who wanted to buy the land. None of that sat very well with me, so I dropped out of college to start my business."

"Did you save the farm?" Snow asked.

"I can't actually say we *saved* it," Sarah said, picturing the ramshackle buildings, her aunt Bess with her ancient treadle sewing machine, "but so far he's been able to keep it. Together we just about cover the taxes."

"Your father must love you so much," Snow said.

"I'm not really sure how he feels," Sarah said.

"Ask him," Snow said.

Sarah tried to smile. "He's a man of strong opinions. And most of them collide with mine."

"Difficult," Will said, looking as if he understood.

"That's no reason not to try," Snow said. "He's a person too. If I'd given up on you, Dad, I'd hate to think of where we'd be. Talk about difficult."

"Hey," Will said. Was he kidding or hurt? Sarah couldn't tell.

"Worse than difficult," Snow said, glancing at Sarah.

"Fathers don't have it easy," Sarah said, although for some reason her thoughts slid to Zeke, who had had it about as easy as it got. From the minute Sarah had told him about her pregnancy, he had never wanted to see her again. Her father had gone crazy.

"They don't *make* it easy," Snow said.

"What did I do," Will asked, taking a cruller, "to get myself in such trouble?"

"I happen to be referring to the fact that you quit the navy and dragged me and Mom way the heck into these ridiculous boondocks," Snow said, glaring at him. Then, afraid she was offending Sarah, she touched the back of her hand. "I'm sorry. They're nice for some people, but we need the ocean."

"I understand completely. My son used to say the same thing to me, and he was right. I moved us away from Boston to here."

"If I had a family farm to run away to, I just might go there."

"Don't run away," Will said.

"He's right, Snow. It's not worth it," Sarah said, feeling suddenly cold. She had worn a silk jacket, and she pulled it around herself.

"I don't see why not," Snow said. "Mike took off, and you're following him out there for Thanksgiving so your family can be together. The way it's supposed to be."

"That's a nice thought, but the reality's going to be a little different," Sarah said. "My father hasn't celebrated a holiday for years—not since my mother died."

"Then why did they ask you?"

"Her son asked her," Will said, although she hadn't told him.

"He did," Sarah said. "He knows I love Thanksgiving more than any other holiday."

"Why do you love it so much?" Will asked.

"It started the year my son was born," Sarah said, looking into Will's eyes. "I just never knew how incredible it would be."

Will nodded. "Having children."

"Having Mike made me a different person. I fell madly in love with him," Sarah said, her eyes shining. "The world made sense. I'd watch red finches at the bird feeder and imagine God made them for me and Mike. I felt so grateful, and when Thanksgiving rolled around that year, it became my favorite holiday."

"And you told Mike?" Will asked.

"Every year. All the time."

"You can't tell them enough," Will said. "You have to tell them you love them all the time."

Sarah bowed her head. "That's why I'm going to Maine."

"It's been too long," Will said.

She nodded. Composing herself, she looked up. "I'm afraid the farm is wrong for him. It's very isolated. His father was from the island, but he's dead, and my father . . . Well, losing my mother made him unhappy. He never got over it. Never. I'm afraid his misery will rub off on Mike. My aunt Bess used to be the smilingest person you know when she lived in Providence, but when her husband died, she moved back to the island, and you should see her now. Living alone with my father all this time has turned her into an old prune. I felt guilty for leaving, but I had to."

"Did you take care of your mother?" Will asked.

"I did," Sarah said quietly.

"And now you're going back," Will said, "for Mike."

"Exactly." Sarah's hand strayed up to her head, where the cancer had been. "I want to set him straight before it's too late."

"Before he turns into a young prune," Snow said.

"Before he forgets why you love Thanksgiving," Will said.

"Fuel up the big plane, Dad," Snow said. "I'm coming with you."

"No," Sarah said. "The island's a mess. There's not enough heat in the house; the geese smell terrible." She felt worried, not wanting this to become a big excursion.

"You can't come, honey," Will said. "It's my job, not a vacation. And your mother needs you with her for Thanksgiving."

"She has Julian," Snow said. "Dad, I—"

"No, Snow. You're staying. That's all there is to it."

THE day before Thanksgiving, Sarah woke up with a slight fever. Her muscles ached, and her throat hurt. "Please, not today," she said. She could not come down with the flu right now. Before dark tonight she would see Mike. Slowly she got out of bed. Pushing back her curtains, she could see the sky, clear and brilliant, bright blue.

By the time she took a shower and drank some orange juice, she felt all better. The flu had merely lighted upon her instead of settling in for a real bout. It reminded her of being very sick, of all she had to be grateful for. Sarah had grown to believe in the small miracles of life, and she knew she had just received another.

Meg Ferguson picked her up at nine to drive her to the airport. Sarah was ready, dressed in traveling clothes: jeans, an Irish fisherman's sweater, a long navy wool jacket.

With her head in the trunk as she rearranged things to make room for the bags, Meg didn't see Sarah right away. When she looked up, her mouth fell open. "Oh, my," she said.

"Is it ridiculous?" Sarah asked, covering her head with her hands. She could hardly look at Meg.

"It's gorgeous. Let me see."

Meg, who wasn't exactly the done-hair type, stood back and gazed appraisingly at her friend. Sarah had bleached her hair, thanks to the curious package Snow had left on her desk. Meg had straight brown hair and bangs pushed off to one side. She wore her usual uniform of a skirt and sweater covered by a white lab coat. But she looked at Sarah as if she were a world-famous stylist. "I can't believe the difference. I mean, it's like Paris."

"Is it too much? Do I look like myself?"

Meg said, "You do look different. You've got that model's bone structure anyway, and now with that white-gold hair . . . Wow. Very chic, Sarah. With you looking like that, Will Burke had better keep his eyes on the sky."

Sarah shook her head, embarrassed. "What would it matter to him? He's just a nice pilot flying me to Maine."

"Sure," Meg said, grinning. "Mimi took a picture of you two at the fair. The look in his eyes . . ."

"He was just being nice," Sarah said, wishing she could see that picture. "Some kids had swiped my hat."

"Well, you don't need any hat today. Ready to go?"

"All set," Sarah said, climbing into the car.

"Dr. Goodacre gave you the green light?"

"Yes," Sarah said, wondering if she should mention the fever.

"Anyway, you feel fine, and that's what counts."

"If it came back," Sarah said, "I couldn't stand it."

"Oh, Sarah," Meg said.

They had talked this over before. Sarah knew that when tumors like hers recurred and metastasized, the survival rates plummeted. The new treatment would be just as aggressive as the last, and the outcome would be uncertain. The thought filled her with dread.

"I won't, you know," Sarah said.

"Won't what?"

"Have any more radiation or chemo." Sarah shivered. "This is my chance, and I'm going to grab it."

THE twin engines hummed loudly. The sky surrounded them in endless blue. Sunlight turned the wings silver, and even though she wore dark glasses, Sarah couldn't stop squinting. They flew along in silence, watching the land unfold. A radio crackled, and voices spoke to them. Sarah had the sense of being passed from tower to tower, as if the air-traffic controllers were a benevolent order, overseeing their progress from New York to Maine.

"Snow said you were in the navy," Sarah said.

"Yes, I was."

"But it's not where you learned to fly?"

"No. I've always loved flying. I grew up in Waterford, Connecticut, near a small airport, and I learned how to fly before I could drive. My first job was taking charters out to Block Island."

"Snow is so proud of you," Sarah said.

Will was silent for a while. "I don't know why," he said.

Sarah could hear the self-hatred in his voice. Why was he spending his holiday flying her to Maine instead of with people who loved him? "It doesn't matter why," she said. "Why they're proud of you, why they love you. All that matters is *that* they do."

"Is that how it is with you and Mike?" Will asked.

"I do the best I can and try to let go of the results," Sarah said. "Look!" There in the far distance was a line of silver. "Do you know how long it's been since I saw the sea? Three years. At least."

Will stared at the Atlantic Ocean. It had appeared as a silver thread on the horizon, and it was spreading into a silver-blue sheet glistening with bright light. "I know exactly when I last saw it," he said. "When we moved up from Newport five years ago. Right after I left the navy. I haven't seen the ocean since."

"Well, you're seeing it now," she said gently, watching him. After he'd mentioned Newport, the lines in his face hardened with pain. He felt her staring, so he looked over. Reaching for his hand, she pulled her sunglasses down to make sure he could really see her eyes. She smiled.

"I haven't wanted to go back," he said. "I see it, and I think of him in there. My son, Fred. He drowned in the Atlantic."

"I'm sorry," Sarah said.

Will nodded. The lines in his face relaxed. He looked straight at Sarah and nodded again.

They were getting closer. Sarah could see waves breaking over rocks. Small towns dotted the coves. Will called in to a tower and announced plans to land and refuel at Portsmouth, New Hampshire.

Sarah closed her eyes. What did it cost to survive? Breathing deeply, she said a prayer for Will and a boy she had never met.

SNOW couldn't hold back another minute. She had taken an extra-large hit of her inhaler just in case of an inopportune allergy attack. She'd had some tense moments. All she needed was one big sneeze, and her father would be turning the plane around. The plane had touched down. Snug in her hiding place behind the back seats, covered with an old green blanket, she flexed her muscles. Poking her head up, she looked around.

There was Sarah walking into the hangar and her father talking to the fuel-pump guy. Snow really had to use the ladies' room. She figured that was where Sarah was heading, and if she timed it perfectly, she could sneak in.

Using other planes to hide behind, she ran into the hangar and found the ladies' room. Sarah was in one of the stalls. Snow went into a stall at the far end.

Hearing Sarah flush the toilet, she knew she had very little time to sneak back aboard the plane. Peeking through the crack in the stall door, she caught sight of something that made her gasp out loud. Sarah stood there, her hair bleached and very short, looking gorgeous.

"Hi, Snow," Sarah said.

"How did you know it was me?" Snow asked, still peering through the crack.

"I recognized your voice."

"Sarah, are you mad at me?"

"That's beside the point."

"Are you going to tell my father?"

"I think I should. How long were you planning to hide?"

"Just till it was too late to turn back."

Sarah closed her eyes and bowed her head. "We're not turning back," she said.

"Did you know I was aboard the whole time?"

"It occurred to me as a possibility," Sarah said, not sounding very friendly.

"I'm sorry." Slowly Snow opened the door. Sarah's angry mood confused her, but now that she was truly facing her, she could get a good look. Sarah's hair had come out white and silky, so fine you just wanted to touch it. "I gasped because I can't believe how great you look," Snow said quietly.

"Oh," Sarah said, looking doubtful, glancing in the mirror.

"You really do. It's like a makeover in *Vogue*."

"Thank you," Sarah said, surprising Snow by sweeping her into a tight hug. Snow closed her eyes and hugged back. When it was time to quit, Snow didn't want to let go. She was so glad Sarah didn't hate her. She hung on, feeling tears in her throat.

"I would never have had the courage if it weren't for you," Sarah said. "Let's go see your dad."

They started walking toward the plane. Stepping into the bright sunshine, Snow saw her father standing by the Piper Aztec with his back turned. "One thing," she said to Sarah. "How did you suspect that I was aboard? Did you see the toe of my shoe or something?"

Sarah shook her head, for the first time really starting to smile. "No," she said. "It's just something I would have done."

"WE HAVE A STOWAWAY," Sarah said quietly.

Will turned around, came face to face with his daughter. He tried to control his expression, to make it seem stern. "Susan!"

"Dad, don't make me go back."

"What's going on here?"

"I want to be with you, that's all. I was *worried* about you."

"I made a promise to your mother, Susan. She wants you with her on holidays, and that's that."

"It's just Thanksgiving, Dad. You know she only cares about Christmas. Please let me come with you."

Sarah looked from one Burke to the other. Snow had her father's eyes. Both faces were full of guarded hope. "If you fly this young lady all the way back to Fort Cromwell, we'll waste half the day. I hired you because you were the best pilot around." Sarah pointed at Snow. "She told me so herself. Now I have a mission to accomplish. I want to see my son. I'd like you to fly me to Maine. Now." Sarah stepped back, folding her arms.

"Mom will understand," Snow said, stepping closer to her father, tugging his sleeve. "She will."

"You'd better call her, then. Tell her what's going on; then let me talk to her."

"Sorry about almost screwing up your charter."

"Just don't let it happen again," Will said. His voice was stern, but a flash of serious delight was in his eyes.

MIKE Talbot kept looking at the sky. He was sweeping out the picking shack, shutting it down for the first time since coming to the island. Grandpa was a driven man. He probably planned to work on Thanksgiving, but Mike had other ideas.

"What going on here?" Grandpa asked, following two geese down the snowy path. His face was windburned and wrinkled. Gelsey, the lame collie, limped along by his side.

"Closing up," Mike said.

"Who told you to do that?"

Mike felt his face redden. "Thought of it myself."

The old man's eyes narrowed. "Never considered you as being

dim-witted before, but what kind of goose farmer shuts down the day before Thanksgiving?"

"They're not turkeys, Grandpa. Besides, Mom's coming—"

"Fowl is fowl, Mike," Grandpa growled. "Some folks like their birds nice and gamy, not all dried out like those big stupid turkeys. All white meat. Makes me sick." Frowning, he sat down on the chopping stump to catch his breath.

"You okay, Grandpa?"

"Course I'm okay," he said darkly, rising to his feet again. He picked up the axe, looked around for any goose.

Snow had fallen every day that week, so the white birds blended in. Mike saw them pecking for grain down by the bay. After all this time he couldn't help wishing the dumb birds would just waddle down to the water and swim away.

"I'll get them, Grandpa," he said. Still wearing his bloody hip boots, he nearly lost his footing on the icy trail. The geese honked loudly. Mike came around behind. "Go," he hissed so Grandpa couldn't hear. "Take off, you stupid birds. Fly away!"

Of course they didn't fly away; they never did. They padded along trustingly to the picking shack.

"We'd better get busy," Grandpa said brusquely. "Some fellow from Mayport Inn's bringing his boat to pick them up."

Grandpa staggered a little from his arthritis. He almost lost his balance, so Mike steadied him. George Talbot had once stood nearly six feet tall, but old age had hunched him over.

Still, George moved fast. He grabbed a goose, laid its neck on the stump, and with one horrible whack he cut its head off. The second goose was always worse, because Mike believed it knew what was coming. But it was over before you could blink.

They carried the dead geese into the picking shack. His grandfather pulled on his hip boots, and they both put on gloves. Mike started the generator, and the feather machine began chugging. Grandpa worked so fast Mike could hardly keep up. He rotated the goose over the machine as it worked like magic fingers, wiggling the feather tips out of the skin. Loosened by the machine, the feathers came out easily by hand.

"Mom should be here anytime," Mike said.

"Surprised she's bothering to come at all. What time's she getting here anyway?"

"Sometime before dark. That's all she said."

"She's always been that way," Grandpa said. "Never could pin her down. If something comes along, she's on to the next thing."

"Huh. I don't know. If Mom says she'll be here, she will. That's what counts."

"Lots of things count in this world, Mike," Grandpa said. "She couldn't get off the island fast enough after her mother died."

Mike didn't even want to look. Practically every time his grandfather mentioned his wife, he got hoarse. "You okay, Grandpa?" he asked.

The old man blew his nose. "Well," he said, "we'll feed her good while she's here. Muskrat stew. It'll put some meat on her bones and get her back some health."

"She is healthy," Mike said.

Grandpa gave him a funny look. "That what she told you? That's what her mother kept saying," he said. "People sicken and die, and that's that. Hasn't your time out here taught you anything realistic?"

"I'm realistic," Mike said.

His grandfather laughed. "You got a long way to go."

Chapter 4

MIKE hung back, watching his mother's plane land. Twice that day he had plowed the grass landing strip himself. The shaky little plane jounced along something fierce, hitting every rut left by his snowplow. Until the aircraft came to a complete stop, Mike couldn't let himself really breathe.

Starting up the big Jeep, he drove through the snow to the end of the strip. He parked beside the plane, then climbed out. His mother had her door open and was waving at him like crazy, but she couldn't get her seat belt off. "Hi, Mike," she called.

"Hi, Mom," he called back.

The pilot gave him a sort of wave, coming around the plane to unhook his mother's seat belt. The guy was really tall, with big shoulders and a dark five-o'clock shadow, just like some movie pilot. Mike watched how tenderly he acted and figured he was probably in love with her. Another man. Big surprise.

"Mike," she said, barreling through the snow at him.

He folded his arms. He didn't mean to; the action took him by surprise. He didn't understand why he suddenly felt like walking away. "Hi, Mom," he said again.

She stopped short. "Mike, you grew three inches," she said. Her blue eyes were darting back and forth. She was looking at his eyes, his hair, his skin, taking everything in. "Your hair looks great. Grandpa's making you keep it short?"

"I want to." He shrugged.

He let his arms fall to his sides. It was okay with him if she hugged him now. But she didn't. She was looking very serious.

"What?" he asked.

"I'm looking at you," she said. "That's all."

The wind had picked up, and it was whipping snow across the field. The pilot was tying the plane down with stakes and a mallet. The beam from the lighthouse flashed across the sky. Mike nodded at the pilot. "He's staying?"

"Yes," Sarah said. "It didn't make sense to have him drop me off, then come all the way back to pick me up."

Mike didn't say anything. He just walked over to watch the pilot whack the stakes into the frozen ground, thread lines through the wings and wheels, tie them down with a sailor's precision. "Need a hand?" he asked.

"Thanks," the pilot said, handing him a line, a stake, and the mallet. "Want to run this aft?"

"Sure," Mike said.

"I'm Will Burke," the pilot said.

"Mike Talbot," Mike said.

They shook hands. The guy didn't smile too long. His handshake was firm. Mike felt his stomach relax a little. He estimated the proper distance, drove in the metal rod, eased the nylon line through the eye, and tied a solid sheepshank. When he looked up, his mother had those proud eyes that made her look sleepy, like she was about to cry at the national anthem or something.

"I'm so"—she swallowed—"glad to see you."

"Yeah," he said. "Me too."

"Then hug me," she said.

Mike did what she asked. They stayed there, with the wind rocking them from side to side. His mother felt small, built like a bird, ten pounds lighter than the last time he'd seen her. She was crying. He felt her shaking. Tears felt hot in his own eyes.

"Hey, Mom," he said. "Don't, huh?"

"I know." Taking a half step back, she fumbled in her pocket. Mike reached inside his jacket, then handed her a handkerchief.

"Thanks," she said, blowing her nose like a goose. She handed the white square back to him. It was stiff with starch. "No one does laundry like Aunt Bessie."

"Nope," he said. Returning the handkerchief to his inside pocket, he was just about to suggest driving home, when he lost his breath. Totally, football-in-the-solar-plexus, couldn't breathe.

"Who's she?" he asked, looking over his mother's shoulder.

This beautiful young girl was climbing out of the plane. She wore a big navy jacket, tight jeans, brand-new sneakers. Her fingernails were painted brown and orange. Catching sight of Mike, she smiled and started walking over.

"That," his mother said, smiling too, "is Snow."

"Snow?" Mike asked.

"You must be Mike," Snow said.

"Yeah," Mike said. "Hi."

"We're friends of your mother's," she said. "My dad and I."

"Good friends," his mother said, placing her arm around Snow's narrow shoulders.

"Your mother couldn't wait to get here," the pilot said.

"I couldn't!" his mother exclaimed, hugging Snow tighter.

Mike saw how happy her eyes looked. He took a step toward her. "You look different," he said.

"Sarah, can I ask him if he likes . . ." Standing on tiptoes, Snow whispered something in his mother's ear.

"Go ahead," his mother said.

"Do you like her hair?" Snow asked.

"Huh?" Mike asked, frowning. His mother's hair was really short and really blond. He smiled. "Yeah, it's okay."

"My idea," Snow said, beaming.

"Huh," the pilot said, smiling like Mike. "It does look good."

"Dad, you are so blind. All the way to Maine and you're just noticing *now?*"

Mike stared at Snow. He noticed her wide eyes, her long chestnut-brown hair. Swallowing, he looked away. "It's cold," he said. "I'll drive everyone home."

THEY all pulled up in front of the old farmhouse. Sarah and Will walked ahead of the kids. The memories of her entire childhood swept over Sarah. She had lived in this house until she went to college. Her mother had died upstairs in the front bedroom.

"I can't believe I'm here," she whispered.

"You sound scared," Will whispered back. "It's your home."

"That's why," she said, and it sounded so funny, she laughed. Will put his arm around her. They stood still on the stone walk, letting her get her breath. She looked the old place over. It was an ancient saltbox, one of the oldest houses in Maine. The white paint was peeling. One front step had cracked.

"I haven't gotten around to replacing that yet," Mike said.

"You?" Sarah asked, surprised. Maintaining the house had always been her father's job. She hadn't seen her father in several years, and all of a sudden she realized that she was afraid of what she was going to find.

"You ready?" Will asked, his hand on Sarah's arm.

"Yes," she said, giving three knocks on the big brass door knocker, then turning the knob and walking in.

George Talbot stood right inside the front hall. Sarah stared at him. He's gotten old, she thought. My father is an old man.

"Well," he said, looking at her. "Well, Sarah."

Sarah felt the blood rush to her face. "Hi, Dad," she said.

"What did you do, bring the troops?" he asked, glaring at Will and Snow.

"I'm Will Burke, sir," Will said, shaking his hand. "And this is my daughter, Snow."

"How do you do? You're the new boyfriend?"

"The pilot, Grandpa," Mike said, stepping in.

"Your daughter hired me to fly her up here," Will said.

"Pretty expensive, a private pilot all the way from New York."

"That shows how much she wanted to get here," Will said.

"Oh," George Talbot said.

Sarah watched the confusion cloud his eyes. He had such little contact with other people. He was terribly shy, but it always came out as hostile. She took his hands. She squeezed them gently, looking into his eyes. The gray hair he had had for as long as she could remember had gone all white. "Hi, Dad," she said again. "My friends are going to fly me home on Sunday, so I thought it would be better for them to stay. I'll make up some beds for them—"

"You come all this way, and you're only staying four days?"

"Yes. I don't feel right leaving the shop for longer."

Her father regarded her, then shifted his gaze to Snow. "You like muskrat stew, young lady?"

"Who, me?" Snow asked. "Um, I'm a vegetarian."

George appeared perplexed. "Aren't you worried about her having a balanced diet?" he asked Will.

Will laughed. He shook his head. "She has a mind of her own."

"I know what that's like, Mr. Burke," George said, glaring at Sarah. "Well, we'd better get down to dinner. Bessie's deaf as a doorpost, or she'd have been up to welcome you. We don't want to leave her out." Shuffling toward the stairs, he started down to the kitchen. He paused. "Seems strange your mother isn't here, doesn't it, Sarah? I never get used to it, no matter how much time passes."

THE BASEMENT KITCHEN RAN the entire length of the house. Five large windows overlooked Elk Bay; a window seat stretched beneath them. A fire crackled in the big stone hearth.

The table was hewn from one enormous fallen oak. A large cast-iron kettle held the stew. Aunt Bess stood by the stove supervising Mike, doling the food into rough crockery bowls. Aunt Bess, as plump as her brother was gaunt, wore her special-occasion navy-blue dress with white polka dots.

"It's so nice to have some girls around," she said.

"It's good to see you, Aunt Bess," Sarah said.

"The same to you, Sarah." Looking from Snow to Will, she said, "Sarah's like the daughter I never had."

"Sarah had a mother," George said, frowning at Bess.

Sarah couldn't look at him. Aunt Bess had set her mouth, but at Sarah's glance she shrugged her shoulders. The mood at the table was as tense as Sarah had remembered.

"This stew is delicious," Will said.

"A Maine specialty," George said. "Don't know what you're missing, young lady," he said to Snow.

"My dinner is just fine," Snow said, eating the plate of carrots and kale Bess had steamed for her.

"This is real New England eating," George said.

Snow paused, tilted her head. "We never ate muskrat stew, and we're from New England."

"Oh, really? I thought Sarah said Fort Cromwell," Bess said.

"Snow was born in Newport, Rhode Island," Will said. "When I was in the navy."

"Newport? Oh, my goodness, my husband and I lived in Providence, and we just loved Newport. Oh, I—"

"Navy man, eh?" George asked, cutting Bess right off.

"Yes, sir."

"See any action?"

"Some."

"The Persian Gulf," Snow said proudly.

Will looked across the table at George. "Sarah told me you served in World War Two."

"That's right. Army Air Corps, Eighth Air Force, in Europe."

"Grandpa flew in the lead plane," Mike said.

"On D-day he was one of the first planes over Normandy," Sarah said, feeling as proud as Snow.

"Surprised you remember," George said.

"Oh, I remember," she said softly. Sarah kept his medals—the Air Medal, the Distinguished Flying Cross—in a small pink satin jewel case back in Fort Cromwell.

"Persian Gulf, eh? What was your rank?" George asked Will.

"Commander."

Sarah watched her father's face fall. He hated being outranked. She wondered whether he would offer the information that upon discharge from the Air Corps he had attained the rank of first lieutenant, but he didn't. Pushing his chair back, he went to the refrigerator and took out a big pitcher. He poured himself a tall glass of milk and one for Mike. "Anyone else?" he asked.

"I'll take one, sir," Will said.

George gave him a sidelong glance as he filled another glass with milk. He had heard the "sir," the tone of respect, and was deciding whether to forgive Will for being a commander. Sarah watched her father replace the pitcher, his eyes hard with anger.

"George was only a few years older than Mike is now when he went off to war," Bess said to Snow. "He was so brave, and we were all so afraid for him. My father cried like a baby when we drove Georgie to the train."

"Bess, that's enough," George said, but this time he couldn't ruin her mood of nostalgic affection.

She gazed at him with love, her brother who had gone to war.

"She doesn't mean anything by it," Snow said.

"What?" George asked.

"She's just teasing you. It's what sisters do. They don't do it to hurt you," she said.

George gave a long, exasperated exhalation. With awe and admiration Sarah watched Snow in action. "You're very lucky to still have each other," she said. "At your ages."

"Lucky?" George snorted. "She's a millstone around my neck!"

Even Bess couldn't take it. "Lucky he still goes to work every day," she said. "I pray to God I die before he retires."

Will caught Sarah's eye, trying not to smile. Mike was openly grinning.

"You don't want to say that," Snow said confidentially to Bess. "You'll miss him when he's gone."

Bess raised her gaze to meet her brother's. He stood there frowning at the outspoken child. A log collapsed in the fireplace, sending a galaxy of sparks up the chimney.

"Hear what she says?" George said, looking at Bess. "You'd better start being nicer to me."

"Take your own advice. Your own daughter walks in after ten years, and you're acting as mean as a black bear in a thicket. We have houseguests, and we're bickering like blue jays."

"We're nothing like blue jays," George said, his tone softening by way of almost apology. "Are we, Mike?"

"Not at all," Mike said. He and his grandfather exchanged manly nods, and Sarah sensed something protective toward Bess in the gesture. Mike had become part of this Elk Island household, and he wanted to make sure everyone knew it.

THANKSGIVING morning was crystal-clear and very cold. The sun came up like thunder here, and Sarah made sure she woke up in time to see it. Again she felt the ripple of fever. It ran through her body as she got dressed, but by the time she had pulled on thermal underwear, jeans, turtleneck, and a heavy sweater, she felt normal again. She paused outside Mike's bedroom door, listening for his deep, steady breathing. She walked down the snowy path to the bay.

The stars were still out. Sarah stood by the water in the darkness, her hands stuck in her pockets. But she wasn't alone. Hearing her footsteps, a man sitting on a rock rose and walked across the tidal flats. She saw him coming, silhouetted against the cold auroral fire. Looking up into his kind face, she smiled.

"Good morning," Will said.

"You're up early," she said. "Do you mind company?"

"No," he said, standing beside her. "Not at all."

His leather jacket crinkled as he unfolded his arms. Waves broke over rocks fifty yards away. Boulders changed shape and slid into the bay, and Sarah touched Will's hand and pointed.

"Seals," she said. "A whole colony."

"Those rocks?" he asked. The animals, fifty or sixty adults and at least a dozen young, did look rocklike, sleek and gray, the water rising around them. "I'll be darned," he said. "Wait till Susan sees these guys."

"Kids love seals," Sarah agreed. "When Mike was little, I couldn't get him off the rocks. He wanted to chase seals all day long."

"Mike's a nice kid," Will said. "He did a good job yesterday getting the airstrip ready for us. And he's glad to see you."

"Hmm," Sarah said, trying to be strong. But her insecurities got the better of her. "Why do you say that?"

"I can just tell. The way he mentioned fixing that step last night. He wants you to be proud of him."

"I was thinking that he wants me to see he doesn't need me at all. He's adopted my father and Bess as his new family."

The sun had broken out of the sea. It was a red ball, shining through the outer islands dotted throughout the bay, turning the tall pines black and spiky against the golden light. "Why is he here?" Will asked quietly.

"He ran away."

"From home?"

Sarah paused. "From me." She thought of their last, and worst, fight. "He had his things packed," she said, closing her eyes as she remembered. "Ready to hitchhike to Maine to catch the ferry out here. We fought, and then I caught up with him on the highway. I asked him to think of his future, stay with me just until he finished high school. He just looked at me and said he couldn't. He wouldn't even listen." She took a breath. "He looked like he hated me."

"Why would he?"

"Lots of reasons," Sarah said.

Will didn't speak right away. He seemed to be watching the seals. "He doesn't hate you," he said. "A boy who hates his mother doesn't ask her to spend Thanksgiving with him."

"He didn't want to be with me last year. I found out I had cancer, and he couldn't get away fast enough."

"He was scared," Will said. "He wouldn't want to lose you, Sarah. No one would."

Watching the sky turn from dark gray to blue, they walked slowly up the frozen path to the dark house.

WHILE all the adults were busy fixing Thanksgiving dinner, Snow decided she needed a tour of Elk Island. She bundled into her parka and checked all the rooms in the crooked little house. Finally she found Mike down by the bay, coming out the door of a tiny little shack. He looked guilty the minute he saw her. He held a bushel basket full of feathers.

"What's in there—secret treasure?" she asked, walking straight over to the shack.

"Uh, no," he said.

"Then how come you look so afraid I'll open the door?"

"Believe me, you don't want to," he said.

Snow stood very still, looking him over. She hadn't spent twenty minutes in front of a bathroom mirror for nothing that morning. Zero eight hundred, out of bed, and beautifying, here in the wilderness of deepest, darkest Maine, thinking how cute Mike Talbot was.

"Why not?" she asked. "What is it?"

"The picking shack. It's kind of gross. It's where we take the feathers off the geese."

"Really?" she asked, her eyes lighting up. "Are there a bunch of naked little geese running around in there?"

"No. They're dead."

"Dead?" she asked, unbelieving. "You have to *kill* them? To get their *feathers?*"

"Well, yeah."

"Oh, no!" Snow said. This threw new light on Sarah's shop. Snow hated killing animals. She couldn't believe this of Sarah.

"Are you okay?" Mike asked.

"No, I'm not," Snow said. "I just can't believe it. I just can't." Snow felt sick. Compared to all the other adults she knew, even compared to her own mother, Sarah was the best person in the world. But here she was, selling products that required the slaughter of beautiful birds. A pair of geese waddled by, nuzzling against Mike's boots. "Go on," Snow said, scaring the geese. She waved her arms, chasing the birds down the path to the water's edge.

"They can't fly," he explained. "Their wings are clipped."

"More cruelty," she said. "They die for their feathers? For quilts?"

"We kill them for food," Mike said. "My grandfather and aunt would starve if we didn't have the geese to sell."

"No one should starve," Snow said nobly. "But quilts!"

"I know how you feel," Mike said. "If we didn't need the money so badly, I'd never kill another goose."

"Stop the death. You have to stand on your principles."

"That's what I'm doing," Mike said. "Keeping the farm alive."

Suddenly he reminded Snow so much of his mother. His eyes were really beautiful, deep and full. Snow felt she could almost peer inside his soul. "You don't have to kill geese anymore," she said softly. She took a step toward him. "You can come home with us. When we leave on Sunday. There's room on the plane."

She could see by the way Mike looked away that he was very nervous. "I can't," he said, his voice nearly a croak. "I have things I have to do here."

"Oh," Snow said. And then they didn't talk any more until they heard Aunt Bess ringing the bell, telling them that Thanksgiving dinner was served.

THE main course was goose. It was roasted golden brown, its skin crackling. Sarah had made her mother's apple stuffing, and Will had mashed the potatoes. They had turnips and parsnips from the root cellar, and Bess had prepared prunes soaked in brandy and stuffed with goose liver.

"Isn't this a little swanky?" George asked, frowning at the spread. He seemed particularly upset by the candles, tall white tapers Bess had unearthed in one of her boxes from Providence.

"It's a holiday celebration, George," Bess said.

"I don't like candles. I like to see what I'm eating."

"The Pilgrims ate by candlelight. I think it's romantic," Snow said, and Sarah noticed Mike starting to blush.

"Will, come carve the goose," Bess called.

Everyone had changed into their best clothes. Her father wore gray flannels and a white shirt. Sarah watched him limp around the kitchen, knocking the fireplace tools over as he added another log to the fire.

"Damn it," he said, burning his hand as he pulled the poker out of the flames.

"Come here," Sarah said, pulling him over to the sink, turning on the faucet. Water, icy from the well, came gushing out, and she held her father's hand in the stream.

"Can't see a thing with those blasted candles," he said.

"Dad, it's only three o'clock. It's broad daylight. If it makes Aunt Bess happy to have candles, let her."

"It's hoity-toity," he grumbled. "Just to let the company know she used to live in grand style with old What's-his-name."

"Uncle Arthur."

"The executive. Blow those candles out, will you, Sarah?"

"Mom loved candlelight," Sarah said.

Her father's rough hand went suddenly slack. His whole body relaxed. "Yes, she did," he said.

"Especially around the holidays," Sarah said. "We always had candles for Thanksgiving, remember?"

"They had to be white," her father said. "Boats and candles, she always said, had to be white. I miss her every day."

"I know you do, Dad."

His anger was back, or something close to it. George Talbot peered into his daughter's eyes as if he wanted to catch her in a lie. "How's that sickness of yours?" he asked.

"It's fine."

"What d'you mean it's fine? It can't be fine. It's over or it's not. But it can't be fine."

"Dad, medicine has come a long way since Mom died," Sarah said. She had turned off the cold water, but she continued holding his hand. She noticed Mike across the room, looking over at her, listening intently. "I'm fine," she said again.

Her father waved his hand. "What a bunch of double-talk. Blow them candles out, Bess. I mean it. Now."

But the candles stayed lit. The families sat at the big table, in the seats they had claimed last night. Already it felt like a tradition. Will had been honored to be asked to carve the goose. He had thought that Snow would miss her mother, but he shouldn't have worried. She was lost in adolescent rapture for Mike Talbot, unable to take her eyes off him.

Will felt the same way about Sarah. She wore a long, beautiful green velvet dress that hugged her body perfectly. She took the seat across from him. Will had not felt anything close to all right for several Thanksgivings now, but he felt that way today. All right. Sitting near Sarah made him happy. She calmed him and excited him at the same time, in a way he couldn't remember feeling for a long time. He felt as though he'd known her forever and she knew him too.

"I'd like to say grace," Sarah said.

George slouched, a sullen look on his face, but everyone else folded their hands and bowed their heads.

"Bless us, O Lord," Sarah said. "Thank You for the food we are about to eat. Thank You for our health. Thank You for bringing us together on this island. Thank You for one another. Thank You for everyone we love, especially those who can't be with us."

"Fred," Snow whispered.

"Fred," Will repeated.

"Mom," Sarah said.

"Yep," George said. "My Rose."

"Arthur," Bess said.

"Can I say something?" Mike said.

"Of course, honey," Sarah said.

"Just this." Mike bowed his head even lower. "I'm thankful you're well. And you're here." He paused, then stared at her very hard. "Okay?"

"Okay," Will said because suddenly Sarah could not speak.

"Amen," they all said.

LATER, WHEN THE HOUSE WAS quiet and everyone had gone to bed, Sarah came down to sit by the fire in the kitchen. She felt too churned up to sleep. Staring at the glowing embers, she sat on the window seat.

"I thought I'd be the first one up and the last one to bed, but you have me beat," Will said, surprising her as he entered the room.

"Can't sleep?" she asked.

"I haven't tried yet," he said. Coming closer, she saw he was wearing his parka and boots, both dusted with snow. "A storm's starting. I was just outside."

"Get warm," Sarah said, sliding down the window seat.

Will slid off his boots and placed them by the door. He hung his jacket on the coatrack. "I keep interrupting your solitude," he said.

"That's good. I have enough of it in Fort Cromwell."

The snow had begun to fall. It blew against the windows, driven off the sea by the wind. Across the room, the dying fire crackled. "This is nice," Will said.

Sarah smiled. "I know. I'm glad you came in."

"No, I mean all of it. Thanksgiving with your family. Thank you for inviting us."

"You're welcome. I've been feeling guilty about bringing you all the way out here. Is there somewhere you usually go?"

Will paused. "Well, we used to have Thanksgiving with my parents. Alice and I lived in Newport, and they lived in Connecticut, so it was easy. Every year we'd drive down."

"Sounds wonderful," Sarah said, curious about Alice.

"It was. I miss them. My parents died within six months of each other, about five years ago."

"That's recent," Sarah said, looking over.

"It is. I feel it today," Will said. "My mother went first, a sudden heart attack one spring morning. My father just didn't want to live without her. He died in his sleep one night in September."

"My father didn't die after my mother did," Sarah said, "but he changed. He wasn't always so . . . hard," she said finally, trying to think of the right word.

Will nodded. They listened to the storm for a few minutes.

"Did Alice take over Thanksgiving after your mother died?"

Will shook his head. "Alice isn't much of a traditionalist," he said. "And by the time my mother died, so had Fred. Thanksgiving kind of faded away. We didn't last long afterward, Alice and I."

"I'm sorry," Sarah said.

"I believed in marriage," he said. "I thought it was supposed to carry people through. Ours just fell apart."

"Do you know why?" Sarah asked.

"I couldn't save Fred."

Sarah waited. The snow slanted against the windows. Could it be that simple? Could the end of an entire marriage really be condensed into those four terrible words?

"She was there too. She got to watch me not save her son."

"What happened?" Sarah asked.

"We were sailing, all four of us. The boom came across, and Fred didn't see. It hit him so hard, it— It would have knocked anyone over, and he just fell in."

"Oh, Will," Sarah said.

"He was such a great kid. He loved sports. Baseball, hockey. He was a great sailor, loved the water. Living in Newport, he got his feet wet every day. You know? He'd skip school to go fishing, and I couldn't even get mad. Whenever I was away, which was often, he'd look after his mother and sister."

"What a good son," Sarah said. She looked at the fire. She supposed Will was thinking about his marriage. What was Alice like? she wondered. She found herself feeling jealous of the ex-wife of a man she hardly knew, and she blushed. "I don't know much about marriage. You asked me this morning why I think Mike hates me. That's part of the reason. I didn't marry his father. I had Mike when I was very young."

"That bothers him? Lots of kids have parents who live apart."

"I know, but we were never together at all. Married, anyway." She cringed, remembering how hurt she had been, how she had cried her eyes out. Her father had stood across this very kitchen, waving a poker and threatening to kill Zeke. All these years later the shame was still damaging Mike. Wondering what Will thought of her, she looked over at him.

"I'm sorry," Will said.

Sarah shrugged, tried to smile. "Poor little kid," she said. "He didn't like it when I was away from him. I worked a lot, and . . . I was young. I had boyfriends. His friends had nice, stable homes, and he wanted that too."

Will was staring at her. He reached over and gently brushed his hand against her cheek. At the sound of footsteps on the stairs they both looked up. Mike walked into the kitchen.

"Hi," Sarah said, her heart rising at the sight of him.

Mike jumped. "Wow. You scared me," he said.

"Hi, Mike," Will said. "I'm keeping your mother company."

"Huh," Mike said, sounding sullen.

"What brings you downstairs, honey?" Sarah asked.

"Just checking the fire," he said. "I heard the wind start, and there's something banging down by the dock. I want to tie down the tarp better."

"I'll help you," Will said, rising.

"It's no big deal," Mike said flatly. "I can do it myself."

"I know you can," Will said, pulling on his boots. "But I'd like some air, if you don't mind company."

"Whatever you want," Mike said. He sounded indifferent, but he was staring at Will. Sarah's heart twisted.

"In the navy," Will said, "we always sent two out on deck, especially at night. In storms like this—always."

"There's nothing dangerous out there. What do you think? Something might fly out of the picking shack and attack us?"

This was so familiar to Sarah: the men she knew trying to be nice to Mike, him acting tough and rude, her right in the middle.

"Are you always such a jerk to your mother's friends?" Will asked.

Mike just stared. He seemed shocked by Will's words. For years he had mouthed off at men, and usually they had disappeared rather than talk back. "I wasn't mouthing off," he said, glancing at his mother.

"Don't worry about it," Will said. "I was in the navy a long time. I've heard people be rude before. You seem like you might grow out of it."

Mike didn't speak. Grabbing his gloves and a flashlight, he led Will out the back door.

Chapter 5

SNOW quilted Elk Island from the north cliffs to the bay. All the barn cats had come into the house seeking the warmth of the fireplace, and they lay curled in their secret places: on top of the bookcases, inside the piano. Gelsey, the ancient collie, lay at Aunt Bess's feet, right on the braided rug she was working on.

All these animals and so many feathers, and Snow hadn't had one allergy attack! She felt the peace and love of Elk Island taking over her body, and she imagined never leaving. She could live here forever. Lying on the sofa, reading by the fire, she watched the snow coming down and considered the logistics.

Her dad would stay with her. He and Sarah got along very well, so he'd have a friend his own age. Plus, he and George had their military days in common. Aunt Bess liked everyone. Sarah would be like a mother to Snow, a kind of maternal best friend and eventual mother-in-law. Snow was going to marry Mike.

Everyone was gathered around, waiting for the storm to pass. Mike lay across the room, stretched out on the floor with a pillow over his eyes. Snow watched him carefully, the way he flexed every muscle in his arms. Sarah and her dad sat at a card table by the window, their heads bent over a jigsaw puzzle. Her father whispered something, making Sarah laugh.

Had she ever seen her parents having so much fun? Snow racked her brain trying to remember. Silence, anger, unspoken accusations, and then *spoken* accusations. Those she recalled. Still, way back, when Fred was still with them, they had loved each other. Snow sighed, thinking of her mother.

Sarah glanced over, alert. "Are you okay?" she asked.

"Mmm," Snow said, smiling back.

"Bored?" Sarah asked.

"Not at *all,*" Snow replied. Did Sarah know how wonderful this was, being snowbound on an island with people who cared about her? Snuggled under a scratchy plaid blanket, surrounded by mangy cats, Snow wondered if Sarah knew that she was the center of everything, the person who had brought everyone together. She was Mike's mom, George's daughter, Bess's niece, Snow and her father's friend. It seemed like such a generous existence, regardless of the goose killing.

Thinking of her mother all wrapped up in Julian and their self-ish life made Snow feel sad. She shrunk inward, and for the first time since coming to the island, she started wheezing.

"Why don't you try calling your mother?" Sarah asked quietly, as if she could read Snow's mind. How had she done that?

"It's a good idea, honey," her father said.

"The phone's in the hall," Sarah said.

"I'll show you," Mike said, easing himself off the floor.

She smiled at him, her brown hair falling across her eyes, hoping she looked alluring and mysterious. "You will?" she asked, her voice low and miraculously wheeze free.

WHEN the main snow stopped, the sky stayed white, and flurries continued to fall. Housebound for too long, everyone but George and Bess put on warm clothes and went out for a walk.

The mudroom contained snowshoes and cross-country skis, but not enough pairs of either to go around. The men strapped on snowshoes while Sarah and Snow took the skis. They all pushed off, aiming for the trail that would lead them to Great South Head. Sarah felt overjoyed to be outside and moving. She gave Dr. Goodacre a passing thought, telling herself she would stop if she got tired.

Mike led the way. He and Will made snowshoeing look effortless, which it was not. Will walked beside her, never letting her get too far ahead. Forging along through unmarked snow, they crossed a wide field, mounted a headland with the pine forest on their left and a rickety rail fence on their right, and the trail became narrow. The land rose gradually.

The old fence needed mending, and at certain spots it had broken down. The cliff dropped one hundred feet to the sea. Sarah shielded Snow, shouldering her closer to the trees. She was almost afraid to look at her fearless son, who was racing ahead, uphill. Suddenly he stopped.

"Hey, Mom," Mike said. Waiting for her to catch up, he pointed at the sky. "There he is."

"Who?" Snow asked.

Circling overhead was a bald eagle. He lived in the cliffs at the far end of the island, but he had come down to fish the bay.

Sarah stood beside Mike, catching her breath. "Oh, Mike! Do you remember?" Sarah asked. Her body ached from exertion, and her chest hurt with each deep breath.

Mike knew what she meant. "When we first saw him? Yeah."

He had been just a boy. They'd spent a whole amazing week lobstering and eagle watching. "It can't be the same guy," she said.

"Eagles live a long time," Mike said. "He's always been missing a few pinions. See?"

The long, fingerlike feathers at the ends of his wings. Mike was right; Sarah could see a wide space. She nodded, gulping for air. "I am out of . . . shape," she said.

"You're doing great, Mom," he said.

"I am?" she asked, loving his praise.

"Yeah," he said. "A mile in the snow? Better than great. Did you and Dad ever ski? Or snowshoe?"

Sarah shook her head. "No. He was always lobstering."

"Everyone here remembers him," Mike said.

"It's a small island," Sarah said carefully.

"Why do you always put him down?" Mike asked hotly.

"Mike, I'm sorry," she said quickly.

Suddenly Snow squealed. Pointing her ski pole seaward, she began to jump up and down. Gazing out, Sarah saw the wide, dark bay. The only movement was a series of large concentric rings rumbling outward from an earthquakelike epicenter.

Sarah and Mike glanced at each other, old Maine hands, knowing exactly what they were seeing. The whale came clear out of the sea. Its sleek, gigantic body launched skyward and landed with a violent splash.

"Oh!" Snow yelled. "What is it?"

"It's a humpback whale," Will said, a big smile on his face.

"How can you tell?" Snow asked.

"The white flukes," Mike said. "Those long white fins."

"Angel wings," Snow said. "That's what those white things looked like to me."

"Angel wings," Sarah said. She stood back, watching the three of them stare at the sea for a whale who had disappeared.

"My father set his pots in there," Mike said, pointing at the bay.

Mike had never seen them, so someone must have told him, Sarah thought.

"Elk Island lobstermen only go out in winter," he said.

"They must be tough," Will said.

Mike eyes narrowed. "The toughest lobstermen in Maine."

AT THE top of Great South Head they turned inland. Will and Sarah hung back, letting the kids lead. Sarah seemed tired. "Do you want to rest?" Will asked.

She shook her head. Her cheeks were pink, her eyes bright. She looked amazing in her black stretch pants, a bulky red sweater patterned with snowflakes, and a black headband around her short white hair. Her eyes were big and dark. "I'm fine," she said.

"So am I," he said, smiling.

She nodded. "You and my son have called a truce," she said. "Thanks for what you said about Elk Island lobstermen."

"I meant it."

"He was really off-base last night."

"He's protecting you, that's all." The bad manners of a seventeen-year-old meant nothing to Will. All he could think of was Sarah. He was glad the kids had gone on ahead.

He and Sarah kept on. At first they could hear the kids' voices, but after several minutes the forest was still. They came to a fallen tree, and Will dusted off a patch of snow. They sat down. Sarah closed her eyes and let out one long cloud of breath.

Will gazed at her. "Do you always arrange to have eagles and whales show up?"

"Only for you," she said.

Will took her ski poles. He laid them beside the log. Sarah seemed to smile, as if she knew what he was going to do. Which was odd, because Will hadn't known himself.

He slid his arms around her. He kissed her. She felt so small, as delicate as a child, but her embrace was so strong he felt her heart beating through her thick sweater.

They smiled at each other, leaning back a little, still holding tight. He kissed her again, reaching up to hold her head. His fingers found a long, hard scar under her hair. His heart jolted, but she didn't flinch. She was kissing him with all her heart. He drew her against him.

"This is very interesting," she said after a minute. She had her hands pressed against his cheeks. She spoke with humor, but there was great seriousness as well. "They asked me who you were, what you were doing here with me, my father and my son, and I told them with total honesty that you were my pilot. And also my friend."

"Definitely your friend," Will said.

"But oh," Sarah said. "Will."

"More than friends?" he asked.

"Don't you think so?"

A scream shattered the peace. It was Snow, far off, crying for help. On their feet, Will and Sarah ran and skied as fast as they could.

THE kids were a quarter mile ahead. Will followed the tracks; Sarah skied behind. They emerged from the woods into a white field spreading across the island. Snow stood alone at the edge of a sunken circle covered with snow. Will could tell it was a pond.

"Mike went through the ice!" Snow cried.

Will doubled his strides. He was unstrapping his snowshoes even before he reached his daughter. She was hysterical, her eyes panicked. She stared at Sarah with horror. "I told him not to go!"

Sarah grabbed her hand. "When? How long?"

Will didn't hear the answer. Untying his boots, he kicked them off. He dropped his parka on the snow. Throwing his heavy sweater aside, leaving only his jeans and T-shirt as protection against the frigid water, Commander William Burke, rescue swimmer for the United States Navy, dived into the hole in the ice.

FOR exactly ten seconds Mike thought it was funny. Trying to show off, clear the ice so Snow could slide around on her skis, he had gone crashing into the pond. He had expected it to be frozen solid. He sank and sank. The water was unbelievably cold. His heart seemed to stop. Landing on the bottom, he tried to swim up, but his snowshoes were anchoring him down. Within ten seconds his lungs were about to explode.

SARAH ran back and forth along the pond's edge. "How long, Snow?"

"A minute, Sarah. I think about a minute."

Sarah eased out on the ice. It held firm under her feet. She inched out more. The ice creaked, and she stepped back.

"A branch," Snow yelled. "They can grab it!"

Sarah and Snow ran to the closest pile of fallen timber. Sarah grabbed the fat end of a long oak branch, and they used all their might to drag it free.

Sarah stepped back onto the ice. It creaked, but it didn't give way. "Slide it out," she said. Snow gave the branch a shove. "More! Hurry," Sarah commanded, wild inside.

Snow pushed the crooked branch hard, hitting Sarah's boot. As Sarah hopped over it, the ice cracked. The sound was loud, like fabric tearing, and Sarah went straight through. Standing in water to her knees, she heard a groan of agony: her own voice.

"I'm sorry. I'm sorry." Snow wept.

Slogging onto land, Sarah wanted to scream her guts out. Snow grabbed her. The child was shaking violently, and Sarah found herself stroking her back. "Shhh," Sarah said, trembling. They clung to each other, staring at the hole in the ice. "Do you pray, Snow? Pray now!"

"I'm too scared. I don't know what to say."

"But you do," Sarah said. "You just think you don't."

Sarah stared at the black hole as if her gaze alone could pull her son and Will from the ice. "Please pray," she whispered. "Please."

"Oh, Freddie," Snow said.

How long could a man survive underwater in such freezing temperatures? How long could two? Holding the girl, Sarah closed her eyes and thought of her brain tumor. She had prayed to live, and God had seen fit to let it be so. She had been given so much in her life—why not this one other thing? Why not Mike? Standing by the pond, Sarah knew she would take back her sickness if Will could just save Mike.

Sarah would trade her life for Mike's in one instant. She knew it had to be so. God couldn't take her beautiful child.

Snow sobbed beside her, melting into her arms.

"It's okay, Snow," Sarah whispered.

"No," Snow said. "It's been too long."

"Wait," Sarah said.

The black water rippled, and the surface parted. Gulping for air, the humans sounded more massive than whales. One head emerged, then the other. Will had Mike in a lifesaving tow hold. He sidestroked to the edge of the pond, breaking the ice with his fist.

"Dad," Snow yelled. "Oh, Dad!"

Wet, dripping, their hair already turning to ice, Will and Mike lay on the snowy ground. Mike threw up pond water, choking for air. Will pulled him higher onto safer ground while Snow struggled to get the snowshoes off his limp feet.

"I saved him," Will said, looking into Sarah's eyes.

Sarah crouched to kiss first her son, then Will Burke.

"I saved him for you," Will said, tears pouring from his eyes.

"I know you did," Sarah said, her eyes warm with joy and unending gratitude and something that felt like love. "I'll never forget it."

Back at the house Aunt Bess made hot chocolate, and George dragged heavy blankets into the kitchen. Mike lay as close to the fire as they could get him. Snow sat by his feet.

"We've got to take him to a hospital," Sarah said.

"What hospital?" George snapped. "The ferry ride would freeze him even worse."

Sarah sat beside Mike, rubbing his ice-cold hands. Will stood beside her. Even though he was half frozen himself, he wouldn't lie down, wouldn't leave her side. On the way home they had had to just about carry Mike. He had almost lost consciousness by the time Will got to him. Flailing his arms as he tried to swim to the surface, he'd socked Will in the eye.

"I'll fly him," Will said, trying to keep his teeth from chattering.

George threw him a blanket. "You're in no condition to do anything but dry off and warm up."

"Not those old scratchy blankets," Aunt Bess wailed. "Get them some nice soft quilts."

"Shush, Bess." George tucked blankets around Mike. "We need big, weighty wool right now to hold the heat in and force it into the bones. There, boy. How's that?"

"Good, Grandpa," Mike tried to say.

"Sweetheart," Sarah said. "I was so—"

"Mom," Mike said, shaking his head. "Come on, okay?"

"Let the boy warm up," George said more gently than he usually spoke to Sarah. "Why don't you tend to Will?"

"No, I . . ." Sarah couldn't finish her own sentence.

She felt Will's hands on her shoulders. Pulling her slightly, he eased her to her feet. "He'll be fine," Will said.

"Thank you," Sarah said. "I mean it. Thank you."

"You're welcome," Will said.

"Your lips are blue," she said.

He nodded, a great shiver running through his body.

Sarah reached down for a blanket. Standing on tiptoe, she wrapped it around Will's shoulders over the one her father had just thrown him. He smiled. "Better?" she asked.

"Much," he said.

Her father, Snow, and Bess were huddled around Mike, checking his color, rubbing his hands and feet. Sarah glanced over, but Will reached out to take her hands.

"You have a black eye," she said.

"You should see the other guy," he said.

Sarah tried to laugh, but Will held her hands a little tighter. She took a step closer. Her face was tilted up, looking straight into his eyes. The whole family was at their feet, but she felt as if she were alone with him. She heard her father telling a joke, Mike laughing.

Will didn't say anything. He just slid his arms around her. The wool blankets felt scratchy against her cheek. They were outside blankets—for picnics, boat rides, stargazing. How many times had she lain on them with Mike when he was a baby?

The memories were sweet and strong, and they made her cry. Will held her, letting her sob silently in his arms.

WHEN Mike was out of danger, they moved him upstairs. Aunt Bess finally got her way, putting the men to bed and covering them to the nose with down quilts. That was okay with Will. He lay on his back, letting massive shivers pass through his body.

"Dad, you look like you're possessed," Snow said. "Your body's shaking like crazy."

"That's how it warms up," he said, feeling another tremor run down his back. "I'll be fine. Why don't you check on Mike?"

Will felt guilty for wanting to get rid of his daughter, but Sarah was standing in the doorway right behind her. Sarah smiled in a way Will had never seen before. "Why don't you, Snow?" she said, stepping forward. "I know he'd like to see you."

Snow looked over her shoulder with complete affection in her eyes. "Hi, Sarah," she said. "Forgive me?"

"For what?"

"For luring Mike to the pond. For having that stupid idea about the branch. I don't know!"

Sarah shook her head. "Mike's falling in had nothing to do with you, and the branch wasn't stupid. Go see him."

Kissing her father, Snow started out the door. She paused, kissed Sarah, then kept going.

"Wow," Sarah said. "That was nice. I have to threaten Mike to get him to kiss me. Or bribe him. Come to think of it, neither has worked for years. I'm sorry I lost it downstairs."

"You didn't lose it," Will said.

"Crying like a lunatic," she said. "Considering how happy I was. Am. You know."

"I know." He smiled, reaching for her hand.

"I mean, you saved his life. It was unbelievable," Sarah said. "You're my hero."

"I'm no hero," he said.

"You have no say in the matter."

"I'm an old navy guy," Will said. "I had no choice doing anything different." But he was thinking, This time it worked.

Pulling Mike to the surface of the pond, he had known he was alive the whole time. The kid had fought him tooth and nail, boxing in the desperate manner of all drowning men. Dragging Mike to shore, Will's heart had been full of Fred. Lying in the soft, warm bed, he closed his eyes and pictured his son.

LESS than five minutes after entering Mike's room, Snow watched old George just push out of his chair and walk down the hall. He didn't even say good-bye.

"How come your grandfather left like that?" she asked.

"Guess he had something to do," Mike said.

"You're at my mercy," Snow said, sitting at the end of his bed. "I'm going to torture you."

"How?" he asked, sounding intrigued.

She didn't really have an answer for him. She was just so happy to be sitting there watching the blood come back to his cheeks, feeling his feet move under the quilts. "Were you scared?" she asked.

"No," he said.

"Did you think you were going to make it?"

"Not in the last minute." He paused. "Your dad was pretty cool. Pilot, ice diver . . . What else does he do?"

"He could have been a secret agent," Snow said, "if he hadn't left the navy."

"Why'd he leave?"

"Oh," Snow said. "Because of Fred."

"I kind of wondered who Fred was," Mike said. "You mentioned his name during grace."

"He was my brother, and he drowned," Snow said. "I was with him when it happened."

"I'm sorry," Mike said. "Was it cold, like today?"

"Oh, no. It wasn't winter," Snow said, picturing the bright September day just outside of Newport harbor.

"Couldn't he swim?"

"He was a great swimmer," Snow said. "We were sailing—my parents, Fred, and I. A storm blew up, and we were heading back to port, and my dad let Fred take the helm. A big gust came along, and we jibed. The boom swung across, and everyone except Fred ducked. It hit him right in the head and knocked him overboard."

"Snow, that's terrible," Mike said.

"My father swam and swam, and my mother and I stood up, trying to see where Fred had gone, but we couldn't. Two days went by before he . . . washed up. My father just about died. I mean it." Snow's voice was hollow. She could still hear her father wailing behind his study door when they came to tell him. "My dad's a rescue swimmer, so you can imagine what it did to him."

"Yeah," Mike said, the reality dawning in his eyes.

"And you can probably imagine how incredible it was for him to pull you out today."

"Nothing could make up for your brother."

"No," Snow said.

"Fred Burke?" Mike said, asking his full name.

Snow wiped the tears out of her eyes and nodded. "Fred Burke," she said.

ON SATURDAY morning everyone had breakfast, then went off to do their own things. Will and George took the Jeep across the island to make sure the storm didn't do any damage to the plane.

Mike went out to one of the sheds, and after a while Sarah went after him.

She sat on a tall crate, watching him take an old lobster boat engine apart. He had installed a woodstove, and he had the old shed very warm. Sarah arched backward, trying to get comfortable. She had woken up with an ache in her lower back.

The lapstrake boat took up most of the space. Dressed in navy-blue work clothes, Mike was covered with grease from head to toe. Frowning as he worked, he reminded Sarah so much of his father that she blinked hard to shake the vision.

"Are you sure you're warm enough?" she asked.

"Mom," he said warningly.

"Well, sorry. It's not every day my son falls through the ice." The conversation stalled, but Mike didn't seem to notice. "You like old lobster boats," she said. "Like your father."

Mike nodded. He didn't say anything.

"Is he the reason you came out here?" she asked.

Mike shrugged.

"I'd rather think that than what I've been thinking all along."

"What's that?" he asked.

"That you hate me."

He exhaled impatiently. Reaching for a wrench, he knocked over a whole tray of lug nuts. Crouching down, he began to locate the nuts with his right hand, place them in his left.

"Mike?"

"I don't hate you, Mom."

"Then why'd you run away?"

"I didn't run away."

"You did! You quit school just like that, walked out of our house with your backpack, and started hitchhiking."

"I wasn't running away," he said. "I was *coming* here."

"Because of your father?"

"He's dead," Mike said. "Why would it be because of him?"

"To find out where he was from?" Sarah asked.

"I don't know," Mike said. "I've found out a lot. But you can tell me more."

Sarah nodded. Ezekiel Loring had been the sun, the moon, and the stars to her for a hundred days. She had counted them one time, from their first date in the spring of her freshman year in college until the day he wrapped his truck around an oak on Birdsong Road.

"Zeke could fix anything," she said. "He was funny, irreverent, smart. He was a beautiful boy. I know I should say handsome, but that doesn't do justice . . . He was beautiful, Mike. Like you."

"Huh."

"We'd known each other forever, but we met again one night in April. I was home for school break, walking along the bay. There was a half-moon, and I was staring at it. I remember hearing an engine. It was Zeke on his motorcycle. He pulled over, and I got on. Just like that. He drove me all over the island, looking at the moon."

"Yeah?" Mike said.

"Did you find his little house? Over by the Hollow, in from his parents' farm? I showed you once when you were young."

"I remember," Mike said. "It's just a little fishing shack, abandoned now. Weeds growing inside."

"Really?" Sarah asked, surprised by how that made her feel sad. "I loved it there. We fixed it up. Mike, we loved each other. We fought like crazy, but we wanted to be together."

"Was that where we were going to live after I was born?"

"I wanted him to come back to Boston with me. I was starting the shop, you know? He wasn't making much of a living out here, but he loved it. I guess it's why he stood me up. We hadn't done a very good job of talking things through." Sarah spoke mildly, as if to counteract the devastation of that last day, being left at the church. She had wanted to take her island lobsterman and fix his life. She remembered all the plans and dreams.

"He wanted to stay here instead of moving to Boston?"

"Instead of marrying me, I think."

"I don't get it."

"We were too young to get married, Mike," Sarah said gently. "But we had you coming."

"He knew about me?" Mike asked, looking scared.

Was he afraid of hearing the answer? That Zeke had known he

was going to be a father and abandoned them anyway. That he had died in a road accident while he was with another woman.

"That I was pregnant, yes. But he didn't know about you, honey. If he'd known you, it would have been different," Sarah said, lying now, unable to stand the hurt in Mike's voice. She doubted that any baby could have induced Zeke to stay. He was on a wild ride, and a wife and child weren't invited along.

"Life would have been better if he'd been with us," Mike said. "We could have been happy together."

"It didn't happen that way," Sarah said sharply. "Your father had other plans."

"You're the one who wanted to leave the island!"

"He wouldn't have stayed anyway. He wasn't ready to marry me."

"We could ask him, Mom," Mike said, turning back to the engine. "But he's dead. I saw his grave."

Sarah sat still. Her son's shoulders were so stiff, his voice so hard. He was banging on the engine as if he wanted to demolish it. Pain shot through her own back, making her flinch. "I'm sorry, honey," she said softly.

"In the churchyard. Have you ever seen it?"

"I've seen it," Sarah said.

"That's where you're going to be buried, isn't it?"

"Yes." Sarah had never seen Mike this upset before.

"Mom," Mike said dropping his hands to the workbench. "Why'd you get sick?"

Sarah stood and walked around the broken-down old boat. Mike was crying now, trying to hide it. "Mike," she whispered, putting her arm around him.

"Are you better?" he asked. "Because Grandpa says you're not."

"I am! Look at me. I'm here, aren't I?"

"That doesn't mean anything."

"Look at me," she said, holding his face between her hands. His cheeks were streaked with tears and grease. "Yeah?"

"Platinum blond," she said.

"Is that supposed to be a joke?" he exploded.

"No, Mike. I was just—"

"You don't know me at all," he said. "You never have. You think bringing some turkey around is gonna make up for not having a father, and you think joking about your hair is gonna make me forget you have cancer!"

She shook her head. "I don't—"

"Say what you want, but you do," he said. "You do."

"I want to talk to you. More than anything," Sarah said, breathless. "I want our relationship to be better. I want you to come home, finish school. If you had any idea how much—"

"I'm staying, Mom," Mike said flatly.

"I'm only asking you to think about it," she said.

"I'm staying," he said.

WILL and Sarah's father had been out brushing snow off the plane. When they walked through the back door, Sarah met them in the hall. Feeling upset about Mike, she tried to sound upbeat. "Aunt Bess says she and Snow have planned a celebration for tonight," she said. "She sent over to Hillyer Crawford's for some lobsters, but Hillyer is too busy to drive the lobsters over. Can I take the Jeep to pick them up?"

"The brakes are spongy," her father said doubtfully. "Mike hasn't had the chance to put the new pads on yet."

Sarah smiled. "I'll be careful," she said.

"I'll go with you," Will said.

"You drive, Will," her father ordered. "She'll show you the way."

"Okay," Sarah said. She and her father had so many battles, this one hardly counted.

Moments later Will backed the Jeep out of the driveway. Several geese had gotten out of the barn. Waddling around, they were right in the way. Sarah rolled down her window to wave her arms. The pain in her back shot down her leg. "Aah," she said, seeing stars.

"What's wrong?" Will asked.

Straightening out, she felt the pain go away. "Nothing."

"That was a loud yell for nothing," he said.

"I might have a pinched nerve," she said. "Or maybe it's tension. I had a fight with Mike."

"What was the fight about?"

"Me." She smiled so he wouldn't see how hurt she was.

She directed Will north along the single-track road that bisected the island. Sarah pointed out the Island School, where she had gone through twelfth grade; the best places to pick blueberries; the road leading down to Kestral Point, where all the big summerhouses were and Zeke's summer girl had lived. They bounced down Harbor Road to the Lobster Wharf and bought a crate of two-pounders from Hillyer, with some clams thrown in.

"Show me somewhere else," Will said. "I want to know all the important places."

"Let's go visit my mother," Sarah said.

"Which way?" Will asked, and Sarah pointed east.

They passed the northern cliffs that housed the bald eagles. Sarah told him to turn left onto a narrow track that meandered through a forest of tall oaks, their branches interlocking overhead.

They emerged at the edge of the Atlantic Ocean. A stone chapel stood alone, surrounded by snowy fields. Beside it, enclosed by a wrought-iron fence, was a small graveyard. Will parked the car, and they walked through the snow.

The chapel was dark stone, small and medieval. Its sturdy steeple held a stone cross attached to the slate roof by strong wires to withstand the Atlantic winds. Three granite steps led to an arched wooden door. Someone had hung a fir wreath decorated with silver bayberries and a purple ribbon.

"My father was here," Sarah said, her eyes bright.

"George hung the wreath?"

"He puts one up every year, the day after Thanksgiving. My mother loved Christmas. He does it for her."

Will lifted the latch, letting the iron gate clank behind them. The wind whipped off the sea, blowing salt spray and loose snow. Sarah knelt by her mother's grave. She looked so beautiful, lost in memories and prayer. The monument was intricately carved, with a small angel flying over the sea, the name Rose Talbot chiseled over the dates of her birth and death. "Mom, I miss you," Sarah whispered. "I miss you very much."

The wind blew hard, bringing tears to their eyes and turning Sarah's cheeks pink. Will wrapped his arms around her, pulled her to her feet. "It's cold," he said. "I want to get you warm."

"Should we go inside? I know where to find the key."

Sarah unlocked the heavy door. Inside, the old church was dark and musty. Six rows of carved oak benches filled the space. The stained-glass windows were dark blue and wine, depicting saints and boats. A plain wooden cross stood behind the altar. Sarah looked around. She walked over to a pew, ran her fingers along the oak. The expression in her eyes was angry and confused.

"What's wrong?" Will asked.

"I don't know," she said. "Twenty years apart, Mike and I were baptized right there." She pointed to the marble baptismal font. It was shaped like a clamshell. "I was nearly married here too."

"To the lobsterman?" Will asked.

"He didn't show up," Sarah said. "He didn't want me."

"He was an idiot."

Sarah shrugged. "He's buried outside," she said softly. "I know he's the reason Mike came out to the island."

"Mike's a good kid," Will said. "He's going to be fine."

"He is, but he doesn't believe it yet. He came all the way out here to learn the ways of a dead man. Island life, it's so crazy. . . . There's no future. I want him to come home with us."

"Let him be," Will said, holding her. "That's all you can do."

"I tell myself that, but how?" she asked. "I'm his mother."

Sarah sobbed in his arms, and Will stroked her hair, thinking of Fred. How did you let your child go? Alive or dead, it was impossible. But Will had learned the secret: You don't really have a choice. They don't belong to you, your children. They are entrusted to you for a short time. You do your best.

"You love him from wherever you are," Will said. "You know that already."

"I do?"

"Look at you and your mother," Will said.

"I love her from where I am," Sarah said, sniffling.

"You already know how to do it as a daughter." He smiled, wiping her tears. "Now you just have to do it as a mother." Walking her back down the aisle, Will stopped at the door. He gazed into her eyes. Then he kissed the woman who had never been a bride. Pushing open the door, they stepped outside into the cold wind.

SNOW called her mother in Fort Cromwell, but she got the answering machine instead. She heard Julian's ask-me-if-I-do-voice-overs voice: "Alice and I are out dashing through the snow, or *very* possibly watching the car win at Monza, so please do us the kindness of leaving your message."

"Hi, Mom, it's me," Snow said. "We're still on Elk Island, flying home tomorrow. Don't worry about picking me up. I'll just get Dad to drive me, so you don't have to. Love you. Bye."

Hanging up the hall phone, Snow had a terrible feeling that something was wrong. Why hadn't her mother answered? Snow had the feeling she was terribly mad and hurt.

Dialing her number one more time, she prayed for her mother to answer.

"Hello?" her mother said. "Susan, is that you?"

"Yes. Hi, Mom. I've been calling you. I haven't talked to you since I called from Portsmouth airport, remember?"

"I remember," her mother said dryly.

"How've you been? How was Thanksgiving?"

"We've been fine. Julian has a little cold." Alice paused. "How was *your* Thanksgiving?"

"It was okay," Snow said, toning it down. She didn't want to tell her mother how wonderful it had been.

"I'm glad," her mother said, and Snow could practically see her lips disappearing into a tight, tight line.

"What's wrong?" Snow asked.

"It's just . . . It's just . . . That was our first holiday *apart*," her mother said, bursting into tears, "since you were a baby."

"I'm sorry, Mom," Snow whispered. Suddenly she heard Julian's voice in the background. "What's wrong?" Snow asked.

"Nothing," her mother said, and now it seemed to Snow that her words were colored by Julian's presence, as if she was putting on a certain kind of show for him. "Except I'm disappointed in the way you chose to do this. If you had asked permission properly, some arrangements could have been made. As it is, I'm very disappointed."

"I know," Snow said, catching sight of Mike at the other end of the hall. "Mom, I'm sorry."

"There will be consequences," her mother said ominously. "Now hold the line. Julian wants to say happy Thanksgiving."

"I have to go, Mom," Snow said quickly. "Someone has to use the phone. Love you. Bye." She placed the phone in the cradle as if it were burning her hand.

"I wasn't waiting to use the phone," Mike said apologetically.

"Oh, I know," Snow said. "It was just a white lie so I wouldn't have to talk to my stepfather."

"You've got a stepfather?" Mike asked.

Snow nodded, feeling miserable. "I hate him," she whispered. "I shouldn't hate anyone, I know, but I do—"

"Sometimes you can't help it."

"If I had an island to run away to, I would. Like you."

"You're here," Mike said. "Aren't you?"

Trying to smile, Snow let Mike lead her down the hallway. They walked up the back stairs. Dark and dusty, every stair tread held a sleeping cat. They came to a closed door. Mike opened it, and they were in the attic. The open space was filled with old beds, trunks, and boxes. At the far end, blankets hung from lengths of fishing line.

Mike let Snow enter first. "It's so cozy," she said.

"Yeah," he said, pleased.

A space heater threw plenty of heat. He had covered an old mattress with down quilts. Three shelves were filled with books. A small window overlooked the front, the fields leading down to the bay. "What's this for?" Snow asked.

"It's where I come to get away."

"Your island on the island?" she asked.

He nodded. He leaned his forehead against the windowpane, scanning the yard. His grandfather was standing outside the picking shed, warming his hands over a brazier.

"Why'd you run away?" Snow asked.

"I keep telling everyone I didn't run away," he said. "I wanted to come here. It's where my family's from, you know? Both my parents. I didn't know my father, though."

Snow nodded. Standing there in his secret island room, she thought of them as two kids who had been through a lot. He had never met his father; his mother had raised him alone. Snow's parents had gotten a terrible divorce; her mother had married a jerk. And then there was Fred's death, Sarah's illness. Reeling from just thinking about it all, Snow flopped down on the mattress. "How do normal kids do it? Don't they get bored?" she asked.

"What do you mean?"

"You and I could keep two shrinks working overtime for the next ten years."

He laughed. "Did they ever send you to a shrink?"

"Of course. Right after Fred drowned, then again during the divorce. Did Sarah send you?"

"She tried, but I hardly ever went."

"You asked if they *sent* me." Snow corrected him. "I didn't say I *went*. Well, I did go some of the time, but I had the faux flu a lot. I faked being sick." She gave him a sample of a phony coughing fit. "Was yours a psychiatrist?"

"Yeah. Dr. Darrow, and he'd just sit there with this—"

"Dr. Darrow?" Snow asked. "You went to Dr. Darrow? Tall guy? Stickpin under his tie? Never says a word?"

"All his diplomas right behind his desk so you can't miss noticing he went to Princeton and Cornell?"

"Pictures of him and his wife on vacation in the Bahamas with their perfect twin sons?"

"Yeah. Everyone smiling, so you can't help noticing how happy the Darrows look compared to your family." Mike laughed. "I can't believe you went to Dr. Darrow."

"Why'd Sarah send you in the first place?" Snow asked.

"I had a problem with school."

"Your grades?" Snow asked.

"No," Mike said. "Going."

"At all," Snow said, cracking up. "I hear you."

They leaned back, laughing till their sides hurt. Shoulders bumping, they were lost in the hilarity of being fellow patients of the silentest psychiatrist in Fort Cromwell.

GEORGE stood in the basement kitchen waiting for Sarah to get the crate of lobsters open. She was such a beauty, just like her mother. Sarah's face could stop a man's heart.

Her hair was another story. George had remembered it long and dark, full of luster, but here it was, too bright and sticking up every which way. Understanding that Sarah's hair had something to do with her cancer treatment, he had said nothing. Rose had never got far enough to lose hers. The cancer had taken her quick.

Finally Sarah had the crate opened. George pulled out one at random. "Darn Hillyer," he muttered. "He knows she-lobsters have the sweetest meat. Figures he'd send males."

"I don't think he did it on purpose," Sarah said.

"Bet he did." He hated being taken advantage of. His heart was pounding, and he tapped his chest and sat down.

"You get yourself so upset," Sarah said. She quietly began taking his pulse.

George felt like slapping her fingers away, but he didn't have the oomph. With his daughter now sitting right beside him, he got a good look at her eyes. They were so deep and blue, but they were surrounded by fine lines. His baby had been mighty sick. The signs were right there. "Why don't you come home where you belong?" he asked.

"I have a business to run, Dad."

"Business. What's business compared to your family?"

"I'm here, Dad," she said. "Aren't I?"

He scowled. "You'd be better off staying. You got Mike to think of. He seems happy here, you know." He patted his pockets, looking for his pipe. He didn't have an inkling about talking to a daughter, never had. "Stay," he said, keeping it basic.

"I can't. And I want Mike to come home with me."

George stared at her. He had expected as much. His heart

banged around a bit but not as bad as before. "You look like your mother," he blurted out.

"I do?" she asked.

George nodded. He reached over, touched her cheek. Her skin was so creamy soft. She had been born in this very house, right upstairs. George had boiled the water himself at the stove behind him. He had held her in one hand; she was hardly as big as a small goose. Their eyes had met, and that was that.

He colored, caught dreaming about the past. How happy they had been, the three of them. George, Rose, and Sarah. This was their island. "Do you have happy memories?" he made himself ask.

"Oh, Dad," she said, smiling. "The best."

"You do?"

She nodded. Putting her arms around him, she rested her head on his shoulder. She had done that so many times as a little girl. In the Jeep, driving around the island, in the boat going out fishing. He felt a big lump in his throat and couldn't swallow past it.

THE sun began to set. It was Saturday, their last full day on Elk Island, and Sarah stood at the kitchen window watching the violet shadows lengthen on the snowy field sloping to the bay. She saw her father limping through the yard with Gelsey, waving his arms to herd the geese into the barn. Gelsey barked, hobbling just like her master. The geese waddled ahead, honking loudly.

Slowly Sarah walked up the kitchen stairs. The house was quiet. Aunt Bess was taking her afternoon nap, and the kids were up in the attic. Sarah could hear music playing, the sounds of Mike and Snow laughing. Feeling clandestine, she knocked on Will's door.

"Come in," he called.

Sarah slipped inside, letting the door close softly behind her. The room was dark, the only light coming from windows overlooking the sea. Will lay on the bed. Perhaps he had been reading, fallen asleep. A book lay open beside him. "Everything okay?" he asked.

Nodding, she stood by the side of the bed.

Will moved over. He held his arm out, and Sarah lay down beside him. He wrapped her in his arms.

"You know what's amazing?" he asked, stroking her back.

"What?" she whispered.

"I was hoping you'd come up."

"You were? I feel funny sneaking into your room."

"I know," he said, squeezing her. "We're acting more like kids than the kids." He kissed her forehead, her cheeks. "How much time do we have before dinner?"

"Hours," she said. "At least two."

He pulled her sweater over her head, and she unbuttoned his chamois shirt. They fumbled with each other's clothes, slid under the quilt. The bed was warm, heated through by Will's body. Sarah felt his fingers tracing her back. They kissed.

Will's hands moved up toward Sarah's shoulders, and then they found the scar. Sarah froze the minute he touched it. Her eyes opened wide, and she felt ashamed. "Just pretend it's not there."

"If it's part of you, it's beautiful."

She shook her head. No one but doctors and nurses had seen Sarah's scars. During radiation treatments she had developed an infection in her scalp. It had spread to her skull, turned into osteomyelitis. Dr. Goodacre had had to debride the bone, remove a portion of her skull. He had to make a large incision to get to the skull and supply a blood source from her back. And although she had had plastic surgery, the scars on her back remained.

"Show me," he said. "You can, Sarah."

Sarah reached past him. She pulled the cord, turning on the bed-side lamp. Holding her with one arm, Will leaned back to look. She could feel him draw a breath. "Oh, Sarah," he said.

It was horrible. Bowing his face, he kissed her back, her shoulders, the side of her neck. His face was wet with tears, and she tasted them as she met his lips. "It's awful, isn't it?" she asked.

"It saved your life, didn't it? Then it's beautiful. Just as I said." He caressed her body, letting her know that he loved her. She felt it in his hands. They touched her as if she were precious, as if it were his responsibility to see that she was never hurt again.

Sarah felt herself letting go bit by bit. She had been so betrayed by Zeke she had never really trusted anyone since.

Placing his lips against her ear, Will whispered, "Stay with me, Sarah."

That was all she needed to hear. She and Will were in it together, loving each other with their hearts and souls and bodies; it was all the same thing, Sarah understood now, the great link of two spirits in love, finding each other after an eternity of searching. She hardly even noticed the words coming out of her mouth, out of Will's.

"I love you. I love you."

ON ELK Island there was only one way to cook lobsters: steamed in rockweed. The tide was out, so Mike and Snow offered to go down to the bay to gather seaweed and mussels. Everyone teased Mike, telling him to make sure he wore a life preserver. Sarah was happy, and surprised, to see him taking the banter so well.

"It's a new sport," he said. "I'm going to the next Olympics."

"Pond walking!" Snow said. "Mike Talbot takes the gold for pond walking," she continued, speaking into a salt shaker.

"Maybe," Mike said, "the gold should go to your dad."

Sarah said nothing, flabbergasted.

"That's a nice thing to say," George said. "But the tide's flooding in, and if you don't move fast, you'll never get that rockweed."

"Come with us, George," Snow said, pulling his hand. "Show us the best spot for mussels. Let's take a walk down."

WEARING thick rubber boots, Mike waded into the tidal pool, filling a bushel basket. Here they were, almost as far north as you could get on the Atlantic coast, and the sea still held its warmth. The old lobstermen had told him the Gulf Stream swept in here.

Mike wasn't interested in lobstering, but sometimes he thought about being an oceanographer. He loved the sea so much. He wanted to study tides and currents, lobsters and whales. Mike had plenty of dreams. His grandfather subscribed to *National Geographic,* and Mike spent hours looking through back issues. Cultural anthropology appealed to him a lot. Or maybe he'd just take over the farm.

"Hey." His grandfather clucked at Snow. "Over here."

She sloshed through the shallow pool. "Mussels!" she gasped.

"Biggest colony on the island. Don't tell anyone."

Mike smiled. His grandfather was amazing. He ruled his land like a king. He knew where everything was. The mussels were blue-black, the color of the evening sky. Everyone picked a few, throwing them into a separate basket from the seaweed. This could be his, Mike knew. This life of mussel picking at the edge of the Atlantic.

"Everyone, look," his grandfather bellowed.

They stopped what they were doing and gazed at the sky. It danced with cold fire. There in the north, just over the house, was the aurora borealis. "What is it?" Snow asked reverently.

"Never seen it before?" Grandpa asked.

Shaking her head, she didn't speak. Mike moved closer. The air shimmered gold and green. If he were an oceanographer, Mike thought, he could study the phenomenon. Any seaside activity, even atmospheric, would be fair game.

"What is it?" Snow asked again.

"The northern lights," Mike said. "The aurora borealis."

"No way!" Snow said. "The aurora borealis!" She peered at her watch. It was too dark to see it, but she kept trying.

Mike stepped in. His mother had given him a Timex Indiglo for his fifteenth birthday. All it took was the push of a button, and the time appeared, flooded in blue light.

"Eighteen hundred hours!" Snow said. "I first saw the northern lights at eighteen hundred hours on November thirtieth." She held on to Mike's wrist even after she was finished looking at the time.

"Let's go get your mother," Grandpa said, already starting for the house. Mike hung back. Snow stayed with him, watching his grandfather go.

"Snow," Mike said.

"What?" she asked breathlessly.

"Nothing," Mike said, bending down to kiss her. It wasn't the first time he'd kissed a girl, but it was the first time he'd kissed Snow. Forget the aurora borealis: Mike was seeing stars.

Moments later the whole family stepped outside to see the northern lights, but thank goodness there was no way anyone could read Snow's mind. She was thinking, My first kiss, first kiss, Mike Talbot. She was standing between Sarah and her dad, just a few steps from Mike, and she couldn't stop smiling.

"Oh, my," Aunt Bess kept saying, clasping her old hands.

"It's not like we don't see it plenty," George said.

"Every time is like the first time," Bess said.

"You're not a young girl, Bess," George scowled. "First time, nothing. Don't we see it plenty, Mike?"

"It's amazing," Mike said.

Snow smiled at his diplomacy. He was so mature. Inching toward him, she found his hand, touched his fingers.

Mike laced fingers with her.

"We'll be seeing the aurora till April up here, won't we, Mike?" George asked, staring at Mike's and Snow's hands as if he had X-ray eyes and wanted to pulverize the connection.

"I don't know, Grandpa. We saw it in May last year." Mike wasn't making any promises about staying on the island.

"And we'll see it again!" George exclaimed. "Come spring, we'll be out here looking at the sky while all the people in New York State are gazing at the pollution. Right, Mike?"

"Aurora is a good name," Snow said, partly to get Mike off the hook. She hadn't decided what she was going to call herself next, and she liked Aurora, but it didn't have any connection to Fred.

"Right, Mike?" George asked again, his voice tight.

Aunt Bess clapped her hands. "All right, everyone," she said. "We've got lobsters to cook. Let's get back inside."

THE clams and mussels were done first, piled into one steaming bowl and set on the table with pots of melted butter. The lobsters came next. There were baked potatoes for everyone.

"Maine lobsters, Maine potatoes. Ever been to Aroostook County?" George asked.

"Not me," Snow said.

"Lot of potato farms up Aroostook way," George said. He leaned over toward Mike. "I'll take you there come spring. We'll herd up the extra cats and drop them off. Good ratting up in Aroostook."

"Which are the extra cats?" Snow asked politely, looking around the kitchen. Cats of all sizes and colors had swarmed in, smelling the lobster. They lurked in the shadows.

Sarah smiled. "These cats are all descendants of Desdemona, the kitten my mother had when she was young." She broke off a shred of lobster meat and fed a scrawny black cat.

"I saw that," her father said ominously.

"Sorry," Sarah said.

"Feeding animals was always your specialty," he said.

"Which *are* the extra cats?" Snow asked, sounding upset.

"They're all extra," George said. "If every one of them fell down the well, it'd suit me just fine."

Sarah heard the bad mood closing in fast. This was their last dinner together, and her father was feeling it. He took a bite of claw meat, grimacing. "Blech," he said. "Garbage. Hillyer knows that she-lobsters are sweeter. Here, kitty." He put his plate on the floor.

"George!" Bess said, dismayed.

"I thought you weren't supposed to feed the cats, Grandpa," Mike said jokingly.

"What's it to you?" he asked, pushing his chair back. "Don't quote house rules unless you're planning to stay in the house."

"Grandpa . . ." Mike began, turning red.

"Dad," Sarah said softly. "What's gotten into you?"

"What's gotten into *him*?" he asked. "That's more like it!"

"Nothing, Grandpa," Mike said. "Come on, let's finish dinner."

"Why, on account of it's your last?"

Mike didn't reply. Sarah felt her heart pounding. He had made up his mind. She could see by the way he was gazing at his grandfather with such love and regret. "Grandpa," he said.

"Love gets folks into trouble around here," George said, glaring from Mike to Snow. He looked at Sarah. "Doesn't it? Tell him."

"Dad, stop. Mike has to finish his education. You want that for him, don't you? You know how important it is," Sarah said.

"That what you want, Mike?" George asked, his eyes steely. "You want more school?"

Mike shrugged. "Maybe," he said.

"You do, honey?" Sarah asked, her heart flooding with surprise.

"Yeah," he said. "I've been thinking maybe I do."

Sarah couldn't take her eyes off her son.

"That's marvelous," Aunt Bess said. "Finishing high school is admirable, and a college education is priceless."

"I thought you were happy on the farm," George said.

"I am. All I wanted was to come to Maine. See where my parents were from. I was sick of school, and sick of—"

"What?" George asked.

"Life," Mike said, looking apologetically at Sarah.

"Who wouldn't be, without any ocean around?" George asked.

"When I came here, I got interested," Mike said. "That's all I know. We're just this little island in the middle of nowhere, and it's so incredible. You have to practically be a scientist to lobster right. And the northern lights. Everyone thinks they happen when the air is cold. Last May the air was eighty degrees—"

"They occur at high latitudes," George said sullenly. "The aurora's got nothing to do with air temperature."

"That's the kind of stuff I mean," Mike said. "You tell me all these things, and I want to learn more."

Sarah blinked, unable to move.

"Like your *National Geographic*s, Grandpa. . . . They're so interesting."

"Glad to be of service," George said. "Go on up in the attic and read them all you want."

"I'm coming back," Mike said. "That's my plan. I want to go to college, and I want to come back and run the farm."

"Round about the time we're dead?" George asked.

"George, you look pretty healthy to me," Will said.

Tears were running down Sarah's cheeks. She was overwhelmed. Mike was coming home. That was all she wanted, but she couldn't stand to see how hurt her father was. She leaned toward him. "Thank you, Dad," she said.

"For what?" he asked.

"For helping Mike the way you have."

Chapter 6

THE day had come. It was time to leave the island. That was Sarah's first thought. Her second thought was, I have a fever. Sleep had not eased the pain in her back. She had fought this for a week. She took vitamins and drank juice, breathed fresh air, and fell in love. A dark corner of her mind harbored fears of cancer, but this felt like the flu. The imminence of departure had lowered her resistance. Sarah dreaded the sadness of leaving her father and Aunt Bess one more time.

At least Mike was coming with her. Rising from her warm bed, she found her slippers on the cold floor. She had a bottle of Tylenol. She'd take an extra, just to take the edge off her back pain. They would be taking off in just two hours.

GEORGE stood in the kitchen waiting for the coffee to perk. The fire had died down during the night, leaving the place as cold as a tomb. If it were Monday, he'd already be about his chores, killing geese for restaurants throughout New England. Forgetting all about the crap with Sarah and Mike.

Perking hard, the coffee started spitting all over the stove. George got to it just before it boiled over. A moment later, not even bothering to put on his jacket, he opened the kitchen door and headed outside to check the geese. George moved stiffly over the frozen ground. Just thinking about a long winter without Mike to help out made him walk slower. Reaching the barn door, he grabbed the handle. The latch was frozen.

"Damn it," George said, yanking hard. He wedged his foot against the boards, trying for a better grip. He threw all his weight behind one last tug and landed flat on his back.

"You okay, Grandpa?" Mike asked, looking down at him.

"I'm fine," George said.

Mike reached down a hand. Taking hold, George pulled himself up. Mike stared off at the sun rising, pretending nothing had happened. George felt furious at himself, embarrassed and old. While he brushed himself off, Mike opened the barn door.

"What are you doing out here?" George asked.

"Feeding the geese, Grandpa," Mike said, walking into the barn without another word.

ONE by one they all helped themselves to breakfast. There was a big pot of oatmeal on a back burner, a pitcher of orange juice, and the battered old pot of coffee. Will ate by himself at one end of the kitchen table, gazing across the snow at the sea. In about an hour they'd fly away. He had left the Atlantic before, but this time it was different.

Staring at the sea, Will felt his son was right beside him. Coming to Maine, he had fallen in love with Sarah Talbot. He had spent time with Snow, the first four full days since the divorce. But in some ways this trip had been as much about Fred as anyone. Will had found a way back to his son.

Pushing back his chair, he washed his bowl and coffee cup, left them to dry beside the porcelain sink. Everyone was busy preparing in their own ways to leave or stay, to say good-bye. He could hear footsteps upstairs, Snow's voice down the hall. Aunt Bess had set a pile of finished quilts by the door. Will pulled on his leather jacket and carried them out to the Jeep. The plane would be fuller this trip, with Mike and the quilts.

SARAH walked into the room where Will had been sleeping. He was downstairs loading the car. Walking straight to the mahogany dresser, she picked up her mother's wedding portrait.

"Mom," she said out loud. She knew it was crazy, but there was something in the air. Sarah felt that she was not alone.

Sitting on the edge of the bed, she looked around. This was where her mother had lain. The things Sarah was seeing were the things her mother had seen—the same wallpaper, the paintings on the wall, the white curtains.

Rising, she walked to the window. She leaned against the narrow sill, watching the early sun throwing orange light on the snow. Thanksgiving was over. In just a few weeks Christmas would be here, her mother's favorite holiday.

For that last Christmas her mother was too sick to get out of bed much, let alone leave this room. Sarah had spoken to her father about a tree. Bitter and full of fear, he had said it wouldn't be proper, that her mother couldn't get down to the parlor to see it anyway. But Sarah wanted her to have a tree. That Christmas night she had come to this room. After placing a chair by the window, she had supported her mother for the achingly hard walk over.

Sarah remembered her mother's gasp. She had stood there, fingers pressed to her lips. Sarah had placed candles in the snow and on the branches of the white spruce tree. The pathway blazed from the back door, and the Christmas tree itself was lit with fifty flickering lights.

"Our Christmas, Mom," she said now, standing at the window, remembering. Kissing her mother's picture, she took a deep breath. Then she went downstairs to find her son and take him home.

AUNT Bess decided to stay home, so everyone said good-bye to her in the front hall. She kept her dignity, hugging Mike only a minute longer than the others, telling him to be sure to write.

George was quiet. He crammed the luggage into the back of the Jeep. Gelsey needed a little help getting in, and George gave her a shove under the rump. Climbing behind the wheel, he sat there silently, like a reluctant chauffeur. Will got in back with Mike and Snow. Sarah got in front, and Gelsey climbed onto her lap.

They drove across the island. Sarah watched the landscape go by. She had such mixed feelings. Was it greedy to hope for her father to see it her way and feel happy?

"Dad," she said in a low voice.

"Hmm," he growled.

"He'll be back."

No comment. He just gripped the steering wheel tighter, pressed the pedal harder.

"We're here!" Snow exclaimed as they turned the last corner and the plane came into sight.

George parked the Jeep, and Will and Mike unloaded it. Sarah's fever seemed to be getting a little worse. Her back ached. Tylenol, chicken soup, and bed, she was thinking, watching everyone bustling around the plane.

MIKE stowed everything carefully in the cargo area. He wanted to make sure he did things right. He had heard about bags coming loose when small planes hit turbulence. In small planes you really got the sensation of flight. You were a bird, soaring into the clouds. Thinking of birds, Mike looked up and saw the eagle. "Mom," he called, smiling. She was still in the Jeep. She smiled in return and waved, and he pointed at the sky.

His mother looked up. She had that expression on her face, that what-have-I-done-to-deserve-something-so-wonderful look that only she got. Mike got a lump in his throat. He worried because he knew how sick she had been. He felt the smile drain from his face. She looked so happy. All she wanted was to make sure he wasn't going to turn out a loser. Mike could understand that.

"Hey, where's yours?" Will asked, counting the bags. "That's the same number we had coming out."

"I know," Mike said.

His mother got out of the car, moving slowly. Snow bounded over, put an arm around her, practically danced her over to the plane.

"You'd better get going," Grandpa said.

It was a perfect day. The sky was bright blue, the sun brilliant. Mike knew it would be a beautiful flight back to Fort Cromwell. Looking at his grandfather, he kept his gaze steady. His grandfather couldn't do it alone, Mike knew. That morning when Mike had found him lying on the ice, he had realized how bad it was.

"What's the story?" Will asked, lowering his voice.

"I'm not leaving," Mike said.

"Look," Will said sharply, "don't do this to your mother. She thinks you're coming home with us."

"I can't," Mike said. For him that was all there was to it. He couldn't live with himself if he got on that plane and left his grandfather and Aunt Bess alone. They'd die this winter without him.

Will looked like he wanted to kill him. His eyes were flashing, his jaw set tight. "Then tell her," he said. "Don't leave her hoping. Tell her right now."

Mike nodded. Turning around, the first person he saw was Snow. Mike remembered kissing her last night. He blushed, and Snow noticed. She smiled wider.

Will stepped between Mike and his mother. He put his arm around her. Mike saw his expression, somber and watchful, and felt glad his mother wasn't alone. "I'm not going," Mike said.

His mother didn't reply. She cocked her head slightly, as if she hadn't heard him right. But Snow got it right away. Her smile disappeared all at once. "You have to," she said.

"Mike?" his mother asked.

"I'm sorry, Mom," he said. He stepped forward, wanting to make her feel better. He wanted to hug her or hold her hands, or something, but all he could do was stand there.

"What about school?" she asked, her voice trembling. "You said you wanted to finish. What about your future, honey?"

"I'll finish, Mom."

"When?" Sarah asked, growing agitated.

"Soon," Mike said.

"It's your life that you're throwing away," his mother said. "Don't you see that, Mike? Life is so short. You think you have time, but a year will pass and you'll never go back."

"Sarah," Will said, holding her close. "He'll be fine."

"He won't," she said, pushing him away. She walked straight to Mike and held his hands. He couldn't stand to see the tears rolling down her cheeks. "Come home," she said. "Please."

"You should listen to your mother," his grandfather said half-heartedly. "Finish your schooling."

"Come with us," Snow begged. "We'll have fun."

"I can't," Mike said. "I'm staying on the island."

His mother wasn't being strong at all. She had pulled her hands back, bowed her head, and started weeping into her palms. Will was holding her again. Snow just stood there staring at her feet. Mike reached into the cargo hold for a small pouch he'd stuck in with Snow's bag. "Here," he said.

"What is it?" Snow asked sullenly.

"One of the extra cats," he said.

Unable to stop herself, Snow reached into the sack and pulled out a black kitten. It was the smallest one Mike could find, with a white throat and bright blue eyes. "Wow," she said. She kissed the cat's nose. "What's its name?"

"I don't know. You're good with names. It's a boy."

"Dr. Darrow," Snow said, her smile flooding back.

"Yeah," Mike said, smiling at her. "Dr. Darrow." He looked at his mother, and his smile died. She looked pale, her eyes dull.

"Sarah, are you okay?" Will was asking.

"My back," she said, "hurts a little."

"Mom," Mike said. "I'm going to finish school. I promise. Even if it's just a GED. I'll write the high school. There's plenty of time."

Tears were welling in her eyes again. She was staring into Mike's face as if she wanted to memorize every detail. "I want you to be right," she said.

Mike nodded. "Bye, Mom," he said, kissing her cheek.

She caught him with her arms. Hugging him so hard, he could hardly believe his mother had that kind of strength, she said something he couldn't quite hear.

"What?" he asked.

"I have to tell you something," she said slowly. "I have never loved anyone as much as I love you."

"Mom—" Mike said.

"No one, Mike. From the minute I saw you, that was it. True love and forever. You changed my world."

"Yeah," Mike said, his throat hurting because he had something to say but didn't know what it was.

"I know you love me," she said. "Don't ever think I don't."

EVERYONE WAS QUIET. SNOW sat in the back of the plane, playing with Dr. Darrow, wishing Mike were beside her. She looked at things out the window and imagined how great it would be to be seeing them with him.

Sarah was just sitting there, all clenched up.

Dr. Darrow cheered Snow up. He was so adorable, no bigger than a coffee mug with legs. Snow picked him up. She held him against her throat, his body resting on her collarbone. It was nice and warm there, and closing her eyes, Snow felt the kitten purring against her neck. When she opened her eyes again, they were just leaving the coastline behind. She had to turn to watch the Atlantic recede into a thin golden line.

As they flew inland, she felt the wheezing start, and she fumbled in her pocket for her inhaler. Her chest tightened.

THEY stopped to refuel in Lebanon, New Hampshire. Everyone went into the hangar to use the bathrooms and get coffee or hot chocolate. Sarah felt like she was in a fog. Her head was thick from all the tears she had cried. Every time she thought of Mike, her eyes welled up. Will brought her coffee. Sarah smiled as their fingers touched. She hated the way she was being. Since leaving Elk Island, she had been unable to talk. "I'm sorry," she said.

"For what?" Will asked.

She shook her head. "For being so upset."

"I don't blame you. He's not my son, and I feel the same way. I'd like to stick him in the back seat and fly him home whether he likes it or not."

Sarah couldn't drink her coffee. Not wanting to hurt Will's feelings, she held the cup. She felt pale, and she knew she had beads of sweat on her forehead. Her back was getting worse.

"What is it?" Will asked. He took the cardboard cup out of her hand and placed it on a window ledge. The air was freezing cold, even inside the hangar. Sarah shivered uncontrollably.

"Nothing," she said. She made herself smile.

He put his arms around her. "Let's go. The sooner we take off, the sooner I get you home. I'm coming over, by the way."

"You don't have to," Sarah said. "You've spent the last four days with me. Aren't you sick of me by now?"

"Not even slightly," Will said, still hugging her.

TAKING off just before noon, they encountered headwinds.

"Hang on," Will said. "It's going to be bumpy."

"Aah!" Sarah exclaimed.

"What is it?" Will asked. When he looked over, her face was pure white. She was clutching her seat. "Sarah," he said, alarmed.

"My back hurts," she said quietly. "That's all."

"Did you strain it? Lifting the bags or something?"

"I don't know," she said. "I don't think so." The pain was intense. Her hip was numb, and her leg tingled. She pictured Dr. Goodacre. On her last visit to him she had felt so reassured. What had he said about numbness?

New tears came to her eyes. She had wept all morning for Mike, but now she was crying for something else. She had fought so hard, been filled with so much hope. Her birthday had been a dream. Flying over the mountains with Will, so grateful to be alive, to feel healthy again, Sarah had imagined it going on forever.

WILL looked down and saw Fort Cromwell. Picking up the radio, he called the tower at Brielmann Field. "This is 2132 Tango. We're coming in at three o'clock, and we need clearance to land."

"We got you, 2132 Tango. Using runway one today."

Attempting to put the landing gear down, Will needed two green lights and got one. He had a main-gear light, indicating that the main landing gear was down and locked, but he wasn't getting a nose-gear light.

Will didn't say anything. He could see the airport now, the runway shining black in the sun. Running his hand under the panel, he found a wire and jiggled it. No light. Exhaling hard, he glanced over at Sarah. "Sarah, we're almost home."

"Hurry," she said. She was in terrible pain.

Okay, calm down, he told himself. The nose hydraulics weren't working. But there was a CO_2 cartridge he could activate to blow the gear down. He found the handle. He knew this method functioned best with minimal airspeed, and he pulled back on the throttle. Pulled back more, slowing the plane down.

"Dad, I think you'd better land right away," Snow said, sounding scared. "Sarah's sick."

"I know that," Will snapped.

Sarah was silent, but the look on her face was excruciating. Will tried to concentrate. He had slowed down as much as he could, but he pulled the handle too soon. The cartridge went off. Nothing happened. "Damn," he said.

"What's wrong?" Snow asked. "What's going on?"

He ignored her. Circling the airport, he tried to think about the problem. His palms were sweating.

"Brielmann Field, this is 2132 Tango. We're experiencing problems with our nose gear. Not getting a green light."

"Fly by the tower, Will. We'll take a look."

Banking right, Will flew back toward the airport. He spied his own hangar, Burke Aviation. He saw his car parked in the parking lot. And there was the tower manned by his friends Ralph and Dave. He saw Dave in the window watching the plane fly by.

"Your main gear's down, Will," Dave radioed back. "Nose gear's hanging limp, does not appear to be fully extended."

"What's that mean?" Snow asked.

Will didn't answer.

The fuel gauge registered under a quarter, and the needle was dropping fast. He needed to almost run out of fuel, but not quite. Without nose gear they were going to go in hard. There would be lots of sparks, a chance of fire. All he wanted to do was land for Sarah, but to save her life right now, he had to fly.

EVERY air pocket sent jolts down Sarah's spine. She had lost all feeling in her legs, but the pain in her back shocked her. Will had taken a big loop north, and now they were coming in.

"Get ready," Will said.

"Oh, Dad," Snow cried.

Aiming at the runway, Will stared straight ahead. Sarah could see flashing lights everywhere. Police cars, fire engines, ambulances. Snow covered the land, and white foam coated the runway.

"Okay," Will said. "I want you to put your heads down."

Snow wept. "Daddy, Dr. Darrow wiggled out of my hands."

"Leave him," Will said sharply.

Sarah had the impression of Snow stretching for the cat in the back seat. Will slapped the seat to get her attention. "Susan, let the cat go. Put your head down! Arms over your head, you hear me?"

"I'm scared," Snow cried.

"It'll be over in just a minute," Will said. "We'll be fine."

"Daddy . . ." she said, her voice breaking.

"Are you listening? As soon as we stop, undo your seat belts. And get out fast. Run away fast, okay? You both hear me?"

"Fast, Dad," Snow said. "I hear you."

Sarah must have spoken, but she didn't know. She was in such a cloud of agony. Bending over stretched whatever was hurting her spine, made it jab deeper and harder.

"Sarah," Will said. "Snow. I love you."

"I love you, Daddy," Snow called.

I love you, Sarah thought. The plane hit the ground. It landed with a roar, scraped the surface raw, skated left and right. Will held on, arms iron straight. Sarah heard him cursing and praying, heard metal ripping. Glass shattered. Sparks flew.

And then they were stopped.

Will was out of the plane before Sarah could get her head up. Snow tumbled onto the tarmac clutching the kitten. Will shoved her away, yelled for her to run. He flew around to Sarah's side, undid the door. Sarah saw foam spraying into the air. She heard firemen calling, shouting for everyone to move clear of the plane.

"Come on, Sarah," Will said, undoing her seat belt.

"Out of the way, Will," one of the firemen commanded.

Will stayed by Sarah.

"Move it, Will. Your plane's gonna explode!"

Will stood still, as if he had all the time in the world. He held out his hand, crouched down to bring his face close to Sarah's.

"I can't move my legs," she said, looking into his blue eyes.

"That's okay," he said. Reaching into the plane, moving as tenderly as he could, he eased her arms around his neck. He lifted her, and she pressed her face against his chest.

THEY were on the evening news. Snow sat in the library, covered with a blanket and holding Dr. Darrow, watching the whole thing. Channel 3 had caught them on film from the moment the plane had started to circle over the airport. Snow could hear the disaster excitement in the reporter's voice. "They must have been pretty sure we were going to die," she said, riveted.

"Don't say that," her mother said. "It was awful. Julian and I were right here, waiting for you to come home, and the tower called to tell us what was going on. I couldn't believe it."

"We turned on Channel Three right away," Julian said.

"We landed fine," Snow said quietly, stroking Dr. Darrow.

"Thank God," her mother said.

"We thought it would be a big 'I told you so,' " Julian said.

"What's that?" Snow asked.

"You know, run away from home, and bad things happen. I told you so," he said, smiling.

Snow wanted to ignore him. She stared at the TV. Her mother was being so nice, not punishing her yet, not saying anything mean about the kitten, but Julian wanted to pick a fight. She felt a coughing fit coming on. "I didn't run away. I was with my father."

"There's Will!" her mother said, sounding strangely excited, as if she had just spotted a movie star. With the zoom-lens view, Snow could see her father at the controls, so handsome and intense. The camera stayed on his face. Snow couldn't believe how calm he looked. "That's not how it seemed," Snow said with wonder. "It was scary, horrible. But look—" The camera panned over to Sarah. Sarah's face was viciously contorted. Snow hadn't realized she was in that kind of pain.

"She's not cool." Julian chuckled. "She's panicking."

"She was just as brave as Dad," Snow said.

"Is she his girlfriend?" Alice asked.

"I don't know," Snow said, knowing she wasn't going to tell.

"Something must be going on. He won't leave her side."

Snow just nodded. Her mother and Julian had picked her up at the hospital because Sarah had a pinched nerve or something and the plane crash had made it worse.

"So cool and collected," her mother said as the camera went back to Will. "He always was. In the worst emergencies."

Snow thought it was weird to hear her mother talking like this in front of Julian. "What do you mean?" she asked.

"Just look at him," Alice said. "He thought he was about to crash with his daughter on board. He's calm."

"Like the day Freddie died," Snow said.

"No one died today," Julian said.

Her mother nodded, ignoring him. "Like that day," she said. "I thought he should have been more upset, but look . . ."

"My little emotional wreck," Julian said, tugging her hand.

A frown creased Alice's forehead. Reaching across the sofa, she took Snow's hand. "I sold him short," she said. "I really did."

"Dad's not cold," Snow said softly.

"He's got that navy training," Alice said. "We don't, you and I, and we really lost it. Didn't we, honey?"

"We did," Snow said, amazed. She had always wanted to talk about the Day of Fred, and her mother never would.

"He's a loose cannon," Julian said resentfully. "I have the crooked nose to prove it. How'd you feel up in the plane?"

"Scared?" her mother asked.

"Yes," Snow said.

"I'm pretty sure your dad was scared too," Alice said. "Even though he never shows it."

"Some people collapse after the fact," Julian said. "I mean, if you can't be there for your wife and daughter—"

"He was there," Snow said. "He was there for us, wasn't he, Mom?" Snow's chest ached. Her throat burned.

Her mother bowed her head. When she raised it again to look at the TV screen, she shook her head. Her eyes looked sad, but there was a hint of mad in there too. "No. Uh-uh, he wasn't."

Snow wheezed deeply. Dr. Darrow's little claws scrabbled across her sweater, getting caught in the yarn.

"Good Lord, Susan!" her mother exclaimed, grabbing Dr. Darrow. "You're allergic to that animal."

"Give him back," Snow tried to say.

"It's ridiculous," Julian said. "Letting her bring home a cat. Weren't there any grown-ups on that island? You have a serious respiratory condition."

"Give . . . him . . . back," Snow pleaded.

Her mother handed her the inhaler. Snow pumped it, stuck it in her mouth, reaching with one hand for the kitten. The TV showed the crash again. The plane hit hard, sending the foam spraying everywhere. Sparks flew like crazy. Mesmerized, her mother handed Snow the kitten. Julian sighed.

"Is IT still bad?" Will asked.

"It's better," Sarah said, lying still.

Was she telling him the truth? Gazing at her, Will tried to see. She hadn't walked yet. She wore a blue hospital gown, but she looked so beautiful Will wanted to lift her into his arms and carry her home right then. Being in the hospital made him nervous.

"They called him?" Will asked. The nurses needed clearance from Dr. Goodacre, Sarah's main doctor, to let her go. They had given her Demerol to take the edge off her back pain. The radiologist had determined that she had a pinched nerve. She had a fever, and that was from the swelling. Nothing serious.

"They called him."

"How long does it usually take?" Will asked. Sitting on the edge of Sarah's bed, he held her hands.

"Sometimes," Sarah said, putting her arms around him, "a long time. He's very busy."

"So am I," Will said. "I want to get you home."

"That sounds very good," Sarah said.

Will looked straight into her eyes. They were almost too bright.

The door opened. Dr. Goodacre walked in, all business. In his dark suit with a yellow tie he looked like a banker.

"Dr. Goodacre," Sarah said, sounding delighted to see him.

"Sarah," he said.

"This is Will Burke," she said. "The hero! I'm sure you heard about the plane crash. Well, this is the guy . . ."

Dr. Goodacre raised his eyebrows. He didn't shake hands.

"I'll leave," Will said.

Dr. Goodacre nodded, but Sarah put out her hand. "No, you don't," she said. She sounded almost playful. "Please stay."

"Of course," Will said, moving closer than he had been.

"Sarah, I've seen your films," Dr. Goodacre said.

"I'm sorry to haul you out for a pinched nerve," Sarah said. "You're way too busy for that, and all I can say is, I was upset about my son, and I guess I got so tensed up . . ."

Dr. Goodacre stood there, his hands folded, listening to her carry on. Will watched him. A glimmer of compassion was showing through in the way he didn't want to speak.

Dr. Goodacre cleared his throat. "The CT scan showed what we've been fearing," he said. "The tumor is back."

Sarah's smile didn't change. "No," she said.

"I'm sorry, Sarah," he said. "A nerve is being pinched, yes. The tumor is located in the lower region of your spine."

"It metastasized," Sarah said. Her eyes filled with dread.

Dr. Goodacre nodded. "I'm sorry," he said again.

Will stood. He faced the doctor eye to eye. "What do we do?"

Dr. Goodacre shifted his gaze to Sarah. "We've discussed this."

"It's like . . . we said?" she asked.

"It's extensive. The films show spread to the liver, the lymph system. I'd like to do an MRI to check for recurrence in the brain."

"But what do we do?" Will asked again.

"Surgery?" Sarah asked.

Dr. Goodacre shook his head. "No," he said. "The cancer is just too invasive. It's growing fast, like a vine around the spinal column."

"You're saying no?" Will asked. "She wants you to operate, and you're telling her no?"

Not replying, Dr. Goodacre just stood there.

Will couldn't believe it. He wanted to slam the doctor against the wall. Just shutting down on Sarah after giving her news like that. He felt his heart pounding. Stay calm, he told himself.

Sarah had tears in her eyes. "How much time?" Will heard her ask. The question took his breath away.

"Two weeks," Dr. Goodacre said.

THE night was long, and it seemed to never end. Nurses came and went, surprised to find Sarah awake as they went about their jobs. Lying in her bed, Sarah said hello. They nodded and smiled.

Sarah asked for a glass of water. The nurse who brought it to her looked familiar. "Can't you sleep?" she asked.

"No, not really," Sarah said.

"I can give you something for sleep," the nurse said, checking her chart. "Dr. Goodacre has it down."

Sarah wanted to stay as alert as possible. "No, thanks," she said. "Can I ask your name?"

"Oh. It's Louise. Sorry. I couldn't find my nametag tonight."

Louise smiled, waiting for Sarah to say something more. But that was all. Sarah just wanted to know her name. She knew that calling someone by name was one of the most important things people could do. It made them feel connected, made them feel alive.

Sarah closed her eyes. For some reason she thought of her shop. Cloud Nine. She had loved the name, thought it celestial and full of hope. It had reminded her of her mother, sending her blessings down from heaven. Sarah had designed the logo herself, a gold 9 on a beautiful summer cloud.

"I read your chart," Louise said.

Sarah swallowed, nodding.

"It's hard," Louise said. "Have you talked to your oncologist, discussed your options? They're doing a lot with chemo these days, getting better results all the time."

Sarah shook her head. Medicine couldn't save her from her own body. She didn't want to be hooked up to machines. She didn't want to be part of any experiments. "All along I've thought I would know when the time came."

"Know what?" Louise asked gently.

"How . . . to leave."

"Yes?"

Sarah nodded. Tears ran into the corners of her mouth. "How do I leave?" she asked. She was trembling now, sitting with this kind stranger in a room on a hospital floor where everyone else was asleep. Louise held her hand. Biting her lip, Sarah tasted salt and felt the pain burning through her last pain shot. She thought of Mike, and she thought of Will.

WILL hadn't slept. All he could think of was Sarah, alone at the hospital. He had wanted to stay with her, had sat on the edge of her bed until the end of visiting hours. The nurse had hesitated, deciding whether to kick him out. "Haven't you seen Sarah's chart?" Will wanted to ask. "We don't have enough time." But the rules won. The nurse told him to go, and Sarah didn't try to stop him.

Just after dawn Will got up. He could think only of getting to the hospital, changing Sarah's mind. Two weeks wasn't enough. He needed much more time with her. They could have their forties, fifties, sixties, seventies together if she could get healthy.

Drying off after his shower, he checked his watch. Nearly six thirty. He made coffee and drank it at his kitchen table. The kitchen was small, impersonal. Moving into this apartment, he hadn't cared about fixing it up. Sarah would make this place beautiful, he thought.

Checking his watch again, he saw it was inching toward seven. Three more hours till he could visit her. Had news about the plane crash reached Elk Island? Needing a connection with Sarah, he reached for the phone and called her family.

GOING to school that Monday morning, Snow hadn't realized it was a half day. The teachers had conferences on statewide reading scores, so classes were dismissed just before lunch. Riding her bike down through town, Snow wondered why they had even bothered having school at all that day.

All the stores had their Christmas decorations up. Wreaths and garlands were everywhere, white lights twinkling. Parking in front of Cloud Nine, she stared at the dark window. No lights, no garlands. Snow was surprised; she had thought Sarah would decorate right away. Was she still in the hospital? A white paper had been taped to the inside of the window. Snow read the note: "Cloud Nine will be closed until the Monday after Thanksgiving. Until then, stay warm and sweet dreams!"

Snow frowned. Sarah had written that note before they'd left for Elk Island, which meant she was still in the hospital. Was her back that bad? Snow had a few bruises from the plane crash, but nothing serious. Suddenly she had an awful thought: What if Sarah's illness had come back? Jumping onto her bike, she pedaled home as fast as she could.

Zooming up Windemere Hill, Snow prayed that everything would be okay. All her insecurities crashed in, filling her with such dread that by the time she reached the top, she collapsed against the front door. She found her inhaler and used it, then went inside.

"You're home early," her mother said.

"Hi . . . Mom," Snow said, wheezing. "Teachers' conferences."

Her mother stood there, arms folded across her chest.

Snow tried to get a good breath. She wanted to tell her mother why she was so scared. Sensing that her mother didn't like Sarah, she didn't want to come on too strong. She exhaled and spoke. "Mom, you know Sarah Talbot? I'm kind of worried about her. She isn't at her store. Do you think she's still in the hospital?"

"You stopped by her store on your way home?" her mother asked, frowning. "Did you ask permission? Susan, when are you going to learn you have to let me know where you are? My heavens! If you'd had an accident, or if someone snatched you— You're grounded, Susan. I was going to wait for Julian to tell you, but now seems like the time."

"Grounded?"

"Do you have any idea how much you worried me?" her mother asked, her face getting all red. "When you didn't come home last Wednesday? And then to get a phone call from New Hampshire? On your way to an island with a family I've never even *met?*"

"You know Dad," Snow said.

Her mother shook her head. "Don't be fresh. Go to your room

and think about this. I'm not grounding you for the fun of it. I love you more than anything, Susan. And Julian—"

"Don't even say it," Snow said, backing away.

"I will say it. Julian is your stepfather. He is my husband. You might not like him, but he cares about you."

"Aargh!" Snow wailed, putting her hands over her ears.

"He does! Do you know how hard it's been for us? He's your stepfather, honey. He might not be perfect, but he tries so hard with you. Do you know what he said about that cat? 'Let her keep it,' he said. I was fit to be tied."

"Dr. Darrow?" Snow asked, her nerves tingling. "Where is he?"

"I took him to the pound," her mother said. "You're allergic to him. You can't have a cat. You know you can't—"

"The pound?" The words tore out of Snow's chest. She didn't want to hear the rest. Flying upstairs, she ran into her room.

SARAH was waiting. After such a short time she had grown used to counting on Will. When he came through the door, she lay with her head on the pillow and smiled. Just seeing him made her feel content, and she sighed.

"Hello," he said, coming over to sit beside her.

"Hi, Will," she said.

"How are you? Is the pain as bad?"

"No," she said. They were giving her medication.

"Have you seen the doctor?" he asked.

"Yes. He was here this morning. I had my MRI, and I guess he'll be back later. I missed you."

"Oh, Lord, I missed you," Will said, giving her a hug. Closing her eyes, Sarah felt his strength. She didn't want him to let go.

"Have you called Mike?" he asked.

"Shh," she said, hugging harder.

"Because I did," Will said.

Sarah's eyes sprang open. "You didn't . . . tell him?"

"I did."

"Will!" Sarah struggled to sit up. "Tell me you're kidding."

"Why would I kid, Sarah? I—"

"You don't just tell Mike something like this. I don't want to drive him further away when I've just started to get him back."

"He wanted to come," Will said. "To see you."

"He did? Come to Fort Cromwell?" Sarah asked, her eyes filling with tears. It was all she could imagine wanting. "Mike?"

"Yes. And your father."

"Oh, Will," Sarah said. She could hardly imagine it—Mike returning home, and *anything* getting her father off the island.

"If you want them to come here, I'll go get them. But I was thinking about something else."

"What?" she asked.

"I know you're in pain. I know it would be a lot to ask you to sit there for the time it would take, but if you'd like, Sarah, I'd like to take you home."

AN HOUR later Dr. Boswell, the oncologist, gave her okay and upped the dosage of Sarah's pain medication for the trip, switching to morphine because the pain could get worse. Will was a guy with a mission. He took directions from the doctor. He had called Meg Ferguson, and she was there, giving him various instructions as the hospital nurses got Sarah ready for the flight.

"Don't worry that you're giving her too much medication," Meg said, crying. "If she asks for it, give it. When you get to the island, do you have a nurse?"

"Sarah's aunt is on that now. She called a hospice in Maine, and they're setting everything up with a visiting nurse."

"Good. Hospice, Will. Hospice for Sarah. You know what that means, don't you?"

"I do know, Meg," Will replied patiently. Meg sounded bossy and kind of harsh, but she was wiping her eyes.

"Damn it, Will. I thought she was going to be okay."

"So did she."

"I've been carrying this around with me for a month," Meg said, reaching into her bag and pulling out a picture. "I've been meaning to give it to Sarah." She handed it to Will. It showed Will and Sarah together at the fair, at the hot dog stand. They were embracing like long-lost lovers, and the expression in Will's eyes amazed him. He had looked madly in love even then.

"Mimi took it," Meg said.

Will stared at the picture. "Can I keep it?" he asked.

"Sure," Meg said.

"What else do I need to know?" Will asked. They were standing in the hospital corridor, and he had his eyes on Sarah's door, waiting for the nurse to come out and say she was ready to go.

"That it isn't going to be easy," Meg said.

"I'm losing Sarah," Will said, the harshness in his voice suddenly matching hers. "I don't want it to be easy, Meg."

ON THEIR way to the airport Sarah looked at Will. "I want to say good-bye to Snow," she said.

They were at a stoplight. Will took her hands. The drugs were taking hold. Sarah had to struggle to focus.

"She'd want to come with us," he said.

"I know. But I have to say good-bye."

"Sarah," Will said. "The flight's going to be hard enough. It's going to upset you, seeing her. It's going to upset *her.*"

"Please, Will." Sarah didn't have the strength to argue. "She didn't get to say good-bye to Fred. Think of how she'd feel."

"DAD!" Snow yelled, tearing into the library. "They took Dr. Darrow to the pound!"

"Honey," her father said, stopping her short. He put his hands on her shoulders and looked at her.

"What, Dad?" Only then did Snow see Sarah sitting on the burgundy velvet love seat under the portrait of Julian's grandfather. Snow walked across the room. "Hi, Sarah," she said.

"Hi, Snow."

"We meet again," Snow said, beaming. Julian and her mother were standing there, looking pained. Her father's face was grave.

"We do," Sarah said, smiling.

"Did you hear about Dr. Darrow?" Snow asked, lowering her voice. "My mother thinks I'm allergic to him, but I'm not."

"Susan, you have terrible allergies," Julian said with a very master-of-the-house tone to his voice. "I think we all know that."

"She didn't test positive for cats," her father said. "She knows I wouldn't have let her bring home a cat if she did."

"I'm getting him back," Snow said straight to Sarah, as if to reassure her that the Elk Island kitten would be properly loved despite the rocky homecoming. It suddenly struck Snow as extraordinary that all the important adults in her life had gathered in this room. Smiling, she caught Sarah's eye. Snow started to laugh. "Is this weird?" she asked.

Sarah said, "I don't think so. We're here because of you."

Snow realized something was happening. "This isn't about Dr. Darrow, is it?" she asked, sitting beside Sarah.

Sarah shook her head.

For the first time, Snow noticed how pale she was. "What is it, then?" Snow asked.

"I've come to say good-bye," Sarah said.

"Where are you going?"

"Back to the island."

Snow's father took a step forward. "With me," he said.

"What?" Snow asked, looking around the room. "Can I go? I have to! If you're going, so am I. Tell Dad I can, Mom—"

Sarah put her hand on Snow's wrist. "No, Snow, you can't."

"What do you mean? Why are you going?"

"Susan," her mother began, her voice thin. Julian put his arm around her.

"I'm sick again," Sarah said.

"No!" Snow said, clapping her hands over her mouth.

"I want to be with Mike, and your father is going to fly me."

"This isn't fair," Snow said.

Sarah was the only one who knew what she meant. Snow wasn't talking about going to the island. She meant it wasn't fair that Sarah was sick.

Again Sarah reached out her hand. Her hair looked so great. A cap of cool, iridescent white-gold. "Your hair looks pretty," Snow said, lacing fingers with Sarah.

"Thanks to you," Sarah said.

Snow lowered her head. "Will I see you again?" she asked, so quietly only Sarah could hear.

"I don't think so," Sarah said.

Snow nodded. With her eyes closed, she savored Sarah's presence. She's right here, Snow thought. Soon she'll go, but for now she's *right here.* Snow had never had that with Fred. "I have some things of my brother's." She clutched Sarah's hand tighter. "Names have been important." She kept her voice steady. "To remind me of him. He loved snow."

"I know."

"I've been wondering what to call myself next. It has to begin with S because that gives me serenity. I've been thinking of Sarah." Snow gripped both of Sarah's hands. "I know you never knew Fred, but it seems like you do. When we saw that whale, when I said he had angel wings, you knew I was thinking of Fred."

"I did," Sarah said. She was holding on just as tight.

"You would have loved Fred," Snow said.

"I believe I would have."

"Don't be sick, Sarah." The words just came out, and they made Snow start to cry. She leaned right into Sarah and held on tight.

"I loved that whale," Sarah whispered, stroking Snow's head.

Snow cried hard for a few minutes, then leaned back. "I want to be called Sarah," she said. "It's your name, but it's about Fred too."

"I'm honored," Sarah said. "But how would it be if, instead, you took another name?"

"Like what?"

"Like Susan," Sarah said.

"Susan?" Snow just stared.

"It's a beautiful name," Sarah said.

"But it's not *enough.* It doesn't remind me of anyone."

"Fred knew you as Susan," Sarah said gently.

"But I miss him," Snow said, her face twisting. "And Sarah, I'm going to miss you."

"Oh, I know," Sarah said, smiling. "That's why I wanted to see you. Because I'm going to miss you too."

Bowing her head, Snow bit her lip. Sarah's eyes were sparkling, and Snow wanted it to last forever. But when she picked her head up, the clouds were back. Just a few, off in the distance, at the back of Sarah's bright blue eyes.

"We have to go," her father said, reaching out his hand.

Snow's mother stepped forward. She put her hand out too. "Honey?" she said. She didn't have jealousy in her eyes for Sarah being there. She didn't have anger at Will for their situation. She didn't even have insecurity about Julian. She only had love, pure and simple, for her only daughter.

A feeling of peace settled over Snow. Staring into Sarah's eyes, she could see Elk Island—the dark bay, the northern lights, Mike.

The big clock in the hall chimed: fourteen hundred hours.

"Honey?" her mother said again.

"The name's Susan," Susan said softly, giving Sarah one last hug, possibly the best one she had ever given, before letting go of Sarah's hands and allowing her parents to pull her to her feet.

Chapter 7

HOME. The word held Sarah together, kept her focus, filled her mind all the way from Fort Cromwell to Elk Island. The drugs made her groggy. The hospital nurses had installed a Port-A-Cath in her arm, a little portable IV that hid under her sleeve. Meg had pumped her full of morphine. As the pain recurred, Will did the same thing. Home, Sarah thought. Home.

"Are we almost there?" she asked, hearing her own voice speak out loud. There was her hand on her knee, her other hand on the cold window. She could feel the cold on her fingertips, but she had no pain in her back or anywhere else.

"Yes, Sarah," Will said. His resonant voice blended with the

motor noise in a way that reminded her of dreams, of strange
movies from the '60s. Sarah was taking drugs, that's why. She was
high as a kite.

"This has to stop," she said.

"What?" Will asked.

She knew she had alarmed him, by the quick way he turned his
head. Sarah herself couldn't feel it. She was wrapped in fog. Her
tongue was thick, her eyelids heavy. The sea had come into sight,
but she was too numb to care. "No more drugs," she said.

"Sarah, the pain will be too bad," he said.

"I want to be alert," she said.

Will didn't agree or disagree. He just flew the plane.

THEY had a welcoming crew for her. Will landed the plane as
softly as he could, mindful that Sarah's medication had to be wearing off fast. George and Bess were there, as grim-faced as the couple in *American Gothic*. Mike stood still, hatless and trying to smile.
A stolid nurse stood beside him, a navy-blue jacket over her white
dress, hands gripping the handles of a wheelchair.

Helping Sarah out of the plane, Will felt her arms around his
neck and felt her breath on his cheek. Lowering her into the wheelchair, he kissed her hair.

"Sarah," George said, his voice all gravelly and his face looking a
hundred years old.

"Hi, Dad," she said. "Aunt Bess, hi."

"Sarah, darling." Aunt Bess leaned down for a hug. When she
straightened up again, Sarah smiled at Mike.

"Well, there," she said.

"Hi, Mom," Mike said. He hung back, frowning and shy. Will
wanted to shake him. Sarah opened her arms. Reluctantly Mike
bent over. But midway through, his hug turned real, and Will could
see he didn't want to let go.

"How's she doing on meds?" the nurse asked Will. She was
about fifty, short and stout, with salt-and-pepper hair.

"She doesn't want to take any," he said.

The woman crouched down beside Sarah. "I'm Martha. If there's anything you need, anything at all, I want you to let me know."

"Oh, the visiting nurse," Sarah said with trust in her eyes.

"Are you ready for some medication?" Martha asked.

"I don't want any more," Sarah said clearly, looking Martha right in the eyes as if she expected Martha to try to talk her out of it.

"Many people decide they don't," Martha said.

"Are you sure, dear?" Bess asked.

"I'm sure," Sarah said, and Will saw her watching Mike.

THE house was just as they had left it the day before. Sarah caught glimpses of the kitchen. The fire crackled, and cats scattered as the door slammed open and everyone trooped in.

"I'd like to lie down," Sarah said.

Mike picked up her bags. Will lifted her into his arms. The drugs had just about worn off, and her body was alive with pain. On the other hand, she noticed everything. The smell of her childhood was everywhere. Aunt Bess had washed the windows, and they gleamed. Gelsey was jumping on Martha. Mike was scared. Sarah saw it in the downward cast of his eyes.

Mike led the procession upstairs, into Sarah's room.

"Not this room. That one," she said, pointing. Will's room on Thanksgiving. The room where her mother had died.

"I can stay in your old room," Will said.

"Stay with me," Sarah said. "Please, Will?"

He squeezed her very gently, hardly pressing at all.

Mike pulled down the covers of the big bed. Will laid her carefully on the mattress, easing her legs under the sheet and quilt. He stepped back, and Sarah caught sight of her son's face. His eyes were filled with terror. "Come here," she said, patting the bed.

Very gingerly Mike lowered himself to sit on the edge of the bed. He was so big, a full-grown man. Sarah never got over it. It made her laugh.

"What?" he asked, hurt.

"I'm happy."

"How can you be?" His voice was hoarse, his expression injured.

"I'm with you."

"Is this . . ." he began, hardly able to talk. "Because I wouldn't go home with you? You getting sick again?"

Sarah shook her head. All she had ever wanted was to see her son on a shining path, but she hadn't known what that path was. Now she did. She felt so proud of her son.

"No, Mike. You were right all along. This is home," she said. And then she was so tired she had to sleep.

DURING the evening Martha checked her. Or was it her mother? Pain did mysterious things. Grimacing in sleep, Sarah felt the cool hand on her warm brow. Slender fingers caressed her hair.

"It hurts," Sarah cried.

"I know, love," the woman said.

Outside the window the moon was full. It shone on the new snow, making a silver path into the dark bay. Tracks of gold-green fire glowed in the sea. The pine tree Sarah had decorated for her mother had grown taller, but it sparkled with candlelight from top to bottom, decorated again.

The pain was unbearable. Tentacles reached out, strangling her bones and organs in a death grip. She cried, reaching out for the woman's soft hand. "Please," she begged. "Make it stop."

"I will, darling. I'll make it stop," the woman promised.

WHEN Will went upstairs after dinner, he found Sarah standing by the window. She wore a white nightgown, and she was staring toward the sea. Seeing her up shocked him. He stopped in the doorway, his heart pounding. "Sarah?" he asked.

She turned, as beautiful as the first time he'd seen her. Her skin glistened. For a moment, viewing her in the moonglow, he thought he was seeing a ghost. But she walked to him, pressed her warm body against his, kissed him with human passion.

"The pain's gone. I don't know why, but it's gone."

Leading him to the bed, she gently pushed him down. They undressed, slowly at first and then, as Will felt more confident that he wasn't going to hurt her, more urgently. Her skin felt hot, as if she had a fever. She pulled him close, and Will gave himself to

Sarah, everything he was feeling, from the deepest part of his heart.

When one of them started falling asleep, the other would whisper their name.

"Will," Sarah said.

"Hi," Will said, wide-awake again. Downstairs, the grandfather clock chimed four. They had kept each other up all night.

"I can't sleep," she said. "I don't want to sleep."

"Me neither." He didn't want to waste a minute.

"Will, I had a strange dream about my mother. It seemed so real. Was Martha up here?"

"Once or twice," Will said, stroking her hair. Sarah seemed so content and carefree, as if she weren't sick anymore.

"Maybe it was Martha," Sarah said, "but I don't think so. I think it was my mother."

"Maybe it was," Will said. She felt so beautiful in his arms, so warm and sleepy. Pressing closer, she kissed his shoulder.

Will remembered meeting her for the first time. The birthday flight over the autumn hills. Had he known then? Had he loved her already? It almost seemed possible that it was meant to be from the very start. Pushing back the covers, he gathered her into his arms. "Can you stand?" he asked.

"Yes, why?" she asked.

Climbing out of bed, he tugged off the quilt. He held Sarah close, pulled the quilt around them. His heart beat fast as he led her to the window. Together they stood still, feeling the cold air around them.

"It's so beautiful," she whispered, staring at the moon's silver path on the blue-black bay.

"You are," he said. "Sarah . . ."

She looked up at him, her eyes wide and shining.

"Will you marry me?" he asked.

"Oh, Will—"

"In the island chapel. Today. Will you marry me?"

"I WISH I were there," Susan whispered, too bereaved to talk in a normal voice.

"I know you do," her mother said.

"We're glad you're here," Julian said.

He was trying so hard Susan couldn't even bear to shoot him a hateful look. They were all sitting at the breakfast table, staring at their bowls of oatmeal and not eating. The baby bear, the mama bear, and the dorky stepfather bear. Susan checked her watch. "I have to go to school," she said.

"Um, no, you don't," Julian said.

"We're keeping you home today," her mother said quietly.

"Why?" Susan asked, a pit in her stomach. "Did you hear something about Sarah?"

"No," Julian said quickly. "We would have told you if we did."

"We've made an appointment for you," her mother said. "With Dr. Darrow."

"Please, no," Susan said with horror, picturing those scary twins, the Darrow family pictures hanging on the wall.

"I've been a little blind," her mother said.

"Moving in here," Julian said. "Getting a new stepfather. We know it hasn't been all Mardi Gras."

"All? Try none," Susan muttered. In about ten seconds she was changing her name back to Snow. Maybe she'd go for Sleet. "You don't know the half of it, Julian."

"Tell me, then," he said.

"DOF, divorce, getting a new kitten and having him taken to the pound."

"What's DOF?" Julian asked, intensely earnest.

"Death of Fred," Susan said.

"Wish I'd known him," Julian said.

"Many people feel that way," Susan said, looking down at her socks. They were the ones Fred used to wear with black jeans.

"That kitten," Julian said. "He was pretty cute."

"Dr. Darrow," Susan said bitterly. "They trusted me, giving him to me. His great-great-great-grandmother was Desdemona."

"Good bloodlines," Julian said, stirring his oatmeal.

"Maybe we acted rashly," her mother said. "Your father's right. Your allergy tests didn't come up positive for cats."

Susan's head snapped up. "You mean I can have him back?"

Her mother nodded. "Yes," she said.

"Oh, Mom," Susan said. "Thank you!"

"You're welcome, honey."

"Can we go now?" Susan asked, jumping up.

Her mother smiled. "On our way to the real Dr. Darrow's."

"Oh, no," Susan said. "You're making me go?"

Her mother nodded.

"If your mother says you have to go," Julian said, putting an arm around her shoulders, "you might as well put your coat on."

SARAH woke up. She was in the midst of a small miracle, and she knew it. Today was her wedding day. Will had woken up an hour ago, if he had fallen asleep at all. He'd kissed her, then had gone downstairs to get everything ready. Stretching, she tested her body. Her pain hadn't come back. She walked to the window, and with every step she knew, Today I'm going to die.

Yesterday's brilliance had worn off, and the sky looked close enough to touch. It was a snow sky, lacy with fine clouds. At the sound of a knock Sarah turned around. Aunt Bess opened the door a crack. When she saw that Sarah was up, she came into the room carrying a large box.

"Sarah," she said, her face turning pink. "When Will told us the news, I couldn't believe it. But we're so happy. All of us." She laid the box on the bed and walked to the window.

"Thank you, Aunt Bess," Sarah said, allowing her aunt to fold her into her arms.

"Will's dear," Aunt Bess said. "I love him."

"So do I," Sarah said.

"I've waited a long time for this day," Aunt Bess said, walking over to the bed. She opened the box. "Your mother was so beautiful," Bess went on, lifting the white satin dress from the box.

Sarah gasped. She touched the fabric of her mother's wedding dress. The white satin felt creamy against her skin. "I hope it fits," she whispered, holding the dress against her thin body.

"It will," Aunt Bess said.

"Aunt Bess, my pain is gone," Sarah said suddenly.

"I know, honey."

"What do you think it means?" Sarah asked.

"It means you have something important to do," Bess said.

THE geese honked and waddled around the yard. George and Mike stood by the Jeep in their church clothes, waiting for Sarah, Bess, and the nurse to come out. Will paced the walk. He looked like some navy flyboy in his bomber jacket.

"You've given this some thought?" George asked.

"A lot of thought," Will said.

"Not enough so you thought to bring a suit," George said, narrowing his eyes.

"I had a few things on my mind leaving Fort Cromwell."

"She's my only daughter!" George exploded.

"Grandpa," Mike said. "She wants to marry him."

"Yes, well," George sputtered. "She hasn't always been so wise about picking men in the past. Now you swoop into our lives, and everything's all topsy-turvy."

"What's all topsy-turvy?" Will asked.

"Well, the fact you nearly killed her in a crash, for one thing."

"It was mechanical failure. The nose gear wouldn't engage."

"Don't you service your planes?" George asked.

"I service my planes, George. I'm sorry, all right?"

"No, not all right. You think a little apology's going to make up for everything?"

"The plane crash. What else?"

"Her getting sick again," George yelled. "That's what!"

Will stood still. George had shocked him; that was sure.

"Getting herself all stirred up," George said, breaking down. "That's what happened. Her system just can't take it." He turned away so the others wouldn't see him crying. He'd lost Rose the same way. Tried to keep her lying down, free of emotions, but no, she'd wanted to get herself involved in everything.

"Sir?" Will asked, standing behind George's left shoulder.

"What?" George snapped.

"Something I forgot to ask."

George gathered himself together. His throat ached. He turned and gave Will a rough nod.

"George, I'd like to ask you for your daughter's hand in marriage."

Standing there, feet planted in the snow, George blinked up at the sky. Snow was starting to fall.

"Please, George," Will said. His tone was soft.

Slowly George nodded. "Yes," he said. "I give you my blessing."

"I love your daughter."

George squinted at Will Burke. "I know you do, son," George heard himself saying. He pulled his future son-in-law over, gave him a backslapping hug just as the door opened and Sarah walked out. Will was crying, and George kept him turned away from her.

After all, George knew, it was bad luck for him to see the bride before the wedding.

BY THE time they crossed the island, snow was falling hard. The dark stone church sat on the edge of the sea, low to the ground, the green wreath still on the door. George led Will into the church. Will still hadn't seen Sarah. Bess had made a big production of making sure he sat in the front of the Jeep while Sarah sat in back.

She sat there now beside her son while the others went inside.

"You okay?" Mike asked. "Warm enough?"

"Yes," she said, although she was shivering.

"I drove over a while ago to turn on the heaters."

Sarah turned, smiling. "You're so thoughtful," she said.

Mike shrugged.

"Snow wanted to come. I know she'd love to hear from you."

"Maybe I'll call her," Mike said.

Sarah nodded. "She likes you," she said, and that was the moment it hit her: She wasn't going to be around to find out what happened. She wouldn't see Mike turn eighteen, wouldn't find out whether he went to school again. If he fell in love with Susan, she wouldn't be around to see it. "Mike," she said, staring at him.

"What, Mom?"

"Honey," she said. "I want—".

"I know, Mom," he said.

"No, you—" She paused to regain a shred of composure. "Be happy, Mike," she managed to say.

He looked worried. Her face showed everything. It always had. She had dressed for the wedding, put on a little makeup, but it couldn't disguise what was happening.

Mike stepped out of the Jeep, came around to her side, and helped her out. They walked up the stone walk. Pausing at the steps, Sarah hugged her son. He supported her with strong arms, holding her steady.

"Mike, will you tell . . ." Something in his eyes made her know she could ask. "Will you tell your kids about me?"

"Oh, Mom," he said, smiling with great strength. "Look where I am. I'm on Elk Island. It's where I want to be, and that's because of you. I love it here, Mom. It's our home." He held her close, then took her hand. "Come on," he said hoarsely but with gentleness. "Let's go in."

They opened the door. Stepping inside, Sarah drew a deep breath.

There he was. Will stood by the altar. His shoulders were so broad they strained at his jacket, and he leaned slightly forward in a posture of yearning.

Reverend Dunston stood there in black and purple robes. He smiled. Aunt Bess and Martha sat in the front row, beaming.

Sarah's father stepped out of the shadows, took her left arm. "Rose's dress," he said softly, bending his forehead to touch hers. "Are you ready, sweetheart?"

"Yes, Dad."

"Okay, Mom," Mike said. "Here we go."

The music was Bach. Old and beautiful, it played in high, reedy notes from an old tape recorder. Candles filled the church, their smoke mingling with incense. A miracle had brought Sarah this far. She was so close, she didn't have much further to go.

Her eyes never left Will's.

Very slowly Sarah began to walk down the aisle. Her father and her son were by her side, her arms solidly in theirs.

Love. Sarah Talbot felt it with all her heart. The candles blazed around her. Dim snow light came through the blue stained glass, the saints looking on. She had two strong men at her side. Only a few steps more to go. Sarah kept her eyes straight ahead, trained on Will's face. His eyes were deep blue, pools of love and sorrow. "Be joyful," she wanted to cry. "It's our wedding day!" Life was so short. Every moment was precious.

Reaching the altar, Mike and her father paused. Sarah looked her father in the eye. She kissed him, and she heard him whisper, "My beautiful child."

She turned to Mike to receive his kiss, saying, "My beautiful child."

Will took her hand. They gazed deeply into each other's eyes, and Sarah felt his love to the depths of her soul. Her body shivered uncontrollably. Taking her in his arms, Will held her.

"Sarah," the minister said. "William."

Will nodded.

"Love one another, but make not a bond of love. Let it rather be a moving sea between the shores of your souls. . . ."

Time went so fast. So much love, such alarming and radiant joy, Sarah thought. Her family had gathered around. Her body felt tired, heavy. Faltering, she leaned harder on Will. His eyes were so very sad.

Reverend Dunston looked from Sarah to Will. "Do you, William, take Sarah, whom you hold by the hand, to be your true wife, to love, honor, and cherish in joy and in pain, in sickness and in health, forsaking all others, until death do you part?"

"I do," Will said.

"And do you, Sarah, take William, whom you hold by the hand, to be your true husband, to love, honor, and cherish in joy and in pain, in sickness and in health, forsaking all others, until death do you part?"

"I do," Sarah whispered. Tears running down her face, she was staring at Will.

"Stay," he whispered, as if he couldn't help himself.

Will was supposed to be the brave one. The strong man, the bridegroom faking happiness for Sarah's sake. Sarah was dying, leaving him, and he was supposed to be stoic and brave.

"Oh," Sarah wept. *Till death do you part.* She felt it coming. It was peaceful, and it was terrible.

"What emblems do you have of your love and regard for one another?" Reverend Dunston asked.

Her father handed her mother's gold wedding band to Mike, who handed it to Will. Will placed the ring on Sarah's finger. Repeating after Reverend Dunston, he said, "With this ring I thee wed, and with all my love I thee endow."

Aunt Bess stepped forward. She pressed something hard into Sarah's hand. "Darling," she whispered. "It belonged to your uncle Arthur."

"Bless you, Aunt Bess," Sarah said. Sliding the ring onto Will's finger, she held his hand, repeating, "With this ring I thee wed, and with all my love I thee endow."

They clasped hands, and Sarah felt her heart soar. They smiled and smiled. She was never going to let go.

"Sarah and William," Reverend Dunston said. "By the power vested in me by the church and the state of Maine, I now pronounce you husband and wife. You may kiss the bride."

Tilting her head back, Sarah felt Will kiss her lips. The kiss was tender. Her lips met his, and his arms encircled her body, and they were husband and wife. "Will," she said, smiling.

"Husband and wife," Will said, grinning, making her remember how he had looked that first time they met, on her birthday flight. The ride had lasted a long time—longer than it was supposed to—but their time was almost done. Time was a gift, and she and Will had loved every minute. They had been on a journey, a secret path, and for Sarah it led back home.

Her son was there, standing behind them. Susan, Sarah thought. Snow. Wherever you are, hello, my daughter. Her heart fluttered. Angel wings moved the air. Her mother was beside her, and Fred. Sarah could hardly breathe. Tears blurred her vision. Life . . . oh, life. "Till death do us part," Sarah whispered.

"Forever," Will said.

"Forever," Sarah said. She gazed at her husband to memorize his face. Forever.

Epilogue

I T WAS Labor Day, and all the island grasses were golden. They tickled Susan's legs as she walked along the path. She had set out from the house nearly an hour before, passing places she had first seen the previous November, when the island was covered with snow.

The church stood straight ahead. She felt nervous about what she was doing, although she had been planning it all along. Her knapsack felt heavy, bumping her back with every step. The discomfort didn't bother her.

The chapel was beautiful, the dark stone steeple rising into the blue sky. A bouquet of wildflowers was tied to the door, and Susan wondered who had put it there. Walking around the side, she went through the gate to the small churchyard. She felt shy, as if she were meeting someone important for the first time. Palms damp, she wiped her hands on the sides of her jeans.

She looked at the small cluster of graves. One stone was so much newer than the others, there was no mistaking it. Susan walked toward it. Brushing the smooth granite with her fingers, she lowered herself to her knees. "Hello, Sarah," she said.

The gravestone was small and humble, the carving deep and sharp. Seeing the name etched in stone made everything so real: SARAH TALBOT BURKE. BELOVED OF THE ISLAND.

"Not just the island," Susan said, frowning. Did Elk Island think it was the only place Sarah had been loved? She felt the resentment, a big knot in her stomach. But suddenly she could almost hear Sarah's gentle laugh.

"I've missed you," Susan said, gazing fixedly at Sarah's name. Settling down, she took off her knapsack. A bouquet, identical to the one on the church door, lay at the base of the stone. Sticking out from beneath the tangle of asters, goldenrod, and Queen Anne's lace was a note in her father's handwriting.

"Dad's here too," Susan said. "I know he was out here early this morning. I heard him leave the house. He misses you too, Sarah." Her heart shrank a little, and she curled inward and wept.

"A lot," she said when she could talk again. "He kind of shut down for a while. Even I couldn't get to him. But Sarah . . ." Swallowing hard, Susan touched the stone again, tracing the letters with her fingers. "He had to go through it. He explained everything to me on our way out here. It's like what I went through with Fred. Love is the greatest blessing there is, and when you love someone as much as he loved you, you can't let go lightly. You just can't."

They had come to pick up Mike. Did Sarah already know? Was she sitting somewhere, radiant and smiling, because Mike had decided to finish his senior year, live with Will until next summer?

"Your father had a fit at first," Susan said, smiling. "He and my dad had these long-distance phone battles. Poor Aunt Bess. She'd call back when George wasn't around, to apologize."

Laughing, Susan bowed her head. "The funny thing was, in the end he accepted it. Good old George!" Her hands shaking slightly, she untied the cord on her knapsack. Carefully pulling out the plaque, she sighed.

"Everyone loves you," Susan began. "Everyone. Your father and Aunt Bess, Mike, my dad. Sarah, my dad loves you so much. You were such a gift to him. You have no idea how much you taught him . . . to love—but, even more, to hope. My dad has so much hope now. He gets up every day, and he lives it for you."

Susan caught her breath. "Remember, Sarah? When we first met? I mean, I'd seen you at your birthday flight, but we didn't actually meet until that day in your shop when I came in freezing cold." A shadow passed across the grave. Susan wanted it to be the eagle, but it was only a cloud gliding across the brilliant sun. "I wanted you to be all mine. When those college girls came in, I felt jealous. But you are mine. You knew me, Sarah. Really knew me."

Making a place beside her father's flowers, Susan stood the

plaque she had made against the gravestone. It was a small blue wooden oval, a magical cloud with a golden 9, feathers falling like snow—a tiny replica of the sign at Sarah's shop.

"My father helped me make this," she said. "We did it in his workshop at the airport all last winter, after you died."

For a minute she remembered the cold hangar, the silence as they worked the wood on the long tool bench, both feeling the loss of Sarah. But by the time the sign was ready to paint, spring had filled the orchards surrounding the airfield with apple and pear blossoms. Susan and her father spent those long hours together.

"When I was making the sign," Susan said, tears making her throat ache, "I was thinking that that was our place—your shop, Cloud Nine. But Sarah . . ." She looked around. Waves broke on the rocks below, and seagulls cried, sounding exultant. "You're with me all the time. That's the amazing thing. Cloud Nine is just where we started, but I have you with me always." She read Sarah's stone again. "Sarah Talbot Burke. Beloved of the island," she said out loud.

Looking up, she saw the eagle. He circled once, a tight bend overhead. Then he ranged out over the moors, around toward the bay, dipping low before he was lost to sight. It didn't matter. Susan knew he would be back. She and her father would take Mike home, and next summer they would all return to the island. The eagle would be here, and so would Sarah.

Standing, Susan brushed bits of grass from her palms. She checked to make sure her plaque was solidly wedged against Sarah's grave to keep her company while Susan, Mike, and her father were away. It wasn't going anywhere. "Beloved," Susan whispered, touching the letters one more time, "of the island."

This time the words didn't seem so hard to say.

LUANNE RICE

"People sometimes ask me what my novels are about, and I always say the same thing: love. It is an easy answer but, like life itself, far from simple." Luanne Rice, the author of seven highly acclaimed novels, traces her love of writing to her mother, an English teacher, who used to hold writing seminars for Luanne and her two sisters. "She'd give us exercises to do— write twenty words to describe a cloud, compose three haiku about starfish," recalls the author. Rice's mother died a few years ago, but her influence remains. As Rice wrote *Cloud Nine*, she says, "I had the feeling that my mother was with me."

THE SIMPLE TRUTH

DAVID BALDACCI

It happened twenty-five years ago: A young soldier committed a heinous crime in full view of witnesses.

He was tried, convicted, and put away for life.

For twenty-five years the truth was that simple.

Until today . . .

AT THIS prison the doors are inches thick, steel. Once factory-smooth, they now carry multiple dents. Imprints of human faces, knees, elbows, teeth are harvested large on their gray surface. Prison hieroglyphics: pain, fear, death—all permanently recorded here. The doors have a square opening at eye level. The guards stare through it, use the small space to throw bright lights at the human cattle on their watch. Without warning, batons smack against the metal with the pop of gun reports. The oldies bear it well, looking down at the floor in a subtle act of defiance, not that anyone notices or cares. The rookies still tense when the pop or light comes, but they soon get over it, fight down the push of schoolboy tears. If they want to survive.

On this night a thunderstorm grips the area. When a lightning bolt dips from the sky, it splashes illumination into the cells through the small Plexiglas windows. During the passage of such light a man's face emerges from the dark, as though suddenly parting the surface of water. Unlike those in the other cells, he sits alone, thinks alone, sees no one. The other prisoners fear him; the guards too, even armed as they are, for he is a man of intimidating proportions. His name is Rufus Harms, and his reputation at Fort Jackson Military Prison is that of a destroyer. He will crush you if you come at him.

Twenty-five years of incarceration have taken a considerable toll

on the man. The ruts of scars on his skin, the poorly healed frac-
tures of bone on his skeleton are a chronicle of his time here. Worse
damage lies within the soft tissue of his brain: memory, thought,
love, hate, fear—all tainted, turned against him. But mostly memory.

Harms is a living oxymoron: a gentle man, respectful of others,
faithful to his God, irreversibly cast in the image of a heartless killer.
Because of this, the guards and the other prisoners leave him be.
And he is content with that. Until this day. The letter his brother
has brought him. A package of gold, a surge of hope. A way out of
this place.

Another burst of light shows his eyes brimming with deep red,
as though bloodied, until one sees the tears that stain his dark,
heavy face. As the light recedes, he smoothes out the piece of paper.
Lights have been extinguished for several hours now, but the darkness matters little. He has already read the letter, absorbed every
word. Each syllable cuts him like the quick bite of a shiv. The in-
signia of the United States Army appears bold at the top of the paper. He knows the symbol well. The army has been his employer,
his warden for almost thirty years.

Until he read the letter, he had only two memories of that night
twenty-five years ago: the little girl and the rain. It had been a punishing storm, much like tonight. The girl's features were delicate,
her staring eyes blue and innocent. Her skin was white, unblem-
ished except for the red marks crushed upon a neck as fragile as a
flower stem. The marks had been caused by the hands of Private
Rufus Harms, the same hands that now clutched the letter.

Whenever he thought of the dead girl, he wept, but he did so
silently. The guards and cons were sharks—they sniffed blood,
weakness, an opening from a million miles away.

He was kneeling beside her when the MPs found him, wet and
shivering, his knees sunk deeply into the mud. The next day he
would come to learn the little girl's name, Ruth Ann Mosley. Ten
years old, from Columbia, South Carolina. She and her family had
been visiting her brother, who was stationed at the base. On that
night Harms had only known Ruth Ann as a corpse: small—tiny, in
fact—compared to the stunning breadth of his six-foot-five-inch

three-hundred-pound body. The blurred image of the rifle butt that one of the MPs smashed against his skull represented the last mental sliver Harms carried from that night. His face in the mud, Rufus Harms saw nothing more. Remembered nothing more.

Until tonight. He swells his lungs with rain-drenched air and stares out the half-open window. He is suddenly that still rare beast: an innocent man in prison.

He had convinced himself over the years that such evil had been lurking cancerlike within him. He had even thought of suicide, to make penance for stealing the life of another, more pitiably a child's. But he was deeply religious and not a fleeting jailhouse convert. He thus could not commit the sin of suicide.

Now he understands that his decision to live has been right. The Lord has kept him alive for this moment. With stunning clarity he recalls the faces of the men who came for him that night at the stockade, the way they circled him, like wolves. What they did that night caused Ruth Ann Mosley to die.

Twenty-five years of terrible, wrenching guilt have relentlessly taunted Rufus Harms until he is just barely in possession of a ruined life. He knows that it is now their turn to suffer. He grips the worn Bible his mother gave him, and he promises this to the God who has chosen never to abandon him.

CHAPTER ONE

 HE steps leading up to the United States Supreme Court building were wide and seemingly endless. Trudging up them was akin to laboring toward Mount Olympus to request an audience with Zeus, which in a real sense you were. Engraved above the main doorway were the words "Equal Justice Under Law."

Since 1935 the majestic four-story building had been the professional home to nine men and, since 1981, to at least one woman, all of extraordinary achievement. They were the defenders and interpreters of the United States Constitution. These nine people could declare an act of Congress unconstitutional. They could force a sitting President to turn over tapes and documents that would ultimately lead to his resignation and disgrace. Crafted alongside the legislative authority of the Congress and the executive power of the presidency by the founding fathers, the American judiciary, headed by the Supreme Court, was an equal branch of government. It bent and shaped the will of the American people by virtue of its decisions.

The elderly man striding through the marble Great Hall carried on this honored tradition. He was tall and bony. His hair was nearly gone, and he walked with a slight limp. Still, Chief Justice Harold Ramsey had energy and a peerless intellect that more than compensated for any physical slide. He was the highest-ranking jurist in the land, and this was his Court. The Ramsey Court, the media had long deemed it, and he ran it tight and true.

Ramsey let out a contented sigh. Another Court term had just begun. Things were going smoothly. But there was one hitch: Ramsey knew he was close to meeting his match with Elizabeth Knight. She was as smart as he and just as tough perhaps. A young-blood female on a court of old men. He had tried to place her under his wing, to guide her, but she had shown a stubborn independent streak. He had watched other Chief Justices grow complacent, let their guard down, with the result that their leadership had been usurped. Ramsey was determined never to join that group.

"MURPHY'S concerned about the Chance case," Michael Fiske said to Sara Evans. They were in her office on the second floor of the Court building. Michael was six two and handsome, with the graceful proportions of the athlete he once was. Most clerks did a one-year stint at the Supreme Court before moving on to prestigious positions in private practice, public service, or academe. Michael was beginning an almost unprecedented third year as senior clerk to Justice Thomas Murphy, the Court's legendary liberal.

Michael was the possessor of a truly wondrous mind. He could mentally juggle dozens of complex scenarios. At the Court he happily labored over cases of national importance. He really didn't want to leave. The outside world held no appeal for him.

Sara looked worried. The previous term Murphy had voted to hear the Chance case. Oral argument was set, and the bench memo was being prepared. Sara was in her mid-twenties, about five five, slender, but her body possessed subtle curves. Her face was nicely shaped, the eyes wide and blue. Her hair was thick and light brown; it still turned blondish in the summer. She was the senior clerk for Justice Elizabeth Knight. "I don't understand. I thought he was behind us on this. It's right up his alley. Little person against a big bureaucracy. What does he want?"

This was how it went most of the time—the famed clerk network. They hustled and scrounged for votes on behalf of their Justices like shameless political hucksters. It was beneath the Justices to openly lobby for votes, but it wasn't for clerks. The process was akin to an enormous, never-ending gossip column with national interests at stake. In the hands of twenty-five-year-olds at their first real job, no less.

"He doesn't necessarily disagree with Knight's position, but he's not going to give away the farm. He was in the military in World War Two. He holds it in the highest regard. He believes it deserves special consideration. You need to know that when you're putting together the draft opinion."

Sara nodded her head in appreciation. *United States* v. *Chance* was one of the most important cases on the docket for this term. Barbara Chance, a private in the army, had been bullied and frightened into repeatedly having sexual intercourse with several of her male superiors. After leaving the military, she had sued the army for damages. The case had slowly worked its way through the proper legal channels, Chance losing at each stop, until it had eventually been plopped like a big tuna on the doorstep of this place.

The current law said that the military was virtually immune from suit by its personnel, but the Justices could change what the law said. And Knight and Sara Evans were working hard to do just that.

Michael stood and looked down at her. It was at his urging that

Sara had signed up for another term at the Court. Raised on a small farm in North Carolina and educated at Stanford, Sara had, like all the clerks here, a wonderful professional future waiting once she left the Court. Having a clerkship on one's résumé was a gold key to entry just about anyplace. That affected some clerks in a negative way, giving them inflated egos. Michael and Sara, though, had remained the same people they had always been. Which was one reason, aside from her intelligence and good looks, that Michael had asked her a very important question a week earlier. A question he hoped to receive an answer to soon. Perhaps now.

"Have you given my question any thought?"

Sara had known it was coming. She had avoided it long enough. "That's all I've been thinking about."

"They say when it takes that long, it's a bad sign." He said this jokingly, but the humor was obviously forced.

"Michael, I like you a lot."

"Like? Oh, boy, another bad sign."

She shook her head. "I'm sorry."

He shrugged. "Probably not half as sorry as I am. I've never asked anyone to marry me before."

"And I can't tell you how flattered I am. You've got it all."

"Except for one thing." Michael looked down at his hands as they quivered a bit.

"You'll find someone, Michael. And that woman will be very lucky." Sara felt so awkward. "I hope this doesn't mean I'm losing my best friend in the Court."

"Probably." He held up a hand as she started to protest. "Just kidding." He sighed. "I don't mean this to sound egotistical, Sara, but this is the first time anybody's really turned me down for anything."

"I wish my life had been so easy." Sara smiled.

"No, you don't. It makes rejection a lot harder to accept." Michael went over to the doorway. "Talk to you later."

"RUFUS?" Samuel Rider cautiously pressed the phone to his ear. "How did you track me down?"

"Ain't many lawyers up these parts," Rufus Harms said.

"I'm not in the army anymore."

"Being on the outside pays good, I guess."

"Some days I miss the uniform," Rider lied. He had been a terri-fied draftee, fortunately with a law degree in hand, and had chosen a safe role in the office of the judge advocate general—or J.A.G.—over toting a gun through the jungles of Vietnam.

"I need to see you," Rufus said. "Don't want to say why over the phone. You still my lawyer, ain't you?"

"Rufus, my schedule's kind of tight, and I don't usually travel over that way." Rider's hand tightened on the phone.

"Tomorrow, Samuel. You think you owe me that?"

Rider now got defensive. "I did the best I could back then. Re-member, they could've executed you. At least you got to live."

"Tomorrow, Samuel. Around about nine a.m. Thank you. Thank you kindly. Oh, bring a little radio with you." Before Rider could ask him why he should bring such a device or why he should even come to see him, Harms had hung up the phone.

Rider eased back in his very comfortable chair and looked around his spacious wood-paneled office. He practiced law in a small rural town near Blacksburg, Virginia. He made a fine living: nice house, new Buick every three years, vacations twice annually. He had put the past behind him, particularly the most horrible case he had ever handled in his brief career as a military lawyer.

Rufus Harms had sounded bitter over the phone, but he *had* killed that little girl. Brutally. Right in front of her family. Rider had been persuaded not to put on much of a case. He had agreed with the prosecutor not to bring in character witnesses from the outside. He had also agreed to rely on the official record instead of at-tempting to find fresh evidence.

That was not exactly playing by the rules, but Rider had gotten Rufus Harms life. That was the best any lawyer could have done.

So what could Rufus want to see him about? he wondered.

DEFENSE attorney John Fiske was at a suburban county jail meet-ing with one of his clients. His practice often took him outside Rich-mond, Virginia, to the counties of Henrico, Chesterfield, Hanover, even Goochland. He was not particularly pleased about his ever-expanding pool of work, but it was like the sun rising—it would continue until the day it stopped for good.

"I've got a plea to talk to you about, Derek. The assistant commonwealth attorney has offered malicious wounding, class three felony."

"Why not class six?"

Fiske stared at him. Derek Brown was a light-skinned black with tattoos of hate and poetry running down his arms. He had been in and out of the criminal system so often he knew the criminal code better than most lawyers.

"Class six is heat of the moment. Your heat came the next day."

"He had a gun, and I ain't got mine. You stupid?"

Fiske wanted to reach across and wipe Derek's attitude right off his face. "Sorry. They're not budging from class three."

"How much time?" Derek said stonily.

"Five, with time already served."

"Five years for cutting somebody with a little pocketknife?"

"Stiletto, six-inch blade. And you stabbed him ten little times. In front of witnesses. You're lucky you're not looking at murder in the first, Derek."

"He was messing with my woman. Ain't that a defense?" Derek leaned forward and popped his bony knuckles.

Derek had a good-paying job, Fiske knew, albeit an illegal one. He was a first lieutenant for the number two drug distribution ring in Richmond. Turbo was the boss, all of twenty-four years old. His empire included the façade of legality with dry-cleaning operations, a café, and a stable of accountants and lawyers. Normally Turbo would have one of his three-hundred-dollar-an-hour lawyers take care of Derek. But Derek's offense was unrelated to Turbo's business, so that accommodation had not been made.

"The ACA doesn't care what he was doing to your girlfriend."

"I can't believe this. Buddy of mine cut up somebody last year and he got two years, half that suspended."

"Did your buddy have a prior felony conviction?" Was your good old buddy one of the top men for one of Richmond's worst diseases? Fiske wanted to ask. But it would be wasted breath. "I tell you what—I'll go back with three and time served."

Now Derek looked interested. "You think you can get that?"

Fiske stood up. "Don't know."

On the way out, Fiske looked out the barred window and watched as a new shipment of inmates climbed from the prison van. Most were young blacks or Latinos. Some of these young men were probably the sons of men Patrolman John Fiske had arrested ten years before. The dialogue he had had with arrestees tended to repeat itself.

"Kill you, man. Kill your whole damn family," some would scream at him, drug-faced, as he put the cuffs on.

"You have the right to remain silent. Think about using it."

"Come on, man, ain't my fault. My buddy done it."

"You have the right to an attorney," he would calmly tell them.

And now that attorney was John Fiske.

After a couple of court appearances in downtown Richmond, Fiske headed down Ninth Street toward the James River. His office, in Shockoe Slip, was located in a cavernous building that had once been a tobacco warehouse. Its oak and pine guts had been given the new ribs of multiple-office drywall, but the reek of the tobacco leaves forever lingered.

Fiske's office was one room with a small attached bathroom, which was important, since he slept here more often than he did at his apartment. He hung up his coat and put on a pot of coffee.

At six feet, John was a couple of inches shorter than his younger brother, and unlike Michael Fiske, his features were far from classically handsome. He had chubby cheeks, a too sharp chin, and a twice-broken nose—one time from high school wrestling, the other time a carryover from his cop days. However, his black hair was swept over his forehead in an unkempt manner that somehow managed to be attractive, and his brown eyes housed an intense core.

John sat down abruptly. The burn started slowly. It usually did. He sensed its march from his belly up to his chest, then spreading, like lava, down his arms and into his fingers. Fiske locked his office door and stripped off his shirt and tie. Through the cotton of his T-shirt his fingers touched the thickened scar. It began just below his navel and followed the meandering path of the surgeon's saw, until it ended at the base of his neck.

Fiske dropped to the floor and did fifty push-ups, the heat in his chest surging and then diminishing with each repetition. He followed the push-ups with an equal number of stomach crunches. The scar rippled and flexed with each bend of his body, like a serpent unwillingly grafted to his torso. What lurked beneath that fused skin would eventually overtake him, kill him, but for now, the heat faded. The physical exertion seemed to frighten it off.

He cleaned up in the bathroom and put his shirt back on. As he sipped his coffee, he looked out the window. From this vantage point he could barely make out the line of the James River. He and his brother had often floated down that river in truck-tire inner tubes on hot summer days. That had been years before. This was as close as Fiske got to the water these days. Leisure time was over. He had no space left for it in his shortened frame of life. He wasn't a Supreme Court super-lawyer like his brother. He would have no money or grand reputation when he died, but he believed he would die reasonably satisfied, reasonably fulfilled.

LIKE a brooding hawk, Fort Jackson Military Prison was perched on the desolate topography of southwestern Virginia, in the middle of a remote scrap of coal country. There had never been an escape, and even if an inmate could manage to achieve his freedom without benefit of a court ruling, such liberty would be short-lived. The surrounding countryside represented a prison of even greater menace, with jagged-faced strip-mined mountains and dense unyielding forests laced with copperheads and rattlers. Along the waterways awaited their more aggressive cousin, the water moccasin, anxious for panicked feet crashing its borders.

Attorney Samuel Rider passed through the fort's main gate, received his visitors badge, and parked his car in the visitors lot. It took him twenty minutes to go through the screening procedure, which included a pat-down of his person and a search of his briefcase. The guards suspiciously eyed the small transistor radio but allowed him to keep it after confirming that it contained no contraband. He took a deep breath as a guard escorted him to the visitors room.

Alone for a few minutes, Rider eyed the dull brown of the walls in the room. He mentally signaled his heart to calm down and wondered why he had come. Rufus Harms was in no position to make him, or anyone else, do anything. But here he was.

Rider stopped his musings as Rufus Harms, towering over the two guards trailing him, entered the visitors room. Harms was the largest man Rider had ever personally encountered, a giant whose arms were thicker than some trees. He wore shackles on his hands and feet. He had to be close to fifty but looked a good ten years older. Rider noted the facial scars, the awkward twist of bone beneath Harms's right eye, and wondered what other telling evidence of abuse he carried under his clothing.

Harms sat down across from Rider at a wooden table. He didn't look at Rider just yet but instead eyed the guard who remained in the room.

Rider caught Harms's silent meaning and said to the guard, "Private, I'm his lawyer, so I'd be obliged if you could stand farther away. Attorney-client privilege. You understand?"

The guard didn't answer, but he did move to the far end of the room. Finally Rufus looked over at Rider. "Take out the radio and turn it on, would you?"

Rider did so. The room was immediately filled with the mournful tunes of country-western music. When the lawyer looked at him questioningly, Harms glanced around the room. "Lotta ears around this place, some you can't see."

"Bugging the conversations of an attorney and his client is against the law."

Harms moved his hands slightly, chains rattling. "Lot of things against the law, but people still do 'em. Right?"

Rider found himself nodding.

The inmate leaned forward and started speaking in a tone so low that Rider had to strain to hear him above the music. "I thank you for coming. I'm surprised you did."

"Surprised me to hear from you. But it got my curiosity up."

"I won't waste your time. I got something I want you to file in court for me."

Rider's astonishment was clear. "What court?"

Harms spoke in even lower tones, despite the cover of the music. "Biggest one there is—Supreme Court."

Rider's jaw went slack. "You got to be kidding."

With smooth increments of motion, despite the restraints of the manacles, Harms slid an envelope out of his shirt. In an instant the guard stepped across and snatched it.

Rider protested immediately. "Private, that is a confidential attorney-client communication."

"Let him read it, Samuel. I got nothing to hide," Harms said.

The guard opened the envelope and scanned the contents of the letter. Satisfied, he returned it to Harms and resumed his post.

Harms handed the envelope and letter across to Rider, who looked down at the material. When he looked back up, Harms was leaning even closer to him, and he spoke for at least ten minutes. Several times Rider's eyes widened as Harms's words spilled over him. Finished, the prisoner sat back. "You going to help me, ain't you?"

Rider could not answer, still digesting all that he had heard, but finally he nodded. "I'll help you, Rufus."

He put the paper back in the envelope and tucked it and the radio away in his briefcase. The lawyer had no way of knowing that on the other side of a large mirror that hung on the wall of the visitors room, someone had watched the entire exchange between prisoner and attorney. This person now rubbed his chin, lost in deep, troubled thought.

"BOY, Ramsey was efficient this morning," Sara remarked. She and Michael were in the Court's cafeteria. "He sliced up that university's lawyer in about five seconds."

Michael swallowed a bite of sandwich. "I admire Ramsey. He sticks it equally to the poor and the rich, the state and the individual. He doesn't play favorites. And by the way, what was Knight trying to do in there today, talking about rights for the poor? Is she posturing for something down the road?"

"I can't believe you're asking me that. It's confidential."

"We're all on the same team here, Sara."

"Michael, I really can't go into it. You don't have to know everything that goes on at this place. I mean, you already know more than most of the Justices. How many other clerks go down to the mailroom at the crack of dawn to get a jump on the appeals coming in?"

"I don't like to do anything halfway."

She looked at him, was about to say something, but then stopped herself. Why complicate things?

He sighed and picked at his meal. "We're just pulling away from each other at all points, aren't we?"

"That's not true. You're just trying to make it seem that way."

He suddenly grinned. "Maybe it's for the best. We're both so headstrong, we'd probably end up killing each other." He fiddled with his drink and eyed her. "But if you think I'm stubborn, you really should meet my brother."

Sara didn't meet his gaze. "I'm sure. He was terrific during that trial we watched."

"I'm very proud of him."

Now she looked at him. "So why did we have to sneak in and out of the courtroom so he wouldn't know we were there?"

"You'd have to ask him that."

"I'm asking *you.*"

Michael shrugged. "He's got a problem with me. I actually don't know all the reasons. Maybe he doesn't either. I do know that I've walked in his shadow all my life."

"But you're the boy genius with a limitless future."

"And he's a heroic ex-cop who now defends the very people he used to arrest. He also has a martyr quality about him that I never have been able to get around." Michael shook his head. All the time his brother had spent in the hospital, none of them knowing if he was going to make it. He had never known such fear—the thought of losing his brother. But he had lost him anyway, it seemed, and not because of death. Not because of those bullets.

"Maybe he feels like he's living in your shadow."

"I doubt that."

"Did you ever ask him?"

"We don't talk anymore." He paused and then added quietly, "Is John the reason you turned me down?" He had watched her as she observed his brother. She had been enraptured with John Fiske from the moment she saw him.

She flushed. "I don't even know him. How could I possibly have any feelings for him?"

"Are you asking me or yourself?"

"I'm not going to answer that." Her voice trembled. "What about you? Do you love him?"

He abruptly sat up straight and looked at her. "I will always love my brother, Sara. Always."

CHAPTER TWO

 IDER wordlessly passed his secretary, fled to his office, opened his briefcase, and slipped out the envelope. He withdrew the letter from inside and tossed it in the wastebasket. In the letter, Rufus Harms had written his last will and testament, but that was just a dodge, something innocuous for the guard to read.

Rider plugged in his hot plate, and within a few minutes steam poured out of his teakettle. Gingerly grasping the envelope by its edges, he held it over the steam and watched as the envelope began to come apart, just as Rufus Harms had told him it would. He now held two pieces of paper: one handwritten, the other a copy of a letter from the army.

As he turned off the hot plate, Rider marveled at the device Rufus had managed to construct—an envelope that was actually a letter— and how he had copied and then concealed the letter from the army in it as well. Then he recalled that Harms's father had worked at a printing press. It would have been better for Rufus if he had followed his father into the printing business instead of joining the army.

He let the pieces of paper dry out for a minute and then sat behind his desk while he read what Rufus had written. It didn't take long—the remarks were fairly brief, though many words were oddly formed and misspelled. There wasn't a trace of saliva left in Rider's throat when he had finished reading. Then he forced himself to read the official notice from the army. Another body blow.

"Unbelievable!" He sank back in his chair and rubbed a trembling hand over his bald spot. The fear spread like a mutating virus. Rider looked once more at the notice from the army, the stark lie of the past now firmly revealed. This information should have been in Harms's military file at the time of the murder, but it wasn't. It would have constituted a completely plausible defense. Harms's file had been tampered with, and Rider now understood why.

Harms wanted his name cleared and his freedom, and he refused to entrust his appeal to the army. That's what he had said while the country-western music covered his words. And could Rider blame him? Harms should be heard, and he should be free.

But despite that, Rider remained immobile. If he did as Rufus asked, he would be the attorney of record in Harms's appeal. He had planned to retire in a few years to the condo he and his wife had on the Gulf Coast. Their kids were grown, and Rider was weary of the frigid winters. However, as enticing as that retirement was, it wasn't quite enough to prevent Rider from helping his old client. Some things were right and some things were wrong.

As he took out a sheet of paper from his desk drawer, sunlight from the window glanced off his square gold cuff links, sending bright dots around the room helter-skelter. He pulled over his ancient typewriter. Rider was unfamiliar with the Supreme Court's technical filing requirements, but he assumed he would be running afoul of most of them. That didn't bother him.

When he had finished typing, he started to place what he had typed into a mailing envelope. Then he stopped. Paranoia, spilling over from thirty years of practice, made him hustle out to the small workroom at the rear of his office suite and make copies of both Harms's handwritten letter and Rider's own typewritten one. This same uneasiness made him decide to keep, for now, the letter from the army. He hid the copies in a drawer and locked it. He returned the originals to the envelope, looked up the address of the Supreme Court in his legal directory, and typed up a label. That done, he put on his hat and coat, and walked down to the post office at the corner, silently praying that he was doing the right thing, and knowing in his heart that he was.

JOHN Fiske walked into the building located in the West End of Richmond. The place was officially called a rest home, but plain and simple, it was a place for the elderly to come to die. It had taken all the resolve he and his father had in order to move John's mother into this place. Michael Fiske had never faced up to the fact that their mother's mind was gone, eaten away by Alzheimer's.

"How is she today?" he asked the administrator at the desk.

"She's had better ones, John, but your being here will perk her up," the woman answered.

"Right," Fiske muttered as he walked to the visitors room.

His mother awaited him there, dressed in housecoat and slippers. Her eyes wandered aimlessly. When Fiske appeared at the doorway, a smile broke across her face. He walked over and sat down.

"How's my Mikey?" Gladys Fiske asked, tenderly rubbing his face. "How's Momma's baby?"

Fiske took a deep breath. It was the same damn thing for the last two years. In Gladys Fiske's devastated mind he was Mike.

He gently touched her hands, doing his best to quiet the frustration inside him. "I'm fine. Doing good." He then added quietly, "Johnny's doing good too."

Her stare was blank. "Johnny?"

Fiske attempted this every time, and every time the response was the same. Why did she forget him and not his brother? He had been the son who had always been there for his parents. He had helped them as a boy, and continued to be there for them as a man. But Mike, always the favorite, always the one to go his own way, his own selfish way, Fiske thought, was always hailed as the great one.

"Mikey?" she said anxiously. "How are the children?"

"They're fine, growing like weeds. They look just like you." Having to pretend that he was his brother and had fathered children made Fiske want to collapse to the floor bawling.

She smiled and touched her hair.

He picked up on that. "Looks good. Pop says you're prettier than ever." Gladys had been an attractive woman. She would have been terribly upset with how she looked now, Fiske knew.

He held out a package he had brought. She seized it with the glee of a child and tore off the wrapping. She touched the brush delicately. "It's the most beautiful thing I've ever seen."

She said that about everything he brought her—tissues, lipstick, a picture book. The most beautiful thing she had ever seen. He loved his mother so much. He would rip from her the Alzheimer's that had destroyed her brain if he could. Since he couldn't, he would spend time with her. Even under another's name.

IT WAS early in the morning as Michael Fiske quietly hummed his way through the broad, high-ceilinged hallway toward the mailroom. "Any con mail?" he asked a clerk as he entered the room. He was referring to the ever-growing number of petitions from prisoners, most of which were filed in forma pauperis, literally, in the form of a pauper. Michael knew that some of the most important Court decisions had resulted from IFP cases—thus his early morning ritual of panning for appellate gold in the mail piles.

"From the hand scribblings I've tried to decipher so far, I'd say that was a good bet," the clerk responded.

Michael dragged a box over to one corner. Within its confines was an array of penned miseries of varying content and description, many from death-row inmates. For them the Supreme Court represented the last hope.

For the next two hours Michael dug through the box. He had not found much of great interest and was thinking of heading up to his office when his hand closed around the plain manila envelope. The address label was typewritten, but the envelope had no return address. That was strange. There was, however, the left side of a postal return receipt card affixed to it. He slid open the envelope and removed the two sheets of paper. The forms required to achieve indigent status included a motion for leave to file as a pauper and an affidavit signed by the prisoner, basically swearing to the person's impoverished status. Neither was in the envelope, Michael quickly noted. The appeal would have to be kicked back.

When Michael started reading what *was* in the envelope, all thoughts of any filing deficiencies vanished. After he finished, he could see the sweat from his palms leach onto the paper.

"Hey, Michael, Murphy's chambers just called down for you," the clerk said. When Fiske didn't answer, the clerk said again, "Michael? Justice Murphy is looking for you."

Michael nodded. When the clerk turned back to his work, Michael put the pages back in the manila envelope. He hesitated an instant. His entire legal career, his entire life could be decided in the next second or so. Finally he slipped the envelope into his briefcase. By doing so before the petition had been officially processed, he had just committed theft of federal property—a felony.

The rest of the day moved at a glacial pace. Michael repeatedly found himself staring at his briefcase, thinking of the contents. Late that night, his day's work at the Court finally completed, he furiously rode his bike back to his apartment on Capitol Hill. He locked the door behind him and took out the envelope once more. He grabbed a yellow legal pad from his briefcase and carried everything over to a small dinette table.

An hour later he sat back and stared at the notes he had made. He decided to attack this problem as he would any other. He would check out the information in the petition as carefully as he could. If it seemed legitimate, he would return the appeal to the mailroom. If it was frivolous, he had made up his mind to destroy it.

He had never heard of Rufus Harms. The man had been incarcerated when Michael was five years old, according to the dates in the letter. The spelling was abysmal; the penmanship resembled a child's. The typewritten letter explained some of the background of the case and was obviously composed by a far better educated person—a lawyer perhaps. The language had a legal air to it. A notice from the army, according to the typewritten letter, had requested certain information from Rufus Harms. However, Rufus Harms denied ever being in the program the army's records apparently indicated he was in. It had been a cover, Harms was alleging, for a crime that had resulted in a horrific miscarriage of justice.

All of his life Michael had believed in a person's inalienable franchise to have access to the law, no matter how rich or poor. But this case was different. Even if false, it could still do terrible damage to the reputations of some very important people. But if it was true?

He suddenly wondered if he should seek his brother's advice. John was savvy in ways his younger brother was not. He might know how to handle the situation better. It also might be a way back into his brother's life.

He picked up the phone and dialed. He got the answering machine, a result that pleased a certain part of him. He left a message asking for his brother's help but revealing nothing.

Toward the early hours of the morning Michael drifted off to sleep, growing ever more confident that he could handle this potential nightmare, however it turned out.

JOHN Fiske hustled after the woman walking down the hallway of the court building. "Hey, Janet, got a minute?"

Janet Ryan was a very experienced prosecutor currently doing her best to send one of Fiske's clients away for a long time. She smiled when she turned to him. "For you, two minutes."

"About Rodney—"

"Wait. Refresh my memory. I've got lots of Rodneys."

"Burglary, electronics store, north side."

"Firearm involved, police chase, priors—now I remember. Your case stinks. Your guy is a career crim, and I'll get a jury who'll put him away for a long time."

"So why waste the taxpayers' money, then?"

"What's your deal?"

"Plead to the burglary, drop the firearm count. We end up with five years, with credit for time served."

Janet started walking. "See you in court."

"Okay, okay, eight, but I need to talk with my guy."

She turned around and ticked off the points on her fingers. "He pleads to all of it, he gets ten years, and probation for another five. If he goes to trial, you're looking at twenty. And I want an answer right now."

"Come on, Janet, where's the compassion?"

"Saving it for somebody who deserves it. Yes or no?"

Fiske tapped his fingers against his briefcase.

"Going once, going twice," Ryan said.

"Okay, okay, deal."

"Good doing business with you, John." She walked off humming, while Fiske leaned against the wall and shook his head.

An hour later he returned to his office and tossed down his briefcase. He picked up the phone and checked his messages at home. When he heard his brother's voice, he erased the message. It was rare but not unheard-of for Mike to call. Fiske had never called him back.

A FEW days later Sara Evans knocked and then opened the door to Michael Fiske's office. It was empty. Michael had borrowed a book, and she needed it back. She looked around the room but didn't see it lying anywhere. Then she spotted his briefcase underneath the kneehole of his desk. She picked it up and opened it, and immediately saw two books and some papers inside. Neither book was the one she was looking for, though. She was going to close the briefcase but then stopped. She pulled the papers out and then looked at the envelope they had come in. Addressed to the clerks' office. She had just glanced at the handwritten page and then the typewritten letter when she heard footsteps. She put the papers back, closed the briefcase, and slid it back under the desk.

A moment later Michael walked in. "Sara, what are you doing here?"

She did her best to look normal. "I just came looking for that book I had lent you last week."

"I've got it at home."

"Well, maybe I can come over for dinner and get it."

"I'm kind of busy. I'll bring it tomorrow," he said a little angrily. "Now, I've really got a lot of work to do." He looked at the door.

Sara went over and put her hand on the knob, then looked back. "Michael, if you need to talk about anything, I'm here for you."

"Yeah, okay. Thanks." He ushered her out, and closed and locked the door.

LATER that night Sara pulled her car down the gravel drive and stopped in front of the small cottage located off the George Washington Parkway. The cottage was the first thing she had ever owned, and she had put a lot of work into fixing up the place. A stairway led down to the Potomac, where her small sailboat was docked. She and Michael had spent their rare free time on the river. It was a haven of calm for them both, but Michael had turned down her last offer to go sailing. In fact, he had turned down all of her get-together ideas the past week. At first she thought it was due to her rejecting his marriage offer, but after this last encounter at his office she knew that was not it. She struggled to remember precisely what she had seen in the briefcase. It was a filing, she was sure of that. And she had seen a name on the typewritten letter. It was Harms.

She had gone directly to the clerks' office to see if any case with the name Harms was logged in. It wasn't. Had Michael taken an appeal before it had been processed? If he had, that was a serious crime.

She went inside, changed into jeans and a T-shirt, and walked back outside. It was already dark. Supreme Court clerks rarely made it home while it was still light. She walked down the stairs to the dock and sat on her boat. If only Michael would confide in her, she could help. She felt more depressed than she had since her father had passed away, leaving her all alone.

That's when she had sold the farm in North Carolina and bought this place. She thought of her father, a farmer and also the town's justice of the peace. He had had no fancy courtroom. He often dispensed sound and fair justice while perched on his tractor in the field or while washing up for dinner. To Sara that was what the law was—a search for the truth, common sense. She sighed. But it was never that simple. She hoped Michael knew what he was doing.

Her next thoughts turned to the other Fiske: John. Michael's comment about his brother had been close to the mark despite her protests. At the very first instant she had seen John Fiske, something had clicked. Every movement he made, every word he spoke, every time he laughed, smiled, or frowned, she felt as though she could watch him forever. She almost laughed at the absurdity.

And that wasn't her only observation of the man. Unknown to Michael, she had gone down to Richmond once more during the summer and watched John at a sentencing hearing. She listened to him argue forcefully for his client. As soon as he had finished, the judge put the man away for life. Outside, Sara had watched as Fiske attempted to comfort the man's family. She could almost feel what he was thinking. Finally Fiske had loosened his tie and walked off. That had been the last time she had seen him.

She couldn't be in love with John Fiske, since she didn't even know the man; infatuation was far more likely. Maybe if she ever did meet him, it would destroy her impression of him.

Sara stared at the sky. She felt like going for a sail. She wanted to feel the wind in her hair, the tickle of water spray against her skin, the sting of rope against her palm. But right now she didn't want to experience any of those things alone.

CHAPTER THREE

OW are you, Mom?" Michael Fiske touched his mother's face. It was early in the morning, and Gladys was not in a good mood. Her face darkened, and she pulled back from his touch.

"I brought you something." He opened the bag he carried and pulled out a gift-wrapped box. When she made no move to open it, he did so for her. He held out the blouse—her favorite shade of lavender—but she wouldn't take it. It was like this every time he came to visit. His gifts were never accepted.

He sat back and sighed. His mother would never treat John that way, Michael knew. To her he was the golden child. Michael Fiske could win the Nobel Prize, and in her eyes he would still always be second to his older brother. He left the blouse on the table, gave his mother a quick kiss, and left.

Outside, the rain had started to come down. Michael pulled up the collar of his trench coat and got into his car. He had a very long drive ahead of him. The visit to his mother was not the only reason he had driven south. He was now headed to southwestern Virginia. To Fort Jackson. To see Rufus Harms. For a moment he debated whether to stop and see his brother. John had not returned his phone call, which was no surprise. But then he shook his head. John Fiske was a very busy attorney, and he didn't have time to run around the state chasing his younger brother's wild theories. He would just have to deal with this alone.

As SHE often did, Elizabeth Knight rose early, did some stretching exercises on the floor, and then ran on the treadmill in the spare bedroom of the luxurious Watergate apartment she shared with her husband, Senator Jordan Knight.

The Supreme Court's most junior associate, she was in her mid-forties, of average height, with a slender body and long black hair tied back in a bun. Her face possessed sharply edged features, and her skin was unlined. Knight had quickly established a reputation as one of the most hardworking of all the Justices.

She and her husband had a good life together. They were routinely touted as the capital's number one power couple. And in a way they were. She carried that mantle as well as she could, even as she combated the isolation that each Justice had to endure. When you went on the Court, people treated you differently, were careful, guarded in what they said around you. Knight had always been gregarious, outgoing. Now she felt much less so. She clung to her husband's professional life as a way to lessen the impact of this abrupt change. Sometimes she felt like a nun with eight monks as her lifelong companions.

As if in answer to her thoughts, Jordan Knight, still dressed in his pajamas, came up behind her and gave her a hug. "You know," he said, "there's no rule that says you have to start every day at the crack of dawn. Snuggling in bed is good for the soul."

She stepped off the treadmill to give him a hug back.

"I don't recall you being a late sleeper either, Senator."

"We should both make a concerted effort to do it. I've heard that sex is the best defense against aging."

Jordan Knight was tall and heavily built, with thinning gray hair and a tanned face scored with lines. He was considered handsome even with the wrinkles and the extra pounds, and he cut quite a fig-ure on national TV shows, where political pundits were regularly overwhelmed by his wit and intelligence.

"You certainly have some interesting opinions. Maybe you should be President?"

He shrugged. "I think the U.S. Senate is challenge enough for me. Who knows? This might be the last roundup for yours truly. To tell you the truth, I'm getting kind of tired of the game, Beth."

She let out a troubled laugh. "I'm afraid I signed on for life." She started to say something and then stopped. Beth Knight had jumped firmly into the "game" of the Supreme Court. Only now was she seeing what a very great impact she could have. The re-sponsibility that came with such power humbled her. Still, there was no other way she would rather be spending her life.

Jordan kissed her on the cheek. "Go get 'em, Ms. Justice."

MICHAEL Fiske's wipers struggled to maintain visibility in the face of the pouring rain. Up to this point he had made good time be-cause the trip had been all highway. Once he had exited Interstate 81, that changed abruptly. Now the terrain was rugged and unfor-giving, the roads narrow and serpentine. Over the next hour or so, he traveled through miles of back roads, over corroded wooden bridges blackened by weather and car exhaust, and past battered house trailers tucked into narrow crevices of the foothills of the Ap-palachians. He was passed by muddy pickup trucks with miniature Confederate flags flapping from radio antennas. As he drew closer to the prison, the weathered faces of the few people he saw grew more and more taciturn, their eyes filled with suspicion.

He glanced over at the briefcase next to him on the front seat, drawing a long breath as he did so. He had learned a lot since reading Rufus Harms's plea for help.

Harms had murdered a young girl who was visiting the military base where Harms had been stationed at the end of the Vietnam War. He had been in the stockade at the time but had somehow gotten out. Those facts were uncontroverted. Michael had used all his information resources in compiling the background facts. However, the military wouldn't acknowledge that such a program as described in Harms's petition even existed. If only Harms or his attorney had included the letter from the army in his filing.

Michael had finally decided that he needed to hear the account from its source: Rufus Harms. If an innocent man was in prison, it was Michael's duty to see that that man became free.

And there was a final reason for this trip. Some of the names listed in the petition were people well known to Michael. If it turned out Rufus Harms was telling the truth . . . Michael shuddered as the nightmarish scenario rolled through his thoughts.

As he rounded a curve, the prison facility loomed before him—stone walls, towering and vast, like a medieval castle. He explained his purpose to the guard at the main gate.

"You're not on the visitors list," the young guard said. He eyed Michael's dark blue suit with contempt. A fancy rich boy from the city, Michael could read in the man's eyes.

"I called several times, but I never got through to anyone who could tell me the procedure for being put on the list."

"Up to the prisoner. Generally speaking, if he wants you to visit, you do. If he don't, you don't. Only control these boys got." The guard cracked a grin.

"If you tell him that an attorney is here to see him, I'm sure he'll put me on his visitors list."

"You're his lawyer?"

"I'm involved with an appeal of his right now," Michael said.

The guard looked down at his ledger. "Rufus Harms," he said. "He just received a visit from his lawyer not too long ago. And that person wasn't you."

"Is that right? Was his name Samuel Rider?" The guard didn't answer, but the momentary surprise on his features made Michael smile inwardly. His hunch had proved correct. "A person can have more than one lawyer."

The guard stared at him for a few moments. He picked up the phone and spoke into it, and then hung up. Five minutes passed before the phone rang again. When the guard put it back down, he nodded at Michael and said curtly, "He'll see you."

WHEN Rufus Harms appeared in the doorway of the visitors room, he looked confused as his gaze settled on the young man. He shuffled forward. Michael rose to greet him and was met with a bark by the guard behind Rufus. "Sit down."

Michael did so immediately.

The guard watched closely until Rufus took a seat across from Michael, and turned to the lawyer. "The rules of conduct during visitation are posted clearly right over there." He pointed to a large sign on the wall. "No physical contact is permitted, and you are to remain seated at all times. Do you understand?"

"Yes. Do you have to stay in the room? There is such a thing as attorney-client confidentiality. Also, does he have to be chained like that?" Michael asked.

"You wouldn't ask that if you'd seen what he did to a bunch of guys inside this place. Even all chained up he could snap your neck." The guard moved closer to Michael. "This is an unscheduled visit, so you got twenty minutes before the big bad wolf here has to go to work cleaning toilets. And we got some real messy ones today."

"Then I'd appreciate your letting us get started," said Michael.

The guard moved to his post against the door. Michael looked at Rufus and found the big man's gaze squarely on him.

"Good afternoon, Mr. Harms. My name is Michael Fiske."

"They said you were my lawyer. You're not my lawyer."

"I didn't say I was. They just assumed that. I'm here because I received your appeal." Michael lowered his voice. "I work at the United States Supreme Court."

Rufus's mouth fell open.

"I read your appeal. It makes a number of very damaging allegations against some very prominent people, but it also had a number of technical deficiencies that would have caused it to be denied processing. I want to try to help, but I need to talk to you."

Rufus looked over at the guard, then turned back to Michael. "You got a radio in your briefcase?"

"A radio?" Michael shook his head.

Rufus lowered his voice even more. "Then you got a pen?"

Michael nodded dumbly.

"Pull it out and start tapping on the table. They've probably heard all they need to hear by now anyway, but we'll leave 'em a few surprises."

When Michael started to say something, Rufus interrupted. "No words, just tap. And listen."

Michael began to tap the table with his pen. The guard glanced over but said nothing.

Rufus spoke so softly that Michael had to strain to hear him. "You shouldn't have come here. You don't know the chance I took to get that piece of paper out of this place. If you read it, you know why. Killing some old black con who strangled a little white girl—people wouldn't care."

Michael stopped tapping. "That was all a long time ago. Things have changed."

Rufus let out a grunt. "Start tapping, and don't stop."

Michael did so. "Believe it or not, I want to help you."

"Why you care about somebody like me?"

"Because I care about the truth," Michael said simply. "If you've been wrongly imprisoned, then I want to help you get your freedom. That's all."

Rufus didn't say anything for a minute, as though attempting to gauge the sincerity of the young man's words. When he finally leaned forward again, his features were softer. "It ain't safe to talk about this stuff here."

"You made reference to a let—"

"Shut up!" Rufus said, looking around. "Wasn't it with what was filed?"

"No."

"Tap louder."

Michael picked up the beat.

Rufus glanced around again and then began speaking. "I'll tell my attorney to talk to you. Whatever you need to know, he'll tell you."

"Mr. Harms, why did you file your appeal with the Supreme Court?"

"Ain't no higher one, is there?"

"No, but there are other avenues you have to pursue in the lower courts before your appeal can be heard there."

Rufus shook his head wearily. "I been in this place half my life. I ain't gonna spend years messing around with lawyers and courts. I want out of here just as fast as I can, and them big judges—they can get me out. They sent you down here, didn't they?"

Michael stopped tapping and said nervously, "Actually, they don't know I'm here."

"What?"

"I haven't actually shown anyone your appeal, Mr. Harms."

"You're the only one that's seen it?"

"For now, but like I said—"

Rufus looked at Michael's briefcase. "You didn't bring my letter with you, did you?"

Michael followed his gaze to the briefcase. "Well, I wanted to ask you some questions about it. You see—"

"Lord help us," Rufus said so violently that the guard braced himself to pounce.

"Did they take your briefcase when you come in? Because two of the men I wrote about are at this prison. One of them is in charge of this whole place."

"They're here?" Michael went pale.

"Did they take your briefcase?"

Michael stammered, "Just—just for a couple of minutes. But I put the documents in a sealed envelope, and it's still sealed."

"You done killed us both," Rufus screamed. Like a hot geyser, he exploded upward, flipping the heavy table over as though it were made of balsa wood. Michael leaped out of the way and slid across the floor. The guard blew his whistle and grabbed Rufus from behind. Shackled as he was, the giant prisoner flipped the two-hundred-pound guard off as though he were a bothersome gnat. A half-dozen other guards poured into the room and went at the man, swinging their batons. Rufus kept tossing them off for a good five minutes, until he finally went down. Right before they dragged him from the room, he stared at Michael, horror and betrayal in his eyes.

After an exhausting struggle that had continued all the way down the hallway, the guards managed to strap Rufus to a gurney.

"Get him to the infirmary," somebody screamed. "I think he's going into convulsions."

Even with the shackles and thick leather restraints on, Rufus wildly gyrated, the gurney rocking back and forth. The guards gathered around him, holding him down, but even with their combined weight it was barely enough.

The group burst through the double door into the infirmary.

"Good God!" The physician on duty pointed to a clear space. "Over here, men." To a nurse he said, "Get an IV over here, an amp of lidocaine, stat, before he goes into cardiac arrest."

They ripped his shirtsleeve up, exposing his sinewy forearm, the veins strong and pronounced. Rufus shut his eyes and then opened them again as he saw the shiny needle coming his way. He shut his eyes one more time. When he opened them, he was no longer in the infirmary at Fort Jackson. He was in the stockade in South Carolina a quarter of a century before. The door burst open, and a group of men walked in like they owned the place, like they owned him. He expected to see the batons come out, to feel the sharp thrusts into his ribs. It had become a morning and evening ritual.

Instead, a gun was placed against his head. He was told to kneel down on the floor and to close his eyes. That's when it happened. He remembered the surprise, the shock he had felt as he stared up at the grinning, triumphant group. The smiles vanished when a few minutes later Harms rose, threw off the men as though they were weightless, burst through his cell door, bowled over the guard on duty, and was out of the stockade, running wild.

Rufus blinked again, and he was back in the infirmary, looking at the faces, the bodies bearing down on him. He saw the needle coming closer to his forearm. He was looking up, the only person doing that. That's when he saw the second needle puncture the IV bag, the fluid from the hypodermic flowing into the solution.

Vic Tremaine—the second-in-command at Fort Jackson—had carried out his task calmly and efficiently, as though he were watering flowers instead of committing murder. Rufus jerked his head back and eyed the IV needle held by the doctor. It was about to puncture his skin, discharging into his body whatever poison Tremaine had chosen to kill him with. They had taken half his life already. He was not about to let them take the rest—not yet.

Rufus timed it as best he could. He ripped free from the restraint, grabbed the doctor's hand, and whipped it across his body. The IV stand came tumbling down; the IV bag hit the floor and burst. A furious Tremaine took the opportunity to quickly leave the infirmary. Rufus's chest suddenly tightened, and his breathing became constricted. When the doctor managed to stagger up, he looked at Rufus. "He could be going into shock." He turned to a guard. "Get a medevac helicopter up here. We're not equipped to handle this kind of situation. We'll stabilize him and then fly him to the hospital in Roanoke. But we need to move fast."

ESCORTED by an armed guard, Michael Fiske walked unsteadily down the hallway. Waiting at the end of the corridor was a uniformed officer holding two pieces of paper. "Mr. Fiske, my name is Colonel Frank Rayfield. I'm the commanding officer here." The man was in his fifties, with the lean build, calm but serious manner, and closely cut gray hair that helped mark him as career military.

Michael licked his lips. Frank Rayfield was one of the men Rufus had named in his appeal. The name had meant nothing to Michael at the time. Inside this prison it meant that he was going to die. He suddenly found himself wishing that his big brother would appear to help him. He looked on dully as Rayfield handed him the papers and motioned the guard to leave.

"I'm afraid my men were a little overzealous," said Rayfield. "We don't usually photocopy documents in a sealed envelope."

Michael looked down at the papers. "I don't understand. The envelope was still sealed."

"The envelope is a very common one. They just put it back in a new one and sealed it." Rayfield broke into a chuckle.

"What's so funny?" Michael demanded.

"This is the fifth time Rufus Harms has named me in some cockamamy lawsuit, Mr. Fiske."

"Excuse me?"

"He's never gone as high as the United States Supreme Court before, but Harms is slick. Looks like he conned his old military lawyer to help him this time. Sam Rider should know better."

"You're saying Rufus Harms makes a practice of filing frivolous lawsuits?"

"Last year he accused the President of the United States of conspiring to frame him for murder. And two years ago he claimed it was Agent Orange that caused him to do it. And you know what? Rufus Harms was never exposed to Agent Orange, because he was never in combat. He spent most of his two-year army career in the stockade for insubordination. Still, a nuisance suit is a nuisance suit, and quite frankly, I'm getting tired of them." He gazed at Michael, who was looking down. "Now take your little papers, go back to Washington, and let it work its way through the system."

"You're just going to let me go?"

"You're not a prisoner here. I've got real inmates to worry about, including one that just beat the crap out of three of my guards. Now if you'll excuse me . . ." Rayfield turned on his heel and walked off.

He went directly to his office. Rufus's suspicions had been well founded—a listening device had been planted on the underside of the table in the visitors room. Some of the conversation had been disrupted by Michael's tapping his pen, but Rayfield had heard and read enough to know that potentially they had a big problem. He picked up the phone and placed a call. In concise sentences Rayfield recounted the events to the party at the other end.

"I can't believe this. You've had twenty-five years to kill him, Frank."

"It's not like I haven't tried. Tremaine tried to do him today in the infirmary, but it's like the guy's got a sixth sense. He just won't die."

"All right, all right. There's no use us arguing about it. You're sure we were all named in the letter? How is that possible? He didn't even know who I was."

Rayfield didn't hesitate. The person he was speaking with had not been named in Rufus's letter, but Rayfield wasn't going to tell him that. Everybody was on the hook for this one. "How should I know? He's had twenty-five years to think about it."

"And of course, you don't have this mysterious letter from the army, do you?"

"No. I mean, not yet."

"It must be in his cell." The voice was again accusatory. "And what about this Michael Fiske? Is he the only other one who knows besides Rider?"

"I think so. He came here to check out Harms's story. Didn't tell anybody. At least that's what he told Harms. We caught a big break there," Rayfield said. "I gave him the song and dance about Harms being a jailhouse lawyer. I think he bought it."

"You don't know that. And you don't know what new information Rider might have found out. But the biggest hole in all this is that Harms *isn't* a jailhouse lawyer. He's never filed anything else in court. If Fiske checks out your claim, he'll find out you lied. Then everything blows up."

"It's not like I had a lot of time to think up a plan," Rayfield said.

"I'm not saying otherwise. But when that wall of lies comes down, you're going to be on the other side of the prison-cell door. That sound good to you, Frank?"

Rayfield took a weary breath. "I'd take Nam over this any day."

"I guess we all got a little too comfortable. Well, it's time to earn your money, Frank—you and Tremaine. You're going to take care of Fiske and Rider. Remember, we survive together, or we all go down together."

MICHAEL left the prison building and walked in the light rain to his car. What a sucker he'd been. He felt like tearing up the appeal papers, but he wouldn't. Still, he felt sorry for Rufus Harms. All those years in prison had taken their toll.

As Michael pulled out of the parking lot, he had no way of knowing that most of his radiator fluid had been collected in a bucket and poured into the nearby woods. Five minutes later he looked on in dismay as steam poured out of his car. He got out, gingerly raised the hood, and then jumped back as a cloud of steam momentarily engulfed him. He thought for a moment. He could walk back to the prison, use the phone, and call a towing service.

As he looked around, his spirits brightened. A van was approaching from the direction of the prison. He waved his arms to flag it down. As he did so, he looked back at the car, steam still pouring out. Funny—he had just had it serviced in preparation for the trip. As he looked back at the van, his heart started to beat rapidly. He turned and sprinted away from the van. It sped up and quickly overtook him, blocking his way. He was about to race into the woods when the window came down and a gun was pointed at him.

"Get in," Victor Tremaine ordered.

CHAPTER FOUR

 IT WAS Monday, and John Fiske sat at his desk digesting yet another arrest report. The knock on his office door startled him. His right hand slid open the top drawer of his desk. Inside was a 9-mm, a leftover from his cop days. His clients were not the most trustworthy.

"Come on in. Door's unlocked," he called out.

The police officer who stepped through the doorway brought a smile to Fiske's lips. "Hey, Billy, how you doing?"

"I've been better, John," Officer Billy Hawkins said.

As Hawkins came forward and sat down, Fiske saw the multi-colored bruises on his friend's face. "What happened to you?"

Hawkins touched one of the bruises. "Guy went nuts at a bar the other night, popped me a couple of good ones." He added nervously, "That's not why I'm here, John."

"It's not anything with Bonnie or the kids, is it?" Fiske asked.

"It's not about *my* family, John."

Fiske's gut clenched. He slowly stood up, his mouth instantly dry. "My mom? My dad?"

"No, John. We got a call from the police up in D.C."

Fiske looked confused for an instant. "D.C.?" As soon as he said it, his body froze. "Mike?"

Hawkins nodded. "It was a homicide, John. Looks like a robbery gone bad. They found his car in an alley."

Fiske let this horrific news sink in for a long minute. His thoughts were interrupted by Hawkins's next words. "They've requested an ID from next of kin, John."

As a police officer, how many times had Fiske told a grieving parent that same thing?

"I'll go on up."

"I'm so sorry, John."

"I know, Billy. I know."

Rufus Harms slowly opened his eyes. The room was dim, shadowy. He shifted slowly on his hospital bed. His arms and legs were still in restraints. He thought back to his last hour at Fort Jackson. He wondered if Michael Fiske had even made it out before they killed him. Ironically, Rufus's near heart attack had saved his life. At least he was out of Fort Jackson. For now. When his condition improved, they would send him back. And then he would die.

For the next two hours he watched people come and go, scrutinizing each of the doctors and nurses attending him. Every time the door to his room opened, he would look at the guard outside—a young kid, looking very self-important in his uniform and wearing his gun. That was good. That meant he had a chance. Leaving a single guard, they must think him pretty well incapacitated, Rufus figured. Only he wasn't.

He heard the door swing inward, and then the light came on.

The nurse carried a metal clipboard and smiled at him as she checked his monitor. She was in her mid-forties, he guessed. Pretty, with a full figure.

"You're doing better today," she said.

"I'm sorry to hear that."

She stared at him, openmouthed.

"Where exactly am I?"

"Roanoke, Virginia."

"Never been to Roanoke." His nose wrinkled up as a scent touched it. At first Harms did not realize that he was simply smelling the woman's scent, a mixture of slight perfume and moisturizing lotion. Oh, my! What else had he forgotten about living a real life? A tear started to tremble at the corner of his right eye as he thought this.

The nurse looked down at him, her eyebrows raised, a hand on one hip. "They told me to be careful around you."

He looked at her. "I'd never hurt you, ma'am." His tone was solemn, sincere. He shifted his body slightly. The shackles pinged against the metal sides of the bed. She drew back.

"Can you call somebody for me, ma'am?"

"Who? Your wife?"

"I don't got no wife. My brother. His name is Joshua. Joshua Harms. He goes by Josh. I can tell you his phone number. Just tell him where I am. Who knows? He might come on over and see me."

"It does get lonely here," she said a little wistfully. She looked down at him, at his tall, strong body, all covered with tubes and patches. And the shackles—they held her attention. "What'd you do anyway to be in prison for?"

"What's your name?"

She hesitated for a moment, looked around at the door and then back at him. "My name's Cassandra," she said.

"Real pretty name." His eyes passed over her figure. "It fits you."

"Thank you. So you're not going to tell me what you did?"

"I killed somebody. A long time ago."

"Why'd you do it?"

"Didn't know what I was doing. Was out of my mind."

She drew back a little. "Isn't that what they all say?"

"Happens to be the truth with me. You gonna call Josh?"

"I don't know. Maybe." She looked at him curiously. "You don't act like a murderer."

"You got to make up your own mind on that."

She considered this for a moment. "So what's your brother's number?"

She took it down, slipped it into her pocket, and turned to leave.

"Hey, Ms. Cassandra?"

She turned back around.

"You're right. I ain't no killer. Come back and talk to me some more if you want." He rattled the shackles. "I ain't going nowhere."

She eyed him from across the room, and he thought he saw a smile flicker across her mouth. Then she turned and went out the door. Rufus lay back and inhaled deeply, letting the remnants of her scent soak into him. A few moments later a smile spread across his face. As did, finally, the tears.

IT WAS an unusual gathering of all of the clerks and the Justices, looking stonily around the table in the large room. Elizabeth Knight dabbed continually at her eyes with a handkerchief. When Harold Ramsey rose from the head of the table, his deep voice was oddly subdued. "This is terrible, terrible news." He surveyed the room, his tall frame shaking. He took a heavy breath. "Michael Fiske is dead."

The Justices obviously already knew. All the clerks, however, collectively missed a breath.

"The details are sketchy right now, but apparently Michael was the victim of a robbery." He looked down for a moment, until Elizabeth Knight rose.

"I know this has been a terrible shock. Michael's loss touches us all, especially those who were close to him." She paused and looked at Sara Evans for a moment. "If any of you wish to talk about anything, please feel free to stop by and see me."

She rallied herself enough to call an end to the meeting, and the room quickly cleared. Except for Sara. She sat there, numb, tears freely streaming down her face. Michael was dead. He had taken an appeal, acted very strangely for over a week, and now he was dead. Murdered. A robbery, they said. She didn't believe the answer was that simple. But right now it didn't matter. She put her head down on the table as the sobs burst from her.

From the doorway, Elizabeth Knight watched her.

"YOU'RE sure you covered your tracks?"

Rayfield nodded into the phone. "Every record of his being here has been expunged. I've already transferred all the personnel who saw Fiske to other facilities."

"And no one saw you dump the body?"

"Vic drove his car back. I followed him. We picked a good place. We took his wallet, his briefcase too. The police will think it was a robbery. Of course, we filled the radiator back up with fluid."

"And Harms?"

"He's still in the hospital. Looks like he's going to make it. But don't sweat it. When he comes back here, we'll deal with him. Weak heart and all, you never know what might happen."

"No mistakes, Frank."

Rayfield laughed. "I'll call you when he's dead."

JOHN Fiske identified his brother's remains. His official duty as next of kin was completed. He could go home, tell his father, make the funeral arrangements, bury his brother, and then get on with his life. That's what everyone else did.

Instead, Fiske pulled himself out of his car and into the muggy air, and entered the building at 300 Indiana Avenue, which was home to the D.C. Police Homicide Division. After passing through security and being directed by a uniformed police officer, he stopped at a desk. He looked down at the card the attendant at the morgue had given him. "Detective Buford Chandler, please," he said to the young woman behind the desk.

"And you are . . ." The sharp angle of her neck and her superior tone immediately rubbed Fiske the wrong way.

"John Fiske. Detective Chandler is investigating my brother's— my brother's murder. His name was Michael Fiske."

"Is Detective Chandler expecting you?"

He spoke in a low voice. "Not exactly, but—"

"Then I'm afraid he's not in," she said, cutting him off.

Fiske leaned forward until his face was only a couple of inches from the woman. "Let me make you understand something. I came up from Richmond to identify the remains of my brother at Detective Chandler's request. Right about now the medical examiner is cutting a Y incision in my brother's chest so that he can lift out his insides, organ by organ. Now, I thought I'd come and have a chat with Detective Chandler and see if he and I can come up with some leads on who might have killed him."

She said coldly, "I'm sure Detective Chandler will be in touch if he needs you." She turned away from him.

Fiske gripped the edge of her desk and took a deep breath. "Look, all I want to do is talk to the man!"

"Am I going to have to call a guard or what?"

"I'm Buford Chandler."

Both Fiske and the receptionist turned. Chandler was black, in his early fifties, with curly white hair, a matching mustache, and a tall, thickened frame that managed to retain a certain athleticism from his youth. He looked Fiske up and down from behind a pair of trifocals.

"I'm John Fiske."

"I heard." He hooked a finger at Fiske. "Let's talk."

Chandler and Fiske made their way through busy hallways to a small cluttered office. "Have a seat." Chandler pointed to the only chair in the room other than the one behind his desk. There were files stacked on the chair. "Just put those on the floor."

Fiske moved the files while Chandler settled behind his desk. "Okay, first things first. I'm sorry about your brother."

"Thank you," Fiske said in a subdued manner.

"So you were in law enforcement?" Chandler casually remarked, then smiled at Fiske's surprise. "The average citizen doesn't usually know about Y incisions. With the manner in which you carry yourself and your build, I'd say you were a patrolman."

"Past tense?"

"If you were still on the force, the folks in Richmond would've told me when we contacted them."

"Right on all counts. I'm glad you were assigned to this case, Detective Chandler."

"This and forty-two other active cases." Fiske shook his head, and Chandler continued. "Budgetary cuts and all. I don't even have a partner anymore."

"Then how about a little unofficial help? I worked a lot of homicides down in Richmond."

"Officially, that's absolutely impossible."

"Officially, I absolutely understand."

"You got a number where you can be reached?" Chandler asked. Fiske passed across his card after writing his home number on the back. In return Chandler handed him a card with a series of phone numbers on it. "Office, home, beeper, fax, cell phone—when I remember to carry it, which I never do." Chandler opened a file on his desk and studied it.

Reading upside down, Fiske saw his brother's name on the label. "I was told he was killed during a robbery."

"That's what the prelim indicated." He closed the file and looked at Fiske. "The facts of this case so far are pretty simple. Your brother was found in an alleyway with a gunshot contact wound to the right side of his head. Looked to be fairly heavy caliber. We have not found the slug, but that search continues. The alley where he was found is a high-use drug area. To your knowledge was your brother a drug user?"

"My brother set the highest goals for himself with everything he did. Drugs did not enter into that equation."

"Any reason why someone would want him dead? Jealous boyfriends? Money problems?"

"No. But I'm probably not the best source for that. We haven't seen each other much the last few years."

"When did you last speak with your brother?"

"He called me over a week ago."

"What'd he say?"

"I wasn't in. He left a message—said he needed my advice."

"Did you call him back?"

"No. It wasn't high on my priority list."

"Is that right?" Chandler twirled his pen between his fingers. "Tell me something. Did you even like your brother?"

Fiske looked at him squarely. "Somebody killed my brother. I want to catch whoever did it. And that's really all I'm going to say."

The look in Fiske's eyes made Chandler decide to move on. "Maybe he wanted to talk about something to do with work?"

"Meaning, is his murder related to the Supreme Court?"

"It's a long shot, absolutely, but you said he wanted some advice. Maybe it was legal."

"Well, you can always make a trip to the Court to see if there are any conspiracies going on up there."

"We have to tread lightly, you know."

"We?"

"I'm sure your brother has personal effects there, and it would not be unusual for next of kin to visit his place of work." Chandler checked his watch. "We have just enough time to get to Court, Counselor."

RUFUS watched the door as it slowly opened. He braced himself for the sight of a mass of men in green fatigues moving in on him, but then his apprehension slid away when he saw who it was.

"Time to check me again?" he said.

Cassandra came and stood at the foot of the bed, checking monitors, making notes on his chart. "I called your brother."

Rufus's expression grew serious.

"He said he'd be coming to see you."

"He say when?"

"Sooner than later. Today, in fact."

"He tell you anything else?"

"I found him to be a man of few words," Cassandra remarked.

"That's Josh."

"Is he as big as you?"

"Nah. He's a little guy. Six three or so, not much over two hundred pounds."

Cassandra shook her head and turned to leave.

"You got time to sit and talk?" Rufus asked.

"I'm supposed to be on my break. I've got to go." She seemed a little unfriendly.

"You okay?"

"Even if I'm not, there isn't anything you can do about it." Her tone was now edgy, rough.

Rufus asked, "Is there a Bible around here?"

She looked over at the table next to the bed, went over, and pulled out a Gideon Bible. "I can't give it to you. Can't get that close. The people from the prison were real clear on that."

"You don't have to give it to me. If you would, I'd appreciate if you could read a passage to me."

"Read to you?"

"You don't have to," he said quickly. "You may not even be interested, you know, in the Bible and churchgoing."

She looked down at him, one hand on her hip, the other closed around the green Bible. "I sing in the choir. My husband, God rest his soul, was a lay minister."

"That's real good, Cassandra. And your kids?"

"How do you know I have kids? Because I'm not skinny?"

"Nope. You just look like you're used to loving little things."

His words startled her, a smile quickly breaking through the cloud over her features. "I *am* going to have to watch you. What do you want me to read?"

"Hundred and Third Psalm."

As she read, Cassandra glanced at him. His eyes were closed, but she saw his lips moving. Rufus was silently mouthing the words she was saying. She stopped, but he continued to the end of the sentence. "You know the psalm by heart?" she asked.

He opened his eyes. "Know most of the Bible by heart. All the Psalms. I've had a long time to work on it."

"Why did you want me to read it to you, then, if you already knew it?"

"Looked like you were a little troubled. I thought visiting the Scriptures might help you some."

"Help me?" Cassandra looked down at the page and read to herself: *He forgives all my sins. . . . He surrounds me with loving-kindness and tender mercies.* Work was depressing. Her teenage children were more and more beyond her control every day. She was on the north side of forty, fifty pounds overweight, and there wasn't an eligible man in sight. With all that, as she watched this prisoner, this chained-up killer, she felt like bursting into tears in the face of his kindness.

The Hundred and Third Psalm also held special appeal for Rufus, one line in particular. He mouthed it to himself: *He gives justice to all who are treated unfairly.*

THE United States Supreme Court was large and intimidating, but what really engaged Fiske's attention was the quiet, so extreme as to be unsettling. He thought of the last very silent place he had been today: the morgue. He said, "Who are we meeting?"

Chandler pointed to a group of men coming down the hallway. "Them." As they drew nearer, their collective footsteps became the boom of cannon in this acoustical tunnel. One of the men wore a suit; the other two were in uniforms and carried side arms.

"Detective Chandler?" The man in the suit extended his hand. "I'm Richard Perkins, marshal of the United States Supreme Court." Perkins was about five nine, skinny, with white hair combed straight over his forehead like a frozen waterfall. He introduced his companions. "The Supreme Court's chief of police, Leo Dellasandro. His second-in-command, Ron Klaus." Dellasandro was about five ten, with a layer of fat over a muscular physique. He had a wide face, a pug nose, and black-and-gray hair. Klaus was trim and professional in appearance.

"Good to meet you," Chandler said, and he watched Perkins look expectantly over at Fiske. He added, "John Fiske. Michael Fiske's brother."

All of them rushed to provide their condolences. Fiske managed an appreciative demeanor in the face of all this instant sympathy.

"Mr. Fiske is helping me with some background information on his brother," Chandler explained.

Perkins's office was right off the hallway leading to the court-room. At a side table sat a man in his late forties. His blond hair was cut very short, and his long, narrow face carried an unshakable air of authority. When he rose, he was well over six feet.

"Detective Chandler?" The man extended one hand and with the other flashed his identification card. "FBI special agent Warren McKenna."

Chandler looked at Perkins. "I wasn't aware that the Bureau had been brought in on this."

Perkins started to say something, but McKenna said briskly, "As I'm sure you know, the FBI is authorized to investigate the murder of any person employed by the United States government. How-ever, the Bureau is not looking to step on your toes."

"That's good, because even the tiniest bit of unwanted pressure, and I just go nuts." Chandler smiled.

McKenna's expression remained unchanged. "I'll try to keep that in mind."

Fiske held out his hand. "John Fiske, Agent McKenna. Michael Fiske was my brother."

"I'm sorry, Mr. Fiske. I know it must be tough for you," Mc-Kenna said, shaking his hand.

Chandler asked a half hour's worth of questions, trying basically to establish if any case Michael Fiske had been working on could have led to his murder. The same answer kept coming back to him from each of the Court representatives: "Impossible."

McKenna asked few questions but listened intently.

"The cases pending before the Court are so well insulated from the public that there would be no way anyone could know what a specific clerk is working on," Perkins said.

Chandler looked unconvinced. "What's the average age of the clerks here? Twenty-five? Twenty-six?"

"Something like that," Perkins said.

"They're kids. You telling me that it's impossible that they might let something slip? Not even to impress a date?"

"I've been around long enough to know better than to use the word impossible to ever describe anything."

"I'm a homicide detective, Mr. Perkins, and believe you me, I got the same problem." Chandler glanced down at his notes. "Now, why don't we have a look at Mr. Fiske's office," he said.

JOSHUA Harms glided cat-smooth down the corridor. He was six feet three, lean but strongly built, with wide shoulders fanning out from a thick neck. He had a long and narrow face; the skin was chestnut brown and smooth except for deep tracings of lines at the eyes and mouth. As he approached the end of the hallway, the soldier sitting next to the doorway of the last room rose and held up a hand. "Sorry, sir. This area is off-limits."

"My brother's in there," Harms said. "And I'm going to see him."

"I'm afraid that's impossible."

Harms eyed the soldier's name tag. "I'm afraid it ain't, Private Brown. Now you let me in there, or I'm gonna go over to Fort Jackson and tell 'em you refused to allow a family member to visit a dying relative. They'll all take turns kicking your butt, soldier boy. Did I mention I spent three years in Vietnam and got me enough medals to cover your whole damn body?"

An unnerved Brown looked around for a minute, unsure of what to do. "What's your name?"

"Josh Harms." He pulled out his wallet. "Here's my license."

Private Brown stared at him and the ID for a few seconds. "Turn around," he said finally.

Josh did so. Brown started to pat him down. Right before he reached his front pants pocket, Josh said, "Don't get excited, but there's a pocketknife in there. Just pull it out and hold it for me. You hold it good and tight, son. I'm right partial to that knife."

Private Brown finished the pat-down and straightened. "You got ten minutes, and that's it."

The two men locked eyes.

"Thank you kindly," Josh said. He entered the room and closed the door. "Rufus," he said quietly. He went over to the bed and stared down at his brother. "What in tarnation happened to you?"

"Ain't sure you want to know. But I'll tell you this. I go back to Fort Jackson and they're gonna kill me soon as I step inside."

"Who's 'they'?"

Rufus shook his head. "I tell you, then they gonna just come after you." Rufus thought for a minute. "Look, Josh, that letter from the army, when I got it, I remembered everything that happened that night. I mean everything."

"You talking about the girl?"

Rufus was already nodding. "It wasn't my fault."

His brother looked at him skeptically. "Come on, now, Rufus, you did kill that little girl. No way around that."

"Killing and meaning to kill's two different things. Anyway, you read the letter?"

"Sure I did. Came to my house, didn't it? Guess that was the last civilian address the army had for you."

"Well, I was never in the program they said I was."

Josh eyed him hard. "How you mean?"

"Just what I said. Somebody put me in the records. They wanted me to look like I was in it to cover up what they did to me. They thought I was going to be dead."

Josh took this in slowly until the truth hit him. "Lord Almighty. If I had known that, I sure as shootin' would've kicked some butt."

"You were busy with the Vietcong. But I go back to prison now, they gonna make sure they get me this time."

Josh looked at the door and then down at his brother. "Woman who called me said you had some kind of heart problem. Look at you, all strapped to this crap. How far you think you can run?"

"I need your help to do this, Josh."

"You bet you do, Rufus."

"What I'm asking ain't fair, I know that. You got yourself a good life. You can turn and walk straight out of here. I'd understand."

"Then you don't know your brother."

Rufus slowly reached out and took his brother's hand. They gripped each other tightly, as though trying to give strength and resolve to one another for what lay ahead.

"Anybody see you come in?"

"Nobody except the guard. I worked on repairs at this hospital for two years, know it like the back of my hand. Way I came in is supposed to be locked, only the nurses taped over the lock. They sneak their smokes out there."

"How you wanta work it, then?"

"We just go back out the way I came in. It's right down the hall. Don't pass no nurses station or nothing. My truck's outside the door. I got a buddy owes me a favor. I'll borrow his rig for a while. We hit the road and don't look back. Just the two of us again. Make Momma happy if she was alive."

Rufus raised his manacled hands. "What about these?"

His brother was already sliding something out of his boot. When he straightened back up, he was holding a slender piece of metal with a slight hook at one end.

"Don't tell me that boy didn't search you?"

"Like he knew where to look. Once he took my pocketknife, he didn't even bother to do my boots." Josh grinned and then inserted the metal in the lock on the restraints.

OUT in the hallway, Private Brown looked at his watch. The ten minutes were up. He cracked open the door to the room. "All right, time's up." He pushed the door open farther. "Mr. Harms?"

Brown heard a small groan. He drew his pistol and pushed the door all the way open. "What's going on in here?"

The groaning became louder. Brown looked around for the light switch. That's when he stumbled over something. He knelt down and touched the man's face as his vision focused. "Mr. Harms? Mr. Harms, you okay?"

Josh opened his eyes. "I'm fine. How 'bout you?"

A fist clamped down on Brown's gun and stripped it clean away. Another fist collided with his jaw and knocked him out.

Rufus put the guard in the bed, covering him with the sheet. Josh put the restraints around his arms and legs. Then he used adhesive tape he found in one of the cabinets to tape his mouth shut. The last thing he did was search the soldier and retrieve his pocketknife.

As Josh turned toward him, Rufus wrapped his arms around his brother and squeezed tight. Josh returned the hug. His eyes moist, Rufus shook a little as Josh pulled away.

"Now, don't get too mushy on me. We ain't got no time for that."
Josh put a hand on his brother's shoulder. "You ready?"

Rufus had already put on his prison pants and shoes. He had left
off the shirt, opting for just his T-shirt instead. He had one thing
clutched in his hand: the Gideon Bible. "Twenty-five years' worth
of ready."

CHAPTER FIVE

ICHAEL Fiske's office was large, with high ceilings and
half-foot-wide moldings. There were two massive
wooden desks, each with a computer workstation;
shelves filled with volumes of lawbooks; and a portable
book caddy. Stacks of files were on the desk.

Marshal Perkins looked at Chandler. "Detective, there has to be
someone from the Court present while you search. There are many
confidential documents in here."

Chandler said, "Well then, get somebody down here, because I'm
going through this office."

Perkins cast an unfriendly glance at him. "Let me see what I can
do," he said. "I'll have to lock this door until I get back."

Chandler took a step closer to Perkins. "Look, Richard, I'm the
police. Now, maybe I'm wrong, and you don't mean what I thought
you did by that very stupid remark."

Perkins's face flushed, but he left the door unlocked and walked
off. Dellasandro stayed behind, talking to McKenna.

Chandler went over to Fiske. "I get the feeling this has all been
scripted out long before we got here."

"McKenna knew your name before you were introduced."

"They've obviously done some digging. I'm gonna go over and
talk to him," said Chandler. "Never know when we might need a
favor from the feds."

Fiske leaned back against the wall and checked his watch. He still hadn't reached his father. Suddenly all of his attention was trained on a pair of people walking toward him. His focus, actually, was on only one. Despite her obvious physical attractiveness, the woman looked, Fiske concluded, like the tomboy next door. Someone you could play touch football or chess with. And end up losing.

Sara Evans had seen Fiske come into the building and guessed what he was there for. She had stayed close by in case they needed one of the clerks. That's why Perkins had "found" her so quickly. She stopped directly in front of Fiske, causing Perkins to abruptly do the same.

"Oh," he said. "John Fiske, this is Sara Evans." He then walked over to Chandler and McKenna.

"You're Michael's brother?"

They shared a firm handshake. Her voice sounded tired, Fiske noted, and she clutched a handkerchief in her other hand.

"I'm very very sorry about Michael," she said.

"Thank you. It came as a tremendous shock." Fiske blinked. Was there something in her eyes when he said that? Something that said it wasn't all that shocking to her?

Before he could say anything, Perkins rejoined them. "All right. Detective Chandler from D.C. homicide is waiting, along with a gentleman from the FBI," Perkins said to Sara.

"Why do they want to search Michael's office?"

"It's part of the investigation, Ms. Evans," Fiske explained, "in case there's a connection with his murder."

"I thought it was a robbery."

"It was a robbery, and the sooner we can convince Detective Chandler that it had nothing to do with the Court, the better," Perkins said huffily. "As I explained on the way down, your task is to ensure that no confidential documents are seen or taken."

"Shouldn't I be involved in that, Richard," came a new voice, "or is that outside my jurisdiction?"

Fiske easily recognized the man approaching them. Harold Ramsey strode toward them like a vintage ocean liner grandly pulling into harbor.

"Chief, I didn't see you there," Perkins said nervously.

"Obviously not." Ramsey looked at Fiske. "I don't believe we've met."

"Michael's brother, John Fiske," offered Sara.

Ramsey held out his hand. His long, bony fingers seemed to wrap twice around Fiske's. "I cannot tell you how sorry I am. Michael was a very special young man. I know that you must feel his loss terribly. If there's anything we can do, please let us know."

Fiske acknowledged Ramsey's sentiments, feeling like a stranger at a wake. "I will," he said solemnly.

Ramsey looked at Perkins and inclined his head toward Chandler and McKenna. "Who are those men, and what do they want?"

Perkins explained the situation in a fairly efficient manner, although it was clear that Ramsey had already thought five steps ahead by the time Perkins finished his account.

When introductions had been made, Ramsey turned to Chandler. "It seems to me that the better way of approaching the problem is to take an oral inventory of the cases on which Michael was engaged. I only ask that any documents pertaining to the Court's work be set aside until you have done that. Then should there appear to be a connection between a case and Michael's death, arrangements can be made for you to investigate the link thoroughly."

"All right, Mr. Chief Justice," Chandler said.

McKenna quickly agreed with this approach.

"I'll also make available the Court's legal counsel to assist you." Ramsey turned to Sara. "You'll be available tomorrow, won't you? You were close with Michael."

Fiske eyed her. How close? he wondered.

Ramsey once again extended his hand to Fiske. "I would also appreciate being advised of funeral arrangements." Then he turned to Perkins. "Please come to my office."

After Ramsey and Perkins had left, Chandler watched as McKenna looked into Michael Fiske's office. "Chief Dellasandro," Chandler said, "to be as least disruptive as possible, I'll bring a team in tomorrow, so we'll only have to search it once."

"We'd appreciate that," Dellasandro replied.

"However, I want this door locked until I come back," Chandler continued. "Nobody goes in, and that means you or Mr. Perkins or"—he looked pointedly at Agent McKenna—"anybody else."

McKenna glared at Chandler as Dellasandro nodded agreement.

They heard a beeping sound. Chandler reached down to his belt, held up his pager, and looked at the number on its screen. "Can I use a phone?" he asked Sara.

She led the way.

Chandler rejoined Fiske and Sara a minute later and shook his head wearily. "Couple of new customers for me to interview. Shotgun wounds to the heads. Lucky, lucky me."

"Can you take me back to the station so I can pick up my car?" Fiske asked Chandler.

"Actually, I was heading the other way."

"I can drive you," Sara said quickly. Both men looked at her. "I'm finished for the day." She smiled a little wistfully.

"Grab some dinner or something," Chandler suggested. "You two might find a lot to talk about."

Fiske glanced around, clearly uncomfortable with this suggestion, but he finally nodded. "You ready?"

"Give me a minute." She shook her head wearily. "I have to tell a clerk that he has to work all night," she said, and headed off.

Chandler said, "John, find out what you can. She was close to your brother." He added, "Unlike you."

"I'm not real good at spying," Fiske said, feeling guilty.

As if he were privy to Fiske's thoughts, Chandler said, "John, I know she's smart and pretty, and she worked with your brother, and she's shook up about his death. But remember one thing."

"What's that?"

"Those are not reasons to trust her." With that parting comment Chandler walked off.

SENATOR Jordan Knight stood in the doorway of his wife's office and watched her. Elizabeth's head was bowed as she sat at her desk. Several books were open in front of her, but she was obviously not reading any of them.

"Why don't you call it a day, honey?"

She looked up, startled. "Jordan, I thought you had a meeting."

He came over and stood next to her, massaging the back of her neck. "I canceled it. And now it's time to go home."

"But I have some more work to go. We're all behind. It's so hard, and now Michael's death."

Jordan Knight cupped her chin in one hand. "Beth, are you somehow trying to blame yourself? Michael's being in an alleyway in a bad part of town has nothing to do with you or the Court."

"Sometimes I think we're too hard on the clerks. Expect too much from them." After a while she added, "Just now I had to go speak to Steven Wright about his bench memo on Chance. I need it by tomorrow. He'll be working through the night."

Jordan Knight put a hand under his wife's arm and helped her up. "Beth, no matter how important it is, it's not that important. Let's go home," he said firmly.

She smiled, touched his face. "You take much too good care of me, you know."

He smiled. "When you have something precious, that's the only way to go."

A few minutes later they were being driven in a government car to their apartment.

"I CAN'T imagine what you're going through, John. I know how badly I'm feeling, and I'd only known Michael for a short time."

They were in Sara's car and had just crossed over the Potomac River into Virginia. Fiske wondered if she was trying to impress upon him that she had little information to provide.

"So how long did you two work together?"

"A year. Michael talked me into coming back for two."

They pulled into the parking lot of a restaurant in northern Virginia. They went inside, got a table, and ordered their drinks and food. A minute later Fiske took a swallow of his Corona; Sara sipped on a margarita.

Fiske wiped his mouth. "So, do you come from a family of lawyers? We tend to run in packs."

She smiled and shook her head. "I'm from a farm in North Carolina. Single-stoplight town. But my father was the justice of the peace for the area."

"Is that what got you interested in law?"

She nodded. "Dad looked more like a judge sitting on his John Deere tractor in the middle of the field than some others I've seen in the fanciest courts."

"I bet he was good. Common sense. Man of the soil."

She glanced at him to see if he was being sarcastic, but Fiske's look was genuine. "That's exactly what he was. He mostly dealt with poachers and traffic tickets, but I don't think anyone walked away feeling they had been treated unfairly."

"You see him often?"

"He died six years ago."

"I'm sorry. Is your mom still around?"

"She died before Dad. Rural life can be rough." She seemed relieved to see their food arrive.

"It just occurred to me that I haven't eaten today," Fiske said as he took a large bite of his tortilla.

"I do that a lot. I think I had an apple this morning."

"Not good. You don't have a lot of excess on you."

She looked him over. Despite his broad shoulders and full cheeks, he almost looked gaunt. "Neither do you."

Twenty minutes later Fiske pushed away his empty plate and sat back. "I know you're busy, so I won't waste your time. My brother and I didn't see a lot of each other. There's an information void I need to fill if I'm going to find out who did this."

"I thought that was Detective Chandler's job."

"Unofficially, it's mine."

"Your cop background?" Sara asked.

Fiske arched his eyebrows.

"Michael told me a lot about you."

"Is that right?"

"Yes, that's right. He was very proud of you."

Fiske rubbed his hand across a water ring on the table. "You spent a lot of time with him?"

"Quite a lot. We had drinks, dinner, outings."

"Something tells me Mike's death didn't seem to surprise you all that much. Is that true?"

Sara dropped her casual manner. "No. I was horrified."

"Horrified, yes. But surprised?"

The waitress stopped by and asked if they would like some dessert or coffee. Fiske asked for the bill.

Then they were back in the car and heading toward the District. A light rain had begun to fall. Fiske looked at Sara expectantly. She caught his gaze, took a breath, and started speaking slowly. "Recently, Michael did seem nervous, distracted."

"You think it was related to something at the Court?"

"Michael didn't have much of a life outside the Court."

"Other than you?"

She glanced at him sharply but said nothing.

"Whatever you can tell me will help, Sara."

She slowed the car slightly. "Your brother was funny. Do you know that he would go down to the clerks' mailroom at the crack of dawn to get an early jump on any interesting cases?"

"I'm not surprised. Michael never did things halfway."

"The clerks' mailroom is where the petitions are opened and processed. They're divided up among the Justices' chambers, and the clerks are assigned to do pool memos on them. We might get in a hundred or so appeals in a week's time. There are nine Justices, so each chamber gets roughly a dozen appeals. Of the dozen sent to Justice Knight's chambers, I might write a memo on three. That memo is circulated to all the chambers."

"So the first person to actually see an appeal filed with the Court would be someone in the clerks' mailroom?"

"That's normally the case."

"What do you mean, normally?"

Sara let out a muffled groan but quickly composed herself. "I can only tell you this in confidence, John."

"I'm not going to promise you something I can't deliver."

Sara sighed and in concise sentences told Fiske about finding the papers in his brother's briefcase.

"I remember Mike telling me that clerks sometimes take files home. Maybe that was the case here."

She shook her head. "This wasn't set up like a normal case file. There was no return address on the envelope, and one of the pages was handwritten, the other typewritten, no signature."

"Did you see any name on the papers?"

"I did. The last name was Harms. That's why I knew Michael had taken a filing. As soon as I left Michael's office, I checked the Court's filing database. There was no one by that name listed."

"Okay. So why one handwritten page and one typed page?"

"Two different people. Maybe someone wanted to help Harms."

"From all the appeals the Court gets, Mike takes this one. Why?"

She glanced at him nervously. "If it turns out that this had anything to do with Michael's death . . . I never thought . . ." She suddenly looked as though she would burst into tears.

"I'm not going to tell anyone about this. For now. You took a risk for Mike. I appreciate that." They drove along in silence until Fiske finally asked, "How was Michael perceived at the Court?"

"Highly respected. He was incredibly motivated. I guess all of us are, but Michael seemed incapable of turning it off."

"Mike was always that way," Fiske said a little wearily. "He started at perfection and moved up from there."

"Must run in the family. Michael told me that you went to college while working as a cop."

Fiske impatiently tapped his fingers against the car window. "It is possible to become a lawyer even if you're too dumb to score high on the law boards."

"You're not dumb. We watched you do a trial."

He turned to look at her. "Excuse me?"

"In the summer Michael and I came down to Richmond and watched you do a trial in circuit court." She was not going to mention her second trip to watch him in court.

"Why didn't you let me know you were there?"

Sara shrugged. "Michael thought you'd be upset." When he said nothing, she continued. "I was really impressed. I think you might have motivated me to become a criminal defense lawyer someday."

"You think you'd like to do that?"

"Why not? The law can still be a noble calling. I'd love to hear about some of your cases."

"Would you really?"

"Absolutely," she said enthusiastically.

He settled down. "Look, Sara, I'm no white knight. Most of my clients are guilty. I know that, they know that, everybody knows that. If somebody actually came to me proclaiming their innocence, I'd probably die of a heart attack. I'm not a defender of anybody. I'm a negotiator of sentencing. But don't worry. You're never going to see it. You'll be teaching at Harvard or working at some gold-plated New York law firm."

They drove on in silence until they pulled up in front of the homicide building. "I'm parked right in front," Fiske said.

Sara looked at him in surprise. "Pretty lucky. In two years I don't think I've ever found an empty space on the street."

Fiske stared at one spot. "I could've sworn I parked right here."

She glanced out the window. "You mean next to that towaway-zone sign?"

Fiske looked at the sign and then at the space where his car used to be. "I really can't believe this day."

"They have a number you call to get your car back, but you're not going to get it tonight."

"I can't go to sleep until my dad knows."

"Oh." She thought for a moment. "Well, I'll drive you."

Fiske stared out the window at the pouring rain. "You sure?"

She put the car in gear. "Let's go find your dad."

"Can we make one stop first?"

"Sure. Just tell me where."

"Michael's apartment. I've still got a key from when I helped him move."

"John, I'm not sure that's a good idea."

He looked at her. "Don't worry. You're staying in the car. If anything happens, just take off."

"And if maybe the person who killed Michael is there?"

"You got a tire iron in the trunk?"

"Yes."

"Then it's my lucky day."

WHEN they reached Michael's apartment, Sara pulled into a parking space around the corner. "Pop the trunk," Fiske said before getting out.

She could hear him rummaging through the compartment for a moment. Then she watched him head around the corner, noting the tire iron in one hand and a flashlight in his other. She picked up her cell phone and held it ready. If she spotted anything remotely suspicious, she'd call the apartment to warn him.

FISKE closed the door behind him, clicked on the flashlight, and looked around. He saw no obvious signs that anyone had searched the place. He entered the small kitchen, which was separated from the living room by a waist-high bar. He found a couple of plastic Baggies in a drawer and covered his hands with them so as not to leave any prints. He went through the living room. The floors were worn tongue in groove, and the creaks followed him with each step. He pushed open the bedroom door and looked. The bed was unmade, clothes here and there. There was a small desk in the corner. Hidden behind the desk he saw a power cord plugged into the wall, but he didn't see the laptop computer the cord should have been attached to. Or his brother's briefcase.

He moved back toward the kitchen. He stopped for a moment, listening intently. As he did so, he raised the tire iron. With a sudden lunge he jerked open a closet door.

The man burst out and hit Fiske right in the stomach with his shoulder. Fiske held his ground and managed to clip the man across the neck with the tire iron. He heard a pained cry, but the man recovered quickly, lifted Fiske off the floor, and threw him. He landed hard and felt his shoulder go numb.

The guy was on his feet and through the door in a few seconds. Fiske finally lurched up and raced after him. He heard feet clattering down the steps. Ten seconds later he was out on the street. He looked right and left. A horn blew.

Sara rolled down her window and pointed to the right. Fiske sprinted hard through the rain in that direction and turned the corner. Sara put the car in gear but had to wait for two cars to pass, and then she spun tires after him. She turned the corner and saw Fiske standing in the middle of the street, sucking in air.

He was furious that the man had gotten away. He stomped around in tight circles. "I can't believe it!"

"What was that all about?"

Fiske calmed down. "He was in the closet." He rubbed his shoulder and eased into the car. "And now comes the hard part." He took her cell phone and pulled a business card from his wallet. "Telling Chandler."

Fiske paged Chandler, and the detective called back a few minutes later. When Fiske told him what he had done, he had to hold the phone away from his ear.

"Slightly upset?" Sara asked.

"Yeah, like Mount Saint Helens slightly erupted." Fiske brought the receiver back to his ear. "Look, Buford, do you want the description of the guy or not?"

After Fiske finished, Chandler said, "I'll get a squad car over there right now to secure it, and I'll request a tech team ASAP."

"My brother's laptop and briefcase weren't at his apartment."

"Okay, so we got a missing briefcase, missing laptop, and a dumb ex-cop who I've got half a mind to arrest this instant."

"Come on, you guys already towed my car today."

"Put Ms. Evans on the line."

Fiske handed the phone over to a perplexed Sara.

"Yes?" she said nervously.

"Ms. Evans," he began politely, "I don't appreciate you two making my job even more difficult. Where are you?"

"Near Michael's apartment."

"And where are you headed?"

"To Virginia. To tell John's father about Michael."

"Okay, then you drive him to Virginia. Don't let him out of your sight. Do I make myself clear?"

"Yes, Detective Chandler. Absolutely."

"Good, Tonto. Now put the Lone Ranger back on."

Fiske took back the phone. "Look, I was only trying to help."

"Do me a favor. Don't help anymore unless I'm with you. Okay?"

"Okay."

"And John, give my condolences to your father."

Fiske put down the phone.

CHAPTER SIX

I N HIS friend's pickup truck Josh Harms drove along the deserted country road. The dense forest bracketing the narrow lanes gave him a certain comfort. Isolation, a buffer between himself and those who would hassle him, had been Josh's one constant goal in life. As a carpenter of considerable skill, he worked alone. When he was not working, he was either hunting or fishing, again alone. He did not desire the conversation of others, and he very rarely offered any of his own. All of that had changed now. The responsibility he had just acquired had not yet fully sunk in, but he knew it was considerable. And he also knew his decision had been the right one.

The truck had a camper, and his brother was back there. Rufus was supposedly resting, although Josh had doubts as to whether the man could really be sleeping. The back of the camper was also filled with a month's worth of food, two deer rifles, and a semiautomatic pistol, in addition to the one he had tucked in his belt. That arsenal was insignificant compared to what would soon be coming after them, but he had faced long odds before.

Josh lit a cigarette and blew the smoke cleanly out the window. They were already two hundred miles from Roanoke, and he was putting as much distance between it and them as he could. The escape would have been discovered by now, he knew. The boys in green had a big advantage in manpower and equipment, but Josh had fished and hunted around this area for the last twenty years. He knew all the abandoned cabins, all the hidden valleys. His plan was to hide out for a while and then hit the road again when the pressure died down. Maybe get to Mexico and disappear.

Josh wasn't leaving all that much behind. A disintegrated family, a carpentry business that was always in the red despite his skill. He guessed Rufus was all the family he had left. And he was certainly all Rufus ever would have. If they survived. He tossed out the cigarette and kept on driving.

In the back of the camper Rufus was indeed not asleep. He lay on his back, a black tarp partially over him. He tried to stretch out a little, relax, but the motion of the truck was unsettling. He had not been in a civilian automobile since Richard Nixon had been President. How many Presidents ago was that?

Rufus tried to peek out at the passing night. Freedom. He often wondered what it would feel like. He still did not know. People, lots of them, were looking for him. He half rose and slid open the window of the camper. From this angle he could see his brother's face in the reflection of the rearview mirror.

"I thought you were sleeping," Josh said.

"Can't."

"How's your heart feel?"

"My heart ain't troubling me none. If I die, it ain't gonna be because of my heart."

"Not unless it's a bullet ripping through it."

"Where we headed?"

"A little place in the middle of nowhere."

"Sounds good."

The two stayed quiet for a while. Josh was naturally reserved, and Rufus wasn't used to having anyone to talk to. The silence was both liberating and oppressive to him. He had a lot he wanted to say.

"I don't think I ever asked you: You been back home?"

Josh shifted in his seat. "Home? Why would I want to go back to that place?"

"Momma's grave is there, ain't it?" Rufus said quietly. "Who's keeping it up?"

"Look, Rufus, Momma's dead, okay? Ain't no way she's knowing nothing about how her grave looks. And I ain't going down to Alabama to brush some leaves off the ground, not after what that town done to the Harms family. I hope they all burn for it. If there is a God, and I got me some big doubts on that, then that's what should happen."

There is a God, Rufus wanted to tell his brother. That same God had kept him going all these years. And one should respect the dead. If he lived through this, Rufus would go see to his mother's grave.

"I talk to God every day."

Josh grunted. "That's real good. I'm glad He's keeping company with somebody."

They fell silent again as the truck rolled on.

FISKE was driving when they stopped at an all-night convenience store. Sara waited in the car. A rusty Esso sign clanked back and forth from the force of a semi sailing past and made her jump. When Fiske got back into the car, Sara stared at the two six-packs of Budweiser. "You intend to drink your sorrows away?"

He ignored the question. "Once we get down to Dad's place, there's no way for you to get back by yourself. It's pretty remote."

"I'm prepared to sleep in the car."

About thirty minutes later Fiske slowed the car and turned into a narrow gravel drive of a trailer park. The mobile homes were laid out along a riverbank. Most of them had flagpoles either attached to the trailer or porch, or sunk into concrete. They passed late-blooming flower beds of impatiens, and red and pink mums. Everywhere Sara looked were outdoor sculptures of metal, marble, and resin.

"This place is like a little gingerbread town built by gnomes," Sara said. She eyed the numerous flagpoles and added, "Patriotic gnomes."

"A lot of the people are from the American Legion and V.F.W. crowd. My dad has one of the tallest flagpoles. He was in the navy in World War Two."

"Did you and Michael grow up here?"

"No. My folks owned a house on the outskirts of Richmond. This was our summer place. Pop moved down here full-time after Mom went into the nursing home."

Fiske stopped the car in front of a trailer painted a soothing muted blue. His father's Buick, with a SUPPORT YOUR LOCAL POLICE bumper sticker, was parked next to the trailer in front of a flagpole that went a good thirty feet into the air.

Fiske eyed the Buick. "At least he's here." He got out of the car with the two six-packs. Sara didn't move to join him. He looked at her questioningly.

"I thought you might want to talk to your dad alone."

He looked over at the trailer and felt his nerves slowly disintegrate. He turned back to her. "I could sort of use your company."

She nodded and got out of the car. As they headed up the wooden porch, she smoothed down her dress and fiddled with her hair.

Fiske took a deep breath and knocked on the door. He waited and knocked again. "Pop." He waited a moment and knocked again, louder this time. "Pop," he called out, and kept knocking.

They finally heard movement in the trailer, and then a light came on. The door opened, and Fiske's father, Ed, peered out. Sara looked at him. He was as tall as his son and very lean, with vestiges of the powerful musculature shared by both his boys.

"Johnny? What the heck are you doing here?" A broad smile cracked his face. When he registered Sara, he looked startled.

"Pop, I need to talk to you."

Ed Fiske glanced over at Sara again.

"I'm sorry. Sara Evans . . . Ed Fiske," John said.

"Hello, Mr. Fiske." She awkwardly held out her hand.

He shook it. "Call me Ed, Sara. Pleased to meet you." He looked back at his son curiously. "So what's up? You two getting married or something?"

John glanced at Sara. "No! She worked with Mike at the Supreme Court."

"Oh, well, where are my manners? Come on in." They went inside. Ed pointed to a worn sofa, and Fiske and Sara sat down there. Ed pulled a metal chair from the small dinette and sat down opposite them. Sara looked around the cramped space. It was paneled with thin plywood stained dark. Several stuffed fish were mounted on the wall. There was a worn recliner in one corner, a TV across from it.

Ed pulled a pack of Marlboros from a knicked-up side table and deftly popped a cigarette into his mouth, taking a moment to light up, then blew the smoke toward the nicotine-coated ceiling. He put his hands on his knees and leaned forward. "So what brings you two down here so late?"

Fiske handed his father a six-pack. "Not good news."

The elder Fiske tensed. "It's not your mom. I just saw her. She's okay." He shot a glance at John. "Just tell me, son."

"Mike's dead, Pop." As he finished saying it, it was as though he were hearing the news for the first time. He could feel his face grow hot as though he had leaned too close to a fire. Perhaps he had waited to see his father, to join his grief with his father's. He watched as devastation washed over the man.

Ed took the cigarette out of his mouth, his fingers shaking. "How?"

"Robbery." Fiske paused and then added the obvious, since he knew his father was going to ask. "Somebody shot him."

Ed tore off one of the beers from the plastic holder and popped the tab. He drank it down almost in one swallow, crushed the can against his leg, and threw it against the wall. He stood up, went over to the small window, and looked out, his big hands closing and opening, the veins in his forearms swelling.

"Do they got whoever did this?"

"Not yet. They're working on it. I'm sort of helping."

"D.C.?"

"Yes."

"I never liked Mike being up there. People kill you for nothing up there. Crazy lunatics."

Sara managed to find her voice. "I liked and deeply respected your son. Everyone at the Court thought he was wonderful. I'm so, so very sorry about this."

"He was wonderful," Ed said. "He sure was. Never figured out how we turned out such a one as Mike."

John looked down at the floor. Sara picked up on the pained expression on his face.

Ed looked around the trailer's interior, memories of good times with his family nudging him from all corners. "Got his mother's brains." His lower lip trembled for an instant. Then a low sob escaped from his mouth, and he slumped to the floor.

Fiske knelt down next to his father and wrapped his arms around him, their shoulders shaking together.

Sara looked on, unsure of what to do. She was embarrassed at witnessing such a private moment and wondered if she should wait in her car. Finally she simply looked down and closed her eyes, silently releasing her own tears.

THIRTY minutes later Sara sat on the porch and sipped on a warm can of beer. She was barefoot, her shoes next to her. She swatted at a mosquito and contemplated getting into her car, cranking up the A.C., and trying to fall asleep.

The door opened, and John appeared, holding two beers.

"How is he?"

Fiske sat down beside her. "Sleeping, or at least trying to." He handed her a beer. "This one is cold."

She popped it open. It felt good going down and managed to lift her spirits a little. She held the can next to her cheek. "Does he want to come back with us?"

Fiske shook his head. "He's going to come over to my place tomorrow night." He glanced at his watch. "I mean tonight."

Sara looked at the river, where a floating dock moved up and down with the lap of the water. "What river is this?"

"It's called the Mattaponi." He looked out at the water. "Mike and I used to race each other across. The river gets pretty wide at some points. Couple of times I thought one or the other of us was surely going to drown. But one thing kept us going."

"What was that?"

"We couldn't bear the thought of the other winning."

Sara turned to him, smoothing out her hair as she did so. "Do you mind a really personal question?"

Fiske stiffened slightly. "Probably."

"Why weren't you and Michael closer?"

"There's no law that says siblings have to be close." Fiske sipped his beer.

"John, I'm really not trying to pry."

"I'm not in the mood to talk about it, okay?"

They sat there, silent amid the noise of the cicadas. The name Harms kept reverberating in Fiske's head. An in forma pauperis petition probably would have come from a prisoner, if that's what the handwritten document amounted to. If Harms was a prisoner, finding him would be easy. The country kept track of cons, and most of the information was on a computer database. He turned and studied Sara's face in silence for a moment, then looked past her at something in the sky. She turned her head to look too. Pink swirls were lapping against the dark edges of the sky as dawn began to break.

"It's beautiful," she said in a hushed tone.

"Yes, it is," he said.

She raised her hand slowly. Her fingers touched his chin, his beard stubble rough against her skin. Her hand moved higher, tracing his cheeks, his eyes, each touch gentle, unhurried. As she gripped the back of his neck and pulled his head toward her, she felt him flinch.

"My brother's dead, Sara," he said simply, his voice shaking slightly. "I'm really messed up right now."

Self-consciously she removed her hand. She looked down, as though searching at her feet for the right words. "And I'm sorry."

He looked away.

She stood up, wrapped her arms around her shoulders. "I'm a little cold. We should go back inside now, shouldn't we?"

Behind them the owner of a glowing cigarette had left his place at the window. "You coldhearted bastard!" Ed shouted. "You and that slut get out of here! You hear me?"

"Pop, what are you talking about?"

Enraged, Ed rushed out the door. "I saw you, damn you both. Kissing while your brother lies dead on some slab. Your brother!"

John's voice cracked as he realized what his father had seen. Or thought he had seen. "Pop, nothing happened."

"You heartless son of a . . ." He swung wildly at his son.

John wrapped his arms around his father, holding tight. "Stop it, Pop. Stop it. You're gonna have a coronary."

The two men began to struggle fiercely. "My own son doing that. I don't have a son. Both my sons are dead. Both my sons are dead." Ed spat out the words in a crescendo of fury.

John let his father go, and the old man spun around and dropped to the ground in exhaustion. "Get the hell out of here. Both of you. Now!" Ed screamed.

Fiske gripped Sara's arm and pulled her up. "Let's go, Sara. He doesn't know what he's doing. I'm sorry."

As they got into the car, Fiske and Sara could still hear the screams of the old man.

SAMUEL Rider arrived home early after being away a few days on business. The airport limo dropped him at his front door, and he entered his house. His wife was not there. It was just as well. Rider wanted to be alone. He picked up his phone and called Fort Jackson, identified himself, and asked to speak with Harms.

"He's no longer here."

"Excuse me? He's serving a life sentence. Where exactly could he have gone?"

"I'm sorry, but I'm not allowed to give out that information over the phone. If you would like to come down in person or make an official inquiry in writing—"

Rider slammed down the phone and collapsed in a chair. Was Rufus dead? Had they somehow discovered what he was up to? Once Rider had filed the appeal with the Supreme Court, Rufus should have had instant security.

Rider clamped his fingers around the edge of his desk. *If* it had reached the Court.

He grabbed the receiver and asked directory assistance for the number of the Supreme Court clerks' office. The voice on the other end delivered a perfunctory message. "We have no case with the name Harms, sir, either on the regular or in forma pauperis docket."

"But I sent the appeal by registered mail."

The polite answer Rider received did not sit well with him. He yelled into the phone, "A man is rotting in the stockade, and you can't keep track of your mail!" He threw down the phone for a second time.

Somewhere between its arrival and the point where a case was actually placed in the official system, Rufus Harms's filing had apparently disappeared. And so had Rufus Harms.

Rider suddenly felt chilled. Then another thought hit him even harder: If they had killed Rufus, they surely wouldn't stop there. They would know that Rider had played a role in it. That meant he could be next on their hit list.

Well, he wasn't waiting around for them to come get him. When his wife got home, they could drive to Roanoke, hop a commuter flight, and take it into Washington or Richmond. From there they could go anywhere. He would explain it to her by saying he was just being spontaneous, something she had said he never was and never could be. Good old steady, reliable Sam Rider. Did nothing more with his life than work hard, pay his bills, raise his kids, love his wife. I'm already writing my obituary, he realized.

He wouldn't be in a position to help Rufus, but he figured the man was probably dead anyway. I'm sorry, Rufus, he thought. But you're in a much better place.

A sudden thought struck him. The copies of the filing he had made for Rufus were back at the office. A few minutes later he was in his garage. His wife's car was next to his.

As he passed by, he glanced at the front seat. His feet seemed to sink right into the concrete floor. His wife was lying facedown in the front seat. Even from where he was standing, Rider could see the blood pouring from the head wound. That was the next to last memory Rider would have. The hand came around and clamped across his face a large cloth that had a sickening medicinal odor. Another hand slipped something into Rider's hand. As the lawyer looked down with eyes that were already beginning to close, he saw and felt the still warm pistol as his fingers were wrapped around it by a pair of latex-gloved hands. It was Rider's pistol, one he used for target shooting. The one he now also knew had been used to kill his wife. As he finished this thought, Samuel Rider's eyes closed for the last time.

DRIVING down the George Washington Parkway south of Old Town Alexandria, John Fiske glanced at the woman sleeping beside him. The sunlight pouring through the car window fell full upon her face, accentuating the sensual margins of her lips. Her hair was limp from sweat, and the little makeup she wore had long since lost its life. Her entire body was pushed to the point of exhaustion. And yet Fiske had to fight the impulse to reach over and stroke her face. The scuffle with his father had not been mentioned on the drive back. It was as though they had silently agreed not to discuss it.

Fiske nudged Sara awake, and she told him where to turn off the parkway. With Sara directing, he drove down another blacktop road and then turned right, onto the gravel lane that ran steeply down to her cottage. The two black sedans flashing in front of their car made Fiske slam on the brakes. Sara screamed. Fiske jumped out of the car. He stopped as soon as he saw the guns pointed at him.

"Hands in the air," one of the men barked.

Fiske immediately put his hands up.

Sara climbed out of the car in time to see Perkins emerge from one vehicle and Agent McKenna from the other.

Perkins spotted Sara. "Are you all right?" he asked.

"Of course I'm all right. What is all of this?"

"I left an urgent message with you."

"I didn't call in for my messages. What's wrong?"

McKenna pointed at Fiske. "Is this man holding you against your will, Miss Evans?"

"Will you stop with the melodrama?" said Fiske. He lowered his hands and caught a sucker punch in the gut from McKenna. Fiske dropped to his knees, gasping. Sara raced to him, helping him lean back against the car tire.

"Keep your hands up until the lady answers the question." McKenna reached down and jerked Fiske's hands up in the air.

Sara screamed, "Leave him alone! He's not holding me. Stop it." She pushed McKenna's hands away.

Another sedan pulled up, and Chandler and two uniformed police officers climbed out, guns drawn.

"Everybody freeze!" Chandler boomed out.

McKenna looked around. "Tell your men to put away their weapons, Chandler. I've got the situation under control."

Chandler walked right up to McKenna. "Tell your men to holster their weapons right now, McKenna. Right now, or I'll have these officers arrest you on the spot for assault and battery."

McKenna didn't move.

Chandler leaned directly into his face. "Right now, Special Agent Warren McKenna, or you'll be calling the Bureau's legal counsel from a Virginia lockup. You really want that in your record?"

Finally the man flinched. "Holster your weapons," McKenna ordered his men.

"Now move away from him," Chandler ordered.

McKenna very slowly edged away from the fallen Fiske, his eyes burning into Chandler's with every backward step.

Chandler knelt down and gripped Fiske's shoulder. "You okay?"

Fiske nodded painfully, his eyes on McKenna.

"Will someone please tell us what is going on?" Sara cried out.

"Another Supreme Court clerk was found murdered—Steven Wright," Chandler said.

CHAPTER SEVEN

 HE shack rested in the center of a heavy forest in a remote part of southwestern Pennsylvania, where it notched into West Virginia. A muddy, tire-gouged strip of dirt was the only way in or out. Josh Harms came in the front door, his 9-mm poking out of his waistband, red clay and pine needles sticking to his boots. The truck was parked under a leafy shield of a soaring walnut tree, but Josh had taken the added precaution of covering the vehicle with camouflage netting. His biggest worry was being spotted from overhead. Luckily the nights were still warm. He couldn't risk building a fire—you couldn't control where smoke went.

Rufus sat on the floor, his broad back resting against the wall, his Bible in his lap. "Everything okay?" he asked Josh.

"Just us and the squirrels. How you feeling?"

Rufus smiled. "Happy as can be. Feels good to be free, sitting here, not having to worry about somebody trying to get the jump on me."

"The guards or the other cons?"

"What do you think?"

"I think both. I was on the inside for a while too, you know. We could probably write us a book."

"How long we gonna stay here?"

"A couple of days. Then we'll head down to Mexico. Got some old army buddies who live there. They'll set us up. Find us a boat, do some fishing, live on the beach. Sound good to you?"

"Living in the sewer would sound good to me." Rufus stood up. "Got a question for you."

His brother leaned against the wall and started carving up an apple with his pocketknife. "I'm listening."

"Your truck was full of groceries, two rifles, and that pistol."

"So?"

"So you just happen to be carrying all that stuff when you come visit me?"

Josh swallowed a slice of apple. "I got to eat. That means I got to go to the store, now, don't it?"

"And you always carry all them guns with you?"

"Maybe I'm still screwed up from Nam, got some syndrome or other."

"Josh, you came ready to bust me out, didn't you?"

Josh finished working on his apple and then threw the core out the window. He wiped the apple juice from his hands before facing his brother. "Look, Rufus, I never knew why you killed that little girl. But I knew you weren't right in the head when you done it. You been in prison for twenty-five years. Let's just say I took it on myself to say that was long enough. If you hadn't wanted to come, I was going to make you. It's what I made up my mind to do."

The two brothers looked at each other for at least a minute without speaking.

"You a good brother, Josh."

"You right about that."

Rufus sat on the floor again and picked up the Bible, his hands gently turning the pages until he found the part he wanted.

Josh eyed him. "You still wasting your time reading that stuff?"

Rufus looked up at him. "The word of the Lord kept me alive all these years. That ain't no waste of time."

Josh shook his head, looked out the window and then back at Rufus. "The Lord ain't the one busted you out. I did."

Rufus went back to his reading.

Josh managed to tune in a radio station from southwestern Virginia. Rufus Harms had been mentioned in the news the day before. All the military authorities would say was that Harms was a convicted murderer who had a history of violence inside prison. He had escaped with the help of his brother, a violent man in his own right. Both men were believed to be armed and dangerous. Translation: No one should be surprised or ask any questions when the authorities dragged their corpses in.

Just then the afternoon news came on the radio. A late-breaking story made both brothers stare at the radio. Josh hustled over and turned up the sound. The story only lasted about a minute, and when it was over, Josh turned the radio off. "Rider and his wife," he said.

"Made it look like he killed her and then turned the gun on himself," Rufus added, his head shaking slowly in disbelief. "Man comes to see me, and now he's dead."

Josh knew exactly what his brother was thinking. "Rufus, you can't bring him back."

"But I asked Samuel to come down to the prison. He'd be alive except for me."

"Supposing that's true, you can't do nothing about it."

Rufus shook his head stubbornly. "Nobody should be able to get away with what they done."

Josh stared at him. "Well, exactly what are you gonna do? March in to the police and say, 'Listen up, boys. Y'all come on help me put these big, important white folk away'?" Josh spit on the dirt floor. "You're crazy, Rufus."

"I need to get me that letter from the army."

"Where'd you leave it?"

"I hid it back in my cell."

"Well, you try going back to the prison, I'll shoot you myself."

"I ain't going back to Fort Jackson."

"What, then?"

"Samuel was a lawyer. Lawyers make copies of things."

Josh arched his eyebrows. "You wanna go to Rider's office?"

"We got to, Josh. If I can get that letter, then maybe I can get it to somebody who can help."

"Yeah, look at all the good it done you last time. Them big judges just come running to help you, didn't they?"

"Josh, you ain't changing my mind. I got to do it."

Josh spit again and looked out the dirty cracked window. "You crazy. Prison's messed you up for good. Dang!"

"Maybe I *am* crazy."

Josh glared at him. "Where the blazes is Rider's office?"

"Somewheres outside Blacksburg. Tha's all I know. Shouldn't be hard to find out where exactly."

Josh violently kicked the wall and then turned to his brother. "Okay, we'll wait until nightfall and then head on out."

"Thanks, Josh."

"Don't thank me for helping us both get killed."

THE flag at the United States Supreme Court was flying at half-mast. Newspaper, TV, and radio reports nationwide were filled with accounts of the two murders. The phones in the Court's public information office refused to stop ringing. Supreme Court police, reinforced by fifty D.C. police officers, national guardsmen, and FBI agents, ringed the Court's perimeter.

The hallways were filled with clusters of people nervously talking. Most of the Justices were secluded inside their chambers, their minds far from the advocates and issues before them. Justice Knight sat at her desk, her gaze downcast. She had just finished reading the Chance bench memo, and it had suddenly dawned on her what she had done. She had instructed Steven Wright to work late, all night if necessary. He had done so, left the building late, and someone had killed him. Her precious bench memo. She had never really focused on this chain of events before. A gush of air came out of her lungs so hard it almost choked her.

She looked around the spacious beautiful room. Here she had sat and contemplated her little strategies, her philosophies of life. And it had cost a young man his life. She covered her face and wept.

VIC Tremaine set the army helicopter down in the grassy field. As the circling of the copter blades slowed, he and Frank Rayfield looked over at the sedan parked near the edge of the tree line. They lifted off their seat harnesses, climbed out, and, torsos bent forward as they passed beneath the blades, headed toward the car. When they reached it, Rayfield sat in the front seat, while Tremaine slipped into the back.

"Glad you could make it," said the man in the driver's seat, turning to face Rayfield.

Rayfield's jaw fell. "What happened to you?"

The bruises were purplish in the center, leaching out to yellow around the edges. One clung to the side of his right eye; the two others spread out from his collar.

"Fiske," he answered.

"Fiske? He's dead."

"His brother—John," the man said impatiently. "He caught me at his brother's apartment."

"Did he recognize you?"

"I was wearing a mask."

"What was he doing at his brother's apartment?"

"Same thing I was—looking for anything that the cops could use to find out the truth."

"Did he find anything?"

"Nothing to find. We'd already gotten Fiske's laptop." He looked at Tremaine. "And you got his briefcase from his car before you killed him, right?"

Tremaine nodded.

"Where is it?" the man asked.

"A pile of ash."

"Good."

"Is this brother a problem?" Rayfield wanted to know.

"Maybe. He's an ex-cop. He and one of the other clerks are snooping around, helping investigate the murders."

Rayfield started. "Murders?"

"Steven Wright."

"What the devil is going on?" Rayfield demanded.

"Wright saw someone come out of Michael Fiske's office. He also heard something he shouldn't have. I had to bluff him out of the building and kill him. We're okay on that one."

"Are you nuts? This thing is totally out of control," Rayfield said angrily.

The man looked at Tremaine. "Hey, Vic, tell your superior to stay cool. I think Nam took away some of his nerve."

"Four murders, and you say stay cool?" Rayfield said. "And Harms and his brother are still out there."

"So we've got two more bodies to go. The two most important. You understand that, don't you, Vic?"

"I do," Tremaine answered. "And what about John Fiske and this clerk?"

"They're on a real short leash. And they'll stay there until we decide what to do with them."

"Meaning?" Rayfield asked.

"Meaning we might have four more bodies to go instead of two."

SARA sat in her new office. Chandler had declared the space she had shared with Wright off-limits, but he had allowed Court personnel to move Sara's computer and work files to her new space. She had taken a list of federal and state prison agencies Fiske had given her and started calling. At the end of half an hour she hung up the phone, depressed. There was no one with the last name

Harms in any prison. It was maddening that she couldn't remember anything more. Finally she gave that up.

Her head sank to the desktop. What if there really was some psychopath targeting clerks? Was it just chance that Wright had been killed instead of her? For a minute she sat there, frozen. Come on, Sara, she urged herself, you can beat this.

She stood and walked out the door. A minute later she entered the clerks' office and went over to a clerk who was manning a database terminal. The question she was about to ask was one she had asked earlier, but she wanted to be absolutely certain. "Could you check and see if there's any case at the Court with the name Harms as one of the parties?"

The clerk nodded and started tapping buttons. After about a minute he shook his head. "I'm not finding anything."

Just then another voice spoke up. "Did you say Harms?"

Sara stared at the other clerk. "Yes. Harms was the last name."

"That's strange."

Sara's skin started to tingle. "Why?"

"I got a call early this morning from a man asking about an appeal, and he used that name."

"Harms? You're sure?"

The clerk nodded. "That's right—Harms. Rufus Harms. I told him we didn't have any filing under that name."

"Did the caller identify himself?"

"No. He got pretty upset. He said something about the guy rotting in a stockade."

Sara raced out and sprinted up the stairs to her office. She grabbed a card from her Rolodex and dialed the number for Military Police Operations. Fiske had covered the federal and state prisons, but he had not thought of the military. She knew very well what a stockade was: Rufus Harms was a prisoner of the United States Army.

She got through to Master Sergeant Dillard, the corrections specialist on duty. "I don't have his prison ID number, but I believe he's incarcerated at a military facility," she said.

"I can't give you that information. The official procedure is to send in a Freedom of Information Act request."

"The thing is, I really need the information now. I'm calling from the United States Supreme Court."

"Right. How do I know that?"

Sara thought for a moment. "Call directory assistance for the general number for the Supreme Court. Then call the number they give you and ask for me. My name is Sara Evans. Please, Sergeant Dillard, it's really important."

There was silence on the other end of the line for a few seconds. "This is highly unusual. Give me a few minutes."

Five very long minutes later the call was put through to Sara's phone. "You know, Sergeant Dillard, I've gotten information from your office before without going through FOIA process."

"Well, it wouldn't be a problem with any other prisoner."

"I don't understand. Why is Rufus Harms so special?"

"Haven't you been reading your newspaper?"

"Not today, no. Why?"

"Rufus Harms has escaped from Fort Jackson." In concise sentences Dillard filled Sara in, and she wrote down the details.

"Now I got a question for you, Ms. Evans. Why is the Supreme Court interested in Rufus Harms?"

"He filed an appeal with the Court."

"What sort of appeal?"

"I'm sorry, but that's all I can tell you. I have rules to go by too. Thank you so much, Sergeant Dillard. You've been a huge help."

Using an Internet search engine, Sara typed in Rufus Harms's name. A few minutes later she was reading the latest news accounts about him, his background and that of his brother. She printed out all of these. One of the stories had a quote from the newspaper editor in Harms's hometown. She looked up the man's number. He still lived in the same small town near Mobile, Alabama, where both brothers had grown up.

The phone was answered after three rings. Sara introduced herself to the man, George Barker, still editor of the local paper.

"I already talked to the papers about that," he said flatly.

His deep southern drawl made Sara think of braying bloodhounds and jugs of moonshine.

"Who are you with again?"

"An independent news service. I'm a freelancer."

"Well, what exactly do you want to know?"

"I've read that Harms was convicted of killing a young girl on the military base where he was stationed—Fort Plessy."

"Killed a little white girl. He's black, you know."

"Yes, I know," Sara said curtly. "Do you know the name of the attorney who represented him at trial?"

"Wasn't really a trial. He did a plea arrangement."

"So you know the name of his attorney?"

"Have to look it up and call you back."

Evans gave him her home number. "If I'm not there, just leave it on the answering machine. What else can you tell me about Rufus?"

"Well, the most noticeable thing about him was his size. He must have already been six foot three by the time he was fourteen. From what I recall, he wasn't a good student, but he was real good with his hands. He worked at a little printing press with his daddy. I remember one time the press at my newspaper broke down. They sent Rufus over to fix it. I gave him the manual for the machinery, but he wouldn't take it, said words just messed him up. Within one hour he had the whole thing running good as new."

"That's pretty impressive."

"And he was never in trouble with the police. His momma wouldn't have let him. She worked at the meat-processing factory here. She took care of her boys."

"What happened to their father?"

"He was a good man, worked hard. Too hard. Heart attack."

"What about his brother?"

"Now, Josh was a different story. Hotheaded, arrogant."

"I read that he fought in Vietnam and was actually a war hero."

"Sure, that's right," Barker conceded. "He was the most decorated war hero to ever come out of this town by a long shot. People were surprised about that. He could fight. I'll give the man that. And Josh actually graduated high school." Barker's voice changed. "But where he really showed up everybody was in sports. He got a slew of scholarship offers. Bear Bryant even wanted him at Alabama, that's how good he was. Probably would've been a star in the NBA or the NFL. But he got sidetracked."

"How so?"

"Well, you know, his government asked him to defend his country in the war against communism. Shipped to Vietnam."

"Did he come home afterward?"

"Oh, sure. About the time when Rufus got in all that trouble."

"Did Rufus killing the girl surprise you? I mean, had he ever been violent that you knew?"

"He never hurt anyone that I know of. A real gentle giant. If it had been Josh, I wouldn't have blinked twice, but not Rufus."

"Did Josh keep living there?"

"Well now, that's a troubling part of this town's history. I'd rather not talk about that."

Sara thought quickly. "It can be off the record."

"Is that right?" Barker sounded wary. "Well, I guess it doesn't matter anymore." He cleared his throat. "The story of what Rufus had done got around town. A bunch of boys started drinking, got together, and decided to burn Mrs. Harms's house to the ground."

"How horrible! Was she in it?"

"She was until Josh pulled her out. And let me tell you—Josh went after them boys. Must've been ten against one, but Josh put half of them in the hospital, until the rest beat him up bad, real bad."

"It sounds almost like a riot. Didn't the police come?"

Barker coughed in an embarrassed fashion. "Well, it was rumored that a couple of the boys, you know . . ."

"Were the police," Sara finished the sentence for him.

"And the police sort of put together this story about him resisting arrest and all. Well, the long and the short of it was he spent some time in jail, and his momma died soon after."

It was all Sara could do not to start screaming at the man. "Mr. Barker, why didn't you use the power of the press?"

Barker sighed deeply. "Frankly, this is my home, Ms. Evans."

"Well, I guess that's partly what the courts are for: to keep people like those in your town from hurting people like Josh Harms. Please do call me back with the name of Harms's lawyer."

She hung up the phone. Her whole body was tingling with rage. As she hurried down the hallway in search of Fiske, she wondered if they would ever find out the truth. If the army caught up to the brothers first, the truth might very well die with them.

FISKE was standing outside his brother's office while Chandler was overseeing the evidence-collection team under close supervision of the Court's staff counsel. When they finished with Michael's office, they would start on Steven Wright's, down the hall.

Fiske looked over at his brother's office door and then back at Wright's. An idea began to percolate in his head. He went over to Chandler. "Where was Wright's body found?"

Chandler flipped open his notebook. "By the way, I got your car out of impound. It's at my office in a nice, legal parking space."

"Thanks for doing that for me."

"Don't thank me. With the tow and fine and all, it's gonna cost you about two hundred bucks."

"Two hundred bucks for a lousy parking ticket?"

"Well, maybe I can pull a few strings, you know, do you a favor. But you'll have to work it off. I got some painting that needs to be done at my house." Chandler cracked a smile and then stopped leafing through his notes. "Okay, here we are. Wright was found in Garfield Park. That's at F and Second streets. It's about a half-dozen blocks from the Court."

"Was it on his way home?"

Chandler tilted his head as he studied his notes. "Not really."

"Does it look like he was killed at the park or maybe somewhere else and dumped there?"

"The grass had blood on it. No shell casings found yet."

"Bullet still in the body?"

Chandler nodded. "Hope we lay our hands on a gun to match it against."

"Considering what happened at Mike's apartment, you should probably have someone posted at Wright's."

"Gee, now, why didn't I think of that?"

"Sorry. Any idea when Wright left the Court last night?"

"My people are still checking that with the guards on duty."

"Doesn't this place have surveillance cameras?"

"We're checking the tapes right now." Chandler scanned his notes once more. "Motive's also going to be tough on this one."

"But his wallet was missing."

"Yeah. I thought about that. It's a little too convenient, like somebody wants to make us think both murders are connected."

"I believe they are connected but not for the reasons everyone probably thinks," Fiske said.

Chandler looked intrigued. "So what's the real reason?"

Fiske hesitated. Keeping the stolen appeal a secret was beginning to become very awkward. "I don't know, but let's say his death might have served a dual purpose."

At that moment Sara joined them, trying very hard to conceal her excitement. "John, can we talk for a minute?"

"Ms. Evans," Chandler said with a broad smile.

"Hello, Detective Chandler," she said quickly. "John, I really need to talk to you."

"Can I catch up with you later, Buford?"

"And you can tell me your theory."

As they walked off together, Chandler's smile faded. He was wondering if he had just lost his "unofficial" partner to Sara Evans.

BACK at her office, Sara spent the next thirty minutes filling Fiske in on everything she had found out.

"It complicates matters that the guy's escaped," John said.

Sara had a sudden terrifying thought. "You don't think Michael was somehow mixed up in that, do you?"

"My brother would not be part of anything illegal. Besides, Harms apparently escaped after Mike's body was found. I do think I know why Wright was killed, though."

"Why? Because he knew about Harms? About what Michael had done?"

"No. Because he saw something he shouldn't have."

Sara drew her chair closer to his. "What do you mean?"

"Wright's office—your former office—is right down the hallway from Mike's. Wright was working all night. Well, I think he saw someone go into Mike's office looking for something."

"Like what?"

"Who knows? Something to do with Harms's appeal."

"But there's security here twenty-four hours a day."

"Well, if the person knew the police were going to search the office thoroughly the next morning, he'd only have a limited amount of time to do it."

"That makes sense."

"So Wright hears something, or he's finished his memo. He comes out and runs right into whoever."

"If your theory is correct, do you think Steven knew the person who killed him?"

Fiske took a deep breath and sat back. "He had to. I saw them lock the door to Mike's office. There's no sign of forced entry. The person had a key."

"So it might be somebody Steven trusted."

Fiske looked at her. "Like one of the Justices?"

Sara stared back, horrified. "I'll accept a lot, but I can't accept that." She had a sudden thought. "Maybe it was McKenna? Steven would have trusted him—FBI and all."

"How could McKenna be involved in this?"

"I don't know. He's the first one who occurred to me."

"Because he's not with the Court and he slugged me?"

Sara sighed. "Probably." Then she remembered something and tore through the papers on her desk until she found it. "I can tell you about what time Steven left." She picked up the Chance bench memo that Wright had prepared. Across the top was a date and time stamp. She flipped the papers around so Fiske could see it. "This was printed out at one fifteen this morning. That's when Steven finished the memo, then presumably left."

"And saw whatever he saw."

"So where does that leave us?"

Fiske shrugged. "We need to see Harms's military file. Until we know who's involved in all this, I want as few people as possible to know we're looking around."

WHILE SARA WENT BACK TO work, Fiske telephoned a lawyer friend at the office of the justice advocate general and requested the file of Harms's court-martial proceedings and a list of the personnel stationed at Fort Plessy during the time Rufus Harms was there.

When Fiske rejoined Chandler, he related his theory of why Wright had been killed. Chandler was impressed. "We can only hope somebody saw or heard something." Chandler stared intently at the young man. "So did you find out anything interesting from Ms. Evans during your time together last night?"

"I think she's a good person. A little impulsive, very smart."

"Anything else? She know any reason why your brother might have been killed?"

"You might want to ask her that."

"Well, I'm asking you, John. I thought we were a team."

Fiske looked away, thinking how best to handle this. Withholding information was not the best course. "Can we get some coffee around here?"

"In the cafeteria. I'll even buy."

A few minutes later they were in the ground-floor cafeteria. Fiske sipped on his coffee while Chandler watched him.

"John, it can't be that bad, unless you tell me you're the one running around popping people."

"Buford, if I tell you something, then you have very specific rules as to what you do with that information and who else learns that information."

"That's true. But my job is to collect facts. If we're not talking facts but just theories—like your theory of why Wright was murdered—then I have no obligation to report it to anyone."

Fiske looked down at his coffee cup.

"John, the bottom line here is finding out who murdered your brother and Wright. I thought that's what you wanted."

"Okay, Buford, let's discuss theories for a minute. Let's suppose that somebody took an appeal before it was put into the Court's system and that somebody else saw this appeal, discovered that it wasn't on the system, but didn't say anything about it. Let's further assume that the person who had filed the appeal was a prisoner."

"Where is this prisoner?"

"I don't know."

"What do you mean you don't know? If he's a prisoner, he has to be in some prison somewhere, doesn't he?"

"Not necessarily."

"What the hell does that—" Chandler abruptly closed his mouth and stared across the table. "Are you saying this person escaped from prison?"

"I'm not saying that." They had already gone well beyond theories now, Fiske knew. He shook his head. "Buford, I'm not going to say any more."

"You know you're taking a risk here, John."

"I do." Fiske finished his coffee and stood up. "I'll grab a cab back to pick up my car."

Chandler watched him leave the cafeteria. "I hope she's worth it, John," the detective said quietly.

CHAPTER EIGHT

OSH Harms assumed the police would now be covering the back roads, so he had taken the unusual tactic of driving on the interstate. It was dusk, though, and with the windows rolled up, a police cruiser would have a tough time seeing inside. But despite all his precautions, he knew they were steering toward disaster.

Funny, he thought, that after all his brother had been put through, he would even think about wanting to do the right thing. Still, you had to admire a person who could fight all that. Maybe the truth *will* set you free, Josh thought. Suddenly out of the corner of his eye he saw something in the truck's side-view mirror.

"Rufus," he called through the open window connecting to the camper, "we got a problem."

Rufus's face appeared at the window. "What is it?"

"Stay low! Stay low!" Josh cautioned. "Trooper's passed us twice and then dropped back."

"You speeding?"

"Five clicks under."

"So, what, then?"

"Look, Rufus, I'm a black man in a real nice-looking vehicle. Cops think I stole it." He looked in the side mirror again. "Looks like he's just about to hit his light."

"What we gonna do? I can't hide back here."

Josh didn't take his eyes off the mirror. "Get down on the floor and pull that tarp on top of you. Do it now." Josh stuck out his chin and pushed his bottom lip out, giving the impression that he had no teeth. He let his strong frame collapse. Then he rolled down the window and stuck his arm out, motioning in long, slow waves for the police cruiser to pull over. Josh eased the truck off the road, and the cruiser quickly pulled in behind, it's roof lights throwing off a startling, ominous blue into the darkness.

Josh waited in the truck. You let the boys in blue come to you, no hurried movement. He heard the boots crunching on the bite of gravel. As the footsteps stopped, Josh looked out the window.

The state trooper stared back at him. "What's the matter, sir?" the trooper asked.

Josh pointed down the road. "Dis a'ight for Luzzana?"

The puzzled trooper crossed his arms. "Where?"

"Luzzana. Bat' Rouge."

"Baton Rouge, Louisiana?" The trooper laughed. "You're a long way from there."

Josh scratched his neck and looked around. "Got me chil'ren on down dare ain't seen they's daddy in a while. Man say I gone git dare from dis here road."

The trooper's expression turned serious. "Well, the man didn't tell you exactly right. But we're close to the exit you need to take. You follow me there, and then you're on your own. How's that sound?"

"A'ight." Josh touched the bill of his cap.

The trooper was about to return to his cruiser when he glanced through the side window of the camper and saw the stacked boxes. "Sir, you mind my taking a look in the camper?"

Josh didn't flinch. "Hell, no."

The trooper went to the rear of the camper and opened the upper glass door. The wall of boxes stared back at him. "What you got in here, sir?" the trooper called out.

"Food," Josh called back, leaning out the window.

The trooper opened one box, shook a soup can. "Lot of food. The trip isn't that long."

"Axed my chil'ren what dey want. Dey say food. You got chil'ren?"

"Two."

"A'ight, den."

"Have a safe trip." The cop walked back to his cruiser.

Josh pulled back onto the road after the cruiser did.

Rufus appeared at the camper window. "I was sweating a river back there."

Josh smiled. "You got to take it cool. You play bad, they cuff you. You act too polite, they figure you scamming, and they cuff you. Now, you be old and dumb, they don't give a hoot."

"Still a close call, Josh."

"THAT was a big oversight on your part, Frank. You take out Rider and his wife, but you didn't search his office?"

Rayfield gripped the phone tighter. "Maybe we'll do it tonight."

"Have you found the letter Harms got from the army?"

"Not yet." He broke off as Tremaine burst into his office, waving a piece of paper. "Hold on."

Tremaine slid the paper in front of Rayfield, who went pale as he read it. He looked up at a grim Tremaine. "Where'd you find it?"

"That s.o.b. hollowed out one of the bed supports. Pretty slick," Tremaine grudgingly conceded.

Rayfield spoke into the receiver. In terse sentences he conveyed the contents of the letter.

The voice sighed. "So now we know what triggered Harms's memory. And maybe Rider had a copy of this letter. That's all the more reason for you to go over his office tonight."

Rayfield looked up at Tremaine and then said into the phone, "All right. We'll hit it tonight. Fast and hard."

JOHN Fiske collected his thoughts on his way from the cafeteria to the Great Hall of the Supreme Court building. The hall was crowded, and his progress was slow. Suddenly Elizabeth Knight powered by, and it was as though the crowd automatically parted for her.

A hand pressed against his shoulder. "Meet me outside the building in ten minutes." It was Sara, but by the time Fiske turned around, he could only see her disappearing into the crowd.

Surprised, he stood for a minute. Then he made his way out of the lobby and down to the street. He looked around but didn't see Sara. A horn beeped, and he saw her car ease up beside him. He climbed in and looked over at her. "Where are we going?"

"To the airport."

"What are you talking about?"

"We're going to see Samuel Rider, Esquire."

"And who is Samuel Rider, Esquire?"

"Rufus Harms's attorney. George Barker called back with the name. I looked Rider up. He practices outside Blacksburg. I tried his office, but there was no answer."

"So why are we flying out there, then?"

"It's not a big town: We should be able to find him. And if we're right about his involvement, he could be in danger. If something happens to him, we may never find out the truth."

"You really think he's the one who called the Court? The one who filed the appeal?"

"I wouldn't bet against it."

CHANDLER walked around Michael Fiske's apartment. He knelt down and examined the gouge mark in the floor caused by John Fiske's swing with a tire iron. Chandler rose and shook his head. His men were putting the finishing touches on the apartment. Black carbon dusting powder lay everywhere in piles. They had taken Michael Fiske's prints for purposes of elimination. They would have to get his brother's as well. And Sara Evans's, he figured. She had undoubtedly been here too.

John Fiske's unwillingness to confide in Chandler had cost him. Chandler had cut off the flow of information to him and had passed along what he had to McKenna. He had also informed McKenna of the missing appeal Fiske had told him about. As if on cue, he heard a sound at the front door, and the FBI agent walked into the room.

"You're working late tonight, Agent McKenna."

"In the Bureau you get double kudos if you solve the crime in time for the evening news." McKenna flashed a rare smile, although it was as though his mouth didn't know quite how to manage it, because the effect came off as lopsided.

Chandler wondered if the man did it on purpose to throw people off. Because he'd had a weird feeling about the guy, Chandler had discreetly checked out Warren McKenna. Before his career at the FBI, he had done a brief stint in the military, then college. His career at the Bureau was first-rate in all respects.

"You're lucky Fiske hasn't slapped you with a lawsuit yet."

"Maybe he should," McKenna said. "I would if I were him."

"I'll be sure to tell him that," Chandler said.

McKenna's gaze darted all over the place for a couple of minutes, seemingly absorbing every detail like a Polaroid, before he glanced back at Chandler. "What are you anyway? His mentor?"

"Didn't know the man until a couple of days ago."

"You make friends a lot faster than I do, then." McKenna inclined his head at Chandler. "Mind if I look around?"

"Go ahead. Try not to touch anything."

McKenna nodded and stepped carefully around the living room. He noted the mark on the floor. "Fiske going after his purported attacker?"

"That's right. Only I didn't know he was purported."

"He is until we have a corroborating account."

Chandler popped a piece of gum into his mouth. "What do you have against the guy? You don't even know him."

McKenna's eyes flashed at him. "That's right, Detective Chandler, and you know what? Neither do you."

Chandler wanted to say something back but couldn't think of anything. In a way the man was right. This thought was interrupted by one of his men.

"Detective Chandler, we found something I think you might want to see."

Chandler took the sheaf of papers from the tech and looked down at it. McKenna joined him.

"Looks like an insurance policy," McKenna said.

"We found it with his tax returns, bills, and stuff like that."

Chandler flipped rapidly through the pages. "Half a million bucks' worth of life insurance." He got to the end. "Michael Fiske was the insured."

McKenna's finger suddenly stabbed at the bottom of the page. "And John is the primary beneficiary."

The two men looked at each other. "Would you like to take a walk and hear a theory of mine?" McKenna asked.

Chandler shrugged. "You got five minutes."

The two men walked out onto the sidewalk in front of the row house. McKenna took a moment to light up a cigarette and then began talking. "I found out that Fiske doesn't have an alibi for the probable time his brother was murdered."

"Might be something in his favor. If he killed his brother, he would've worked hard to establish one."

"I disagree. There is no such thing as a perfect alibi. If you're guilty, then a hole will come up in it eventually. Fiske was a cop and now a lawyer. He knows all about alibis." McKenna took a long drag on his cigarette and looked up at the few stars visible in the sky. "I checked him out. He's got a two-bit law practice in Richmond, defending the scum of the earth. He's third-rate at best. Mid-thirties. Unmarried, no kids, a real loner. Oh, and he left the Richmond police force under a somewhat dark cloud."

"How do you mean?" Chandler asked sharply.

"Let's just say that there was a shooting incident that was never fully explained other than the fact a civilian and another police officer were dead as a result."

Chandler turned to him. "What about Sara Evans? She said she

saw a guy running out of Michael Fiske's building. You say she's lying too?"

McKenna took a last puff of his cigarette and then crushed it out
on the sidewalk with several twists of his foot. "I'm not saying she's
in on the whole thing. I'm saying maybe she has a thing for Fiske,
and she's doing what he tells her to."

"Why do you have such a thing against Fiske?"

Now McKenna erupted. "What am I supposed to think? He's
got no alibi for the night of the murder, and now we find out he's a
half million bucks richer because his brother is dead."

"Okay, you've made your point. Maybe I have been too lax with
him. Rule number one: Don't trust anybody."

"Good rule." McKenna walked off, leaving a very shaken Chandler staring after him.

THE building was small and at this hour pretty much deserted.
The office they were looking for was one of the half-dozen on the
second floor. Stenciled lettering on the glass door read SAMUEL
RIDER, ATTORNEY-AT-LAW.

Fiske squinted through the glass. "Dark inside."

"He's probably at home," Sara said.

Fiske clasped the doorknob, and it turned easily. He and Sara exchanged a significant glance. He pulled her away to the exit stairs and
whispered, "If you hear anything, run to the car and call the cops."

She grabbed his arm and whispered back, "And if you go in there
and get killed, what exactly is that going to accomplish?"

"Maybe you're right."

"Lady is for sure right."

Fiske and Sara whirled around.

Josh Harms stood there, his pistol aimed at them. "Wall's mighty
thin. Figured when we heard all that whispering, you two were going to go for the cops."

Fiske studied him. He was big, but not as big as the news reports
described Rufus. Unless they had run into a routine burglary, this
man had to be the brother.

"You must be Josh. My name is John Fiske. This is Sara Evans with the United States Supreme Court. We're here to help you."

Behind him, from the open doorway leading into Rider's office, appeared a man of such huge proportions that both Sara and Fiske knew he could only be Rufus Harms. He had obviously heard Fiske's words.

Josh kept his pistol tightly on the pair.

"Why don't we talk inside the office?" Fiske motioned to Sara. "After you, Sara." Out of the brothers' line of sight, he gave her a reassuring wink. He only wished he felt as confident on the inside.

Sara walked into the office, with Fiske behind her. Josh and Rufus eyed each other quizzically. Then they followed the pair inside and shut the door behind them.

"We came here to talk to Sam Rider," Sara explained.

Josh looked over at her. "Well, unless you're gonna put on a séance, you're gonna have a real hard time doing that."

Fiske and Sara looked at each other and then back at Josh.

"He's dead?" Sara asked.

Rufus nodded. "He and his wife. Made it look like a murder and suicide."

Fiske noted a file clutched in Rufus's hand. "Is that what you sent to the Court? Sam Rider filed that for you, didn't he?"

"I ain't answering no questions."

"Okay, I'll just tell you what we know. Rider filed it. My brother, Michael Fiske, got it and took it out of the Court's system. Then he ended up dead in an alley in Washington. Now Rider is dead. Another clerk was killed too." Fiske stopped talking and studied the two men. "That's all we know."

"You with the cops?" Josh demanded.

"I'm helping the detective in charge."

"See, Rufus, I told you. We got to get out of here. Cops probably on their way right now."

"No, they're not," Sara said. "I saw your name in the papers Michael had, Mr. Harms. I don't know why you filed it."

"Why does a prisoner file something with a court?" Rufus asked.

"Because you want out," Fiske said. "But you have to have grounds to do that."

"I got me the best grounds of all: the simple truth," Rufus said forcefully.

Josh edged toward the door. "Rufus, we stand here talking to them and the cops are closing in."

"They killed his brother, Josh."

"You don't know if he really is his brother."

Fiske pulled out his wallet with his driver's license. "This'll at least prove we have the same last name."

"I work at the Supreme Court, Mr. Harms," Sara said. "I know all the Justices. If you have evidence that shows you're innocent, then I promise you it will be heard."

Fiske added, "The detective on the case knows something is fishy. If you tell us what was in your appeal, we can go to him and get him to explore that angle."

"Rufus, don't you answer that, dammit!" Josh yelled.

Rufus ignored him. "Something the army sent me—a letter."

"Did you kill the little girl, Rufus?" Fiske asked.

"I did," he said, looking down. "At least my hands did. The rest of me didn't know what the hell was going on. Not after what they done to me."

"What do you mean by that?"

"They messed with my head, that's what," Rufus said.

Fiske eyed him sharply. "Are you pleading some sort of insanity? Because if you are, you don't have a prayer." He watched Rufus intently. "But it's more than that, isn't it? Because my brother took whatever was in that appeal very seriously. Seriously enough that he broke the law and lost his life. Tell me what it was."

Josh put one big hand on Fiske's chest and pushed him back. "Look here, Mr. Hotshot, Rufus here didn't ask your brother to do nothing. Your brother was the one that blew this whole thing up sky-high. He had to come check Rufus out 'cuz he's some old black man sitting in some old prison for some old crime." He moved the pistol closer to Fiske's face.

"Please stop," Sara implored. "Please, he's just trying to help."

"Josh, this ain't the way to handle things," Rufus said.

"Oh, so now you know the way to handle things?" said Josh.

The screeching of rubber against asphalt made them all look toward the window. Rufus went over and cautiously looked out. "It's Vic Tremaine and Rayfield. Vic's got a machine gun."

As they listened, heavy boots clattered into the building. In another couple of minutes they would be there.

Fiske's eyes were squarely on Rufus. "Rufus, maybe I can get you out of this if you'll trust me. My brother came to help you. Let me finish what he started. Come on, Rufus, give me a chance." A bead of sweat trickled down Fiske's forehead.

Finally, almost imperceptibly, Rufus nodded.

Fiske launched into action. "Get in the bathroom, both of you."

Josh started to protest, until Rufus cut him off and pushed him toward the private bath adjoining the office.

"Sara, you go with them."

She looked at him, stunned. "What?"

"Just do what I say. If you hear me call your name, flush the toilet and then come out."

Sara's face was pale. "John, I can't do this."

He gripped her shoulders hard. "Sara, you *can* do this. You are going to do this. Now go." He squeezed her hand, and then she and the Harms brothers went into the bathroom and Sara shut the door behind them. As the boots boomed down the hallway, Fiske raced to the small conference table set up in one corner. He sat down and pretended to study some of the papers as the door opened. He stared up into the faces of the men.

"What—" he started to say, until he saw the machine gun.

"Who are you?" Rayfield demanded.

"I'm here for a meeting with Sam Rider."

Rayfield edged closer. "Little late for a meeting, isn't it?"

"I have a busy schedule. This was the only time I could meet. The meeting's been planned for weeks."

Tremaine's face flushed angrily. "Well, you're going to have to get another lawyer," he said.

"I'm happy with Sam's work."

"That's not the point. The point is, Rider's dead. He committed suicide. Killed his wife and then himself."

Fiske stood up, trying to make his expression as horrified as possible. "I can't believe it," he said, slowly shaking his head. "But no one told me. The door to his office was unlocked." He pushed the papers away, then looked up sharply. "So what are you two doing here? Why is the army involved?"

Tremaine and Rayfield exchanged glances. "There's been an escape from the military prison nearby. Rider was the escapee's lawyer. We're here to look around, catch the guy if he's here."

Fiske watched with a sinking heart as Tremaine headed to the bathroom door.

"Susan, can you please come out here?" Fiske said in a loud voice.

Tremaine stared hard at Fiske as they all heard the toilet flush. And then the door opened partially, and Sara came out, trying her best to look astonished. "John, what's going on?"

"You're not going to believe this, but Sam Rider's dead."

"What?"

"Susan is my assistant."

She nodded at both men.

"These men are from the army. They're looking for an escaped prisoner they think might have had something to do with Sam."

"Oh, please, John, let's just get out of here."

"That's not a bad idea," Tremaine said. "We can search the place a lot faster with you two out of the way." He once again looked over at the bathroom door.

"Well, I can tell you there's no one hiding in there," she said.

"If you don't mind, ma'am, I like to see these things for myself," Tremaine said curtly.

Fiske watched Sara. He was sure she was going to start screaming. Come on, Sara, hold on. Don't lose it.

Behind the door of the darkened bathroom Josh Harms had his pistol pointed directly at Tremaine's head through the slight gap between the door and doorjamb. No way could he miss.

"I can't believe it," Fiske said. "First two black guys almost run us over, and now this."

Tremaine and Rayfield jerked around and stared at him. "What two black guys?" they said in unison.

Fiske turned to them. "We were coming in the building, and they ran by us, almost knocked Susan down."

"What'd they look like?" Rayfield asked, edging closer to Fiske. Tremaine quickly moved away from the bathroom door.

"One of them looked like he was ex-NFL or something. You remember how big he was, Susan?"

She nodded and then started breathing again.

"I mean, he was huge. The guy with him was pretty big too, and they were running like wildfire."

"Did you see which way they went?" Tremaine asked.

"They jumped in some old car—green, I think—and took off on the main road heading north." He suddenly looked frightened. "You don't think it was the escaped prisoner, do you?"

Tremaine and Rayfield didn't answer, because they were rushing out the door. As soon as Fiske and Sara heard the outer door open and the boots running down the hallway, they looked at each other and then collapsed onto the sofa. They reached for each other and huddled together.

"Glad I didn't have to shoot. You think fast on your feet."

They looked up at the grinning face of Josh Harms. "We're both lawyers," Fiske said hoarsely, still clutching Sara tightly.

"Well, nobody's perfect," Josh said.

Rufus appeared behind his brother. "Thanks," he said quietly.

"I hope you believe us now," Fiske said.

"Yeah, but I ain't gonna take your help. Everybody's tried to help me up till now is dead except Josh. You two stay out of this."

"I can't do that. Michael was my brother."

"Suit yourself, but you're gonna do it without me." He motioned to Josh. "Let's get going. No telling when they might get the itch to come back."

As the two men started to turn away, Fiske reached into his pocket and took out something, which he held out to Rufus. "This is my business card."

Fiske looked surprised as Sara lifted the card from him and wrote something on the back. She held it out to Rufus. "That's my home number on the back. Call either of us day or night."

Slowly the huge hand reached out, took the card. Rufus slipped
it into his shirt pocket. In another minute Sara and Fiske were alone.

AS THE jeep raced down the road, Tremaine scrutinized the passengers of each car they passed.

"Of all the luck," Rayfield moaned. "We couldn't have missed
them by more than a few minutes."

Tremaine ignored him, focusing instead on the car in front of
them. The dome light of the car came on as they passed, revealing
the driver and passenger. The passenger was unfolding a map.

As Tremaine stared at the car's interior, he hit the brakes, ripped
the jeep to the left, and went across the median. The vehicle
bumped and jostled in the grassy ditch before the tires found asphalt again, and they were heading back toward Rider's office.

Rayfield grabbed Tremaine's shoulder. "What are you doing?"

"They suckered us. That story was bull."

"How do you know that?"

"The light in the bathroom."

"The light? What about it?"

"It wasn't on. She was in there in the dark. It hit me when I saw
the dome light go on in the car back there. There was no light coming from under the bathroom door. She was standing in there in the
pitch-dark. And guess why?"

Rayfield's face went pale. "Because Harms and his brother were
in there too. Could the guy have been John Fiske?"

"And the girl was Sara Evans. That's what I'm thinking. You better call and let the others know."

Rayfield picked up the cell phone. "We'll never catch up to
Harms now."

"Yes, we will."

"How?"

Tremaine drew on thirty years of army training, studying what the
other side would do in a particular scenario. "Fiske said he saw them
get in a car. Opposite of a car is a truck. He said it was an old car.
Opposite of that is a new truck. He said they were going north, so
we go south. It's only been five minutes. We'll catch them." He nod-

ded at the phone. "Now you make that call. We'll take care of Harms and his brother. They'll have to deal with Fiske and the woman."

BECAUSE of the high-profile nature of the case, the FBI had offered the use of its laboratory to perform analysis on a slug found in the alley where Michael Fiske's body had been discovered. After comparing tissue samples taken from the slug with Michael Fiske's remains, it was deemed to have been the bullet fired through the victim's brain. The slug was a 9-mm of a type typically carried by law-enforcement personnel.

With that information Agent McKenna sat down in front of a computer terminal at the Hoover Building and typed in a high-priority request to the Virginia State Police. Within a few minutes he had his answer: John Fiske had a 9-mm SIG-Sauer registered in his name, a carryover from his cop days. Within minutes McKenna was in his car. Two hours later he turned off Interstate 95 and drove through the darkened streets of downtown Richmond. His car rumbled over the aged and uneven streets of Shockoe Slip. He parked in a secluded area near the old train station.

Ten minutes later he was standing in John Fiske's office, having picked the locks with ease. It took only a couple of minutes to find it. The pistol was relatively light and compact. Wearing gloves, McKenna palmed it for a moment and then put it into his pocket.

He cast his thoughts backward. He had led a long, productive career on the side of law enforcement, but that had not made up for one event that had caused him great shame ever since. It had happened so many years ago and yet was still one of the clearest memories he possessed. What he had done back then was today compelling him to frame John Fiske for a crime.

He took a long breath as the darkness clung to him. Penance was a lifelong responsibility.

THE plane touched down and taxied to a stop. A few minutes later Fiske and Sara were headed toward the parking garage at National Airport. "We flew all the way out there, nearly got slaughtered, and we came back empty-handed," she muttered.

"That's where you're wrong," Fiske said. "We learned a few things. One, my brother visited Rufus in prison. Two, we saw Rufus face to face. I think he's telling the truth, whatever the truth happens to be."

"You can't be sure of that."

"He came to Rider's office to get the appeal when he should be doing his best to get out of the country. Why would he do that unless he believed it to be true?"

"I don't know," Sara admitted. "If it was his appeal, why not just write it again?"

"Rider had filed his own document with it. That was something Harms couldn't duplicate. He also mentioned a letter he got from the army. What sort of letter would the army be sending a con?"

"Do you think the letter somehow triggered this?"

"It could have had some information that Harms didn't know about before. Then Rufus maybe fakes a heart attack, gets taken to the nearest hospital, and that's where Josh breaks him out."

"That works."

"And those army guys didn't come there to look for Rufus Harms. They came there to search Rider's office for the appeal."

"How do you know that?"

"They didn't even ask us if we'd seen anyone suspicious, anyone who looked like Rufus. I had to volunteer the information. So I'm thinking whatever was in that appeal had something to do with those guys personally."

"But we don't even know who they are."

"Yes, we do. Rufus told us their names: Tremaine and Rayfield."

Sara shook her head. "And if Rayfield and Tremaine work at the prison, then Michael walked right into the lion's den. Even though you two weren't close, I'm really surprised Michael didn't try to call you for help. He might still be alive if he had."

Fiske froze at her words and then closed his eyes. He said nothing more until they reached Sara's cottage.

THEY were out on the small rear deck that looked out over the river, sitting on a faded wooden glider.

"You made a good choice in housing," he commented.

"The first time I saw it, I could see myself living here forever." She watched the car lights pass over the Woodrow Wilson Bridge in the distance. Then she stood up. "Want to go sailing?"

He looked up at her in surprise. "A little late for that, isn't it?"

"We'll just do a lazy circle and come back in." Before he could answer, she disappeared into the cottage. Within a couple of minutes she came back out wearing jean cutoffs, a tank top, and deck shoes, her hair pulled back in a bun.

Fiske glanced down at his dress shirt, slacks, and loafers. "I didn't bring my sailor suit."

"That's okay. You're not the sailor. I am." She had two cold beers. They walked down to the dock. It was miserably humid, and Fiske quickly broke a sweat helping Sara ready the sails.

The water was flat, no shore wind evident. They motored out into the middle of the river, where the sails finally caught a breeze. Sara looked over at him and smiled. "It feels magical to catch something invisible and yet so powerful, and compel it to do your bidding, doesn't it?" The way she said it, so girlish, with so much frank wonder, he had to smile. They drank beer and talked about things unrelated to present events, and both felt relieved to be able to do so even for a short time.

"You have a nice smile," Sara remarked. "You should use it more often."

By the time they headed back in, the wind had started to pick up as a late-night storm rolled in. They watched as the clouds turned black-edged and pops of lightning appeared on the horizon. Sara shivered, and Fiske put his arm around her. She leaned into him.

Then a few drops of rain hit. With Fiske's help Sara docked the boat and snapped vinyl covers into place across the open compartment. They walked up to the cottage, running the last few feet as it started to pour.

"Long day tomorrow," Sara said, looking at the kitchen clock while patting her wet hair with a paper towel.

"Especially after no sleep last night," Fiske added, yawning. They turned the lights off and headed upstairs.

Sara said good night and went to her room. Fiske watched through the doorway as she opened the window, letting the breeze in along with some of the rain. A shaft of lightning flared across the sky and connected with the earth somewhere. The boom was deafening. Fiske went down the hallway to the other bedroom. His room was stuffy, but he made no move to open a window. A clock hanging on the wall ticked the seconds at him. He caught himself measuring his pulse against it.

FISKE awoke early, just as the first shafts of sunlight were dropping over the windowsill. Behind the storm had come waves of deliciously chilly air and a sky that would transform fully from pink and gray to a deep blue in another hour. He made coffee and stood on the rear deck as the sound of the shower started upstairs. Dawn always seemed so much purer over water, as though these two essential elements of life—heat and water—produced a near spiritual performance.

But then came the blunt clarity of morning. Fiske lifted the coffee cup to his lips, but then quickly put it back down. If he had called his brother back right away, Mike would be alive right now. Fiske could never dodge that truth. He would, in fact, have to live with it forever.

CHAPTER NINE

 OSH Harms finished his sandwich and then idly smoked a cigarette as he watched his brother doze in the front seat of the truck. They were parked on an old logging road in a dense forest. Driving through the night, they had finally stopped because Josh could barely keep his eyes open, and he didn't trust his brother to drive, since Rufus hadn't been behind the wheel of a vehicle for almost thirty years. Rufus had kept watch while his brother had dozed, and now Josh was playing sentry.

They had talked during the drive about what they were going to do. Much to his own surprise Josh found himself arguing that they shouldn't go to Mexico.

"What's with you? I didn't think you'd want any part of that. You said you didn't," Rufus had said in wonderment.

"I didn't. But once we made up our mind, we should stick to it. Fiske and that woman—maybe they're shooting straight."

Rufus had stared at him. "I can't figure you out, Josh."

"You ain't got to figure me out. I ain't figured me out."

That had done it, and as soon as his brother woke up, they were going to head back toward Virginia, hook up with Fiske, and see what they could do. Josh checked his watch. Another ten minutes, and they would have to be on their way.

He looked back out the window and squinted as the sunlight reflected off something. He sucked in his next breath, spit his cigarette out the window, started the engine, and put the truck in gear.

"What the . . ." Rufus said as he was jolted awake.

"Keep your head down," Josh hollered. "It's Tremaine."

Rufus gripped his pistol and ducked down.

Tremaine charged from the woods and opened fire. The first shots from the machine gun hit the tailgate of the truck, blowing out one of the lights and riddling the frame with holes.

Josh cut the wheel to the left, and the truck went off the road and into a dry creek bed.

Rayfield came flying down the road in the jeep from the other direction, trying to box the truck in. Rayfield stopped to let Tremaine climb in, and they came after the truck.

"How'd they catch up to us?" Rufus wondered aloud.

"Ain't no sense wasting time thinking about that. They're here," Josh yelled, glancing in the rearview mirror. "They should've shot our tires out first thing. That was their second mistake."

"What was the first?"

"Letting the sunlight hit their binoculars. I saw that long before I spotted that little lizard."

Back in the jeep, Tremaine hung out the side and fired his

weapon, but the machine gun wasn't really worth a spit long-range. He pulled out his side arm instead. "Get as close as you can," he barked to a very nervous-looking Rayfield.

Josh cut the wheel to the right and then to the left to avoid several trees that had toppled across the creek bed. Then he drove through a narrow cleft in the trees and brush, leaves and slender branches slapping and tearing at the truck. The maneuver had its intended effect. Tremaine had to duck back inside the jeep to avoid having his head torn off by a tree limb.

The jeep slowed down. The narrow lane ahead opened up a little, and Josh decided to take advantage, hoping Rayfield was losing a little of his nerve. "Hold the wheel," he shouted to his brother.

Rufus gripped the steering wheel hard, alternating between looking at his brother and eyeing where the truck was heading.

Josh pulled his pistol and scanned the trees ahead. Doing his best to figure distance and speed, he selected what he wanted: a thick oak branch high up on a forty-footer. The branch was at least twenty feet long and four inches thick. It hung directly over the narrow creek bed and was so long and heavy it had started to crack where it was attached to the trunk.

Josh slid his arm out the window, took aim, and started firing. The first bullet hit the tree trunk directly above where the branch joined it. Having now gauged the trajectory, Josh continued to fire, and each bullet after that hit squarely at the juncture of branch and trunk as the truck hurtled closer. The heavy branch dropped a couple of inches as its support weakened.

Tremaine saw what he was doing. "Gun it, gun it."

Rayfield hit the gas.

Josh kept firing. Finally gravity took over. The branch broke free and started coming down. Josh slammed on the accelerator and took the steering wheel back, passing by the tree as he did so.

Rayfield slammed on the brakes as about a thousand pounds of tree branch smashed into the middle of the narrow lane directly in front of them. Tremaine was almost thrown from the vehicle. "Why'd you stop?"

Rayfield was breathing hard. "That thing would've crushed us."

Josh swerved left and gunned the motor. The truck broke free from the brush, lifted a little off the ground as it went over a shallow gully, and landed in a clearing. Rufus's head hit the top of the cab's interior as the truck came back to earth.

"Josh, what're you doing?"

"Just hold tight."

Josh slammed on the gas again, and Rufus looked up in time to see a small shack ahead. Where there was a shack in the woods, there usually was a road. Josh pulled the truck around onto the other side of the old structure. Both brothers' hearts sank. There was a road there, all right. But it had a large steel barricade blocking any passage. And on either side of the barricade were impenetrable woods. Josh looked back. They were trapped.

A minute later the jeep scaled the gully and shot around the corner of the shack. Instantly both men saw that the road was blocked off, and Rayfield slammed the jeep to a stop. With a roar the truck, which had been hidden on the far side of the shack, exploded forward and hit the vehicle broadside, knocking it over on its side and flinging Rayfield and Tremaine out. Rayfield landed on top of a pile of rotted stumps, his head at a vicious angle. He lay still.

Tremaine took cover behind the overturned jeep and opened fire, forcing Josh to back the truck up, his head below the dashboard. Finally the truck engine died, steam pouring out from the hood, the front tires flattened by the machine-gun fire.

Josh came out the driver's side, dropped down, and rolled to the rear of the truck, and then he peered out. Tremaine hadn't moved from his position. Josh could see the tip of the machine gun. He sprinted from the truck and made it behind the shack.

"Rufus," he hollered, "on the count of three."

"Start counting," Rufus shouted, tremors of fear in his voice.

Three seconds later Josh opened fire on Tremaine, the bullets pinging off the jeep's frame. Rufus hustled to the back of the truck. He was stopped there, however, when Tremaine managed to fire a burst between the truck and the shack.

Josh and Rufus looked at each other, and then Josh cracked a smile, sensing the rising panic in his brother.

"Hey, Vic, buddy," Josh yelled out, "how 'bout you throw down that little widow-maker and come on out with your hands up?"

Tremaine responded by blowing a chunk of wood off the shack above Josh's head.

"Okay, okay, I hear you. Now you be cool, you hear me, little buddy? Don't you worry. We'll bury you and the other guy. Ain't gonna leave you for the bears to chew on. Animals eating dead bodies. You saw that in Nam, didn't you? Or maybe you was running too fast the other way to see that." While he was talking, Josh was motioning for Rufus to stay put and then pointing around the shack to show his brother what he was going to do.

Rufus nodded to show he understood. Josh was going to try to flush the man into his brother's field of vision and let Rufus cut him down. Rufus gripped his gun and slipped in a new clip, grateful that his brother had taken the time to show him how. Rufus was afraid. He had fought many men in prison in order to survive—with his hands only. But a gun was different.

In a half crouch Josh made his way across the front of the shack, stopping at intervals to listen intently. He pointed his pistol directly in front of him. Machine gun against pistol, a hundred rounds to one.

He moved forward another foot. Then he heard the machine gun open fire again and listened as the bullets tore into the pickup truck. He raced forward and rounded the corner. While Tremaine was busy firing at Rufus, Josh could outflank him.

This plan vanished when he went around the corner, for Tremaine was standing there, his pistol pointed at Josh's head. An astonished Josh stopped so abruptly that his feet slid in the gravel, and his legs went out from under him as the bullet slammed into him. His momentum carried him forward and his legs clipped Tremaine's, and they went down hard, both their pistols sailing out of reach.

Tremaine pulled a knife from his belt. In the background the machine gun stopped firing. Josh yelled out as Tremaine lunged into him, and both men hit the wall of the shack, shaking the primitive structure right down to its wooden joints. Josh felt the knife cut through his shirt and into his side, and he started to lose consciousness. The pain from this fresh wound was barely felt, so overwhelmed was it by the first. He could hardly make out the image of Tremaine pulling the knife free from his body and rearing his arm back for a final thrust.

The knife never made its downward plunge. The bullet hit Tremaine square in the back and dropped him on the spot.

Rufus raced over and knelt next to his brother. "Josh! Josh?"

Josh opened his eyes and looked over at Tremaine's twisted body, both relieved and sickened by what he saw. He looked back at Rufus. "You done good, little brother. I'd be dead if you hadn't killed him."

Rufus ripped open his brother's shirt and looked at the wounds. The knife had only cut a slice in his side. Probably hadn't hit anything vital. The bullet, though, was something else. He saw the blood dripping from his brother's mouth, the rising glaze to his eyes. Rufus could stop the outside bleeding, but he could do nothing about what was going on inside. And that's what could kill him.

Josh's eyes closed, and he didn't seem to be breathing.

Rufus shook him gently. "Josh, Josh, don't go to sleep on me."

Finally Josh opened his eyes. "You got to get outta here, Rufus. All the shooting—people might be coming. You got to go. Now."

"*We* got to get out of here. That's right."

"Rufus, get yourself out of here," Josh said again. "You crazy."

"Yeah, I'm crazy. Let's leave it at that." He gently lifted his brother, but the movement sent Josh into a coughing spasm. Rufus carried him over to the truck and laid him down next to it.

"Hang it, Rufus. This thing ain't going nowhere," Josh said desperately, looking at the battered truck.

"I know that." Rufus pulled a bottle of water from the camper, twisted it open, and put it to Josh's lips. Josh gripped the bottle and drank a little.

Rufus rose and went to the overturned jeep. He pulled the machine gun free from where Tremaine had wedged it between the seat and the metal side of the jeep. The man had used wire, a piece of metal, and a string to rig the trigger for full automatic fire while he set up his ambush of Josh. Rufus eyed the situation for a moment and then tried to push against the hood to right the vehicle, but he couldn't get any leverage that way, and his feet slipped in the loose gravel. He studied the situation some more. There was really only one way that he could see.

He put his back against the edge of the driver's-side seat and then squatted down. He dug his fingers into the dirt and gravel until they got underneath the jeep's side, and then he clenched the metal, giving one good pull to gauge what he was up against. Thirty years ago this wouldn't have been much trouble.

He hunkered down again, closed his eyes, and then opened them. He looked skyward, where a big black crow lazily circled. Not a care in the world. As sweat poured off Rufus's face, he clenched his eyes again and did what he always did when he was troubled. He prayed. He asked the Lord to please grant him the strength he needed to save his brother's life.

He tensed his massive shoulders and legs. His long arms began to pull; his bent legs began to straighten. For a moment jeep and man were suspended in a precarious equilibrium, moving neither up nor down. But then Rufus slowly started to fall back a little. The weight was too much for him. He opened his mouth and let out a terrible scream that forced tears from his eyes. As Josh looked on at the impossible thing his brother was trying to do for him, tears started to fall down his exhausted face.

Rufus's eyes opened again as he felt the jeep rise inch by agonizing inch. His joints and tendons afire, Rufus pulled and heaved. Pain snapped perilous signals through his trembling body. The jeep fought him every punishing inch. But then he was standing upright, and he gave the hunk of metal one last heave. The jeep cleared the point of no return and fell hard to earth, rocking upon impact and then coming to rest on all four wheels.

Josh looked on in silent wonderment.

Rufus's heart was racing hard now. He clutched at his chest. "Please," he quietly said. "Please don't." A minute later, his body still shaking, he slowly walked over to his brother and carefully lifted him into the jeep. He gathered up as many supplies as he could from the truck, including his Bible, and put them into the back of the jeep, along with the weaponry. He stopped and looked over at Tremaine and Rayfield. Then he stared up once again at the circling crow. In less than a day the two dead men would be picked to the bone if left out in the open.

Rufus slid first Rayfield's body and then Tremaine's into the shack. He said a few simple words over both men before closing the door. He climbed into the jeep, gave Josh a reassuring look, and started the engine. Gears grinding as Rufus got a quick lesson in driving a stick shift, the jeep jolted forward, and the brothers left this impromptu battlefield behind.

FISKE made his way to police chief Leo Dellasandro's ground-floor office, knocked on the door, waited. He knocked again and then opened the door and peered inside. He was looking at the anteroom to Dellasandro's office, where his secretary worked. That space was empty. Probably at lunch, Fiske assumed. He stepped into the office. "Chief Dellasandro?" He wanted to know if anything had turned up on the surveillance videos.

He approached the inner-office door. "Chief Dellasandro, it's John Fiske. I was wondering if we could talk." Still no answer. He slipped into Dellasandro's office and over to his desk. He picked up a piece of paper and a pen, and scrawled a brief note. As he turned to leave, he looked around the office.

Hanging on the back of the door was a jacket. It had to belong to Dellasandro. Obviously, part of his Court uniform. As Fiske passed by it, he noticed several smudges on the collar. He rubbed it with his finger and examined the residue: makeup. He went out into the anteroom and looked at the photos on the desk. He had seen Dellasandro's secretary once—a tall brunette with memorable features. There was a photo of her and Chief Dellasandro. His arm was around her shoulder; they were both smiling. There was something in the eyes, how close they were standing together, suggesting something more than a platonic relationship.

Fiske glanced back into Dellasandro's office at the photo on his credenza—of his wife and kids. A very happy-looking family. Only on the surface, obviously. As he left the office, he concluded that it pretty much summed up how this place and the world in general operated: Surface appearances could be very deceiving.

SARA WAS IN HER OFFICE WHEN she received the urgent summons from Elizabeth Knight. She was surprised. On Wednesday afternoons the Justices were usually in conference, going over the cases heard on Monday. As she entered Knight's chambers, Sara greeted Knight's secretary, Harriet. Normally cheerful and friendly, Harriet spoke in a cold tone. "Go right in, Ms. Evans."

Sara paused at the door. She turned around and caught Harriet staring at her. Harriet quickly turned back to her work. Sara took a deep breath and opened the door.

Within the office, either standing or perched upon chairs, were Ramsey, Detective Chandler, Perkins, and Agent McKenna. Seated behind her antique desk, Elizabeth Knight was nervously fiddling with a letter opener when she saw Sara. "Please come in and sit down."

Sara sat in an upholstered wing chair carefully positioned so that it allowed everyone in the room to directly face her. She looked at Knight. "You wanted to see me?"

Ramsey stepped forward. "We all did, Ms. Evans. Detective Chandler?" Ramsey was as stern as Sara had ever seen him.

Chandler sat down across from her. "I've got a question I need to ask you, and I want the truth in return," he said quietly. "Have you ever heard the name Rufus Harms?"

Sara closed her eyes for a moment. "Let me explain—"

"Yes or no, please, Ms. Evans," Chandler said.

She nodded, then said, "Yes."

Chandler continued. "You've been asking questions at the clerks' office about an appeal he filed. Why?"

Sara let out a deep breath and looked once more at the army aligned against her. "One day I happened to see what looked like an appeal with Rufus Harms's name on it. I checked at the clerks' office because I didn't recall seeing it on the docket."

"Where did you see this appeal?" Ramsey interjected.

"Just somewhere," Sara said, looking miserable.

"Sara," Knight said harshly, "tell us the truth. Don't throw your career away for this."

"I don't remember where I saw it. I just saw it."

McKenna spoke up forcefully. "Listen, Ms. Evans, it is in your interests to cooperate and stop protecting the Fiske brothers."

"What are you talking about?"

"We have reason to suspect that Michael Fiske took that appeal," Chandler informed her. "And you are running around asking questions because John Fiske put you up to it."

"This may come as a shock to you, but I can think and act all by myself, Detective Chandler," she said hotly.

McKenna's next words almost put her on the floor. "Did you also know that Michael Fiske was killed by a slug fired from a nine-millimeter?" He paused for effect. "And that John Fiske has a nine-millimeter registered to his name?"

Sara looked at Chandler. "I don't believe this."

Chandler nodded thoughtfully, his arms crossed. "Ms. Evans, a Master Sergeant Dillard from Military Police Operations has informed us that you phoned him about Rufus Harms. You were checking into his background."

"There's no law that says I can't make a phone call to clarify something, is there?"

"So you admit having called him," Perkins said triumphantly. "That means you admit to having used Court facilities and Court time on a personal investigation."

"I admit to no such thing. It was Court business."

"Ms. Evans, if someone at this Court stole an appeal before it was filed and if you know who it was, you have a duty to this institution to tell us." Ramsey was staring at her just as he peered down at the lawyers during oral argument.

Summoning a reserve of strength she was unaware she possessed, Sara rose slowly. "I think I've answered enough questions, Mr. Chief Justice."

"Then Sara, I have to ask you to voluntarily resign your clerkship, effective immediately," Elizabeth Knight said, her voice breaking as she made this announcement.

Sara looked at her with very little surprise. "I understand, Justice Knight. I'm sorry it's come to this."

"Not nearly as sorry as I am. Mr. Perkins will escort you out. You may gather your personal belongings from your office." Knight abruptly looked away.

As Sara turned to go, Ramsey's voice boomed out again. "Ms. Evans, be advised that if your actions cause this institution any harm whatsoever, all appropriate action will be taken against you."

Sara Evans fled the room before she burst into tears.

FISKE was waiting for Sara in her office. When she appeared in the doorway, he rose and started to speak, but then Perkins appeared behind her. Sara went over to her desk and started cleaning it out.

"Sara, what happened?"

"This is none of your concern, Mr. Fiske," Perkins said.

Sara finished packing her things into a large shopping bag and wordlessly pushed past Perkins.

On the way down the main hallway, the group slowed as Chandler and McKenna approached from the other way.

"I need to talk to you, John," Chandler said.

Fiske looked at Sara. "I'll catch up with you."

"I'll meet you in the garage," Sara whispered.

She and Perkins walked off.

"You wanted to ask me something?" Fiske said.

"That's right." Chandler looked at Fiske. "Your brother was killed by a nine-millimeter slug."

"Really?"

"You own a nine-millimeter pistol, don't you?"

"Yes. I own a nine-millimeter—SIG-Sauer P226. It's in my office, back in Richmond."

"We'd like to have it."

"Buford, this is a waste of time."

McKenna said, "We can have a search warrant issued in about one hour."

"You don't need a warrant. I'll give you the gun." Fiske looked at Chandler. "I assume I'm not part of the unofficial team anymore, but one thing: Have the video cameras been checked for the night Wright was murdered?"

"I would advise you to say nothing to him, Chandler," McKenna said.

"Advice duly noted." Chandler looked at Fiske. "For old times' sake, the film from the video cameras was checked and showed nothing out of the ordinary."

"Okay, let's get back to the gun," McKenna said. "I'm going with you to your office."

"I'm not driving anywhere with you."

"I meant I'll follow you down."

"Do whatever you want, but I want a uniformed Richmond police officer there, and I want him to take the gun into custody. I will not let you be anywhere near the chain of custody."

"I really don't like what you're implying."

"Fine, but that's the way it's going to be."

Chandler spoke up. "Okay, anybody in particular?"

"Officer William Hawkins. I trust him, and so can you." Fiske looked down the hallway. "Just give me a half hour. I need to talk to somebody."

Fiske hustled off in search of Sara. He caught up with her in the parking garage. It didn't take her long to explain what had happened.

"Sara, maybe I can go and talk to Ramsey and Knight, try and explain things to them?"

"Explain it how? What they're alleging I did, I did. And I assume they told you about your gun?"

Fiske nodded. "McKenna's giving me an armed escort to my office so I can hand it over." He looked at her closely. "So what are you going to do now?"

"I don't know. But I've suddenly got a lot of free time on my hands. To tell you the truth, I feel pretty good. Maybe I'll go for another sail." She stroked his face. "Come by my place tonight."

As Sara drove off, it suddenly occurred to her that she did have something very important to take care of. She needed to see somebody. And today was as good a day as any. She got into her car and pulled out of the garage.

When she drove past the columned façade of her old place of work, a great wave of relief swept over her. It was so sudden that it left her breathless. She accelerated down Independence Avenue and didn't look back.

JOHN Fiske sat in his car. He felt numb. He had gotten Sara fired and was being set up for murdering his brother, all in less than an hour. In any realm other than total lunacy, that would be called a bad day. He had no desire to drive to Richmond and watch McKenna try to put the finishing touches on the destruction of his life.

His eyes widened as he saw Elizabeth Knight tapping on his car window. He rolled it down.

"I would like to talk to you," she said.

He composed himself as best he could. "What about?"

"Can we talk in the car?"

Fiske finally nodded, and Knight slipped into the front seat.

"I feel terrible about Sara," she said.

"Join the crowd. She tried to help my brother and then me. I'm sure she just loves the day she ran into the Fiske brothers."

"Well, at least one of you anyway."

"What does that mean?"

"Sara liked and respected your brother. But she didn't love him, although, quite frankly, I think he was in love with her. Her heart lies elsewhere."

"Is that right?"

"John, it's clear to me Sara is in love with you."

"Your womanly intuition?"

"Something like that." Knight put her hands in her lap and looked out the window. "However, that's not why I wanted to talk to you." She looked at him. "I wanted to ask you in private about Michael's and Steven's deaths? Is there anything to this story of the missing appeal?"

"Why ask me?"

"Because you seem to know more than anyone else."

Fiske sighed and sat back. "Michael was killed because he knew what that appeal said. I think Wright was killed because he was working late and saw someone at the Court going through my brother's office."

She turned pale. "You believe someone at the Court murdered Steven?"

Fiske nodded.

"Can you prove that?"

"I hope so."

"That can't be, John. Why?"

"There's a guy who's spent half his life in prison who'd like to know the answer to that."

"Does Detective Chandler know all this?"

"Some of it. But Agent McKenna has pretty much convinced him I'm the bad guy."

"I'm not sure Detective Chandler believes that."

"We'll see."

As she climbed out of the car, Knight said, "If everything you suspect is true and someone at the Court is involved in this—" She stopped, unable to continue for a moment. "Do you realize what this could do to the Court's reputation?"

"I'm not sure of a lot in life, but I'm certain of one thing." He paused and then said, "The Court's reputation isn't worth an innocent man dying in prison."

WHEN Fiske and McKenna arrived at Fiske's office, the FBI agent said, "Let's get to it."

"We wait for the police," Fiske said firmly.

Just as he said that, a police cruiser pulled up, and Officer Hawkins climbed out. "What's going on here, John?" Hawkins asked.

Fiske pointed at McKenna. "Agent McKenna thinks I killed Mike. He's here to get my gun so he can do a ballistics test."

Hawkins looked at McKenna with hostile eyes. "If that's not the biggest bunch of hogwash I ever heard—"

"Right, thanks for your official assessment . . . Officer Hawkins, is it?" McKenna said, coming forward.

Before Hawkins could do something foolish, Fiske grabbed his sleeve and said, "Now let's just go get this over with." As they walked into the building, Fiske commented, "Your face looks a lot better, Billy."

Hawkins smiled, embarrassed. "Yeah, thanks."

"What happened?" McKenna asked.

Hawkins looked at him sullenly. "Guy decided to take a ride on drugs. He was a little difficult to arrest."

Fiske was staring at Hawkins. "What's that, Billy?" He pointed at Hawkins's neck and collar.

"What's what?"

Fiske touched Hawkins's collar with his finger and then held it up for the man to see.

Hawkins blushed a little. "Oh. Well, that was Bonnie's idea to cover the bruises. That's why my face doesn't look so beat up."

"Then you're saying it's—"

"Yeah, it's makeup," he said sheepishly.

Despite the revelation that had just occurred to him, Fiske tried his best to appear calm.

There was a stack of mail and packages in front of his office door. He picked them up, stuffed them into his briefcase, and unlocked the door. They went inside, and Fiske walked over to his desk and slid open the top drawer. He stuck his hand in and fumbled through the contents. "It was right in this drawer. I actually saw it the day you came to tell me about Mike, Billy."

McKenna crossed his arms and eyed Fiske sternly. "Okay, has anybody else had access to your office? Cleaning crew, secretary?"

"No, nobody. Nobody has a key except for the landlord."

"Well, it looks like we have a little problem here. Your brother was killed by a nine-millimeter. You have a nine-millimeter registered to you. Now that pistol is missing, and you have no alibi for the time of death."

Fiske edged closer to McKenna. "If you think you have enough to charge me, then do it. If not, then get out of my office."

Hawkins looked over at McKenna. "You ready to leave? Because I want to lock up. Don't want anybody else coming in here and stealing any more stuff."

The way Hawkins said it made McKenna blink. The guy couldn't know that he had taken the gun, could he? Still, he felt guilty about it. But he had bigger things to feel guilty about. Far bigger.

SARA PARKED HER CAR NEXT TO the trailer and got out. She took a deep breath. The Buick was there. When she knocked on the trailer's door, it was jerked open so quickly she almost fell off the stoop. Ed Fiske must have watched her drive up.

"I got nothing to say to you." His tone was cold, but at least he wasn't screaming at her.

"But I have a lot to say to you."

"You can tell Johnny that it's no good sending you over to try to mend things."

"He doesn't know I'm here."

He looked surprised.

"What you saw the other night wasn't John's fault. It was mine."

"It takes two to tango, and you ain't telling me no different."

"May I come in?"

After a long moment Ed finally moved aside and let her pass. He closed the door noisily behind them. "You want something to drink?" he asked grudgingly.

"Only if you're having something."

"I'm not." Ed motioned to the sofa, and Sara sat down. He sat down in a chair across from her. He crossed his arms, waiting for her to start talking.

"Michael and I were very close friends."

Ed's face started to flush.

"The fact is, Mr. Fiske"—Sara swallowed hard, her own face reddening—"Michael asked me to marry him." She hesitated for a moment. "I told him no." She shrank back a little, but Fiske just sat there, trying to digest this.

"I take it you didn't love him."

"I didn't, not like that anyway. I'm not sure why. He seemed perfect. Maybe that scared me—sharing my life with someone like that, trying to keep my standards that high for a lifetime." She looked past him, out the window, where a cardinal flitted by and settled on the branch of a weeping willow. "You know, I always thought I'd be able to tell almost instantly this is the person I want to spend my life with. Seems silly, doesn't it?"

A tiny smile creased the man's face. "The first time I saw Gladys, she was waitressing at this little diner. I walked in the door, and it was like it was just me and her in the whole world. Couldn't get her out of my head."

Sara smiled. "I'm well acquainted with the stubbornness of John and Michael Fiske. So I doubt if you just left it at that."

Ed smiled too. "I went to that diner for breakfast, lunch, and dinner for the next six months before I got up the courage to ask her to marry me. I swear I would've done it that first day, but I thought she'd think I was crazy or something." He paused for a moment. "Is that what happened to you when you saw Johnny?"

Sara nodded.

"Did Mike know?"

"I think he figured it out." Sara tensed. "So that night what you saw was me pushing myself on your son. He had been through the most nightmarish day imaginable, and all I could think about was myself." She looked directly at him. "He turned me down flat. That's what I came to tell you. If you want to hate anyone, hate me, not your son."

Ed studied the floor for a minute. "I've thought a lot about that night. As mad as I was, I never should've hit him."

"He's pretty tough."

"Did Johnny ever tell you why he left the police force?"

"He said he had arrested some pathetic young kid for a drug offense and decided to start helping people like that."

Ed nodded. "Well, he didn't actually arrest him. That boy died at the scene. And so did the officer that backed Johnny up."

"What?"

"Johnny never talked about it. I got the story from the officers who arrived after it all happened. Johnny stopped the car for some reason. It was stolen, I think. He got the two boys out. That's when his backup came. Right before they were going to search them, one of the boys dropped like he was having a seizure. Johnny tried to help him. His backup should've kept his gun on the other, but he didn't, and the other fellow, Darnell Jackson—I'll never forget that name, Darnell Jackson—pulled a gun and killed him. Johnny managed to fire, but Darnell Jackson put two rounds in him.

"They both went down. The boy with the seizure had been faking. He jumped up and took off in the car. Darnell Jackson and Johnny were both bleeding like crazy."

"How horrible!"

"They found Darnell dead and Johnny next to him, his arm around him. Some of the cops didn't like that, what with one of their own lying dead because of the kid, but they checked everything out and Johnny was cleared. It was the other cop's fault. Johnny was in the hospital for about a month—his insides were ripped to shreds."

Sara's face took on a stricken look. "He's fully recovered, isn't he?"

Ed shook his head sadly. "They patched him up, but just about every one of his organs was damaged for good. Docs say eventually things inside him are just going to stop working. They said it was like diabetes. You know, how a person's organs get worn out and all?"

Sara nodded as her own stomach started to churn.

"Well, the docs said those two bullets will cost Johnny about twenty years." Ed paused. "I tell you this so you'll see that Johnny doesn't really have the same goals as you might. Never got married, never talks about having kids of his own." Ed looked down, his voice catching. "Never figured I'd outlive Mike. I pray I don't outlive my other boy."

Sara finally found her voice. "I appreciate your telling me this. I realize it was hard for you."

Sara rose to leave. As her hand touched the doorknob, Ed spoke one last time. "You still love my son?"

Sara walked out without answering.

IN THE powder room of Jordan and Elizabeth Knight's Watergate apartment, Beth Knight splashed water on her face. She gripped the edges of the sink, composed herself, opened the door, and moved slowly down the hallway.

She could still hear Jordan in the shower. She looked at her watch. She went out into the lobby and down the elevator to the reception area of the building and waited by the main entrance. Time seemed to pass slowly. Finally a man she didn't recognize, but who clearly knew her by sight, appeared and handed her something. She looked down at it. When she looked back up, he had already disappeared. She put what he had given her into her pocket and hurried back up to her apartment.

"Where's Jordan?" she asked their housekeeper.

"I believe he's in the bedroom getting dressed. Are you all right, Ms. Knight?"

"Yes, I . . . I'm fine. I decided to do some window-shopping downstairs, get some fresh air. Would you mix up some cocktails and put them out on the terrace?"

"It's starting to rain."

"But the awning's up. And I feel very claustrophobic," she said. "Make Jordan's favorite, will you?"

"Beefeater martini with a twist. Yes, ma'am."

"And the dinner, Mary—please make sure it's absolutely wonderful. Just perfect."

"I will, ma'am." The housekeeper headed to the bar with a puzzled look on her face.

Elizabeth Knight squeezed her hands together to fight the waves of panic. She just had to stop thinking about it. If she was going to make it through this, she had to merely act, not think. Please, God, help me, she prayed.

CHAPTER TEN

FISKE gazed moodily through the car windshield at the dark clouds, trying to make sense of all the information he'd learned. He was halfway back to Washington when he pulled off the highway to look for pen and paper to make notes. He got his briefcase from the back seat. He popped it open and pushed through the stack of mail, until his hands closed around a bulky package. "Wow, that was fast," he said aloud.

It was Harms's service record and the personnel list from Fort Plessy. Fiske tore the package open and started reading. Ten minutes later he called Sara's cell phone.

"Would you like to guess why Rufus Harms was so insubordinate, wouldn't take orders, was always in trouble?"

"He was dyslexic," Sara answered promptly.

"How did you know that?"

"When I talked to George Barker, remember he told me about Rufus fixing his printing press? Well, Rufus didn't want to look at the manual—he said that the words would just mess him up. I went to school with a girl who had dyslexia. She told me more or less the same thing."

Fiske looked back at the records. "Looks like he was diagnosed with it after the murder. Maybe Rider discovered it. Preparing a defense requires some client cooperation."

"Dyslexia is not a defense to murder."

"No, but I know what is."

"What?" Sara asked excitedly. "What?"

"First a question. Leo Dellasandro—is he having an affair with his secretary?"

"I doubt that, because she just got married. Why do you ask?"

"He had makeup on his coat collar. I think he was wearing it."

"Why would a man—a chief of police, no less—be wearing makeup?"

"To cover the bruises he got when I hit him in my brother's apartment." Fiske could hear Sara catch her breath. "I'm looking at a list of personnel stationed at Fort Plessy when Rufus was there. Luckily, it's alphabetized." He turned toward the end of the roster. "Sergeant Victor Tremaine." He turned another page. "Captain Frank Rayfield." He flipped back through some pages, stopped, and said triumphantly, "And Corporal Leo Dellasandro."

"Then Rayfield, Tremaine, and Dellasandro were the men in the stockade that night?"

"I think so."

"But what did they do to Rufus Harms?"

"I think they—"

The car phone cut off, and before Fiske could redial, it rang. He picked it up. "Yes, I'll accept the call. Hello? . . . What? . . . Okay, calm down, Rufus. Where are you?"

Rufus was inside the jeep, parked next to a pay phone. He had one hand on the phone, the other on Josh, who was now slipping into longer periods of unconsciousness. "Richmond," he answered. "I'm two minutes from the address on the card you gave me. Josh is hurt bad. We need a doctor, and we need him quick."

"Okay, okay, tell me what happened."

"Rayfield and Tremaine caught up to us. They're dead, and my brother's about ready to join 'em. We need help."

Fiske thought quickly. "Okay, Rufus, I'll meet you at my office. I'll call an ambulance. Describe the car to me and give me the intersection where you are right now."

Rufus did so.

"Leave Josh in the car. Take any ID he has on him. As soon as you hang up, walk to my office building. Go in the front door and down the flight of stairs on your left. You'll find a door marked Supplies. Get in there and sit tight. I'll be down quick as I can."

"I'm trusting you. Please don't let me down."

"Rufus, I'm trusting you too."

When Rufus hung up, he looked at his brother. He thought Josh was completely unconscious now, but when Rufus brushed his shoulder gently with his finger, Josh opened his eyes.

"Josh—"

"I heard." The voice was weak.

"I'm gonna stay with you, Josh."

"You stay, all this is for nothing."

"I can't leave you alone. Not like this."

With a painful grimace Josh sat up. "You ain't leaving me alone. Give it to me."

"Give you what?"

Josh said, "The Bible."

Without taking his eyes off his brother, Rufus slowly reached behind the seat and handed him the book. In return Josh held out his pistol. "Fair swap," he said hoarsely.

Rufus thought he saw a smile flicker across his brother's lips before he climbed out of the jeep. He looked back once more and then left his brother behind.

FISKE finally reached Hawkins at home and arranged for the ambulance. "Billy, I can't tell you who it is. For now he's a John Doe. Stall the paperwork." Fiske hung up and called Sara back. "I'm meeting Rufus," he told her. "You have to make a phone call for me, to my friend Phil Jansen at the J.A.G."

"What about? And you still haven't told me what you think happened in that stockade twenty-five years ago."

"*U.S.* v. *Stanley*. An innocent soldier and LSD," Fiske said. "Only this was worse," he added.

As FISKE headed back south toward Richmond, traffic was heavy. It was almost three hours before he pulled the car up to his office building. He had already checked in with Billy Hawkins. Josh Harms was in surgery. It didn't look good, Hawkins had told him.

Fiske went to the lower level and approached the supply room. He tapped on the door. "Rufus?" he said quietly. "It's John Fiske."

Rufus cautiously opened the door.

"Let's get out of here."

Rufus gripped his arm. "How's Josh?"

"He's in surgery. All you can do is pray."

They went out the rear entrance, walked quickly to Fiske's car, and climbed in.

"Where we going?" Rufus said.

"Tell me about the letter from the army? They wanted to follow up on the phencyclidine testing, right?"

Harms stiffened. "Phen what?"

"You know, PCP."

"How did you know about that?"

"Same thing happened to a guy in the army named Stanley. They used LSD on him."

"I wasn't in no PCP program even if they said I was. They'd been out to get me for a while—Tremaine and Rayfield."

"And Dellasandro? Corporal Leo Dellasandro?"

"Yeah, him too. I guess they didn't take too kindly to me sitting nice and snug in the States, even if it was in the stockade. They came in one night. Leo had a gun. They made me close my eyes, get on the floor. The next thing I knew, they stuck something in me. I opened my eyes and saw the needle coming out of my arm. They all stood there laughing, waiting for me to die. I could tell, from what they said, that was their plan—OD me on the stuff.

"I remember getting up, and it felt like the room wasn't big enough to hold me. I tossed 'em all aside. They left the door unlocked. The guard came running up, but I hit him like a truck, and then I was running free."

"And you ran into Ruth Ann Mosley?"

Rufus slammed his fist down onto the dash. "If only the Lord had struck me down before I got to that little girl. Why'd it have to be a child? Why?" Tears streamed down the man's face.

"It wasn't your fault, Rufus. PCP can make you do anything. Anything. It wasn't your fault."

In answer Rufus held up his hands and bellowed, "These did it. No matter what they put in me, ain't nothing gonna change the fact that I killed that beautiful little girl. Ain't nothing gonna make that go away. Is it? Is it?" Rufus's eyes blazed at Fiske.

Fiske tried to keep calm. "And you remembered nothing until you got the letter?"

"All those years the only thing I remembered from that night was sitting next to this dead little girl." He wiped the tears away.

"But you pleaded guilty to the murder anyway?"

"There was a bunch of witnesses. Rider said if I didn't take the deal, they'd execute me. What was I supposed to do?"

Fiske thought about that for a moment and then said quietly, "I guess I would've done the same thing."

"But when I got that letter, it was like somebody turned a light on inside my head." He took a deep breath, watched the rain falling over the darkened skyline, and then looked over at Fiske. "Now you know everything I know. So what are we going to do?"

"I'm not sure," was all Fiske could manage to say.

Sara picked up the cell phone for the tenth time and dialed Phil Jansen's home number. She was relieved when he finally answered. She quickly introduced herself. "I don't have much time, Mr. Jansen, so I might as well get to the point. In the past has the army been involved in PCP testing programs?"

Jansen's voice tensed. "Why exactly are you asking that?"

Sara recounted all that she and Fiske had deduced, along with what they had learned from Rufus Harms at Rider's office. "Harms recently received a letter from the army asking him to participate in a follow-up test to determine the long-term effects of PCP. We think a group of army personnel forcefully administered PCP to Harms but not as part of any program. We think they intended to kill him. Instead, he broke free and committed a murder."

Jansen said, "Wait a minute. Why did the army send him a letter saying Harms was in the program if he wasn't?"

"We think whoever gave Harms the PCP enrolled him in the program. If they killed him and there was an autopsy, the substance would have been found in his bloodstream. So they enrolled him to cover that up. Mr. Jansen, did such a program exist?"

"Yes," Jansen conceded. "It's public information now. It was run jointly by the army and CIA in the '70s. They wanted to determine if PCP could be used to build supersoldiers. If Harms was listed in the program's records, he would have recently received a follow-up letter."

Sara thanked Jansen and hung up. Then a sudden thought hit her. She dialed the number. After three rings a woman answered. It was the housekeeper.

"Is Senator Knight in? It's Sara Evans."

A minute later Jordan Knight's voice came on the line. "Sara?"

"I know this is terrible timing, Senator."

"I heard what happened today." His tone was cold.

Sara struggled to hold her nerves in check. Every second counted now. "I need a favor."

"A favor?" Jordan sounded perplexed. "Sara, I hardly think this is appropriate."

"Senator, I will never, ever call you again, but I really need to know the answer to a question, and with all your resources and clout you're the only person I can think of to ask. Please?"

Jordan pondered this for a moment. "Well, I was just settling down to a late dinner with Beth."

"But you could call your office or maybe the FBI." She hurried on. "I need to know if Agent McKenna ever served in the army. Specifically at Fort Plessy during the '70s."

"Why in the world do you need to know that?"

"Senator, it would take me far too long to explain."

He sighed. "All right. I'll see what I can do. I'll have someone from my office check and then call you. You'll be at home?"

"Yes."

"Sara, I hope you know what you're doing."

When he went back into the dining room about fifteen minutes later, Elizabeth asked, "What in the world did Sara want?"

"The strangest thing. You know that FBI agent fellow?"

She tensed. "Warren McKenna? What about him?"

"She wanted to know if he had ever served in the army. I told her I'd check and that I'd have somebody get back to her. That's what I was doing, calling my office."

"Where is Sara?"

"At home, waiting for the answer."

Elizabeth got up, her face pale.

"Beth, are you all right?"

"A headache just hit me. I need some aspirin."

A worried-looking Jordan Knight watched his wife go down the hallway. Elizabeth Knight did indeed get some aspirin, since she did have a very real headache. Then she picked up the bedroom phone and dialed a number.

"Hello," the voice said.

"Sara Evans just called from home. She asked Jordan if you had ever been in the army."

Warren McKenna loosened his tie and took a sip of water from the glass on his desk. "And what did he tell her?"

"That he'd check and get back to her."

McKenna grabbed his coat. "Thanks for the information, Justice

Knight. It might prove to be even more valuable than one of your opinions."

Elizabeth Knight slowly hung up the receiver and then picked it up again and dialed. She couldn't leave it like this.

"Detective Chandler, this is Justice Knight. Please don't ask me how I know, but you have to get to Sara Evans's house. I think she's in grave danger. Please hurry."

Elizabeth Knight slowly put down the receiver. No matter how this turned out, her life was going to be devastated. How ironic, she thought, that justice would end up destroying her.

SARA had been nervously pacing her bedroom, constantly checking her watch and waiting for a phone call from Jordan Knight's office. A jet passed overhead, and then the complete silence returned in its wake. Silence so profound she could clearly hear the side door of the cottage open. She jumped up and raced to the stairs. "John?" There was no answer, and when the downstairs light went out, a shiver of fear hit her spine.

She ran into her bedroom, shut and locked the door. Her chest heaving, her own pulse bursting in her eardrums, she held her breath as she saw the doorknob slowly turn until the lock halted the movement. Something hit the door with a solid blow. She instinctively jumped back, a small scream escaping her lips. She scanned the room before her gaze settled on the four-poster bed. She raced over and grabbed one of the pineapple-shaped finials off one of the bedposts. The finial was solid wood and weighed at least a pound.

She held it in one upraised hand and stepped quickly to the door. It shook as another blow landed. She reached over, quietly unlocked the door, and then stood back. With the door unbolted, the next blow sent it and the man, with a ski mask pulled over his face, flying into the room. Sara's arm came down, and the finial hit flesh. She raced through the doorway and down the hallway. The man she had struck lay on the floor, holding his shoulder and moaning.

She navigated the stairs in two jumps, grabbed her car keys off the table, and threw open the door on her way to the car. She let out a shriek of terror.

A second man stared back at her. Calmly, coolly Leo Dellasandro pointed a pistol at her. The other man came racing down the stairs, his gun trained on her as well. The ski mask came off, and Richard Perkins glared at her. Then he smiled at her obvious astonishment.

She stared at him angrily. "The marshal of the Supreme Court and the chief of its police, parties to a despicable crime."

"Harms killed the girl, not me," Dellasandro said.

"Have you made yourself believe that, Leo? You killed her just as sure as if your hands were around her neck."

A smirk appeared on Dellasandro's face. "I don't see it that way."

"How's the face, Leo? John really popped you. He knows everything, of course."

"We'll just have to visit him too."

"Your two buddies, Tremaine and Rayfield, are dead." Sara's smile emerged as Dellasandro's faded. "They ambushed Rufus and his brother, but just like last time, they couldn't finish the job," she added tauntingly.

"Then I hope I get the chance to do it for them."

Sara stared him up and down, and finally shook her head in disgust. "Tell me something, Leo. How did vermin like you ever get to be a police chief of anything?"

He slapped her across the face and would have hit her again if Perkins hadn't stopped him. "We don't have time for this, Leo." He gripped Sara by the shoulder. That's when the phone rang.

Perkins looked at Dellasandro. "Fiske?" He looked again at Sara. "Fiske is with Harms, isn't he?" She didn't answer. Perkins stuck his pistol under Sara's chin.

"Yes! Yes, he's with him."

He shoved her to the phone. "Answer it. If it's Fiske, pick a place to meet."

She hesitated.

"Do it!"

She slowly picked up the phone. Perkins stood next to her listening, his gun pressed against her temple.

"Hello?"

"Sara?" It was Fiske.

"Where are you?"

"I'm with Rufus. We're halfway to D.C. Look, it's time we went to Chandler. Rufus and I have talked it over."

Perkins shook his head and pointed at the phone.

"I don't think that's such a good idea, John. I've . . . I've found out some things that you need to know first."

"Like what?"

"I can't tell you over the phone. It might be bugged. Can we meet someplace? Then we can go to Chandler."

They arranged a meeting place off the GW Parkway. She wrote it down on a pad by the phone and ripped off the top sheet.

"Are you sure you can't tell me over the phone?"

"I talked to your friend at the J.A.G." Sara whispered a silent prayer for what she was about to say next. If Fiske reacted the wrong way, she was dead. "Darnell Jackson told me all about the PCP testing."

Fiske stiffened. *Darnell Jackson.* He answered quickly, "Darnell's never let me down before."

Sara let out an inaudible breath and hung up.

Perkins grinned malevolently. "Good job, Sara. Now let's go see your friends."

FISKE made one more phone call. The news was not good. Not good at all. Then he got back into the car and looked at Harms. "He's got Sara."

"Who's got her?" Harms asked.

"Your old buddy—Dellasandro. He's the only one left."

"What you talking about, the only one left?"

"Rayfield and Tremaine are dead. That leaves Dellasandro." Fiske stopped and stared at Rufus. "Rufus, how many men were in the stockade that night?"

"Five."

Fiske slumped back. "Who are the other two?"

"Perkins. Dick Perkins."

"Richard Perkins is the marshal of the Supreme Court." Fiske thought he might be sick. "And the fifth man?"

"Didn't know him. Never seen him before."

"That's okay. I think I know who it is." Fiske had finally figured it out. Warren McKenna's image appeared starkly in his thoughts. That's why the FBI agent was trying to frame him. It all made sense.

"Where we going?"

"They want us to meet them at a place off the GW Parkway in Virginia. I tried to get hold of Chandler, but he wasn't in. I left a message telling him where we'll be. I hope he gets it in time."

In response Rufus slid a pistol out of his pocket and handed it to Fiske. "You know how to use one of these things?"

"I think I can manage," he said.

IT WAS well after midnight, and the parkway was deserted. Fiske eyed the exit signs until he found the one he wanted. He spotted Sara's car parked in the otherwise empty parking lot. Beyond he could make out the deeper darkness that was the Potomac River.

Rufus was crouched in the back seat. They had devised a plan of sorts on the way up. Fiske passed a bend in the road that took them beyond the line of sight from Sara's car. The back door opened, and Rufus quickly disappeared into the surrounding trees and headed through the woods toward the parking lot.

Fiske drove into the parking lot and pulled up a couple of spaces from Sara's car. He slipped the pistol into the back of his waistband and slowly got out. "Sara?"

"Over here, Fiske," Dellasandro said.

Fiske did his best to look shocked.

"Where's Harms?" Dellasandro said.

Fiske made a show of rubbing his cheek. "He had a change of heart. Didn't want to go to the cops. Hit me and took off."

"And left you the car? I don't think so."

"I'm telling you the truth. You know he's been in prison all these years. He didn't take the car, because he can't even drive." He stepped toward Dellasandro and Sara. "Are you all right, Sara?"

She nodded. "I'm sorry, John."

"Just shut up," Dellasandro said. "Exactly where did Harms get away from you?"

"When we got off the interstate. We came up Route 1."

"Why don't I believe a word you're saying?"

"Maybe because you've been a lying sack of garbage all your life and you figure everybody is the same way."

Dellasandro pointed his gun at Fiske's head. "It's gonna be so much fun blowing you away."

"Perkins is here too," Sara blurted out.

"Shut up!" Dellasandro yelled.

"I knew it. I think I can guess who the other partner is."

"Run your theories by the fish. Let's go."

They all started to move toward the riverbank. Suddenly a bullet hit the dirt next to Dellasandro's leg. He shouted and moved the pistol away from Fiske's head.

Fiske hit him hard in the belly, doubling him over, and clocked him in the head with his fist. Before Dellasandro could recover, Rufus exploded from behind a tree and hit him with the force of a runaway tank. The man sailed down the bank and into the water. Rufus was about to go after him when more shots zipped past them, and everybody hit the ground.

Fiske had one protective arm over Sara. "See anything, Rufus?"

"Yeah. I think those shots came from two different places."

"Great. Both his backups are here." He clenched his pistol. "Look, Rufus, here's the plan. I'm going to move to my right about ten yards. I'll fire two shots and draw their fire so we can see where the muzzle flashes are coming from. Then I'll cover you, and you take Sara, get to her car, and go get Chandler."

Fiske started to move away, but Sara clutched at his hand, unwilling to let him go. He wanted to say something confident to her, to show he wasn't scared. But he was. "I know what I'm doing, Sara."

She stared at him as he crawled off, convinced it would be the last time she would see him alive.

A minute later the shots began. Rufus half carried Sara as they raced for the car. They made it, and Rufus threw open the door and pushed Sara inside before climbing in.

Fiske moved slowly through the underbrush, the smell of hot metal and flamed gunpowder clinging to him. As the car cranked up, he didn't hear the sound behind him until it was too late.

Dellasandro, dripping filthy river water, pointed the gun at him. When the shot came, Fiske watched in stunned silence as Leo Dellasandro pitched forward and lay still.

Fiske looked up. What he saw made him wish Dellasandro had been able to get off his own round. McKenna looked down at him. Fiske shook his head. Why couldn't it have been Chandler? Why couldn't he catch a break just once? "You sleazebag!" Fiske said.

"Actually, I thought you'd want to thank me," McKenna said.

The man's next actions absolutely astonished Fiske. He pulled another gun from his pocket, flipped it around, and handed it to him. "Here's your gun. I just happened to find it." Then he put a hand out and helped Fiske up. "Chandler's on his way. I managed to catch him at Sara's house. I got there just as Perkins and Dellasandro were leaving with her. I figured they were using her to set you up. I followed along as your unofficial backup. Perkins took off. He was the other guy firing."

Fiske just stared at him in disbelief. "I thought you were one of the five guys in the stockade that night," he said.

"I was, but there were six men there other than Rufus."

Fiske looked bewildered. "I don't understand."

"I was the guard on duty that night, John. I could have stopped this whole thing." He looked down. His body seemed to sag for a second as his mind went back to the past. "But I didn't."

Fiske studied the man for a moment, still reeling from this last development. "Well, you're doing something about it now."

"Twenty-five years too late."

"Rufus is going to be free, isn't he? That's all he cares about."

McKenna looked up. "Rufus is free now, John. No one will ever put him back in prison. If they try to, they have to go through me first. And believe me, they won't be able to."

Fiske looked toward the road. "What about Perkins?"

McKenna smiled. "I know exactly where Perkins is going. He's going to see the sixth person who was in the stockade that night."

"Who? Who was it?"

"You'll find out. Soon you'll know everything."

WHEN THE WOMAN OPENED the door, Richard Perkins burst in past her. "Where is he?"

"In his study."

Perkins raced down the hallway and threw open the door. "Everything's gone down the tubes, and I'm getting out of here."

Jordan Knight sat back and shook his head. "If you run, they'll know you're guilty."

"They already know I'm guilty. Leo is dead, and Rufus Harms is still out there. I saw him."

Jordan's face darkened. "Ah, the celebrated Mr. Harms."

"He killed Frank and Vic."

"Two fewer people to worry about, then."

"Why you cold-blooded— You were the one who told them to kill Michael Fiske. You got all this started."

Jordan Knight looked thoughtful. "I still don't know how Rufus Harms was able to identify me in that appeal. He knew all of you. I wasn't even in the army."

"He didn't ID you."

Knight looked shocked; then there was a glint of hope in his eyes. Perkins explained. "I talked to Tremaine. Rayfield lied to you. You weren't named in the appeal. Just the four of us."

"So I'm still unknown." Knight stood up and looked at Perkins. That meant he still had a way out. Only one more thing, one more person to deal with, and this nightmare was over.

"But for how long? All this for what? We shoot Harms up with PCP, and it comes down to this."

"You actually shot him up, Richard."

"Don't get high and mighty with me. It was your idea to use the PCP, Mr. CIA."

"Well, naturally. I was there conducting the testing, listening to all of you complain about Harms. Just trying to do you a favor."

"Well, I'm not hanging around for the axe to fall."

"I suppose you'll need money?" Jordan took a key from his pocket and unlocked his desk drawer. "I have some cash here. Fifty thousand to start?"

"That sounds good. To start."

Knight turned and pointed a pistol at Perkins.

"What are you doing, Jordan?"

"You burst in here, clearly out of your mind. You threaten me. I manage to get out my gun and kill you."

"You're crazy. No one will believe that."

"Oh, they will, Richard." Jordan pulled the trigger, and Perkins dropped to the floor. He heard a scream from the hallway. "It's all right, Beth," he called out. "I'm all right." He turned, and froze as Rufus Harms stared back at him. Behind Rufus were Chandler, McKenna, Fiske, and Sara.

McKenna stepped forward. "Senator, you don't remember me, do you? I mean outside the FBI?" Jordan stared at him. McKenna edged closer. "Perkins and Dellasandro didn't remember me either. It's been a long time, and everybody was pretty drunk that night. Everybody except you."

"I have no idea what you're talking about."

"I was the guard on duty the night you and your friends came calling on Rufus at Fort Plessy. It was my first and last time pulling guard duty at the stockade. Probably why nobody remembered me. I let you in to see Rufus. And I've lived with the guilt of that mistake all these years. But I got off easy." McKenna looked over at Rufus. "I'm sorry, Rufus. I was weak, a coward. It probably doesn't make any difference to you, but there hasn't been a day gone by that I didn't hate myself for it."

Jordan cleared his throat. "Very touching, Agent McKenna. However, if you think you saw me in the stockade that night, you're mistaken."

"CIA records will show that you were at Fort Plessy conducting PCP tests on soldiers stationed there," McKenna said.

"That program was perfectly aboveboard and legal, as my wife could certainly tell you."

"*U.S.* v. *Stanley?*" Sara said bitterly.

Jordan's gaze did not leave McKenna. "Quite a coincidence that you claim to have been in the stockade and now you're involved in this matter," he said.

"It was no coincidence. It was intentional," was McKenna's surprising reply. "After I left the army, I finished college and then went to the FBI Academy. I kept tabs on you and the others. Guilt is a very strong motivation. Rayfield and Tremaine moved around with Rufus. Perkins and Dellasandro moved around with you. When you were given a seat on the Senate Judiciary Committee a few years ago, you got them their positions at the Court. Real nice of you. When I got wind of Michael Fiske's murder and discovered Rufus was connected somehow, I prayed all those years of following you were going to pay off."

He pulled a cell phone from his pocket, spoke into it, and listened to the response. "I'm going to read you your rights now."

"I'll have you in the FBI equivalent of Siberia by dawn," Knight said. "You have no proof of anything."

"Actually, I'm basing my arrest on your own words." While everyone watched, McKenna knelt under the desk kneehole, probed for a moment, and pulled out a listening device. "Your statements came through loud and clear in the surveillance van parked outside."

Jordan was furious. "That is completely illegal. There's not a judge in this city who would have given you a warrant for that."

"We didn't need a warrant. We had consent."

The blood drained from Jordan's face as his wife stepped into the room.

"You?"

"I live here too, Jordan. I gave that consent."

"In heaven's name, why?"

Elizabeth held his gaze for a moment, then touched the sleeve of Rufus Harms. "This man is why, Jordan. This man is the only reason strong enough to make me do what I did."

"For him? He's a child killer." He stabbed a finger at Rufus. "This man deserved to die."

Moving faster than his bulk would seem to have allowed, Rufus reached Jordan, his big hands encircling the Senator's neck.

McKenna and Chandler grabbed Rufus, but it was like pulling on a mountain.

"Rufus, stop," Sara yelled.

Fiske stepped forward. "Rufus? Rufus!" Fiske took a quick breath and then just said it. "Josh didn't make it." Rufus instantly loosened his grip on Jordan's throat and stared at Fiske. "He's dead, Rufus. We both lost our brothers. If you kill him, you'll go back to prison, and Josh will have died for nothing."

Rufus relaxed his grip even more as tears wound down his face. A gasping Jordan Knight slumped to the carpet.

JORDAN did not look at his wife as he was led away in handcuffs by McKenna. An hour later the forensics team had completed its work, and Perkins's body was removed. Chandler, Rufus, Sara, and Fiske remained behind. Elizabeth Knight was in her bedroom.

"So how much did you know?" Fiske asked Chandler.

"Some of it. McKenna and I had talks. He knew the people involved, but he didn't have any proof. He had to make them think you two were the primary suspects. He took your gun and made sure Perkins and Dellasandro knew it was missing. He hoped they would feel safe and slip up. He had already told Justice Knight that he knew her husband from Fort Plessy, so when the Senator told her he had to call to get that information, she knew he was lying."

"Justice Knight's quick thinking saved my life," Sara said.

Chandler nodded in agreement. "McKenna knew Perkins would make a run for it and need Jordan's help. Jordan killing Perkins was not in the game plan, but I'm not going to lose any sleep over that." Chandler looked at Rufus Harms.

"I want to see my brother."

Chandler nodded. "I can arrange that."

As they walked to the door, Elizabeth Knight met them in the hallway. She reached out her hand to Rufus Harms. "It can't possibly be worth anything to you after all you have suffered, Mr. Harms, but I am so sorry. So very very sorry."

He took her hand gently. "It's worth a lot, ma'am."

As they headed out the door, Elizabeth Knight looked at them all and said with finality, "Good-bye."

When the three men stepped into the elevator, Sara hesitated. "I'll catch up with you later," she said. She raced back to the apartment.

The housekeeper opened the door.

"Where's Justice Knight?"

"She went into the bedroom. Why—"

Sara flew past her and burst into the bedroom. Sitting on the bed, Elizabeth Knight looked up at her former clerk. The Justice's hand was clenched in a fist; a prescription bottle lay empty next to her.

Sara walked slowly over to her, sat down, and took her hand. She opened it, and the pills spilled out. "Elizabeth, that's not the way to deal with this."

"Deal with it?" Elizabeth said hysterically. "My life just walked out that door in handcuffs."

"Jordan Knight just walked out that door. Justice Elizabeth Knight is sitting here next to me, the same Justice Knight who will be leading the Supreme Court into the next century."

"Sara . . ." The tears spilled down her face.

"It's a lifetime appointment, and you have a lot of life left." Sara squeezed her hand. "I'd like to help you if you'll have me back."

Elizabeth clutched at the young woman's shoulder. "Will you stay with me, Sara?"

"I'll stay as long as you want."

CHAPTER ELEVEN

N THE strength of his being the possessor of the Silver Star, Purple Heart, and Distinguished Service Medal, former sergeant Josh Harms was entitled to burial with honors at Arlington National Cemetery.

And thus, on a cool, clear day in October, he was laid to rest in ground that was so covered with white crosses that it looked like an early snow had fallen. As the honor guard fired off its salute and the bugler launched into taps, the simple coffin was lowered into the ground. Rufus received the flag, folded tricornered, from a somber and respectful army officer while Fiske, Sara, McKenna, and Chandler looked on.

Later Rufus prayed over his brother's grave. His heart was sad, but his spirits were lifted. He knew that his brother had passed on to a better place. And for as long as Rufus lived, Josh Harms would never be forgotten. And when Rufus went to join his Lord, he would also, once again, embrace his brother.

Two days later Michael Fiske was buried at a private cemetery on the outskirts of Richmond. Ed Fiske, dressed in an old suit, his hair neatly combed, awkwardly stood next to his surviving son and received condolences from each Justice of the United States Supreme Court, together with many of Virginia's political and social elite. Harold Ramsey spent an extra minute giving comfort to the father.

Looking at Ramsey made Fiske think of what lay ahead for Rufus. Fiske had encouraged him to sue everybody he could think of.

Rufus had refused. "All of 'em except for Knight are in a far worse place than any judge on this earth could send 'em to," he had said. "That's their true punishment. And Knight's got to live with what he done. That's enough for me. I just want to live as a free man, go see my momma's grave. That's all."

Fiske had tried to get him to change his mind, until he realized that the man was right.

But there were two things that he, with the assistance of J.A.G. attorney Phil Jansen, was going to accomplish for Rufus: an honorable discharge and a full military pension and benefits. Rufus Harms wasn't going to scrape for an existence, not after all he had been through.

As Fiske finished this thought, Sara walked up with Elizabeth Knight. "I feel deeply responsible for this," Knight said.

She and the Senator, Fiske knew, were divorcing. The government, the army in particular, wanted to keep all of this quiet. Important strings in Washington were being pulled. That meant that Jordan Knight might not go to prison for what he had done. Even

with Elizabeth Knight's consent the legality of the electronic surveillance of the man had already been drawn into serious question
by the Senator's very skillful lawyers. The thought that Jordan
Knight would go unpunished made Fiske want to visit the man late
at night with his 9-mm. But the man had already suffered and
would continue to do so. The wiretap had carried some leverage.
Jordan had resigned his Senate seat and, more devastatingly, lost the
woman he cherished.

"If there's anything I can ever do for you . . ." Elizabeth Knight
said.

"You have the same offer from me," Fiske said.

Thirty minutes after the last mourners were gone, Fiske watched
as the coffin was lowered and the slab was laid over the vault. Then
the dirt was shoveled on top. Fiske spoke with his father and Sara
for a few minutes and told them he would meet them back at his
father's house. He watched them drive off. When he looked back
over at the fresh hump of earth, he was startled. On his knees next
to the new grave, eyes closed, Bible clutched in one hand, was
Rufus Harms.

Fiske walked over and put a hand on the man's shoulder. "Rufus,
you okay? What are you doing?"

"Praying."

"Oh."

"How about you? Have you prayed over your brother yet?"

"Rufus, I haven't been to Mass since high school. I don't remember any prayers."

"Then don't pray. Just talk plain words."

Fiske looked around to see if anyone was watching. Then he awkwardly knelt. At first he didn't even close his eyes, but then they just
seemed to do so on their own. He felt the moisture from the ground
soak through his pant legs, but he didn't move. He felt the comfortable presence of Rufus next to him. He didn't know if he could
have remained there without it.

He focused on all that had happened. He thought of his mother
and his father. With a smile he thought of Sara. Fifty, sixty, maybe
seventy years old? Why not give himself the benefit of the doubt?

He had a life to live. Potentially a very satisfying one. Particularly when it included Sara. He tilted his head up and smelled the wet air, caught the scent of leaves burning somewhere.

Finally, with difficulty, he thought of his brother. He felt the burn in his chest. It was not the underbelly of his scar come calling. This pain was not capable of killing him, but it was worse by legions than that inflicted on him by the two bullets. Mike was not coming back. He had lost him.

He felt his body start to give on him. The tears suddenly poured with such force he thought his nose was bleeding. He started to go down, but a strong hand grasped him, easily held him up. Through the blur of tears he looked at Rufus. The man had one hand under Fiske's arm, propping him up. Yet his eyes were still closed, his head looking to the sky, the lips still rising and falling as he continued his prayers.

Right then John Fiske envied Rufus Harms, a man who had lost his own brother, a man who really had nothing. And yet in the most important way Rufus Harms was the richest man on earth.

Fiske looked away from Rufus and stared down at the grave. He dug his knees into the earth, closed his eyes, bowed his head, placed his hands firmly together, and started making his peace. With his brother below. And with whatever lay above.

DAVID BALDACCI

David Baldacci has written a best seller a year for the last four years. Is it getting to be a habit? Baldacci's answer is an emphatic "No!" In fact, if there's one thing he wants to avoid, it's formulaic writing. "I want to be able to write about whatever interests me, and I have a lot of interests." For *The Simple Truth* he drew on five years' experience as a trial lawyer and on the insights he gained as a student in Richmond, where he attended Virginia's first integrated public school. Today Baldacci shares the secrets of his craft with teenagers at writing workshops he conducts in that same school. He lives in Virginia with his wife, Michelle, and their two children.

THE CAT WHO SAW STARS

LILIAN JACKSON BRAUN

Catnaps on the lakefront porch . . .
Elegant vittles with old friends . . .
Reporter Jim Qwilleran and his feline
family, Koko and Yum Yum, had been
looking forward to a peaceful vacation.

But the whiskered trio finds peace
elusive. Instead, fur flies when the cats
uncover murder, mystery, and mayhem
at their rustic hideaway.

ONE

WORLD-SHAKING news was seldom broadcast by WPKX, the radio station serving Moose County, four hundred miles north of everywhere. Local baseball scores, a fire in a chicken coop, and death notices were the usual fare. In late June listeners snapped to attention, then, when a Sunday evening newscast included this bulletin:

"An unidentified backpacker of no known address may or may not be a missing person, according to Moose County authorities. The Caucasian male, thought to be in his early twenties, stowed his camping gear on private property in the Fishport area three days ago and has not returned. He is described as fair-haired with blue eyes and of medium build. When last seen, he was wearing cutoff jeans, a white T-shirt, and a camera on a neck strap. Anyone seeing an individual of this description should notify the sheriff's department."

Since the description might fit any number of vacationers in Moose County, the listening audience ignored the matter until the next day, when it was reported in the *Moose County Something*.

MISSING HIKER BAFFLES F'PORT

Magnus Hawley of Fishport, a veteran on the commercial fishing boats, flagged down a sheriff's patrol car on Sunday and told a curious tale. Hawley and his wife, Doris, live in a trailer home surrounded by flower beds on Lakeshore Road near Roaring Creek.

"T'other night," Hawley said, "me and m'wife was watchin' TV when there come a knock on the door. It's a young feller with a big backpack, wantin' to pitch his tent down by the crick. He says he's gonna do some hikin' on the beach."

Doris Hawley approved of the stranger. "He reminded me of our grandson—nice smile, very polite. He said he was mostly interested in taking pictures. We told him he could camp near the picnic table at the bottom of the hill."

The stranger said his name was David. "I never knew a David who wasn't trustworthy," she said.

She gave him some of her homemade gingersnaps and filled a jug with fresh water from the well. Shortly after, they saw the young man heading for the lakeshore with his camera.

"After that we di'n't see hide or hair of the feller," said Hawley. "I went down to the crick in a coupla days to see if he'd cleared out. The water jug was still on the picnic table, full up! And his pack was underneath. On'y the cookies was gone."

A sheriff's deputy and a state trooper inspected the campsite but found no identification. A description of the hiker, as given by the Hawleys, was broadcast Sunday night, but no response to the bulletin had been received at press time.

Following the appearance of the story, the local gossip mill started grinding out idle speculations and sensational details. Abduction was a possibility, many said. A few busybodies suspected the Hawleys of foul play. "Don't eat any gingersnaps" was the popular quip in bars and coffee shops.

One who listened to the gossip without contributing to it was Jim Qwilleran, a longtime journalist now writing a twice-weekly column for the *Something*. Qwilleran's own reaction to the backpacker's disappearance was an educated curiosity. Formerly a crime reporter in major cities around the United States, he had retained a Sherlockian interest in solving mysteries.

Qwilleran was a popular man-about-town in Pickax City, the county seat (population 3000). His column, "Straight from the Qwill Pen," rated more readership than the daily horoscope. Wherever he went in the county, he drew attention, being a good-looking fifty plus and a well-built six feet two with a mustache of outstanding proportions. It accentuated his melancholy demeanor, and his eyes had a brooding intensity. Yet friends knew him to be amiable, witty, and fond of taking them to dinner.

There was something else in Qwilleran's favor: He was a philanthropist of incredible generosity. Earlier in life he had been a hardworking journalist Down Below, as locals called the high-population centers around the country. He lived from paycheck to paycheck. Then a strange happenstance made him the most affluent individual in the northeast central United States—he inherited the Klingenschoen estate, a fortune that had been amassed when the area was rich in natural resources.

To Qwilleran all that money was a burden until he thought of establishing the Klingenschoen Foundation, or the K Fund, as it was known. Now financial experts in Chicago managed the fortune, distributing it for the betterment of the community and leaving him free to write, read, dine well, and do a little amateur sleuthing.

Qwilleran's oversize mustache was a landmark in Moose County, admired by men and adored by women. What no one knew about was its peculiar sensitivity. Whenever faced with suspicious circumstances, he felt a nudge on his upper lip that prompted him to ask questions. Needless to say, it was not something he cared to explain.

With the disappearance of the backpacker, a nagging sensation on his upper lip was urging him to visit Fishport, a modest village near the resort town of Mooseville, where he had a small log cabin and a half mile of lake frontage. Although it was only thirty miles from Pickax, Mooseville, with its hundred miles of lake for a vista, was a different world. Even the pair of Siamese with whom he lived responded to its uniqueness.

A propitious fate had brought the three of them together. The female had been a poor little rich cat abandoned in a posh neighborhood when Qwilleran found her. Because of her sweet expression and winning ways he named her Yum Yum. The sleek male had simply moved in—at a time when Qwilleran was trying to get his life together. Kao K'o Kung had been his name before being orphaned. Now called Koko, he had a magnificent set of whiskers and remarkable sensory attributes.

The day after the newspaper story about the backpacker, Qwilleran drove downtown to the *Something* office to announce his vacation plans and hand in his copy for the "Qwill Pen" column. He found the managing editor's office decorated with crepe paper streamers and a sign with the message HAPPY BIRTHDAY, JUNIOR. TODAY YOU ARE 16! Junior Goodwinter was past thirty, but slight stature and boyish features gave him the look of a perennial schoolboy.

"Happy sixteenth," Qwilleran said, dropping into a chair. "You don't look a day over fifteen. Any coffee left?"

The editor swiveled in his chair and poured a mugful. "Did you see our story on the backpacker, Qwill? A teacher in Sawdust City called and laid us out for quoting the fisherman verbatim instead of correcting his grammar."

"Pay no attention. She's a crank," Qwilleran said.

"The woman wants us to start running a column on correct speech instead of 'wasting so much space on sports.' I quote."

"No one would read it."

"It would have to be chatty, like Ann Landers," Junior said. "Well, anyway, what are you doing for the Fourth?"

"Leaving for a month's vacation at the beach. Reading, loafing, biking, walking on the beach."

"Can you fax your copy from up there?"

"What? You forget I'm going on vacation."

"But the readers have fits if your column doesn't run."

"Well . . . only because it's your birthday."

"Did you read our piece about the new restaurant up there?"

"Yes, and I'm looking forward to checking it out. The new summer theater, too."

"Friday is opening night," Junior said. "How'd you like to review the play for us?" He caught Qwilleran's dour glance.

"I'll think about it."

BEFORE LEAVING THE building, Qwilleran stopped in the publisher's office. He and Arch Riker had been lifelong friends and fellow journalists Down Below. Arch's florid face glowed with midlife contentment, and his paunchy midriff was getting paunchier. His wife, Mildred, was food writer for the paper.

Qwilleran asked, "Have you two moved to your beach house?"

"Sure have! It's a longer commute but worth it."

"I'm packing up the cats and moving up there myself this afternoon. Polly will be gone all month, you know," Qwilleran said.

Riker had his Mildred, and Qwilleran had his Polly Duncan. She was the director of the Pickax Public Library, and the possibility of their marriage was widely discussed in the community. Both preferred their individual lifestyles, however, and let it be known that their cats were incompatible.

Riker said, "Why don't you come and have dinner with us tonight? The Comptons will be there, and Mildred is doing her famous coddled pork chops."

"What time?"

"About seven. . . . What do you think about the Fishport mystery? Have you heard the rumor about the Hawleys?"

"Yes."

"Personally," Riker said, "I think it's all a publicity stunt trumped up by the chamber of commerce to promote tourism."

QWILLERAN could never leave downtown without stopping at the used-book store. Currently he was interested in Mark Twain.

A bell had tinkled on the door, and Eddington Smith, the old gray bookseller, came out eagerly. "Mr. Q.! I've found three more: *Connecticut Yankee, A Horse's Tale,* and *Jumping Frog.* Mark Twain lectured up here once, so his books were popular."

"Well, keep your eyes peeled for the titles I want, Ed. I'm going on vacation for a few weeks."

"Do you have plenty to read? I know you like Thomas Hardy, and I just found a leather-bound edition of *Far from the Madding Crowd.*"

Qwilleran bought the Thomas Hardy book as well as the others and was leaving the store with his purchases when the bookseller called after him. "Where are you going on vacation, Mr. Q.?"

"Just up to Mooseville."

"That's nice. You'll see some flying saucers."

Qwilleran bristled at the suggestion but said a polite, "Maybe." Both he and Arch Riker, professional skeptics, scoffed at the UFO gossip in Mooseville. Locals blamed aliens for every quirk of weather or outbreak of sheep fly. Qwilleran, to his dismay, had found several believers in the interplanetary origin of UFOs—including such persons as Riker's wife and the superintendent of schools.

THE last stop on his morning round was Amanda's design studio, where Fran Brodie, second-in-command, was back from vacation. She had done a small design job for Qwilleran's new guesthouse, and she was redesigning the interior of the Pickax Hotel, but her greatest passion was the Pickax Theater Club. It had been her idea to do summer theater in a barn near Mooseville. They were opening with a comedy, *Visit to a Small Planet*.

"Are you going to review our opening night, Qwill?"

"I'm afraid so."

"Do you know the play?"

"Only that Gore Vidal wrote it a long time ago."

"It's a fun production," Fran said. "A flying saucer lands in front of a TV commentator's house, and a visitor from outer space proceeds to stir things up."

"Who's playing the visitor? Were you able to draw from a pool of small green actors?"

"That's our big joke, Qwill. We've purposely cast actors under five feet nine for all the earthlings, so the visitor comes as a shock. He's six feet eight!"

"Derek Cuttlebrink!"

"Isn't that a hoot?"

"Where did you find a barn suitable for a theater?" Qwilleran asked.

"Avery Botts is letting us use his dairy barn for nine weekends. Each play will run three weekends."

"Good," said Qwilleran. "See you Friday night. Break a leg!"

Driving home to collect the Siamese for the Mooseville expedition, Qwilleran considered what he would need to pack in his van. For himself he would require only the automated coffeemaker, polo shirts, shorts, and sandals, plus writing materials and a few books. There was no point in taking the revolutionary high-tech recumbent bike presented to him by the community as a token of their esteem. The rider reclined in a bucket seat, pedaling with elevated feet. It was such a sensation in Pickax that he seldom ventured out on the highway; instead he displayed it in his living room as a conversation piece.

The cats' vacation needs were more complex. He would have to take the turkey roaster that served as their commode, grooming equipment, their special dishes for food and water, and a few cans of red salmon, lobster, and smoked turkey.

Right now it was time for their midday snack, and they would be waiting, waving eloquent tails, raising eager blue eyes. When he unlocked the door, however, both were asleep on the sofa.

"Treat," he said in a stage whisper.

Two heads popped up.

"Yow!" came Koko's clamoring response.

"N-n-now!" shrieked Yum Yum.

After the luggage was packed and the van loaded, and after Yum Yum had been captured and pushed into the cat carrier, Koko was found sitting in the bucket seat of the recumbent bike, looking wise. Oh, well, Qwilleran thought, I might as well take it along. I can practice on the back roads.

THE two passengers in the cat carrier on the back seat jockeyed for position, then settled down as the brown van picked up speed on the highway. The route to Mooseville lay due north.

At Ittibittiwassee Road the Siamese perked up, stretched their necks, and sniffed. They smelled the lake, still a mile away. Their excitement increased as the van traveled along the lakeshore road. On the right Qwilleran saw glimpses of the lake between the trees; on the left a solitary stone chimney, all that remained of an old one-room schoolhouse; on the right the letter K on a post.

This was the old Klingenschoen property, a half square mile of ancient forest on ancient sand dunes, with a sandy drive winding into a clearing, where a cabin overlooked a hundred miles of water. Built of full-round logs interlocking at the corners, the small cabin seemed anchored to the ground by its enormous stone chimney. Eighty-foot pine trees surrounded it like sentinels.

Before bringing the cats indoors, Qwilleran inspected the premises. The interior space was limited: a single large room with two cubicles at one end and a stone fireplace spanning the other. What suggested spaciousness was the open ceiling that soared to the peak of the roof and was crisscrossed by log beams and braces. As soon as blinds were opened, the large window facing the lake and the three skylights in the roof filled the interior with shafts of light.

Only then was the carrier brought indoors, its occupants yowling loudly. The tiny door was unlatched, and suddenly they were quiet and wary.

"It's safe," Qwilleran reassured them. "No lions or tigers. The floor has been cleaned and polished, and you can walk on it with impunity." The more you talk to cats, he believed, the smarter they become.

Immediately they remembered the back porch with its concrete floor warmed by the sun's rays. They rushed out to curl and uncurl on its rough surface.

While the Siamese lounged alfresco, Qwilleran unpacked the van. First the recumbent bicycle, which he parked on the kitchen porch. Whether he would have the nerve to ride such a curiosity in tradition-bound Mooseville was yet to be decided.

Other baggage from the van made itself at home: clothing in the sleeping cubicle, writing materials in the office cubicle, books on shelves in the main room. Two exceptions went on the coffee table: the Thomas Hardy novel because of its impressive leather binding and *Mark Twain A to Z* because of its large size. Koko liked to sit on large books.

There was a second screened porch on the lakeside—with a magnificent view and plenty of afternoon sun. The cabin perched on a lofty sand dune, its steep slope anchored by beach grass and milkweed. A sand ladder led down to the beach; it was simply a framework of two-by-fours filled in with sand for treads.

Qwilleran, dressed for dinner in white shorts and black polo shirt, stood at the sand ladder and noticed that the beach had changed. Normally deep dry sand, it was now a hard pebbly surface, while the loose sand had blown up into a ridge at the foot of the dune.

He walked along the shore to the Rikers' beach house. The first half mile bordered his own property. Then came a row of cottages. The golfing Mableys called their place The Sand Trap. The Bah Humbug could belong only to the Comptons; Lyle was superintendent of schools, a grouch with a sense of humor. Last in the row was the Rikers' yellow frame bungalow, called Sunny Daze.

Arch was serving drinks; Mildred was serving canapés. The Comptons were already there. Mildred was wearing a caftan intended to disguise her plumpness. Her husband's leisure garb did nothing to camouflage his well-fed silhouette, but he was happy and relaxed. By comparison the superintendent of schools looked underfed and overworked after three decades of coping with school boards, teachers, and parents. Lisa Compton was as pleasant as her husband pretended to be grouchy.

Mildred announced, "Qwill has built a guesthouse."

"Expecting a lot of company?" Lisa asked.

"No, it's strictly for emergency overnights," he said.

Lisa asked about Polly Duncan; she and Qwill were usually seen together at dinner parties.

"She's traveling in Canada with her sister during July."

"A whole month? You'll miss her," Mildred said.

He shrugged. The truth was he already missed their nightly phone calls and he would miss their weekends even more. "Has anyone tried the new restaurant?"

No one had, but they had read about it on the food page of the *Something*. A couple had come from Florida to run it during the summer months; the wife was the chef, with a bachelor's degree from a culinary institute. It sounded promising.

While Arch uncorked another bottle, Lyle asked if Qwilleran had brought his weird bicycle.

"Yes, I brought it, but I plan to ride only on back roads. Mooseville isn't ready for state-of-the-art technology."

"And what do you intend to read?" Mildred asked.

"Chiefly old editions of Mark Twain."

"He came through here on a lecture tour," Lisa said. "My great-grandmother had a crush on him. She fell for his mustache. I have her diary. The pages are brown, and the ink is fading, but it's full of fascinating stuff."

Qwilleran made a mental note for the "Qwill Pen": Lisa Compton's great-grandmother's diary.

Mildred invited them indoors to the table. With the coddled chops were twice-baked potatoes, a broccoli soufflé, a pinot noir, and a toast from Lyle Compton: "Thursday's Independence Day. Let's drink to the genius who single-handedly dragged the Fourth of July parade from the pits and launched it to the stars!"

Mildred blushed. "Lyle, I didn't know you could be so poetic."

"Speech! Speech!" the others shouted with vigor.

"Well, our parades were getting to be all commercial and political," Mildred said. "This year's parade will have marching bands, floats, and a little originality. Athletes from Mooseland High will march, carrying banners with a single letter of the alphabet. Each row will spell a word: Peace, Truth, Honor, and Trust."

"Very clever," said Lisa. "Who's the grand marshal?"

"Andrew Brodie, in Scottish regalia, with his bagpipe."

"There's something about bagpipe music that makes me limp with emotion," Lisa said.

"The floats will be sponsored by the chamber of commerce, parent-teachers, commercial fisheries, private marinas, and the Friends of Wool." Mildred referred to a new coalition of wool-growers, spinners, knitters, and other fiber artists. "Barb Ogilvie is our mentor—very talented. She teaches knitting, started the knitting club, runs a knitting day camp for kids. In high school she was considered a bit wild, but she's settled down. Did Arch tell you he's learning to knit socks?"

Qwilleran turned to his lifelong friend in astonishment. "Arch! Why were you keeping this dirty little secret from me?"

"What the heck. It's one of the things you do when you're middle-aged and in love."

There was a moment of silence, which Qwilleran interrupted by asking, "What are the Friends of Wool going to do on a float?"

"We'll have two spinners spinning and six knitters knitting—four women and two men, if Arch will consent. Dr. Emerson, the surgeon, has agreed, and I think it would add prestige if the publisher of the newspaper were on the float, knitting a sock with four needles."

As all eyes turned to Arch, he said, "To quote Shakespeare: I don't wanna, I don't hafta, and I ain't gonna."

His wife smiled knowingly at the others.

After an old-fashioned Waldorf salad, Black Forest cake, and coffee, Mildred said, "Qwill, I'd like to ask you a favor. The parade opens with a 1776 tableau on a float—the signing of the Declaration of Independence—and it ends with a flock of bicycles. Wouldn't it be a terrific finale if you brought up the rear with your high-tech recumbent bike?"

Qwilleran hesitated. "I'll pedal with my feet up in the air if Arch will ride on your float, knitting a sock."

TWO

ORDINARILY Koko was a feline alarm clock at eleven p.m., reminding the world at large that it was time for a bedtime snack and lights-out, so his behavior on his first night at the cabin made Qwilleran wonder. The three of them had been lolling on the screened porch in the dark, watching the fireflies. While Qwilleran and Yum Yum enjoyed the luxury of cushioned chairs, Koko huddled on the porch table, perhaps because it gave him an elevated view of the dark beachfront.

Eventually Qwilleran consulted his watch and announced, "Treat." Yum Yum scampered after him, but Koko stayed where he was. Something's down there, Qwilleran realized—something I can't see. It was a pleasant night, so Qwilleran left the door to the porch open when he retired to his sleeping cubicle.

The next morning Qwilleran found Koko none the worse for his nocturnal escapade. He ate a good breakfast and then wanted to go for a ride on Qwilleran's shoulder. He kept jumping at the latch on the screened door of the porch.

"Not now," Qwilleran told him. "Later."

BEFORE setting off for Mooseville in his van, Qwilleran inspected his new guesthouse. Hidden in the woods, it was the same size as the toolshed and built of the same green-stained cedar. But the snuggery, as he called it, had windows and indoor plumbing. Modular furniture, including a double-deck bunk, made the utmost use of every inch of space.

From there he drove to Mooseville, a quaint resort town two miles long and hardly more than a block wide. It was squeezed between the lake and a high wall of sand called the Great Dune. On the lake side of Main Street were the municipal docks, private marinas, and the Northern Lights Hotel; on the other side, the bank, post office, hardware store, Shipwreck Tavern, and so on.

The Great Dune, which had taken ten thousand years to form, was revered in Mooseville. It towered protectively over the downtown area, crowned with a lush forest. There were no structures up there. Only one thoroughfare sliced through the Great Dune, and that was Sandpit Road, at the east end of downtown.

On the first day of Qwilleran's vacation he always made the rounds, renewing his acquaintance with businesspeople. On this morning he had breakfast at the hotel and shook hands with the owners. He shook hands with the bank manager and cashed a check. He shook hands with the postmaster and told her he expected to receive mail addressed to general delivery. At Grott's Grocery he shook hands with the whole family and bought some boiled ham for sandwiches.

At the Shipwreck Tavern he shook hands with the bartender. "Still drinkin' Squunk water?" the man asked. "Have one on the house."

"I believe in supporting local products," Qwilleran said. It was a mineral water from a spring in Squunk Corners. "Any developments in the case of the missing backpacker?"

"Nah. I say it's a lot of hokum, like the two-headed raccoon a coupla years back. Gives folks somethin' to talk about."

Next Qwilleran went to Huggins Hardware for mosquito repellent and shook hands with Cecil Huggins and his great-uncle.

"What can you tell me about the new restaurant?" Qwilleran asked.

"It's on Sandpit Road," Cecil replied. "A couple came up from Florida to run it for the tourist season. The chamber of commerce ran an ad in Florida papers—business opportunity with special perks. The guy's name is Owen Bowen. His wife's the chef."

"What were the special perks?"

"Pretty generous, we thought. The landlord gave him a break on the rent. The Northern Lights Hotel gave him a suite for the price of a single. Chamber members pitched in and painted the walls, cleaned the kitchen, washed the windows before the Bowens got here. You'd think he'd be tickled pink, wouldn't you? But no! He came to a chamber meeting bellyaching about this, that, and the other thing. He talked down to us as if we were a bunch of hicks."

Qwilleran said he hoped the food was better than Owen's personality. "Have you tried it?"

"Not yet, but they say it's good. They say his wife's nice. Too bad Owen turned out to be disagreeable."

"He's a horse's tail!" said Unc.

After the formal handshaking, Qwilleran ambled over to Elizabeth Hart's boutique on Oak Street at the foot of the Great Dune. A Chicago heiress, she had visited Moose County, met Derek Cuttlebrink, and decided to stay. They were good for each other. She had convinced him to enroll in restaurant management at Moose County Community College, and it was Derek who had named her boutique.

Elizabeth's Magic featured exotic wearables, crafts by local artisans, and such mystic paraphernalia as tarot cards and rune-stones. There was also a coffee dispenser in the rear of the shop and a ring of chairs in aluminum and black nylon.

When Qwilleran walked in, Elizabeth was busy with customers but waved a greeting and said, "Don't go away. I have news for you." For a few minutes he joined the browsers, then gravitated toward the coffee dispensary. After a while Elizabeth joined him, leaving an assistant to keep an eye on customers.

"Are you going to the parade tomorrow, Qwill? I designed the chamber of commerce float—the signing of the Declaration of Independence, based on the John Turnbull painting."

"I know it," Qwilleran said. "It's in Philadelphia. Is Derek going to be in the parade?"

"No. The play at the barn opens Friday, and he has the title role. He's concentrating on that. But the big news is that he has a job! Assistant manager at the new restaurant. They have a sophisticated menu, so he hopes he'll learn something."

"Have you met Owen Bowen?"

"Only at a C of C meeting. He's middle-aged, quite handsome, rather supercilious, and ever so tan," she said disdainfully. "I consider him a bit of a pill, but Derek can handle him."

"I believe it." Derek's height—six feet eight—coupled with his swaggering but likable personality appealed to young girls, bosses, grandmothers, and cats and dogs.

Qwilleran looked at a sailboat in the craft display. It was hand-crafted entirely of copper and labeled SLOOP RIGGED WITH TOPSAIL, MAINSAIL, JIB, AND SPINNAKER—BY MIKE ZANDER.

"Does the pedestal go with it?" Qwilleran asked.

"I dunno, but the guy'd sell it to you, I bet."

When Qwilleran drove away, he had bought a copper sculpture and a railroad tie pedestal. And now he could tell Arch he had bought a sailboat and would watch his old friend's jaw drop.

Before going home, he drove out to Fishport to see Doris Hawley. At her trailer home a sign on the lawn said HOME BAKES. That meant muffins, cinnamon rolls, and cookies. Mrs. Hawley was watering her extensive flower garden when Qwilleran pulled into the side drive.

"Beautiful garden, Mrs. Hawley," he called out.

"Oh, hello, Mr. Q." She turned off the spray and dropped the nozzle. "What can I do for you?"

"Do you happen to have any cinnamon rolls?"

"Half pan or whole pan? They freeze nicely." She was a gray-haired woman with a gardener's slight stoop and the energy of a much younger person.

When she went into the house, Qwilleran looked toward the rear of the property and saw a picnic table on a grassy bank. "Have you heard anything about the young man you befriended?" he asked when she returned.

"Not a thing. The police were here twice, asking questions. They act as if we're holding something back. It makes me nervous. And some nasty people are saying my cookies were poisoned. I haven't sold a one since that rumor started. I worry about the whole thing."

"You have nothing to worry about, Mrs. Hawley. The nasty people will choke on their lies. As for the police, they are trained to investigate in certain ways. I'm sorry your act of kindness boomeranged."

"You're very kind, Mr. Q. Are you going to the parade tomorrow? Four generations of our family will be on the sidelines, including my widowed mother-in-law, who's a great fan of yours. She's embroidering a sampler for you!"

"That's thoughtful of her." He mustered as much enthusiasm as he could. Devoted readers liked to send him useless knickknacks made by their own hands, and he always sent a handwritten thank-you. "That's something to look forward to, isn't it?"

DRIVING home, Qwilleran watched automatically for the old schoolhouse chimney, then turned left into the long K driveway. Halfway up the twisting dirt lane he could hear Koko yowling. The noisy welcome could mean that the phone had been ringing or something had been knocked down or there was a plumbing leak.

"Cool it, old boy. Nothing's wrong," Qwilleran said after inspecting the premises, but Koko continued to frisk about. When he jumped up at the peg where his harness hung, the message was clear: He wanted to go for a walk. Qwilleran obliged—and later recorded the cat's antics in his personal journal. This report was headed "Mooseville, Wednesday, July 3."

> Koko did it again! He solved a mystery. Nobody but me will ever know. If the media discovered this cat's psychic tendencies, they'd give us no peace.
>
> What happened: Koko wanted to go for a walk on the beach, meaning that I walk and he rides on my shoulder. Smart cat! He wears a harness, and I keep a firm hand on the leash.
>
> We hadn't gone far before a strange growl came from the cat's innards and his body stiffened. Keeping a taut leash, I let him get down on the sand. When he reached the sand ridge, he climbed up the slope, slipping and sliding. By the time he reached the top, he started to dig. What was he after? I started to get suspicious.
>
> "Look out!" I said, pushing him aside. I saw something shining in the hole. It was the face of a wristwatch! I grabbed Koko and ran back to the cabin.

After calling 911, Qwilleran gave Koko a treat. In a matter of minutes a patrol car came through the woods, and a deputy in a wide-brimmed hat stepped out. Qwilleran went out to meet her.

"You reported finding a body?" she asked impassively.

"Down on the beach, buried in the sand. I'll show you."

She followed him down the sand ladder and along the shore to Koko's excavation. "How'd you find it?"

"Just walking on the beach."

Unhooking her phone, she called the state police. Qwilleran said he would go back to the cabin and direct whoever responded.

In the next half hour the clearing filled with vehicles. First, the state police car with two officers. Second, the ambulance of the rescue squad. Then, another sheriff's car with two passengers in the back seat. Magnus and Doris Hawley were escorted down the sand ladder by the deputy.

Soon the helicopter from Pickax landed on the hard flat sand near the water. That would be the medical examiner, Qwilleran presumed.

He ducked indoors. Eventually a sheriff's car left with the Hawleys. Then the ambulance left and the helicopter lifted off, taking a blue body bag on a stretcher. When the state troopers drove away, only the deputy remained, and Qwilleran went out to size her up. Though not bad-looking, she was stony-faced.

Getting out her pad, she said, "You must be Mr. Q."

"Yes, but are you aware of the department's policy?"

"We don't release your name."

"That's right."

She nodded, and the tassels on her hat bobbed.

Now Qwilleran knew why Koko had stayed up all night. Most cats had a sixth sense, but Koko's perception of right and wrong went beyond catly concerns. Qwilleran could attribute his talents only to his magnificent whiskers. Yum Yum had the standard forty-eight; Koko had sixty.

Qwilleran had reasons for being secretive about Koko's special gifts and his own involvement, and he was relieved to hear the six-o'clock newscast on WPKX:

"Acting on a tip from a beachcomber, the sheriff's department today found the body of the backpacker missing since Friday. The deceased was identified by Magnus and Doris Hawley as the hiker who had come to their house asking permission to camp on their property. Cause of death has not been determined. Identification was found on the body but is being withheld pending notification of family."

Qwilleran proposed to reward the Siamese with a session of reading aloud. He suggested *Far from the Madding Crowd*. "You'll like it," he said. "It's about sheep and cows."

After the reading, he unpacked the sailboat that he had bought. A foot tall, it was constructed of sheet copper that had been treated to retain color and brilliance, and it was dazzling in the light from the windows. To stabilize the lightweight object, there was a heavy base of wood, with the keel cemented into a groove.

Qwilleran carried the sailboat to the porch, only to discover that Koko had taken possession of the pedestal, where he posed like an ancient Egyptian cat.

"Jump down," Qwilleran said foolishly, knowing that Koko never jumped down when told to jump down. So he left the sailboat on the table and went to write some more in his journal.

THE Fourth of July parade was scheduled to start at one p.m., and Qwilleran reported early to scout around. The staging area was beyond the town limits, with parade units assigned to specific open fields. Marchers were close to the starting point, and mechanized units were farthest away. In between were the bikers. They were a colorful troupe. Qwilleran himself wore white shorts, a blue-and-white-striped T-shirt, and a red baseball cap. There were trail bikes, school bikes, plenty of racers, and one old-fashioned high-wheeler.

As parade time drew near, the official starter in his tricolor top hat ran up and down the highway, waving his arms and yelling. Standing by was the sheriff's car that would precede the parade. Highly visible was Andrew Brodie, the Pickax police chief. As grand marshal, the Scots bagpiper would lead the parade in full Highland regalia. He was a big man in any uniform but a giant when swaggering in his lofty feather bonnet, with a shoulderful of plaid and an armful of pipes.

The sheriff's car started to roll. After giving it a fifty-yard head start, the piper began his slow, swinging gait and skirling rendition of the national anthem. The color guard snapped to attention. One by one the floats and marchers moved out.

Finally the Parade of Bikers was given the signal. The first to take off was the high-wheeler, followed by neat rows of bikes pedaled by girls and boys in helmets. Bringing up the rear was the most prominent man in the county, reclining in a bucket seat with his feet elevated. Everyone recognized the mustache, and while they cheered, Qwilleran pedaled with unflappable cool.

Whether the acclaim was for the bike or the famous mustache or the man behind the K Fund, that was anyone's guess.

QWILLERAN had invited Andrew Brodie to stop at the cabin for a drink following the parade. At four o'clock he had a beverage tray on the porch, along with some Gorgonzola and crackers. When Brodie arrived, he was still in piper's garb, except for the feather bonnet and shoulder plaid.

Koko was again on the pedestal, and Yum Yum was sniffing insects on the outside of the screen.

"Your beach is a lot different this year," Brodie said. "What's that burned circle?"

"Some trespassers apparently had a bonfire before I got here," Qwilleran said. "At least they didn't leave any beer cans."

Brodie gave Qwilleran a sharp look. "I hear you're the one that found the body on the beach."

"Well, if you must know . . . yes." He refrained from mentioning Koko's involvement. Brodie had heard about "that smart cat" from a detective Down Below but believed only fifty percent of it. Yet he valued Qwilleran's interest in certain cases.

They sat in silence for a while, until Qwilleran asked, "Were they able to identify the backpacker?"

"Oh, sure. He had an ID on his person—Philadelphia address—age twenty-five—no next of kin, but the name and phone number of a woman."

"Homicide or natural causes?"

"Homicide hasn't been ruled out. The coroner can't determine cause of death. They've flown the body to the state forensic lab."

"That's strange."

"Stranger than you think. Everything points to the time of death as midnight last Friday, a few hours after he called at the Hawley house; but"—Brodie paused uncertainly—"there was no decomposition. Almost like he was embalmed. He'd been dead four days."

"Does anyone have a theory?"

"If they do, they're not talking. The state bureau has clamped down. This is all between you and me, of course."

"Of course."

"And now I've gotta take off. Thanks for the refreshments."

After Brodie had driven away, Qwilleran came to a decision: Koko would never give up the railroad tie as his pedestal. The sailboat sculpture would have to go on the fireplace mantel.

Late that night the three of them sat on the porch in the dark: Koko gazing at the constellations, Yum Yum fascinated by the fireflies, Qwilleran thinking his thoughts. Brodie's remarks about the backpacker piqued his curiosity. Tomorrow he would drive to Fishport to buy some of Mrs. Hawley's home bakes and find out how she and Magnus felt about identifying the body.

THREE

FRIDAY was a gala day in Mooseville, as vacationers and locals looked forward to opening night of the barn theater. Qwilleran had promised to review the play and would first have dinner at Owen's Place; he wished Polly could be with him.

Meanwhile, he had to finish a "Qwill Pen" column and take it to the bank to be faxed before noon. He found Main Street in the throes of a holiday weekend. Throngs of vacationers sauntered along the sidewalks, looked in shopwindows, and were mesmerized by the waterfront: the lake lapping against the pilings, boats gently nudging the piers.

Next on his schedule was a drive to Fishport. What would Doris Hawley have to say about the grim task of identifying the backpacker? As soon as he crossed the Roaring Creek bridge, however, he realized it was the wrong time to ask questions. Two police cars were parked in the driveway—one from the sheriff's department and the other from the state troopers' post. Furthermore the sign on the front lawn was covered with a burlap sack, a signal that there were no baked goods for sale. He made a U-turn and returned to Mooseville.

Back in town he went into the post office and found some post-cards from Polly. He had complained, while driving her to the airport, that she never kept in touch while on vacation. She had replied, with a cryptic smile, that she would do something about it. Doing something about it meant mailing six cards a week—a kind of playful overkill.

In the lobby of the post office he saw Sharon Hanstable—plump, good-natured, and pretty—a young version of her mother, Mildred Riker. She was also the wife of Roger MacGillivray, a reporter for the *Moose County Something*.

"What are you doing here?" he asked. "Shouldn't you be at home, homeschooling your brats around the kitchen table?"

"I work part-time at the Great Dune Motel," she explained, "and Roger's home with the kids today."

"If you're on your way to work," he said, "I'll walk with you and carry your mail."

They pushed through the heavy pedestrian traffic on Main Street and walked down Sandpit Road. Sharon said, "Did you hear that they found the backpacker? It'll be in today's paper. Roger's been on the story since Wednesday. There's something unusual about the death." She lowered her voice. "Mother and Roger and I think it has something to do with the visitors from outer space."

"Is that so?" he murmured.

"Don't mention it to Arch. You know how he is."

They had reached the Great Dune Motel, and he handed over her tote bag. "Have you been to lunch at Owen's Place?"

"Too expensive. I carry my lunch."

Owen's Place stood alone on the west side of the highway, although its stained cedar siding and white louvered shutters in the large front windows matched the motel, antique shop, and fudge kitchen on the east side. With the Great Dune as a noble background, the restaurant looked elegant. A recreation vehicle with a boat hitch and Florida tags could be seen at the rear of the building.

Walking back toward Main Street, Qwilleran went into Arnold's Antique Shop. There were several customers, either buying or browsing. Arnold himself was everywhere at once. He was an age-less man with tireless energy, but he had a weathered face that looked like the old wood carvings he sold.

A long-haired white-and-black dog wagged a plumed tail. "Good dog. Good dog," Qwilleran said to him.

"Hi, Mr. Q. Do you like our pooch?" Arnold asked. "He just wandered in one day. A friendly soul. Brings in more business than an ad in your newspaper!"

Arnold went off to take a customer's money. A man was buying a rusty iron wheel, four feet in diameter, with sixteen spokes.

Meanwhile, Qwilleran poked through baskets of arrowheads, Civil War bullets, and old English coins. "What's that guy going to do with the wheel?" he later asked Arnold.

"Hang it over the fireplace in his lodge on Grand Island."

"Hmmm. I could use one of those myself." He was thinking of the gable end above his own fireplace, a large blank wall.

"There were two of them, from a field combine," Arnold said. "The other one's in my main store in Lockmaster. I'll have it sent up here, but it'll take a couple, three days."

"No rush. I'll come back in a couple of days," Qwilleran said. "What do you know about the restaurant across the way?" he added as Arnold accompanied him to the door.

"I hear the food's good."

"Have you had contact with Owen Bowen?"

"Only through Derek. He's working there part-time, you know. Derek said the entry needed some spark. So I lent them a setup for the summer months—some Waterford crystal in a lighted china cabinet. And that so-and-so from Florida never picked up the phone to say thank you, let alone sending over a piece of pie. Our dog has better manners than Owen Bowen!"

QWILLERAN'S watch told him that the lunch hour had ended at Owen's Place, and his intuition told him that Derek would be heading for Elizabeth's Magic. Qwilleran headed in the same direction, stopping for two copies of the *Moose County Something*.

When Qwilleran opened the door to Elizabeth's Magic, an overhead bell jangled and two persons turned in his direction: Elizabeth and Derek Cuttlebrink. "Just got off work," Derek announced. "Five hours till curtain time." He loped to the rear of the store. Qwilleran followed after giving Elizabeth one of his newspapers.

The two men sat in the sling chairs with cups of coffee.

"How's business over at Owen's Place?" Qwilleran asked.

"Great at lunchtime. I'm not there at night."

"Do you and your boss hit it off well?"

"Oh, sure. We get along. He needs me, and he knows it." He lowered his voice. "I know more about the food business than he does. Owen happened to marry a great chef. She's a creative artist, trained at one of the best chef schools. Besides that, she's a nice person—much younger than he is. And not as stuffy. He expects to be called Mr. Bowen. She says, 'Call me Ernie.' Her name is Ernestine. She works like a dog while he goes fishing."

"Whatever he happens to reel in, I suppose, goes on the menu as catch of the day. At market price."

"Well, no. He fishes for the sport. Whatever he catches, he throws back. The guy's nuts!"

"Hmmm," Qwilleran said, smoothing his mustache. "What's your best seller at lunchtime?"

"Skewered potatoes, hands down."

"What are they?"

Derek yelled, "Liz, got any skewers left?"

"A few," she said, and showed Qwilleran the foot-long needles of twisted iron. At the opposite end each had a decorative medallion for a finger grip. She said, "If you bake potatoes on skewers, the baking time is shortened and they're flakier."

"Here's why they're popular," Derek said. "The potatoes are unskewered and dressed at tableside for dramatic effect. Dining in a fine restaurant is part showbiz, you know. I put on a good show. Come and have lunch someday."

"I'll do that. Meanwhile, I'm having dinner there tonight before the play."

"That reminds me . . ." Derek jumped out of his chair and headed for the front door.

"Break a leg!" Qwilleran shouted after him.

"Qwill, have you seen today's paper?" Elizabeth asked. "Look at the announcement on page five."

He unfolded his newspaper and read a boxed announcement:

YOU AIN'T SEEN NOTHIN' YET, HARDLY

Do you have pet peeves about English as she is spoken?

Do you think "whom" should be eliminated from the English language?

Are you confused about him and me and he and I?

ASK MS. GRAMMA

Her column starts next week on this page.

"Well, that's a surprise, to say the least," Qwilleran said. "What's your reaction, Elizabeth?"

"The people who need it most won't read it."

Qwilleran said, "My question is, who will write it?"

BEFORE going to dinner and the theater, Qwilleran fed the cats and treated them to a reading session, until the phone rang.

"Excuse me," he said, dislodging Yum Yum from his lap.

The caller was Sarah Plensdorf, the conscientious office manager at the *Something*. "I'm sorry to bother you on your vacation, Qwill, but I had a request for your phone number from a woman in Fishport who had an urgent message for you."

"Give me her number. I'll call her," he said.

"You're to ask for Janelle."

When he phoned the number, a soft, whispery voice said, "Safe Harbor Residence."

He had to think a moment. Was this the home for widows of commercial fishermen? He said, "Is there someone there by the name of Janelle?"

"This is Janelle," she said. "Is this Mr. Qwilleran?"

"Yes. You called my office. You have an urgent message?"

"It's from one of our residents. The widow of Primus Hawley. She's made a lovely gift for you."

He huffed into his mustache. That would be Doris Hawley's

mother-in-law. She was embroidering something for him—probably Home Sweet Home bordered with roses. He glanced at Koko, who was at his elbow, listening. "Very kind of her," he said.

"Would it be too much trouble to pick it up? She's ninety years old. She'd be thrilled to meet you."

Koko was staring at his forehead, and Qwilleran found himself saying, "No trouble at all. I'll drop in tomorrow afternoon."

After promising to be there at two o'clock, Qwilleran hung up and was surprised to see Koko running in circles. "If you could drive," he said to Koko, "I'd send you to pick it up."

WHEN Qwilleran arrived at Owen's Place, the first thing he noticed in the small foyer was a lighted case of sparkling cut crystal. Otherwise the interior was mostly white, with accents of pink and yellow and a great many potted plants and indoor trees.

Half the tables were taken, and there was a hum of excitement from showgoers headed for the opening-night performance. As Qwilleran stood waiting in the entry, several heads turned in his direction and hands waved.

Owen Bowen, handsomely tanned, came forward with a frown wrinkling his fine features. "Reservation?"

"No. Sorry."

The host scanned the room. "How many?"

"One."

After painful cogitation he conducted Qwilleran to a small table. The menu was unusual by Moose County standards: veal loin encrusted with eggplant, spinach and roasted red peppers with sun-dried tomato demiglaze—that sort of thing. Qwilleran played it safe with a lamb shank osso buco on a bed of basil fettuccine. The soup of the day was a purée of cauliflower and Gorgonzola served in a soup plate, with three spears of chives arranged in a triangle on the creamy surface.

While a self-conscious wait staff took orders and served the food, the host seated guests and served drinks with an air of zero hospitality. Latticework in the rear of the room screened a window into the kitchen, where Qwilleran caught glimpses of a young woman in a chef's towering toque. Her face had a look of extreme concentration and a kitchen pallor.

OTHER diners started leaving at seven fifteen, saying they were concerned about parking facilities. When Qwilleran arrived at the Botts farm, vehicles lined both shoulders of the highway as far as one could see, and others were being directed into designated pastures. He himself had a press card that admitted him to a lot behind the dairy barn. Showgoers gathered in the barnyard, reluctant to go indoors. It was a beautiful evening, and this was a festive celebration. The Rikers were there. "How was Owen's Place?" they asked.

Qwilleran was pleased to report that the food was excellent. "The chef is nouvelle, but not too nouvelle. The host is a cold fish. I suggest you go for lunch, when Derek is on duty."

"Curtain time!" an usher shouted to the crowd.

There was no curtain in the theater, and there were no backs on the seats. Bleachers, providing good sight lines, filled one end of the barn, while an elevated stage occupied the other.

The lights dimmed, and the play began—with headstrong characters insisting that UFOs were figments of the imagination. Meanwhile, a spaceship was landing in a rose garden offstage with green lights spilling onstage. Enter, a visitor from outer space, almost seven feet tall. The audience howled as they recognized their favorite actor. He wore a Civil War uniform and sideburns and explained to the earthlings that he had miscalculated and landed in the wrong century. It was a challenging role.

Derek was stealing the show. All his groupies were there, overreacting to every line. After the last tumultuous applause it was a joyful crowd that poured out into the barnyard.

"Apart from the hard seats, how did you like the show?" Qwilleran asked Arch.

"I hope it's not going to stir up a lot more UFO fever. People have brainwashed themselves."

"Well, I listen to their conversation politely," Qwilleran said, "but I don't buy it, of course."

"I've stopped being polite. Enough is enough! Our cat, Toulouse, sits staring into space, the way cats do, and Mildred insists he's watching for visitors."

"Qwill, would you like to stop at our place for a snack?" Mildred asked.

"Thanks, but I want to go home and grapple with my review while the show's fresh in my mind."

"We're parked half a mile away," Arch said. "Where are you parked?"

"Behind the barn. Reviewer's privilege."

"Lucky dog! I run the paper, and I have to walk half a mile."

"I'll make a deal," Qwilleran said. "You write the review, and I'll drive you to your car."

It was no deal.

QWILLERAN had never known his grandparents. His extended family consisted of his mother's friends and Arch Riker's parents. Pop Riker was as good a father as he had ever known. Now he often wondered about his forebears. Who were they?

He thought about it on the way to his Saturday afternoon appointment. Before he knew it, he had reached the Fishport village limits, and the landmark mansion called Safe Harbor loomed ahead.

Safe Harbor was a three-story frame structure in the Victorian style, with porches, gables, a turret, and a widow's walk. There were many bedrooms upstairs, and the stately mansion was now a retirement home for widows of commercial fishermen.

When Qwilleran arrived and rang the bell on the front door, it was immediately opened by a breathless young woman with a sweet smile. A mass of auburn hair cloaked her thin shoulders. "I'm Janelle Van Roop," she said. "It's so wonderful of you to come, Mr. Qwilleran. All the ladies are waiting in the parlor."

Janelle led him to a room that was bright and cheerful, with white lace curtains on the tall narrow windows. As they entered, applause came from twelve pairs of frail hands. Widows with silver hair and pretty blouses sat in a circle.

"Good afternoon, ladies," Qwilleran said in a mellifluous voice.

"It's a great pleasure to meet so many loyal readers, looking so festive and so . . . fetching."

There was a general murmur of excitement.

As he and Janelle moved clockwise around the room, he cupped each extended hand in both of his. He paid compliments, asked questions, and proffered greetings from Koko and Yum Yum. The exploits of the Siamese were often reported in the "Qwill Pen" column, and many of the women inquired about their health.

A few women had canes by their sides; the last in the circle was in a wheelchair. She was introduced as Rebecca Hawley.

"I've made something for you, Mr. Q.," she said, and handed him a roll of linen tied with a red ribbon, like a diploma.

He unrolled it slowly, then stared at it in disbelief. The painstakingly embroidered words stared back at him—his own words:

CATS ARE CATS . . . THE WORLD OVER!

THESE INTELLIGENT, PEACE-LOVING FOUR-FOOTED FRIENDS—
WHO ARE WITHOUT PREJUDICE, WITHOUT HATE, WITHOUT
GREED—MAY SOMEDAY TEACH US SOMETHING.

—THE QWILL PEN

"I'm overwhelmed," he said. The words were from a column published the previous fall. "If it had been chiseled in marble, it couldn't have been more of an honor. I'll think of you every time I see it."

"Oh, my!" Mrs. Hawley put her bony hands to her face and rocked back and forth in pleased embarrassment.

Janelle spoke up. "Thank you, Mr. Q., for paying us this visit."

"My pleasure," he said, throwing a final salute to his fans.

In the foyer Janelle seemed nervous. "Please, Mr. Q., somebody wants to see you privately. She's waiting in the office."

The office was a small space, equipped with desk, filing cabinet, and two institutional chairs. Perched primly on one of the hard seats was Doris Hawley. She jumped to her feet.

"Mrs. Hawley! What a surprise," he said. "I've been wondering about you."

"This was the only way I could think of to talk to you without being seen. Do you mind if I close the door?"

"I'll close it. But why the secrecy, Mrs. Hawley?"

"The state troopers don't want us to talk to anybody—Magnus and me—and if we talk to the media, we could be arrested."

"You identified the hiker's body?"

"Yes. Magnus asked them why we couldn't talk, but all they'd say was 'State bureau of investigation orders.' "

"It seems like high-handed treatment," Qwilleran said. "I suggest you remove the burlap sack from your sign and get back into the baking business. And if there's a single objection from the police, phone me."

Mrs. Hawley was grateful to the point of tears.

As he walked to his van, Qwilleran pondered the small intrigues that occur in small towns. The SBI had overreacted, assuming that townsfolk would panic if faced with something hard to explain.

ON THE way back to town Qwilleran's watch told him that Derek might be at Elizabeth's Magic, cooling off after his steamy lunch hour at Owen's Place. Derek had a play to do that evening; there would be theater talk as well as restaurant talk.

Derek had not yet arrived. Elizabeth said he was rearranging the tables as a surprise for the boss.

"Have you met Ernie?" Qwilleran asked. "What's she like?"

"Very nice, but she's a person with an intense drive. Here comes Derek."

He blustered into the shop with his usual energy. "I'm thirsty. Got anything cold?" He bounded to the rear, where there was a small refrigerator beneath the coffeemaker, then flopped into a chair with a bottle of chilled grape juice.

Qwilleran joined him. "Do you have any problem shifting gears from cuisine to showbiz?"

"Nah. It's all showbiz."

"Too bad Ernie can't take an evening off to see you act."

"She'd never go to the theater. She's a workaholic," Derek said. "Did you see that big recreation vehicle behind the restaurant? It's full of cookbooks."

Derek knew Qwilleran liked to hear the story behind the story.

"The way it works, I report at ten thirty a.m. Owen is there to check me in. We count the cash together, and I sign for it. Then he takes off with his bait bucket for a few hours of fishing—or that's what he says. But there's liquor on his breath already! Makes you wonder what's in the bait bucket."

Qwilleran said, "Does Ernie ever go out in the lake with him?"

"Only on Mondays, when we're closed. And then I'll bet she takes cookbooks. I think she worries about his drinking. She made two mistakes last week because she wasn't concentrating—like making a BLT without the T. Then a Monte Cristo with mushroom sauce didn't have the sauce. Well, I've gotta go home and make an adjustment from dumb earthling to smart alien."

DRIVING home along the shore, Qwilleran saw a vehicle approach from the east and turn into his drive. He stepped on the gas. It was a green van he could not recognize, and he was wary of uninvited visitors. Yum Yum had been kidnapped once, and he had never forgotten the horror of coming home and finding her gone.

By the time the van pulled into the clearing, Qwilleran was right on its tail. He jumped out to confront the driver.

"Bushy!" he shouted. "Why didn't you let me know—"

Stepping out of the green van was a young man in a baseball cap: John Bushland, photographer for the *Something*.

"I phoned. No answer, so I took a chance. I had a shoot in the neighborhood—the Ogilvie family reunion."

"Well, come in and have a gin and tonic."

Bushy leaned on the bar while Qwilleran mixed his drink and opened a ginger ale for himself. "Where are the cats?" Bushy asked.

"Asleep somewhere."

"Then I can speak freely. Those guys are finally licked. I've sent for the trick lens."

For years Bushy had been trying to take a photo that would land Koko and Yum Yum on the cover of a cat calendar, but they had thwarted his efforts. Now Bushy had tracked down a trick lens for photographing reluctant subjects without their knowledge.

"Good," Qwilleran said.

They carried their drinks to the porch and absorbed the view: blue sky, blue lake with white sails skimming across the horizon.

"Did you know I've got a new boat?" Bushy said. "Twenty-four-foot cuddy cruiser. I'd like to take you for a cruise."

"Okay, I'll put my life on the line," Qwilleran said.

Bushy said, "I was thinking about tomorrow. The weather's going to be perfect, and I thought we could pick up some pasties at the Nasty Pasty and have lunch on board."

Qwilleran was inordinately fond of pasties. "What time? Where?" he asked.

AFTER Bushy had left, Qwilleran phoned Mitch Ogilvie, a goat farmer he knew. "I hear you had a family reunion today, Mitch. Would you happen to know the two Ogilvie women who do hand spinning?"

"Sure, that would be Alice and her daughter. Her husband has the sheep ranch on Sandpit Road."

"If I wrote a column on hand spinning," Qwilleran asked, "would Alice make a good interview? Is she an authority?"

"Definitely. She sells her yarn to weavers and knitters all over the country. Her daughter has started a knitting club."

Next Qwilleran phoned the sheep ranch, but there was no answer. He chose not to leave a message, but applied himself to his theater review for Monday's paper. He sprawled in a lounge chair on the porch, writing on a legal pad while the Siamese napped.

Every once in a while Qwilleran looked up from his pad, and his eyes fell on Koko. In one of these interludes he saw Koko raise his head suddenly and crane his neck toward the lake. A few minutes later a figure came into view: a young woman in black tights, a leopard shirt, black baseball cap, and jogging shoes. She was not the usual beachcomber in shorts and T-shirt.

Qwilleran walked to the top of the sand ladder. When she came close enough, he called out, "Good afternoon. Beautiful day."

Startled, she looked up, nodded, and labored on. In half an hour she was back, trudging without looking to right or left.

FOUR

WHEN Qwilleran went to the drugstore Sunday morning to pick up his *New York Times*, who should be doing the same thing but Arch Riker. "Had your breakfast?" Qwilleran asked him.

"Sure have! Pecan waffles and sausages. But I'll have a cup of coffee with you if you're getting something to eat."

They crossed the street to the Northern Lights Hotel and took a table in the coffee shop, overlooking the harbor. Mrs. Stacy rushed forward to greet them. As co-owner, her job was to keep guests happy; her husband, Wayne, solved the problems.

"Could I bring you gentlemen some coffee?"

Qwilleran ordered ham and eggs and country fries without consulting the menu.

"What have you heard from Polly?" Riker asked.

"Just a shower of postcards. She and her sister are whooping it up in Ontario. . . ." Qwilleran's attention wandered.

"What are you staring at?"

"A woman sitting alone at a table in the corner. She's the same one who walked along my beach yesterday, looking aloof. She still looks as if she wishes she were somewhere else."

Qwilleran stood up and tossed his napkin on the chair seat. "I'll be back in a minute." He crossed to the table where the woman was preparing to leave. "Excuse me," he said respectfully, "but are you Dr. Frobnitz from Branchwater University?"

"No," she said curtly.

"I'm sorry. I was sure you were—"

"Well, I'm not!" she snapped, standing and shouldering her handbag with pointed annoyance.

"Please forgive the intrusion," he called as she left. To Mrs. Stacy, who had observed the encounter, he explained, "I thought she was someone else. Do you know who she is?"

"She's not registered here, but she's been coming here for meals. She must be staying at the motel. She's very standoffish."

Qwilleran looked smug as he returned to his table.

"What was that performance all about?" Riker asked.

"I just wanted to hear her say a few words. I thought she might be from the SBI, investigating the backpacker case, but she sounds more Main Line than bureaucratic."

"For your information, Qwill, that case is dead. The closure will be in tomorrow's paper: death attributed to natural causes."

"Hmff," Qwilleran murmured. There was more to the mystery than the cause of death, according to Andrew Brodie.

Riker said, "Millie is making lamb stew and inviting singles to dinner tomorrow night. Why don't you join us? Lisa Compton will be there because Lyle has a conference in Duluth. Roger is coming because Sharon and the kids are taking an overnight bus trip to a hands-on museum in Lockmaster."

"What time?"

"Six, for drinks."

AFTER breakfast Qwilleran was ready for his boating date. He went down the pier to *The Viewfinder*. It was a sleek white cruiser with V hull and open cockpit. Bushy was pumped up with pride.

"Neat craft," Qwilleran said. "Great deck space."

Bushy pointed out the two-person helm station and amenities belowdecks: four berths, a slick head, and galley with refrigerator, stove, and sink. "I've gotta work a lot harder to pay for this baby," he admitted.

With both men seated behind the windshield, the craft moved slowly out of the dock, putting on exhilarating speed when open water was reached.

"This bucket really moves," Qwilleran said.

"And steers like a dream," Bushy boasted.

"What's our destination?" Qwilleran asked as the boat skimmed over the glassy lake.

"I thought it would be nice to go to the lighthouse," Bushy said. He pointed out islands, shoals, and fishing banks.

Near the Pirate Shoals they spotted a cabin cruiser and a speedboat lashed together starboard to starboard.

"Looks like some kind of hanky-panky," Bushy said.

Training binoculars on the tête-à-tête, Qwilleran reported, "No one visible in either boat. Maybe they're below in the galley, making bacon, lettuce, and tomato sandwiches."

"Ha!" Bushy said in derision. "Can you see a name on the transom of the cruiser?"

"It looks like *Suncatcher*. Does that ring a bell?"

"Nah. I'll circle so you can see the name on the speedboat."

It was an older craft. Its name was *Fast Mama*. There was no registration tag visible. Qwilleran said to Bushy, "Let's take off before they get the idea we're tabloid journalists and start shooting at us."

The Viewfinder moved quietly away and a few minutes later passed the south end of Grand Island, where there was a marina with yachts and sailboats from Chicago. Beyond that were the palatial "cottages" of summer people from Down Below. At the north end the lighthouse stood on a rockbound promontory.

"Here's where we'll anchor," Bushy said.

Pasties were a perfect picnic food, and the Nasty Pasty had also packed apples, coconut cupcakes, and a thermos of coffee.

Qwilleran said, "You once told me about some kind of incident when you were out fishing."

"Yeah. It was my old boat. I was on the lake all by myself, fishing for bass. All at once I had a strange feeling I wasn't alone. I looked up, and there was a silver disk with portholes! Before I could get out my camera, the thing disappeared in a flash."

Qwilleran listened with his usual skepticism, although he tried not to show it.

"I have a theory," Bushy said. "You know how the beach has changed this summer—not just in front of your cabin but for miles along the north shore? The loose sand has blown up into a ridge, all the way from Fishport to Purple Point. Okay, now flash back to the time when the spacecraft was right over my head; when it zoomed away, there was a rush of air more powerful than anything I've experienced in a hurricane. It lasted only a second or two."

"Are you suggesting that one or more spacecraft followed the line of the shore, rolling up sand like a carpet?"

"You've got it!" Bushy said with a look of triumph that was followed by silent indecision. Qwilleran waited for the next revelation. "I don't know whether I should tell you this," the young man finally ventured. "It's confidential, but . . . Roger MacGillivray has access to the sheriff's office, and there was something unusual about the backpacker's body when it was found. It was found in the rolled-up hill of sand, so . . . You can put two and two together."

"I see what you mean," Qwilleran said, meaning just that and nothing more. He could have revealed who found the body. Instead he said, "Bushy, this has been a great outing. Thanks for inviting me."

The Viewfinder skimmed across the miles to shore. The Sunday afternoon skippers were now swarming over the lake. Qwilleran was thankful to be back on dry land.

Driving back to the cabin, he looked forward to the sanity of the domestic scene, and he received an ankle-rubbing welcome. Koko had been on the bookshelves and had dislodged a book as a subtle reminder that they were entitled to a Sunday afternoon reading session. It was a Mark Twain novella, *A Horse's Tale,* about an army horse who saved a young girl from wolves. It was a good choice, lending itself to the sound effects that would excite the Siamese: neighing, whinnying, snorting, and, of course, the howling of a wolf pack.

ON MONDAY morning Qwilleran faxed his theater review for that day's edition. Next he called Alice Ogilvie at the sheep ranch. The woman who answered the phone had a vigorous voice and outgoing personality. He accepted her invitation to come for coffee and doughnuts, and drove to the ranch, which was on Sandpit Road, two miles south of the shore.

When Qwilleran drove up to the Ogilvies' sprawling old farmhouse, he was met by Alice, in jeans and a western shirt. She ushered him through the side door into a large kitchen, where they sat at a table for coffee and doughnuts. They were real friedcakes, prepared that morning because Alice was taking them to a coffee hour at the church.

Qwilleran said, "I've been reading *Far from the Madding Crowd* and find myself identifying with sheepkeepers."

"Our family," Alice said, "has worn out three copies of that book over the years. It's surprising how little sheepkeeping has changed in two centuries."

"What do you spin other than wool?" Qwilleran asked.

"Silk, cotton, angora from rabbits, even a little dog hair blended with other fibers. It's hard-wearing. For socks, you know. Want to see the spinning studio where I give lessons?"

The spinning wheel caught his eye. It had a ten-spoke flywheel, tilted bench with treadle underneath, and a post holding a cornhusk bobbin. A hundred years old, Alice said.

On a table was a thick blanket of fleece, exactly as it came from a ewe on shearing day—white on the inside, weathered on the outside. Alice said it would be torn apart and laundered before being carded and fluffed up. Finally it would be combed and rolled into rovings to feed into the spinning wheel.

She demonstrated at a contemporary wheel—compact, with a well-engineered head assembly and a proper bobbin. Treadling with a foot, she pinched fibers from a roving to feed with rhythmic movements of both hands while talking of ratio, tension, ply, and texture.

Outside the window a pickup truck came to an abrupt stop, a door slammed, and footsteps came down a hall.

"My daughter," Alice explained. "She's been in Pickax renewing her driver's license." She appeared in the doorway. "Qwill," her mother said, "this is my daughter, Barbara."

"Call me Barb," the young woman said. "I hate Barbara."

Her mother smiled and shrugged. "By any name she's my one and only daughter and a very talented knitter. She'll tell you all about it. I have to take my doughnuts to the church."

As soon as she had left, Barb said, "Do you smoke? Let's go out on the porch. Alice doesn't let me smoke indoors."

They went to the side porch, where Barb sat cross-legged on a glider. She had long, straight blond hair and sultry eyes that were heavy with makeup. She shifted her eyes from side to side as she talked—half smiling when Qwilleran complimented her on the knit vest she was wearing. It was white with a multicolor pattern of fireworks in the stitchery.

"Tell me about the knitting club," he asked.

"It's unisex. We get together once a week around our big kitchen table, and we laugh a lot—and learn. Then I have a knitting day camp for kids every Saturday."

"What do they knit?"

"Socks. Goofy socks. Socks are a good way to begin knitting." Barb jumped off the glider. "I'll show you. I make 'em to sell at Elizabeth's."

She returned with a boxful of mismatched pairs in wild mixes of colors and patterns: stripes, plaids, zigzags, and confetti dots.

"Do people actually buy these?"

"As fast as I can knit them. I also have non-goofy stuff on display at Elizabeth's—vests, scarves, mittens, hats."

"Where have you been hiding your talent?" he asked.

"I've been living Down Below. I came home a couple of winters ago," she said with a shrug of dissatisfaction.

"Why did you leave in the first place?"

"You really wanna know?" She slouched down on the glider. "My girlfriend and I decided there weren't any interesting guys around here, so we went to Florida. I met a cool guy who was a balloon chaser." Her eyes swiveled pleasurably at the recollection.

"What kind of balloons did he chase?"

"Hot-air balloons. They lift off and drift away, and the chaser follows in a truck so he can pick up the passengers, the envelope, and the basket. I worked weekends in the support crew."

Qwilleran said, "It seems to me that the pilot has all the fun and the chaser does all the work."

"No, no. It's exciting!"

"If you found it so thrilling, why did you come home?"

She lowered her eyes. "My balloon chaser wasn't all that interested in a country girl. Then I started dating an older man who really liked me, only I found out he was married. So I came home."

Another truck turned into the driveway.

"Here's Alice," she said. "Gotta empty the ashtray."

QWILLERAN drove back to town thinking that the plight of an ex–balloon chaser was more interesting than the operation of antique spinning wheels, though less suitable for his column.

In Mooseville he proceeded to wait for the newspaper truck from Pickax; the Monday edition would carry his theater review and the closure of the backpacker case. The truck from the printing plant was always late on Mondays. Fortunately, one could kill time at the Northern Lights Hotel. Qwilleran mounted the broad flight of wooden steps to the wide porch that overlooked Main Street.

"Coming for lunch?" Mrs. Stacy greeted him in the lobby.

"I might have a sandwich," he said. "What's the chopper doing over the lake?" The sheriff's helicopter could be seen in the distance, making wide circles.

"Looks like a boating emergency. I hope it's nothing serious. By the way, you know that woman you spoke to in the coffee shop yesterday? She's been in twice more."

"She must like your food," he said.

"I don't know about that. She eats like a bird."

Qwilleran had a ham-and-cheese sandwich and a cup of tomato soup, and still the Monday papers had not arrived, so he sat on the veranda and watched the activity on the waterfront.

The helicopter was still hovering, and after a while an ambulance drove to the end of the main pier and waited. A cabin cruiser was heading for shore at a fast clip. When it docked, a sheriff's deputy jumped to the wharf and conferred with the two medics. A wheelchair was rolled out, and a young woman in deck wear and a visored cap was helped off the boat and wheeled to the hotel's side door on the lower level.

Qwilleran's curiosity exceeded his interest in Monday's paper. He returned to the lobby in time to see an elevator door open and one of the medics hurry to the manager's office; the other stayed in the elevator with the woman, who was wearing dark glasses. Mrs. Stacy was brought to the elevator, and a pantomime ensued: questioning, advising, urging. Mrs. Stacy hurried back to her office, and the elevator ascended with the patient and the two attendants.

Now captivated by the melodrama, Qwilleran stationed himself where he could see both elevator and office. Mrs. Stacy was making urgent phone calls. The elevator signal indicated that the car had stopped at the second floor. Soon after, Mrs. Stacy left her office and ran up a nearby flight of stairs, whereupon the elevator came down with the emergency personnel and wheelchair.

Qwilleran saw Derek Cuttlebrink rushing into the building and bounding up the stairs, after which Mrs. Stacy came slowly down the same flight, looking disturbed.

Qwilleran called to her, "Mrs. Stacy, what's wrong?"

"Come in the office, Mr. Q., and have a cup of coffee," she said. "I need one. I feel so sorry for that poor woman." She peered across the lobby. "There's my husband. Wayne, come in here!"

The hotelkeeper joined them, nodding to Qwilleran. "Just got back from Pickax. What happened?"

"One of our guests drowned," his wife said. "Owen Bowen."

"No! Any details?"

"Nothing much. He and Mrs. Bowen were boating on their day off, and she radioed for help. The helicopter's been searching for more than an hour."

"Where is she now?"

"Upstairs. She asked me to call their assistant manager."

Wayne Stacy, who was president of the chamber of commerce, said, "I wonder if there's something the chamber can do for her. The restaurant may never reopen. Darn shame!"

Qwilleran spoke for the first time. "The chef is called the kingpin of a restaurant, and this one is dedicated to her profession. I predict the operation will continue after a suitable hiatus."

"I hope so," Mrs. Stacy said. "They say she's a wonderful chef."

NEXT QWILLERAN WALKED TO Elizabeth's Magic. Although it was closed on Mondays, she would be there, totaling the previous week's receipts. He rapped on the glass, and she ran to the door.

Her first breathless words were, "Qwill, have you heard—?"

"Shocking, isn't it? How did you find out?"

"Mrs. Stacy was trying to locate Derek, and he happened to be doing some work for me. He rushed over to the hotel."

"Do you expect him to come back?"

Before she could answer, Derek charged into the shop, saying, "Weird accident. You won't believe it."

The three of them huddled in the chairs at the rear as he told what he knew. "They went out in the boat and anchored somewhere and had a picnic lunch. Ernie had some red wine and got tipsy, so she went below for a nap, leaving Owen to do some fishing. Suddenly she woke up because the boat was rocking violently. She called to Owen, and he didn't answer. She climbed up the ladder, and he was gone! Then she radioed for help. That's all I know."

Qwilleran said, "Did she explain his disappearance?"

"Yeah. He'd been drinking a lot. She thinks they got caught in the wake of another boat and he fell overboard."

"Could be," Qwilleran said, although a nagging sensation in the roots of his mustache was telling him, Not so. Not so.

Derek said, "I imagine she'll want to sell the boat; it was Owen's plaything. What she likes is the RV. It has all her cookbooks, and it's kind of cozy."

"Well, I've got commitments to take care of," Qwilleran said. "I'll leave you two to finish your work."

HALFWAY between the unhappy news about Owen Bowen and the happy prospect of dinner with the Rikers, Qwilleran received a phone call that left him with mixed reactions.

Wetherby Goode, the WPKX meteorologist—whose real name was Joe Bunker—had been his neighbor in the Indian Village condominiums, and he was good company. An unstoppable extrovert, he played cocktail piano at parties and boasted about being a native of Horseradish in Lockmaster County, once the horseradish capital of the Midwest. Like Qwilleran a divorced man, he lived alone—with a male cat named Jet Stream.

Earlier in the year Wetherby had talked about his cousin, Dr. Teresa Bunker, a corvidologist. She wanted to produce an animated feature film about crows and was looking for a collaborator. In a weak moment Qwilleran said he would be interested.

Wetherby had said that his cousin would be coming up to visit her family in the summer and would like to meet Qwilleran and discuss a scenario for the film. Now summer was here, and Wetherby was calling to say, "She's coming. She's coming."

"Who's coming?" Qwilleran demanded.

"My cousin Tess. She's driving up. She's already left. I don't know her itinerary, but I gave her your number at the beach so you two can plan a meeting."

"Tell me something about your cousin," Qwilleran asked, thinking he should have asked the question a few months earlier.

"Well, she's a little younger than I am. A lot of fun. Likes to do things on the spur of the moment."

Fighting his compunctions, Qwilleran said, "Okay, I'll expect her call. By the way, what does Dr. Bunker drink?"

"Anything, but she's crazy about mint juleps. And call her Tess. She likes to be called Tess."

QWILLERAN fed the cats early and announced, "I'm having dinner with Uncle Arch and Aunt Mildred. I'll be home around dark, and we'll sit on the porch and look at the stars."

He started down the beach, marveling at the lake. The sky and water were turquoise, and a low cloud bank on the horizon resembled a mountain range.

At Sunny Daze, Arch was waiting at the top of the sand ladder, and Qwilleran handed him two bottles of wine from a canvas bag. Qwilleran asked Lisa Compton, who was there without her husband, "How's life without Lyle?"

"Serene," she answered promptly.

Mildred served zucchini fritters with a dill-yogurt dip, and

Qwilleran presented her with a set of rune-stones he had purchased. She promised to tell fortunes the next time they met. Roger MacGillivray hoped the stones would predict rain.

"It's dangerously dry. I worry about forest fires," he said. "Even the Sand Giant is worried. People think they're hearing distant thunder, but it's really the old boy growling in his cave."

Qwilleran, who was collecting local legends for a book to be titled *Short & Tall Tales,* said, "Would you explain the Sand Giant to me? I just happen to have my tape recorder here."

"Sure," Roger said, relishing an audience. "The history of the Sand Giant goes way back. The first explorers in this region arrived by sailing ship and made camp on the beach at the base of a huge wall of sand. Strangely, they claimed to hear rumbling inside the dune, and some nights they could see a large gray shape moving among the trees on the summit. Being superstitious in those days, they decided a giant lived in a cave inside the dune. They often saw things that weren't there."

"Still do," Riker muttered. Qwilleran nodded and chuckled.

"Through the years," Roger went on, "the Sand Giant continued to prowl and growl. In the mid–nineteenth century wealthy lumbermen got the idea of building fine houses on top of the Great Dune, as it was then called. As soon as they started cutting down the ancient hardwoods, a giant sand slide engulfed the lumber camp, killing everybody. Old-timers said the lumbermen had offended the Sand Giant. My grandparents believed that absolutely."

"Great story," Qwilleran said, turning off the recorder.

"Interesting," was Arch's reluctant comment.

"Dinner is served," Mildred announced. It was squash bisque, lamb stew, crusty bread, and green salad. Dessert and coffee were served on the deck, during which Qwilleran and Arch entertained everybody with a tell-all session about growing up in Chicago. The evening ended with laughter.

When Qwilleran returned to his cabin, the Siamese were waiting with the tranquillity that indicated some mischief had been done. Polly's postcards, which had been stacked on the bar, were now scattered about the floor.

THE day after the Owen Bowen incident Qwilleran fed the Siamese and thawed the last one of Doris Hawley's cinnamon rolls. He telephoned, and she answered cheerily—a good sign. There were cinnamon rolls in the oven, she said.

"Save a whole pan for me," he requested. "I'm heading for Fishport."

There the Roaring Creek was reduced to a gurgle by the lack of rain and the Hawleys' lawn looked sadly thirsty. The burlap sack had been removed from the home-bakes sign, however. He rapped on the side door; Doris Hawley answered his knock. "You haven't heard the latest, Mr. Q. Come in the kitchen and have a cup of tea."

The kitchen was heady with the aroma of baking gingersnaps.

"Sunday afternoon," she began, "a woman came to the door wanting to talk to the last ones who saw David alive. She was his partner, she said. She'd come from Philadelphia to claim the body and his belongings."

"What was she like?" Qwilleran asked. "I think I saw her at the hotel and walking on the beach."

Doris's description matched his. "She was kind of stiff at first but softened up when I talked about David and what a nice young man he was. He worked with computers, she said, but his hobby was UFOs, and he'd heard we had lots of sightings here."

Qwilleran huffed into his mustache.

"The SBI had taken the film from his camera and wouldn't give it to her, and they warned her not to discuss the matter—the way they did us. What do you think about UFOs, Mr. Q.?"

"I try to keep an open mind," he said, "but I think official attempts at cover-up are a trifle absurd."

THE TRUTH WAS THAT QWILLERAN was beginning to find the topic tiresome. When he returned to Mooseville, however, he found the townsfolk debating another hot topic: the Owen Bowen incident. At the drugstore, he bought the newspaper. A news item on the front page read:

M'VILLE MAN LOST ON LAKE

The owner of a new Mooseville restaurant was reported missing Monday, following an unexplained incident aboard his cabin cruiser. Owen Bowen, forty-eight, proprietor of Owen's Place, sailed from the municipal pier shortly before noon. With him was his wife, Ernestine, twenty-seven, chef at the restaurant.

They anchored and had a picnic lunch aboard, after which Bowen dropped two lines off the stern. His wife took a nap in the cabin below. She woke to find the craft rolling violently and her husband missing from the open deck.

The sheriff's marine patrol responded immediately to her call for help but found no trace of Bowen.

A spokesperson for the sheriff's department said, "After an exhaustive search and investigation the conclusion is that the twenty-five-foot craft was caught in the wake of a larger boat and Bowen was thrown off-balance. Only a few minutes in the icy water north of the lighthouse can cause death by hypothermia."

Owen's Place, a summer operation of a Florida restaurant, will remain closed until further notice.

QWILLERAN huffed into his mustache when he left the drugstore and walked around town. Eventually he found himself on Sandpit Road in front of Arnold's Antiques. In the window was his rusty wheel, and Qwilleran went in.

As he expected, Arnold's first words were, "Well, we lost our quirky neighbor. Do you think the Sand Giant got him?"

"I don't try to fathom the mysteries of this daft community, Arnold. I just came for my wheel."

Arnold took it from the window. "What'll you do with it?"

"Hang it in my cabin, over the fireplace." Qwilleran said he would bring his van, which was parked behind the bank.

On the way to the bank he realized there were no nails at the cabin. He detoured to the hardware store.

"Help you?" asked Cecil.

"Yes. I'm in the market for a couple of nails. I've bought an antique wheel to hang over the fireplace."

"What kind of wheel? How large? I'd better talk to our construction specialist. Unc, we have a technical problem."

The old uncle ambled over to the nail bin and went into a huddle with Cecil, discussing the kind of wall, number of spokes in the wheel, and width of the wheel rim.

"How much do I owe you?" Qwilleran asked when the experts had made their decision.

"No charge," said Cecil.

"That's generous of you."

The two storekeepers walked to the door with their customer, and Cecil said, "Can you believe that we've lost Owen?"

The old man said, "If he hadn't been soaked to the gills, it wouldn'ta happened."

Qwilleran asked, "How is his wife? Does anyone know?"

"She's better off without that horse's tail," the old man said.

In a flash an idea struck Qwilleran: Koko knew about Owen's death before and after the fact. Else, why his sudden interest in *A Horse's Tail?* The connection between a book title and an epithet bestowed on Owen Bowen would seem far-fetched to anyone but Qwilleran. Though Koko's communications were coincidental in the extreme, they always proved to be accurate.

HANGING the four-foot wheel over the fireplace was no easy task, and Qwilleran tackled it Wednesday morning when he was fresh. He climbed up a ladder, eyeballed the space, penciled two dots, hammered the nails into the wall, and hung the wheel. While up there he noticed a crack in the mantel, a square-cut, hand-hewn timber that spanned the width of the room. The crack was just wide enough for wedging postcards upright. More than a dozen had come from Canada, each with Polly's hurriedly scrawled message on the back. Together they made a pictorial frieze several feet long.

Polly and her sister had seen four plays: *Oedipus Rex, Macbeth, Major Barbara,* and *The Importance of Being Earnest.* The cards pictured a grotesque mask used in Greek drama, a sketch of Shakespeare, a portrait of George Bernard Shaw, and the Toulouse-Lautrec caricature of Oscar Wilde. Other cards had been mailed as they motored east: Niagara Falls, parliament buildings, a mountain lodge, and more.

As soon as Qwilleran opened the porch door, Koko bounded in to see the exhibit, walking behind the upstanding cards. He sniffed each like a connoisseur of fine wines. The cat finally gave his seal of approval, a gentle fang mark, to the two cards that were third and fourth from the left end of the row: portraits of the two Irish playwrights. Qwilleran thought, That cat. Now he's getting interested in dramaturgy.

AT THE Northern Lights Hotel, where Qwilleran went for a cup of coffee and some scuttlebutt, he was stopped in the lobby by Wayne Stacy. The hotelkeeper said, "Qwill. Just the guy I want to see. I have a favor to ask. Saturday we have the annual dogcart races sponsored by the chamber of commerce. Wetherby Goode usually announces them, but this year he's got a conflict—wedding or something. Could you help us out?"

"What does it entail?"

"You just announce each race, name the winners in each class, and hand out the trophies. You've got the voice for it."

Qwilleran appreciated compliments on his vocal quality. "What time on Saturday?"

"Eleven a.m. Come early and have breakfast with us."

"Okay," Qwilleran said. "And now tell me: How's Mrs. Bowen?"

"I haven't seen her. She has her meals sent up to her. But last night she ordered dinner for two and champagne!"

Qwilleran thought, Who was up there helping her drink the champagne? Derek? Qwilleran changed his mind about having a cup of hotel coffee and hustled to Elizabeth's Magic.

Derek was there, working. Barb Ogilvie was there, too, arranging a window display of her hand knits.

Elizabeth said, "Qwill, you should buy one of Barb's lovely vests for Polly as a welcome-home gift. When is she due to return?"

"I pick her up at the airport Monday."

"Barb could do a custom design for you. Barb, conference, please." To Qwilleran she whispered, "She's not herself today. Something's wrong. A special order might perk her up."

Elizabeth explained to Barb that Qwilleran's friend was returning from a long vacation on Monday and he wanted a very special gift for her. She would be thrilled with a Barb Ogilvie original.

"I'll see what I can do," said the knitter, and after some aimless puttering, she left and drove away in her pickup.

Qwilleran thought, She's argued with Alice about smoking, or she's having man trouble again.

Elizabeth, on the other hand, was elated. "We've had some good news," she said. "Ernie called Derek this morning. She wants to open next Tuesday—with a whole new menu, except that skewered potatoes will still be featured at lunchtime. Why don't you buy some skewers, Qwill? I know you don't cook, but they're decorative when hung on the kitchen wall."

"Whatever you say," he agreed.

"You're a dear, Qwill," she said. "I'll give you a set of five."

Qwilleran found Derek. "Hi, Mr. Q. I'm trying to finish some work for Liz before the restaurant opens Tuesday."

"Save me a table for two Tuesday night."

Derek approached Qwilleran in a confidential manner. "Ernie needs some cash flow, and she wants to sell the boat. I wish you'd have a look at it. Maybe you know somebody interested in a good deal."

"Where is the boat?"

"Near the marina office. It's the *Suncatcher*."

"*Suncatcher?*" Qwilleran stroked his mustache.

"Yeah. You'd think Owen would call it *Bottoms Up!*"

Clutching his package of skewers, Qwilleran walked briskly to the marina, and there was the *Suncatcher,* gleaming in the sun. Its pristine whiteness was marred only by a faint stain on the deck—about the size of a spilled glass of red wine.

What interested Qwilleran was whether or not it had been involved with *Fast Mama* and why. What was Owen's game? And was the speedboat again in the vicinity on the day he disappeared? Could Owen have been abducted while Ernie was sleeping off a wine jag below deck? And if so, was Owen murdered?

These were questions to discuss with Andrew Brodie over a nightcap at Qwilleran's Pickax address, and the sooner the better. Driving away from town, Qwilleran made his plans. This was Wednesday. He could move his household back to Pickax on Thursday, then drive to the shore briefly on Saturday morning to announce the dogcart races. On Monday he would pick up Polly at the airport, and Tuesday evening they would celebrate at the opening night of Owen's Place.

It was neat planning, but Robert Burns was right: The best-laid plans go off-line.

WHEN Qwilleran arrived at the cabin, the Siamese were lounging on the coffee table in a shaft of sunlight, their fur glistening. Qwilleran took a moment to admire them. "You are two gorgeous brutes." Koko, who was keeping the Mark Twain reference book warm, stared with meaningful intensity.

Qwilleran patted his mustache. On an impulse he phoned Hixie Rice, a promotion director for the *Moose County Something*.

"Hixie! I've just thought of a sensational idea to promote the city of Pickax—and the newspaper, too."

"Is it as big as the Great Food Explo?" she asked dubiously.

"Bigger."

"As big as the Ice Festival?"

"Bigger and guaranteed not to melt. How about meeting me for lunch tomorrow? I'd suggest Owen's Place, but you know what happened."

"How about Linguini's? The food is wonderful!"

"You might also bring Fran Brodie, if she's available."

"We'll be there, I promise," Hixie said.

After breakfast the next morning Qwilleran hung the skewers on the log wall above the kitchen counter. Koko sniffed the finger grips and touched the thin twisted skewers with a nervous paw. "Stay away from those," Qwilleran warned him. "They're for skewering potatoes, not members of the family."

Shortly before noon he set out for his lunch date. At the restaurant he was greeted by Mrs. Linguini. "Sit anywhere," she said.

Qwilleran took a table for four, and soon his guests bustled in excitedly, saying, "There he is. . . . Qwill, you look wonderful. . . . Your vacation agrees with you."

Standing to pull out their chairs, he responded with a frown. "I haven't had a minute's rest since coming to the beach. I do more loafing in Pickax. You two look as if you'd won the lottery!"

"We're excited about your secret project," Hixie explained.

"We've been making wild guesses," Fran added.

In Qwilleran's opinion they were the two most glamorous women in the county. The publicity woman was recklessly vivacious; the interior designer was coolly dynamic.

"First some wine," he said. It was immediately served in squat tumblers, with grape juice for the host. After they ordered, Qwilleran presented his proposition.

"Moose County has never been associated with a prominent literary figure. So I suggest we adopt one and observe his birthday. Mark Twain made Pickax one of his stops on a lecture tour, and the locals flocked to hear him speak. So I propose an annual Mark Twain celebration."

Fran said, "The theater club could do readings from his books or dramatizations from *Tom Sawyer* and *Huckleberry Finn*."

"We could have a parade—with floats!" Hixie said ecstatically.

"Why not rename a street Mark Twain Boulevard?"

Hixie squealed with delight. "We could have a Mark Twain Look-Alike Contest, and Qwill would win!"

"Qwill is handsomer. And sexier."

He huffed into his mustache. "Here comes the *nutrimento*."

Mrs. Linguini came from the kitchen, balancing three plates. She banged one down in front of Fran, saying, "Stuffed manicotti, very good." The next landed in front of Hixie. "Veal marsala, very good." Qwilleran got the third. "Lasagna, the best!"

After the frenzied brainstorming, they enjoyed lunch quietly, with only desultory conversation.

Fran shocked them with the news—confidential, of course—that Amanda Goodwinter was quitting the city council and running for mayor. Qwilleran said he would campaign for her.

Then Hixie said she had seen proof sheets of the first "Ask Ms. Gramma" column and had brought a set with her. "I think she wrote it with a pitcher of martinis on her desk," she said.

At her suggestion Qwilleran read it aloud at the table:

> "Dear sweet readers, Ms. Gramma was thrilled by your response to last week's announcement. It shows you care about saying it right. Stick around, and we'll have some fun, too.
>
> Dear Ms. Gramma, My two grown sons are educated and know better, but they still say 'he don't' instead of 'he doesn't.'— Pauline, in Pickax.
>
> Dear Pauline, Some men think 'he don't' is macho. Give up, my dear. The male animal is as stubborn as a mule—and we all know about mules, don't we?"

Fran interrupted. "Who's writing this column?"

"Only Junior Goodwinter knows," said Hixie.

"Well, I think it's a man."

"I do, too," said Qwilleran. "I also think it's not very good. Do you think it was written by a staffer or a freelancer?"

"I won't rest until I find out," Hixie said.

"Don't waste your time on Ms. Gramma," Qwilleran told her. "Apply your brain to a Mark Twain celebration."

SATISFIED with the lunch hour and looking forward to a return to Pickax, Qwilleran planned his exodus while driving back to the cabin. He bought a frozen dinner at a roadside convenience store and started watching for the old stone chimney. When he spotted the historic landmark, he also saw a yellow vehicle turning into the K driveway. It was a school bus!

Qwilleran was indignant. The bus was already in the clearing when he drove up and parked directly behind it. He jumped from the driver's seat, expecting to see a yardful of noisy kids. The only sign of life was a tall figure at the top of the sand ladder, gazing at the lake. Qwilleran noted a straw hat, jeans, field boots, and some kind of inscription on the back of a T-shirt.

"Hello, there!" he shouted with a note of annoyance.

The uninvited guest turned, revealing a life-size crow on the T-shirt. "You must be Qwill," she said. "I'm Tess, Joe Bunker's cousin."

"Oh! If I'd known you were coming, I'd have been here to welcome you," he said. "Go on the porch and make yourself comfortable while I put my purchases in the freezer."

Only then did he realize that the yellow vehicle, a minibus, was boldly labeled REPUBLIC OF CROWMANIA. Indoors, he briefed the cats. "We have company. Don't sniff her boots; it's considered impolite."

When he opened the door to the lake porch, Tess was sitting, with her hat off, her dark hair sleeked back into a bun. Her features were clean-cut, with thin lips and high cheekbones.

"How far have you traveled today?" he asked.

"From my aunt's house in Bixby. I tried calling you, and when there was no answer, I decided to take a chance and come anyway."

"Would you explain your bus?"

"I'd love to! It's used for field trips with students. As Joe may have told you, I believe crows are the next big craze. The crow is a noble bird—intelligent, rather handsome, well organized, cooperative, and focused. What's your reaction to crows, Qwill?"

"They all look alike."

"On the contrary, they have different personalities, physiques, and body language. Why don't we bring in my luggage, and I'll unpack, and then we'll talk some more."

Luggage? Joe had said nothing about her coming as a houseguest!

"Joe tells me you don't cook. I'd be glad to prepare meals while I'm here."

Meals? How long does she think she's staying?

"Just tell me what you like to eat," she said. "I make a fantastic macaroni and cheese with horseradish."

"First let's bring your luggage in," he said.

Together they carried two enormous duffel bags to the guesthouse. "It's small, but it has indoor plumbing," he said.

"It's cute," she said. "I love it!"

Qwilleran rushed back to the cabin to make his first mint julep. A few minutes later Tess came through the woods in a fresh denim shirt.

"How would you like a mint julep?" he asked.

"I love mint juleps!" she exclaimed. "But the doctor won't let me have anything stronger than wine. What are you drinking?"

"Ginger ale."

"Then I'll have the same." She wandered about, admiring the fireplace, the copper sailboat, the Mark Twain collection. She commented on the row of postcards. "There are two on the floor."

"They probably have fang marks in the corners," Qwilleran said. "Just put them on the coffee table." He had a hunch which two they would be: George Bernard Shaw with his beard, and Oscar Wilde with a posy in his buttonhole.

SIX

QWILLERAN took his houseguest to dinner at the Northern Lights Hotel, apologizing for the ordinary menu. They ordered Swiss steak and carrots. Qwilleran found Tess well read, well spoken, and not a bad-looking dinner date. They discussed cats—she had two—and journalism, but not a word about crows. Yet the sooner the crow-show was off the docket, the sooner he could take off for Pickax. For breakfast they would have coffee and rolls and then spend the morning talking crow, after which he would hope to see the tail-lights of the yellow bus disappearing down the driveway.

"Do you have any assurance that your film will be produced?" he asked.

"Definitely! The university has the grant. My responsibility is to provide the scenario. I left a dossier on your bar—papers I've written for scientific journals. You can read them tomorrow while I run into town. Do you have a market that sells good meat? One of my specialties is lamb shank with beans, lumberjack-style."

That was one of Qwilleran's absolute favorites. Okay, he thought, she can stay a second night. He said, "Grott's Grocery cuts meat to order and cheese from the wheel."

Then a surge of hospitality prompted him to say, "Would you like to see a play at the barn theater tomorrow night?"

"I love barn theater!" she said.

FRIDAY morning Qwilleran served a continental breakfast on the kitchen porch. He thawed cinnamon rolls and pressed the button on the automated coffeemaker. The Siamese joined them, looking for warm concrete on which to sun. Koko stretched out full length to do his grooming in solarized comfort.

"He's a ham," Qwilleran explained to Tess. "He likes an audience for his morning ablutions."

"Stop and think: For centuries, cats have been washing up in the same way, while we go on inventing revolutionary improvements that may or may not be successful or even necessary," Tess said.

"Avoid radical theories in Mooseville," he advised. "Incidentally, while you're there, be sure to visit Elizabeth's Magic on Oak Street."

AFTER the yellow bus had wheeled down the driveway, Qwilleran took the file of crow literature to the lake porch and read it carefully. There was nothing that made crows seem glamorous or heroic. They had repulsive feeding habits. They enjoyed pulling the tails of dogs, sheep, and birds. Some of their hobbies bordered on the kinky, like encouraging ants to run through their feathers.

"Please!" he said in repugnance. Qwilleran threw the dossier aside and drove into Mooseville to buy red wine and fruit juices for sangria. He found Tess's yellow bus on the hotel parking lot, surrounded by excited tourists. Tess stood on the bottom step of the bus and answered questions.

Qwilleran went to Elizabeth's Magic to inquire about his special order.

"Barb assured me she'll finish it on time," Elizabeth said. "And thank you, Qwill, for sending me that delightful Dr. Bunker. She loved everything in my shop and bought several things."

"Did she talk about crows?"

"Enthusiastically! I said I would be willing to sell T-shirts like hers if the proceeds went to scientific research."

"Good for you!"

TESS would be returning to the cabin to prepare dinner, and Qwilleran intended to stay out of sight lest he be asked to peel potatoes. He sat on the hotel veranda to consider the crow scenario. He was definitely cooling off, but how to break the news to Tess? He would conclude the matter after the play. Then she could leave after breakfast, and he could return to Pickax after the dogcart races.

All went well that evening: Qwilleran thought the lamb shank superb; Tess loved the play. Afterward he served sangria on the lake porch and said, "Tess, your visit has been memorable. I only wish I could work on your project. Unfortunately, I have other commitments. But I can visualize the possibilities and decisions."

"I understand," she said. "What kind of decisions do you mean?"

"In regard to the plot: Who or what will provide the conflict? Other species of birds? Other wildlife? Humans? Mechanical equipment? Scarecrows?"

Tess asked, "What about dialogue?"

"Well, you might have all the animals in the cast speak in their own voices—with a human voice-over translating their caws and clucks and woofs."

"What language do you suppose scarecrows speak?"

"That's one for the language department at your university." Qwilleran smoothed his mustache as an idea began to form. "The scarecrow's job is to protect the crops from the crows, right? Suppose he makes friends with the crows and starts an underground movement in their behalf."

"I love it! I love it!" she cried.

"May I refresh your drink, Tess?"

It was a happy corvidologist who took the electric lantern and found her way to the snuggery. Before saying good night, she said, "Do you realize you have thimbleberries behind the toolshed? I could make thimbleberry pancakes for breakfast."

"Splendid idea," Qwilleran said.

"And Grott's Grocery had some beautiful rib-eye steaks. I bought two, thinking we could have steak au poivre tomorrow night—with skewered potatoes." Before Qwilleran could react, she said, "Do you realize one of the skewers is missing? There were five."

AFTER the thimbleberry pancakes Qwilleran drove to Mooseville for the dogcart races. He had never seen so many kids in one place. Both hotel lots were cleared for official use: one marked as a race-track, the other serving as a paddock.

Wayne Stacy spotted Qwilleran and explained the system. Forty youngsters would ride in forty toy wagons hitched to forty family pets. The dogs wore boleros in the family's racing colors. Wagons were decorated with crepe paper, and the young drivers were in costume. There were astronauts, ballerinas, cowboys and -girls mingling with the dogs, adults, and numerous harassed officials.

When Qwilleran went to the mike, the first whistle blew. Spectators cheered their favorites and screamed at unexpected happenings. Once, a basset hound left the track in midcourse and trotted to the sidelines for some sociability. Another time, two dogs started to fight and dumped their drivers.

The grand champion was a black Labrador in a red, white, and blue bolero, with a seven-year-old astronaut for a driver.

Qwilleran said to the astronaut's father, "Nice dog you've got."

"Right! Einstein is a retired G-dog, trained to do drug search. Very intelligent. When he detects somethin', he just sits down."

"Is that so?" Qwilleran patted his mustache. "I just had a crazy idea," he said. "There's a boat over here that I'm thinking of buying. Would Einstein give it a sniff?"

"Sure. He'd probably enjoy it."

The two men and the dog walked over to the *Suncatcher* and went aboard. Einstein gave a passing sniff at the stain on the deck, but it was the cabin that interested him. They took him below. He inspected everything—and sat down.

"He's tired," said the father. "He's had a hard day."

DRIVING back to his cabin, Qwilleran pounded his mustache with his fist. Now he had something pertinent to discuss with Brodie: first the rendezvous of the *Suncatcher* and *Fast Mama,* then Owen's disappearance, then Einstein's behavior.

As for his houseguest, he would drop some leading remarks into the dinner conversation about her leaving on Sunday morning.

The excellent dinner was served on the porch, and Qwilleran dropped his hints as planned.

During the soup course (she made gazpacho): "I hope you've found this trip worthwhile."

With the steak: "They're expecting violent weather tomorrow."

With the dessert: "How long does it take to drive to Horseradish?"

Immune to Qwilleran's dropped hints, she said, "Do you realize that Grott's Grocery carries duck eggs? I couldn't resist buying four for breakfast. We'll have mushroom omelettes. I also bought some of their cheddar for macaroni and cheese. I'll prepare a casserole after breakfast, and we'll have it for lunch."

She had touched the two most vulnerable spots in his considerable appetite. Defeated, he mumbled, "Sounds good."

ON SUNDAY morning the sun was shining despite the weather warnings of rain, and Tess came from the snuggery in shorts, sandals, and a T-shirt depicting three nest-builder crows.

"Everyone out of the kitchen!" she ordered cheerily. "The poor man's Julia Child is about to perform miracles. By the way," she added as she picked up a skewer from the countertop, "one of these skewers keeps falling off its nail."

"It's no accident," Qwilleran said. "Koko thinks it's a toy. It was a mistake to hang them there."

Qwilleran got out of her way and went onto the lake porch to wait for the omelettes. From the kitchen came aromas of melting butter, brewing coffee, sautéing mushrooms, and toasting muffins.

With great feelings of satisfaction, he prefigured his reunion with Polly. She would be pleased with her new vest and would undoubtedly bring him something from Canada.

When breakfast was served, Qwilleran paraphrased Dickens. "There never was such an omelette!"

"Thank you," Tess said. "I admit that I make the world's best."

After breakfast, when Tess was assembling the casserole, Qwilleran went into town for *The New York Times* and sat on the hotel veranda for a while. He was surprised to see a sheriff's deputy looking at the *Suncatcher*. If Einstein's owner had tipped off the authorities about the dog's behavior, that was good. If an investigation would implicate Ernie in wrongdoing, that was bad.

When Qwilleran returned to the cabin, he found Tess on the porch, reading about ravens.

"Would you like a glass of sangria?" he asked.

"I'd love it! And while you're in the kitchen, would you turn on the oven to preheat? Set it at three fifty."

Eventually the casserole went into the oven to bake for forty minutes, and what happened in that brief time was best described by Qwilleran's own notes in his personal journal:

Sunday, July 14. Beautiful day, storm predicted.

At 1:15 Tess and I are on the porch drinking sangria and cranberry juice respectively. Suddenly the cats are alerted. I see a red pickup pull in, and out steps Barb Ogilvie carrying a package. "I brought your vest," she says moodily. "Elizabeth said you had to have it today." I offer her sangria and introduce her to Tess.

At 1:30 I mix another batch of sangria. At 1:35 I hear a tooting behind the cabin. It's an airport rental car, and out steps Polly. In shock, I say, "Your plane isn't due till tomorrow!" She says sweetly, "I couldn't wait to get home. I flew in on my broomstick." I take her around to the porch and introduce her to the two young women. She's somewhat surprised.

At 1:40 Tess takes the casserole out of the oven. At 1:45 the sun disappears behind cloud cover.

At 1:50 the phone rings. I answer, and a man shouts, "Where is that woman?" I say calmly, "Which one do you want?" It's Joe Bunker. Tess is supposed to be in Horseradish as guest of honor at a family reunion. Fifty relatives have come from all over to meet the Bunkers' first Ph.D. I tell Tess, "It's for you." As she rushes to the phone, she's saying, "Oh, no! Oh, no!"

At 1:55 she returns to the porch. "I've got to leave! I'm going to pack. There's a car blocking the drive!" It's the rental car, and I offer to move it, but Polly wants to go home.

At 2:00 Polly leaves, saying she'll phone me.

At 2:05 Tess leaves in embarrassment and remorse.

At 2:10 Barb leaves, looking troubled. I ask if something's wrong. She nods, but says she can't talk about it.

At 2:25 the sky turns yellowish gray. Koko goes into a tizzy, racing around, knocking things down.

At 2:35 it's really dark. Lights have to be turned on. I sit down to wait for the storm to hit. But where are the cats? Nowhere in sight! Where's the macaroni and cheese? I yell, "Koko!" From the pantry comes a yargle—half yowl and half swallow. The two of them are on the counter devouring the casserole.

THE wind and rain that bombarded the shoreline communities on Sunday afternoon was a true squall. Wind-lashed rain slammed into the cabin, rattling the window glass. The good news was that the power and the telephone had not failed. Qwilleran called Polly in Pickax. "Just checking to see if you got home safely."

"Luckily I was indoors before the onslaught. How about you?"

"We're getting a thorough drenching, but the worst is over. Make a cup of tea," he advised. "And let me know if there's anything I can do. You'll need groceries, and I expect to be back tomorrow."

The storm continued all night, pounding the cabin roof and alarming the cats. Qwilleran allowed Yum Yum to crawl under his bedclothes, and eventually brave Koko followed.

On Monday morning it was still raining steadily, and roads outside Mooseville were flooded. Qwilleran would have to stay at the cabin one more day, and the cats were moping.

It was a dull day, and it inspired Qwilleran to telephone the florist in downtown Pickax. He recognized the silky voice of Claudine, a gentle young person with innocent blue eyes. "Good morning," he said. "Is it raining cats and dogs where you are?"

"Sounds like Mr. Q.," she said.

"Have your new flowers come in?"

"They're unloading the truck right now. What would you like?"

"A mixed bouquet for Polly, to be delivered ASAP."

"What do you want the card to say?"

"Just 'the grocer boy.' No name," he said. "I also want to send a large bouquet to a restaurant in Mooseville tomorrow. The roads should be open by then. It's Owen's Place on Sandpit Road. Just say 'from a well-wisher' on the card."

WITHIN an hour Qwilleran received a phone call, and a woman's cheery voice said, "Is this the grocer boy? I'd like a dozen oranges."

"With or without seeds?" he replied.

"Qwill, dear, the flowers are lovely. Thank you! It's good to be home. We'll have much news to exchange tomorrow night. Is it still raining at the beach?"

"It's pouring! The book I've been reading is so soggy, I've retitled it *A Damp Yankee in King Arthur's Court.* See you tomorrow."

Hanging up the phone, Qwilleran found two reproachful cats huddled on the coffee table, giving him an accusing eye, and two postcards on the floor. He thought about his belief in Koko's prescient talents. Not only did Koko sense that the backpacker was buried in the sand hill, but he managed to lead Qwilleran to the site. And how to explain the cat's obsession with the postcards?

"Wait a minute!" he shouted. "What's wrong with me?" He dashed to the two cards on the floor. Why had he not thought to turn them over? He had not read Polly's messages since they arrived two weeks ago!

"We have tickets for *Major Barbara* tonight—not my favorite Shaw play, but it will be beautifully done."

"A male actor plays Lady Bracknell in *The Importance of Being Earnest*. Always a delightful comedy."

The scrawled messages brought to mind Barb Ogilvie and Ernestine Bowen. It was pure coincidence, and yet . . . He looked at Koko.

"Yow!" said the cat, squeezing his eyes.

Did the two women know each other in Florida? Did Barb work in the Bowens' restaurant? Was Owen the older man who had entered Barb's life when she was feeling low? Answers might explain Barb's depression in the days following Owen's disappearance.

Qwilleran was in deep contemplation when the telephone rang.

It was Tess, calling from Horseradish. "Sorry to leave so abruptly yesterday. I was having such a wonderful time. Thank you, Qwill, for your hospitality."

"How was the family reunion?" Qwilleran asked.

"The usual. Family gossip. A potluck supper. It was held in the community hall, and cousin Joe played the piano and sang." Then she asked the inevitable question: "How did you like the macaroni and cheese?"

"I've never tasted its equal!" he said with a slight bending of the truth.

ON TUESDAY morning the sun was shining. Qwilleran dashed off a thousand words about the dogcart races and took the copy to the bank to be faxed. The downtown streets swarmed with vacationers.

Shortly after two o'clock Qwilleran went to Elizabeth's to have Polly's vest gift wrapped. There were quite a few customers buying skewers and raving about the potatoes at Owen's Place and the personable young man who dressed them at tableside. "There he is!" they cried when Derek burst in the front door. They applauded, and he bowed graciously before striding to the rear of the store.

Qwilleran followed. "How was the kickoff? Was Ernie pleased with the turnout?"

"Sure was! And she was bug-eyed over the flowers from a wellwisher. I knew they were from you, but I didn't tell." Derek glanced toward the front of the store. "Here comes Bad News Barb. Something's wrong with her."

The knitter walked solemnly toward the two men, carrying a box of goofy socks. "These need price tags," she said to Derek.

He took them into the stockroom, and Qwilleran asked her, "Do you knit vests for men? I wouldn't mind having one for myself in olive green—with some kind of interesting knit."

"I could show you samples," she said.

Before he could reply, there was a moment of silence in the store as the building vibrated. Then came a thunderous boom, followed by crashing and screaming.

"Earthquake!" Derek yelled. "Get out! Everybody out!" He ran through the store shoving customers toward the exit.

OAK Street was in turmoil. Frightened customers and workers streamed from the stores and huddled in the middle of the street. On Main Street, half a block away, sirens were wailing and emergency vehicles with flashing blue lights were speeding eastward. To the east a cloud of dust or smoke billowed upward.

Qwilleran made a dash for Main Street. He found official vehicles turning into Sandpit Road, while scores of individuals fled away from the Great Dune Motel and surrounding establishments. Yellow tape defining danger zones was stretched in all directions. He showed his press card to a deputy guarding the entry.

"Sorry, Mr. Q.," she said. "Security orders."

"Is it an earthquake?"

"Sinkhole. Step aside, please." A sheriff's car drove through.

Among the many flustered persons swarming up to Main Street was the antique dealer, and Qwilleran shouted, "Arnold! Where's the sinkhole?"

"Back of the restaurant. Huge cave-in. Cars swallowed up!"

At the same time, the earth rumbled like thunder and the east end of the Great Dune crumbled, engulfing the rear of Owen's Place. Giant trees came tumbling end over end.

Thank God, Qwilleran thought, that the restaurant was closed after lunch. Then the question struck him: Where was Ernie?

In the milling crowd he spotted Derek, head and shoulders above the rest. He yelled, "Derek! Was she in the RV?"

"I'm positive! The police took an S-and-R dog in!"

"Was anyone working in the kitchen when you left?"

"The prep cook and the dishwasher. But I'm sure they'd get out when the building began to shake. Ernie, though, had gone to the RV to plot the dinner procedure." Derek's face was pale. "The dog will find her, dead or alive. I wish I could be more optimistic, but I've got this gut feeling that she's gone."

Qwilleran stroked his mustache with a heavy hand. "Let's go into the hotel for a cup of coffee."

They sat in the coffee shop, and Derek said, "Ernie was so professional. I'm the only one in town who got to know her. She was swell."

Qwilleran asked, "Do you think she really grieved about losing her husband?"

"Well, she went through the motions, but to tell the truth, I didn't get any good vibes between those two." Derek got up. "I should go and try to find Liz." He shuffled out of the coffee shop with none of the bursting energy that was his style.

WHEN Derek left, Qwilleran remembered his dinner date with Polly at Owen's Place. He phoned her from a public booth in the lobby. "Have you heard the news on WPKX?" he asked.

"I haven't been listening to the radio. What is it?"

"A sinkhole behind the restaurant where we were supposed to have dinner! And it caused a catastrophic sand slide—the east end of the Great Dune."

"Qwill, I can't believe this!" she said in horror. "I hope there was no loss of life."

"That hasn't been announced, but I have fears for the chef."

"Qwill, this is such depressing news. Perhaps we should postpone our dinner until tomorrow night."

"I'm definitely moving back to Pickax tomorrow morning. I'll call you at the library as soon as I get in."

With that matter settled, Qwilleran returned to his van and tuned in WPKX. He heard this:

"One casualty has been reported in the Mooseville disaster. Ernestine Bowen was killed in her recreation vehicle when it dropped into the sinkhole and was buried under tons of sand."

Parked near Qwilleran's vehicle was John Bushland's van. The photographer was getting photos. Qwilleran wrote a note on his business card and wedged it under Bushy's windshield wiper.

WHEN Qwilleran arrived at the cabin, the Siamese met him with expressions of concern; they knew something was wrong. He fed them and gave them a good brushing to calm their apprehensions. They were basking in the late afternoon sun on the porch when the green van pulled into the clearing.

Bushy jumped out, waving the card. Qwilleran had written, "Good for G and T at the K ranch. Q."

"I need one," Bushy said. "I've exposed a lot of film in the last hour. They're giving the story most of the front page tomorrow."

"Well, I've got the gin and tonic. Have you got the trick lens?"

"I've got the lens. Have you got the cats?"

"They're on the porch in the sun, freshly fed and brushed, so they should be receptive. We'll take our drinks out there and talk about anything but cats and cameras. Don't even think about taking a picture; they read minds."

The two men took porch chairs facing the lake. To their left, visible from the corner of an eye, were the Siamese: Koko striking aristocratic poses on his pedestal; Yum Yum stretched full length on the warm glass top of the snack table.

Bushy stood up slowly, raised his camera, and clicked it while facing the lake. Yum Yum, without knowing it, was facing the camera with a contented look.

"That does it!" Bushy announced with satisfaction. "If that doesn't win a prize, I'm going to give up photography."

"What about Koko?" Qwilleran asked.

"Forget that tyrant. He's missed his chance. He'll never be famous." Having heard the click, click, click, Koko had jumped from the pedestal to the floor.

WEDNESDAY WAS MOVING DAY. Packing had to be done surreptitiously; although Koko was usually eager to jump into the carrier, the sight of it sent Yum Yum scurrying to places unknown.

On this occasion she was captured and caged, but Koko—instead of panting to join the expedition—vanished suddenly. Impatiently Qwilleran yelled, "Treat!" There was only a faint murmur in the upper reaches of the cabin. Twenty feet above the floor, in the peak of the roof, the cat had elongated himself on a narrow shelf created by the ridgepole and rafters.

Qwilleran sat down to think. At that moment the phone rang, and he answered with a curt, "Yes?"

It was Polly. "Qwill, I'm calling an emergency meeting of the library board tonight. My assistant has resigned, and the roof is leaking. We'll have to postpone our dinner date again."

"We have a crisis here, too. I'll keep in touch," said Qwilleran.

Replacing the receiver, he heard a thump, thump, thump as Koko descended from his perch to the floor.

"Okay, young man, you've had your joke. Now let's go."

As Qwilleran rattled the latch of the carrier, the phone rang again, and Koko flew back up to the peak of the roof.

This time it was Junior Goodwinter. "Qwill, how are you coming with Operation U No What?"

"Slowly and painfully."

"Could you meet today's deadline? A hole just opened up."

"Will it blow my cover if I fax it?"

"Use an alias. Thanks a lot, Qwill."

Qwilleran hurried to the van and retrieved his typewriter. Then, releasing Yum Yum from the carrier and forgetting about Koko, he pounded out his copy:

Dear sweet readers—Your charming, sincere, intelligent letters warm Ms. Gramma's pluperfect heart! Sorry to hear you're having trouble with the L words. The safest way to cope with lie, lay, lied, laid, and lain is to avoid them entirely. Simply say, "The hen deposited an egg. He fibbed to his boss. She stretched out on the couch." Get the idea? But if you really want to wrestle these verbs to the mat, use Ms. Gramma's guide.

1. Today the hen lays an egg. Yesterday she laid an egg. She has laid eggs all summer. (Ms. Gramma likes them poached, with bacon and hollandaise sauce.)

2. Today you lie to your boss. Yesterday you lied to him. You have lied to the old buzzard frequently. (Tomorrow you may be fired.)

3. Today you lie down for a nap. Yesterday you lay down for a nap. In the past you have lain down often. (See your doctor, honey. It could be an iron deficiency.)

There was more. Ms. Gramma tackled such bothersome partners as who and whom, that and which, as and like, and less and fewer. And the copy made it to the fax machine at the bank on time.

AFTER that ordeal Qwilleran treated himself to a pasty for lunch and reviewed his "vacation." There had been one incident after another, and a tremor on his upper lip convinced him there were more to come. Perhaps Koko had sensed some forthcoming development and was trying to stop him from leaving.

He walked back to Main Street, where his van was parked. On the way he heard running footsteps behind him and a throaty voice calling, "Mr. Q., Mr. Q." It was Barb Ogilvie.

"I was just thinking about you and my vest," he said.

"I'll dye some yarn samples as soon as I get back on track," she said. "I've had a bad time."

"Sorry to hear that."

Swiveling her glance, she said, "I don't want to impose, Mr. Q., but I wish I could talk to you about something serious. You're the only one I know who's cool enough to understand."

The compliment, coupled with his unbridled curiosity, led him to suggest talking over coffee somewhere.

She hesitated. "I don't dare talk about it in a public place. How about at my family's ranch?"

"Four o'clock?" he suggested. "We'll take a walk."

"Wear boots. It could be muddy."

SEVEN

WHEN Qwilleran drove into the Ogilvie farmyard, Barb met him and told him where to park. The driveway tapered into a wagon trail and then into a footpath. "Nice day for a hike," he said.

They tramped across pastures and past grazing flocks. When the trail ended, they selected two horizontal rocks and sat down.

"Now what did you want to tell me?" Qwilleran said.

"Well, I told you about Florida and the balloon chaser, didn't I? After I chalked him off, I started dating my boss. He took me out on his boat, and I think he really liked me. I liked my job, too."

"Where were you working?"

"At his restaurant. The trouble was the other waitresses were jealous. The boss gave me the best tables, so I got bigger tips. One day another waitress backed me into a corner and said, 'We all know what's goin' on, honey, and you'd better quit this job or we'll tell his wife, and she'll come after you with a cleaver!' His wife was the chef! I thought they were brother and sister. How could I be so dumb?"

"It happens," he said.

"I decided in a hurry that Florida was a dead end for me. A year ago last winter I came home and started being a country girl again. Everything was okay until this summer. Then they showed up in Mooseville—the Bowens!"

"Did they know you lived here?"

"I talked about my hometown a lot when I was Down Below."

"Did Owen try to contact you?"

"No, and I stayed away from Sandpit Road. Then, after he died, Ernie called and wanted me to have dinner with her at the hotel. She said I was the only person she knew within two thousand miles. So I went to her suite. She had two dinners sent up and champagne in an ice bucket. She threw her arms around me and cried a bit. At first we just talked about Florida. When they decided to come up here, they drove the RV, towing the *Suncatcher*. On their first day off after opening the restaurant, they were out on the lake when a speedboat started following them and finally flagged them down."

Fast Mama, Qwilleran thought.

"Owen told them to buzz off. He said the *Suncatcher* was not for sale. But Ernie was suspicious. You can't live in Florida without knowing what goes on, drugwise, and she had seen some locked suitcases down in the cabin. She figured that Owen had a commission from a Florida drug ring and was supposed to open up a new market. He told her to keep her eyes and mouth shut. If she didn't, he told her, she'd never cook another meal."

"What did she do?"

"What *could* she do?" Barb said. "She didn't want to be a dead chef. But it was driving her crazy. She started making mistakes at the restaurant."

"I heard about the mistakes," Qwilleran said. "Derek thought she was worried about Owen's drinking."

"Ernie told me she'd made a deal with the devil. Owen would put her through chef's school, and she'd run his restaurant. She didn't care if he drank a fifth a day and chased women. She hoped he'd die of cirrhosis, and the restaurant would be hers. Suddenly she got an idea that would get her off the hook with Owen, and she could start her own business." Barb stopped and gulped.

"Go ahead," Qwilleran said. "I'm listening."

"It was their second day off. There aren't many pleasure boats around on a Monday, and Owen said they wouldn't be bothered by customers, because the deal was, never on Monday. He said some stupid guy had got his signals crossed the week before. So they anchored at Pirate Shoals. Ernie ate her lunch, and Owen drank his. Finally Owen flaked out on the banquette in the stern. As soon as he started snoring, she got a potato skewer from the picnic basket and stabbed him in the ear, then rolled him over the railing."

There was silence. After a while Qwilleran said, "Wouldn't there be a lot of blood—from an artery?"

"She sopped it up with towels and stuffed them in the bait bucket. Then she threw it overboard, along with the locked suitcases. She moved the boat about a mile before calling for help."

"One question, Barb. Why did she tell you all this?"

"I don't know. I didn't know what to do! I went around like a zombie for a week, and then—"

"And then the Sand Giant came to your rescue," Qwilleran said, "except that you have information on a homicide that could enable police to effect a closure, and it's your duty to report it."

A commotion among some crows—frenzied cawing, fluttering, and squabbling—signaled the end of the conversation.

ARRIVING at the cabin, Qwilleran found all five skewers hanging on their brads. Either Koko was tired of his new toy or it was his way of saying "case closed." The cat was now lounging contentedly in a patch of sunlight coming through a roof window. After feeding the Siamese, Qwilleran opened the lakeside door, and the three of them moved gratefully onto the porch with its idyllic view. "This is your last chance, guys, to watch the twilight bird ballet and the nighttime show of stars!"

Qwilleran read to the Siamese until the light began to fade. He enjoyed twilight, those moody moments between light and dark. What poet had called it *l'heure bleu?* Polly would know. He missed her for reasons he had never put into words: her loving smile, merry laugh—and their shared interests. There would be much to talk about over dinner: her trip abroad and his adventures at home.

Darkness always came reluctantly to the lake, but eventually it was total. Koko studied the stars from his pedestal, while Yum Yum stared into the shrubbery, and Qwilleran, stretched in a lounge chair, let his thoughts drift. All three were so enthralled by the magic of the night that they stayed on the porch well after midnight.

It was then that an uncanny incident occurred—something Qwilleran would later record in his journal. When it happened, he was too unnerved to write about it. He paced the floor, unable to sleep, and in the morning he was dressed and ready to leave the cabin. Before the cats were really awake, he stuffed them into the carrier and took them to the van. Luggage, coffeemaker, bike, and so forth were already loaded, and they took off for Pickax.

At home, after a phone call to Polly confirming their dinner date, he felt better. He reserved their favorite table at the Old Stone Mill, and at six o'clock he and Polly walked into the restaurant looking happy. Each carried a flat gift-wrapped package.

First they toasted each other affectionately—Polly with a glass of sherry, Qwilleran with Squunk water. Then he presented his gift. A printed card inside said AN ORIGINAL BARB OGILVIE DESIGN, HAND-KNITTED IN POINTILLÉ CALE STITCH, USING UNBLEACHED, HAND-SPUN WOOL FROM LOCAL SHEEP. Polly was thrilled.

Qwilleran gingerly opened his souvenir of Canada. It was something made of fabric in the Mackintosh clan tartan. It was a vest!

"Now we have a vested interest in each other," he said.

Altogether, it was a memorable evening. When Polly was back in Indian Village and he was back home, it was late, and he was sufficiently relaxed to write in his journal:

Pickax. Thursday, July 18.

Last night was our last at the cabin. We were sitting on the porch after midnight with the lights turned off, indoors and out. The cats sensed something irregular and fussed nervously. Soon Yum Yum ran indoors.

Was it my imagination, or was the sky turning green? Suddenly a strong gust of wind stirred up papers and whatnot on the porch, and Koko jumped onto my lap and dug in with his claws. It lasted only a few seconds, though.

At the same time a large round disk floated downward, throwing shafts of light on the beach. I could feel Koko's fur standing on end. His tail bushed. Next thing I knew, he was at the screened door, pawing the latch.

I leaped out of my chair, but he slipped outside and headed for the beach, straight down the side of the dune.

Just as I was about to go after him, I saw small creatures tumbling out of the disk and sliding down the shafts of light. They had four legs and long tails! He was going to meet them!

Desperate, I plunged headlong in a flying tackle and landed on top of him. For a second I saw stars, then blacked out.

When I came to my senses, I was pinned down under a heavy weight—in total darkness. Where was I? My eyes were open, but I couldn't see, and there was a throbbing in my chest.

Then something wet touched my nose. Koko was on my chest, purring loudly, and I was back in my lounge chair. How did I get there? My mind was muddled. The green light had disappeared, and the beach was dark.

Still I felt stunned. It was a dream, I told myself . . . or was it? Koko's fur was sandy, and when I stood up, I brushed a shower of sand off my clothes.

It had been twenty-four hours since the incident, and Qwilleran still felt uneasy about the experience. He might be a fool, but he could not swear it was only a dream.

One thought caused a spasm in his mustache. Was this a clue to Koko's abnormal sensory perception? What were the cat's origins? No one knew. One day he had simply appeared.

Previously Qwilleran had attributed Koko's superior intelligence to his sixty whiskers. Perhaps the secret was something more unthinkable—the intelligence of an alien race who were not little green men, but little green cats!

As for Sixty Whiskers himself, he had not changed a whisker since the incident. He was still a handsome, intelligent, companionable, unpredictable, somewhat imperious and frequently exasperating feline. But Qwilleran had changed. He was willing to concede that Koko was not seeing stars when he gazed at the sky; he was seeing fuzzy green blobs.

LILIAN JACKSON BRAUN

"Every day they do something that gives me an idea," says Lilian Jackson Braun, explaining the influence of her cats, Koko III and Pitti-Sing, on the famous kitties in her best-selling mystery series. "They are very creative." Koko and Yum Yum aren't her only characters with real-life counterparts. Feline-loving sleuth James Qwilleran is based on a number of men Braun has known over the years. Today she and her husband live in North Carolina, far from Moose County, her fictional setting that is "four hundred miles north of everywhere."

The volumes in this series are issued
every two to three months. A typical volume
contains four outstanding books in condensed
form. None of the selections in any volume has
appeared in *Reader's Digest* magazine. Any reader
may receive this service by writing to
The Reader's Digest Association (Canada) Ltd.,
1125 Stanley Street, Montreal, Quebec H3B 5H5.

ACKNOWLEDGMENTS

Pages 362–363: Bob Wickley/SuperStock.

The original editions of the books in this volume are published and copyrighted as follows:
Rainbow Six, published by G. P. Putnam's Sons,
distributed by BeJo Sales Inc. at $38.99
© 1998 by Rubicon, Inc.
Cloud Nine, published by Bantam Books, a division of
Bantam Doubleday Dell Publishing Group, Inc.,
distributed by Bantam Books Canada Inc. at $29.95
© 1999 by Luanne Rice
The Simple Truth, published by Warner Books, Inc.,
distributed by Fenn Publishing Company Ltd. at $30.00
© 1998 by Columbus Rose, Ltd.
The Cat Who Saw Stars, published by G. P. Putnam's Sons,
distributed by BeJo Sales Inc. at $32.00
© 1999 by Lilian Jackson Braun